Lay IT DOWN

Bastards MC Series Boxed Set

CARINA ADAMS

LAY IT DOWN

This book is a work of fiction. Names, characters, places, and incidents are the product of the author's imagination or are used fictitiously. Any resemblance to actual events, locales, or persons, living or dead, is entirely coincidental. The author acknowledges the trademarked status and trademark owners of various products referenced in this work of fiction, which have been used without permission. The publication and use of these trademarks is not authorized, associated, or sponsored by the trademark owners.

BOOKS BY CARINA ADAMS:

THE 'BAMA BOYS SERIES:

Forever Red

Out of The Blue

Black (Coming 2019)

Sidelined: A Bama Boy Spinoff

THE BASTARDS MC SERIES:

Unfinished Business

Lay It Down

STANDALONE TITLES:

Almost Innocent

Lucky

Ruffles & Beaus

For **JENN H.** and **JENNIFER S.**

Because you believed,

Supported me when no one else did,

And loved Matty

Always Been Mine

For **BAMBINO**

You and me against the world,

In sunshine or in shadow.

ONE

It was raining again. Again. So far, the whole summer had been a washout. Normal rain I could handle, but this dreary want-to-go-back-to-bed weather made me cranky. Well, I could *try* to blame my mood on the weather.

The parking lot was almost empty this morning. I was always one of the first people at the office, but it looked as though the other early birds had decided to sleep in. I didn't blame them. I'd thought about sleeping in, but the hotel room was too quiet, and if I was going to be miserable, I might as well be miserable at work. I parked in my usual spot, locked my doors, and ran for the three-story brick building, trying to avoid getting absolutely soaked. I was inside and waiting for the elevator, looking out the glass door at the growing puddles, before I saw the familiar car parked near the building.

My mood instantly improved. Matty was never here before eight. And today was Thursday, the one day we both had full office days. Barring an emergency, there were no meetings to go to, no parent visits to supervise, and no kiddos to see. A full eight hours of my best friend, even though we were working, made me happy. I was grinning by the time I got off the elevator and walked to our cubicles.

"Good morning!" I smiled at his back, removing my raincoat.

"Hey." He didn't turn around, and his normally energetic voice seemed flat.

Thinking he was on the phone, I started my computer and turned on my light. He didn't say anything else, so I glanced at his desk; his phone was still on its cradle.

"What's wrong?" I sat in my chair, turning toward him.

We'd been friends for years, co-workers for even more. When you spend forty hours a week with someone, you get to know them pretty well. Add our Friday lunch ritual, the time our families spent together, hours of phone conversations, and hanging out almost every Saturday morning for the last few years, and I could honestly say that I knew him very well. He always greeted me with a smile—unless there was a problem.

When he didn't answer, I reached out and touched his shoulder. "Matty." I wasn't demanding, just insistent.

"Not gonna leave it alone, are you Joes?" He sounded annoyed, but he turned and offered me his signature lopsided grin. I shook my head, grinning back. "Taylor stuff."

Of course it was. I felt slightly annoyed that I hadn't pegged that one. Matt's girlfriend, Taylor Butler, was the prettiest woman I'd ever met. She was absolutely model perfect from the top of her platinum-streaked head all the way to her impeccably manicured toes. She was flawless, at least until you got to know her. Then you realized that she was one of the most spoiled, self-centered, and pretentious people on the planet. The epitome of beautiful on the outside, ugly inside.

I was biased, of course, but I couldn't stand her. I hated the way he acted around her. He spoiled her rotten and overlooked her crappy attitude. They'd been together for well over a year, and we'd learned a few months into their relationship that we couldn't talk about Taylor. Matty would vent sometimes, but only when he really needed it, and I would just listen, biting my tongue.

"Need an ear?"

"Nope. Don't want to think about her right now. I needed a distraction." He motioned toward the thick blue files scattered on his desk.

I scanned the piles of chaos; they hadn't been there last night when I left. "What time did you get here?"

"Five thirty-ish." He shrugged. Apparently, the Taylor issues were big this time.

"Did you get breakfast?"

He raised an eyebrow; his normal breakfast consisted of a protein shake that would put hair on even the most feminine chest. It made me nauseated just thinking about it.

"Come on, I'm taking you to Denny's."

He smiled. "I said I needed a distraction, not a heart attack."

I rolled my eyes. "You'll be okay. Besides, what could possibly be better, or more distracting, than having a nasty grease-filled breakfast with me? You'll be so busy worrying about your girlish figure and how much exercise you'll need to burn off all those awful calories that you won't have time to think about other things." I moved just in time to avoid the highlighter he tossed at me, and I giggled at the annoyed look that crossed his face.

2

"I'll drive." He grinned as he stood.

My breath caught, and I looked away. He had the best smile, and when it was genuine, his entire face lit up, even his eyes twinkled and creased. Lately I'd noticed that my heart beat a little faster when that happiness was directed at me.

It shouldn't have been a surprise. Whenever Matty smiled, women noticed. I'd seen him use his charms more than once. My reaction to it, however, was new, and I blamed it on my husband, Will.

Our families, along with a couple of other co-workers' families, had gotten together for our annual Memorial Day cookout the month before. Taylor had worn strappy heels, so she couldn't play in our traditional soccer match after lunch. Will offered to sit with her, making the teams even. I didn't argue because I sure as hell didn't want to sit with her.

My team was winning, and I was about to kick a goal when I was lifted into the air and spun. I screamed and kicked, batting at the strong arms around my waist. The kids stopped playing the game and came to either help me or help Matt keep me from scoring more points.

Everyone was laughing, and one of the kids tackled us. Before I had really figured out what had happened, I was on the ground and looking up into Matty's face, his body heavy on mine, his hand under my head. The kids thought it was the perfect time to pig pile, and without warning, they were all climbing on us at once. Matty was grinning down at me like a fool, and I couldn't stop laughing long enough to catch my breath.

He pushed himself up, knocking off anyone who tried to keep him down, and reached a hand to me, pulling me up. "You okay?" His hand ran through my hair, touching my scalp, as if checking for bumps.

"Yeah, I'm fine. Something broke my fall," I answered, trying not to start laughing again. "Thank God it was soft."

Matty popped an eyebrow and his features twisted in confusion as he patted his arms and then flexed, showing me his muscles. "Nope, nothing soft here."

I giggled.

He smirked, moving his mouth next to my ear so only I could hear, "Part of me had an amazingly soft landing though." His hand tapped my butt in the innocent way athletes do. "Great game!"

3

He winked before turning back to the kids and was busy playing tag before his words sank in. The soccer game forgotten, I walked toward the table where my husband sat. I was still laughing and looked up just in time to see Taylor giving me a nasty look.

On the way home, Will brought up the game. "She really doesn't like you."

I knew who he was talking about without even asking, and I scoffed at him. "Well, the feeling is mutual."

"Careful, honey. That's dangerous ground." He tilted his head at me. "I know you don't think she's good enough for him, but he loves her and that should be enough for you. Female friends of men tend to get catty when said friend dates a woman they don't approve of." He shook his head when I tried to interrupt. "You know what I'm talking about."

I did. He'd heard all of my Taylor induced rants, and I had no doubt that catty was the nicest way to phrase my opinion of her. I just didn't like her.

When I didn't say anything, he continued. "There is nothing worse than a jealous woman. You can't choose who he loves, and you can't change his mind. He adores you. That won't change because of her behavior. It could change because of yours though."

My husband had a way of looking at most situations that made me reassess. I still didn't like her though. "I don't understand why she hates me so much."

"Really?" He sounded genuinely surprised. "You have no idea?"

I wanted to make some comment about not being able to understand the thought process of a self-absorbed beauty queen, but I kept quiet and shook my head.

"I don't know," he mused, looking at me in amazement. "Maybe you just don't notice it the way the rest of us do. When Matt sees you, he stops what he's doing and smiles. He touches you every chance he gets. His eyes follow you when you walk by. Christ, whenever you laugh, even if you're across the room, he finds you. I'm not blind, and neither is Taylor. I see how you look at him and how you react to him. You two have a connection that leaves the rest of us out."

I didn't know what to say. At work we both listened to music on our headphones, so it was easier to touch his shoulder to get his attention than to yell. We were comfortable with each other. And he

4

was one of the nosiest people I knew. He needed to know what was going on at all times and most likely wanted to know what was funny.

I would have pointed out each of these arguments, but the thing that I was most concerned with at that point was Will's lack of emotion. "And none of that bothers you?"

Will gave me a small smile. "Honey, how Matt feels about you is really the least of our issues, don't you think?"

He'd been right of course. Matt and his overly familiar tendencies toward me were the smallest problem Will and I had. Now, a few weeks after the picnic, our kids were spending the summer with their grandparents and I was living in a hotel room five miles from work. Trying to save our marriage wasn't even the biggest problem Will and I had; figuring out if it was worth saving was.

"Hey, where'd you go?"

I shook off the memories and realized we were pulling into the restaurant.

"I thought breakfast was a distraction for me." Matty nudged my left arm. "In order to do that, you have to actually talk to me."

"Wait. Are you actually complaining about me being quiet?" I sassed, trying to cover my sadness.

He stuck out his tongue. "There's a first time for everything." He opened the restaurant door for me, putting his hand on my lower back and guiding me in before him.

The woman who greeted us made no attempt to hide her distasteful ogling. Her eyes roved slowly over my friend, all six feet three inches of him, from his head to his feet and back to his face. Meeting his eyes, she gave him a flirty grin before showing us to our table. Her gaze followed him again as he slid into the booth.

"Your waitress will be here in a few minutes. Can I get you anything?" Her tone implied she wanted to give him something— like her phone number.

I moved into the booth across from him, knocking my knee into his.

He raised an eyebrow in my direction but answered the waitress, "I'll take a coffee, black. And we'll both have iced water— hers with lemon."

The girl looked at me as if she'd just realized I was there.

5

I nodded at her, moving farther back in the booth to avoid the legs invading my side of the table. "Thanks."

A leg bumped mine suddenly, and I turned away from the girl to glare at my companion.

His head was buried in the menu, so I bumped him back. "Get those knobby things on your side of the table."

"Listen, shrimp, if you don't need the space, you can share."

"Shrimp? Really? And I do need the room!" I wanted to kick him but settled for another knee nudge.

He moved the menu enough for me to see his smile, but he didn't budge his legs. I didn't know why he was reading the menu; we both ordered the same thing every time we came. A few minutes later, the waitress brought his coffee and our waters and took our order. I was debating distracting small-talk topics when he cleared his throat.

"Taylor..." He broke off as though he didn't know what to say. His brow creased, and I could tell he was searching for the right words. He sighed. "Taylor can be a miserable witch sometimes."

I almost choked on my water. Never, not one time, had he ever said anything like that about her. He'd complain about her spending habits, her criticisms of him, and her complete lack of knowledge about kids. After he complained, he would defend her and boast about all her "redeeming" qualities. Blah, blah, blah.

"Not one word." The way his jaw tightened and his eyes narrowed told me that I'd regret not keeping silent. "She wants to have a baby, says"—his voice got high, mimicking Taylor's— "that it will fix all our problems." He shook his head, lowering his voice back to normal. "Because bringing a baby into our house will fix everything." The anger had taken over, and his face was contorted as if in pain. "I'm thirty-six for Christ's sake. I don't want to start over!"

I couldn't keep quiet. "She hates kids!"

"Yep." He glared out the window. "She said a baby would ruin her body, so she made me get fixed, remember?"

I couldn't forget even if I wanted to. I'd gone with him because Taylor hated hospitals. She was supposed to pick him up after the surgery but had "lost track of time" and couldn't make it, so I took him home and kept him supplied with a steady stream of frozen peas and Advil while watching the first season of *Sons of*

Anarchy and listening to him complain about how fake it was. Good times, really.

"Now she wants me to get it reversed so we can have our own baby."

I didn't know what to say. I had no words of wisdom. Hell, I couldn't save my own marriage.

"I'm sorry." It wasn't much, but I could offer empathy. I had to many burning questions to stay quiet though. "Why now?"

"She wants a 'grand gesture.'" His hands made air quotes around the words. "A real commitment. Something to prove I'm going to stay with her, even with all our problems." He sighed. "I think I'm going to ask her to marry me."

The bomb left me speechless. There was so much to say, but the words wouldn't form. I searched his face, looking for his telltale smirk or a wink that would prove he was just kidding. All I saw was sincerity.

There were probably thousands of reasons why he thought marriage was the answer, but I was positive that I could easily rebut most of them. In fact, I had plenty more why he shouldn't. One was more glaringly obvious than the rest.

"Have you told Sam you want to marry her?" If anyone disliked that woman more than I did, it was Matt's son.

"Sam's nine, Jo. He still wants his parents to get back together."

I didn't blame the kid; I did, too.

"When I talked to Becky, she said I should ask you what you thought." His eyes burned into mine.

I fought to keep the shock hidden. "You already talked to Becky?"

"Of course I did." He scoffed as if that was the most absurd question he'd ever been asked. "If she ever decides to do something stupid, like move that loser in, I know she would talk it over with me first."

"Loser? Did she and the vet break up?" I changed the subject, welcoming the distraction.

His lips tipped up. "Nope."

I shook my head, fighting a smile. "Some habits are just hard to break, huh?"

I had adored Becky when they were married—but just like every other possession in a divorce, friends were split up evenly.

Matty was the lucky party who got me. I still spoke to his ex every chance I got, but it wasn't the same. She was more reserved, and it was very clear she knew my loyalty was with Matt.

The last time I'd seen her, she'd been out with her long-time partner. The "loser" vet was anything but. He owned his own practice, was known for both his dedication to animals and for having a big heart, was easy on the eyes, and most importantly, adored Sam. I'd liked him instantly. But Matt would find something wrong with a saint if that saint was dating his ex-wife.

"Whatever." He rolled his eyes. "What do you think?"

"About the vet? Or about you getting married?"

He tipped his head slightly, giving me an annoyed look.

"I think getting married because you want your girlfriend to feel secure or because you want to prove you're not going to leave her when the next floozy comes along is stupid. It's something you would have done in your twenties."

He graciously ignored my floozy comment. "I'm not getting married tomorrow. I'm talking about getting engaged. That way she'll know that I'm committed, but we'll have plenty of time to work out the kinks."

Kinks? They had more than a few kinks to work out, but I was really the last person who could judge. The waitress appeared at our table, handed out our food, and after making sure we were all set, left just as quietly as she'd come.

I watched her go, making sure she was far enough away to not hear us. "I didn't know you were having trouble."

He dove into his eggs; I was sure he was going to ignore me.

"It's over stupid shit." He took another bite. "You piss her off."

"Me?" I almost dropped my fork. "What in the hell did I do this time?"

He chuckled. "We piss her off. I spend too much time with you and she gets insecure."

I fought a sigh. It was the same old argument. "I thought her attitude had changed now that we don't go out Saturday mornings."

Our Saturday mornings used to be spent at the local Y. While the kids had swim lessons or a baseball clinic, the two of us would use the cardio room, go for a run, or sit and have coffee. He'd brought Taylor once. After that, Becky had started to bring Sam, even on his dad's weekends. Matty might pick him up, but

8

Taylor was always with him. Her argument had been that she'd felt like a third wheel, which she was, and that I got to see him enough.

"Yeah, well, now she says I'm in a bad mood every weekend."

"That's my fault how?"

He shrugged. "It's the only two days of the week I don't see you."

That made no sense. I frowned into my omelet. "We talk all the time on the weekends though."

"Yeah. She doesn't know that."

"No wonder I piss her off. I'm your dirty little secret." I teased, my tone light as I glanced up at him.

His head snapped up, sky-blue orbs finding mine. "You are." He had a serious look, his usual crooked smile and twitching lip gone. He looked almost sad. I didn't see this side of him very often, and I couldn't pull my eyes away. "Well, one of them anyway."

He must not have shaved last night; a dark five o'clock shadow ran along the sides of his square jawline and chin. His heart-shaped lips weren't full enough to be feminine, but they were just pouty enough to make most women ache to kiss him. The small rectangle patch of thick, dark hair right below the middle of his bottom lip should have looked out of place, yet it fit him. The indent above his upper lip was pronounced and led to a perfectly centered, long, thin nose.

When you looked at him from the side, you could see a little bump right between his eyes where his nose had been broken when he was younger. From my view though, all I could see was a straight line to his eyes. Black lashes that would make any woman jealous surrounded hooded eyes. Dark thick eyebrows topped each bright blue eye; those eyes were peering at me now. The left side of his forehead creased slightly as he watched me study him.

He looked like a Greek God. A Greek God I wanted to do unholy things with. The thought came out of nowhere, and my heart pounded as I realized exactly what I was thinking. I stared down at the table, hoping he couldn't read my thoughts.

This was Matty! My best friends. The one constant I had in my ever changing life. I didn't want more from him.

I could deny it all I wanted, but the truth was that I was extremely attracted to him. I bit the inside of my cheek, trying to figure out if I had always been or if it was new. He was pretty, sure, but he was my person. The one I could always count on and trusted more than anyone. That was a line I couldn't cross.

I simply needed more sleep. My mind was foggy and playing tricks on me because I'd been to stressed to get much shut eye. When I peeked back up, his eyes were glued to me, concern clear on his face.

"You really are beautiful." *Awesome. Open mouth, insert foot.* But it was the first thought I'd had.

The lips twisted into crooked smile. "I know." His voice was husky, and for a second, all I could focus on was his mouth. He laughed merrily, breaking the spell. "Where'd that come from?"

I shook my head.

"I think your ability to say whatever is on your mind is my favorite thing about you, Josephine." He grinned again, shaking his head. "It's good genetics, that's all." He ran his hand down his cheek, rubbing his chin. "Poor Sam."

I raised an eyebrow. Poor Sam? Other than having his mom's brown eyes and dimples, Sam was the spitting image of his dad.

Matty nodded. "It's hard to be this pretty. It's a ton of work to maintain." He was joking, but I knew for a fact how much effort he put into staying fit. "Plus, he doesn't have a best friend like you in his corner to talk him through everything. How does one survive without a Joes?"

He always knew just what to say, the bastard. I was as bad as the other women he had eating out of his hands.

"Do you love her?"

He took the last bite of his egg, nodding. "Yeah, I do."

"What about a promise ring?"

His eyebrows rose, and he smirked. "I'm an adult, not a teenager who doesn't want his girlfriend sleeping around."

I opened my mouth to argue, but snapped my mouth closed when I realized he had a point. Will had been right; it was not my place to say the person Matty loved wasn't good enough for him.

"If you love her, and really want to marry her, and it isn't for some other reason, then you should ask her." *Go ahead. Give her the validation she clearly needs.*

He beamed at me. "You really are the best friend ever." His knee bumped mine once again as he pulled it away from my side of the table.

The rain had disappeared by the time I left work, but my mood had gotten worse. I couldn't shake it off—I wasn't sure I wanted to. It didn't bother me if I snapped at everyone who got within a two-foot radius. My head was pounding from sleep deprivation, lack of caffeine, or too much of Matty's obnoxiousness and the handful of ibuprofen I'd managed to swallow hadn't touched it. I needed to go home and sleep.

Home.

My heart raced, and I felt the panic rise. I didn't have a home to go to anymore. Will was at the house and the kids were gone. I'd call them as soon as I got back to the hotel and pretend that just hearing their voices would make everything better.

It wouldn't. My life was changing and nothing could make it better. I was at a crossroads and needed to make the difficult and life-altering decisions no adult wanted to make.

We'd been through this before, and I'd told Will I could never do it again. I definitely couldn't handle it a third time. I would never trust him to not make the same mistake again.

Yet, I didn't know how to live without my family. No, I'd never have to live without my kids. It was Will... I didn't know how to live without him.

Will and I had been together forever; at least it felt that way. Seventeen was a lifetime ago for a thirty-three-year-old. I'd loved him almost half my life.

While my friends planned to go to local universities, I spent my time searching for colleges close enough to the people I loved but far enough away that I could have the freedom I craved. Boston University was on the top of my list. The psychology program was decent, and I loved the city – it felt like home to me.

After my acceptance letter came, my parents insisted we go for a weekend visit and take the whole bells-and-whistles guided tour so they could ask embarrassing questions about crime rates and the probability that I would be flashed. I hadn't dressed up, instead wearing jeans, a golden-yellow T-shirt with a green-and-yellow plaid over it, and sneakers. My mother was furious, but I argued that she didn't understand late-90s fashion. She had seemed to buy my argument until another family arrived at the meeting point with a teenager dressed in a pencil skirt, sweater set, pearls, and stylish flats. My parents had been debating whether we should leave so I didn't embarrass them any further when our guides walked in.

William Walker, or Billy, as he liked people to call him, was adorable. Dressed in a polo and khakis, he oozed charm out of every pore. His smile lit up his whole face, and my mother seemed as taken with him as I was. He was the perfect escort, giving my parents the attention they needed, not laughing at any of their silly questions, and showing us everything we could have wanted to see. At lunch, we discovered that he'd volunteered to take us around because he was from Maine too and missed home. He'd thrown me a wink when he reminisced about his own parents' visit the year before. Later that afternoon, the other guide took the parents to talk to the financial aid office, and Billy took little miss Sweater Set and me for a walk.

I loved his laugh. It was deep and made his Adam's apple bob. Sweater Set asked a ton of questions and, for once, I was quiet, content just to watch him. His whole body changed when he talked about his life. The curly blond hair bounced on his forehead when he moved, reminding me of an excited little boy. He loved living in Boston but wanted to move home after getting his degree in economics. He spent every second he could outdoors, mostly on the Charles River as a member of the BU Crew. He wanted to hike the full Appalachian Trail after he was done with school. And he was single. He'd laughed when Sweater Set asked him that, telling us there was no time for girlfriends in rowing.

He asked us questions too, about our majors, what we planned to do after school, why we wanted to live in Boston. Sweater Set talked so much that I tuned her out and took in the sights and sounds around me. I couldn't wait to move. The campus was beautiful and had a busy energetic current, as if something important was going on at all times.

I was happy to let her talk because I was the girl with the lame answers. I'd picked psych because people fascinated me. I didn't know what I was going to be when I grew up. I wanted to come here to get the hell away from my parents and be surrounded by culture. When she did stop talking and Billy coaxed my answers out, she scoffed. Billy smiled and told me it sounded as though I would be a good fit.

By the time we got back to our parents, Sweater Set was practically throwing herself at him and I was mildly disappointed to realize he seemed interested. I understood it though. She was cute and little and bubbly. I was the chubby girl, out of place in jeans and flannel. When he said good-bye to my parents and turned to me, I was shocked that he asked for my phone number and email. He said that he was coming home for summer vacation and wanted to know if we could get together because it would be nice for me to have some friends before school started.

He didn't wait for summer but emailed me a week later. We talked all spring. He was brilliant and funny and saw the world completely differently than I did. He came to Maine for a few weekend trips, and by the time my high school graduation came, he had me and everyone I knew wrapped around his finger.

We spent the summer falling in love and talking about our future. We had nothing in common except our feelings for the other. We laughed because we were different from all the other couples we knew. There was no drama or games, no major fights in front of an audience. There was no great love story where one of us broke the other's heart; we were a team that agreed to face the world together and talk through every problem that could arise. We were the boring couple, and we were both okay with that.

When we left for school in the fall, everyone told me to not be upset if it didn't work out, that summer relationships never last. Billy was "a handsome and popular upperclassman," after all, and I was "the geeky freshman"—at least, those were my mom's words. As the days past, Billy was overloaded with school, work, and crew, and I struggled to keep my head above water, but he called me every night before bed and woke me up every morning with a Dunkin' Donuts coffee. Each weekend he would sneak me into his dorm, and while our friends partied the days away, we'd spent every second we could wrapped in each other's arms, talking about everything or nothing at all. Time flew.

There was never a question of if we would get married, just when we'd tie the knot. By the time Billy was a senior, everyone assumed he'd ask me to be his wife. We had other plans though. He would take an internship in Boston and get an apartment close to campus so I could stay with him as much as possible while finishing my degree. After I graduated, we were going to take six months off to hike the Appalachian then discover the continental states before settling back in New England. Once we had our careers figured out, we'd talk about marriage.

May was rough for me that year. End-of-semester projects and preparing for finals were brutal, and I was so overtired and run down that I caught every bug going around. To top that off, Billy and I were struggling. I'd missed all of his races and couldn't go to any of the senior functions he'd expected me attend, leaving him openly bitter about my absences. I was frustrated with him because he had morphed from supportive boyfriend into party frat boy. I hated the change.

I spent the weekend before his graduation immersed in textbooks and writing papers; my parents and Billy's family were coming down at the end of the week, and I wanted to dedicate as much time to them as I could. I hadn't seen my boyfriend in days, so when he knocked at my door early Sunday morning, I was surprised. That surprise grew to worry when I opened my door. There were giant black smudges under his pale gray eyes, sweat dotted his forehead, and his skin was a light yellow. I'd never seen him look so unhealthy. I was terrified that he was sick.

Before I could react, his arms surrounded me and he yanked me him, declaring how much he loved me. Then after shutting my door and sitting on my bed, he ran his hands through that beautiful curly blond hair and told me about his mistakes over the last few weeks. He'd been seeing someone else. When he'd woken that morning and seen her and not me, he'd run straight to me to beg my forgiveness. He vowed to spend the rest of his life making it up to me, if I could forgive him just that once. He'd gotten down on his hands and knees, showing me the most beautiful diamond ring. The princess-cut single-carat stone shone in the light. He claimed he'd gotten it months before and had been waiting for the right moment.

That was not the right moment. It couldn't have been a worse time.

It took me a few minutes for his words to sink in. I fell to the floor because my legs couldn't support me anymore, not even to walk to the chair. Not my Billy. We weren't like those other couples. We didn't fight. We didn't cheat.

Yet, Billy had.

I needed to know how many times it had happened, but I was afraid to ask. I couldn't wrap my head around the words he was saying, and eventually drowned him out completely. Instead, my mind replayed all of those times that I'd seen another girl smile knowingly at him, or look at me with pity. I'd assumed I was reading too much into them, that it was my insecurities shining through. So, I'd stayed quiet.

I had been a damn fool. Not wanting to hear another word out of his lying mouth, I told him to leave. Instead, he'd sat next to me and pulled me into his arms, telling me over and over that he was sorry. I did what any young girl in love would do—I forgave him.

Stupid, clueless girl.

The memory devastated me. If only that girl hadn't given in, hadn't forgiven him, hadn't built a life with him, I wouldn't be where I was.

I needed to vent—to get everything I'd been holding in, out. I couldn't say the words yet because then it would be real. My marriage wasn't over—we just needed to regroup and figure out how to move forward.

Will needed some time to to get his shit together and his head on straight. I wanted time to learn to forgive him. More important was that we had to spend time away from each other to remember how we felt about the other. Absence makes the heart grow fonder and all that jazz. We could save this.

I wasn't sure I wanted to.

I was sure that I needed a good weep. A full-blown pity party breakdown was due. There was nothing wrong with crying. It didn't mean I'd given up, it just meant I needed an outlet for my feelings.

I needed sad music or a Hallmark movie and a pint of Ben & Jerry's. I'd exhaust myself with tears and start over in the morning. Having a plan made pulling into the hotel alone much more bearable.

Not finding anything sappy enough on cable, I pulled out my laptop, changed into pjs, and ordered Thai from my favorite restaurant. I was twenty minutes into *The Notebook* when my phone rang. Pressing pause, I sat up and answered.

"What are you doing?"

I smiled. Normal people would say hi or ask how I was—not him. "I'm about to watch a movie. Thought I'd lay down and try to get rid of this headache."

Matty had left the office a few hours before I did, but it had been obvious I was getting a migraine.

"Oh." He had a tone I couldn't place. "You gonna watch it alone?"

Not sure why he was asking, I nodded knowing he couldn't see me. "Mhm."

"I just got home from grocery shopping."

I wondered for a brief minute if all of our conversations were this weird or if I was overly easy to annoy because I was cranky.

"I ran into Billy and asked him if you were feeling any better."

My heart sank.

"Imagine my surprise when he told me he didn't know. Then picture the look of shock on his face when he realized I didn't know why he wouldn't know. Why in the hell didn't you tell me?"

There wasn't a good answer. I told Matty everything. But I hadn't told him this because I didn't want anyone to know. "I...I..." I fought for words, not knowing what to say. Nothing I could tell him would make him feel any better. Honesty was the best bet. "I don't know. I guess..." There was a knock on my door. "Shit. Hold on a second, okay?"

I grabbing my wallet off the little table by the entrance and yanked open the door. Instead of finding the normal delivery guy, I came face-to-face with my best friend. He narrowed his eyes slightly and held up my bag of Thai. When I didn't say anything, he moved past me into the room, dropped the bag on the coffee table, and turned to face me. "I brought food."

I shut the door, leaned against it, and tossed wallet and phone on the stand. "I was expecting the food. Not you."

"Yeah. So you can sulk. But what fun is eating takeout alone in a dark and depressing hotel room"—he turned back to the table and pulled out a takeout box—"when you could be sharing the same takeout with your best friend?" After grabbing the fork out of the bag, he lifted the Styrofoam container, opening it as he walked to the couch and sat down. "Come sit and eat with me."

I didn't move. The chicken pad Thai smelled heavenly, and my stomach growled in defiance. "How'd you know where I was?"

The ass slurped a forkful of noodles before answering. "Billy." He twirled his fork in the box, pulling out another heaping pile. "He was extremely surprised to learn that I didn't know where you were or what was going on. He wouldn't tell me much." He took a bite and chewed. "But he did tell me you were here when I insisted I wanted to check on you." He swallowed loudly. "I'm hungry enough to eat it all"—he held up the container again—"but I'll gladly share with you if you hurry."

I glared at him. That was my food and this was my sulk night. I was going to eat junk food, not care if I got fat, and watch heartbreaking love stories until I cried myself to sleep. No part of that included the goofy buffoon sitting on *my* couch eating *my* noodles. "Why are you here?" My tone was terse.

"Because you need me." He shrugged. "If someone"—he gave me a sharp look—"had let me do my job, I'd have been here earlier."

"I don't want you here." I was sure I hadn't thrown a full-blown temper tantrum reminiscent of a two-year-old in almost thirty years, but I was pretty close to having one then.

He leaned forward and put the container on the table before standing. He'd changed from his dress pants and shirt into a pair of jeans and a black Harley tee, one that showcased the glorious ink he he had covering both arms. I cautiously watched as walked toward me for a few seconds before I realized that he was leaving and that I was in his way. I stepped to the side, away from the door, surprisingly sad at the idea of being alone.

He didn't reach for the door. Instead, his hand grabbed my upper arm and yanked me against him. Solid arms came around me, holding me tight. My face was squished into his chest and I had to turn my head so I could breathe.

He was so warm that I didn't try to resist; instead I melted into him, trying to drive away the chill that went to my bones. His chin came down on my head, enveloping me, sheltering me from my reality. I couldn't remember the last time I'd been held, and the thought devastated me because Will used to hold me all the time.

Before. Before we fell out of love. Before my world fell apart. Before *her.*

Tears burned my eyes. One of Matty's giant hands cupped the side of my head, covering my ear and holding me closer. He was talking. I could hear the rumble in his chest but couldn't decipher the words. It was such a soothing gesture, and it made me miss my husband.

As soon as the thought hit me, I realized that Will probably didn't reciprocate those feelings. In fact, he was probably holding another woman at that exact moment.

It was too much to bear. I threw my arms around Matty and bawled like a baby. He pulled me even closer, giving me the support he knew I needed.

He never let go. Not while I sobbed, shook, and tried to catch my breath. If it had been anyone other than Matt, I would probably have felt like an idiot. But he knew me better than most.

After an eternity, he pulled back, moving his hands to my cheeks and tipping my face up toward his, the rings on his hand were cold against my hot skin. Leaning forward, he kissed my forehead. It was unexpected and sweet, and I could feel my eyes filling with water again.

His met mine, searching. "I'm right here."

I nodded. A runaway tear escaped down my cheek, but his thumb caught it, wiping it away.

"Hey. Shh. Shh." He pulled me close again, this time his hand rubbing my back, soothing me.

My stomach growled loudly, making us both laugh.

"Ugh." I groaned. "I'm a mess." I stepped back, breaking our embrace, and ran my hands over my face.

Some women could cry and look absolutely stunning, both during and after. I was not one of them. I was an ugly crier. I knew my face was red and tear-stained and my hair was a rat's nest. I just didn't care.

When Matty looked down at me, it was as if he didn't see the wreck in front of him. Grabbing my hand, he gave it a squeeze. "Let's get you some dinner."

I felt better than I had in days. Weeks maybe. Matty was on one end of my couch and I was on the other, my legs stretched on the cushion between us. We'd enjoyed dinner, chatting while we ate, talking about everything from pop culture to office gossip. I knew he was trying to keep me distracted, and I appreciated the gesture.

The breakdown had calmed me and given me the clarity and peace I always felt after a good cry. Sitting there with my best friend, talking about normal things, made me feel like me again. It was nice.

Matt hadn't mentioned Will, yet I could tell by the way one of his eyebrows arched every time I broke the silence, as if he was preparing himself for whatever I was going to say, that he had questions. I didn't know how to start that conversation, but I knew I needed to say *something*. The elephant in the room was taking up so much space, it made me more uncomfortable than talking about my failing marriage ever could.

"I don't know where to start." I blurted out suddenly.

Eyes that reminded me of the ocean on a calm breezy day searched my face. "How about at the beginning? That's always a great place to start."

I snorted. "I don't think you have that much time."

He grabbed my big toe in a playful manner, giving it a reassuring squeeze. "I've got all night. Take as long as you need."

There was so much more to it though. I sighed. "I don't know if I can talk to you about Will."

Matt's eyes narrowed slightly and he crossed his arms over his chest. "Why not?"

"Because you're our friend. I refuse to put you in the middle. I don't want you to feel like you have to take sides."

His forehead creased as he frowned at me. "I'm not his friend, Jo. I'm yours." He sounded almost angry.

I shook my head, ready to argue. I'd been where he was. I refused to force him into that position. "Mat-,"

He cut me off. "No. Nothing you can say right now will change that." He glanced away from me, twisting his lips. "I think he's a total asshat. You, I care about. I don't give two shits what in the fuck happens to the douche you're married to. I'm here to support you—end of story." He adjusted himself on the couch, bending a knee and pulling one of his legs onto the center cushion with mine. "You're here"—he motioned around my room—"so obviously something serious happened. Can you please just tell me what in the hell is going on? Because right now, my imagination is running wild and I want to kill him."

I stared at him, trying to figure out if he was being sincere, still unsure of where to start.

When I didn't answer right away, he lifted a hand to his chin and pinched his chin. "Is it me? Are you fighting because of me?"

I wanted to groan. Or throw something at him. "Good lord, you really are self-absorbed sometimes. The world doesn't revolve around you. You know that, right?" I sounded harsher than I meant to, but he was something else. "Not everything is about you." I sat up, dropping one foot to the floor and pulling the other closer to me.

Anger flashed in his eyes and he shot me a dangerous look. "I know that!" He argued "That isn't what I meant. Billy's a guy, and sometimes men can sense..." He snapped his mouth closed, shaking his head slightly. He turned away, but I could tell I'd hit a nerve by the way his jaw ticked. After a few seconds he squinted at me over his shoulder. "I know how Taylor feels about us being so close. I imagine that Billy feels the same way."

I shook my head. "That would mean he'd actually have to pay attention to me and what I'm doing."

I pushed myself off the couch and walked to the mini-fridge, desperate to delay the conversation. I grabbed a bottle of water and held it up, tossing it to him when he nodded, before grabbing another for me. It was a long story that I didn't want to share, but I knew needed to.

"Will cheated on me while we were in college."

Matty couldn't hide the disgusted surprise on his face. I fell onto the couch, folded my legs under me, and told him the whole sordid truth. The words I didn't want to admit to me, let alone my friend, were bitter on my lips, but I got them out.

"People cheat. I know that. We're not monogamous creatures," I lifted my shoulder. "I told him I would forgive him that once, because we all make mistakes. But, if it ever happened again, I would leave."

I bit my lip. It was harder to say the next words than to think them, but I needed to explain, desperate to defend my husband. "Our love life has never been normal. When it's good, it's great, and nothing can touch us. When it's bad, it's awful. Sometimes we go months without him touching me. If I try to initiate anything sexual, he complains that I'm too needy or just pushes me away. It is such a blow to my ego." I took a deep breath. It killed me when Will didn't want me to touch him, and I couldn't begin to count the nights that I'd cried myself to sleep because of his refusals.

"The first time was after I had Benjamin. I'd gained a ton of weight through the pregnancy, and when Will didn't want to have sex, I assumed it was because I'd gotten fat. I was too tired to exercise, so I went on an extreme diet. I was convinced that if I was smaller, if I could fit into my pre-pregnancy clothes, that he would want me again. He didn't."

Matt tensed beside me, his fists clenching.

"I took that rejection harder than the others. I'd worked my ass off to lose the weight for him, yet he didn't care. I still repulsed him. I got so depressed that I blew the diet, ate junk, and got bigger. I was shocked a few months later when he couldn't keep his hands off of me. He said he loved my curves."

I laughed bitterly. "That became the vicious cycle of our lives. When he was in a funk, he didn't even want to hug me. And instead of getting mad at him, I pointed that anger inward, chastising myself, trying every diet I could think of. When he continued to ignore me, and I'd yoyo and gain more weight. And then I'd hate myself." I hated myself for the way I'd acted. "You know that the doctor told me I needed to lose the weight or I would be insulin dependent by forty."

Of course he knew. I'd gone to work crying after that appointment, and Matty had been my biggest supporter. He'd run pavement with me, gone to the gym on our lunch break, and helped me stick to a diabetic diet. With his help, I'd lost sixty of the extra pounds I had packed on since Ben's birth. And he had helped me keep most of it off.

"During all my changes, I came to terms with Will's behavior. I woke up one morning and realized that it was his issue, not mine. I needed to get healthy for me and the kids, and if it made my sex life better, then it was an unexpected benefit. If it didn't, I wasn't going to worry about it.

"Part of me always thought that if I lost the weight, the old Will would appear and we'd be okay. When that didn't happen, I begged him to get help for his..." I stumbled, not sure what word to use. "issues. He talked to a doctor, but nothing changed. Will was never mean to me. He wasn't cruel. He is just indifferent. That killed me. I wanted him to notice that I was making this huge change in my life and that it would ultimately be a huge change in *our* life.

"When he didn't, I got passive aggressive. I got upset of the dumbest things. In turn, he'd get mad at me over equally stupid shit. For the last six months, we've been at each other's throat constantly. We've argued about everything, even things we never argued about before. Like how to parent the kids, how to spend our money, and our jobs. He'd been working on a mysterious big project that he never talks about and he was gone practically all the time. When he was home, he was annoyed with me constantly.

"In early May, his parents asked if they could take the kids over summer break. I guess Will had told them he was working extra hours, and with my schedule, they wanted to help. We never see them since they moved, and we thought it was a great idea. After talking about it, we decided to send the kids to his parents' for the first six weeks and then to mine for the last six. I looked at it as a chance to work on us. I was convinced that we'd have a chance to go on dates and get to know each other again. I was positive that we would fall back in love.

"Instead, we grew further apart. It seemed to happen overnight. One day I realized that we weren't talking about anything anymore, not even the kids, and somewhere along the way, we'd stopped laughing with each other and them. I was miserable. By the time school was over, the kids knew something was wrong. I tried to hide it, but children are smart. They pick up on the subtleties adults sometimes miss. I didn't want them to know, so I happily packed them and sent them away, just so they wouldn't be caught in the middle.

"The night his parents came into town, Will stayed at work all night. He claimed that he had to finish his presentation. I knew better. He never missed the chance to see his parents. He likes to put on a show, make people think everything is perfect. Maybe he was afraid they'd realize something was wrong. Maybe he just didn't care. He came home the next morning, showered, and ate breakfast with us all before the kids left. He kissed them and his mom good-bye, and as soon as they pulled out of the driveway, he left too. He acted like I wasn't there, which I foolishly chalked up to him being preoccupied with the presentation.

"I was getting ready for work when I found his phone tucked in the towels. I didn't go through it—that thought never crossed my mind. I put it with mine so I could take drop it off before I headed to the office. While I was in the shower, he came home. I was so happy to see him, excited, thinking about what we were going to do with no kids around." I didn't want to say any more. I didn't want to admit his mistakes, let alone my own foolishness. "He started to yell, angry that I'd moved his cell. He demanded to know what I'd looked at, what I'd seen."

I took a deep breath, trying to steady my breathing. I refused to cry over him again, yet my heart was tearing wide open again, the shock and pain too strong. "I didn't want to fight with him, so I jokingly asked him what was so important in his phone that I couldn't see. I made some comment about pictures of naked women or dirty text messages, because that's the last thing Will would have on his phone. His face got red, and I knew." I could see him now, standing in the middle of our kitchen in his pristine suit, his face the color of an apple, sputtering.

Matty hadn't moved, barely breathing. "He cheated."

I nodded. "He'd been cheating. For months." I smiled, even though there was nothing remotely amusing or happy about the situation. "He sat at our kitchen table, looked me right in the eye, and told me he loved her. She makes him laugh. She's a happy, sexy, fun person who always has time for him." The bitterness in my tone was clear. "Of course she is. She doesn't have two kids and a husband to clean up after or any responsibilities that tie her down."

"You know who she is?" Matt's tone was a mixture of surprise and anger.

I nodded. "Yeah. Her name is Rachel. They work together. I've met her at corporate outings, and I really liked her. The kids thought the world of her. And, Will's right. She is beautiful and young and fun. She is everything I am not." I chewed on my bottom lip. So many things about this made me made angry. "Everyone knows he's married and has a family! Someone they work with will figure it out. As much as I would love to blame her for getting involved with a married man, it's his fault. He took a vow, he made promises, and he broke them.

"He tried to validate it, of course, telling me that he couldn't help whom he loves. Maybe he can't. Maybe I can't help that I love him still. However, he had complete control over his body. He didn't have to kiss her. He didn't have to sleep with her. Not when he had me, right here, begging him to touch me."

I lifted a hand toward my friend. "What is it about me that repulsed him so much? Why didn't he want me? Can you please tell me from the male perspective?"

Matty slid closer, looping his arm around my shoulders. "I don't know, Joes. I don't fucking get it. I don't understand why anyone would put energy into a new relationship when they could put the same energy into saving their marriage. I cannot imagine why anyone would give up their family for an infatuation. I had to start over and it almost destroyed me. I can't fathom doing it by choice."

"There's one difference between you and Will. He—"

"Yeah," He scoffed, cutting me off. "There's a hell of a lot more than that! I think I know where you're going, and don't you dare." He straightened, agitation clear. "You were right when you realized Billy's problems were his own. They're still his own. He'd have cheated if you hadn't been angry with him or if you looked different. A man who loves his wife doesn't love her body—he loves her soul. Don't you take his shit on and make yourself feel worse." His face softened. "This is not your fault."

I knew that. Really. But my head was in a constant conflict with my heart.

"Why are you here instead of him? Why didn't you kick his cheating ass out?"

I wrinkled my nose "I couldn't stay there. How could I sleep in my bed not knowing if she'd been there?"

"Why didn't you ask?"

"I didn't want to know. I still don't. It doesn't matter. I can't change the past. That truth will only make me more upset. As soon as he told me, I ran upstairs, packed the things I knew I'd need, told him I was coming here, and I left. I haven't talked to him since."

There. I sighed. It was out. It wasn't a secret anymore.

"He hasn't called?" Matty's voice dripped with doubt.

"Oh, he's called. My cell, the room, work. I just don't answer. I don't want to talk right now."

"I can talk to him for you if you want." He smirked. "With my fist."

I laughed. Leaning into him, I dropped my head onto his shoulder and let his arms pull me tight. Matty always knew what I needed.

"I'm serious. It wouldn't hurt my feelings at all."

"Thanks for offering, but I'll talk to him soon enough."

"Not too soon though. Make the fucker sweat it out."

FOUR

"You're feeling better." The excited statement was followed by a little squeal and a clap.

I couldn't help but smile at Teagan as she slid into my cubicle and sat on Matty's filing cabinet. My headache *was* gone. For the first time in days, I was listening to music while I caught up work. I pulled off my headphones, and turned to face her.

Teagan Murphy-Jones was one of my favorite co-workers. She'd been a caseworker with the department since she'd earned her degree, had seen it all, and was one of the women who had terrified me when I first started. Not only did she have a great physical presence, but she also had a bullshit monitor that could detect a lie from ten miles out and had no tolerance for anyone who even tried to get one past her.

Teagan was tall, almost six feet, with legs that went on for miles and shoulders that were wide enough to carry the weight of the world. But it was her hair that made her stand out. Curly and naturally mahogany, it was breathtaking and the envy of every woman around. She once told me that she had gotten her looks from her dad, who got his from his Celtic warrior grandfather. Seemed legit, but sometimes a person had to take what Teagan said with a grain of salt. That BS gauge of hers worked well for a reason.

"Is it that obvious?"

She grinned. "Your color isn't all pasty." She wrinkled her nose and made a face. "You don't look like you might start crying at any second." She tipped her head sideways,.. "Basically, you don't look like shit."

Coming from anyone else, it might have been an insult. Teagan always told it like it was.

"Thanks," I laughed.

Her eyes moved over Matty's empty desk. "Where's Biker Boy?"

"Court."

Her dark brown eyebrows raised in silent question.

"Contested TPR," I explained.

"He'll be there all day." The disappointment in her voice was barely masked, but I nodded.

Terminating a parent's rights to their child was a hard decision for a child welfare team to make and an even harder court hearing for a caseworker to testify at. After over a decade at this job, I still didn't know what was worse: a contested hearing where a parent lost their child against their will or a parent voluntarily giving up their child. I couldn't imagine the pain of having to do either.

"So," she continued, "since he's gone, want to do lunch with me? We can catch up."

"Absolutely. When are you leaving?"

She stood. "Now."

We settled on a favorite local pub. The restaurant was on the second floor and had a covered deck that overlooked the river. We sat out there, enjoying the bright and warm summer day.

Teagan always had the best stories. A single mom with two teenage girls, she had just entered the dating scene again, only to find it severely lacking. The men she met, and the problems she had, would have been the perfect comedy relief in any movie. When she told me about her latest date failure, I laughed until my sides hurt.

"Have you or Billy talked to the kids recently?" She took a bite of her sandwich and waited for me to catch my breath.

"I talk to them every night." I smiled. "They're having a blast—getting spoiled by Grandma and keeping busy." Smiling, I relayed Lily's stories of meeting the fairies and Belle at Disney World, and Ben's excitement over seeing St. Augustine. I picked at my salad. "I miss them and wish I could be there with them." I'd been so focused on my problems with Will that I hadn't realized just how much I missed my littles.

She snorted. "Enjoy the break, kid. Right now you can go home and nap, or read a book, or go to the beach and actually lay in the sun without someone annoying you every five seconds. Before you know it, they'll be back home and driving you nuts. You'll be up to your eyebrows in laundry, running to football practice and field hockey, and mediating fights. And telling them they're too young to date." She waved a fry in my direction. "I'm jealous. Do you know what my two heathens are up to now?"

She relayed the girls' shenanigans, making me laugh again. The company was as good as the food, and lunchtime flew by. As we walked back to the office, I realized that life was finally getting back to normal.

I was surprised to see Matt at his desk when I got back.

"Court on lunch?" I asked after I greeted him.

"Nope. We won. Dad's case was weak, and Judge G saw right through it." His relief was clear. The case had been a rough one for him, and I was thankful for him that it was over. "I drove out to the Smiths' right after court to give them the news in person. They are beyond excited. Pam cried."

Teddy and Pamela Smith were some of the best foster parents I had ever worked with. When Matty placed Todd, a two-year-old who had been severely physically abused, with them almost two years ago, they had fallen in love. Of course they had—the doe-eyed blond was so small he was mistaken for a child half his age and stole your heart the moment he smiled at you. As a result of their gentle guidance and constant love, Todd was now a feisty little four-year-old.

Matty had worried about this TPR hearing for weeks. Todd's dad had made some great progress over the last several months and while there was no doubt that he deeply regretted what had happened and cared about his son, he was still failing random drug tests and had not completed a single anger management classes. If he won and the court didn't terminate his rights, Todd's adoption would be delayed and Matty would have to start facing the possibility that Todd might have to go back to live with the man who had hurt him.

Todd loved his biological parents and still saw his mom, who had voluntarily terminated her rights last year. To Todd, they were only people he visited with once in a while. The Smiths were his parents. I was glad it was finally over, for everyone involved.

"Oh, Matty! That's fantastic news! If I'd known, I would have waited to go to lunch. We could have celebrated."

"I'm actually headed out early, but why don't you come over for a celebration dinner tonight?"

That actually sounded fun. Something unusual to get me out of the tiny hotel room. "What time?"

"Six. Will that work?"

"Yep. What can I bring?"

"Preferably not Will." He gave me a small smile when I laughed. "Just bring you, Jo. That's all I want."

28

FIVE

I was a few minutes early, but I didn't think Matty or Taylor would care. There weren't any other cars in their driveway, so either I was the first one there or the only one coming. I parked behind Taylor's gorgeous silver Audi TTS coupe. I had to give it to her—her taste in cars was as good as her taste in men. For a brief second, I allowed myself to be jealous of both of the beautiful things that belonged to her.

Then I imagined trying to fit both kids and all their gear in the sporty little two-door that barely had a backseat. I could see it now, very similar to a game of phone booth, where I had to buckle in each child then pack their backpacks and sports equipment on and around them. I laughed picturing a field hockey stick hanging out of the passenger window and Lily's little face peering at me from the backseat, the rest of her buried underneath stuff while I tried to pacify her by saying it was okay because at least Mommy had a cool car.

Nope, I'd stick with my Dodge. I unbuckled and grabbed the shopping bag off the seat next to me. I refused to show up empty-handed, no matter what Matty had said, so I'd stopped at the local bakery and bought a bouquet of summer flowers and a box of Matty's favorite cannoli. It was a celebration, after all. I'd thought about buying wine for the lady of the house, but I was a vodka girl and didn't know the difference between white and red, or which went with what food. Taylor would definitely have some sort of alcoholic beverage if Sam wasn't here.

I couldn't remember if it was Matty's weekend to have his son or not, but I hoped it was. The idea made me perk up a little. I adored that kid.

A few steps away from the house I paused, just for a second, and smiled at the adorable house in front of me. The small T-shaped ranch with an attached two-door garage had come a long way in the two years since Matt had bought it. The first time I'd been there, I had actually been afraid to go inside.

I was rooted to the ground, appalled as I gaped at the shack Matty hadn't stopped talking about for days. It was a dump. Half of the shingle siding was falling off and the paint was peeling, the metal roof was dented and destroyed, and I doubted it could barely keep out the rain, the front door was hanging by only the top hinge, and the steps were rotted away. What I could see of the backyard told me it was filled with weeds and grass taller than me, giving it an eerie Children of the Corn *feeling.*

I had turned to my delusional friend, shaken my head, and backed up. "Someone was murdered here."

Matty's proud and excited smile vanished and his eyes moved from me to his realtor. "Really?"

I lifted my hand and pointed toward the disaster in front of us. "Just look at it. It's like a scene from a horror movie!"

For a brief moment he'd stared down at me, the sides of his lips quirking as he fought the smirk. He grabbed my hand. "I promise I'll protect you."

Before I could argue with his patronizing tone, he was striding toward the house of horrors, pulling me behind him and into the bowels of hell.

The inside wasn't much better, yet it wasn't as creepy as I had assumed it would be. Matty was oblivious to the destruction in front of us. He tugged me from room to room, pointing out the solid structure and explaining his plans, I was fascinated. When we left an hour later, I no longer saw the shabby little run-down shack, but instead the home he had been determined to create.

He had built it. The shingles had been replaced with vinyl siding, the metal roof exchanged for shingles, and a beautiful front porch added. He'd transformed the terrifying backyard into a wonderful fenced-in area with gardens and a swing set.

It had taken us weeks, but we'd gutted the entire home, then Matty had built it back from scratch. He'd designed the open floor plan, laid hardwood floors in every room but the bathrooms, installed gorgeous cabinets in the kitchen, and added a sunroom. It was a perfect home for a man and his little boy.

I loved it here.

I paused on the front stoop, about to knock, when Matty pulled open the door and stepped out to greet me. He smiled warmly before his arms closed around me and he held me tight.

"Matt! Don't maul our guest before she even gets through the door!" Taylor's voice, although casual, held a note of annoyance.

Matty stood back, winking at me before glancing into the bag he lifted from my fingers. "Look, Tay, Jo brought desert!"

Taylor scowled at the pastry box as we walked further into the kitchen. "Isn't that nice?" Her irritated pitch betrayed her words. "You'll have to go for a super long run tomorrow if you eat those. One has more calories than an entire meal. And, at your age, the weight doesn't melt off anymore."

I wanted to roll my eyes. Neither of us needed a reminder about age, especially not from the child in front of us. And I sure as hell didn't a reminder about weight.

I forced my lips up instead. "Yeah, but it's a celebration." I looked from her to Matt and couldn't help myself. "I can totally come run with you if you're going to go for a long one. Or"—I smiled as I saw his lips twitch—"we can go for a run in the morning and then a hike in the afternoon. I'm free all day."

Taylor stepped closer to Matt, her hand resting on his arm possessively, and sent me one of her fake smiles. "No need. We have plans, but I'll make sure he gets plenty of exercise tonight." With a toss of her hair, she turned and left the room.

Matty looked from the place she'd been standing and back to me, as if not sure what to say, before deciding a change of subject was in order. "I'll go throw the steaks on."

He grabbed a covered plate, which I assumed had the marinating meat, and headed out the back door. *Great. Leave me with the beast, you brat.*

I smiled at Taylor when she appeared again. "What can I do to help?"

"Nothing." She moved her left hand as if to sweep away my question, and my eye caught the glint of a ring on her hand. She giggled at my questioning stare. "Oh, okay." She slid next to me, holding out her left hand. "I know I'm not supposed to be wearing it, and Matt wanted to keep it on the DL around you because of the whole Billy thing, but isn't it beautiful?"

It was. I'd never seen a diamond that large on a real person before. Her fingers were as tiny as the rest of her, but it took up the whole finger.

I fought to keep my mouth from falling open in shock as I met her eyes, not sure what to say. Not only was it a surprise to see the engagement ring, she obviously knew Will and I were having problems.

"Congratulations?" I knew my voice and expression betrayed me and told her I wasn't happy for her at all.

31

She pouted. "Oh, Jo! I know this must be hard for you, but come on. Be happy for us!"

"Hard for me?" I asked, unease working its way through me. "You mean because of the Will thing?" I tried to keep the agitation hidden. I failed. I had been convinced that Matty would realize the type of person she really was and would leave before he proposed. Instead, he'd told her my secrets. I felt like a fool.

Trying to cover my disappointment, I snatched the bouquet and walked to the cupboard where Matty kept his vases, desperate to keep my hands busy so they didn't start to shake.

"Well, yes." She started slowly. "I know that you two are having trouble. That and—"

"You're so sweet to worry about me." I interrupted her. "Actually, I talked to Will on the phone earlier." I forced a smile as I turned toward her. "We had a nice long chat," I lied, forcing the memories of the actual conversation away. "It's all going to be okay."

"You did?"

I hadn't heard Matty come back in. I turned toward his voice. He was leaning in the doorway, one foot propped over the other, his arms crossed over his chest.

I gave him the happiest smile I could fake. "Congratulations!"

He didn't move, yet his eyes sliced to Taylor. "I thought we agreed that you wouldn't wear that tonight?"

She only beamed back at him.

His eyes came back to me. "When did you talk to Billy?" He looked pissed, but I couldn't tell if he was mad at me or his finance.

"Earlier." I was being vague on purpose.

His nostrils flared. He was mad. He didn't need to say the words because I could always tell when Matt was upset with me. His body language screamed the truth.

I took a deep breath. Turning back to the cupboard, I picked a large lead crystal vase and filled it with water. "Obviously we have a lot to talk about, but I really feel like everything is going to be okay. He wanted to go out to dinner tonight." I turned, carrying the flowers and water back to the island. "I told him my plans were too important to cancel, so we're having dinner tomorrow night. Looks like it's been a good news kinda afternoon."

Matty's breath came fast, and his jaw moved back and forth. I waited for his opinion to come barreling out, but he remained silent, eyes never moving from mine. Finally, he stood up. "Yeah. I'll go check dinner." And he was gone.

There was a tension in the air I couldn't explain. Thankful for the distraction, I leaned against the counter, opening the flowers and arranging them in the water. "So? Any concrete wedding plans?" I didn't care really. I needed her constant babble to drown out the pounding of my heart though.

"Wow. How'd you get him to come back?"

It took a second for her words to sink in. I straightened and jerked my body toward her, on alert. "Excuse me?"

"Matt told me what happened." Her disdain was clear. "I'm just curious what magic words you said to Billy to make him want to come back. Did you bribe him? Blackmail? "

I shook my head in disbelief. There hadn't been any magic words. Dinner had been Will's idea. One that I didn't agree with and one I longed to avoid. It was his, "I love you, I miss you!" in the middle of the conversation that made me feel obligated to go see him. If he truly wanted to work on us, I would try, too.

"Okay. Maybe you really are dumber than you look, but you have to know that now that he's freed himself from you, Billy isn't going to wake up one morning and realize he made a mistake. A man like him isn't going to come running back to a woman like you. You do know that, right?

I took a deep breath, trying to center myself and not react to her vicious words. "I'm not sure what Matty told you, but it wasn't Will who left. I needed some time away. We had a problem, and like a real married couple, we're going to work through it."

"Matt," she stressed the word, correcting me, "told me everything you told him. Like he always does." She smirked triumphantly as my face fell. "There are no secrets between my fiancé and me. I get that you're used to having a marriage where lies and cheating are acceptable, normal problems that real marriages have, as you claim. But, that isn't the norm. Mine isn't going to be like that."

Matty would never cheat; loyalty was everything to him. "You're right. Will made some mistakes, but Matty isn't Will. You don't need to worry."

"Oh, I'm not worried about my fiancé." Her voice was ice cold. "I'm not worried at all. But I want you to know where you stand. There is no room for you in Matty's and my relationship. Whatever you think you're doing, stop now. Before you embarrass yourself."

I laughed. She was really something else. "Maybe it's you who doesn't get it. Matty and I are just friends."

"Sure. And that's what Billy thinks too, right? You and Matt are just good friends with no other feelings getting in the way?"

I tried to hide it, but knew the truth showed on my face.

"There is no such thing as a man and a woman being just friends, Jo. Someone always feels something they shouldn't, and someone always gets hurt. You may not understand it now, but I'm really watching out for you by making these changes."

My mind was working in overdrive as I tried to connect the dots. "What changes?"

"I won't let my marriage fail because of you. I've talked to Matt, and he agrees. We need to focus on us, and you and your drama need to be gone from our lives." She moved her hand, as if pushing me out. "We both know you're in love with him. And as pathetic as you chasing after a married man is, you need to figure it out on your own."

"You're delusional." I shook my head in disbelief.

"No, I'm not. The only one imagining things here is you. Did you think that Matty would leave me for you?" She sounded appalled. "Have you actually looked at yourself lately? Honey, I can promise you, if you can't keep your own husband in your bed, you sure as hell won't be able to get mine there. After tonight—"

"Taylor!" I'd never heard Matt bellow, but that was the only way I could describe the sound he made. The glass plate he'd held made a hollow noise as he shoved it across the dining room table, before stomping toward us. "What in the fuck is going on?"

My eyes darted between them. Taylor had straightened, standing at her full height, almost as if in challenge. Her face wasn't red, her breath wasn't coming faster, and she showed no outward signs of concern. She wasn't scared of him or upset that he'd walked in on this conversation.

Matt, on the other hand, looked as if he'd just seen a ghost. His face had lost all color, and his body almost vibrated in unbridled emotion. I didn't know if it was in fear or anger, but it was clear that these two had obviously had this conversation before. My heart sank.

Not only had my best friend told his girlfriend, a person he knew I hated, the most personal details of my life, but he'd talked about cutting me out of his. I was shocked. Nothing had prepared me for that revelation.

I took a deep breath. I wanted to demand answers from him. To tell him he couldn't get rid of me that easily. We'd been friends long before his girlfriend had come into the picture.

Worst of all was the feeling of ultimate dread creeping in. Will's cheating hadn't hurt this much. On some level, I had always expected my husband to leave me. Matty, on the other hand, was the friend I was going to have until the end.

A life without my husband didn't seem nearly as lonely as a life without Matty. I was that pathetic. I looked up, meeting his worry-filled eyes and realization stabbed me in the gut.

Taylor was right. My feelings for Matt crossed a line. Maybe I wasn't in love with him like she was, but I did love him. And I was definitely attracted to him. I just hadn't realized how obvious that was to everyone except me.

I needed to get my shit together and leave, yet I couldn't look away. I wanted to hug him, tell him I was sorry, and explain that I hadn't realized until that moment. I longed to beg him for forgiveness.

Instead, I forced myself to let him go. "Congratulations, Matty. It was a good win today." I turned to Taylor, who looked delighted. "I have to go." I practically ran for the door.

"Jo!" Matty came across the kitchen and was reaching for me. "What are—?"

I paused, long enough to reach out and squeeze his hand. "Good-bye."

I had never been so thankful for a half-circle driveway before. All I had to do was back up a little, put my car in first, and punch the gas. My heart beat fast as I drove back to my hotel. I thought about calling Will and telling him I'd changed my mind, or even driving straight home and begging him to let me come back.

Neither of those options were what I really wanted, and they only muddy the water even more. Instead, I turned up my music, silenced the ringer on my phone, and tried to convince myself that change was good.

I had other friends. I could transfer into a different unit at work. I would be fine.

I didn't believe a word of it.

There weren't a lot of nights when the idea of being alone was appealing. I usually hated the idea of going back to my hotel. Tonight though, both seemed wonderful. I didn't want to be around anyone.

As soon as I parked, I shot out of my car, leaving everything but my keys and cellphone behind. I couldn't care less if someone stole my purse. I stole a glance at the dark screen before shoving my phone into my back pocket. Matty hadn't called. Not that I thought he would, but I was just so used to him always being there, constantly checking on me, that it made me a little sad.

I was so lost in thought, so absorbed in my own head, that I never heard the bike roaring into the hotel lot. It wasn't until it stopped directly in front of me, blocking my path, that I looked up.

Matty stretched his booted leg out, bracing the bike upright, and cut the motor. "You okay?"

I forced a smile. At least, I hoped it looked like a smile. "Yep. A-Okay." I gave him an overly exaggerated thumbs-up. "You can go now."

"Jo." His voice held a warning note that I rarely heard.

"Go home to your fiancée, Matt. She'll come hunt you down if you don't." I looked at the street, half convinced I'd see Taylor's Audi speeding toward us.

"She knows where I am."

I swallowed, my face falling as I remembered Taylor's words from earlier. "Of course she does. Because you two tell each other everything, right?"

"Joes." He scrubbed his face with one hand, and for a brief moment I saw the confusion and worry on his face.

Wanting to reassure him, I took a deep breath and plastered a smile I didn't feel onto my face. "It's okay. You and I, we're good. You don't need to check up on me anymore. I'm a big girl, with a husband of my own. You can assure Taylor that I won't be stealing hers anymore."

He shifted, pushing his shoulders back. "Taylor doesn't have a husband yet. You're my best friend. I'm yours. Right now, that means that I do need to check up on you. Even if it pisses her off."

He wasn't hearing a word I said. "I don't need you, Matty. You can leave. I have plans."

He squinted. "Did you call Billy?"

Jesus, he was annoyingly persistent. Shaking my head, I admitted, "No."

"So you're gonna go back to your hotel room and wallow?"

I nodded. That was the plan. Wallowing was good. I might even have another cry.

"All by yourself?" His doubt pissed me off.

"Yeah, all alone. Imagine that. No one to betray my trust, no one to make me feel bad about myself, no one to—"

"Cut the shit, Joes! Stop feeling sorry for yourself and get on."

I stepped unintentionally. "Get on?" I scoffed. "The death trap? Yeah, I don't think so."

His eyes rolled and he gave me the annoyed look he wore every time we talked about his Harley. He held out a hand though. "Come for a ride with me."

"You don't even have a backseat."

He chuckled softly and slid forward a bit. "I have a backseat, Jo." He tapped the spot behind him to show me. "I just don't have a sissy bar." Seeing my blank look, he explained, "The bar behind the seat that riders lean against."

I shook my head, horrified. There was no way I could stay on the bike without that bar. He had lost his mind if he thought I would even attempt it.

He sighed, reading my thoughts. "You hold on to me, babe. I won't let you fall."

"I don't have a helmet." Then I realized he didn't have one either. "Where in the hell is *your* helmet?"

"I didn't have a chance to grab it. I had to use the regular door to get my bike out of the garage, not the bay door." He laughed at my look. "Long story."

Hmmm. "Well, you should have taken the extra few minutes to grab it! It's dangerous!"

He gave me his lopsided grin. "I couldn't. I needed to catch you."

I rolled my eyes. "Why don't you have a sissy bar?"

He laughed again, the deep and sincere sound that made me smile. "Taylor won't ride without it. I like to ride alone, and if it's on, she insists on coming with me." He curled his fingers, motioning me. "Come on. Come celebrate with me."

I hesitated. The fact that Taylor never rode his bike made me want to. I was mad at him. Confused, yes, but angry that he had told her all those things. I was spiteful, though. I was tempted to go with him just because I knew how angry she'd be when she found out.

I took a tentative step toward him, ready to throw caution to the wind. I hesitated at the last second. I had no idea how to get on.

Reading me again, Matty explained. "Take my hand, put your left foot on the peg, and swing your right leg over."

Fuck it. I grabbed his hand, followed his directions, and lifted myself up, and straddled the seat. Looking behind me, I noticed how close I was to the back of the bike. "You're sure I won't fall off?"

He glanced over his shoulder as his right hand grabbed my knee. "Scoot closer."

I was already close, my inner thighs touching his butt, but I did as I was told.

He shook his head. "Closer."

I sighed and pushed myself as close as I could get, the front part of my body flush against his back. It felt so intimate, as though we were doing something that wasn't as innocent as it really was. My cheeks burned and my breath caught. God, he smelled fantastic.

His hand slid up to the outside of my thigh, giving it a squeeze. "Now put your arms around me."

I wrapped them tightly around his belly and felt his laugh rumble through him.

"Not so tight, Jo."

I relaxed them slightly.

"Now, where to?"

I didn't care as long as I was with him. "It's your night. Somewhere far away from here."

"It's a gorgeous night. Wanna go to Portland?"

I didn't. The idea of going on the freeway on that little piece of metal scared the crap out of me, but I nodded. Instantly he started the motor. It was loud, but not as loud as I'd thought it would be. The vibrations ran through my entire body.

Matty started out of the lot slowly, pulling up his legs and leaning back into me when we hit the main road. Every now and then, his right hand came back and held onto my leg. I pushed my cheek into his back, right between his shoulder blades, and watched the sights go by.

I wasn't prepared for how relaxed I felt. Or, how much I enjoyed the ride. There wasn't anything between the pavement and me except a bike and Matty, but I hadn't felt so safe in a long time.

SIX

The ride didn't last as long as I thought it would, even though Matty didn't take the freeway. At every stop sign, he turned back and talked to me, checking to make sure I was doing okay. Sometimes he put his hands over mine on his stomach and rubbed them, helping me keep them warm and letting me know he was right there with me. His body completely blocked mine from the coming traffic and wind, and eventually I forgot to be scared and started having fun.

Matty told me once that the most relaxing place in the world was on the back of his bike. I'd argued and said it had to be the white sand beaches on the Virgin Islands, but now I understood. I was completely calm and had forgotten why I had been upset when he backed the bike into a parking spot. And a little sad that the trip was over.

"You okay?" he asked, after he put down the kickstand and turned off the bike.

"Yep." I sighed in contentment. "That was awesome."

"Yeah?"

I nodded.

"Good. Now you can come with me more."

He got off the bike, stretching and slipping the black hoodie over his head. I only had a second to think about Taylor's vicious words earlier while he shoved the sweatshirt into his saddlebag then held a hand out to me. I slid off, and his hand went to my back, rubbing the exact spot where I was sore.

"I know it's hard on your back to sit without a bar; if you want, I'll put it back on."

I shook my head. It was selfish, and completely bitchy, but I had a piece of him that his girlfriend didn't. And I refused to share. "If you do that, Taylor will want to ride."

He looked at me for a few seconds. "Good point."

He reached for my hand but I pulled away, eying it, then him, speculatively.

"Trust me," his voice was low, "it's better if people think you're with me."

"I am with you." I argued, flexing my toes in the flip-flops I wore. Next time I rode his bike, if there was a next time, I was wearing enclosed shoes.

He closed his fingers around mine anyway. "I mean *with me* with me. This can be a rough place."

A rough place? Awesome. I looked up and down the cobblestone streets, but all I saw were many other couples and groups of friends walking under the streetlights. It didn't look scary. Everyone seemed to be having fun and in a hurry to get where they were going. I didn't pull my hand away, though. I liked how his fingers felt entwined with mine. We walked in silence, lingering here and there so I could look into the windows of the little shops that lined the street.

I stopped in front of a quaint Maine Made store admiring the display when angry voices echoed down the practically deserted street. Without thinking about it, I stepped closer to Matty, seeking both his warmth and protection. He automatically draped his arm over my shoulders and pulled me close. In that moment, everything in my world was right.

An angry yell cut the quiet that surrounded us. I would have ignored it, yet Matty tensed and scanned the area over his shoulder. When I peeked around him, I understood his apprehension. At least ten very large, very intimidating men walking toward us. They looked like quintessential bikers—big, brawny, and scruffy, sporting leather vests or jackets, jeans, and boots. Matty dropped his arm and moved in front of me, as if sheltering me from an incoming attack.

For a few seconds I just stood there, watching the swarm approach from all different directions. *Oh, my God. We're getting mugged.* One of the largest walked straight for us, lips and face contorted in a nasty scowl. My fear grew with each step he took.

Matty drew himself up to his full height, puffing out his shoulders as he did, which made him look almost twice as big as he actually was. If I hadn't been so scared, I would have been impressed. My friend was almost as daunting as the rest.

I didn't hear what the big one said to Matty, but his reply was low and vicious. "You looking for a problem, son?" The tone suggested that he wanted the answer to be yes.

The other man raised his head slightly, moving directly into Matty's space, going toe to toe. "I think I found one."

41

I'd lived in Boston long enough to know that his accent screamed Southie. I slid my hand up my hip and into my back pocket, closing my fingers around my phone. debated dialing 9-1-1, but wondered if I should just let Matty handle it. I had a feeling it was too late for the police to help us.

Suddenly, the choice was made.

The other guy grabbed my friend and, to my surprise, pulled him into a hug. "Didn't think I'd see you here, Brothah!"

Matty returned the hug in that manly way, slapping his back and laughing. "What in the hell are you doing here?"

Matty looked around the group of men, hugging some, shaking hands and offering greetings to others. He obviously knew this band of thugs and was very happy to see them. Before I could say anything, or retreat quietly back to the bike, he grabbed my hand and pulled me out into the middle of the street.

"This is Rocker." He motioned to the big guy in front of him.

"Rocker? As in you like to go to the local bar and sing your heart out every weekend?" I surveyed Rocker suspiciously. Up close, he wasn't nearly as frightening as I initially thought. He couldn't have been more than a year or two older than me. He was wearing designer jeans over his beat-up boots and a tight black T-shirt under the vest, which showed off his muscles and a full tattoo sleeve down one arm.

He shook his head. "No, ma'am, it's because—"

I held up a hand, interrupting him. "Wait. Did you just call me ma'am?" I looked at Matty. "He just called me ma'am!" I was completely appalled, but Matt, used to my reaction to that word, just smirked and shrugged. I turned back to Rocker. "Do I look old to you?"

The man had the sense to look ashamed. His whole face fell. "No, ma'a... ugh." He shook his head again. "Fuck. No, you don't."

I grinned, trying not to laugh. I liked him immediately. "Let me guess. They call you Rocker but"—I cast a side glance at Matty— "it's actually Rock. Her." I leaned a little closer. "Like the ladies, huh?"

Rocker's neck got a little red, and the other men laughed.

I held out my hand. "Joey."

Rocker took my hand in a nice, firm handshake. I couldn't help but notice how calloused and cracked his hands were. He either rode a lot, or he worked with his hands.

"Joey?" I liked the way he said it with his voice raising a little on the "ey."

He was looking at Matt, not me, and I knew there was more to the question than just my name. I ignored the way they seemed to be communicating without words and answered him anyway.

"Joey. As in the cute little kangaroo."

Rocker's eyes left Matty and traveled over my body. One of the other men made a comment about me being a kangaroo with boxing gloves, and they all laughed.

Rocker's eyes glowed with humor. "It fits. I like it." He looked back at Matt. "Is she—"

Matty stepped closer to me, his legs and body touching mine, as he laced our fingers together. "Yeah. Something like that.".

A thick current of electricity ran through him into me, or from me into him, jolting me and stealing my breath. It felt like I'd been touched an electric fence. I wondered if he felt it too.

Before I could ask, one of the other men spoke up. "Hey, Mateo, does she kick like a kangaroo when she—"

That one I understood before he finished, and I cut him off. Turning toward the voice, I scowled playfully. "Hey now!" I held up my hand. "If he wants to live, he's not going to answer you with me standing right here."

Matty laughed, shrugging, and leaned in to kiss my temple. "You are amazing," he whispered. "Joey, this is Dean." He pointed at the man who had asked the question.

Matty went around the circle of men, introducing each. I was surprised by their names. Other than Rocker, Tiny (who was anything but, so I didn't want to know where that nickname came from,) and Hawk, they all had normal names. And none of them were nearly as scary as I had first thought.

Rocker nodded at us, giving me a dazzling smile that completely transformed his gruff appearance. "If he gives you any trouble, any at all, you let me know. I'll take care of him."

I jerked my free thumb toward Matty. "This guy? Nah, I've got this one under control."

The group of them murmured their agreement.

Rocker's lips tipped up. "I can see that." As soon as it had come, the pleasantness vanished from his face and he turned somber. "We're headed to the bah down the street. Wanna come?"

"No. We're headed out to dinner. You come all the way up here for drinks?"

"We had a job."

"I should've called me."

Rocker shook his head. "Nah, man, we got this one. Too close to home for you. I'll call you tomorrow to fill you in, yeah?" With a few goodbye waves, the group stated to filter past us. Rocker gave me one last smile. "It was nice to meet you, Little Kangaroo."

I liked the name. "You too, Rocker!"

SEVEN

The tavern Matty took me to wasn't far, but when we got there the line was out the door. I was surprised when the bouncer let us in, acting as if he knew Matty. It reminded me that there was more to my friend than I knew.

I followed him through a packed bar and into a small dining area, dropping into the first open chair I saw.

"Have you been here before?" Matty asked as he moved his chair closer to me.

I shook my head, scanning the menu. I hadn't realized how hungry I was. Everything looked delicious.

"This used to be two separate businesses," he informed me, pointing at the window-sized holes in the walls. From our table, we could see the dance floor perfectly. "in two separate buildings. Neither one had enough space and the code enforcement officer was called all the time. So, the owners reached an agreement and they combined."

It seemed to be working for them. The bar was so crowded I couldn't see an inch of empty space, and almost every seat in the dining room was full, with plenty of people standing around. I was beyond thankful Matty was able to get us in.

"How do you know the bouncer?" I asked.

Matty didn't move his eyes from his menu. "What bouncer?"

I snorted. "The one outside."

He shrugged absentmindedly. "I don't."

"How'd we get in?"

"I lied and told him we had reservations."

I laughed at his sheepish look.

He waited until after we ordered and our first round of drinks had been delivered before turning serious. "Are we gonna talk about it?"

"No." *Not now at least.* "Tell me about Rocker."

"There's nothing to tell really."

"Oh, there's something to tell. Spill it."

"Fine." He gave a small exasperated sigh. "I was in the youth center with him." He paused dramatically, as if waiting for his words to sink in and for me to run away screaming in fear.

I rolled my eyes at his dramatic flair. It was no secret he'd been in a lot of trouble as a kid. I'd known for years that he'd spent the later part of his teen years in Long Creek, a detention center for criminal teens.

"Oh! What did he do? Or can you not tell me?" I lowered my voice so the couple at the table next to us couldn't hear.

Matty met my eyes. "It's his story to tell, not mine."

I wasn't surprised. After all these years, he still wouldn't tell me the specifics that had led to him being locked away, as if it was some terrible thing that would make me hate him. Matty's past made me sad, not scared. Every once in a while he would let something slip, and I had been able to piece together that he'd had a pretty rough time before becoming an adult.

"He was my best friend and had my back through a lot of shit. We went through hell and back together. After we got out—I mean for the last time—we moved to Boston together."

"You moved to Boston with both Rocker and Rob?" I'd heard the stories enough to know that Rob Doyle and Matty had been close, like brothers, and even had matching tattoos. They'd gotten into even more trouble in Beantown. He hadn't talked about Rocker before though.

Matty beamed at me, as if he was happy that I had remembered. "I forgot I told you that. Yeah, Rob is Rocker."

I gaped at him. Nothing about the man I met earlier matched the Rob I had imagined. From the way Matty had talked about him, I'd pictured the Hulk. Someone large, destructive, and always angry, but could turn, in an instant, into Bruce Banner and be calm and collected. Rob, or so I'd gathered from the brief mentions of him, was bad news. Matty had bailed him out of jail more than once. I'd expected a monster who could put on a good show, not a good guy who could be a monster. Rocker had seemed genuinely nice and funny.

"But... Rocker is freaking hot!"

Matty choked on his beer. I stood and pounded him on the back. When his coughing stopped, he glared at me. "Really?"

I shrugged. It was the truth.

"Since when do you think the tattooed guy on a Harley is hot? You don't like the bad guy. The geeky guy with the pocket protector is more your style."

Since you. I blushed at my thought. The waitress chose that moment to deliver our burgers, saving me from answering.

After a few minutes of eating in peaceful silence, Matty lifted his beer to his lips and surveyed me. "I'm sure Rocker's wife would agree with you. I'll have to mention it next time I go for a visit."

I glared at him, speechless.

He smiled slowly. "Sorry." He shrugged. "Too soon?"

"Are you trying to tell me something?"

He shook his head. "Nah. You don't want to talk about it."

"Well, we kind of have to now, don't we?" I snapped. "Fine. Why are you here with me when you told your fiancée"—I spat the word at him—"you were sick of my drama? Why aren't you home celebrating with her?"

His eyes flashed at me. "Why are you here with me instead of with Billy?"

I'd half expected him to deny the drama comment and the fact he'd mentioned Will was a surprise.

"Because it's your night," I snapped back.

He leaned over the table, his face close to mine. "Then why did you run away?"

"You wanted me to stay after Taylor made it perfectly clear I wasn't welcome in her house?"

"Yeah, actually, I did. It isn't her house. It's mine."

"Actually, Matt, it's her house now too. You fucking proposed and didn't tell me!" I was seething, but until that minute, I didn't realize how upset I was about their engagement.

"You told me I should do it!" he shot back, gripping the edge of the table. "I asked you if there was any reason I shouldn't and you said there wasn't! Regretting that now?"

"She's a hag. That should be reason enough. Yet, you're a glutton for punishment because you decided to marry her anyway. Whatever. That's your life you're screwing up. The real issue is the fact that you betrayed the person you claim is your best friend. When in the hell would you tell her why my marriage is falling apart? And agreeing to stay away from my drama? Mine! Do you know how laughable that is? Coming from the woman who threw a fit because you didn't remember her shoe size? Why in the fuck would you tell her that shit? I told you because I trusted you, not so you could have pillow talk."

He took a deep, slow breath, his eyes never leaving mine. "Taylor and I never had that conversation. You'd know that if you had stayed for another five minutes. You ran away before I could explain."

I bit the inside of my cheek, still angry but not sure what to say. I felt like an ass because I was sure he was telling me the truth. And it was just like Taylor to do what she could to cause trouble between Matty and me.

"That's the woman you're going to marry? One who blatantly lies? I doubt it's the first time, but somehow you overlooked it and proposed anyway!"

"Is that really why you don't want me to marry her, Jo? Because she lied?" He was seething now. "Is that the reason you're telling yourself?"

His hint was clear and I realized that Taylor had meant that both she and Matty knew how I felt.

"No! I don't want you to marry her because I knew this would happen! She hates me"—I glared at him again—"and there is no way she's going to be happy until I'm out of your life forever. I've always told you everything—that's what we do—and now I can't tell you anything because you'll run right back to her."

"Bullshit. She talks to Billy; did you know that? I didn't tell her anything about you or him. I told her I came home late last night because he was a fucking asshole and I couldn't stand him. Which led to her defending him; we had a giant fucking fight." He leaned back a little, sighing. "I didn't propose to her, Jo. She went through my shit while I was with you, and she found the ring."

Taylor and Billy had always been friendly. Whenever we were together, the two of them naturally drifted toward each other, like Matty and I did. I assumed it was because they were the two outsiders amongst our friends. I had no idea they talked outside of the parties, though. Or that they still spoke. I felt like Will had crossed another line.

As upset with my husband as I was, it was nothing compared to the way I detested Taylor. Her search of Matty's things was a complete betrayal.

"Seriously? What was she looking for?"

He shook his head. "I dunno. But she found the ring. I told her I wasn't ready for her to have it yet but that I'd ask her soon. She wore it to work today, and when I got home, I asked her to not wear it in front of you. She isn't like this all the time. You just bring out the worst in her." He held up his hands at my hateful stare. "Okay, she's a bitch. And fucking awful around you. The worst part is that I think she planned tonight."

"What do you mean?"

"After you left, I was going to grab my car and follow you. But both sets of keys were gone. My bike keys were there, but the garage door opener had miraculously disappeared." He shrugged, smirking. "I guess she didn't realize that the side door is wide enough for a wheelchair, so my bike can fit through. She knows now." He gave a small laugh. "I almost wish I could have seen her face when I drove the bike out the door and took off. She's gonna be ripshit that her plan didn't work."

I couldn't understand why he would stay with someone who treated him like that.

He reached forward, grabbing my hand. "I'm sorry."

"You have nothing to be sorry for." I squeezed his hand back. "I'm sorry your celebration was ruined."

The lopsided grin appeared. "It wasn't, Jo. It's been better than expected actually."

I smiled back at him, the anger leaving me. The best thing about Matty was that he could be mad at me one second then laughing the next. "Okay. We've talked about it. Can you tell me more about Rocker now?"

He rolled his eyes.

I didn't know how long we sat there, but time flew. Matty kept me entertained with stories of Rocker, some of which I'd already heard, some that were new. It was easy to picture them now that I'd met the man behind the crazy ideas. I would have stayed there all night, listening and laughing, but when Matty yawned, I realized he still had to drive us home.

"Sorry, Jo. I didn't get much sleep last night," he told me when I suggested we go.

Guilt hit me because I'd kept him here so long and because I'd kept him out late last night too. "Will you be okay to drive?"

He nodded. "Yeah, once I'm outside, it'll be better." He stood, barely stifling another yawn. Holding out his hand, inviting me to hold it, he tipped his head toward the door. "Come on."

I stood, grabbing for his hand when someone in the club caught my eye. I dropped my arm, moving slightly to get a better view, assuring myself that my mind was playing tricks because I was tired. I gasped.

Matty slid in behind me and followed my stare. Will was in the bar, and he wasn't alone. Rachel, his cute co-worker, had her arms wrapped around his neck, grinding along to the music with him. He turned her so she was facing us and moved behind her, running his hands familiarly down the front sides of her barely clad body. Her arms went behind her, as if to hold him close, her head falling back on his shoulder.

It was a very intimate, very private moment. We were intruding. I sat down abruptly, my thoughts racing as fast as my heart.

I miss you. I love you. Will's words from earlier echoed in my head. He'd asked me to go out to dinner with him. He'd sounded genuinely disappointed when I'd said no.

Yet, here he was, with her. We never came to Portland. I hadn't even known this pub existed. This would be the last place he expected me to be.

I silently willed him to open his eyes, hoping he would see me. He was so caught up in his moment with her I doubted he'd see me even if I was right next to him. I watched helpless and horrified as his left slid back up, closing around her breast possessively. It a sucker punch I'd never expected.

He'd taken off his wedding ring. The bastard had removed the one piece of me that he had left.

Matty made a feral sound, sliding around me and stomping off in the direction of the bar. I caught his arm right before it was out of reach. "Where are you going?"

He barely stopped, staring down at me, barely holding his anger. "I'm going to go kick his fucking ass."

I shook my head. I didn't want Will to know I'd seen him. I just wanted to go back to my hotel and forget. "Please, Matty. Please just take me home."

He lifted his chin, glaring back at the dance floor and stiffened. I didn't want to know what he'd seen. Then he leaned over in front of me so that we were eye to eye, and cupped my cheeks between his hands.

"Please?" I asked again.

"Can you ride?"

I nodded. He moved, placing me on the the inside, blocking my view of Will, and put his hand on the small of my back before he walked me out of the tavern. It had gotten chilly, and I was shaking by the time we got back to the bike.

"Here." He pulled his hooded sweatshirt out of the saddlebag and slipped it over my head.

"You'll need it." He only had on a lightweight T-shirt, but my lips chattered as I said the words.

"Nah. You'll keep me warm." He smiled as he lifted his leg over the bike and held out a hand for me. "It looks like we're gonna get a storm. I'll hurry."

We made it halfway home before the skies opened and it began to downpour. I'd been cold before I got on the bike, but after a few minutes of riding in the rain, I thought I was going to freeze to death before we made it back to the hotel. I didn't know how Matty could see a thing. The driving drops felt like hail pounding into my flesh, and it dripped from my hair into my eyes, burning as it did.

Matty had told me to lean my head into his back and he covered my hands with one of his, but I felt horrible that he didn't even have a shirt to protect his arms. Not that clothes would have helped much. My sweatshirt and jeans soaked up the freezing water and, mixed with the cold air, gave me a chill right down to the bone. The trip down to Portland had gone quickly, yet the trip home felt as if it took forever.

I sagged in relief when he slowed and turned into my hotel. We were both off the bike as soon as Matty cut the engine. He pushed the kickstand down, and we ran for the door. Our clothes made giant puddles in the elevator, but at least we were out of the rain. I struggled to make my numb fingers work the keycard, but I couldn't get them to do what I wanted and instead handed the card to Matty. The door had barely closed before I yanked off the sweatshirt, my shirt coming with it, trying to get away from the freezing fabric.

"Get out of your clothes before you freeze!" I struggled with the button on my jeans, stopping to flex my fingers a few times, blowing on them to warm them up.

Without thinking, I lifted my head, finding Matty across the room, and instantly forgot what I was doing.

He'd stripped in record time. Standing in the bathroom doorway in nothing but his boxers, he was briskly rubbing his hair with a towel. I couldn't look away.

I'd seen the tattoos on his arms hundreds of times, probably enough to describe each picture in detail. I'd never seen him shirtless, though. He always wore a rash guard at the beach, telling me he didn't want the majority of his tattoos getting ruined by the sun. Seeing his ink now, I was sure the sun wasn't the only reason. He was covered in ink, which he'd told me, but the pictures he'd chosen to forever etch on his body surprised me.

They were beautiful, not the harsh, manly images I had expected. None of them touched the others, with the exception of the giant Claddagh over the front of his right shoulder. It coiled and twined with tribal knots into the sleeve on his arm. A lonely cross with the words, "Only God Can Judge Me" above it, sat in the middle of his chest. A single word, Trust, ran beneath his heart. A giant angel ran around his right side, stretching from hip to just below his armpit. Low on the right side was a picture that looked as though a child had drawn it, but I couldn't tell what it was. Right below his belly button and stretching out onto his stomach, was an anchor. But it was the words low on his right pubic bone that held my attention. I couldn't pull my eyes away.

"Are you any warmer yet?" he asked without looking up. When I didn't answer, he stopped drying his hair and lifted his head. I could feel his eyes on me. "Jo?"

My mind went blank. My lips wouldn't have formed the words even if I'd had them. I knew I was being rude, but I couldn't stop staring.

He cleared his throat. "Enjoying the view?"

I knew I should look away, that I shouldn't ask. But I had to know. "Does that really say what I think it does?"

He snatched the towel from his head and covered the lower part of his torso. The movement was enough to break my trance and I peeked up. I met his eyes, amused to see that he was embarrassed.

He shifted uncomfortably and took a deep breath. "Yeah."

I cackled. His discomfort mixed with the absurd tattoo cracked me up. He narrowed his eyes at my reaction.

I tried to stop laughing. I even bit my lip, hoping the pain would distract me. It didn't work.

"That. Is. Awesome," I gasped between gulps of air. I wanted to know more. I needed to hear the story behind that ink. "Let me see it again! Does it keep going or does it end there?" I stepped across the room, soaked jeans forgotten, and grabbed at the towel.

He shook his head.

"Oh, come on! Is it new?" I demanded, completely scandalized.

He was getting red. "No! I just"—he pulled up the elastic on his boxers while managing to keep me from grabbing the towel—"keep it covered." When my fingertips tickled up his side, a mischievous glint entered his eyes. Before I could move away, his fingers closed around my upper arms and he pulled me close, the towel forgotten as it fell between us. "I'll show you mine if you show me yours." The growl was low and dangerous.

I'd told Matty I had tattoos, but he'd never seen them—they were personal. His hand was on my bare back, running up and down the part of my spine where the words were written, then dipped dangerously close to the top of my jeans. It became painfully obvious that the only things between us were a pair of sopping jeans that clung to every part of my lower body and the soaking wet slips of white cotton that were my bra.

I couldn't breathe. My heart started to race. His body was scorching hot against my frigid skin, but I knew it had nothing to do with the sudden warmth growing low in my body. For a brief moment I wished there was nothing between us.

He leaned down, lips almost touching my ear. "What do yours say, Jo? Should I lean down and take a closer peek?"

I swallowed roughly as my eyelids dropped. There wasn't anything else I'd rather have him do, but I refused to admit that. Fighting the urge to wrap my arms around him and kiss every inch of his body until he begged me to do what his tattoo so crudely directed, I stepped back. I spun around, showing him my back as my fingers traced the spot where the message was.

"It says, 'I am enough.' And this one..." I turned, facing him again, and unbuttoned my jeans, forcing the zipper down as quickly as I could. I forced the rough material over my hips and down my legs before tugging the side of my panties down so he could see all of it. "Says, 'Of all the names I have been called throughout my life, my favorite will always be Mommy.' It's so I can remember that every one of these scars," my other hand slid over the faded stretch marks, "brought me the best gifts ever."

He didn't say anything, yet the way he watched me made me squirm. Unable to handle it anymore, I bent down, grabbing for the towel.

"Are you going in for a closer look, Jo?" His voice was husky and strained, but I could hear the humor.

I snatched the towel, jerking upright, and turned toward the bed. I needed dry, warm clothes. And to get away from him.

He sighed in exasperation. "It says 'Suck My.' That's it."

I giggled as I pulled a shirt out of the drawer and slid it on before I kicked off my jeans and underwear, replacing them with pajama bottoms.

"I love it! How old were you when you got it?" All dressed, I turned back to my friend. He was standing in the same spot, shivering. I forgot the tattoo. "Good lord! Get over here, and get under the covers."

He raised an eyebrow and didn't move.

"For God's sake, I'm not going to molest you." *Not unless you beg me to.* "But unless you plan on putting on wet clothes and riding home in the storm, you're going to have to stay here." I motioned to the bed. "I'll sleep on top if you want. I at least have warm clothes."

He looked at the door and back at me. "Isn't there a laundry room here?"

"Yep. It closed at nine. And then you'd still have to ride home in the rain. Call Taylor and tell her you got stuck in the storm."

He frowned, lips twisting as he contemplated his options. He tipped his head back as if he was asking for divine intervention. Then, deciding to stay, he hurried to the bed, pulled back the covers, and practically jumped in. I couldn't keep the happy smile off my face as I crawled in behind him.

He didn't fight me as I snuggled up next to him, laying my head on his shoulder and putting my arm over his stomach. His shivering subsided after only a few minutes, but I was too tired to move away. I felt him shift, sliding my head to the pillow and my arm from his belly to his side.

"Jo?"

"Hmmm?"

His hand touched my cheek. I fought to open my eyes, but they wouldn't budge. Soft lips pressed against my forehead.

"I thought you were going to be on top?"

The last thing I heard before letting the darkness of sleep take me was his chuckle. It made me happy.

EIGHT

The bright sun rays, sneaking in the window and dancing along my skin, pulled me from slumber. I'd started to sleep in on Saturday mornings after the kids had left because it helped fight the loneliness. However, it had been a long time since I'd felt as refreshed..

I'd slept better than I had in months. Stretching my hands above my head, I arched my back, trying to work out all the kinks. When I bumped into a hard mass of muscle, I jumped, a small squeak escaping my lips, and I forced my eyes open.

Matty, entirely too close for comfort, watched me in amusement. Memories of the night before hit me like a ton of bricks.

"Well, this is awkward," I said as I covered my mouth so he wouldn't be forced to endure my morning breath.

"You snore. Not like a sweet, sexy snore either. I'm talking Hoover vacuum snore. I woke up and thought the maid was in here cleaning before I realized it was just you."

I fought the snort that tried to escape, coughing instead.

"Good morning." He brushed a rough knuckle over the apple of my cheek, pushing back a strand of flyaway hair. "How'd you sleep?"

"Morning." I smiled slowly. "Good. You?"

"You mean other than the snoring and the furnace who insisted she wrap herself around me half the night? Yeah, I slept great." He sat up, stretching his arms above his head, giving me one hell of a view. "What are your plans today?"

I flopped onto my back, wishing I could stay in the moment forever. "I have a dinner date, but I've decided to cancel. I'm going to go to the gym and then maybe the movies. I actually don't know."

Matty laid back down next to me, head on my pillow, shoulder touching mine. "How you holding up after last night?"

I shrugged. I didn't want to talk about it. Hell, I didn't even want to think about it. The two of them dancing that way... I shook my head and closed my eyes, as if that would make the memories vanish. Knowing your husband hadn't been faithful was one thing; having the image burned into your brain was another.

56

Matty's fingers closed around mine. "It just so happens that my plans got cancelled too. I'm gonna go for a run, read a little, and then maybe dinner and a movie. A lazy day. I'd love company."

I let him hold my hand. It was a sweet gesture, and he was trying to offer me comfort. I loved how perfectly my hand fit into his.

The thought of Matty's hands made me think of Will's. It shouldn't have been a surprise that he'd taken off his wedding ring. Most married people probably removed the reminder before they cheated.

I wasn't even sure if he normally wore it when he wasn't around me. Maybe he stuck it in his glove compartment every day before going into his office or out with his friends. For all I knew, Rachel didn't even realize he was still married.

Will was everything a young woman her age could want. He was incredibly handsome, successful, financially secure, and he had all his hair. The only negative he had was the pesky wife and kids. Without that, he was quite the catch.

Rachel was stunningly beautiful. She had a perfect body, one that I would have killed for at her age, and every time I saw her, she was happy. They were quite the pair.

I'd loved him before he'd had the success and money though. Back when he was just an idealistic kid with a dream.

I let go of Matty's hand and rolled toward him, snuggling into his chest. He hesitated, as if he didn't know what to do, then closed his arm over me. I buried my head under his chin. I had so many conflicting thoughts and emotions running through my mind, screaming at me, and I just wanted them to be quiet.

On one hand, I could understand completely. I hadn't given Will enough attention, yet I always made time for Matty. Things had been more than a little strained for year. Plus, it was hard to be judgmental of Will's extracurricular activities considering I was lying in bed with a half-naked man—okay, a mostly naked man—who was engaged to someone else. We'd not only spent the night in the same bed but were locked in what could only be described as an intimate embrace. I sure as hell couldn't cast the first stone.

On the other hand, I'd never had sex with anyone else.

I'd fantasized about Matty over the last few days, sure. I was attracted to him. Yet, it was all a recent development. I would never actually betray Will. I'd vowed to be faithful to him, and I had been.

Taylor and Will didn't seem to agree with me on that theory, though. Their definition of cheating and mine were completely different. I didn't know if I would be as upset about Will and Rachel if their relationship had been emotional instead of physical.

The bitter truth made me feel like an ass. If Will and Rachel were as close as Matty and me, without having sex, I would probably be more upset. Attraction, as I knew from my marriage, came and went. The intimacy of an emotional connection never left.

I was jealous. I wanted Will to look at me the way he'd looked at Rachel last night, to want me as much as he obviously wanted her. Yet, I didn't view Will the same way I saw Matty.

Will and I didn't have anything in common, other than our children. We didn't enjoy any of the same things, from music to movies. Will had never been my friend. And somewhere along the way, I'd unintentionally made the friendship a priority.

I was just as guilty as Will in this whole mess we'd gotten ourselves into.

"That's a big sigh." Matty's lips moved against the tip of my ear. "The world's problems aren't going to get solved here, kid." He rolled over and out of bed. "Come on, let's go clear our minds with a run."

Our clothes from last night were still soaked, but Matty insisted he'd be okay in wet jeans until he back to his house to change. In turn, I insisted we take my car instead of the bike. My stomach was in knots by the time we pulled into his driveway, and I breathed a sigh of relief when I saw Taylor's car wasn't there.

"I told you she'd be gone. She has family get-together." He pushed open the door, pausing when I didn't turn off my car. "You're not coming in?"

"No." It was Taylor's home, too. I was not welcome and I refused to be inside, especially alone with Matty, when she came back.

Matty didn't argue. "I'll be right out."

I kept my car in neutral, just in case I had to make a quick getaway, and my eyes glued to the road. I didn't have to worry long though. Matty was true to his word and came out just a few minutes later, dressed for a run.

He threw a bag into my backseat as he climbed in and grinned at my confused look. "I'm not going to dinner dressed like this. Plus, I want to have something to sleep in tonight other than boxers."

I had started to ease down his driveway but slammed on my brakes, snapping my head around to see him, sure I'd heard him wrong.

He turned away, avoiding my gaze. I heard the humor in his voice as he mumbled, "Just in case."

The beach at Popham Fort was only twenty-five minutes from Matty's. We'd overslept though, and by the time we got there, families were scattered on towels and blankets along the sand and children darted in and out of the cold water. It was one of my favorite places, whether running with Matty or playing with my kids.

Matty was much faster than I was, a fact I blamed on his long legs, and even though he slowed for me, I struggled to keep his pace. By the time we got halfway down the beach, I stopped trying and slowed to a jog. I watched him race to the bend and turn back before I gave up altogether.

When he got close enough I waved my hand, "It's too hot to run."

"It's never too hot to run!" He teased, even though he fell into step beside me. A few steps later his fingers threaded with mine.

I rolled my eyes. "You don't have to hold my hand, you know. I'm not going to be get lost."

"Yeah, but I want to." He paused, giving me a weird look. "If it makes you uncomfortable..."

Holding his hand didn't make me uncomfortable, it was just... new. We'd touched plenty of times, but this seemed more personal. I liked it.

I looked up at him, and couldn't help but smile. He was covered in sweat, hair messed up from the ocean breeze, and was slightly out of breath, but he was completely in his element. And utterly beautiful.

He glanced at me out of the corner of his eye. "Feels great to sweat the stress out, right?"

Sure. That's why I'm smiling. I nodded though, and tightened my grip on his hand, holding it all the way to the car.

The rest of the day flew by. We hung out at the hotel pool, me swimming laps and getting some sun while he read in the shade. My kids called in the early afternoon, and I was excited to listen to each talk about what they'd been doing. Then, we went to a matinee and dinner, and were back at the hotel before eight.

I'd put my phone on the charger before we left and had forgotten it in the room. I was surprised to see eighteen missed calls. I panicked, thinking something happened to one of the kids. Then, scrolling through the call list, I realized they were all from Will.

"I never cancelled with Will!" Appalled that I'd completely forgotten, I hit the recall button instantly.

Matty laughed like it was the funniest thing he'd ever heard, but I didn't see the humor.

"Where in the hell have you been?" The anger coming from the other end of the phone surprised me.

"I'm so sorry! I forgot my phone and—"

"We had plans! I've been calling you for hours!" Will interrupted, seething. "If you were going to blow me off, you should have let me know hours ago. I could have—"

It was my turn to interrupt. "Could have what?" I challenged, barely holding onto my own agitation. *Gone to Portland with your girlfriend again?* I almost let the words slip out.

"It isn't important. It's too late now." He snapped.

"It's barely eight, Will."

"You're right." His voice calmed almost instantly. "I can come pick you up."

I hesitated. I'd had an amazing day. I didn't want to end it with a fight.

Sensing my reluctance, he continued. "We need to talk. I'd prefer to do it face to face."

I knew what he was going to say, yet dread washed over me. "I don't handle your big reveals well in person. Maybe it would be better if you just tell me over the phone."

"Big reveal? Jo, I've already bared my soul. I don't have anything else to tell you. We need to come up with a plan, that's all." I heard him shift. "Why don't you meet me for drinks and we can talk?" His voice was warm and persuasive. "The house is so quiet without you. I'm lonely without you."

I shook my head, annoyed. I didn't know what was worse— his lies or that I'd believed them yesterday and still wanted to believe them today. If I hadn't seen him the night before, I'd be the idiot running home to a cheater. I had though, and I knew I could never trust him again.

"You don't have any other friends who could meet you for dinner or even drinks? Ya know, so you aren't so lonely?"

Matty looked up at my bitter tone, a concerned look on his face. "Joes." He shook his head, as if warning me to stop talking before I said too much.

"Where are you?" Will demanded.

"My hotel."

"Matty is with you at your hotel?"

"He is. He's been here all day." Lying never crossed my mind.

"I see." The anger was back.

Arguing with him would get us nowhere. "Look, I'm sorry I forgot to call you. It wasn't intentional. I'll talk to you later?"

"Jo? Don't you dare hang up..."

I hung up. Before I could drop my phone, he called back. I hit ignore. It immediately buzzed again. I turned it off and tossed it onto the table. Sighing, I met Matty's eyes.

He studied me for a few minutes. "What do you want to do with the rest of our night? Want to go grab a drink?"

I shook my head. "Can we just..." I sighed. "I don't know. Sit here?"

He pulled me down onto the couch and tucked me into his side. I read while he surfed the Internet on his phone and talked to Sam. It was sweet, listening to the two of them talk about their days and read together. I thought Matty would head home at some point, but he claimed that he wasn't ready to see Taylor. I understood completely. Being with someone I felt comfortable around and pushing the inevitable fight from my mind was easy.

Thinking about my husband was not. I couldn't avoid him forever. Will and I had to talk. I'd have to tell him what I'd seen. I just wasn't ready to have that conversation.

I didn't have time to worry about where Matty was going to sleep. He'd put on pajama bottoms while I was brushing my teeth. I came out to find him passed out in my bed. I shut off the lights and crawled in next to him, grateful to not be alone. I was almost asleep when a hand clutched mine.

"Try not to snore so much, 'k, Jo?"

NINE

Sunday was another lazy day with Matty. He woke me up early, the excitement of a little boy on Christmas morning oozing from his pores, and convinced me to go for an all-day motorcycle ride. I had a great time but was exhausted when Matty dropped me back at the hotel late in the afternoon. I stripped off my clothes while walking to the bed, planning to fall in and stay there until morning.

Halfway across the room, Matty's blue bag caught my eye. I rummaged through it until I found one of his shirts. I smelled him on the fabric as I pulled it over my head. Smiling, I crawled into bed.

I hadn't thought about my husband once all day.

I felt as if I'd only slept a few minutes when an insistent knocking pulled me out of oblivion. I stumbled toward the sound, realizing at the last minute that it was probably Will. I didn't want to see him and hesitated as I reached for the handle.

"Jo?" Matty's voice called quietly.

I flipped the lock and yanked open the door. "What are you doing here?"

"Were you sleeping?" he asked at the exact same time.

I nodded, stepping back to let him into the room. He was wearing the same jeans and shirt from earlier and had a garment bag folded over his arm.

"I've been gone for, like, a half hour."

I shook my head, trying to clear the fog. "Really?" It felt so much later. "I didn't know you were coming back." I rubbed my eyes. Grabbing my purse off the table, I pulled out a keycard and laid it down. "Take this. It's my spare. That way you can come anytime you want. Without waking me up."

"Thanks." He smiled. "Taylor's sisters are in town and crashing at my place. They're out to dinner, but I didn't want to deal with them all when they got back."

I didn't blame him. One Taylor was enough, but two more would be too much for any one person to handle.

He opened the closet door, hung up the bag—which I assumed contained tomorrow's work clothes—and turned back to me, frowning. "Is that my shirt?"

It took me a second to remember. Putting my hand on my hip, I tipped my head and teased, "Is this where you tell me I can keep it because it looks so much better on me?"

A slow sexy smile grew on his face, and he shook his head. "Nah. It looks better on me." He tipped his head, mirroring mine. "This is where I tell you I want it back." He lunged, grabbing the hem.

I jumped back, completely surprised, and ran, giggling. There weren't a lot of places I could hide in the little hotel room, and I never had a chance to outrun the daddy long legs. He caught me as I was trying to get into the bathroom. I turned, back to the wall, putting my hands to my sides. I didn't have anything on under his shirt, and I'd be damned if he was getting it back. He leaned into me, laughing with me, hands fighting with my own. I froze as three fingers made it past the cotton and up onto my hip.

I could see the shock on his face when all he felt was bare skin. As if double-checking, he slid his fingers down and back up, then onto my backside. I didn't move; his touch was as light as a feather and incredibly sensual. His eyes focused on mine, head tilting toward me as his hand explored more of my body, looking for something that wasn't there.

"I could be wearing a thong."

The hand stopped moving, but his face was dangerously close. "Are you?" His voice broke.

I shook my head. *Nope.* I was completely bare.

He inhaled sharply, and his eyes dropped to my mouth. He leaned in and I held my breath, sure he was going to kiss me. Instead, he moved his mouth to my ear.

His breath tickled my neck as his fingers moved down my thigh. "Do you always go commando?"

I groaned as fingertips crossed my leg, headed for my inner thigh.

He snatched his hand away suddenly. "What are we doing, Joes?" His voice was low and husky, filled with worry.

I didn't know. But I didn't want him to think about it, and I didn't want him to stop. I lifted my arms, looping them around his neck, attempting to pull him closer. He let me coax him closer, kissing my neck lightly. His hands grabbed fistfuls of the cotton around my waist, pulling it closer to him. I leaned into him, biting my lip to keep from making any noise. I wanted to beg him to touch me again, to kiss me, to do so many other things. But, I was afraid I'd break the spell.

For a blissful moment, his mouth hovered over mine.

"Christ!" Matty shoved away from me, his breath coming fast and hard. "Jo?" His voice plead with me, begging me to help him. But I didn't know what he wanted me to do. He groaned in frustration, combing his hands through his hair. "This isn't... Jo, we can't... this isn't right."

Yes, it is! I wanted to yell, to push him to the bed, to kiss him down his tattoo.

My hands clenched into fists, but I didn't argue. Instead, I cleared my throat. "We're both exhausted, Matty. Can we just pretend this didn't happen?"

Easier said than done, considering I was dripping wet and wanted nothing more than for him to kiss me as he touched me everywhere.

He eyed me warily, taking a few more steps away, then nodded.

"Do you really want your shirt back?"

He looked away suddenly, refusing to meet my eyes. "Nope. In fact, you keep it." He grabbed the pillow from the side of the bed he'd been sleeping on and threw it on the couch. "I'm gonna sleep on the sofa tonight. Tomorrow I'll go home."

Seriously? "Sharing a bed with me isn't a big deal, Matty. We share the same tent all the time."

He didn't look at me as he grabbed the spare blanket and settled on the couch. "I should have been on the couch all weekend anyway." He shook his head. "We both know that. And, I don't trust myself right now." The last part I almost didn't hear because he said it so softly.

I stomped to the bed, frustrated and angry. I listened to him toss and turn and sigh half the night. Each time I was tempted to beg him to come cuddle me. He had slept so well curled up in the bed, and I knew we could keep it PG if he would just crawl in with me. I mentally cursed Will. It was his fault I was here. It took me forever to fall asleep.

TEN

I was late to work the next morning. Matty was already gone when I'd finally woken up, and he was out visiting with clients by the time I got to the office. I didn't know if he was avoiding me or if he was really busy, but I didn't see him all day.

The hotel room was deserted when I got back. The only thing that told me he'd been there was his shirt—the one I'd worn to bed—folded neatly on my side of the bed. I'd taken it off and shoved it into his bag that morning. Even his toothbrush was gone from the sink. Putting my purse on the table by the door, I realized that the extra keycard was missing. I smiled in relief, half tempted to call him, but I didn't want to bother him if he was with Taylor. We'd talk later. Or at least I assumed we would.

Tuesday I was out of the office all day, visiting foster homes and the children on my caseload. Usually when I was driving, I called Matty. Even if he was in the office, we'd chat and it would keep me awake. I wanted to call him but was worried that it would be too weird. Instead, the long drive gave me plenty of time to think. There was no doubt now that he knew I was attracted to him, and while it didn't change how I felt about him—he was still my best friend—I wasn't sure how he would handle it.

There was casual flirting, where two people could laugh and have fun, stealing glances, having inside jokes, exchanging innocent touches. Then there was full-on flirting that was more like foreplay, where if you weren't careful, you ended up half naked in each other's arms, ready to have sex at any minute. We'd spent years in the first category. Maybe we hadn't meant to be there, but after one of us got the other through a serious situation, we always ended up back there.

The last few days had been a whole new thing though. Holding hands in public just so I could touch him, spending the nights wrapped up in each other, my fingers trailing over every part of his upper body, and then last night. I would have slept with him if he hadn't stopped it.

What kind of best friend did shit like that? I'd held Matty's hand and took away the alcohol when Becky left, and he'd held me and tried to make me laugh while I cried over Will. Sharing joys and heartache, being honest with the other even when it hurt, supporting their decisions, having their back even if you disagreed. That was what a best friend did. That was what Matty and I had done for years. We didn't screw with the other's emotions or confuse our relationship for something it wasn't.

Until last night. I wished that I could rewind and do the last few days over. Just so I could have my best friend back. I let memories take over.

I glanced up nervously as he walked around the corner into our cubicles. The man looked like hell, as if he'd been out all night partying. Yet he sauntered to his desk, giving the impression that he was much older than twenty-five.

When he saw me, his eyebrows rose. "Well, hello." He gave me a smile that would melt most hearts and drop most panties. It didn't work on me. "Matthew Murphy."

He held out a hand, but when I put mine in his, he lifted it to his lips. Offering me a smirk that made me want to slap him, he added, "I think you're at the wrong desk, sweetheart. First day?"

I nodded, completely unfazed by his dazzling looks but confused because my boss had brought me to that desk herself.

"I'm getting a new trainee, some middle-aged man named Joe." He whispered, almost conspiratorial.

"I'm Jo." I explained with narrowed eyes. "Not middle aged. And, definitely not a man."

He dropped my hand like it was on fire and took two steps back. His eyes narrowed as if I'd done something wrong. "Not possible."

"You're saying I look like a middle aged man?" I sassed back.

He opened his mouth, but no words came. He snapped it shut. Then, he scowled at me again, crossing his arms over his chest. "No. I mean there's no way in hell you're in the right seat. No one in their right mind would put me with a kid. Especially one fresh out of school."

I started to explain that I'd been escorted here, but he held up a finger silencing me. "Save it. You'll be moving soon." He spun around before I could say anything else.

I'd been appalled and had called Will and told him how much I hated my new trainer. I hoped they would move me. I didn't want to sit by him. Hell, I didn't want to speak to him.

The office scuttlebutt was that Matthew Murphy was a chauvinistic pig who thought every woman worshiped him—he wasn't far off, of course—and although he flirted shamelessly, he avoided office romance as though it was the black plague.

They didn't move me but told Matty he needed to suck it up and deal. None of his charms worked on me, and he was miserable to work with. I hated him for weeks, dreading going into work.

"You're late!" He snapped as I hurried to my desk.

Already flustered, I peered down at my watch. "It's seven twenty-four." I argued. "You told me to be here at seven thirty."

"No," he snarled, "I told you we had to leave at seven thirty." He grabbed his bag and strode off, leaving me to drop my files and rush after him.

He didn't say anything else until we were on the road. "Listen, Sweetie. If you can't do something simple like show up on time, you're never going to make it here. I've been carrying your workload and mine for weeks. Maybe it's time to find another job, yeah? Maybe you could get hired as an admin assistant."

My jaw clenched and my hands clenched around my shoulder belt. It wasn't the first time he'd suggested I quit. In fact, he found a way to drop a not so subtle hint daily.

I'd had enough.

"You know what you sexist asshole?" I snapped. "The only fucking reason you're carrying my cases is because you refuse to let me handle them alone. Which no one understands! I've asked other workers. If you're so eager to get rid of me, then transfer my cases to me! As soon as you do, I can promise you that you will never have anything to do with them again."

"You've asked other workers," he forced out a humorless laugh. "Bet you didn't tell them that you're incompetent as hell. Maybe if you'd spend half as much time learning how to do your job as you do talking to your boyfriend-,"

"Husband." I yelled, holding up my left hand. "I'm married you, idiot!"

He snorted. "What are you, twenty? Yeah, 'cause that will last." He shook his head, lips twisting in that annoying smirk of his. "Maybe you should take a break, Sweetheart. Work on being the good little housewife you want to be instead of trying to play social worker. You're not cut out for this work."

Fuck him. "Yeah, well maybe you should find a job at a bar, where the only people you have to interact with are drunk off their ass or stupid enough to find you funny and attractive. I'm not quitting. Nothing you can say or do will make me any more miserable than you already have."

"That's your comeback? I interact with people just fine, little girl. The only person I have a problem with is you. You know what that tells me?"

It was a rhetorical question, but I answered him anyway. "That you're a judgmental prick who has his panties in a twist because you had a hard on for working with some old guy and got me instead? Your sexuality doesn't offend me, so I'm not sure what your problem is."

"I have a name! If you call me Sweetie, or Sweetheart, or little girl one more time Matt," I hissed, fire shooting through my veins as I reached my boiling point, "one more fucking time, and I'm going to do something so horrific to you that you won't be able to hear my name without shuddering or pissing your pants in fear. You may think I'm a stupid kid, but I can promise you, I'm smart and creative and I will make you rue the day we met Unlike the bimbos you sleep with – who are desperate to get away, I'm not going anywhere!!"

An awkward silence filled the car and I crossed my arms and turned my back on him as I watched out my window. I'd tried to hold my tongue, knowing that I would never survive if I didn't have friends at the office. I didn't need dickheaded friends, though.

I half expected him to turn the car around and drive me back to the office. Or to call our supervisor. I didn't expect him to start chortling.

"Rue the day," he repeated when he caught his breath, breaking down in another fit of laughter. "Jesus, Joes. You kill me." When he finally stopped laughing, he squinted over at me. "There she is. There's that fire I knew you had. You're going to do fine here, kid."

I chuckled at the memory. We'd spent countless hours on the road together after that and I learned there was more to him than just a slutty, pretty party boy. He was funny as hell—most of his humor was dry or self-deprecating but hilarious. He was surprisingly sweet, once you got past the asshole exterior. And he was an exercise junky because he'd been the "fat kid."

He was also a major geek, just like me. When I told him about my weekend marathon of the five Star Wars episodes, he'd looked at me doubtfully and asked me if I knew what a rancor was, other than the name of his first band. He was excited to know someone who could actually appreciate the concepts of the movies. I confided that I'd always wanted to get a Jedi symbol tattooed on one shoulder and a Sith symbol on the other, my version of an angel and a devil. He'd looked at me as if I was crazy then told me he had those exact tattoos.

We'd been best friends ever since. We were such an unlikely pair. Somehow we'd formed an unbreakable bond. Through thick and thin, we had each other's back.

I hoped that I hadn't ruined that.

Taylor's words came flooding into my mind. *"Have you seen yourself lately?"* I couldn't turn on my own husband; there was no way Matty would rather share my bed than hers.

I'd seen the women he had loved over the years, and I wasn't even close to being in the same league. I had never needed to be. I had a part of Matty no one else got.

Realization sank in. The last few days had been about him supporting me, nothing more. He would never leave me when I needed him, because I had never left him. I felt like an idiot. I'd been throwing myself at him, and he'd been catching me and trying to stand me back up on my own two feet.

I sighed at the long stretch of road in front of me. I'd been so upset over Will that Matty had let me use him as a distraction. My stomach churned; I disgusted myself. Sighing again, I pulled over to text Matty. *I'm sorry for being an asshole.*

My phone buzzed back seconds later. *Why? That's why I like you.*

I laughed, looking over my shoulder as I pulled out onto the road. I adored him.

Wednesday, we were both back in the office for part of the day, and things seemed as though they were back to normal between us. It was as if the weekend hadn't happened, like I received the do-over I so desperately wanted. He didn't mention anything about it, so I didn't either.

I was just thankful that I had my Matty back. He didn't look miserable and his mood wasn't all over the chart, so he and Taylor must have worked out their problems. I wondered if she had taken off her engagement ring or if he had caved, but I was refused to ask. We went for a run in the afternoon then talked on the phone for almost an hour that night.

I woke up in a good mood the next morning, knowing that it was my full day with Matty. He strolled into the office right before nine, humming. We were back to normal. Things were good. It was a whistle-while-you-work kinda day.

Before he could sit down, our boss came out of her office. Connie hadn't been our supervisor for very long, but we both had great things to say about her so far. She was easy to read, and right now, something was very wrong.

"I need you in my office, Matt."

He turned and followed her.

"You come too, Jo," she called over her shoulder. "This concerns you both." She closed the door behind me and sat on her desk, her face somber. "The Todd TPR is being appealed."

Matty sputtered and I gasped. I fell into one of Connie's chairs, completely shocked.

"I don't understand." In all my years with the department, I'd never heard of a signed termination being appealed. Not one. "How long does that take? What will happen with the adoption?" I rattled off the questions, barely breathing.

"I don't know." Connie pursed her lips in thought. "We have to wait to see if his dad wins the appeal. If he does, he can get Todd back. If he doesn't win, this will still slow everything down."

The blood drained from Matty's face, but he was gripping the arms of his chair so hard I thought he might break it. "I just told them..."

I knew that he was talking about the Smiths.

A swift knock landed on the door before it opened. Ash, one of our clerks, peeked her head around the corner before anyone had a chance to tell her to come in.

Her eyes landed on Matty and she smiled flirtingly before moving on to me. "Jo, someone is downstairs for you. They say it's urgent."

"Is it a client?" I didn't want to leave Matty if it wasn't something important.

She shrugged. "I don't think so. They asked to speak to Mrs. Walker, and they said they need you to go down now."

70

Twenty different things ran through my mind as I bounded down the stairs. However, being served papers showing that Will had filed for legal separation was not one of them. I walked back to my desk in a daze. First Matty's TPR, now this. I was sure this day couldn't get any worse.

ELEVEN

Hooligans Pub was crazy. For some reason, I had thought it would be at least half-empty. It was Thursday night for crying out loud. People had to work the next morning.

God, I sounded like my mother. I was too young to have that mentality. Looking around at the children crowding in, I realized I was a hell of a lot older than I'd realized.

Matty cleared a path to a corner table, and I quickly followed him, sliding into the chair next to him. It was so loud that if I wanted to talk to him at all, I'd have to be close. He stood as soon as I was in my seat.

"What are you having?"

I shook my head. I honestly didn't know what to order. All I knew was that I wanted to get shit-faced drunk and forget about this awful day.

He smiled that slow sexy grin that made me weak in the knees. "How 'bout the separation special?"

"I have no idea what that is, but if it will get me drunk, then absolutely!"

He hesitated for a moment, then winked before turning and heading toward the bar.

I scanned the room fascinated by the amount of people. I wasn't as out of place as I originally thought. There were more people in their thirties than their early twenties. The realization made me sad. These people should all be home with their families.

"Hey there."

I turned and was startled to see a young man sliding up to my table. Obviously he was lost. He smiled pleasantly in greeting. I gave him a little wave.

He spoke, but I couldn't hear him. He stepped closer, leaning into my space. "Busy in here tonight, right?"

I nodded trying to figure out if I knew him as he pulled out a chair. He looked familiar. Oh, God. I hoped he wasn't a client. Although, that would be my luck.

"I saw you sitting here all alone and sad. Thought I'd come over and cheer you up."

I looked around, expecting to see some of his frat buddies filming my humiliation. He was a kid for crying out loud. I wouldn't have been surprised if he was in here celebrating his ability to drink legally.

"Aren't you out past curfew?"

His snicker was annoying as hell. He reached out and traced the lines of my index finger. "Nah. But if it turns you on to think I'm that young, we can pretend."

I snatched my hand away. *Eww.* I was searching for an appropriate way to tell this child to get the hell away from me when a pink drink slid across the table toward me and a strong hand found my back. Before I could turn around, Matty leaned in and nuzzled my cheek, kissing the side of my mouth.

"Hey, you," he said in a low voice that was sexy as hell. He put a muscular forearm on the table between me and the kid. "Everything okay here?"

I looked up at him, relief washing over me, and touched his cheek. "It is now." I looked back at the young man. "This gentleman said that I looked lonely and sad, so he came over to cheer me up."

Matty's other arm snaked out around my shoulders, pulling me close. "Thanks, guy. I'm back now, so she won't be lonely anymore. You can leave."

The youngster's eyes darted back and forth between the two of us, before he lifted his chin at me. "If you change your mind, I'm here all night." He winked and disappeared into the crowd.

Knowing Matty was going to pick on me unmercifully, I held up a hand. "Don't even," I warned before I grabbed my drink and took a big gulp. I swallowed half of it before coughing.

"Easy there, tiger." Matty chuckled. "I told them to make it strong."

They had obliged. There was more vodka than anything, but I could taste the soda. I didn't know where it got the pink color though. "What is it?"

"A twisted Willie." He chuckled, looking quite pleased with himself. "I thought you'd appreciate it. Raspberry Smirnoff, Sprite, and a hint of Bitter Lemon. Like your husband." He took a long tug off his beer. "Is it good?"

"It's actually really good." I held up the clear plastic cup. "Want some?" He took a sip, wincing. Vodka was not his drink of choice. I giggled at the disgusted face he made. I leaned into him. "Thanks for this."

His day had been just as shitty as mine, but when I had suggested that we get completely wasted after work, he had insisted on being the designated walker. Apparently he thought it was a bad idea for us both to get blistering drunk, and he claimed the end of my marriage warranted a good hangover. He handed me the cup back and I held it up in thanks, then I tipped my head and drained the rest of the glass.

He raised an eyebrow but smiled. "Round two?"

Round two turned into round four. From the taste of my twisted Willies, I assumed he had asked the bartenders to scale them back a bit. Or I'd just had so much to drink that I was used to the vodka. After I'd finished my fourth drink, I made Matty go out on the floor and shake his groove thing with me.

Of course he could dance. I was pretty sure there wasn't a single thing he couldn't do. He was one of the only men on the floor who didn't look like a complete idiot, and women swarmed around him. I couldn't dance but was doing my best to pretend I could, laughing at myself and the look of disgust on his face when another random stranger tried to grind with him. The music was loud and there were tons of people—a perfect place to lose myself.

Or my friend.

I had turned away from Matty, my hands in the air, screaming the words to one of P!nk's girl power songs, swaying from side to side with a couple of other women when I realized I didn't know where he was. I turned completely around, trying to find him. The move made me dizzy, and I took a step backward, laughing.

"Easy. I've gotcha."

I'd backed into someone, and that someone was holding onto my upper arms, keeping me from falling flat on my back. It took me a second to regain my balance, but when I did, he let go and I spun to thank my hero. The man was incredibly handsome. Not quite as tall as Matt, but he was a solid six feet of pure muscle. Realizing how close I was to the giant, I stepped back.

I was still wobbly, and he reached a heavily tattooed arm out and steadied me again. "You okay?"

I held up a hand and nodded like a fool. Holding up my thumb and a finger, a couple of inches apart, I explained, "I think I may have had a wee bit too much to drink." I giggled. Mortified, I put my hand over my mouth and giggled again.

"It happens. Here"—he held out a hand—"let's get you to a seat before you break your leg in those things."

Those things? My confusion must have shown on my face because he looked down toward my feet. I couldn't remember what shoes I had on but knew if I tried to look, I would fall on my face.

I hiccupped and took his offered hand instead. "'Sanks."

There were no empty tables near the dance floor, so I let Andre lead me toward the pool tables. I was surprised by how much quieter it was. He stopped at a small round table and pulled out a chair for me. I hadn't realized my feet hurt as much as they did.

"Having a good time?"

I nodded. At least I tried to.

He looked concerned. "Are you alone?"

I didn't know if I should answer. I wasn't getting a bad feeling from him. I was sure serial killers or rapists would send off a bad vibe.

"No." I looked back toward the crowd but still couldn't see Matty. "Celebrating with a friend. Are you?"

He ignored my question. "What are you celebrating?"

My limbs felt heavy and I had to concentrate hard to get the words out. Yep. I was definitely feeling that fourth drink. "M' divorce."

He looked taken aback. "Oh! Sorry."

I shook my head. "Don't be. It happens."

"There you are!"

Matty looked both worried and annoyed as he strode toward us. The giant next to me stood, and I was worried he was going to keep Matt from me. Instead, he greeted Matt as if he knew him.

When Matty held out his hand, then threw an arm around the big guy in a hug, I realized they did know each other. I couldn't hear what they were saying, but Matty was laughing. I glared at him.

Matty held out a hand for me. "Come on, sweetie. I'll take you home."

"Sweetie?" I snarled. Fuck him and that stupid name. I didn't want to go home.

"Sorry," He eyed me cautiously as he stepped close, helping me to my feet.

"I'll take another drink."

Matty and the giant exchanged a look. Realizing just how much my feet still hurt, I sat back down, not caring what they thought. After what looked like a debate, Matty handed the larger man cash and then sat next to me.

"Did you just let Andre run off with your cash?"

"Who?" His eyebrows pinched together in confusion before he chuckled. "That's Fred." He moved his finger in a circle. "He owns Hooligans. He's bouncing tonight, but he's usually at the bar serving."

Fred who owns a bar and is a bouncer. Because obviously everyone knows Fred, the bouncing bar owner. The thought made me laugh.

Matty frowned. "You're cut off after this one," he told me sternly, which only made me giggle harder.

By the time a waitress brought our drinks, I was crying from laughing so hard. The girl was wearing short shorts and a tiny tank top that showed her perfectly flat belly whenever she moved her arms. Which was often. She squealed when she saw Matt, practically throwing the tray she carried on the table and jumping into his arms. I wiped the happy tears from my face while I eyed the bimbo climbing all over him. She was tall, blond, and obviously worked out all the time. Either that or gravity hadn't caught up with her yet. I hated her.

Matt was talking in her ear, and she was looking at me, nodding. She beamed at me. I glared back.

She leaned over Matty and giving me a great view of her perfect Ds. "Jo! I've heard so much about you! This guy"—she bent her head toward Matt—"never stops talking about you."

It took a second for her words to sink in. Once they did, I started at him in disbelief. He only shrugged.

"This is Darcey." He leaned close to my ear. "Fred's wife."

Oh! Fred was nice. I raised a hand and waved like a loser.

"We ride together sometimes." I didn't understand what he meant. My confusion must have been obvious because Matt rolled his eyes. "Bikes, Jo. They have a motorcycle and we go on rides together."

They were bikers! That made sense.

Darcey handed me another pink drink, but she also slid two shots in front of me and two in front of Matty, along with another beer. Matty looked up at her, and she winked back. "I know a guy. Courtesy of the owner."

I picked up my drink and took a long slow sip. If it was the end, I wanted to enjoy it. I hadn't planned on it being stronger than all the others combined, and I turned toward the dance floor so they couldn't see the look on my face.

After Darcey left, we sat in silence, taking sips of our drinks every now and then, watching the other patrons. I couldn't drink mine fast if I had wanted to—I was sure straight gasoline didn't taste nearly as bad.

"What kind of shot is that?"

"I have no idea. Knowing them, something strong."

I picked one up, sniffing it, not sure I wanted to try it. It didn't smell strong, and I doubted that anything could taste worse than my current drink. I held it up, waiting for Matt to toast with me.

He hesitated before lifting one and holding it out to me. I took a deep breath. "To happy endings."

I downed mine. I was wrong. So very wrong.

It burned all the way down my throat and into my stomach. It was awful. I scrunched my eyes closed, hoping to will away the vile taste, and praying that I kept it down.

I opened one eye, trying to see if my best friend was faring any better. He hadn't drunk his yet.

"That hurts like hell going down." I warned.

"Happy endings? Really?" He lapped his bottom lip before smirking. "Fine. I'm all for that. To happy endings." His voice was full of humor as he upended the glass. The jackass didn't even cringe.

I glared at him. "That wasn't what I meant and you know it!" I snorted at his doubtful expression. "I *meant* that my white prince could still come and knock me off my feet with his horse."

Matty didn't even try to hide his amusement. I tried to glare at him again, but his shoulders were shaking with laughter and I couldn't help but join him.

"Oh, Jesus, Joes. I'm going to take you drinking more often." He finally managed to get out, "You meant that your prince charming could still ride in on his white horse and sweep you off your feet, right?" He leaned forward. "You still want a happily ever after? Even after everything?"

I nodded. "Thas what I meant. Thas what I want. Happily ever after."

Matty lifted the second shot and held it to me. I didn't want to drink anymore of that poison, but I knew he wouldn't let me die. I grabbed the last shot and clinked it with his glass.

"To your happily ever after, Jo."

They say that after the first shot goes down, the next isn't as bad. They're wrong. It was worse.

I coughed, struggling to keep it down as the vile liquid revolted in my stomach. I grabbed my cup and took a quick sip, trying to get the taste of the shot out of my mouth. Big mistake. Gasoline does not get rid of the taste of diesel, and the two don't mesh well.

I closed my eyes and leaned my head on the table. I wasn't getting sick. I wouldn't let myself get sick.

"Joes?" Matty sounded worried.

He moved closer, his hand running up and down my spine again. I held up a hand, hoping I was holding up one finger. I just needed a minute. His hand stayed on my back, comforting me.

I wasn't sure how long it took, but the nausea finally passed and I forced myself to sit up. Big mistake. Everything was rotating, so I turned to him, leaning my head on his shoulder. He immediately wrapped his arm around me, pulling me tight.

It was nice to have him so close. He smelled heavenly, and the world didn't spin so much when I had something to hold on to. From my spot under his arm, I had a perfect view of the dance floor. I watched a cute brunette with red highlights dance with two men, one in front of her, one grabbing her hips from behind. One of those men could be my Mr. Perfect, but as long as a girl who looked like that was an option, neither would look twice at me.

Glancing up at Matt, I realized I had never been as honest with him as I had thought, and with all the wisdom of someone who had had more than enough alcohol, I decided to bare my soul.

"I hate her. Dichya know that?" I picked up my right hand, putting it on his belly.

Matty looked down at me then across the bar, searching for whomever I was looking at. "Who?"

"Taylor." I felt him tense, and I knew I needed to get it all out while I was full of liquid courage. "For so many reasons. She's gorgeous and smart and funny and she's never had to shop in the petite section because she has legs that go on for miles and everywhere she goes, men adore her. She isn't a nice person, not

78

really. But I think I hate her most because she took you." It was a run-together babble, and I wasn't sure he even heard it all.

He was watching me closely, brows knit together. "Took me?"

I sat forward a little and nodded. "Took you. Away from me. You're going to marry her." I laughed bitterly, trying to cover the sadness I felt. "If she's going to look like that and act all bitchy, she should at least leave the good guys for the rest of us. It isn't fair. How many more nights like this do you think we'll have? You already can't do Saturday mornings with me. It won't be long before she has you whipped and you forget about me. She took you, now she has you, and soon I won't have anyone. So I hate her."

He looked away then and picked up his beer. "She doesn't have me, Joes." He took a big gulp. "You do. I've always been yours."

The last words were so quiet that I almost missed them. I didn't understand. He must have meant because he was there, in a bar with me on a weekday night when we both had to work in the morning, so I wouldn't have to deal with the reality of my life alone.

"I know." I sat up, moving back into my own chair. "I'm drunk and being..." I couldn't think of the word. I shook my head again. "You are a great friend." I smiled. "I'd be lost without you. I love you. I hate her. Very simple. And she really doesn't deserve you."

He shook his head, looking back at me. "No, Jo. She doesn't have me." He swallowed, his Adam's apple bobbing in the sexiest way. "We broke up."

I was shocked. "What? When? Why?"

"Earlier this week."

I stared at him, willing him to explain.

He motioned toward the bar with his beer bottle. "Because of this. Because of Friday." He took another drink. "Because I want something I can't have." He put the bottle down before meeting my eyes. "Because of you."

Before I could think about what he was saying, his hands were in my hair and his lips were on mine. It was sweet and soft. I leaned into him, moving my lips against his. His tongue pushed at my bottom lip, and I opened my mouth, letting it in.

He was taking over my senses. I could taste his beer mixed with the alcohol from the shot, all I could smell was his cologne, and the only thing I heard was the pounding of my heart in my ears.

My hands balled into fists in his shirt as I pulled him closer. It wasn't close enough. I wanted more. Much more.

He pulled back slightly. He was as out of breath as I was, and for a minute, he rested his forehead on mine. He sat up, pulling the fabric out of my hands. "Joes? We can't do this. You're drunk off your ass and..." He tipped his bottle to his lips, finishing it off.

Anger took over. "And what? I'm not the girl you want to be making out with in a bar? Afraid someone, like maybe Short Shorts, might see you?"

"No!" he snapped, obviously as irritated as I was. "But I can tell you that you will thank me tomorrow morning."

I was suddenly ashamed. "I get it. I'm the friend. Not the hot hookup."

Matt rolled his eyes. "Now you're being melodramatic and ridiculous."

I was not being dramatic! "Listen, we both know you're here because I'm the burdensome best friend that you have to make sure gets home okay." I stood up and downed the rest of my drink, just for flare. I cringed at the thoughtless act. "Whatever, Matt."

The asshole was trying not to laugh at me.

"Take me home," I said.

The walk back to the hotel was quiet and slow. I wouldn't let him help me walk, and my feet refused to cooperate. I was surprised when we made it back without me falling.

I debated sitting down once we were on the elevator but was sure I wouldn't be able to stand back up. I'd be damned before I'd let Matty help me. Instead, I leaned against the wall and silently begged the world to stop spinning as the elevator climbed.

As soon as we reached my floor, I realized I hadn't brought my purse and didn't have my key. Seeing my face, he pulled his out of his back pocket and waved it at me in that annoyingly sassy way he had.

I let him get off the elevator first and unlock the room. He held the door open for me, and I stumbled into my room ahead of him, kicking off my heels. I turned around to look at him, knowing he was probably angry with me. He could be pissed off all he wanted—I was mad at him too.

One look at him though, and I was completely distracted. He was leaning against the closed door with his hands tucked into the pockets of jeans that fit him just right, watching me as if he expected me to keel over where I stood. He was so unbelievably attractive all dark and brooding. I had to have him.

Staring him in the eyes, silently daring him to stop me, I unbuttoned my shirt slowly and pushed it off my shoulders and onto the floor. His eyes strayed from mine, watching as my hands trailed down my breasts, over my belly, and to the button on my jeans.

"Joes." The voice was confused, unsure of why I was stripping in front of him.

Before I could push the denim over my hips in what was supposed to be a super sexy move, the world started to spin. Laughing, I stumbled back.

"Jesus, Jo!" A hand grabbed my arm, steadying me. "You are beyond drunk." There was no humor in his voice.

"I'm not drunk!" I narrowed my eyes at the chest in front of me, following it up until I met his eyes. "Oh, there you are. Hi!" I smiled, giggling again.

"Of course you're not. Let me help you into bed."

"Only if you're naked and getting into bed with me." I giggled again. "What I meant to say"—I grabbed the top of his jeans under his T-shirt—"is that you can help by getting naked and getting into bed."

"Stop." He moved my hands but didn't let them go. "You need to sleep this off."

I stepped into him, closing the small gap, and slid my hands under his shirt. Oh, my god. My fingers slid upward over hard-as-rock muscle, and I could feel his flesh pimple into goosebumps. "I'm going to bed, but sleep is the last thing I need."

Matty grabbed my arms and pulled them away from him. "You don't want to do this. Come on, babe, you know you don't."

I didn't know that at all. In fact, I knew I didn't need to sleep it off. I knew I needed sex. I needed his arms around me and him to fuck me three ways from Sunday. I needed him to make this all go away.

Then it hit me. "You're not attracted to me." I shook my head, embarrassed. "I really don't turn you on, do I?"

His face softened a little. "Joes." He sighed. "I'm trying to save you from making a mistake. I'm not the kind of guy you want in your bed."

He was the only man I wanted in my bed, but he was doing that stupid Matty trick where he said whatever it took to make me feel better about an awful situation. I had totally read him all wrong. A thought nagged at me. He'd had such an urgency when he kissed me, as if he'd been waiting to do it all night. "Why'd you kiss me then?"

He sighed again, but this time he was annoyed. "You are so drunk." He shook his head as if I was a naughty child and he, as my parent, couldn't believe my unsightly behavior. "We'll talk about this later. When you know what you're saying."

I wanted to talk about it then. "What it is about me that disgusts you so much? I may not be tall and perfect, but I'm not a fucking troll."

"I never said you were."

"Yeah, you kinda just did. Nice try, with the whole 'I'm not the kinda man you want in your bed.' It's not you, it's me, right, Matty? Whatever. You think I'm not good enough for you, the Greek God of... of..." I waved my arm, searching for the right term, but the words never came. "Whatever." I grabbed my shirt and shoved one arm in then the other, sidestepping him as I struggled to button it.

"What are you doing?" He was clearly annoyed.

I had almost reached the door. "I'm leaving. Going back to the bar." I turned and faced him. "I'm horny as hell. I haven't had sex in months. Since I'm not good enough for you to fuck, I'm gonna find someone who will." I reached for my purse.

"The hell you are!"

His hand wrapped around my arm, and he jerked hard, catching me off guard. He pushed me back into the door, and his lips came down on mine. Alarm bells started ringing. This wasn't a soft, sweet kiss like before. This was raw, unrestrained, and dangerous.

He pulled back, and I was surprised to see his sneer. "See? You can't even fucking kiss me back! You're playing with fire here, Jo, and you know it. Make me the bad guy if you want, 'cause that's what I am. If knowing that I'm dangerous helps you walk away, then I'll show you how fucking scary I am!"

He pushed my hands above my head, holding them with one hand while his other roamed over my body, settling on my chest. His mouth descended again, lips rough, demanding. He didn't give me time to kiss him back, moving his mouth to my ear, sucking on

82

the bottom of my lobe and closing his teeth around it. Hard. I hissed.

He moved, grinning at me in sinister triumph. "By the time I get started, you'll be begging me to save you!"

I glared at him. "I don't need you to save me! You don't scare me. I know that you're trying to save yourself from making the mistake of fucking me!" I was shouting and didn't care. "How awful it would be to have to look yourself in the mirror and know that you got turned on by the fat girl."

His eyes widened before they narrowed, his jaw clenching, and for a split second he looked truly dangerous. "Really?" He laughed humorlessly. "I'm the idiot arguing with the drunk moron, but for the record, I've had to look myself in mirror every morning knowing that I want you, knowing that you aren't mine to want, and knowing I would never have this chance. For fucking years. Now that I have it, all I want to do is throw your drunk ass over my shoulder, strip you naked, and make you scream my name until you forget everyone and everything else. If you remember anything from tonight, remember I had to use every ounce of willpower to try to resist you because I don't want you to hate me tomorrow."

I wanted to yell at him, tell him I didn't believe a word. But I couldn't. He was telling the truth. His face was so sincere, it cut through the little bit of a buzz I had left. And my heart broke for him.

His arms were boxing me in, but I could duck under them and hide in the bathroom until he left, then we could pretend this didn't happen. That was probably exactly what he expected me to do. Or I could just take the chance and make him love me tonight.

His face was inches away from mine. I reached up, grabbing him behind the neck, and pulled him down again. My lips touched his and he started to pull back, then suddenly he groaned and pulled my body against his, deepening the kiss. This time, I kissed him back.

His hands traced my body, coming up to my half-open shirt. He grabbed the sides and gave it a quick tug. Buttons flew off as it came open, his hands moved inside, and he pushed the shirt the rest of the way off. His lips moved down my neck to the top of my breasts and back up, making me shiver. He pulled back.

"Joes, I'm not..." His voice was full of need. "This isn't a good idea, but I want you in my bed, your body asking me for more. I want to watch you come apart, hear you beg me to let you come, screaming my name when you lose control. Fucking Christ, Jo, it's taking every ounce I've got to..." He groaned. "This isn't a good idea."

I smiled up at him as I tugged his shirt up and over his head, trying to get to skin so I could kiss him. "Yes, it is."

I kissed the tattoo on his chest. He sucked in his breath.

"It's a great fucking idea." My lips trailed down the anchor, kissing the middle of his belly, stopping right above his pants. "Years in the making."

I reached for the button of his jeans, but he moved just out of reach. I ached to touch him. All of him.

"Once we cross that line, we can't take it back."

Right now, I hated him and his mixed signals. I stood up straight and met his eyes. I wiggled my hips as I pushed my jeans down and kicked them out of my way, then I reached behind me, unbuckled my bra, and threw it in the same direction.

He groaned. "Jesus, Jo."

I shrugged. "Whoops. Line crossed."

His eye darted along every piece of me. "I want to touch you." He groaned. "Being the sober one fucking sucks."

"If you don't stop talking and start touching, I'm going to explode." I grabbed him by the waistband, pulling him hard. He fell against me. "I'm not that drunk," I tried to assure him as I pushed off his jeans. "I know what we're doing, and I want to do it." I kissed him. "I need this."

He cupped my cheeks, kissing me softly. I was terrified he was going to push me away.

"Matty, please just make me forget everything."

His teeth nipped my bottom lip, fingernails digging into my bare hips as he picked me up and carried me to the bed. "I'd do anything for you."

TWELVE

My alarm beeped incessantly, tugging me out of what seemed like a happy dream. Groggily I dragged my hand over the top of the nightstand, trying to find the offending device before it got any louder. I stabbed at the screen, sighing in relief when the noise stopped, wondering if I could sneak in fifteen more minutes of sleep. Falling back onto my pillow, I closed my eyes, trying to will away the dull pounding in my skull as I tried to remember where I'd put my Tylenol.

I was never drinking that much again.

My eyes popped open as memories from the night before assaulted me. Then I recalled where I was. And who was with me.

I rolled over slightly, just enough to see him. We had left the shades open, and the early morning sun was just starting to shine on his side of the bed. It gave his skin a bronze glow, creating a slight shadow in the valley that ran down the middle of his back. I fought the urge to reach out and trace it. He was gorgeous on any given day, right then he was breathtaking.

Lying on his stomach with his arms folded under his pillow, his head was tilted toward me, his chin touching his right shoulder. His dark hair, with the slightest tinge of gray, clumped together in what had been professional spikes just a few hours earlier. A few wisps had escaped and were tickling his forehead. I could just make out the black lines of the tattoos on his back, a few of the indents where his ribs were, and the bulge of his shoulder blade. A small corner of the sheet, flung over his waist, kept him covered just enough to be decent. He looked like an erotic painting or the cover of a steamy smut novel. Somehow he looked both youthful and innocent, as well as the sexy-as-hell bad boy.

His face was emotionless in sleep, but his lips pouted slightly, begging for a kiss. I started to lean forward but stopped suddenly. I didn't want to wake him up yet.

That awkward conversation was not one I wanted to have right then. I didn't want to have it at all. I frowned at him as reality crept back in and I saw my friend and not the sex-god I'd been admiring five seconds before.

I didn't know what in the hell I was going to do. There was no way in hell we could forget. We'd crossed a line that he knew we shouldn't have crossed. There was no way to go back, but I hoped there was a way to move forward.

Well, obviously you didn't think that through well enough, I chastised myself. I didn't know if he would ever forgive me. *Shit, shit, shit.*

I leaned back to my side of the bed as quietly as I could. I didn't want to risk waking him - the idea of talking to him right now terrified me. My heart was pounding so loud that I was sure he would hear it, my breaths coming heavy.

I would laugh about this later, really. Maybe it wouldn't be as awful as I thought. *Ha! It will be.*

I started to turn over, getting ready to slide out of bed, when a muscular arm wrapped around my belly and held me in place. I hadn't heard him move, and I jumped, barely keeping a yelp from escaping.

"Leaving so soon?" his tone was groggy as he moved in behind me, his chin resting on my shoulder.

"Hey, you." I forced myself to sound jolly, willing my heart to stop pounding. "I've gotta get ready for work."

The arm didn't release me as I attempted to get up again. Instead it slid me back into the solid wall that was his chest. "I thought we had all morning." The voice was low and husky and promised naughty times. I shivered as his lips made a trail down my neck onto my back.

"We did. Time's up."

I wasn't sure if he could sense my urgent need to get away from him, but his arm only tightened. In one fluid move, he pulled me into the middle of the bed and rolled on top of me, one of his legs nestled between mine. I knew he was watching me closely, trying to read my thoughts, but I couldn't look at him.

Instead I stared at the Claddagh on his shoulder, and traced the lines lightly with my finger. He didn't move, just stayed propped on his hands, looking down at me until I had gone around the tattoo twice.

"Fine. I need twenty more minutes though." There was humor in his voice, yet I still couldn't meet his eyes. "'Cause twenty minutes is all it'll take."

No explanation was needed as he pressed into me, and I could feel how hard he was.

The muscles in his biceps strained as he held his weight off me. Unable to resist touching them, hand slid from his tattoo over his shoulder and down. I loved these arms. I loved to look at them, and I loved touching them. He wasn't as big as some of his friends, but he certainly wasn't small.

At first glance you couldn't tell how muscular he was. Underneath the button up shirts and the dress khakis, there was an entirely different man. Big, strong, and solid under my fingers, and I couldn't stop myself from reaching my left hand out too. I ran my fingertips down both arms, amazed at how hard they really were. He shivered, giving me an impatient sigh, and pushed himself into my leg again.

"Look at me," he growled.

I met his eyes and knew mine must reflect his. I wanted him to fuck me as much as he wanted to do it. His eyes were the brightest blue that I'd ever seen. When we'd first met, I thought that they were contacts because there was no way that color was natural. I was wrong. Now they'd grown darker—more dangerous, as if a warning sign. Too late, I thought as I arched toward him, remembering that I was just as naked as he was.

The eyes narrowed and his nostrils flared. "Okay. It'll only take five minutes."

I'd never been good at holding my laughter. I giggled when I was nervous and laughed at the most inappropriate times. This was one of those times. A laugh burst out before I could even try to stifle it.

A smile tugged on his lips as his mouth descended on mine. He wasn't forceful, but he wasn't gentle as he demanded a response. I heard a moan and didn't know if it came from him or me. I moved my hands to his hair, curling my fingers in the strands and pulling him down. I wanted him closer, and I didn't want him to stop.

I'd think about the rest later.

He shifted, moving his lips to my neck, trailing kisses up each side and back down again while his hands traced the lines of my body. He was heavy, all of his weight pushing me into the soft mattress. Each action more urgent than the last, and I struggled to hold him still so I could kiss him back. I slid down a little and was able to reach his neck, mimicking the trail his mouth had just taken on mine. When I got to his ear, I closed my teeth around the bottom of the lobe. He moved fast, giving me no time to think, and pinned both my hands above my head with one of his own. His other hand and mouth seemed to touch every inch of me. Every few seconds, his teeth would find skin and he'd bite me softly.

I pulled my hands free and found his hair once again, this time yanking at it every time he bit me. I moved my hips against his legs, trying to show him I wanted more. His hand moved to my breast, fingers squeezing my nipple tightly while his mouth closed over the other and bit down.

Oh, my God.

My entire body was on fire. I rocked my hips against him again, silently begging him to give me what I wanted. What I needed. He didn't.

There was no question who was moaning now. I was so loud the people in the next room could probably hear me. His eyes shot up to mine, and he released my nipple long enough to give me his "up to something" smile as he moved his mouth to the other breast.

"Like that?" His voice was husky, and he didn't wait for an answer, clamping his teeth down harder than he had a second ago.

I cried out. That must have been the answer he was looking for. His arms circled around me, holding me tight before he shifted again, my legs opened wider to let him in. As he moved between them, his mouth found mine and kissed me gently. I wasn't expecting it. It was such a stark contrast to the kisses he'd just given me. My hands fell from his head, clinging to his shoulders.

I didn't want him to do anything but lay there and kiss me like that again. I couldn't remember the last time I had been this turned on. He pushed himself up onto his knees, forcing me to break my hold, and a wave of cold air hit my naked body, making me shiver. I missed him immediately.

His hands slid up the inside of my legs slowly, before he moved just close enough for me to feel his heat. He paused, eyes traveling over my body, devouring me with his gaze. He wasn't seeing me naked for the first time. He'd kissed or touched almost every inch of my body, but for one brief second, I panicked and fought the urge to push him away.

He was perfect; I was not. Rejection on a normal scale I could handle. I'd done it many times before and would again. Having my best friend decide not to fuck me and leaving me this horny was something I could not handle. I moved my hands over my stomach, trying to hide what I could.

His beautiful face turned into a frown, and his eyes narrowed angrily. Grabbing my arms, he pushed both up over my head.

"Don't!" He snarled before his mouth was on mine, all tenderness gone, biting my lip and pushing himself into me.

I didn't have a chance to rise up to meet him, and I gasped—both at the surprise and the hardness that was filling me. He let my arms go, his hands lodging themselves in my hair, pulling my head back roughly, forcing my eyes to meet his once again as he thrust into me harder than I expected, almost angrily.

"Don't do that, not now." His mouth covered mine, stealing my reply.

My muscles flexed around him.

"Christ!" He shuddered, eyes squeezing shut as he leaned his head back.

Oh, no. He was not getting off that easy. I squeezed his dick again.

His eyes flew open and his head snapped up, smirking down at me. "You wanna play that way, huh?" His voice was barely a whisper but held a note of serious threat.

I leaned up, as far as I could without his hands pulling my hair, and bit his chin. He groaned, a long drawn out sound.

His hands found my thighs again before sliding up onto my ass cheeks. He pulled out of me, lifting my body toward him, and slammed back in, pumping harder. Again and again, each time faster, rougher and deeper than the last. His hands squeezed at the flesh hard enough to be painful.

I felt him shift his weight slightly, never missing a beat as he pummeled my tender flesh, his teeth finding my nipple. He bit me hard, harder than earlier. I screamed out, raking my nails up his back into his hair. He hissed, and for a brief second, I was afraid I had drawn blood. Then he suckled the other tenderly.

He continued the assault, being so rough I thought I would cry, and then right when I was on the brink of breaking, he'd turn tender and soft. His teeth marked my flesh, his nails digging so hard I knew I would bruise. Yet, the way he kissed me, like I was his entire world, made me clench around him.

I cried out, my body on sensory overload. He paused for just a moment, letting go of my tender flesh, moving his hands back to my hair. He cupped my face, gazing down lovingly.

"Jesus, Joes."

I couldn't hold on any longer. My legs tightened around his hips as his mouth found mine, covering the cries I made as I came. I trembled around him, my muscles squeezing and milking, trying to draw as much pleasure as possible. I was so wet I knew he must be having a hard time, but he didn't stop.

I didn't realize that I was still moaning until he buried his face in my neck. He kept a steady pace, each pump sending ripples of pleasure through my entire body. Every inch of me was on fire.

"I want to watch you come this time," he whispered, lifting himself up onto his hands.

I didn't understand. My mind was foggy, and I couldn't begin to form words with his steady rhythm. I shook my head. I'd already gone over the edge. It was his turn.

As quickly as he had slowed, he regained the mind-numbing pace from earlier. His hand found my hips, holding me still, before he leaned down to kiss me slowly and deeply. The man never strayed from his rhythm, and even though I wasn't the one moving, I was out of breath in seconds.

I felt the familiar fire—fucking Christ. I was going to do it again. My insides clenched as the orgasm began to build.

His eyes got dangerously dark again as he felt my reaction. He dropped his forehead down onto mine and grabbed both of my hands, twisting his fingers around mine, holding them just above my head. "Come on, baby. Come with me. I want to hear you scream my name."

Fireworks exploded all through my body. My body convulsed in places that didn't convulse. Shaking uncontrollably, back arched off the bed.

I wanted him out of me. I wanted him deeper. I wanted him to kiss me and never stop.

His eyes never left mine. I didn't scream, but I was close. He kissed me, his noises mingling with mine as he finally found his release.

I didn't know how long we lay there, completely entwined, before I realized that I wasn't sure which of us was shaking. We were both soaked and the room was fairly chilly—maybe one of us was shivering. Or maybe it was nerves, because it really was time to face reality.

"That was a big sigh." He backed out of me slowly, dragging me with him as he rolled onto his back and managing to throw a sheet over us. He kissed the top of my head and his fingertips started drawing on my back. I snuggled closer to him. "I would stay right here with you all day if we could. You know that, right?"

Not really the first words I thought we'd share, but I smiled. "I do." The hair on his chest moved slightly every time I breathed, and I reached up to play with the little curlicues. I knew what he wanted me to say, but I didn't know if I could. I lifted my eyes. "I'd stay with you, but I'm not sure we'd get much sleep."

He smiled. "That wasn't what that sigh was though, huh?" His arm nudged me. "We're not going to worry about this, remember?"

He seemed so confident, but I could see the concern creeping into his face. It made me feel even worse. He had enough to worry about, he didn't need to add me and my mistakes to the list.

I'd wanted this. He hadn't. I refused to let this be a problem.

I forced a smile, pretending everything was fine, and pushed up to kiss the spot on his chin that I had bitten earlier. "I do. I'm not worrying. It was a good sigh, silly. But I am late." I wrinkled my nose at him. "And I need a shower."

THIRTEEN

Relief washed over his face. Patting his cheek, I rolled over and slid out of bed, stealing the sheet, heading for the shower. I needed a few minutes alone.

"Fucking Christ!" He snapped, inhaling sharply.

I whipped around, clutching the sheet to my chest. "What's wrong?"

"Baby," He was out of bed, walking toward me. "I hurt you."

"What are you talking about?"

Cool fingertips found my lower back, making me wince as they slid onto my bottom. He made a noise deep in his throat and gently pulled the sheet away from me. We stood there motionless, his body tensing, as he gazed at the marks on my flesh.

"It's fine. Really. I'm just a little sore."

"A little sore?" He scoffed. "Yeah."

I watched as he lightly traced a finger next to a line of red marks trailing down my breast and onto my nipple. I couldn't see the rest of me, but from the look on his face, I had more.

Shame convulsed his features. Followed closed by fury.

Stepping closer, he wrapped his arms around me, yanking me tight against him. "I am so sorry!" He was just tall enough that his chin could rest on my head perfectly.

I was uncomfortably aware that we were both naked, skin pressing into skin. I didn't need to be coddled, especially not like this. I couldn't pull away, though. Not when he seemed genuinely upset.

Instead, I hugged him, trying to offer some comfort. "Hey, I'm okay."

"You must think I'm a monster." I could hear his voice rumble in his chest, mixing with his heartbeat.

I laughed. If by monster he meant a sex-starved beast who had just feasted on my body, making me beg for more, then yeah, he was a monster. A fuck monster.

He went ridged at my laugh, proving to me that he was serious. He thought he was a scary beast, capable of horrible things. I didn't see him that way. There were many things I thought about him, but evil monster was not one of them.

"God, no. I think you're an amazing lover."

"That's what you like? Someone hurting you?" His breath caught. I couldn't tell if he was angry or intrigued.

"To be honest, yes. I like rough sex." I shrugged. There, now it was more than a secret I shared with Will. "But if you're asking if I'm into heavy BDSM shit, I'm not. I don't want to be choked or whipped, or have a man tell me what to do every second of the day. I don't want to be dominated. I don't have Daddy issues. I'm not gonna lie—I like it when a man takes control and tells me in great detail what to do. It drives me crazy. It doesn't have to be like that every time. I enjoyed every second I was with you. Every time." I raised face, staring up at him. "Did you not like it?"

He groaned. "Oh, babe, you have no fuckin' idea. I like it wild, rough." His eyes sparked. "I want to tie you to that bed and do things to you..." He wet his lower lip. "I never, and I mean not one fucking time, have left marls." He pulled me tight again. "You were so... into it. Stopping never even crossed my mind. I wanted you beneath me, screaming and begging..." He trailed off. "It was fucking amazing, but I never meant to hurt you."

I couldn't drop it. I had to know. "Screaming and begging you to stop? Or begging you for more?"

"More. I only ever want you to beg me for more."

My heart stopped. He wasn't disgusted by me, by what we'd just shared. "Is it always like this... with you?" The thought of Matty with anyone else, especially Taylor, turned my stomach. Standing there naked, pressed into him the way I was, I really didn't want to think of him sharing what we'd just had with anyone else. Yet I had ask.

He tensed a little. "Joes." Something in the way he said my name told me he wasn't the kind to screw and tell. He sighed. "No. I lost control, got carried away. That's a first. I'm not even sure what that was."

I smiled against his bare skin. "That, my boy, was you fucking me. Hard." I ran my hands up his back, stopping when I felt welts, surprised. "And I fucked you right back. Does your back hurt?"

He pulled away, walked to the mirror, and turned so he could look over his shoulder. "Shit. Naw, it doesn't hurt." His eyes met mine in the reflection, looking incredibly pleased with himself. "Looks like someone didn't want to let go."

I could see the damage I'd done mixed among the black ink, at least twenty bright red welts, some stretching from waist to neck. Some of the shorter ones, near his shoulders, were bloody. I felt guilty, but the memories of why I had clawed his skin made me blush. "Or wanted you to be closer."

He walked back to me and put his hands on my hips. "Baby, I couldn't get any closer. I tried as hard as I could."

I laughed as he smiled that damn lopsided grin of his. "That you did! I'm sorry about your back though. It looks painful."

"It's fine, really. Just a little sore."

Hearing my words said back to me, I smiled.

His hand moved from my hip, fingertips tracing my neck. He looked sad. "What are you going to tell Will? I think he might notice that his wife has teeth marks all over her and that her ass is covered in bruises."

I shook my head. "Since I don't plan on seeing Will, let alone showing him my ass, I'm not going to tell him anything. This is between you and me."

I almost asked him what he planned to tell Taylor before I caught myself. Even if they hadn't broken up, I didn't want to talk about her. Or Will. Or even the two of us. As long as we were in this room, I didn't have to face reality.

In just a little while though, we'd be forced to face it together. To see if we could really go back to being the friends we had been. After everything that had happened in the last few hours, I had my doubts. But screw that. I wasn't thinking about any of it right now.

I touched his face. "We have to be at work soon, and I need a shower. I think your sexy ass should come wash my back."

I could see the worry on his face, but he grabbed my hand. "Hey, you wash my back, I'll wash yours." Then he quickly added, "As long as you're gentle with me."

He looked so sheepish that I giggled. "Oh, I'll be gentle," I promised.

"Good." He lowered he head to mine, his voice barely a whisper. "Because I won't be gentle at all."

The mirrors in the bathroom were surrounded by bright white lights, and when he turned me toward my reflection, I could see why Matty had been upset. I didn't want to look, but he stood behind me, holding me in place.

I met his eyes in our reflection, suddenly shy. It was hard for me to see the naked couple staring back at us. Matty was tall, athletic, dark, and all kinds of tattooed sexy. I was the polar opposite: short, pale with only a slight tan—even though it was the middle of summer—and I looked like a mom.

Will had told me once that I was annoyingly self-critical, but I preferred to think of it as being realistic. I had always been proud of the fact that what I lacked in appearance I made up for in personality. I pursed my lips at the girl standing in front of my friend. She wasn't hideous, but she certainly wasn't the kind of beautiful girl I would expect to see with Matt. She was normal.

Maybe it was because I had been the fat girl for so long and I'd gotten used to seeing her when I looked at myself. I wasn't obese anymore and was proud of the body I saw in front of me, even though it was covered with stretch marks and scars. It was just hard to see the glaringly obvious contrast between Matty and me.

Without thinking about it, I traced the new marks on my skin lightly. Starting at my neck, I drew a fingertip down onto my shoulder then onto my right breast. They really didn't hurt as much as they looked like they should. My poor nipple though was an alarming shade of purple, and I touched it just to make sure I could still feel.

A tattooed arm slid around my waist, and I glanced up, meeting Matty's eyes once again. They were dark, full of wanting. He bit his lip, and the motion was so erotic, I almost groaned.

Spinning me around, he lifted me onto the counter, and moved between my legs as his mouth found mine. I forgot my thoughts as his lips teased. As if not sure where to put his hands, he ran them lightly over every part of my body. I knew his back was sore, but I couldn't stop myself from running my hands over the welts. I tried to be easy, but when his lips abandoned mine to tug gently on my ear lobe, I dug my fingernails in. Then, as if he suddenly remembered that my back was clear, his hands shot behind me and did the same. Feeling his nails in my skin, I arched my back, pushing away from his fingers and into his chest.

"What the fuck are you doing to me?" He groaned as his lips made their way to mine.

I didn't know, but I knew what he was doing to me, and I wanted more. Burying my hands in his hair, I pushed his head away from my mouth and down my body. I needed him to kiss me everywhere. He fought me for a quick second, looking up into my eyes as if making sure I wanted him to keep going.

I nodded, shoving his head into my chest. I wanted his mouth on me, not caring how sore I already was or how sore I'd be in a little while. He laughed against my skin as his teeth found a nipple. I gasped.

He pulled back suddenly, making me want to cry, and stood in front of me, hands on my cheeks, before he leaned in, coaxing my lips open. As I deepened our kiss, his hands moved down my back, digging in slightly, then they kept going.

I almost winced when he touched my bottom. It was incredibly sore. But his hands weren't rough, and within a few minutes, the gentle massage had me even more worked up.

"God, Matty, please," I begged between kisses.

"Please? Please what?"

I could feel his smile against the side of my mouth, and I knew he wanted me to beg him. Not wanting to give him the satisfaction, I refused to answer. Instead, I trailed kisses down his neck, my fingers just a few steps ahead of my mouth. My kisses stopped at his collarbone, and I swirled my tongue around the indent in his skin, but my hand kept going.

I traced a line down the middle of his chest, the valley between his muscles, and onto his belly. Not stopping there, my fingers danced along his skin, picturing his tattoos, following the deep V of his pubic bone, until I found a patch of hair. My fingers wound into the little curls while my mouth made the return trip back up his neck, biting lightly then running over each spot with my tongue. My fingers didn't stay in the soft locks long, instead leaving them to run lightly down the inside of his thigh and back up. Not all the way up though. As I moved my hand inward, I found what I'd been looking for—soft, sweaty and dangling. I cupped him at the same time my teeth sank into his shoulder a little rougher than I had planned.

Matty had become still at some point during my exploration and was now breathing harder than I'd heard him breathe the last time he'd run a marathon. The idea excited me, and I moved my hand, letting go of him and finding his curls again. This time I pulled at the sensitive hair. It was his turn to gasp, followed by a loud series of moans.

I smiled against his shoulder and slipped my hand down a little until I felt his hardness brush against my fingers. I fisted him, sliding up and down, tracing the tip of him with my thumb.

I tried to push him away with my other hand, intending to lean down and see what kind of reaction I'd get when I put my mouth on him, but he wouldn't let me move him.

He squeezed my ass as he pulled my entire body toward the edge of the counter. I arched my back, wrapping my legs around him in anticipation of what was coming. He didn't pull me down onto him. Instead, he picked me up and carried me out of the room.

"Matty, wha—"

He shook his head, cutting me off. "I'm not making love to you in a hotel bathroom." His growl was low, and the whiskers on his jaw tickled my neck when he talked. "I'm taking you to bed."

When we reached the bed, instead of laying me down, he turned around and sat, pulling me onto him. I gave him my sexiest smile as I kneeled above him, pushing his shoulders back until he was lying on the bed.

"I don't want to hurt you again." His voice was strained as his hands moved up and down my thighs. "But if you want..."

I shook my head, knowing it was only fair. He'd been amazing last night. It was my turn this morning. I wanted more than him just beneath. I wanted him screaming and begging. I moved off him quickly, before his hands could grab me.

He sat up on his elbows, alarmed. "Jo?"

I'd already moved to the end of the bed, between his legs, fingertips finding my target. He watched me as I kneeled, leaning my head close to him, a look I couldn't decipher planted on his features. He shuddered when my tongue circled his tip.

"Do you want me to stop?" My voice came out so much stronger than I felt, and I licked my bottom lip before biting it gently.

He groaned. "Good Christ, no."

His breath caught, and for a few seconds, I was afraid it had stopped altogether. I ran my tongue around him again, very gently, as my fingers found his hair, pulling and tugging at it while my mouth closed over his tip. I felt him flop back onto the bed with a sigh, and I moved my lips down the outside of him to his testicles before kissing each, sucking on them one at a time. Turning my head, my teeth skimmed across the inside of each thigh, lightly but enough so he could feel me teasing him.

I moved back up, groaning as I closed my mouth over all of him, but his sounds drowned out mine. I slid up and down, my hand pumping his base, his noises encouraging me to move faster. One of his hands gripped the sheets as if they were the only thing holding him back while the other grabbed a fistful of my hair and pushed my head down farther, making me take more.

Before I could stop him, both had moved to my arms, tugging at me, as if to pull me off. I ignored them, sitting up on my knees to get better access and taking him as deep as I could.

"Baby, I can't... I can't. Take. Much. More. Please..." His words came in short spurts, as if it took every ounce of energy he had to talk.

I didn't have a chance to ask what he wanted before he began to beg. "Fuck me, Jo. Jesus! Come ride me. Now! I need to be in you."

Matty was beautiful all the time. Matty sprawled naked on my bed was sexy. But Matty demanding and telling me what to do was fucking hot.

I glanced up, half tempted to do what he asked. He was covered in sweat, an amazing feat for someone not doing anything. Lying there, looking like that, commanding me, caused a flutter in my stomach, and I could feel myself getting even more turned on. He was driving me crazy, but I had no intention of giving him what he thought he wanted.

Instead, my fingers slid onto the sensitive section of his inside thigh, digging in every time he tugged on my arms, and I went back to work. Every groan, every word, every swear he uttered made me enjoy my job even more. It wasn't long before I felt his muscles tighten and heard his warning, telling me he was close, ordering me to let him go, to take my mouth off him.

I didn't. Instead, I pulled my hands from his thighs and circled one around his base and one around his balls. My mouth filled with him as he climaxed, his hands yanking at my hair, trying to get my mouth away from his sensitive area again. I pushed down, making sure he'd given me all he had to give before I kissed my way back up his body.

I was surprised when his lips met mine, his tongue pushing its way past my teeth, his hands pushing into my back, forcing me to lie on him.

When I ended the kiss, he moved my head to his chest, sighing as he held me tight. "You will pay for that later."

I smiled at his reaction. I put my hands on his chest and pushed against him, looking into his eyes. He looked exhausted, but he had a goofy smile on his lips.

"Is that what you had in mind?"

The confusion on his face as he tried to figure out what I was talking about made me laugh.

My hand moved down, tracing his right pubic bone, feeling a slight bump in the skin where the words I'd seen last week were forever imprinted on his body. "Is that what you hand in mind when you got this?"

He grinned, realization crossing his beautiful features. "Nope. Never in my wildest dreams did I picture that." He sighed. "What I imagined doesn't even fucking come close to that."

"Good." I smiled proudly, moving my hand up to his heart to trace my favorite tattoo.

"You really like that tattoo, don't you?"

I met his eyes, knowing he wasn't talking about the Claddagh. "I really do." My voice was low. "It makes me want to... do it." I laughed, a little embarrassed. "Now I really need a shower." I pulled back, intent on getting out of bed, but he held me tight.

"If I asked you to call out of work and spend the day with me, would you do it?"

I nodded without even thinking. I didn't want this day to end. "In a heartbeat."

Untangling himself from me, Matty rolled and slid out of the bed. Finding his phone, he punched in a number and held it out to me.

Connie's voice mail answered almost immediately.

"Good morning, Connie. I'm not coming in today." I sighed, not sure what to say. I filled her in on my day's schedule, then told her I'd see her Monday.

Smirking up at Matty in challenge, I handed back the phone. "Your turn, lover. I'll be in the shower." I got halfway across the room before I turned back to find him watching me with that goofy grin still on his face. "Don't make me wait too long."

I glared at my reflection, twisting my lips, turning my head from side to side, looking at my neck from every angle, trying to decide how I could possibly cover the bright red tooth marks. Unzipping my makeup case, I sorted through the containers to see what I had—not much. I could try the concealer, but...

"You look amazing right now."

I snapped my head up, meeting his eyes in the mirror. I hadn't known he was watching me. He had towel dried his hair then wrapped the white terry cloth around his waist, but his shoulders still glinted with water from the incredibly steamy shower we had just taken. He leaned against the counter, facing me.

"Ha!" I shook my head. "You're blind."

He frowned, pushing his hip off the counter and moving to stand behind me. He met my eyes in the mirror again. "Do you see that?" He nodded toward our reflection. "Does that look like a guy who would fuck an ugly girl?"

His lips twitched, the only sign he was kidding, and I burst out laughing. "I love how modest you are."

His arms came around me, highlighting the stark contrast between my pale white stomach and his tattooed sleeves. He leaned in, eyes still on mine in the mirror, and kissed my neck. "And I love to hear you laugh. Nothing makes me happier than seeing you smile."

They were simple words, yet they made my heart beat fast. His mouth moved down toward my shoulder, and my breath caught.

"I thought you were hungry." I narrowed my eyes at his reflection. "If you don't stop that right now, we won't make it out the door."

The corner of his mouth twitched again, before he continued his line of kisses. "I'm sure you've got something I could eat." His words, low and full of innuendo, shocked me.

My mouth fell open in an unflattering way, and I could feel my cheeks glowing red.

He laughed against my skin. "Fine." He backed up, a pout on his face. "But later we're picking this up right here."

I had no doubt that he meant it.

FOURTEEN

There weren't many cars in the lot when we pulled into the restaurant. I wasn't surprised—we were a little early for the typical lunch time rush.

Matty reached for my hand as he came around the front of my car. I took it, sliding my fingers between his as I smiled happily up at him. Before I could pull away, he leaned down and kissed the tip of my nose, making me laugh. The guilt I'd had last week from this type of intimate contact with gone. I was just enjoying him.

He held open the door, just as he did every Friday when we came here, but he never let go of my hand, stepping into place beside me as soon as we were both inside. It was as though he was telling the world that I was his, to back off. The gesture was reassuring. He wasn't ashamed of us.

Taking a minute to adjust to the dimness of the Thai restaurant, I glanced over to the counter where the hostess usually stood. Seeing it empty, I skimmed the dining area. She was at a large table in the corner, filling water glasses for a group dressed in suits. Knowing she'd be over to seat us in a minute, I laid my head on his shoulder and snuggled into Matty's side, watching the fish swim around in the tank in front of us.

Matty sighed happily, letting go of my hand and moving his to the small of my back. I closed my eyes as his fingers drew small circles over my clothes. I was so relaxed that I could have stood there for hours, cuddling with him. I heard the hostess call to us tell us she'd be right over, then I felt Matty stiffen, straightening up a bit. His fingers stopped moving, yet his arm got tighter, holding me closer.

I stood, trying to figure out what had alarmed him. Following his glare, my eyes landed on a familiar face I felt myself tense.

Standing at the table of businessmen, staring straight at us, my husband—soon-to-be ex-husband—was glaring at us. Excusing himself, he walked our way. It wasn't a large space, and I pushed away from Matty as he approached, needing to protect him as much as I could. Matty turned, his eyes burning a hole in my back, but all I could do to offer comfort was wrap my fingers around his in a tight squeeze.

"Joey." Will nodded at me in greeting, giving me a tight smile. Before I could object, his arms were around me and he pulled me close. I froze, and for a minute, we stood there in an awkward pose. His lips came close to my ear. "I haven't told them yet. Please?"

He didn't need to explain further—I knew what he was asking. Sighing, I lifted the hand that wasn't holding Matty's and returned the hug. The company Will worked for prided itself on family values. Things like divorce, broken families, and adultery didn't have a place on their moral compass. It would be one thing if his boss saw Matty and me out together—I would be the adulterous whore. But with Will there, it was a whole other ball game.

Part of me wanted to laugh in his face; he had done this, created this mess, not me. I sure as hell wasn't going to help him clean it up. He was the one who'd had the affair, so why in the world would I help him save face? Another part of me hated his job and didn't care if he did lose it. I'd sacrificed hours and hours of my time with him so he could climb the ladder, be the dedicated employee. Hours that could have been spent working on us, saving us from ending up exactly where we were. If he hadn't been working there, he never would have met her. However, as much as I wanted to—and at that moment I really, really wanted to—I couldn't just hang him out to dry. I didn't have it in me.

Stepping back from his embrace, I plastered a smile on my face and greeted him warmly, loud enough so his if his co-workers were listening, they could hear me. Will's shoulders sagged slightly with what I assumed was relief as his eyes traveled over me. His lips puckered in a scowl and his eyes narrowed as they settled on my neck.

I'd been in such a rush to get Matty out of the hotel that I hadn't completely covered the marks. Instead, I'd dusted powder over them, hiding them as best I could. I hadn't expected to see anyone important.

Will's head jerked toward Matty, unmasked hatred clear on his face. When he held out his left hand, jaw clenched as if greeting my friend was the last thing he wanted to do, the glint of his wedding ring caught my eye. Obviously I'd been wrong about Rachel not knowing he was still married.

Matty dropped my hand and took a step towards Will. The two were roughly the same height with a similar build: broad shoulders, muscular arms, toned chests, and slim waists followed by long powerful legs. That was where the similarities ended though.

Matty was dark and his sun-kissed skin made him look as if he hailed from an island, his short hair almost ink black. Will was the complete opposite. His light skin was much darker than his normal pale complexion, thanks to the hours he spent outside, and his blond curls fell in various lengths over his head.

The differences weren't just in physical characteristics though. Matty was wearing the pair of jeans he'd from the night before—they were frayed in the sexiest places possible and clung to his hips and ass, fitting his legs in just the right way. His black T-shirt wasn't snug, but it was tight enough to show thick arms and a solid chest. He was almost edible.

Will, always the professional, didn't have the words "casual Friday" in his vocabulary. Dressed to impress in one of my favorite suits—a Ralph Lauren charcoal gray-stripe two-button front that he'd paired with a light purple shirt and a gray-and-purple striped tie. He looked like a model, as if he'd been born to wear the ensemble.

Matty took Will's outstretched hand, but I saw him pull back his shoulders, obviously irritated. "Billy." Matty's voice was hard as steel. "Nice tie."

Will's eyes narrowed once again. "Thanks. My wife gave it to me. I'm not sure what happened. She used to have such great taste."

Ouch. I stepped forward, ready to interject. Before I was able to interrupt, Matty yanked on Will's hand, catching him off guard, and Will stepped forward, close enough so the two were almost toe-to-toe.

Matty's voice was low but very clear. "How's your girlfriend feel about that?"

Shaking off Matt's hand, Will shrugged. "About the wife or the tie? I'm not sure. We don't do much talking."

I inhaled sharply, unable to believe the words I'd just heard.

The man I'd married glared at me in defiance. "Doesn't look like you two do either." Turning back to Matty, he sneered, "How's *your* girlfriend feel about that?"

"Ex-girlfriend." Matty never took his eyes off Will, but his hands clenched into fists and his jaw ticked. He only chuckled though. "Jo and I do plenty of communicating. I find her to be very"—he paused—"vocal."

I gaped at him, wondering how long the two of them were going to carry on their pissing contest. They appaled me.

"You're wrong, by the way. From what I've seen, Jo's always had impeccable taste." Matty continued, his face showing pure disgust. "Unfortunately, she had some slips from time to time. Like, choosing a life partner. Thankfully, that's almost over." He leaned in and kissed my temple, whispering, "Do you want to get takeout instead?"

I nodded. There was no way I was going to eat here under the constant watch of Will and his friends.

"I'll order us our usual." He strode toward the counter. "See you round, Billy boy."

I watched him for a moment, before glancing at Will. I didn't know what to say to him. "You don't like Thai." *This was the last place I thought I'd see you.*

"I don't. We're in the middle of brainstorming and needed to refuel. I was out-voted." He blew out a long breath. "We need to talk at some point."

I nodded. I couldn't avoid if forever.

"Do you have plans tomorrow?"

Matty and I hadn't discussed our weekend. I hesitated, glancing over at Matty, wondering if he'd planned to spend another weekend with me in the hotel. He seemed to sense me watching him and turned, giving me a heart-stopping smile. I wanted nothing more than to go put my hands in his back pockets and make out with him as if we were a couple of horny teenagers. I grinned just thinking about it. His smile grew, reading my mind, and bit his bottom lip. I almost groaned, catching myself at the last minute.

Will was staring at me, his mouth tight, cheek muscles twitching. "Well, if you have time, it would be great if you could come home so we can talk." His voice was cold. He held out a hand to me. "Come on, let's go talk to—"

My gasp cut him off. I had reached out to take his hand so he could lead me to his co-workers when one of them stood, glancing our way curiously. I let my hand drop between us.

The petite brunette was pretending to adjust herself in her chair, yet I knew from the way she searched out Will that she was actually wondering what was taking him so long.

"Why didn't you tell me she was here?"

"I told you it was a work meeting." He sighed annoyed. "I should have mentioned that Rachel was here. I'm sorry." He moved his hand to the small of my back, a move that made me glance over my shoulder toward Matty. "You are here with him, though, so we're even. Maybe we could go on a double date some time." His voice was ice cold again.

I glanced at him out of the corner of my eye. I wasn't going to fight with him. "Can we please just get this over with?"

Will nodded and guided me to his table. I was able to greet almost all of his co-workers warmly. I liked this group of men and walked around the table, chatting with each, asking about children and wives, vacations and pets.

Most of them joked with me, asking about the kids or telling me stories about something Will had done recently. The general consensus was that with our children gone, I was keeping him busy with adult activities that made him show up to work extremely tired on Monday mornings and left the bite marks on my neck that they were all graciously ignoring.

By the time I got to Rachel, Matty had joined us. Will practically jumped from his seat, as if to keep me from talking to his whore, and introduced my best friend. I almost laughed as Rachel's eyes traveled over Matty and she licked her lips. Will was still standing, so I stole his chair.

"Hello, Rachel! How are you?"

The young woman smiled politely at me, avoiding my eyes. "I'm well, Jo. How are you? The house must be so quiet without the kids."

My eyes swept slowly over the girl. I wasn't sure how old she was. I'd guess twenty-four, maybe twenty-five. Much younger than me.

She was adorable. Her red sleeveless dress wasn't revealing, but it was form-fitting, with a coordinating belt buckled around her unbelievably tiny waist. The outfit was so different than the one I'd seen her in the weekend before, it was hard to reconcile she was the same person.

Apparently both she and my husband led a different life at the office.

I leaned in close so only she could hear. "I'm not at the house. I'm in a hotel, so any time you feel like going to the house, just stop on by. Will's there alone."

Her chocolate brown eyes widened, as if she didn't know that I was in on their little secret. Her mouth opened as if she was going to say something, then closed. Her hand shook.

She turned her head, seeking out my husband, her anger clear. For a moment, I thought she might slap him.

"He didn't tell you I moved out?"

She shook her head, avoiding my eyes.

Matty chose that moment to step close, offering his hand to the woman next to me.

"I'm Matt," he told her in a low voice, raising a suggestive eyebrow.

She sighed. "Rachel."

Matty's lips shifted into his mischievous I-bet-I-can-get-your-pants-off-in-twenty-minutes-or-less grin, "It's nice to meet you Rachel." Not looking at me, he dropped her hand yet held her eyes. "Our lunch is ready, Joes. We should get back to the office."

I agreed. It was time to go. "It was nice to see you, Rachel." Avoiding looking at Will, I smiled at the rest of his co-workers as I walked around the table towards the lobby. "Have a good lunch. I hope you get loads of work done."

Will moved between Matty and me and grabbed my hand and muttered over his shoulder, "I'm walking Joey out. I'll be right back."

I turned to give them one more smile. Rachel wasn't even looking at Will and me. Instead, it was Matty who held her attention.

Will walked me to my car, holding my hand the entire way, even after we were out of sight of his friends. Apparently he wanted to keep up the charade. I tried to pull away once we were through the door, but he didn't let go.

"Hey." His voice was soft, and I turned to him. "Thank you. I'm sorry to put you on the spot like that."

I almost shrugged, then the irritation I'd been holding burst out. "I come here every Friday, William. If you ever listened, you'd know that."

"I do listen, Joey." He sighed. "Maybe I wanted to see you." His voice was still low, and he stepped closer to me. He ran his fingertips over my cheek and onto the side of my head. "You won't return my calls."

"I saw the look on your face. You were as surprised as I was. You didn't know you'd see me here." I accused, ignoring the hurt in his eyes.

He shook his head vehemently. "I didn't know Matt would be with you! I wanted to see you. Not him. Not you with him. Forgive me if I think seeing my wife with another man is startling."

We were standing closer than we had been a minute ago. He was so close I could smell the cologne. For a brief second, I forgot that we were separated and I longed to step into him and get a hug. Then, I remembered.

"I doubt that." My attitude returned as I took a step back. "Did you want to see how I'd react being in the same room as her? Or maybe you just wanted us side by side, so you could see that you chose the right woman?"

Will tipped his head and took a deep breath. "Joey, I said I was sorry. I wasn't thinking." His hands grasped my shoulders. "I miss you."

The bell on the restaurant door jingled and I glanced over just as Matty came out, holding our bag of food. He stopped short, hesitated a minute, then took two steps right to us.

"Great performance in there, Billy boy. I almost believed you weren't fucking Rachel." He held his palm out to me. "Keys?"

I stepped back, forcing Will's hands to fall, and grabbed the keys out of my pocket, holding them out to my friend. Matty took another step, stopping between us, invading the bubble that Will had just created.

Will's eyes turned to ice as he glared at Matty. "Mind giving me a minute with my wife?"

"I do, actually. Our lunch is getting cold." Matty snapped. "None of them can see you, Billy, so you can drop the loving husband act. It doesn't impress Jo." He chuckled. "Unless you're doing it to make me jealous. If you are, no need. I know who she's going home with." Cocking his head to the side, he sized my husband. When Will didn't say anything, Matty nodded. "Yeah, that's what I though. If you'll excuse us," Matty drawled out slowly, "your estranged wife and I have plans."

The way he said plans made me blush.

107

Will made a snorting sound and moved toward the door of the restaurant. "Call me when you decide about tomorrow, Joey."

Matty turned to me, a weird look on his face. "Tomorrow?"

I walked around the front of the car, to the passenger side, and eased into my seat, explaining as I went. "I told him I wasn't sure. I didn't know if we had plans."

I pulled the seat belt across me, looking up when Matty stayed silent. Before I could question him, his hands cupped my cheeks and he pulled me close, kissing me softly. His lips worked against mine, teeth nipping at me, making me moan. I clutched his shirt, pulling him close, kissing him back. I was breathless before he pulled away.

I opened my eyes, not even sure when I'd closed them, to see him grinning at me. "What was that?"

His smile grew wider. "That was me kissing you. Because I can."

I raised my eyebrow. Matty was so weird sometimes.

"I have Sam this weekend. I would love it if you join us tomorrow, but I understand if you need to work things out with the douchenozzle." He pointed his thumb back at the restaurant. "Right now, I just want to go somewhere I can kiss you."

Not caring where we were, I leaned into him again.

"Yeah, here works." He laughed, pulling me toward him.

Will, or any of his co-workers, could have walked out and caught us, but at that moment, none of them even crossed my mind.

I sang along to the radio as I drove home the next morning. I hadn't been there in weeks, but it had been my home for so many years that I was able to get lost in my thoughts and my car practically drove itself.

Matty dominated my mind, bring a content smile to my face. I couldn't remember the last time I'd had such a fun, relaxing day filled with laughter and kisses. We'd spent the majority of it on my couch, talking and cuddling. It had been wonderful.

I didn't know how to classify what we were. He was my best friend, which explained the ease of our time together and our ability to talk about everything. Or nothing. And now we were *involved*. I laughed at how absurd that sounded. We were best friends enjoying everything the other had to offer.

Everything.

My face flamed at the thought. Thank God I was so comfortable with him. If I wasn't, I would be too embarrassed to ever look him in the eye again.

I was surprised when I turned into my driveway; the trip hadn't taken long at all. I sat there, looking up at the house, and panic filled me.

It didn't feel like home anymore. Instead, the building looked cold and lonely, even though there were planters filled with wild flowers welcoming visitors and it was sunny and already seventy degrees outside.

Will opened the door and stepped through, holding up a hand in greeting. He smiled and bounded down the front steps. "Good morning!"

He had entirely too much energy.

He pulled open my door before I could and stood on the other side, waiting for me to get out. "Did you have breakfast yet?"

I shook my head.

Matty and I had taken Sam to dinner and the movies last night, and because Taylor was still at their house and Matty hadn't wanted Sam in the hotel with us, we'd taken him back to Becky's afterward. Sam hadn't seemed upset that he had to go back to his mom's, but Matty had promised that he'd be there to pick him up before Sam got out of bed. True to his word, Matty had left before I got up this morning.

Will smiled. "Good. I made you some."

He'd made me my favorite breakfast—homemade waffles with fresh strawberries and whipped cream with a side of maple bacon. They were delicious, and we made comfortable small talk throughout the meal. The kitchen looked just as it had when I'd left, and for a few minutes, it was easy to pretend everything was back to normal.

Will didn't waste any time once we were done eating. "We need to talk about the papers."

I put my coffee mug back on the table and looked at him. "What do you want me to say?"

"I want to know if you really want to get divorced."

I gaped at him. "Me?" I scowled. "I'm not the one who served you." I narrowed my eyes at him. "You wanted this. Not me."

He turned his coffee cup in his hands. "You wouldn't talk to me."

"So your answer was to serve me with legal separation papers? To divorce me?" I shook my head angrily. "I needed space. You want freedom. Two totally different things." He tried to interrupt, but I moved my hand, cutting him off. "What—do you want me to tell you I'm miserable? Do you want me to beg you to change your mind?" I stood up, grabbed our empty plates, and walked to the sink. "I won't do that."

"Aren't you miserable? Don't you want me to change my mind?" His voice was curious.

I sighed, putting the plates in the dish tub. "I'm not. And, honestly? I don't know." I shook my head, turning. "I'm confused, I'm lost. I'm not sure what I want to happen. I love you. I love the kids. I want to find a good solution. But right now..." Right now I had Matty, and I was finding myself. I walked back toward the table, meeting his eyes. The flash of anger I saw in his depths made me stop and lean against the wall. "Right now I'm trying to figure things out."

"Alone? You're trying to figure out things alone?"

I didn't answer him, and he laughed bitterly, looking out our window. I didn't know what to say. Silence filled the room, and after a few minutes, his breathing became steady.

"How long have you been fucking him?" Will turned to stare, his tone light and curious, but I could tell he was forcing it to sound that way. I knew the look on his face well. He was barely controlling his anger.

He had some fucking nerve.

"Not as long as you've been screwing around with her," I scoffed at him.

"Try again." He shifted slightly. "I told you I was in love with her, not fucking her."

I narrowed my eyes. Fucking liar. "I don't believe you."

He laughed, an eerie hollow sound. "You don't have to admit it, but we both know that deep down, you know it's the truth." He glared at me. "How long have you been fucking Matt?"

There were so many things I wanted to say to him. I wanted to tell him I knew he was a damn liar. I longed to yell that what I had with Matty was none of his business and that he'd lost the right to question me.

On the other hand, I didn't want to talk about this, and I sure as hell wasn't going to talk about Matty with him. He could fuck off.

"What? Nothing to say?" He sneered. "Did you leave here and run straight to his bed?"

"Go to hell!"

"Oh, sweetheart"—he smiled nastily—"I've been there for years."

Screw him. "You're not the only one, buddy. I've been there right along with you!" I was shouting now.

He gave me a sad, mocking look. "Oh, that's right! I forgot... poor Jo. Her life has been so fucking horrible." His face turned hard, and he raised his voice. "I've given up everything, sacrificed everything I had. For you. To give you this"—his hands swept across the kitchen—"to give you a life you wanted and deserved."

"A life I didn't ask for! A husband who's never home, a family that never spends time together, a job that breaks my heart. You think you're the only one who has sacrificed? That you're the only one who has lost something? You would see it like that!"

"Yeah, well, at least I had enough balls to stay and try to work it out. I didn't run away at the first sign of trouble."

"You didn't run away?" I screamed at him. He couldn't be serious. "Maybe you should have! But no. You had the"—I held up my hands and made air quotes with my fingers—"'big balls' to stay married and go behind your wife's back. You were too fucking busy making a fool out of yourself over a younger woman to even notice you had a wife. And you sure as hell didn't try to make anything work."

"Jesus, Joey, get off your fucking sky-high moral horse!" he screamed back.

The cup of coffee he had on the table went flying through the air. I had all I could do to not jump at the sound of glass shattering.

His voice went ice cold. "You have some fucking nerve talking about the things I do behind your back. I'm not the one who has been having an affair for years."

Really? "You know damn well I didn't have an affair."

"Yeah." He gave me a nasty look, obviously not agreeing. "Maybe you weren't sleeping with him, but you might as well have been. There have been three people in this marriage for a long time now. Me, you, and the asshole you run to about everything. I should have known. The first sign of trouble and you run. Packed your shit and ran away."

"First sign of trouble? No." I shook my head. "I'd say when someone's husband tells her he doesn't love her, it's not the first goddamn sign. I was just too fucking blind to see the others."

"I never told you I didn't love you," he snarled. "I never told you I was going to leave. I never fucking planned to leave!"

"Yeah, okay." I sounded like a petulant child. "So when you sat there"—I pointed at the table—"and got pissed off because you didn't want me to see what was on your phone and you told me that you couldn't help that you loved her, you were what? Just letting me know? Trying to make me jealous? Making sure I knew where I stood?"

He was infuriating. I knew he was trying to piss me off, and I was taking the bait. If he wanted a fight, I'd give him one. I looked around, hoping to find something large enough to throw at him. Not finding anything, I stomped my foot, frustrated.

"You knew fucking well what I would do. I told you years ago if you cheated again, I would leave. This is on you, not me."

"And where did you go? Oh, that's right. Right into someone else's bed. Obviously you were real heartbroken. You left because it was a convenient excuse for you. You could play the victim, saying I hurt you, and no one would be surprised you'd ended up with Matt.

Because Matt always jumps in and saves you, doesn't he? One call from you, and he drops everything. Fuck the fact that you're someone else's wife. He's been waiting for years for me to screw up. Couldn't even give us some time to figure it out. You both forgot one little detail though."

I raised my eyebrows; that man had quite the imagination. This was not all a grand scheme for me to finally be free of him, to be with Matty. Jackass!

"You're my wife! Not his. If you think you can just walk away that easily, you're in for a nasty surprise." He took two steps and was standing right in front of me. The vein in his forehead, the one that showed only when he was beyond controlling his anger, was starting to pop out. His voice was dangerously quiet. "How long have you been fucking him?"

My heart began to pound. He could try to intimidate me all he wanted, but he was still Will, and I wasn't afraid of him. I'd had enough of this conversation; we weren't getting anywhere. "I'm done talking about this."

His hands came up to my neck, and I stepped back. There was nowhere for me to go, and I bumped into the wall. He traced the sore spots where I knew the bite marks were still showing, even though I'd covered them with concealer.

"He's just a friend, huh? A friend who practices vampirism maybe?" His lips curled in disgust. "Did you enjoy it when he did this to you? Did you like him hurting you?"

"Don't you fucking touch me!" I pushed at him, surprised when he didn't budge. Will had suddenly turned from athletic into solid brick. I put my right hand on his shoulder, hoping to keep him from getting any closer. "Get your hands off me!"

He leaned in, pushing on my hand, forcing my arm to bend. "Did you tell him what a freak you are? Did you tell him you like it rough and he gave you what you wanted? Did he like hurting you? Did you get your kicks going out in public with his brands on you?"

I moved my head, desperate to get him to move. His hands only tightened. *Asshole.*

I wanted to hit him. No, I wanted to kick the shit out of him. I'd never been as angry with him as I was right then. A few years ago, I'd been big enough to do it. Now I was barely strong enough to hold him off me. I could hurt him in other ways though.

"Brands? Let's be honest for a minute, shall we? You're pissed that your sweet innocent little girlfriend saw them and will think you're a monster." Using every ounce of courage I had left, I laughed at him. "I saw how she looked at Matt, and I know you did too. Are you worried she isn't as innocent as you think and now you'll never be able to live up to her expectations? 'Cause we both know you never will!"

He inhaled sharply. *There, you ass!* Now he would move and I could leave. He didn't. Instead, he leaned in so close that I could see every pore on his face.

"Did you enjoy another man putting his hands on you, Wife? Did Matty make you scream and beg to come? Or did you have to beg him to take you to bed, like you do me?" His voice was barely a whisper.

What in the hell was wrong with him? I'd never seen Will act like this. I searched his eyes, hoping to find a clue. All I could see was his rage.

I gave him one more shove and brought up my knee, hoping to connect with his obviously large balls, but Will was quick. One hand tightened on my neck and pushed my head back into the wall roughly. The other hand found one wrist, painfully squeezing and twisting it as he pushed my arm over my head and his whole lower body crushed mine, forcing my leg down.

I couldn't move. The grip he had on my neck terrified me, and I was afraid if I fought him too much, he'd break my wrist. Will had lost his fucking mind. Panic set in as I realized I didn't know what to do. I wanted to close my eyes to keep him from seeing how scared I was, but I wouldn't let him win.

Instead, I glared back. "Fuck you!"

"Oh, you will!" The tone was cold and threatening, and a shiver ran down my spine.

His mouth came down on mine, and I jerked against the hand on my neck. He didn't back away, instead moving his mouth to my neck, biting at my skin, pinching it between his teeth then kissing each spot. It didn't hurt, but I struggled against him because I wanted him to get away from me, to leave me alone. His mouth traveled back up and found the tender spot right below my ear. His teeth were sharp, followed by his soft, wet tongue. He bit down. Hard. I cried out.

Will snapped his head back and met my eyes. "Tell me to stop, Jo!" His voice was low but demanding.

I couldn't catch my breath, let alone tell him to stop. I was seconds away from sobbing. He knew I wanted him to leave me alone.

He narrowed his eyes and yelled, "Tell me to fucking stop!"

My entire body shook as fear gripped me.

His eyes moved slowly from my face, down my neck to my chest, taking me all in. Keeping his hand on my neck, he moved the other from my wrist and fondled a breast. His hand slid down slowly under my shirt and lightly up my stomach and into a bra cup.

I cried out, confused by his actions. I didn't know this man. "Will!" It was a hoarse plea, "Please!"

His eyes moved back to mine, and I thought for a moment he was going to let me go. Instead, thick fingers closed around my still sore nipple, and he squeezed. I bit my lip so hard I drew blood, desperate to stay quiet.

I knew this was a scare tactic – and it was working. His eyes were unnerving, glaring into mine. His expression was a mixture of puzzlement and disbelief, and for a brief moment, he looked sad.

Will liked the missionary position. At night. In our bed. And cuddling after sex. He only got authoritative and rough when we had a "sex night" planned, and he'd never been like this. He'd never hurt me; I'd never been scared of him.

This was not the man I knew and loved. Behavior like this would disgust him. I needed to make his see that so he would walk away.

"Billy."

"You liked that. Admit it. It's what you want."

He was wrong—I did like it rough, when I was a willing participant. This was something completely different. His eyes flashed for a brief second, the fingers released my nipple and he pulled his arm from my shirt.

I closed my eyes, hoping it was over.

The hand around my neck tightened for a brief moment, tipping my head back. I could feel his breath and knew that he was close. Teeth tugged at my bottom lip and nibbled down my chin. Warm lips closed over mine and kissed me gently before he pulled away suddenly, and the hand on my throat let go.

I expected him to walk away, to leave without saying a word, and I felt relief at the idea. I wasn't sure I could look at him the same ever again.

The hands that grabbed my upper arms, pulling me forward before shoving me into the wall, were a surprise. It wasn't a hard push, but my eyes flew open in shock. I didn't have time to react; Will's hands were under my shirt, pulling it up and over my head before my mind even registered what was happening. His mouth was on me before my shirt was fully off. He bit my shoulder before pulling me forward and spinning me around.

He pushed me against the wall, more gently than he had earlier, and pinned my arms against my sides. One hand moved to my bra, and my breasts fell slightly as he broke the clasp. His left hand slid between the wall and me and cupped me. His right hand slid under the side of my shorts, grabbing my waist and digging in fingernails. He nipped at my shoulder blade.

The hands changed places, his left grabbing my hip and kneading at it while his right pawed at me. Teeth bit down on my neck roughly. I yelped, as much in surprise as in pain.

His mouth came next to my ear, and he laughed evilly. His left hand grabbed the top of my head and pulled it toward my shoulder, giving him more access, and his teeth dug into me all the way down to my shoulder. It hurt, and I tried to pull away.

"That's what you like, isn't it?" His voice was cold. "To be dominated. To feel like you have no control."

"There's a difference!" I spat out between clenched teeth, pushing against the wall, sure he'd drawn blood.

He let go of me suddenly and whirled me back around. His face was dark with anger once again, and I realized that he'd been playing a game. He stepped back, and the look on his face said it all. He was as infuriated with me as I was with him. The last few minutes had been nothing more than a chance for him to humiliate me. To hurt me.

I glanced down, searching for my clothes. I needed to get away from him, even if we weren't any closer to figuring out our mess than we were when I'd gotten here.

Will's hands moved quickly, grabbing the bottom of his shirt and yanking it over his head. The sudden movement made me jump. I had never even entertained the idea that Will might strike me, but the last few minutes had made me uneasy. I hoped he

116

hadn't seen it because all I needed was for him to think he had power and I was terrified of him.

His shirt hit the floor, and he stepped toward me. Tan, muscular arms wrapped around me, under my arms, hands sliding into the back pockets of my shorts. In one quick movement, he pulled me into him and pushed my back into the wall again. My head thumped against it, making an awful sound and causing me to yelp.

It was the tip of the iceberg for me. I couldn't handle any more. Tears flooded my eyes and streamed down my cheeks. "Stop, Will. Just stop it!"

His fingers were digging into my upper arms when I croaked out the words, and I watched him as they sank in. Anger, shock, and embarrassment showed on his face before he yanked me into his arms, wrapping them around my back and holding me tight as he leaned us back against the wall. My mind struggled to process what was happening.

Ten seconds ago, he'd looked at me as though I was something he wanted to hurt. Now he was holding me as if my life depended on it. The cold smooth wall was such a contrast to the heated skin on his chest that I fought off a shiver as I tried to keep from sobbing.

"Jo?"

His voice was muffled by my hair, but I couldn't look up. My tears had stopped, but I was still trembling, too afraid of what I'd see. I didn't know what to say. I listened to his heart start to beat slower, a more regular pace.

He inhaled deeply. "Jo, please. Please talk to me. I am so sorry."

I didn't want to move, but I pulled back, searching his face. He was gazing down at me, sadness etched in every line on his face, the anger gone.

He leaned his head down, lips meeting my forehead. It was a gentle, soft kiss, nothing like a few minutes ago. I closed my eyes, trying to focus on a better time. A happier time.

Fingertips traced down my spine and back up. The movement reminded me of Matty. I felt my body become rigid as I pictured the smiling, happy man I'd been with just a few hours before. The man who would never treat me this way. It gave me the strength I needed to yank away from Will.

117

He straightened but didn't back away, staring down at me. He looked devastated, and I didn't know if he was upset with himself or me. For a brief moment, old habits kicked in and I wanted to make that hurt go away.

This was Will. *My Will*. The man I had loved him with every part of my being. For so many years, his happiness had been the most important thing to me, and I would have given him the world on a platter if I could see that beautiful smile of his. Will was home. He was the face I looked for in the crowd, the hand I held through every scary movie. We were a team. We had built this amazing life together and made gorgeous babies. His bare chest pressed against mine, and my fingers ached to run over his skin. My body had belonged to him for so long that it felt unnatural to not touch him.

This was also the man who knew I loved him, that I would do what I could to make him happy, that I would forgive for almost anything. And he knew where my limits were. Now he was, above all else, the man who had crossed the one line I had drawn deep in the sand. He was the man who had hurt me.

Everyone wants to focus on the good times. But when you highlight the good and try to forget the rest, you're only cheating yourself. Every fight, every angry word spoken, every stressful situation holds a lesson to be learned. Some are there to teach patience. Others make you see your own flaws and vow to be a better person. And sometimes, you realize just how much you have to lose so you can change in order to keep the things you love. Ultimately, you have to see the whole picture. When one, or both, people focus only on the good and stop learning lessons from the bad, it's time to say good-bye.

The man in front of me had given me so many good days I couldn't begin to count them. Some of them had started bad, some so awful that I was sure I would die from heartache or the pain, but we had dealt with them together and turned them around. Part of me wanted to fight for that now. I could change the parts of me that he was struggling with. I could reach that part of him that obviously still wanted me and make him love me again. That would only prove to him that I didn't think I was good enough the was I was. It would show Will that he could cheat, that when times got hard, he could go to another woman. Those were not healthy thoughts for either of us.

118

"Men don't cheat because they're unhappy with their wives. Men cheat because they're unhappy with themselves." Matty's words from months ago came back to me.

I didn't want to think of Matt right then because I wanted to believe he had nothing to do with this. But he did. He had everything to do with it.

I loved him. The thought made my heart ache. I couldn't be there for Will the way I wanted to be because I loved someone else more. I needed to figure out if my feelings for Matt were real or if they were just a result of friendship mixed with everything that had happened over the last few weeks. Either way, the sudden realization that I was in love with another man but was still standing half-naked in front of Will shamed me even more. The fact that I'd let this happen made me angry with myself.

Will's face showed only concern, as if he knew where my thoughts had gone. I knew that today wasn't what he had planned, that it had gone horribly wrong. He knew about Matty, even if I didn't say the words. He knew me that well. I understood jealousy— that nasty little emotion that made a person behave in ways they never thought they would.

This was more than jealousy, though.

"I saw you with her," I said.

Will's eyebrows lifted and I felt his heartbeat quicken, but he didn't move.

"Last week." It seemed like so long ago. "I'd talked to you that afternoon and I was going to Matty's for dinner." *You told me you were sorry, that you loved me.* I didn't need to say those words. The look on Will's face told me he remembered. "Taylor and I had words and I left not long after I got there. Matty came after me, and we went out to dinner in Portland." And drinks. And a motorcycle ride in the rain. And so much more.

Will swallowed.

"You two looked like a real couple, like you'd been together forever."

He backed away from me slowly.

"And when you left, there wasn't a single person in that club who doubted you were taking her to bed."

He made a guttural sound as if I'd just cut out his heart. "Joey."

119

I shook my head and grabbed my shirt, slipping it over my head, not worrying about my bra. "It really is a small state, William." I sighed. "This"—I ran my fingers over my neck—"this happened yesterday morning after Matty dragged my drunk ass home from a bar. It wasn't planned, and he tried to get me to stop. I got mouthy and told him if he wouldn't sleep with me, I would find someone who would. So you can be happy with the knowledge that yes, I had to beg him to take me to bed." I felt my voice shake at the connection.

Will looked as if I had just slapped him and tried to interrupt, but I kept talking. "Matty isn't any of your business, and I won't discuss him again. Rachel isn't any of mine." I turned toward the door. "I... I can't do this. I'm done." The words came out as a sob. "We need to figure something amicable out for the kids. But you and I are done."

I shut the door behind me and ran for my car before he could stop me.

I was only a few miles down the road before my phone beeped, letting me know I'd gotten a text message. Glancing down, I saw Will's simple words.

I am so sorry, Joey! I love you. Please come back.

I pulled over and let my tears fall. Not for Will. For the kids we'd once been. For the love a foolish girl had once invested everything in. For the woman who had never been strong enough to leave. And for the women who still didn't have the courage.

Something was touching me lightly. I tried to ignore it, but it wouldn't stop. I batted it away, yet it kept coming back.

He was staring at me when I opened my eyes, a slight smile on his face. "Well, hello, sleepyhead."

His voice was low and seductive, but I jumped anyway. The room was dark, and Matty's eyes seemed to glow bright against the black.

He laughed. "Sorry, babe!"

It took me a few minutes to realize where I was. I didn't know how late it was, but by the darkness in the room, I'd say it was well into the evening. I'd come back to the hotel after meeting with Will, taken a shower, crawled into bed in Matty's T-shirt, and cried myself to sleep.

"I wasn't going to wake you, but I couldn't help myself." He smiled slyly at me, leaning in for a light kiss.

 He was sprawled out on the bed next to me, his head on my pillow. I touched his cheek and smiled back at him. I was so happy to see him, I could have cried. I kissed him back warmly, moving into him. He deepened our kiss, putting his arm over me. His lips moved slowly over my jaw, up to my ear, and down onto my neck. When his tongue touched the wounds that Will had left earlier, I flinched and cried out. It hurt like hell.

Matty pulled back, panic in his eyes. "Joes? What...?" He sat up and reached for the bedside table.

The light brightened the room immediately. I sat up, covering my eyes. My wrist ached, my neck was stiff and sore as hell, the light was blinding me, and all too late, I remembered the migraine that had prompted my all-day sleep-a-thon. I rocked myself back and forth, head in my hands, silently begging the nausea to go away, willing my body not to throw up.

Matty had turned back to me, and a quick glance at his face told me he was trying to figure out what was wrong. I felt the bed shift as he moved off the mattress.

"Jo?" His voice was soft as he came around my side of the bed. "What happened?"

I took a deep breath, thankful the nausea had subsided. I opened one eye then the other. He was kneeling on the floor next to the bed, watching me with wide eyes.

"Sorry. Headache."

"I've heard of the headache excuse," he joked, "but no one has ever tried to use it on me before."

I snorted at the absurdity. The movement made my neck hurt and I groaned. I felt as if I'd been run over by a truck, not... how exactly could I classify what had happened with Will?

There were women who let their men do much worse to them, I knew that. I wondered how they felt the next day. It wasn't the physical pain that was making me sick—I'd had much worse. No, it was the stress, the emotions that I couldn't figure out. I was lost. Another wave of nausea rolled over me as I remembered how I'd let Will put his hands on me, how I'd frozen instead of screaming at him to stop.

"Jo? Where'd you go?" Matty's voice cut through my thoughts. He was standing now, and I raised my head to look at him. "Do you have any ibuprofen or Tylenol? I'll go grab you some." He leaned down to kiss me, brushing my hair back off my face. "What the..."

I cringed at his tone. I knew he'd seen the marks. I shook my head. "It's nothing."

He was on the bed, pulling my shirt off my shoulder gently and looking at the bloody puffy lines that Will had left. I moved my hand to swat him away, but he only caught my fingers and swore under his breath. I looked down at the hand he held, realizing too late that my wrist was swollen and had turned purplish blue in a line that resembled a bracelet.

"I'm fine." I pulled away, stood up, and walked toward the bathroom.

"What happened?" I knew he was behind me before his hands fell on my hips. "Did Will do this to you?"

I didn't want to talk about it but knew if I didn't offer some sort of an explanation, he would assume the worst. I turned around, looking down, afraid to meet his eyes.

He squatted in front of me to lower himself to my height. "He," his voice broke over the next words, "hurt you?"

"It really does look worse than it is." I whispered quickly. "I'm just tired and have a headache. It looks bad." I nodded at his scowling face. "I know. Things got out of hand, but—"

I didn't even have a chance to finish before he growled, a feral sound from deep in his throat that made my flesh break into goose bumps. He turned and stalked toward the door.

"Wait! Matty? Where are you going?" Panic gripped me.

"I'm going to kick his fucking ass!" He didn't stop, just threw the words over his shoulder.

I felt a sob coming, and even though I tried to fight it down, some of it escaped. "Please don't leave me alone, Matty. Please!"

He spun around at those words, his face suddenly softer. I was barely standing upright, knowing at any minute I was going to collapse on the floor in front of him like the pathetic damsel in distress I didn't want to be. He practically lunged across the room, scooping me up as if I didn't weigh more than an infant, and pulled me into his arms. He carried me to the couch and sat, cradling me on his lap. I didn't stop crying until I'd soaked his shirt.

He waited until I had calmed before he pushed my matted hair from my forehead and asked, "What happened, Jo?"

In a rush of words, I told him the truth. All of it. The awful fight, the cruel words Will and I had said, the fact that Will's hands touched my body and I hadn't made him stop. I told him how scared I'd been and how I'd thought for a few minutes that Will was actually going to hurt me. I told him that I just didn't understand how any of the day had happened. Somewhere along the way, I dropped the bomb that I thought I was in love with him.

There was so much more to tell, but my head was still pounding, and once I realized that I'd just confessed how I really felt, I slapped my hand over my mouth, terrified of Matty's reaction. I broke into hysterics again, begging him not to leave me, because I didn't know what I would do without him. It was pathetic, but I couldn't stop.

Matty listened, not saying a word, his hand stroking my head and playing with my hair then rubbing my temples. Every so often he would shush me, trying to calm me down. Finally, he shifted us so he was lying down with me, his back against the couch, my back against him. One of his arms cradled my head, the other held me to him.

"I'm here, Jo. I'm right here, and I'm not going anywhere."

I don't know how long we laid there, but I needed a drink and an entire bottle of pain meds.

"I'm sorry," was all I could mutter before heading to the bathroom. I hoped he knew that I meant it for so much more than one thing.

He followed me, bottle of water in his hand, and gave me a slight smile when he saw me struggling with the child-proof cap. He took it from my hands, opened it, and handed me three migraine pills. I gulped them down, closed my eyes, and leaned against the narrow wall next to the shower.

"Hey."

When I opened my eyes, he was leaning back against the sink, long legs stretched out, one propped over the other, hands gripping the edge of the countertop next to him. The worry showed on his face, top teeth gently biting his lower lip in concentration. I didn't know if he was worried about me or thinking about what I'd said. I gave him a small smile, trying to convey that I'd be fine. I hoped that he wasn't going to bring up my confession from earlier—things with him were good. I had him back. I couldn't handle losing him right now.

"You need to get away from all of this for a little while."

Did he mean Will, him, or both of them? I took a deep breath, bracing for the moment he'd tell me he was packing his stuff and leaving to give me space.

"I'm going home next weekend."

Home? I startled in confusion.

His lips twisted into a small smile. "I know it's an entire week away, but I thought it would give you something to look forward to."

I shook my head, not understanding. Matty leaving was not something to look forward to. I closed my eyes again.

"Come to Boston with me."

I pushed off the wall, eyes flying open, meeting his.

"I didn't want to ask like this, but..." He shrugged. "It seemed like the right moment. Will you come?"

I nodded, the movement sending pain through my skull. "Absolutely." My mumbled answer didn't come close to conveying the excitement I felt.

He straightened up, relief clear. "I was afraid you were gonna say no." He reached out for me. "You really okay?"

I smiled and gave him a small nod.

He sighed. "I'm exhausted. Who knew a nine-year-old could deplete my never-ending energy so quickly? He kept me going from the time he woke up until the time I tucked him in." He held out a hand, reaching for me. "And you look like death warmed over, babe. I'd say it's been an exhausting day—both physically and emotionally. I need a bed, a comfy pillow, and your body in my arms. Come cuddle me?"

I grunted my agreement as I took his hand and let him pull me to bed. He pulled back the covers for me before going around to the other side and sliding in.

His legs covered mine as he leaned over me, kissing my temple. "Good night, Joes. I'm right here... sleep tight."

I smiled sleepily. I wanted to thank him for being him, to tell him I loved him. Instead, I closed my eyes and let the medicine work. I was almost asleep when he draped his arm over my body protectively. I leaned into him, feeling his muscles tense.

"Joes"—he was practically whispering, but his tone was hard—"if he ever touches you again, whether he leaves bruises or not, whether you're with me or not, if he ever hurts you again, I will kill him."

I was half-asleep, but the words penetrated deep into my mind. There was no doubt in his tone, only steel and determination. Matty meant every word.

SEVENTEEN

My phone was ringing. I didn't know where it was or why someone would be calling me this early, but I hoped Matty would answer it for me. I reached out to his side of the bed, planning to either grab his hand, pull it back over me to hold me tight, and block out the world, or to shake him until he got up and stopped the incessant ringing. All I felt was the coolness of empty cotton sheets.

I groggily opened my eyes and saw that Matty really wasn't there. I frowned. My phone beeped again. Realizing it might be him, I rolled over to his nightstand and grabbed it, only glancing at the screen before hitting Accept and bringing the phone to my ear.

"'Lo?" The silence on the other end surprised me. I cleared my throat, struggling to clear the brain fog. "Hello?"

"Hi." Will's voice came out breathless. "I didn't think you'd answer. I was waiting for voice mail."

There was a long pause as I tried to get my thoughts straight. "Did you call me a few minutes ago?"

"Uh... no." He was silent for a minute, and I closed my eyes, leaning back on my pillow, wondering if I'd missed Matty's call. "Joey, are you snoring?" There was humor in his voice. "Shit! Did I wake you up?"

I opened my eyes, glaring at the wall across from me. I wanted to be sarcastic, say something mean, but I was just too tired. Leaning my head back on the pillow, I closed my eyes again.

"Yeah." I yawned. "Migraine pills." I explained. He would understand – the things kicked my ass. "I'm awake now." I yawned again, willing myself to open my eyes. "What's up, Will?"

He cleared his throat. "I just..." I could tell he was searching for words. "I just really wanted to... talk to you?" The last part of his sentence came out as a question.

"Talk to me?" I chortled at the absurdity. "You just said you thought you'd get voice mail, that I wouldn't answer. Well, you're talking to me now."

There was silence on the other end of the phone. "Joey, I just..."

I couldn't remember the last time I'd heard Will struggle to find the words he wanted to say.

126

"I'm just... well, I'm really sorry about yesterday."

I let out the breath I'd been holding. I knew he was. I was, as well. I didn't know what to say that could possibly make him feel any better.

My first reaction was to comfort him like I always did. *"I know you are, it's okay. Everything is going to be okay."* But I couldn't say that because it wasn't okay. So I said the only thing I could.

"I know."

"I'm still trying to figure out what I want to say." His voice was soft. "I thought I'd get voice mail and you'd call me back later today or during the week, and I'd have plenty of time to practice what I was going to say." The seconds ticked by and neither of us spoke. "I guess I just thought you'd never want to talk to me again."

It was my turn to search for words as I rolled my eyes. It was too early for his mind fuckery. I popped my jaw in agitation.

"Well, considering you told me yesterday that the reason you filed for separation was because I wouldn't answer my phone when you called, I'm a little concerned about what you might do next. Kinda can't ignore you anymore, can I?"

"Yeah"—his voice was soft, remorseful—"that's true." He let out a long breath. "I don't know how this all got so fucked up. How it got so out of control." He cleared his throat. "All I know is that if I could take back the last couple of months, I would."

He sounded so sad, so lost that I wanted to hug him, assure him that it was all going to be okay. But I just couldn't find the right words, so I didn't say anything. The silence was too much to bear.

"Joey, is there any way that we can get back to what we were? Is there any way I can make this all up to you? Any way we can forget about it? Pretend it was a bad dream?"

I shook my head as if he could see me. We couldn't undo the last four months. Hell, we couldn't even undo the last twenty-four hours. I couldn't forget the way I felt about Matty. And I couldn't change how Will felt about Rachel.

"Will," I started quietly, "we can't change who we are. God! Sometimes I wish I could! But we just can't. I love you, but I don't want to be with you. After yesterday, I'm not sure I could ever be with you again. What about Rachel? Do you just pretend you don't love her? Do you just forget about her and move on with me like none of it ever happened? Do I just forget about Matty? What in either of those scenarios makes us happy?"

"We can be happy together, Jo. We've been happy for years—"

"No, we haven't!" I interrupted, but there was no fire in my voice. "We've been getting by for years. Happy is a little bit of an exaggeration, don't you think?"

"Joey—" His voice held an edge, and I knew an argument was coming.

"No! It's the truth, Will. Look back on our life together. The last six months... when? At what point would you say that we were happy?"

"All of it." He didn't even hesitate. "I know we have problems. Everyone has problems. But, we're a team!"

We had been. I knew that. Yet that team no longer played well together. A sliver of me desperately wanted to run home because that piece of me was one of those wishy-washy girls who would forgive him for just about anything. The other parts of me wanted nothing to do with him though.

"Will. You're not hearing me. I can't do this right now. I can't keep fighting with you. I need space to clear my head."

"With him?" The old argument was back again, along with the bitterness. "You need to space to clear your head—with him."

"Yeah, I do." I was quiet. "He makes me happy."

"I make you happy," he grumbled.

We weren't going to get anywhere like this. Round and round in circles we go... I sighed, biting the inside of my cheek.

"All right, Will. What do you want me to do? In your perfect little world, where do you see this going? In your mind, what do I do now? Do I pack up my stuff? Do I move home while the kids are still gone? Do we try to put this back together before they come home? How do I trust you again?" I scoffed. "Do you take the fact that I told you I was in love with another man, a man who just yesterday you accused me of loving for years, and forget it? Do we just try to put that behind us? And where does Matty fit into all of this? Because without Matty, there really is no me. I don't know how to be who I am without him being a part of my life. If—"

"This is what I'm talking about Joey," he interrupted. "Don't you see it? It's me that you should be worried about learning how to survive without. It's me you should be talking about, saying, 'I don't know how to move on if Will isn't part of my life.' Death do us part, remember?"

"Yeah, I'm pretty sure our wedding vows didn't include the terms 'remain faithful and loving while your husband fucks whomever he wants!'" Silence on the other end meant I'd hit a nerve. I chewed on my lip letting the silence envelop us. "That was uncalled for. I'm sorry."

"We're never going to move past this, are we? I'm always going to hate Matty, and you're never going to forgive my mistake."

I wished I could tell him he was wrong, but he'd hit the nail right on the head. "You don't fall in love with a mistake. You sleep with her once while your girlfriend is working her ass off to pass her finals. A mistake is not someone that you have an emotional connection with, someone you fall in love with over a period of months and then make love to. Rachel was an affair, Will. I forgave your mistake; I can't forgive an affair." He didn't say a word, and I hoped I was finally getting through. "I don't know, Will. I hope we can act like adults at some point. God, I feel like we're teenagers again."

He snorted. "We're long overdue for this. Remember all those times our friends used to tell us if we didn't fight when we were young, then we'd have brawls when we got old? You used to think that was hilarious. Well, I think this is our first brawl."

He was right, and for a minute, I was the old me, talking to my husband who always had a great way of seeing things. "It really is a nasty one!"

"It is." He got quiet again. "Joey, I'm not giving up. I'm going to fix this. You're my family and I'm not stopping until I get you back. I'll do anything."

"Will." I clenched the phone tightly. "You really aren't hearing me, and I need you to listen right now. I love Matty."

He made a disgusted noise.

"I'm sorry if that upsets you, but I do. I don't want to fix us. I want to be with him if he'll have me. You can't love me as much as you think. Not if you were able to so easily fall for someone else. Where does Rach—"

"You said you need time to figure this all out," he interrupted. "That you need time away from me. So that means you really aren't sure yet. That means you don't know. I can give you time. The kids are gone for a few more weeks, and I won't call you again. I promise. Do what you need to do, then come home to me."

I knew what he was saying, even if he didn't say the words. He was telling me to spend the rest of the summer with Matty, to have a full-blown affair, and that at the end of summer, I could come back to him.

Before I could argue and tell him I wouldn't do that to Matty or him, he continued, "Call me when you're ready. I love you, Joey."

He hung up.

I sat in bed for a long time afterward, replaying his words. He insisted he wasn't giving up on us, but he'd already done that. Funny how only two weeks ago, I wanted him back, and as soon as I decided I didn't, he changed his mind.

He hadn't mentioned Rachel. He expected me to spend the summer with Matty, which I assumed meant he'd be spending his with her. I knew that I should be jealous, but all I felt was relief at the notion that if he was spending all his time with her, then maybe, just maybe, he would really leave Matty and me alone.

EIGHTEEN

We took the Amtrak to North Station. Matty gave me the window seat, and I lifted up the arm between us, snuggling into his side as I watched the scenery fly by. Our car was filled with people, some headed to the city for the weekend, some headed home after a long work week in Portland. Their constant chatter, along with the vibration of the train, relaxed me.

Not even a half hour in and my eyes start to close. I forced them open once—feeling Matty's arm come around me, pulling me into him, and his lips warm on my forehead—but he was so comfortable that I fell back into oblivion.

"Jo? Honey, we're here."

I could feel Matty's breath on my neck, his soft stubble tickling my cheek. I didn't want to wake up and instead stretched against him, smiling.

"Come on, babe, you gotta wake up."

I groaned and sat up. We were pulling into the station. The people around us had grabbed their bags, and there was a current of excitement running through each of them.

"I fell asleep."

Matty bit the outside of his lip, trying to keep the smile from his lips. "You did."

I frowned at him, stretching again. "You should have woken me up! I wanted to see the city."

The train came to a complete stop, the doors opened, and everyone rushed out.

Matty stood up, offering me a hand. "You'll see plenty of the city this weekend, I promise." He lifted his bag onto his shoulder, grabbed the handles of mine, and clutching my hand, pulled me off the train. Once we got onto the platform, he pulled me next to him. I reached for my bag, but he held it away. "I can carry it."

I gave him a dirty look. "So can I."

I was going to argue when I heard my name called in a way only a true Bostonian could say it. I turned, surprised.

"Lil' Kangaroo?" the voice asked again as if I was a figment of his imagination.

Rocker was standing right outside the door that led to our tunnel. He smiled at me, opening his arms as he strode toward us, and pulled me into a hug before I could even say hello.

He pulled back, hands still on my shoulders, and looked at Matty then back at me. "When you said you were bringing a surprise, this isn't what I pictured."

"Surprise." Matty's voice was almost flat.

I glanced from one to the other, feeling like I was missing something. There was an undercurrent of understanding between them—I just didn't know what was being said. Silly boys.

"Disappointed?" I asked the man in front of me, pouting for the full effect.

He laughed, pulling me into another hug. "With you? Nevah!"

He let go of me then and threw his arms around Matty in what can only be described as a "man hug." Two grown men, both intimidating in size, wrapped in an embrace, pounding each other on the back attracted some stares. It was a sight to see.

Rocker pulled back, grabbed my bag from Matt, then tipped his head toward the main entrance. "Ready?"

Nodding at his friend, Matty put his hand on my back and led us toward the exit. There was insanity everywhere. Rush hour in Boston - honking horns and the smell of exhaust filled the air. I couldn't keep the excitement off my face.

Turning slightly and catching the look on my face, Matty grinned. Still watching me, he asked Rocker, "Are the boys here yet?"

I didn't know what he was talking about, and I didn't wait to hear the response. I was far too busy taking in the sights and smells. After years away, I'd come home.

A cab slammed on its brakes, double parking, and the trunk popped open. Rocker threw my bag in then opened the door before climbing in the back, yanking me along as he did. I fell into the seat next to him, suddenly crushed into him as Matty squeezed in next to me.

I saw Matty's hand before I felt it, moving slowly toward my leg, then he squeezed my knee before sliding his hand up the inside of my thigh. We had slept together every night but hadn't been intimate since my altercation with Will. His fingers made a pattern, burning my skin through the denim, and I stifled a moan.

132

I was beyond turned on. I pulled my legs together tightly before he could go any farther north. He gave me a sheepish look and shrugged. I scowled back.

Rocker started to laugh, and I turned my glare on him. "You two are wicked cute."

Deciding to ignore them both, I looked out the window. I hadn't heard Rocker give the driver the address, but I assumed we were driving to south Boston. Knowing we'd be in the car for at least an hour with traffic, I leaned back. We got lucky, hitting green light after green light, with no one blocking the road, and fifteen minutes later, we stopped in Back Bay.

Both Matty and Rocker stepped from the car at the same time, out into the summer air. Rob shut his door, but Matty left his wide open. I looked out toward the brick-sided town houses lining the street. I knew this place. We were on Marlborough Street.

Matty peeked his head back inside the car. "Come on, babe."

I slid out, shutting the door behind me, and stared at the large four-story townhouse in front of us. It was taller than the homes on either side, making it appear gigantic. A black wrought-iron fence surrounded a tiny yard on the other side of the sidewalk, just big enough for a tree and some shrubs.

"Where are we?"

Matty didn't answer. Instead, he Rocker up the steps and into a foyer. I trailed behind, completely confused.

The hallway was beautiful; marble floors and mahogany walls led to a single elevator that Rocker had called by waving a fob in front of a sensor. I breathed a sigh of relief, realizing it was an apartment building. I laughed as we stepped into the car.

"For a minute there, I thought this was your house."

Everyone knew that the homes in Back Bay cost at least a million dollars; the homes in this block though cost millions. With an S. Not that an apartment in this neighborhood would be cheap, but for a few seconds, I'd panicked.

Rocker shook his head, smiling. "Nah, it's a duplex. We only own the top two floors."

My mouth fell open. I knew I was gaping, but I couldn't stop myself. My eyes slid to Matty, who was clearly avoiding me.

"Well, top two'n a half floors," Rocker corrected himself, looking at Matty. "Wicked sweet views of the rivah on one side and the city on the othah, so I'm okay not owning the whole place. Plus, the taxes are fuckin' brutal as it is."

The elevator stopped, opening into a hallway similar to the one downstairs, with dark mahogany floors and light yellow walls. There was a giant opening to the left that led into what I assumed was the house, a door just past that in the corner. Directly to the right of the elevator was another door. On the right wall, there were closet doors and another door in the corner.

"We only own the top two floors."

I wondered what Rocker did for work or, better yet, what the other half of the "we" did. Then I remembered what I should have asked when I first saw Rocker at the station. "Is your wife home? I can't wait to meet her."

He was a few feet in front of me, but he stopped mid-step and turned. His eyebrow arched. "My wife?" His eyes looked at Matty over my shoulder. Shaking his head, he continued, "Sorry, Lil' Kangaroo, not hitched." He winked. "Don't even have a girl. I'm a lot to handle."

I stopped abruptly and spun. Matty looked at the table, at the closets, back at the elevator, then past me into the room. I stared at him until he met my eyes.

"Really?" I hissed. The sides of his mouth twitched. "You could have told me he wasn't married, and you could have told me he lived here." My arm stretched out. "I am totally out of my element."

He dropped the bag he carried, snaked out an arm, wrapping it around me, and pulled me into him. His mouth found mine. My arms had a mind of their own, circling his shoulders while my hands tangled his hair around my fingers. His tongue ran over mine playfully, touching my bottom teeth, then it was gone. He pulled my bottom lip between his, nibbling on it. It was all I could do to remember to breathe, pulling him tighter against me.

A throat clearing brought me back to reality, and I didn't try to hold Matty when he pulled away.

As I turned back toward Rocker, I felt Matty's breath on my ear. "If you think this is nice, wait until you see what I have planned for later." His words made a shiver run down my back, and I couldn't wait to see what he had in store for me.

"You two gonna be okay for a minute, or should we go downstairs while you two still have clothes on?"

I felt the blush rise, but Matty just smacked my ass and grabbed my hand.

"This," Matty said, pulling me a few steps into the room, "is the hall. Elevator, stairs to the roof." He pointed at the open elevator and the door next to it. "The washroom is in there too."

I raised my eyebrows at that, and he shrugged, pulling open the door. The little room was bright, surprising me, and I looked up to see the sky through a roof window. There was a circular staircase, and the marble floors continued into a little alcove that held an industrial-sized sink and lots and lots of shelves and pegs with clothes on them.

"It's for when we come back all dirty and gross; we can change and get washed up before..."

I knew what he was going to say. Get cleaned up before going inside. The house was so nice that you couldn't walk inside after work without cleaning up. Yep, way, way out of my league.

He tugged me back to Rocker, pointing out the door in the back left was a "Guest bathroom, no shower," and the door across from it, in the back right corner, was the stairway.

"But it only goes down to the living room and then down to the bedrooms, not outside."

I was impressed before he pulled me through the archway into the apartment, but I was speechless once we were standing in the kitchen. The open room in front of me was huge, magnified by the light wood floors and the wall of windows showing the city's skyline on the other side of the room. It wasn't just a kitchen but also the dining room and living room, and it was exquisite.

A group of men were sitting at a table that had to hold at least twenty. Rocker strode over to them, talking in low tones before Matty dropped my hand and followed him. I reached out to the island in front of me, steadying myself.

Rocker leaned his back against the counter next to me, and I met his eyes.

"They're BbDs."

"Huh?" I shook my head. I knew how idiotic I sounded, but I had no idea what he was talking about.

He smiled a sweet and kind smile. "The counters."

I still didn't understand.

"The counters and cabinets. They're BbDs. The whole house is, actually."

I loved how the Southie accent vanished as he clarified what he'd said, but it wasn't his accent I didn't understand.

Seeing my confusion, he nodded. "Ah. BbD, Boston by Design, although no one ever gets the name right. Some people think it's Beautiful by Design. It's a custom cabinet company." He shrugged. "It's a Boston thing, I guess. The best you can get. We remodeled the whole place a couple of years ago. He's got expensive taste." He tilted his head back toward the table.

I felt one eyebrow rise. I glanced over at the men talking to Matty, some I recognized from a few weeks ago. Then it hit me—his words "we own" and "I don't even have a girl" being laughed at me. Rocker was gay.

"Oh!" I smiled up at him, meeting his almond-shaped eyes.

They were dark brown, almost black, and like Matty's, they were surrounded by black eyelashes that would make any woman jealous. He was a smidge taller than Matty, maybe 6'3", but he was much bigger. I wouldn't be surprised if he tipped the scale at 260, even though there wasn't an ounce of fat on him. He radiated bad boy from the set of his jaw to the way he held himself when he was leaning against the counter, muscles taut and showing.

It would be obvious to anyone within ten miles of him that this man was not someone to be messed with. If they couldn't see how dangerous he was, the sound of his voice would erase all doubt. It was low and rough, almost threatening, even when he was laughing. A picture of the Hulk crossed my mind, and I was reminded of my earlier thoughts of Rob.

There was so much more to this man though. He was beautiful. Not in the old-fashioned Hollywood way Matty was, but more rough-around-the-edges. His black hair was buzzed short, showing his wide forehead and full black eyebrows. He had a triangular face with a pointed chin and wide cheek bones that broke into dimples when he smiled. A long and thick, slightly pointed on the end nose led to full lips that were dark pink and always seemed to be breaking apart into a dazzling smile.

I'd heard him speak numerous times without a hint of an accent, so there was no doubt in my mind that he played it up.

Today, his clothes didn't say biker thug. Instead, they screamed laid-back professional. A long sleeved button-up shirt hid all of his tattoos and another pair of designer jeans hugged his hips in a way that called attention to his perfect ass. I blushed slightly, picturing Matt's ink, and I wondered if Rocker was the same kind of canvas—kinky in all the right places but hidden from the rest of the world. He was barefoot, and I struggled to remember if he'd kicked off shoes at the door or if he'd had any on at all.

I cleared my throat. "Well, they are beautiful." I motioned to the room. "The whole place is." I lowered my voice. "Your boyfriend did a great job. Does he design for others or just you?"

His eyebrows rose as he tipped his head in confusion. Before he could explain what was on his mind, Matty called my name.

As I got closer to the wall of windows, I realized that there were double French doors in the middle, leading onto a patio. The wall to the left of the windows held a fireplace between two built-in bookshelves that were filled. I ran my hand over the back of the overstuffed couch, taking in everything. When my eyes landed on the painting over the fireplace, I stopped and stared. Lee Teter's *Reflections* was Matty's favorite painting. It should look out of place in this bright and beautiful room, but it was perfect.

"I thought you'd like that." Matty was next to me, his own hand gliding over the fabric until his fingers reached mine.

Matty turned me around to face the table, introducing me to his friends once again. There were five of them. Tiny—a man larger than Rocker—was the only one who smiled at me, giving me a cute wink that made me smile back. Hawk and Sean both raised their eyebrows, giving me an entire once-over. Sean refused to make eye contact. Dean looked completely surprised, as though he was unsure how to react, when Matty put his arm around my waist and kissed my neck. Ian, the one I pegged as Rocker's significant other, glared at me, making his beautiful face grow cold.

I was relieved when Matty led me away, telling them he wanted me to see the rest of the house. When we got to the hall, Rocker was holding our bags and propping the stairway door open with his foot. Matty headed down the steps first, and Rocker followed me. It might have been because of their friends' reactions to me or maybe it was because I was so uncomfortable around people with money, but I felt Rocker's eyes on me with every step I took. We stopped at the first landing.

"This is the living room," Matt told me, heading into a room similar to the open area upstairs. The walls were covered with thick white and blue stripes, large windows looked out toward the water, and there were three couches and half a dozen overstuffed chairs spread through the enormous space. A flat screen television sat above the fireplace.

Matty walked back toward the stairs, opening a door off the landing that I assumed was another closet. "The spare room."

I headed in, assuming we were staying there. It was a dark windowless room with deep red walls and two full-sized beds and minimal furniture.

He pointed at two doors across the room. "One is a closet, the other a full bath with our laundry stuff."

His hand was on the small of my back and he ushered me toward the stairs before I could sit on the bed. This time Rocker went first, leading us down another half flight. We stopped at the bottom, and he opened a door to our right.

"Bathroom." Taking a few steps, Rocker opened a door to the left. "This is you." He dropped the bags but turned and blocked the entrance, as if waiting for Matty to keep going. He did.

Matty directed me into a walk-in closet right in front of us, then immediately to the left through an almost hidden door tucked away between the shelves that lined the walls. A set of bunk beds was pushed against one wall, and almost every inch was filled with toys. The windows gave the space a magical glow and I immediately wished my kids were there.

I didn't have long to sulk, because Matty pulled me back through the doors. I was sure we were done with our tour, yet Rocker motioned me to the left, down a hallway. We passed the elevator door and a tiny alcove.

"My office," was all Rocker said as about the small space two steps above the regular floor and enclosed by a half wall before he continued down the hall, pointing at the next door.
"Back stairs. You can't get in that way, only out."

Shoving open the very last door, he stepped inside. "This is me."

Rocker's room had two large windows that looked out on the city, a marble fireplace, and unlike the rest of the house, carpet. A king sized bed dominated the room, two rocking chairs sat next to the windows, but other than a single bedside table, there was nothing else in the room. It was lonely and sad.

Giving Matt a knowing look, Rocker shut his door. "I'll be upstairs."

Matty stepped in close behind me, wrapped his arms around me, and rested his chin on my shoulder. "Hi."

My heart started to beat a crazy rhythm. "Hi."

We walked toward the room we were staying in as one, his thumb drawing circles on my belly as we went. I bit the inside of my lip, fighting to keep my composure. All I wanted was to get his clothes off.

Trying to keep my mind out of the gutter, I gulped air. "This is a beautiful place."

Matty made a sound that I knew was agreement, but he said nothing else, turning his mouth to nibble on the spot where my neck meets my shoulder. I closed my eyes. We needed to get into the bedroom and out of our clothes.

All thoughts of getting him naked vanished when we stepped into our room. I planted my feet, completely surprised.

"Jo?" Matty dropped his arms and stepped back, worry hinging his voice.

I ignored him. The room wasn't as big as Rocker's, but it was close. A marble fireplace was to my left, a queen-sized poster bed to my right, and there two windows looking toward the water in front of me. But it was the little details that had brought me up short. Rocker's room had felt cold and lonely. This one was exactly the opposite. It felt homey and welcoming.

Numerous child's paintings lined the walls. The mantel housed frames filled with pictures. Some of Sammy, a few of Matty with his sister Cris. A cute black sleeveless dress was draped across the back of a chair in front of the windows, a pair of peep-toed black pumps sat in the seat, as if on display. There were throw pillows on the bed. On the nightstand closest to me was the same picture of Matty and me that I had on my desk at work. We were laughing at the camera and looked utterly happy.

I turned to look at him, confusion showing on my face.

"Surprise?" His voice was low, seductive. He kicked the door shut, and walked slowly around the bed, not taking his eyes off mine. He pointed at the dress. "I'm hoping you'll wear it out with me tonight.".

I climbed up on the tall bed, sat cross-legged, and looked at him. "That's not mine." I eyed the small piece of silk.

"Yeah, it is."

"You bought it for me?" I asked in a daze.

He gave me his lopsided smile. "I did. Although I don't know what I'm looking forward to more: seeing you in it or taking you out of it."

The hungry look on his face made my breath catch, and I had to look away before I lunged across the room and ravished him. I eyed the dress. It was almost positive it wasn't my size. "What happens if it doesn't fit?"

He chuckled. "Trust me. It'll fit." He moved toward the bed and into my view, his voice low. "I know your body, Jo, every line, every curve. It'll fit perfectly."

My stomach clenched at his words, a sudden heat appearing low in my body. I didn't know how he managed to get me so worked up with just a few words. I need to change the subject, to ask what I really wanted to know.

"This is your room?"

He nodded.

"Rocker and his boyfriend don't mind saving a room for you? They don't have any other friends who would want to use the space?"

"Boyfriend?" Matty sat up on the bed next to me, and I briefly scowled about the fact that he didn't have to climb up like I did. He pulled a leg onto the bed, bent his knee so his foot was still hanging over the side, and leaned back onto the footboard, facing me. "Rob doesn't have a boyfriend. Does he?" He asked the question in a hushed tone, as though I would know a secret about his best friend that he didn't.

"He said..." I looked away, trying to figure out what I was missing. The dress caught my eye again, and I realized how exquisite it really was for a simple little black dress. There was no way it had come off a rack from a store like Penny's. "It looks expensive."

Matty was cheap, like me, but he liked nice things, so I wasn't really all that surprised. Realization hit me like a ton of bricks. Wow, I was an idiot.

I glared at him. "You have expensive taste."

His face showed his confusion, unsure of why I was angry.

"This is *your* room." I continued. "As in, you're here often enough to have your own room."

He nodded, looking uneasy.

"You live here when you're not home?"

This time he didn't nod, only raised an eyebrow, obviously confused about my line of questions were going.

That made two of us. I was simply grasping at straws. "When you told me you were coming home, you meant it. This is your house, isn't?"

"Partially." He didn't need me to clarify. "I co-own."

I waited for him to explain, but he didn't say anything, making me think the worst. "It's drugs, right? I know you got in a lot of trouble when you were young. Rocker's a drug dealer."

He only raised his eyebrows at me.

"Mobster? Stripper? Male escort?" I silently prayed it wasn't the last one, although that would totally be my luck.

He burst out laughing as if I was the funniest person in the world. "Noooo." He dragged out the word, still chuckling. "All of those are better than what it really is." He shrugged.

"Wait. What?" I gaped at him. I'd expected him to say I was crazy. Matty couldn't have money, and he certainly wouldn't have millions tucked away. I would know. "Then what is it?"

"Inheritance. From my grandparents. They cut off my mom when she married my dad, so my parents ran away. The grandparents didn't know where she was or that she'd had kids until I was a teenager. Apparently they never got over the fact that they didn't help Cris and me. So they left the two of us everything. This"—he motioned around the room—"was their home. My mom grew up here. Now it's mine." He sighed, adjusting on the bed. "I had a life back in Maine, a job I wasn't gonna leave, and I couldn't begin to pay the taxes here, so I put it on the market. Rob convinced me that I didn't want to give up my history, and since he was looking to buy, he bought half. Now we share." He bit his lip, pushing a strand of hair behind my ear, then cupped my cheek. "One more of my dirty little secrets."

"One more?" I was searching for words. "Why didn't you tell me?"

"You know I have a closet-full. It didn't seem important. I don't want anything to come between us. I'm trying, Joes."

I wanted to bat his hand away but didn't. "You have a lot of money, don't you?"

His eyes bore into mine. "I've got enough not to worry. But I'm not quitting my job any time soon, and there definitely isn't a private yacht in my future."

"Does Taylor know?" I thought about the larger-than-life rock she'd had on her finger, and the car she'd told me Matty had bought for her, which I'd assumed he'd financed. Of course she knew. Dread filled my stomach. "She thinks I know... she thinks I'm after your money?" When he didn't answer, I pulled away from him. "Your friends... they do too. Don't they?" I felt sick.

"Hey." His voice was low, calming. He grabbed my chin, making me meet his eyes. "I don't care what other people think. I know you didn't know." He gave me his crooked grin. "You didn't know, and you fell in love with me anyway."

"I've been in love with you for a long time, Matty." My voice was a whisper. "I just never realized it." A tear I didn't even know was coming escaped, rolling down my cheek.

A rough thumb swept it away. He tipped his head. "Really?"

Christ, this was all too surreal. The girl whose life was falling apart only fell in love with the perfect rich guy in romantic movies and romance novels, not in real life. I would give anything for this to be a bad dream, for him to go back to being my Matty.

"Yes." I nodded. "I didn't see it before, or at least I didn't know what it was, but it is so damn clear when I look back." I shook my head angrily. "I can't remember a time when I didn't love you. I know I can't possibly compete with the women you're used to dating. I don't have the model looks or the rich daddy or..." Out of nowhere, I thought of the weekend getaways he and Taylor had taken that I'd assumed were a gift from her parents. "Or even a passport! And I don't wear things like that." I waved at the dress. "I'm simple and boring. I would rather stay home and have a *Lord of the Rings* marathon in my sweats than get all dressed up and go out to a fancy dinner. All I can give you is me." I was making a complete fool out of myself and didn't care.

His blue eyes turned dangerously dark—it was like watching a storm brew on the horizon. I braced myself for the devastation headed my way. This was when he told me I was right, I was just too ordinary and that I should go back to my mundane little life. Christ, why would I think I could ever be enough? I tried to pull away, to save him the trouble of breaking my heart, but his hand refused to let go.

"Do you remember the day you threatened me?" His question was so random, I could only stare. He smiled, making my heart lurch. "I'll never forget it." His lips twisted in humor. "You told

142

me that you had a name, and unlike the bimbos I slept with, you weren't going away, so I might as well learn it. Said that if I ever called you sweetie again, you'd make me pay."

My stomach tightened into knots. Oh, I remembered.

"That was the day I can look back at and say everything changed."

I wasn't following him.

"I called Rob and told him that I was stuck working with the most annoying, uptight, and bitchy girl I'd ever met. He laughed at me. Apparently I bitched about you for a while, and when I was done, he asked when he could meet you. He said if you made that big of an impression, I was obviously crazy about you. I thought he was being an asshole. Over the next few weeks though, I realized how fucking great you are. So that was the day my life changed. Boring and simple are not the words I would ever use to describe you, Joes.

"We have a good thing, you and me. I would have married Taylor and gone the rest of my life being your best friend because at least I could have been a major player in your life. Then Will made the dumbest fucked up move in the history of dumb fuckery, and when I held you that night in the hotel, it hit me. I'm your friend because it's the next best thing. I don't want the next best thing anymore. Fuck, I don't want any of that shit you just said. All I want is you."

He was up on his knees and pushing me back onto the bed before I realized he'd moved. He leaned down, his forehead on mine, lips almost touching mine. "Are you done feeling sorry for yourself now? 'Cause if you are, I'm going to kiss you."

NINETEEN

I stared at the dress and shoes for a long time after Matty left. I'd never had a man buy me clothes before. Hell, I'd been lucky if Will remembered to help the kids buy me cards.

Matty had insisted that they hadn't cost a lot, but I was afraid to look at the label on the dress. The shoes were adorable. I didn't need to see their brand to know they were something I would never wear to work, and because of that, I wouldn't have purchased them for myself.

Yet Matty had bought them for me. Not because I'd asked him to, but because he wanted to take me out and have a special night. He had smiled and offered to return them if I was uncomfortable, and buy me something I picked out. That idea offended me even more though, and I told him I would gladly wear them.

I pushed myself up off the bed and grabbed my bag. Rummaging through it, I found my razor and headed into the bathroom to get ready. Maybe I hadn't bought him a present, but I could make the night special in other ways.

I spent an hour washing, shaving, tweezing, and primping every inch of my body. Afterward, I rubbed a vanilla-scented lotion over my skin, soothing it from the vicious hair removal that had just taken place. When I reached my feet, I was thankful that it was flip-flop weather and that I'd painted my toes a few days ago.

I left my hair down, and after a few minutes with the curling iron, a handful of dark brown curls joined the rest of my shoulder-length hair. I didn't have any jewelry, not that this dress needed it, but as long as my hair was down, my naked neck wasn't as noticeable. That, and long hair hid the leftover bruises from Will.

Thinking we were spending the weekend in jeans and T-shirts, visiting the highlights of the city, I'd neglected to pack my makeup bag. I only carried a few things in my purse, but I did the best I could. I hoped Matty would like the minimal look.

Glancing in the mirror one last time, I grabbed the shoes off the bed, and headed upstairs barefoot.

I heard pieces of a conversation once I rounded the living room landing, but I was out of breath and focusing on actually making it to the top floor without dying. It was no wonder the two of them were so fit; if I had to walk these stairs all the time, I would be, too. It wasn't until I stepped into the hallway that I realized Matty and his friends were having a privae discussion.

I stopped, trying to catch my breath and listen at the same time.

"Alls I'm sayin' is, if you were gonna dump her, you coulda let me know. I'da helped her through the heartbreak. Even with that skinny ass o' hers."

I didn't recognize the voice, but laughter filled the room.

"Yeah, 'cause you didn't creep her out or anything, Sean." Rocker answered, his voice recognizable. "That almost woulda happened. I dunno, Ian might of had some luck—she likes her boys pretty."

There was more laughter.

"She was a wicked bitch, Brothah. I'm glad you got rid of her." I didn't know that voice either. "But I gotta be honest. Betta the devil we know than the devil we don't."

"What the fuck is that supposed to mean?" Matty asked, voice cold and growling.

"Don't get me wrong, Joey seems great. But at least Tay wasn't wearin' another man's ring when you were fuckin' her. It's a big fuckin' risk to take, and I've never known you to do somethin' so fuckin' stupid over a piece of ass."

I bit my lip and stopped breathing completely. They were talking about me. Me and Taylor.

There was a thump, like something was set down hard on the table, followed by the scrape of a chair being pushed back.

"You don't know a fucking thing about Jo, so shut the fuck up before I break your goddamned nose." Matty wasn't yelling, but his voice was even and held a definite threat.

It seemed as if all of them were talking at once, arguing. I stood still, praying no one would come out and find me eavesdropping.

"Hey!" Rocker was screamed. The room quieted almost instantly and it sounded like people were sitting back down. "Jesus, Hawk! Shut your mouth before Mateo shuts if for you." Matty tried to say something, but Rocker kept talking. "No, Mateo! He's got a fuckin' point. They don't know a fuckin' thing about Jo. All they know is that you brought a strange chick home, didn't tell a fuckin' soul she's comin', and then expect them all to ignore the fact she belongs to someone else?" Matty tried to talk, but Rocker spoke over him. "She's wearing a wedding ring. Another man's fuckin' wedding ring is on her damn finger!"

I looked down, almost surprised to see that I was. I rolled my eyes at my stupidity. I'd never thought about taking it off. Did it bother Matty that I still wore it? It would bother me. Fuck.

"We've done a lot of fucked up shit over the years." Rocker sighed. "I get it, okay? I fuckin' get it. It's Joey. Tiny and I could recite her life story. God knows we've heard all about her. We know she means somethin'. But them? They don't know her. You'd be the first one to shit on one of us if we were that stupid. We avoid attention at all costs, not create it. Tell me just one thing." He drew in a breath. "Is there a pissed off husband huntin' you down 'cause you're goin' balls deep in his wife?"

Matty didn't say anything.

Another voice continued, "Jesus, Mateo. Give us something. Does the douche beat her?" The voice wasn't condescending, just curious. "Is she a widow who isn't ready to let go?" Another pause. "I can't think of any other reason you'd bring a married woman here. Especially this weekend."

"It's not like that." Matty argued, but there was no anger in his voice. "He's not looking for her. You can trust her."

"Like I said, I'm not questioning her. If she didn't have that ring on her finger, she'd be a fuckin' keeper. It's your judgment I have a problem with."

I didn't want to hear anymore. They might be talking about me, but it was between them. I needed air. I thought about going out for a walk, but I was in the dress with and didn't have shoes that I could actually function in.

Spotting the roof door, I didn't hesitate. Instead, I sprinted across the foyer. As I got to the other side of the foyer, I glanced back into the kitchen and locked eyes with Rob, who was carrying empty beer bottles toward the counter. Thankfully, he blocked my view of the table. He watched me quizzically for a second before I spun around and yanked open the door, running up the stairs.

The spiral staircase was steep, but that wasn't the reason I was out of breath when I stepped out onto the roof. I shouldn't have been eavesdropping. Their conversation wasn't any of my business.

The humid July air sucked away what little breath I had left making me thankful for the sleeveless, lightweight dress. I didn't know what I'd expected, but the space in front of me wasn't it. I turned around, taking it all in. I was in the middle of the roof, which surprised me, as did the black iron fence that enclosed the entire area. A little building was on the other side of the roof in front of me, but the rest was wide-open space that the boys had decorated to show their style.

There were two black wrought-iron tables, one a little circular two-seater on the side facing the city, the other a monstrous rectangle that had to seat at least ten, overlooked the river. There was a grill surrounded by a small counter, lounge chairs with bright cushions and potted plants scattered around. Set off in it's own corner was a giant hot tub secluded by mesh netting and Christmas lights.

I immediately loved it. This was a place you came to relax and let every worry drift away. A special space.

I walked to the railing, braced myself with my hands, and leaned over to see the city. Millions of lights started to glow against the dusk sky, headlights blurred as cars hurried to their destination, and horns blared in protest. There was life everywhere around me. I let my scattered thoughts float away and focused on a couple walking a dog on the street below.

"It's not you. You know that, right?"

I jumped at the voice and spun. Rocker strode across the rooftop, a beer in each hand. "Sorry. I didn't mean to startle ya."

I didn't answer, but accepted the bottle he held out to me and took a long sip of the bitter liquid.

"We've got nothin' against you. I didn't know you were in the hall.:

I looked out at the city, not making eye contact. "None of my business."

"Matt's not your business? Your marriage isn't?"

I stiffened at his tone. "I'm impressed." I changed the subject and took another sip. "It's a beautiful view."

I heard him swallow his beer then clear his throat. "It is, Lil' Kangaroo. Not in a traditional way. But very beautiful."

I could feel him staring at me and after a few heartbeats I gave in and met his eyes.

"When I met you last week, I was shocked shitless. You aren't at all what I pictured."

"Really? And what exactly did you picture?"

He smirked. "Not some little hot-as-hell firecracker that can keep him on his toes. When he talks about you, he uses words like 'loyal' and 'sweet.' Says you think he's funny instead of annoyin' as shit. When he talks about Tay, or hell, even Bex, he uses physical descriptions, like giant rack, tight ass, lips that—"

"I get the picture," I snapped, glaring. I remembered *that* Matty quite well. I hadn't seen him in a while. "Your point?"

His smile widened. "He talks about you. Not your looks. Hell, you coulda been a fifty-year-old widow, and I wouldn't have known because he never talks about how fuckin' hot you are."

"And you never saw the picture on his nightstand?" I asked, my doubt obvious. His lips twisted but he hid them behind his beer. I rolled my eyes. "Did you need something?"

He leaned his forearms onto the railing, focusing on the city. "We're a private group. We don't trust outsiders as a rule. I feel like I've known you for years, so I don't see you that way. But the guys, well..." he cleared his throat, "The ring, it was a surprise. Another thing Matt never mentioned. They'll get over it though, so don't take that shit personally. How long you been hitched anyway?"

I rolled the bottle between my hands. "A long time. Before I met Matty." I sighed. "I have two kids."

"Really? Wow..." He couldn't hide the surprise in his voice. "I knew about the kids, not the old man." He took another sip then stood straight and faced me. His voice was loud when he spoke, and he offered me a wink. "Not right now—I'm puttin' the moves on this little cutie. Give a guy some privacy, will ya?"

I glanced over my shoulder, expecting one of the others. Instead, my breath caught. Matty was standing a few feet away, head tipped slightly, watching me. I moved my eyes over him slowly, taking him all in. He'd put a few spikes in his hair, leaving the rest of it in a sexy mess and he hadn't shaved, leaving a thin layer of whiskers over his chin and down his neck. Dressed in dark blue jeans and an untucked white dress shirt with a black tie, he looked scrumptious.

I didn't realize that I was biting my lower lip, until he was directly in front of me, his thumb on my chin, pulling my lip free. Then his mouth was on mine, and I couldn't stifle the moan. His other hand cupped my cheek, pulling me closer to him. His hands trailed down my body, onto my shoulders, then fingertips lightly touched my back. Settling on my ass, he moved forward a step, and I thought he was going to pick me up. Instead, his hands grabbed the thin material and started inching it up.

A throat clearing snapped me back to reality and our audience. I pushed at his hands until he stopped tugging at my dress. He growled but let me move his hands, and then, as if remembering where he was, he stepped back.

He took a shaky breath, then scowled at his friend. "Rob? You hittin' on my girl?"

Rocker gave us an evil grin and leaned back on the railing. "Nah. I'm only here for the show."

I giggled, but Matty lifted one hand, flipping him off. Turning his attention back to me, he smiled. "You look amazing. Can I go show you off now? Somewhere without creepy peeping Toms?"

I nodded my agreement, excited about having him all to myself. I laced my fingers in his and waved to Rocker over my shoulder.

"Go have fun kids! But be home before curfew. Don't make me come lookin' for you."

"Fuck off!" Matty called, making me laugh as he pulled me through the door.

As soon as the door closed behind me, Matty wrapped me in his arms and backed me against it. His face was serious as he peered down and for a brief moment, I worried.

"Are you ok?"

"Yeah, he was just playing."

Matty shook his head once. "Not what I meant. You know that."

I forced the conversation I'd overhead from my mind and grinned up at him, my fingertips creeping up the middle of his chest. "I'm just hungry."

"Oh, I'm starved," he nipped at my ear playfully, "but let's get you real food first."

TWENTY

The restaurant was perfect. It looked like a little hole-in-the-wall, but as soon as we were through the door, my opinion changed instantly. It was small, yet what it lacked in size it made up for in charm. Red-and-white checkered tablecloths covered every table, along with a single candle in a tall hurricane jar that cast flickering shadows over the walls. The food was to die for, service was phenomenal, and the wine... well, I blamed that for my current state.

I wasn't drunk, not really. I was feeling good—and maybe a little tipsy. Matty laughed at my constant chatter and singing as we walked along the downstairs corridor of his house to the elevator, his arm around my waist, holding me tight. When we got into the little box, he hit the button and wrapped both arms around me, pulling me into him. He didn't try to kiss me, just held me close.

I tipped my head back, chin on his chest, and smiled up at him. "Tonight was fun. Thanks."

He ran his hand up and down my back slowly. "Mmmmm." He sounded sleepy. Carb coma, no doubt. I giggled at him, and he grinned back. "It's not over yet."

We got off on the top floor and I instantly kicked off my shoes, my feet practically screamed in relief. I watched, amused, as Matty copied me, leaning against one closet door as he peeled off socks and tucked them in his shoes, setting them neatly under the table. There was something about him barefoot that was so damn sexy. Okay, everything about him was sexy.

He pulled me towards the stairs. "You need to see the view of the city at night. It's like nothing else."

I nodded, mind whirling as I tried to figure out how to get him naked and into the hot tub so I could take advantage of him. When we walked onto the roof, I realized I wasn't the only one thinking that way.

Someone, I assumed Rocker, had been busy while we were gone. There were oversized pillar candles everywhere, giving the space a romantic glow. A giant white couch, one I hadn't seen on the tour of the house earlier, was placed so it's occupants could sit and stare out at the city. The small table had a bottle of wine chilling, two wine glasses, and something under a round glass cover.

I turned back to the most amazing man in the entire world, ready to tell him just that, when he reached both hands around me, grabbed my ass, and lifted me. My arms wrapped around his shoulders, and I leaned in, nipping his ear. He groaned and flopped us onto the couch.

I wanted his mouth on me, all of me, and nothing else mattered.

"Joes?" Matty pushed my hair back from my face, meeting my eyes.

I leaned forward, trailing my lips along his jaw and down his neck, as I pressed the lower half of my body onto his. I could feel how hard he was, but he didn't seem interested in more than a make-out session. Every time I reached back, trying to grab my zipper, he pulled my hand back to his head. Sometime over the last few minutes, we had shifted on the couch and he'd lain back, pulling me onto him. He'd balled up my dress, tracing fingertips gently over my exposed thighs, but he hadn't explored anything else. I was soaking wet and the last thing I wanted to do was lie here and kiss like high school kids, but he was taking it slow tonight. Slow frustrated me.

To keep my hands from straying, I alternated between pulling on the tie that was driving me nuts and running them through his hair. We'd been kissing for so long, my lips felt swollen and chapped, but I didn't want to stop.

"Jo?" he repeated. This time, the hands didn't just pull the hair out of my face, they pulled my head back away from his.

I relented, sitting up and leaning back into the legs he had bent up behind me.

"Hey, what's your rush?" He looked up at me, completely serious for a moment.

I shrugged, confused. I wanted him. That was it. He grabbed the back of the couch and sat up, pulling me with him.

"We haven't had dessert." Before I could jump in and tell him exactly what I wanted for desert, he added, "I would kill for a drink right now. You want?" He stood, reaching down for me.

I let him pull me to my feet and followed him to the little table. He poured each of us a glass of wine then lifted the glass lid off our desserts. I clapped once and tipped my head back, laughing hysterically when I saw the cannolis on the plate.

Looking up into his eyes, I teased, "Guess we'll have to go for a run tomorrow." I sipped on my wine.

His eyes twinkled mischievously. "Or get plenty of exercise tonight."

I choked. Matty jumped forward, slapping my back hard. As I coughed, the cool liquid fell out of my open mouth. I was mortified.

He only laughed. "It wasn't that funny, Joes." He gave me a wry smile then walked to the other side of the table. He sat and gave me that serious look of his. "I love you."

He spoke casually, as though it was something he'd say to any friend. I was actually quite positive he'd said it to me before in a laughing manner when I'd done something absurd. I couldn't tell if that's what he was doing then. I stopped breathing, not sure if I should reciprocate or even acknowledge he'd said it.

Before I could respond or overanalyze more than I already had, he put me out of my misery. "I do." Then he added that heart-breaking smile of his. "I love you, Joes." Then for even more clarity, he added, "I am hopelessly in love with you."

I couldn't stop the smile. I wanted to hear it again and again. I would never get tired of hearing those words come out of his adorable mouth. A stray thought drifted through my mind and must have reflected on my face because he stiffened.

His eyes narrowed briefly. "Don't do it."

I raised an eyebrow, unsure of which *it* he was talking about.

"Don't ask me why. Don't think about it. Just say it back."

I shook my head. That wasn't my problem. At least not right then. I vaguely remembered him telling me he wanted me the night we went to the bar, but he'd never said the words that made my heart thump and my belly tighten. I leaned over the table, one eyebrow still raised. "Say it again." I challenged.

He didn't hesitate. "I fucking love you, Joes."

"Then I love you back!" I grinned. Then I shivered.

"You cold? Wanna go in?"

I shook my head. It was beautiful out there. Yes, anyone in one of the handful of tall buildings around could look out and watch us, but I felt as though we were in our own little world. I didn't want to leave.

"How 'bout we take a dip in the tub?" His voice was suddenly husky, and I turned quickly, just in time to see his eyes watching me, dark again.

I stood as I nodded, reaching around to unzip my dress.

"Hey! I told you I wanted to take that off you. Slowly."

I giggled like a little girl as I grabbed his hand and walked to the other side of the roof.

He opened the hot tub and I watched steam rise into the air as the smell of chlorine filled my nostrils. I couldn't wait to sink into the purple-lit water. Stepping up behind me almost silently, he leaned in, pressing his lips against the back of my neck. My breath caught instantly as his mouth blazed a trail down to my nape and onto my shoulder, nudging the silk strap out of the way. His hand wrapped around my hair, twisting it gently and lifting it off my back, before he kissed from one shoulder blade to the other. Then he moved up onto my neck, mirroring his movements from just a few minutes before. I groaned.

He stepped closer, but his body still didn't touch mine. He clutched my waist briefly, then slid his hands up each side of my back, fingers light as they traced the skin at the edge of my dress. When I shivered again, it had nothing to do with the temperature outside. He slid the zipper down slowly and leaned over, trailing his tongue down the middle my back.

When he pulled away, I closed my eyes, unsure of where I'd feel him next. I heard him move, then he was in front of me. Fingers skimmed up my arms, into the shoulders of my dress, and eagerly pulled the material down. He stepped into me and I bit my bottom lip, trying to hold in the sounds my body wanted to make as his pheromones worked their magic on me. He chuckled at my reaction, and my eyes flew open.

I wanted to say something sassy, but as my dress pooled around my feet, his laughter died, and the look on his face made me forget my retort. He didn't move, just stood in front of me, hands slightly out as if he was going to reach for me, staring. I felt more than a little self-conscious as his eyes roamed over my barely clad body.

Hoping that we'd finally be together again this weekend, I'd wanted to make a better impression than the drunk version of me stripping naked in front of him, so I'd gone shopping. The white with black lace strapless bra wasn't a typical choice for me; the cups

CARINA ADAMS

were so short they barely held me all in, but the effect of the plunge was dramatic and made my breasts look bigger than they actually were. The black lace cheeky panties I'd paired with it weren't quite a thong, but they sure as hell didn't cover anything. Together, the lingerie was quite a sight. Not overly naughty, but it definitely screamed "fuck me and do it now" loud enough so even the seemingly clueless man in front of me would get the message.

At least, I'd thought he would. But Matty was still standing there watching me instead of ripping them off with his teeth. I twisted my lips, debating my next move. Propping a hand on one hip, I arched an eyebrow.

"Something wrong?"

Keeping his body motionless, he slowly slid his eyes back up my body until they met mine. After a few seconds, they grew huge, and he looked around frantically, as if he were searching for someone. Then he dropped to his knees in front of me.

I inhaled sharply. Out of all the scenarios I'd played out in my mind, this was not one I'd thought through. His hands ran up my calves, the backs of my knees, then he grabbed my upper thighs hard, pulling me toward him. Hit hot breath tickled my lower stomach before he pressed his lips to my skin. The noise he made in the back of his throat, low and incredibly sexy, made me shake with need. I knew if he kept going, I was going to come apart at the seams.

As quick as he'd appeared, he pulled away, his hands sliding farther up my sides. When he touched my ribs, I realized that he was pulling my dress back up. I gave him a questioning look, not understanding anything that had happened in the last few seconds. His only answer was a wink. Without zipping me up, one arm came up under my legs and he lifted me, carrying me across the open space, down the stairway, then onto the elevator, and across the hall into his bedroom.

It wasn't until the door was firmly shut and locked that Matty set me down. I barely had time to register what he was doing before he moved his hands over my shoulders and the silk fell into a pile around my ankles again. This time though, he let out a low whistle.

I grinned and cocked my body to one side, moving my hip and shoulder into a pose, holding out my hands. "You like?"

154

He stepped back, giving me an appreciative look. Then, smiling, he shrugged. "Yeah, it's okay."

His lips twitched, and I couldn't help but laugh. I stepped into him, my fingers joining his on the buttons of his shirt. I loosened the tie and opened each hole from the top down while he started on the bottom, working up. We met in the middle, and I immediately pushed my hands inside the material and began tracing the pictures and words on his body. Starting at the lonely cross, I worked down slowly until I found the little phrase that drove me wild at the start of his V. He made little gasps and pleasure sounds as my hands discovered him, pushing at his clothes until he was completely naked.

He was hard and as ready as I was, but when I closed my fingers around him, he pulled away. I was in his arms again, this time as he climbed into the middle of the bed. Then he was on top of me, holding my hands above my head as he focused on the little bra and then my nipples after he'd moved the lace out of the way.

His hands trailed down my arms, up to my shoulders, and then my breasts as his mouth traveled south to my belly. By the time he got to the top of my underwear, I was panting. His fingers stopped tormenting me long enough to give my panties a tug, and I heard the delicate fabric give way.

"Holy fuck." Matty said the words slowly, as if he couldn't believe his eyes.

I smiled, shifting my legs open a little. Light-as-a-feather fingertips circled around my belly button and walked slowly down the rest of me to my now hairless sensitive spot.

The mattress dipped under his weight as he moved up over me, legs burrowing between mine, hands next to my shoulders so he could brace himself above me. "Are you trying to kill me, Joes?" His voice broke.

He moved, hard against soft, and I arched, tipping my head back to meet his mouth. His lips, urgent and rough, were gone as quickly as they'd come. He moved hurriedly, pushing himself down me, closing his teeth around a sensitive nub. Waves of pleasure rolled over my body, but I didn't even have time to cry out before he let go and closed his teeth around the other. He met my eyes for a fleeting second, before his hand came up and cupped the tingling area his mouth had just left.

He moved his body down again, this time never taking his mouth off my skin. Alternating between skin-nipping bites and soft wet kisses, he made his way to the soft part of my stomach, then he kept going. As he got lower, I jumped, realizing where he was headed, and I attempted to close my legs. He lifted his head up, resting his chin on my pubic bone, and made eye contact.

He raised one eyebrow seductively, as if in challenge. I didn't care what he wanted. I needed him to fuck me.

I arched my lower body against his chest and begged. "Matty, please?"

He pushed up onto his knees, and I opened for him, digging my heels into the bed. He grabbed my hips, but instead of pulling them up to him, he pushed me down into the bed. His mouth descended, and I gasped as I felt his tongue flit up the inside of my thigh, so very slowly.

Thankfully, he didn't tease me as I had him. I dug my fingers into his hair and lost all conscious thought as his tongue attacked me, circling my clit. He was amazing in bed, but this... this was unbelievable. His tongue deserved an Oscar for the performance.

I bucked against him, pleading for what he was so ready to give me, begging him for more, telling him how much I loved him and what he did to me. Oh. My. God. I didn't want him to ever stop.

He backed away, leaving me hanging on the edge.

"I was so close," I managed to pant. So, so close.

He sat up on his knees, pulled my entire body down the bed to him, and flipped me onto my stomach. Fisting my hair, he forced me onto my knees in front of him.

His body moved into mine, rock solid as fingers dug into my hips, and he yanked me up so that my back was against his chest. "The noises you make drive me fuckin' crazy," he growled.

He slid one hand up my stomach to my breasts and tormented my nipples, making me gasp and cry out. The other hand drifted south, gently slapping the spot where his mouth had just been, sending pleasure rippling through my body.

"Uuuuggghhh. Fuck!"

He laughed, a slow sexy sound. "You are so fucking wet, Jo."

I trembled against him, biting my lip. His hand cupped me, fingers moving into the folds to massage my sensitive clit with a slow, steady pressure. My head flopped back onto his shoulder because I couldn't support myself anymore. It gave him more skin

156

to feast on, and within seconds, I was digging at his arms and biting the insides of my cheeks to keep from screaming.

The bastard laughed again. "Like that?" His breath was hot in my ear, and I couldn't respond. "Bend over. Put your ass in the air." He ordered. "I am going to fuck you hard."

He moved us with lightning speed, pushing me over, cheek to the bed, groaning as he entered me. I cried out, both from how fucking amazing his dick felt and also in frustration. I had been so close again. I gripped the quilt tightly, trying to hold on as he drove us both wild, his fingernails digging into my hip as if he didn't ever want to let me go. He moved hard and fast, unrelenting against my sensitive flesh.

He felt amazing, and I couldn't stay quiet. Every noise I made seemed to penetrate his being, making him pound into me harder. I bit the quilt in front of me, turning my face into the mattress to muffle my screams.

"I wanna hear you, Jo!" The hand around my waist moved to my hair, yanking my head up away from the bed. He continued to drive into me, demanding in a breathless snarl, "I told you I want you beneath me, screaming my name when you lose control. Tell me what you want."

I didn't think, just begged. "I wanna come, Matty. God, please make me come!"

Before I'd even finished the words, I was on my back, spread-eagled, and his mouth was on me. The sounds he made were hot and something you'd hear from someone devouring a sinful dessert, the same he'd tried to contain when I was going down on him. I vaguely felt the hands gripping me, holding me still as he increased both the speed and pressure of his tongue, and then I was there, my entire body stiffening, calling out his name as I came apart.

I wanted to sleep, to drift off into oblivion. Matty, however, wasn't ready to let me go. He was up on his knees, moving into me again, lifting me to meet him. The man had stamina, I'd give him that. His steady thrusts left him gasping for breath, but he didn't slow. Finally recovered, I raked my fingernails over his shoulders, moving with him. He started to curse and leaned forward, closing his teeth over my shoulder, as if to quiet himself, but I could hear his ecstasy perfectly. The sounds he continued to make, mixed with the earth-shattering movements, were my undoing, and I cried out as I came again.

"Come, baby!" he commanded. "Let. Go. Come." I felt him tense as both of his hands entwined with mine and he held them as if his life depended on it. "Good Christ, Jo!" He pushed into me once more, groaning as he tipped us onto our sides.

We lay there, still connected, with his arms wrapped tightly around me, my cheek pressed tightly against his shoulder for what seemed like forever. When he finally pulled away from me gently, it was just for one second, then he was back with a blanket and pulled my head onto his chest.

As my eyes closed, my mind drifting away into oblivion, a random thought struck. I sat up, bracing my hand on his stomach. "We didn't have dessert or close the hot tub!"

Shaking his head, he pulled me back down onto him, chuckling. "I can't even begin to tell you how much I love you, Jo."

TWENTY-ONE

I woke up cold and uncomfortable, one of the wires from my bra was digging into my side painfully. I slid from the bed, hoping not to wake snoring beauty. Glancing out the window, I realized that the glow I could see wasn't the sun coming up, just the lights of the city. It was far too early to be awake.

I stretched, trying to work out the kinks. Knowing I'd never get back to sleep, I grabbed my sweats, I headed for the shower.

I came out completely refreshed. Matty was still sleeping, and while part of me wanted to sit and watch him, or curl up next to him and wake him in a not-so-subtle way, I needed coffee. Matty hadn't shown me around the kitchen, but I could run to the nearest Dunkin. Maybe bring breakfast back.

Except, I realized, I wouldn't be able to get back in. Hmm. Guess I'd snoop until I found what I needed.

I was only slightly out of breath when I made it up to the top floor, and I mentally congratulated myself as I walked through the archway. A black figure moving in the dimly lit space made me jump and I squeaked in surprise.

"Fuck me!" Rocker exclaimed, just as startled to see me.

I smiled at his choice of words. "Good morning to you too."

He snorted. "Someone seems happy this morning. Good night?" Holding up a mug he asked, "Coffee, Lil' Kangaroo?"

"Yes! Thank you!" I slid into a chair on the back side of the island, watching him as he brewed me a K-Cup.

He was wearing a pair of sweatpants and a baggy tee, but his shoulders seemed to sag, and from what I could see, he looked exhausted. Guilt flooded over me; I hadn't been exactly quiet, and neither had Matty.

My eyes slid around the room, wondering if the walls were thick enough so he hadn't heard us. "We, uh... we didn't keep you awake, did we?"

Rob laughed. "From the roof? Nah. I doubt even Mateo's that good."

I laughed with him, not correcting him.

"You always up this early?" I nodded in answer. "No wonder you two work well. I'm surprised lazy bones isn't up yet." He's usually awake before dawn." He handed me a black coffee.

"I'm surprised you two don't have a gym. There doesn't happen to be one in the basement, does there?" I asked hopefully.

"Nope. Rob hates to exercise." Matty, wearing nothing but a pair of running shorts hanging dangerously low, strutted across the room toward me.

I stared, still half shocked every time I saw his colorful torso.

"Besides, it's dark and creepy down there. It's like the dungeon's dungeon. We've got underground parking though, 'cause coming home in the middle of the night and walkin' through Dracula's crypt is exactly what every sane person wants to do." Matty laughed, adding, "Good morning, beautiful!" in a hushed tone before he leaned in to kiss me. "I missed you when I woke up."

Turning back to his friend, "Hey, did you close the hot tub?"

Rob had started out of the room but paused long enough to give me a wink. "Yeah, I took care of it."

"How'd Rob know we weren't upstairs?"

Matty took the seat beside me and shrugged. "I texted him."

Oh, my god. We had kept him awake! My face flushed.

Matty gave me a weird look as he reached for my coffee. "Wanna go for a run? Or maybe we could get a different workout in?"

Forgetting my embarrassment, I laughed.

The day flew. Matty and I held hands and played as we visited all of Boston's tourist traps. When we breezed through the aquarium on our way to Faneuil Hall Marketplace, an ache filled me as I missed my children. I found a quiet spot and called them just to hear their voices. They were still having a blast but missed me, a fact that made me sad.

Matty bought me a chowder bowl for lunch, just to cheer me up, even though he thought eating chowder in late summer went against nature. He did give in and have a few bites, but only after I begged him to share. I was feeling much better when we got back to the apartment later in the afternoon.

"Well, look who the cat finally dragged back home," a lazy voice drawled at us as soon as we stepped off the elevator.

I'd barely taken two steps into the foyer when her arms wrapped around me, pulling me into a tight embrace. Crissia was the last person on earth I'd expected to hug me. Matty's little sister and I had always been friendly, but she wasn't the touchy-feely type. Unless it was with her brother, whom she was clinging to now.

Crissia—pronounced Ca-riss-ah—wasn't as tall as her brother, but at 5'9", she towered over me. She had the same dark curly brown hair, bright blue eyes, sharp cheekbones, and plump lips that all too often were twisted into the same cynical smirk or panty-dropping grin— in her case, the boxer-dropping smile that her brother had. She didn't have the runner's body, but she was toned in a thicker, more pronounced, kickboxer version. There was no denying the two of them were siblings.

The two exchanged colorful sibling banter for a moment before she pulled me downstairs.

"What's going on?" I demanded as she pushed me into Matty's room and saw the clothes and makeup she'd strewn about. It looked as if she had cleaned out Marilyn Manson's closet.

"We're going out." She cocked an eyebrow. "Now, spill!"

I turned from the leather mini-skirt I was eyeing suspiciously. "Hmm?"

Cris propped a hand on her hip, "How in the hell did you get him away from the sea witch?"

I loved the title and grinned evilly. "We should totally call her Ursula from now on." It was fitting. I sighed. "I didn't. Not really. We just..." I stopped, staring at her. I didn't know how to explain what had happened. "We got drunk and slept together."

She tipped her head back and laughed. Hysterically. When she finally composed herself, she cleared her throat and smirked. "She must have lost her shit!"

I shook my head. I wasn't sure. Matty and I hadn't talked about her again.

"If I'd known that was all it would take, I would have gotten you two drunk years ago. Jesus, watchin' him mope around, all love sick over you for the last ten years was enough to swear me off love for good."

My face wrinkled in disgust. "Matty never moped over me, silly, and ten years ago he was with Becky. But thanks for the thought."

She crossed her arms and gave me a pointed look. "Yes, he was with Bex. But he was in love with you before that. Not that he'd change anything, 'cause he's got Sammy." Her brow furrowed.

"Wait, did he really not tell you?" She lifted one of the piles of clothes and cleared a spot and sat on the bed, crossing her legs in front of her.

"You really didn't know?" She pursed her lips and tipped her head the same way her brother did when trying to work out something perplexing, her doubt was clear. "We gotta get ready, or the boys'll leave without us." She grabbed a little skirt, holding it out to me. "Go change."

TWENTY-TWO

"Would you stop fidgeting already? You look amazing!"

I glared into the giant mirror, giving Cris the evil eye. She ignored me, smacking her deep red lips together and playing with her hair.

I didn't look amazing. I looked like a prostitute—and not even the expensive classy kind. I eyed my outfit again in disgust.

Cris hadn't backed down from the leather mini skirt idea until I finally insisted I wasn't leaving unless I was wearing jeans. Sighing, she'd brought me a skin-tight pair with the knees, upper thighs, and the bottoms of the ass shredded—they were nothing like the comfy denim I'd expected. They were too tight and too long, but she insisted they were perfect.

She paired them with a skimpy bright pink flyaway tank, dangly hoop earrings, two chunky black bracelets, and peep-toe hot-pink-and-black stilettos that were so tall I could barely walk in them.

If the ensemble wasn't enough by itself, my makeup screamed, "I charge by the hour!" My cheekbones were defined, eyes heavily painted in smokey shadow, lips dark, and neon pink streaks scattered in my hair. I felt ridiculous as I stumbled off the elevator and into the kitchen.

Matty took one look at me and stopped in midsentence, hurrying toward me. "We're staying home." He declared without as much as hello.

"The fuck you are!" Rocker snapped.

Cris crossed her arms over her chest and pouted. "She looks too good to stay home."

Matty ignored them, stepping closer, his eyes lighting mischievously as he ran a few strands of my hair through his fingers. "Promise me you won't take this out until tomorrow?"

I lapped my lips, fighting a smile. Apparently pink hair made him horny. Before I could answer, he cupped my cheeks and pressed his lips to mine.

"Are we leaving, or are we going to stand around all night?" I pulled away from the boy and glanced at Cris. She waved her hands in the air. "And do that." She wrinkled her nose in disgust.

I might have looked like a two-dollar hooker, but she was channeling a model in leather pants, skirted corset with a chiffon-covered sweetheart bustline, and spike-heeled, leather-buckle ankle boots. Her makeup was flawless and even though my highlights were fake, her purple streaks with real. Also unlike me, she looked completely comfortable, as if she dressed like that all the time.

The boys didn't look bad either. They were all dressed normally in black or blue jeans, boots, and T-shirts. But the leather jackets set them apart.

When Matty turned around, I laughed. "The Bastards— Boston?"

The Bastards, M.C. was in large red print arched across the shoulder blades. Boston was much smaller, in the middle of the bottom. Taking up the majority of the back was a silver figure that I couldn't place; it held two blood-red swords, as if ready to strike.

"What, are you in a bike gang now?" I teased, finding the whole concept highly amusing.

Rocker jerked to a stop, eyes roaming from Matty to me to Cris and back again, as if trying to figure something out.

"Yeah, something like that," was all Matty said before grabbing my hand and pulling me out of the room.

I'd seen that movie *Wild Hogs,* and the fact that my boyfriend was a weekend warrior with a silly name was cute. I wondered which of their girlfriends or wives had sewn on the patches.

"Jo?" Crissia called to me as she knocked on my bathroom stall. "The boys will start panicking if we don't go out soon."

"How are you not sweating your ass off? It's, like, forty billion degrees in here!" I fanned a hand in front of my face as I hurried toward the sink.

She shrugged. "You get used to it."

I was pretty sure I'd never get used to clubbing. Period. The last few hours had been a blast—dinner with Matty, Cris, Rob, and their friends, followed by drinks at a little biker bar. After last call Cris convinced the boys that we needed to go dancing. Rocker refused to let us go alone, safety in numbers or something. She suggested a dance club across the city so we'd walked back to the apartment to get wheels.

There weren't a lot of us—nine on seven motorcycles—but hearing the bikes roar to life and seeing them all in a group, I was impressed. I would definitely be intimidated by this group. They looked rough and mean. Until you heard their playful banter.

When we'd pulled into the club lot, I understood Rocker's reluctance. The old warehouse was huge. With the amount of people—mostly men—coming in and out, the bass-heavy music drifting through the windows and doors, and the lights reflecting on the tar, I knew I would never want to come here alone. As we headed toward the doors, I noticed the worry etched on Rocker's face and the stiffness in his movements. It was clear that he didn't want to be there. Tiny, apparently on the same page, had straightened up to his full height and wore an expression that dared someone to mess with him. Or any of us.

Cris, oblivious, headed straight to the front of the line, leaving us no choice but to follow. The bouncer looked at Rocker and the guys and nodded, opening the door. As we stepped through, the bouncer gave me a once-over and winked. Rocker glared but Matty only laughed and slapped my ass.

"Jo!" Cris snapped pulling me back to reality. "You still look great, really. Can we go dance now? If we don't go out soon, they'll send someone in."

As soon as we stepped out of the bathroom, I spotted Rocker leaning against the wall in front of the stairs. A woman was standing next to him, flirting, but when he saw me, he stepped away from her.

Cris gave me an *I told you so* look and stopped in front of him. "Did my brother send you, or are you so fuckin' paranoid that we can't go to the bathroom alone?"

She had to yell to be heard over the music, but I could sense the unbridled anger just below the surface. She wasn't just angry that he'd followed us. I couldn't shake the nagging feeling that there was some history between the two of them.

Rocker shook his head, eyes narrowing slightly. "I had to piss, so I waited." His jaw clenched, irritation evident.

"Stalked, is more like it." She shook her head and flounced down the steps.

I offered a small smile and a quick wave before I followed her. Matty was deep in conversation with Sean and Dean, the three of them laughing about something, and none of them seemed concerned by our absence. Tiny stood so I could slide around him into my chair and Matty handed me a new drink as I sat, offering me a wink.

I half listened to the conversation as I looked around the table. All of them had a patch on their lapel that said 1%. I had no idea what it meant, but the jackets were pretty cool, and I felt as though people avoided us when they saw them, giving us a wide berth. The privacy was nice.

Cris and Rob were talking in hushed tones, and although I couldn't hear what the words were, it was obvious that they were arguing. His eyes were constantly moving over the crowd, ever vigilant, but when they turned back to her, they were filled with fire. His nostrils flared, his jaw ticking, pissed at whatever she had said. When he leaned in close to her, I yanked my eyes back to my date.

Suddenly, Cris grabbed my hand as she leaned over Tiny, clearly aggravated. "I'm bored. Come dance?"

I glanced at Matty, giving him a quick peck on the cheek before nodding. When Tiny stood to let me out, Cris climbed over Rob, not even waiting for him to move, and ignored him when he tried to talk to her.

He stood to give me room to squeeze behind him, but grabbed my wrist gently as I went by. Leaning down he spoke into my ear. "If you need us, we're right here."

I nodded up at him and his fingers let me go. At the last second I turned back to him and motioned him toward me. "You don't look like you're having fun. Come dance with us?"

He chuckled. "Not a chance in hell."

Rocker did end up on the dance floor a few times. The first was after a couple of guys moved in to dance with us. They weren't being obnoxious, just two friends having a good time. I laughed as one grabbed my waist, pulling me into him.

Seconds later, Rocker and Matty appeared, forcing the duo away. Rocker hurried away, but Matty stayed for a few songs. His hands, running all over my body, made me forget where we were, and I turned, needing to kiss him. We stopped in the middle of the floor, people all around us, and had an impromptu make-out session. It was amazing, and I wanted to find a quiet place and do a lot more than kiss. That was, until Cris made a disgusted noise and pulled me away, farther into the crowd.

Five or six songs later, Rocker and Hawk brought us water. I laughed as they awkwardly danced off the floor, completely out of their element. Matty's friends were funny and very likeable, once they'd decided to stop hating me.

I didn't know how long we'd been out there—my feet were killing me and it felt as if we'd been hoping around for hours—when Cris stopped suddenly and swore. She marched off the floor with a scowl on her face, leaving me to either follow or lose her.

She stopped in front of a sleazy looking Latino man with slick backed hair. "What the fuck are you doin' here, Carlos?" She shoved her hands into his chest. Hard.

He looked annoyed and let go of the blonde he had his arm around. Taking a step toward Cris, his lips twisted into a sinister smile that made me shiver. "Celebrating. Didn't anyone tell you?" He spread his arms wide. "I'm out, baby."

Rage crossed her features. "Who in the fuck did you pay off?"

He shook his head, amusement lighting up his eyes, laughter tugging at his mouth. "No need to pay anyone, Chrissy-yah. The charges were dropped." His smile widened. "No one to testify."

Next to me, Cris started to shake. I couldn't tell if she was pissed or terrified. I looked over my shoulder, hoping to see black jackets headed our way. I wanted to go get Rocker, but I couldn't leave her alone.

"What did you do to her?" Cris's voice had gone ice cold.

"Me?" Carlos asked, in mock astonishment. "I didn't do shit. She knows you're just trying to come between us. I made a mistake and no matter what, I love her. Our family is the most important thing to me."

"Bullfuckingshit!" Cris snarled, turning toward the young woman with him. "Do you have any idea what kind of a monster he is?" She was screaming, and Carlos's arm came out to block her from getting closer to the girl. "Did you know that he beat his girlfriend so badly this time that she's gonna be blind? That the fucker you're with beat the mother of his children with pipe? In front of their kids while they were begging him to stop?"

Carlos grabbed Cris and shook her hard. The hair on my arms rose, and I moved toward them, desperate to protect my friend. Ten or fifteen men appeared out of nowhere, almost as if they'd appeared out of thin air, and they were looking around as if making sure no one interfered with this horrible scene.

Cris swore at Carlos, but he didn't let her go. Instead, he leaned closer, saying something I couldn't hear. She spit in his face. In answer, he raised a hand and slapped her.

She stumbled backward. *Fuck him.* With an inaudible scream, I lunged forward, trying to get to her. She was quick though and was on her feet, throwing a blow back at the man who had struck her.

Fingers closed on my arm, biting into my skin painfully, and I shoved at the stranger who'd grabbed me. He let go, looking at me with a hungry smile as if I was the mouse that had walked into the cats' convention. Warning bells screamed in my head, and I backed away from him quickly.

He had taken one step toward me when an elbow came out of nowhere, catching me in the side of the face. The impact spun me around in time to see another man punch Cris. She fell to her knees and, in a move that gave credit to her training, aimed a fist right at Carlo's nuts. He doubled over.

A pair of arms grabbed me, lifting me. I struggled to get free, kicking out. If these men would beat on two women in public, they would do much worse behind closed doors. I wasn't going to let them take either one of us without a fight.

It was Matty's voice I heard over the crowed, as he yelled at someone. "Get her the fuck out of here! Now!"

Familiar black jackets seemed to be everywhere as a brawl erupted in front of me. I saw glimpses—Rob kicking someone on the floor, Dean taking a punch but coming right back with one of his own—but I didn't see Matty anywhere.

The voice near my ear was talking loudly, telling me everything would be okay. I was too stunned to fight the hands that gripped me tight as I was carried outside. As soon as we were away from the mob of people, he set me down and turned me toward him. I only had a second to register that it was Ian before his arms came around me, hugging me tightly, trying to offer me comfort.

He pulled away, holding my face between his hands, moving it toward the light. "It isn't split, but you're gonna have a wicked fat lip." He shook his head. "Fuckin' rat bastard coward." He glanced back at the door, flexing his fist as if he wanted to be inside. "I hope they fuckin' kick him in the teeth for me." He sighed. "You okay other than that?"

I nodded. "Are they gonna be all right?"

He looked back at me, smirking. "The guys? Yeah." He nodded. "And Cris'll be fine too. She's fuckin' tough. I've seen her beat people bloody in the ring." Sounds of the fight echoed into the lot, and he tensed.

"You don't have to wait here with me. I'm fine."

Ian chuckled. "Mateo would kill me if I left you all by yourself. Not—" He broke off as a siren screeched in the distance. He tensed. "Fuck. Fuck. Fuck!"

I grabbed his hand, terrified of what was happening.

He squeezed back. "It'll be okay."

I watched helplessly as twelve cruisers squealed to a stop on the street and around the parking lot, and police officers swarmed the club. I started to shake but I wasn't sure if it was from the temperature or nerves. Ripping off his jacket, Ian put it around my shoulders.

"I've gotta get you outta here." He started to pull me toward the bikes.

"No, I..." My teeth chattered. "I work with the police on a regular basis. We have to stay and tell them what happened."

He stopped walking and gave me the once-over. "You normally look like that when you're working with 'em?"

I felt my face flush as I realized he was right.

"Come on. Before they see us," he said.

I'd never ridden a bike other than with Matty. Ian's looked a lot meaner, and I hesitated, but then I lifted a leg over and huddled into his back. As we hurried through the city I worried about the ones we'd left behind.

TWENTY-THREE

He parked in the basement and moved me to the elevator quickly. I had only a second to realize that Matty was right; it was eerie as hell down there. I half expected some sort of mythical being to jump out and attack us.

Ian grabbed a spare fob from its hiding spot, guiding me into the elevator when it arrived, then we were upstairs. He swept me up into his arms and carried me to the couch, as if I was some helpless pathetic girl who had just swooned. I bit back my resentment filled retort.

"Thanks for bringing me back." I sighed as I kicked off the heinous shoes and tucked my feet under me, leaning back into the pillows. "But you don't have to hover. I'm fine."

He leaned against the island, facing me and crossed his arms over his chest. Sleeves of tattoos I hadn't noticed earlier covered each arm. The left held a large black tribal design, very similar to Matty's, ending a few inches below his elbow. The right also lacked color and was filled with words and pictures that I couldn't make out, ending abruptly at his wrist.

He adjusted, and I suddenly remembered I was still wearing his jacket. Leaning forward, I shrugged out of the warm leather and held it out to him. He stepped forward, took it, and draped it over a chair. I stared at the picture on the jacket.

"It's Itus." Seeing my confusion, he sighed, tugged on his jeans a little, and sank onto the couch next to me. "The God of protection. He was born a mortal man, a good man. He didn't lie, didn't steal, and his skills with a sword were unmatched. Apollo chose him to be his protector and gave him two new swords to slay the wicked—those who would do harm to others. Later, Zeus made Itus a God so he could spend eternity protecting the innocent." He looked back at the jacket. "That's what we do."

I almost couldn't speak. "Slay the wicked?"

He snorted. "No. Protect the innocent."

"So you're like a real gang? It's not pretend?"

He looked at me, eyebrows high. "We're not a gang. But yeah, we're a real club." He searched my face. "You don't know much about Mateo, do you?" His tone was curious, not snide.

I thought I did. I knew what he was thinking before he did most days. I knew all his favorites, from movies to quotes to food. I knew his expressions, his body language, and now every part of his body. But Ian was right; I didn't really know him that well.

I shook my head, sighing. "Not the version you know."

He gave me a sharp look, glancing at my ring. "We all have secrets, Joey. Sometimes we keep the most important ones, the ones we hate about ourselves or the ones that we know no one will understand, hidden away from the people we love. We're afraid that if they knew the truth, they'd leave. Or worse, if they see who we really are, they won't love us anymore."

I was tempted to laugh at him. He couldn't be older than his early twenties, but this kid had serious insight. "That's a great reason to hide, isn't it?"

He nodded. "Especially if it's from someone you've loved for a long time. You don't want them to run away."

I watched him for a moment, letting his words sink in. I wasn't going to run away. No matter who Matty really was.

"What about you? Do you have someone you're hiding from?"

"Me?" He adjusted slightly. "Nah. I got Ellie. She knows all of me. She's too fucking good for me." His cheeks twitched as he fought off a smile. "But for some fucking reason, she loves me anyway." He turned to me, meeting my eyes. "She teaches high school. Inner city, underprivileged kids. She's one of those truly good people, ya know? Always doing shit for someone else, never asking for anything in return."

As he spoke, telling me stories of his Ellie, I could feel the love he had for her. It was powerful and contagious. By the time he was done, I felt as if I not only knew her but I liked her.

Finally letting his guard down, he yanked his phone from his back pocket and leaned toward me. Beaming, he showed me pictures of them. The small slip of a girl with a shy smile was not what I'd expected. He scrolled to a picture of just her.

"Isn't she beautiful?" His voice was full of pride.

"She is." I agreed as I stared at the picture. Dark blonde hair fell past her shoulders in a frizzy mess, her eyes were hidden by a thick pair of glasses, and her clothes were old fashioned and conservative, but I could see the beauty shining through. "She looks kind."

Ian beamed. "I'm gonna marry her one day."

I had no doubt that he would. I hoped that they would be the exception to the rule, that they would have forever. Love like he had for her was hard to find.

The early light of dawn had just broken the horizon when the boys started to trickle in. We congregated in the main room, making cup after cup of coffee, checking cell phones repeatedly, trying to kill time with small talk. The current of worry that ran around the room was terrifying, even though they all tried to mask it with jokes. Even though I was uncomfortable, I never changed, because I was sure that if I went downstairs, I'd miss something.

Rocker didn't come home until the sun was burning down, warming the city. Exhaustion was etched in every line of his face, with a cut above his left eye, knuckles raw and bloody, he looked like hell. As soon as he walked through the door, he stopped and looked at each of us, as if doing a mental count.

"Cris?" He asked us as a whole. There were murmurs but no one had an answer. "Mateo and Tiny?"

They'd all been held at the station, detained for questioning. But that's all anyone knew.

"I thought I was the last one." He shook his head, tossing his cell phone on the table. "I need a phone. Someone needs to call Barbie and tell her what the fuck is going on."

I tuned out the rest of the conversation. If it wasn't about Matty or Cris, I didn't care. I got the feeling that it wasn't the first time they'd been through this. Then I remembered where Rocker had met Matty and realized it wasn't. Looking over the ragtag bikers who, with the exception of Ian, were all sporting bruises of some sort, it dawned on me that it certainly wouldn't be the last either.

Rob leaned on the back of the couch, looking down at me, "You ok?"

I nodded. "I'm fine. Just worried."

"You and me, too, kid. How sore is that eye?"

"It's fine. Really. I've had worse."

His eyes narrowed and I knew he wanted to argue. Instead, he sighed. "Not quite the night you expected, eh? I—" His voice broke off as Tiny walked through the door.

Tiny tipped his head backward. "They're right behind me." His usually pleasant face was tense, and he looked wary.

Rocker stood, crossing his arms over his chest. "Go home. We'll talk later."

There was a rumble of agreement as all four of the men who had kept me company all night stood and hurried out.

Tiny didn't move, looking from me to Rob. "He's pissed. Angrier than I've seen him in years. Providence pissed."

Rocker stiffened but didn't say anything. Those two obviously knew something I didn't.

"Maybe I should stay." Tiny's eyes rested on me again.

"No."

Without any further explanation from Rocker, Tiny nodded once and followed the rest down the stairs.

I didn't have a chance to ask before I heard the ding of the elevator. Cris came limping into the room, Matty hot on her heels. Seeing me, he hesitated for just a small moment, then he hurried my way, pulling me into his arms.

He moved back, looking over my face. "How sore is it?"

I wanted to tell him it wasn't bad and that I was fine. One look at him though, and I lost all words and my tears started to flow. I lifted my hands, touching his very red, very swollen eye as gently as I could, then moved my fingers down to the dried blood under his nose. "You're hurt!"

His lip looked much worse than mine, and when he smiled at me, he winced. "This? This ain't nothin', babe. As long as you're okay, I'm okay." He shook his head. "Jesus, Joes, when I saw that guy hit you... I... fuck!" His hands ran through my hair gently, and he bent down, pulling my forehead to his. "I could have killed him! I should have been with you, not halfway across the fuckin' bar. I am so sorry!"

Then his mouth was on mine, rough and claiming. It wasn't painful to me, but I tasted blood and knew his lip had cracked again. I pushed him away, intending to get him a cold pack.

He looked over my head at Rob. "Where the fuck were you? You said you had eyes on her!" I watched Matty's face transform from worried boyfriend into a rage-filled maniac.

173

"Back off, Mateo!" Cris jumped in before Rocker had a chance to speak. "I knew it... I fuckin' knew you had him creepin' us! We're not kids, and I don't need a fuckin' babysitter."

Matty turned on her. She was leaning on the counter, obviously exhausted, but she adjusted herself under his glare.

"You fucking happy? Don't you ever get tired of causing trouble?"

She straightened, ready for a fight, her voice ice cold. "What?" Her eyes grew dangerously wide. "I didn't do anything you wouldn't have done! That jerk should be in jail, not out partying it up like—"

Matty interrupted. "We had it under control, Crissia! When are you gonna learn to fucking back off and let us handle shit?"

Cris narrowed her eyes. "You knew he was going to be there? You fucking knew!" She threw her hands in the air, exasperated. "I don't know why I didn't realize. You in town, the guys all here, agreeing to go to the club... you were on a job!"

"Carlos isn't a job! He's a goddamned menace who hurt someone we love! We wanted him to know..." Matty broke off and took two steps toward her, and for a minute, I almost stopped him. He was so intimidating, his rage pouring off him, that I worried for his sister. "Jo was there! You confronted him with Jo right there! You should have come gotten us. It doesn't matter if we knew he was there or not; when you see scum, you get backup. Plain and simple. You don't fuckin' attack someone like Carlos alone!" He raked his fingers through his hair. "What would you have done if he'd pulled a knife or a gun? I can't—"

"Matt." The warning came from Rocker.

My breath caught as two sets of bright blue eyes turned toward me, glaring. I knew they were looking at the man behind me, but a shiver ran down my spine just the same. Matty turned back to Cris, and suddenly they were yelling at each other again.

Fingers wrapped around my arm, and I was led backward. "They'll be at this for a while," Rob's voice quietly informed me. "It's better if we stay outta the way."

From the murderous look each wore, I couldn't think of a better idea. Something crashed and the sound of glass shattering reached us just as we closed the balcony door.

He shook his head. "See?" He sank into the padded patio loveseat, groaning as he leaned back. "Fuck, I'm old."

He lifted a small glass filled with brown liquid to his eye and inhaled through his teeth sharply. I sat next to him, pulling up my knees and watching the siblings through the window. Every now and then I could hear a hint of a shout, but no other sound came out. He followed my gaze, sighing before he looked out at the city.

"Does she know you're in love with her?"

"I'm not." His eyes met mine.

I raised an eyebrow and gave him my mom look. It didn't look like that from where I sat. In fact, the way he watched her constantly, the way he seemed to want to protect her, the way she got under his skin told me he was lying.

"I'm not anymore." He clarified as he shifted his gaze to the glass in his hand. "There's lots of history there. I don't love her because I can't." He swallowed roughly and stared out into the horizon. "Doesn't mean I don't care. I have a wicked hard time remembering that I don't haveta protect her anymore." He looked back into the room, pain evident on his face. "She can take care of herself now, but..." He tipped back the glass, swallowing all of it. "But old habits die hard."

I didn't know what to say. It was none of my business, and Matty had never said anything about the two of them. Maybe he didn't know. I changed the subject.

"I googled you."

He smirked. "Me? I hope you found somethin' interestin'."

I rolled my eyes. "Not you, you. All of you. The Bastards."

Rob's jaw clenched, and his lips moved into a thin line as he inhaled slowly through his nose. Not the reaction I had expected. He was angry, that much was clear, even though it was unexpected. I kept talking, nervously.

"Then I had to look up one percenters, because I didn't know what that was either. That was a surprise." I trailed off.

"What did you find on this search-a yours?"

"There wasn't much," I explained quickly, "but one site said that you are a 'vigilante gang that uses various degrees of violence to protect those they deem as innocent,'" I recited to him. "Another said that you were criminals that hid behind the skirts of the general public, who protect you only because they think that you are a bunch modern-day Robin Hoods."

He snorted. "Yeah, that's what we do, steal from the rich and give to the poor."

"I also read that you help every charity you can, participating in anything that has a cause. However, most police believe that your involvement in those events is only to cover your illegal activities. And according to the web, you've all gone to jail. Sometimes the charge is as simple as assault, but more serious crimes have been committed."

His eyes bore into mine. "And do you believe everything you read, Joey?"

I didn't break his stare. "All I know is that Matty never mentioned any of this shit to me. So I'm asking you, is there anything I should know?"

Rocker looked away then, out over the city. He didn't speak for a long time, and I wasn't sure he would answer.

Finally, he stretched out his legs. "We aren't vigilantes, because we know we aren't above the law." He turned to me. "What would you do if someone hurt your kids? Would you trust the justice system, or would you take matters into your own hands? If you found a grown man touching your child, would you call the police or murder him with your bare hands?" He cracked his neck. "There are people in this world who need help. We do whatever we can, however we can. No one should ever feel alone. Sometimes it's raising cash, sometimes it's us just being there, and sometimes we push the boundaries of the law.

"We sure as shit ain't saints. All of us are bein' chased by our own demons. But we're willing to do almost anything to protect those we can from goin' through the same shit. People are afraid of us for a fuckin' reason. Every one of us has a breakin' point, and we've done some things that would make a lady like you be scared shitless. But we'd do it all again because if we don't help, no one will. That's who we are."

"And Matty? That's who he is?"

Rocker smiled, genuine care crossing his features. "Did you ever wonder why a guy like Matt became a social worker?"

Of course I had. It was an odd fit. Yet, he did it well.

"Did you ever ask him?"

I nodded again. His answer had been simple—*"Because I want to help the kids."*

The memory must have shown on my face, because Rocker gave me a knowing look. "Yeah, that's who Matt is. He may be doing it a different way now, but he is a Bastard through and through."

I looked back into the house, seeing the siblings still arguing. Rocker didn't need to say any more; I knew he was right. Matty wasn't a saint—he had a past that I might never fully know about because he seemed so damned determined to keep me in the dark. So I didn't know about his money, or the Bastards, or even the man he used to be. I knew the man he was now, and I loved that version of him. That was enough.

Hearing Matty bellow at his little sister, startled me. I narrowed my eyes at Rocker, but he just gazed back as if we were having a casual conversation about the weather. "Did he really come down this weekend for that Carlos guy?"

"Cut 'im some slack. There's nothing scarier than realizing you could lose the one person you can't live without."

I knew he meant that I was that person for Matty. I should have taken it as a compliment. I didn't.

It pissed me off that everyone just assumed that I'd leave. Yes, I'd found one more piece to the riddle that was Matty. While I wasn't sure how I felt, I had never done anything to give these people the impression I would just runaway. Yet, twice, in a matter of hours, Matty's friends had hinted that I was going to leave him. Jesus, I hoped he knew me better than that.

"I'm not going anywhere!" I snapped back.

Rob didn't look convinced. "Don't make him a promise you can't keep." It wasn't a threat, more of a plea for his best friend. "There are some things he won't survive."

I bit the inside of my lip to keep from snapping back. We waited for the Murphy's to finish their argument in uncomfortable silence.

TWENTY-FOUR

I was enjoying the quiet. Matty had called out sick, trying to recover—we were both worried that his black eye and split lip would scare his clients. Or at least get the office scuttlebutt stirred up.

It seemed as though I hadn't had a moment's peace in weeks—so different from the life I'd lived just a few months ago. Listening to tunes on my phone, I was kicking ass entering my narrative from my home visits earlier when an email notification from my boss popped up on my screen.

I clicked on it, confused by the "Vacation Time Approval" subject line. I hadn't requested any vacation time. Pulling out my earbuds, I rolled my chair back into the cubicle opening.

"Connie?" I asked loudly, knowing she could hear me.

"Come on in, Jo." I peaked into her office, but she motioned me in with her hand. "Close the door." I shut it quietly behind me and looked at her with confusion.

I was about to ask about the email when she leaned forward and asked, "How is Matt doing today?"

I swallowed. "I guess he had a rough weekend and still wasn't feeling well. I haven't talked to him yet today though."

Her lips twisted, her amusement clear. She knew about us. Shit. I changed the subject. "I didn't request vacation time."

Connie nodded. "I know. But you're going to in a few minutes, and I wanted to make my approval official so there isn't any confusion later on. That's where the email comes in."

"Why am I going to request vacation time?"

My supervisor smiled pleasantly at me. "You need to ask Matt. If you decide you don't want to take any time off, you don't have to. But on the off chance you will, don't delete the email."

I needed to talk to Matty right away. I turned and reached for the door as Connie cleared her throat. "Jo? Tell Matt to check his work email, too. His approval is in there as well."

"What do you mean it's a surprise?" I demanded a few minutes later. I'd snuck into the break room to call him.

"I mean I'm not telling you where we're going until we're on the way. All you need to know is that it's gonna be sunny and hot.

You need swim gear and shorts and sunglasses. Oh, and comfortable shoes. It is somewhere you really wanna be, and we have to fly to get there, so you should just bring a carry-on."

"I did tell you I don't have my passport, right?"

He chuckled. "No passport required."

"Why are we going on vacation? We just got back from Boston."

"Boston was a fucking nightmare." Matty grumbled. We hadn't talked about anything that had happened over the weekend, and at some point, we needed to discuss both the events and the Bastards. I just didn't want to. "This is a mini-vacation to say I'm sorry for that."

"You don't need to take me away to say you're sorry."

"I know." He argued. "I want to take you away so we can have fun and forget ourselves for a little while. Say yes."

I never could say no to him.

Wednesday afternoon came quickly, and before I knew it, we were in my car, two carry-ons packed, and headed for Boston. Wherever our destination, Logan Airport had a non-stop flight and we were going to spend the night at the apartment. But we had to make a quick stop at Becky's so Matty could say good-bye to his son.

I glanced at him with worry as we pulled into Becky's. This was his weekend with Sam, and instead of spending time with his son, he was taking me away. He had seemed so calm about it, eve though I had massive guilt. I figured it would hit him later.

I was wrong again. As soon as we pulled in, the little boy came out of the house, pulling a suitcase behind him.

"I'm ready!" He called, practically bouncing in excitement.

Matty laughed at my confused face. "Surprise!"

It took us almost fifteen minutes to say our good-byes, but then we were on our way again—this time with an extra passenger.

"Okay." I turned in my seat to face the boys. "What's going on? Where are we going?"

Matty just shook his head. Sammy could barely contain his excitement though. He squirmed in his seat, anxiously waiting to let me in on the secret.

"Fine." Matty rolled his eyes playfully. "If you really can't wait, you can tell her, bud."

"We're going to Disney World!"

Disney World? My face fell. I loved Mickey as much as the next girl, but I wouldn't say that was somewhere I really wanted to be. In fact, Florida in July was definitely not somewhere I wanted to visit. *Florida!* My heart stopped beating.

"Is someone else in Disney World?" I grabbed Matty's arm, my voice barely a whisper, not daring to hope.

"Lily and Jamin are coming too!" Sam couldn't wait for his dad to answer, and this time he was actually jumping in his seat, dimples showing. "We're gonna be there all weekend!"

Matty was beaming. He *was* taking me to the one place I really, really wanted to be. God, I loved this man!

TWENTY-FIVE

The flight lasted forever. Okay, even with the security check, boarding, and actual flight, it took us four hours to get from Boston to Orlando. But for a mom who hadn't seen her kids in weeks, it felt as though it lasted forever.

I tapped my foot in annoying eagerness as Matty checked us in at the Polynesian, and I wished the woman behind the counter would move just a little faster. We had adjoining rooms, and the other half of our party—my family—had already checked in. Familiar giggling on the stairs behind me had me spinning around. Seeing their faces, I felt as if I'd won the lottery. Tears burned my eyes and Matty's hand rubbed my back gently as a petite eight-year-old, her wavy blond hair pulled away from her face by a Minnie-ear headband, spotted me and squealed.

"Lily-belle!" I called as she ran full tilt and jumped into my arms. I gave her the biggest hug I could, looking over her shoulder for her big brother.

Much too cool to run to his mom, especially in a public place, my dark haired mini-me strutted across the lobby, giving me a gapped-tooth grin.

"Ben-amin!"

He laughed at my silly nickname, the same way he always did, and leaned in to hug me. "We missed you, Mommy!"

I dropped to my knees, pulling them both close. "I've missed you both so much. I hope you had fun this summer, because you're not leaving me again until you're thirty-two!"

They giggled, and I let go reluctantly, knowing they'd want to see Sam. Lily immediately started telling me all about our rooms, the pool, and how she'd seen Lilo this morning. Her excitement was contagious, and for the first time, I let the fact that I was in Disney World sink in. I'd been so ecstatic about seeing the kids that I hadn't thought about the fact that we were in the House of Mouse. Suddenly, I felt like a little kid visiting the World for the first time.

As soon I stood up, my dad wrapped his arms around me in the comforting way that only a dad can. He kept one arm around me, almost protectively, as he reached a hand out and shook Matty's. He seemed genuinely happy to see us both. My mom, on the other hand, looked as cold and reserved as always, offering me a quick kiss on my cheek. I was so happy that even she couldn't bring me down.

Splashing and the sounds of children's laughter floated to the chair where I was sprawled out, having the sun dry my skin. I moved the brim of the giant floppy hat Matty had bought me, glanced out into the pool, and smiled. Matty was currently under attack from all three kids and was trying his best to fend them off. He picked up Sam, tossing him through the air, and Lily screeched, jumping on his arm. I smiled happily.

"What were you thinking?"

I tore my eyes away from my loves and glanced questioningly at my mom. She looked fabulous for a woman in her mid-fifties, blue swimsuit clinging to a body that she'd taken expert care of over the years. Her hair was graying and was the only thing that made her look like a sweet, loving grandmother. It was funny how her attitude didn't match that image at all.

"You should be ashamed of yourself, young lady! Coming here with *him* while your husband stays home. I'm sure the kids would have loved to see their father."

I rolled my eyes. "I didn't know we were coming, Mom. Matty surprised me."

"Hmm." She turned back to the water, and I saw her glare at Matty. "I'm just glad your father and I have been down here so we didn't have to watch our only daughter ruin her marriage and make an ass out of herself by having an affair. Do you know how foolish you look—throwing yourself at a man like him? No one in their right mind would believe he'd be interested in you!"

I ignored the insult. "So you've talked to Will."

She pursed her lips in answer.

"I hate to break it to you, Ma, but your precious son-in-law isn't the saint he claims to be. Next time you talk to him, ask him who cheated on who."

"Oh, for God's sake, Josephine, grow up! Men have affairs all the time!" She swept her arm dramatically. "Do you honestly think your father had been faithful to me?"

I gaped at her.

She only smiled snidely in return. "It's different for men; they need to—"

"Stop right there!" I interrupted. "You honestly expect me to believe that Daddy cheated on you and you stayed?"

"Well, of course I did! He was nothing when I met him. I didn't put in all the hours of encouraging him and helping him get where he was to leave over a few silly affairs."

A few...? I looked away, unable to believe this woman with the crazy ideas shared my DNA.

"Will felt ignored and did what any man would do." She clucked in annoyance. "I did not raise you to behave so selfishly. You need to end this stupidity now!" Her voice was low and icy.

It never failed. Five minutes alone with my mom, and I felt like I was twelve again. I was sure if we'd had this conversation a few weeks ago, I'd berate myself.

That was before Matty. I turned my head to find him leaning against the edge of the pool, laughing with Ben. I smiled. He looked up, as if sensing me staring, and his eyes lit up as he blew me a kiss.

"Think what you want, Mom, you always do. How I feel about Matty isn't any of your business."

"Joes?" Matty stopped suddenly, staring out into the water.

After a busy few days of park hopping with the kids, he'd somehow convinced my dad, to keep all three kids after a luau dinner show at Ohana's. We'd taken advantage of the privacy and were walking hand in hand down the moonlit beach next to the Seven Seas Lagoon.

"Matty." I was completely content, watching the lights of the Magic Kingdom in the distance and listening to the water lap the shoreline.

He squeezed my hand gently. "I'm having a really good time."

I was too. Disney with three kids wasn't as bad as I'd expected. They'd all been amazing.

"I want this all the time."

"The beach and balmy temps? Yeah, the Caribbean does sound nice."

He chuckled. "You. I want the three of you all the time. I love you. I love them. I want you to move in with me."

I was speechless. We'd never talked about our future. I did want to spend the rest of my life with him, and at some point, we'd have to tell the kids that Will and I weren't together. They couldn't live in the hotel with me, so I'd have to find my own place eventually. Part of me hesitated, the other didn't want to over think it. "Okay."

Matty whooped, jumping in the air like a little kid. "Do you have any idea how happy you make me?"

If it was half as happy as he made me, then I made him delirious. Cutting our walk short, we ran back to the hotel, excited to be alone again. As quietly as we could, so we didn't wake up the family in our adjoining room, we spent the night showing each other just how much we each loved the other.

I said good-bye to most of my family at the hotel. We thought it would be too hard to bring everyone to the airport, and since they had another few days at Disney, my mom distracted the kids by taking them to Animal Kingdom. My dad, on the other hand, had insisted on coming with us.

He and Matty joked and made small talk the entire ride. I tried to enjoy them, but I hated leaving my babies. When we got to the security entrance, I thanked my dad for making the weekend fun. He shook his head and pulled me close.

"I'm gonna miss you, kid!" His lips skimmed my forehead. Pulling back slightly, he looked at me as though he wouldn't see me again for months. "You look happier than you have in years."

"I am." It was the simple truth.

He dropped his voice almost to a whisper. "I've always liked Matt, you know that. I have a whole new respect for him now that he's got my little girl smiling again. Don't listen to your mom. Will wasn't good enough for you fifteen years ago, and he still doesn't come close." He moved so we were eye to eye. "You find out what makes you happy, and you hold onto it."

"Oh, Daddy!" Tears stung my eyes. "Take care of my kids, okay?"

"And you," he turned to Matt, "take care of my little girl."

Matty took the comment very seriously. "I promise, Sir."

I turned and waved as I followed Matty and Sam through baggage check. Watching the father and son in front of me, I realized that I couldn't wait until my kids were home and the five of us were together again. Starting a our new life.

TWENTY-SIX

"You seriously flew to Florida and spent the weekend with my kids and didn't bother giving me a heads-up?" Will was leaning against his car, one ankle propped over the other in a causal manner that contradicted the anger I could see bubbling below the surface.

To a passerby, we were two professionals having a conversation in a hotel parking lot. To me, we were a couple on the verge of a major blowout. The tension was thick

I'd gotten out of work a little early to move my stuff from the hotel into Matty's house. Thankfully, I'd just brought another load to my car when Will pulled in and he hadn't found me in the room. The idea of being alone with him in a small space was terrifying.

I met his eyes, ignoring the vein in his forehead, and nodded. "We only went for a few days."

His nostrils flared. "You really don't see a problem with that?"

I leaned against my own car, parked next to his, trying to ignore my sweaty palms. I knew that I couldn't move any farther away from him, but the urge to back up was strong. *Don't show him any fear, don't show him you're afraid!* I repeated to myself over and over. Being terrified by his presence was such a new reaction that it made it worse.

Lifting my head, hoping he couldn't see how scared I was, I replied as evenly as I could. "No, I don't. Sooner or later, we have to tell the kids. I think they'll realize something's off when they come home and we're living with Matty."

"The fuck you are." He seethed. "My kids are not living with him."

I glared. "We are. I'm taking them at least half the time." I shook my head angrily. "I told you, I'm not discussing this. Your lawyer can call mine."

We'd talked about it on the phone that morning, when I'd told him I was moving into Matty's. I'd wanted to be courteous, to give him a heads-up. It had turned into a screaming match though, and I'd hung up. Apparently nothing I'd said sunk in.

Will stepped toward me. "And I told you that you can get this shit out of your system until the kids come back, and then you are moving home. Don't defy me, Jo. Or I swear to god I'll—"

My mouth fell open, fear forgotten as I interrupted. "Or you'll what, William? Is that a threat?" I shook my head, amazed. "Defy you? Do you think it's 1952?" I laughed humorlessly, appalled. "Are you high? Is that what's going on? Obviously something has scrambled your fucking brain if you think you can tell me what to do!"

"You're my wife!" He snarled. "Since you've been acting like an immature little twit and making decisions that will put both you and my children in danger, I've come to the conclusion that you aren't fit to make any on your own." His eyes flared, daring me to argue. "When you come back to your senses and start acting like the responsible adult you're supposed to be, then you can lecture me on how I talk to you!"

"Fuck. You." I stepped closer to him, my resentment for this man that I'd once loved building with every breath. "I'll use small words to make sure you understand them." I gave him a bitchy smile. "You cannot tell me what to do. I am leaving you and taking my children with me. You are not going to use them to control me, and you are not going to ruin their childhood by being a vicious and spiteful asshole. Keep up your crazy talk and anger issues, and you will be lucky to see them on Christmas and birthdays." I started to walk away, stopping to add, "We're done. If you want to talk to me, call my lawyer."

I was so proud of myself for standing up to him, for pushing back, that I didn't see his expression change until it was too late. It was like watching a switch flip inside of him, and I instantly knew what people meant when they said they saw someone lose their mind. I didn't have time to react before his hands wrapped around my shoulders and he shoved me backward against his car. My teeth slammed down, and iron filled my mouth as I bit my tongue.

Will's face was in front of mine, eyes on fire. "You fucking ungrateful bitch! You will never take my kids away from me!"

He was screaming, and I could barely hear him over the pounding of my heart or the harshness of my breath. He continued to scream, but all I saw was Cris shaking in rage and attacking Carlos at the club, yelling about her friend that he'd hurt.

I was not the girl who let anyone treat her like this. I was not the victim. This was not my life. Fuck him!

The blood pooled with saliva around my tongue. The taste a bitter reminder that this was all too real. I didn't think, just lifted my foot and kicked him in the shin then brought the high heel down on his foot. It did little more than get his attention, but it made him step back a hair. He inhaled as my palm connected with his cheek, and with wide eyes, he backed away.

"What the fuck is wrong with you? You don't put your hands on me!" I yelled, not caring who was watching.

He stood, a look of shock on his face as he met my eyes. He shook his head, looking away. "Jo... I... Those are my kids, Jo," His voice held a note of devastation. "I can't lose them too!"

I was pissed. The dick had some major balls. The horrified look on his face made my heart sink. I'd never seen Will look so scared. For a fraction of a second, I felt guilty for not loving him.

I heard a vehicle pull in on the other side of mine, then the driver's door slam, and I knew Matty was there before I saw him. I couldn't stop staring at Will. For the first time all summer, he looked as if he was processing what had happened. Emotions ran over his face, from humiliation, to amusement, to loss. When his eyes finally slid back to mine, I knew that he understood.

"What's going on?" Matty moved to my side.

His question was rhetorical. Out of the corner of my eye, I saw him turn to me and felt his eyes surveying for damage. Before our trip to Boston, I'd never considered Matty to be aggressive. Intimidating, at times, yes, but I would have sworn he'd never actually hurt someone. I knew better now.

He took a step toward Will. "Did you hurt her?" His voice was a coarse whisper.

Will didn't have a chance to answer before Matty's fist flew through the air. It wasn't like a punch you see in the movies; he didn't raise his arm in threat or pull his shoulder back. Will's head reeled sideways, and before he could right himself, Matty hit him again, this time in his stomach. Will doubled up, and Matty lifted a knee, connecting it with Will's head.

"Matty!" I screamed. "Stop!" I flew between them as Will dropped to the ground and Matty was pulling his leg back. "Jesus, Matty! Stop right now!" I held up a hand as if it would stop him.

I was shocked at the ease with which Matty moved. It seemed natural for him, as though he didn't have to think about what to do next. He just reacted. The worst part was how calm he was. His hands clenched at his sides and I could see his pulse pounding in his neck, but nothing else about him said that he'd just pummeled a man.

"I told you that if he ever touched you again, I'd kill him." Even his voice was void of emotion. "I fucking meant it."

My anger flared again. "I had it under control!"

Behind me, Will was pulling himself up, and I fought the urge to turn to help him. Matty's eyes locked on mine and I saw a small spark of emotion, but I couldn't tell if it was anger or worry. I only glared back into the blue depths, trying to convey that I was fine.

Matty looked at Will, his face showing pure hatred. "I'll leave the happy couple to it then."

I stood there, staring after him long after he had disappeared into the hotel. Will hadn't said anything, but he also hadn't left, as if he was waiting for me. I didn't know what to say, but I knew we needed closure. I took a deep breath, still staring at the hotel, wondering how my life had gotten so screwed up.

"Joey?" Will's voice was full of question when he finally spoke.

I held in the surprise as I looked him over, but I knew it must show on my face. Sitting on the hood of his car, one hand holding a blood-soaked cloth to his nose, the other braced on his knee, Will mused, "He packs one helluva punch."

I reached out, lifting his chin so I could see his nose. "Is it broken?"

"Nope. And I still have all my teeth. See?" He grinned, showing me his pearly whites. "Kinda disappointed. How am I supposed to look like I've been in a brawl if I don't have battle wounds?"

I smiled even though I didn't mean to. "That wasn't a brawl. He went easy on you."

"That's because of my cat-like reflexes. I was just too quick."

Without thinking, I stepped forward, settling between his legs, and put my arms around his belly, cheek to his heart. He sighed, moving his hand to the back of my head, holding me close.

He slid a hand up under my hair, cupping the back of my head in the familiar and comforting way he'd held me to him for years.

"Do you know where I'd go if I had a time machine and could go back and change everything?"

"The end of June?" I deadpanned.

"March of my sophomore year." His thumb stroked my ear. "We were bickering over something stupid and should have had our first big blow-out, but you shut down. I didn't want you to dump me, so I took you home early. All I could think about was how stubborn you were and how I wanted you to yell at me so I could yell back. And then I wanted to carry you to bed, show you how much I loved you, and propose."

"What?" I was shocked. "You hated when our friends fought over stupid shit!"

His thumb continued to move against my hair in a relaxing rhythm. "Couples fight, Joey. They disagree, they yell, they say hateful things. It's a great way to release frustration. Doesn't mean you don't love the other person. In fact, it means you know they'll love you no matter what. You always shut down, backed away from every argument with me. But with everyone else, you were so passionate. I was terrified you'd leave me. I was a kid who loved his girlfriend more than anything else and didn't want her to leave," he sighed. "So I'd go back to that night, have that argument, and then make love to you the rest of the night. I think it would have changed our course."

I pulled away, scowling. "How so? Would you have beaten me into submission back then?"

Sadness crossed his face. "No! Fuck, no." He looked down. "I am sorry. The idea of losing you, of waking up to an empty house for the rest of my life... it kills me. I can't imagine it."

I backed away. "How many times did you cheat in college?" It wouldn't change anything, but I needed to know.

"Once. I'm not proud of it. I made mistakes. There was that one time in school and then..." He trailed off and I knew he was talking about his adorable co-worker. "Rachel wasn't about sex. I got confused." He shook his head again. "I love her." He shrugged. "I love you more. You're my whole world. I never thought you and Matt... not really. I never imagined you would..."

He didn't finish. He didn't need to. He'd said it all before. He never thought I would leave him. Because I was the woman who stayed.

Tears burned my eyes. I was for both of us. "I love him."

"I know. But that doesn't make me love you any less." He looked away. "And that doesn't make him any less dangerous."

I instantly took another step back, defensive again. "Matty isn't dangerous."

"The man who just beat your husband up isn't dangerous?" I started to argue, but he only held up a hand. "I know that's what you think, and I respect your opinion, but-"

"Oh, shut up!" I interrupted. I couldn't begin to count how many times I'd heard those words, his way of avoiding an argument. "If you have something to say, just say it!"

His eyes flashed, and a ghost of a smile crossed his lips before his face got serious. "I think there are a lot of things Matty hasn't told you about his life. He isn't who you think he is." He stood before I could say a word and walked to the passenger side, lifting out a thick manila envelope. "Here."

"What is that?" I asked, refusing to take it.

"This"—he held it out to me—"is Matt. I hired a private investigator. This is who he is."

I shook my head. "No. It's a bunch of shit that you paid someone to dredge up about him. Matt's the man upstairs waiting for me." I turned, suddenly wondering if he'd been watching us. "He's the one who kicked your ass in my defense."

"Take it." He shook the envelope at me. "I know you, Joey. You may think that I don't know who you are, but I do. You need to read this so you can decide if this is the kind of man you want in your life, the kind of man you trust around our kids."

"What?" I sneered, shaking in anger. Matty had been always been part of our children's lives, and other than Will, there wasn't a single person I trusted more around them.

He closed the gap between us, setting the packet in my hands. "I've read it, and I know who he is. I know you won't like what you find."

"It won't matter, Billy. There is nothing in here that he hasn't told me, nothing that would change my mind about him. I'm still leaving you, no matter what that packet says."

"Fine. Then read it and stay with him. We'll let the court decide who gets the kids."

TWENTY-SEVEN

"Jo?"

I jumped. Closing my eyes for a brief second, I reopened them to find my computer screen much less fuzzy. My eyes weren't the only thing tired. Matty and I had spent the early evening moving my things then unpacking me at his—no, our—house, then we'd sat on the porch and talked for half the night.

Well, we'd talked for a few minutes. I smiled at the memory of his body holding mine against the wall as he moaned my name when he found his release.

I turned to my visitor, smile still in place. Teagan looked uncomfortable and worried.

I raised both eyebrows. "Everything okay?"

She shook her head. Looking around quickly to make sure no one could hear her, she moved over to my chair. "I heard a vicious rumor."

I laughed at her seriousness. "I told you, T, there is no way in hell shoulder pads are coming back! Look at these things"—I rolled my shoulders forward—"they cannot handle that craze again!" The giggle died on my lips when she didn't even smile. "Teagan, what's wrong?" My heart started beating faster as I leaned forward, anticipating what she was going to say.

She turned, grabbed Matty's empty chair, and slid it over to me before sitting down. Bracing her hands just above her knees, she leaned in close so only I could make out the whispered words. "Are you sleeping with Matt?"

My breath caught. Teagan never called him Matt. He had always been Biker Boy or Party Prince to her, so I knew she was angry. I wet my bottom lip before scraping my teeth along it and pulling it into my mouth. The answer wasn't simple, especially for her. She wasn't just my friend; she was the friend who had been decimated by a cheating husband. Plus, she was a co-worker. We weren't ready to go public yet. However, that bullshit monitor of hers wouldn't allow a lie.

"It's complicated."

She narrowed her eyes.

I took a deep breath and told the truth. "Yes. I moved in with him."

Teagan turned her head, but didn't break my stare, and drew in a long breath. I could tell she was debating what to say.

I didn't wait for her to ask the questions. "Will and I separated legally earlier in the summer. Matty and I decided to see if we could work a few weeks ago."

"I get it. I do. It's Matty. The two of you..." Her eyes moved from mine to the picture of Matty and me hugging and laughing at the camera.

I knew that would be the general consensus around the office. People had wondered about us for years. Many assumed that we'd had an affair already, and most wouldn't be surprised that we were together.

She leaned forward, putting a hand on my knee. "I need you to promise me you will think about giving your marriage more time." Her words surprised me, and I frowned at her. "Take it from me—it's easy to be mad, to throw a marriage away, but I can promise you'll spend the rest of your life wondering if it was a mistake. Always choose your marriage. Always."

I tipped my head, trying to find the right words. "This isn't about Matty at all. He's my best friend and I love being with him, but even if you take him out of the picture, Will and I are still done." I sat back, shaking my head. "If I stay with him any longer, I'm going to resent him. And one day, sooner than later, I'm going to hate him. I would rather end it now, than wait it out and spend the rest of my life fighting through my children."

Her eyes sparked. "You know I love you and will support whatever decision you make, but please, just think about it."

I didn't know what to say. She tapped my knee in a loving, motherly fashion and offered a small smile as she stood and left. I turned back to my desk, staring at a picture of Will and me from college. The lack of emotion I felt when I saw him smiling down at me surprised me. Teagan was wrong. The only thing I regretted was not leaving months ago.

Matty and I tried to find a balance between our new life and the old. We didn't talk about what had happened in the parking lot. When I'd walked back into my hotel room that night, I discovered he'd packed the rest of my things and was waiting to load the cars.

I didn't miss the look of relief on his face when he saw me and I couldn't bring myself to tell him about the envelope from Will.

We spent all of our free time adjusting to life as a living-together couple. The little things that we'd never known about the other caused some laughing arguments. He left his dirty socks all over our bedroom and never changed the toilet paper roll when it was empty. I kicked off my shoes when I walked in the door and could never remember where they were or where the cover to the toothpaste went. Getting to wake up every morning to his scruffy chin nuzzling my neck and going to sleep every night with his arms wrapped tightly around me was worth every ounce of aggravation.

Saturday, we decided to have a lazy day, lounging in nothing but a pair of pajamas—him in the bottoms, me in the top—while I read and he caught up on Red Sox highlights. We cuddled together on the couch, my head on his lap, reading the same sentence over and over again and struggling to stay awake while he twirled a strand of hair around his fingers. I was happy. Matty's cell, forgotten in another room, rang repeatedly, but he didn't move other than to lean over and kiss my head and tease me about falling asleep.

Will would have answered it. The thought struck me as I hovered between reality and half sleep. It was the truth though; my ex would have been up on the first ring, hurrying to find it.

I opened my eyes, smiling up at the man who held me. He glanced down, a blank look on his face. When he caught me staring, he gave me his lopsided grin, eyes sparkling mischievously. The look had an instant effect on my body, and I moved slightly, intending to show him how much I wanted him.

The phone screeched again. This time, it didn't stop after five rings. There was a brief pause, but it started right in again. Someone needed him, and they needed him badly.

"It could be Sam." He kissed the top of my forehead as I sat up to let him out. "I'll be right back. Don't move."

I stretched out lazily, grabbed the blanket from the back of the couch, and flipped off the TV. I snuggled back into the plush cushions for a quick nap, knowing he'd wake me up when he was done. I'd just started to fall asleep when I heard his string of curses. I sat up, feeling pity for whomever was on the other end of that call.

The porch door slammed as he made his way back inside and headed to our room. Drawers opened and shut loudly as if he was searching for something. Then he was out in the hall, head tipped, pinning the phone between his shoulder and ear, while he buckled the belt on his jeans. "What hospital?"

I perked up at his words, pushing the blanket all the way off, ready to spring into action.

"'K. I'm on my way."

I jumped up, practically running around the couch to step in front of him. Matty stopped short as he tucked his phone in his back pocket, looking at me as if he'd just remembered I was there.

When he didn't offer any information, I clutched at his shirt. "Hospital? Is Sammy okay? You're scaring me."

He nodded quickly, his eyes big. He ran his hands down his face, scrubbing at his whiskers. "Jesus, Joes!" He blew out a deep breath. "I'm sorry, I didn't mean to scare you."

He pulled me into his arms, hugging me almost too tight. He put a hand under my chin, tipping my face to his and I could see his eyes were clouded with worry and tension. One hand slipped behind my head and he pulled me to him, warm lips found and claimed mine in a rough touch that was full of need.

I groaned against the tongue that invaded my mouth, surprised that my hands had found their way to his back and that I was pulling him closer. He made a noise deep in his throat, before grabbing my ass and lifting me. I wrapped my legs around his waist as he moved us to the couch, laying me on my back.

He moved onto me, pushing against me, and I groaned again. He was ready, his hardness straining against the denim of his jeans. His weight on me made my stomach clench, and I felt the familiar need between my legs. His mouth was everywhere, hands pulling up the light cotton of my shir, an urgency in him that I didn't understand.

"Joes," he panted, "I need this. Now."

I wasn't about to deny him anything. He shifted back, weight on his knees, stretched his arms over his head, and yanked his T-shirt off. Before he could move back onto me, I reached out, tracing the tattoos that I knew I'd never get tired of. He paused, letting me run my fingertips over the smooth flesh, pressing his bottom half against mine suggestively. I followed the inked words down to his

196

happy trail, and I grabbed at the zipper on his jeans, struggling to get them open.

He hissed my name as he sprang free and I circled him with my hand. I didn't have a chance to push his jeans down his hips before he grabbed both wrists. In one move, he forced them to the end of the couch above my head and buried himself in me. Letting go of my hands, he grabbed my hips, lifting me up to him as he bucked against me.

We were at a weird angle, his knees sinking into the couch so that my body was higher than his and I could only reach his arms, digging my fingernails in as I struggled to hang on. We'd had crazy hot sex where he dominated every part of me, we'd made love so sweetly I'd wanted to cry, and we'd done the carnal need quickie.

This was different. Stress and worry flowed off him in waves, and he pounded into me as if it was his only salvation. Whatever he'd been told on that phone call was driving him crazy, pushing one of his demons close. I met him stroke for stroke, hoping my body would be enough to calm him.

He moved suddenly, lifting me up onto him so that he was sitting and I was straddling him. He lifted my shirt and tossed it behind him, hands moving immediately to my breasts, pinching at my nipples, nails digging into my back. I gasped, arching into his hands.

"Ride me."

It was a low, gruff command, and I felt the rush of wet heat that surrounded him as my lower muscles clenched at the tone. He sucked in a breath, feeling the tightness as I eased onto him, pulling him into me. He swore. I did what I was told and started to move against him as fast as I could, his rasping sounds of pleasure encouraging me to keep a quick pace. He tensed, close to the edge, and I arched my back against him to take him deeper. The move brought my shoulder near his mouth, and he dug his teeth into me, fingernails raking down my back. I cried out, grabbing fistfuls of hair as he bucked under me.

He moaned then stilled, wrapping both arms around me, enveloping me before buring his head in my nape. The sad sound he made brought me out of my daze instantly.

"Do you have any fucking idea how much I love you—how much I need you?"

His arms were so tight I couldn't move. Hell, I could barely breath. "Matty?" I wheezed, unsure what was wrong. "Baby, what's going on?"

He didn't answer, just held me with a death grip. Finally his hold loosened, and I eased off him. We both winced as I pulled away. He didn't attempt to cover himself, just watched me sink to my knees next to him. He reached one hand out, cupping my face. Tears glistened in his. The tortured expression on his face was not one I'd seen in a long time—not since Becky had left him.

Disbelief mixed with fear. I didn't know what had happened. All I knew was that it was bad.

TWENTY-EIGHT

It was a hot August day, probably high nineties in the sun. I still sat on our sun porch, covered in a blanket and clutching a steaming hot cup of tea that I probably would never drink. The house was quiet, too quiet, and I missed Matty with every ounce of me. I just couldn't get warm.

I kept picturing the beautiful young kid who had been so nice to me in Boston and the glow he'd had when he talked about his girlfriend Ellie. A sob escaped as I thought about the innocent young woman in the pictures. I closed my eyes, but all I could see was the scene Matty had described, and I forced them back open, trying to think of anything else.

I didn't know when he'd be back. He hadn't known if it would be today, tonight, or even tomorrow. I didn't want to think of what could happen to him.

I bit my lip, shaking my head. Nothing would happen. He was going down to support his friends, to get answers, that was it. I knew that wasn't really true. I knew when he left, the way he kissed me, the way he'd called Sam and told him he loved him, that he was going down to be stupid.

"They attacked them, Joes. Fuckin' jumped them while they were taking a walk by the river in a nice part of town!" His hands had fisted, jaw clenched as he said the next words. *"They didn't just hurt one of us, Joes. Ellie was a nice girl, with her whole future ahead of her. They attacked all of us."*

No one knew who the "they" was. That was part of the problem. An unknown enemy. A nameless, faceless foe. That fact terrified them all.

Ian had taken Ellie out last night for a romantic dinner and a moonlit walk when they'd been mugged. Or at least, that's what they'd thought it was. Until five or six men beat on Ian and then held him while they hurt Ellie. He hadn't been wearing anything that told the world he was a Bastard, but my gut told me that it didn't matter. Matty didn't know how badly Ellie was hurt, but I felt as though he was holding something back. He did promise that she would recover from her injuries.

Ian was never going to be the same though. They'd released him from the hospital early this morning, and he'd headed right to Rocker's. The rest of them were taking it just as hard as he was.

I had wanted to go with Matty, to support his friends that I'd become attached to. Matty flat-out refused. He said he didn't know what he was walking into down there, but I could sense his hesitation. There was something else, something I didn't understand. He'd promised he'd call me when he had news, told me to call a friend, then kissed me hard, telling me he loved me.

I shivered and sighed, looking out the window onto the back lawn, wishing the kids were here and laughing and playing. It really was too quiet.

Never a dull minute with my Greek God. My mind connected something it never had before. Itus, the Greek God of protection. That was my Matty.

A knock on the door brought me back to reality. I'd called Teagan, needing to scare away the quiet and because I needed a distraction. I put my forgotten tea on the table and walked to the kitchen.

I stopped short when I saw the beautiful blonde at the door. She had no reason to be here, but I opened the door, eyebrows raised, feeling seriously underdressed in my yoga pants and tank top. I took a deep breath and smiled.

"Where's Matt?" she demanded without smiling back.

"Not here." I was being rude but couldn't stop myself.

She raised her left hand, patting the top of her head, the giant ring on her hand reflecting the sun. It took every ounce of self-control I had not to show the shock I felt at seeing her still wearing the one thing that told the world she was Matty's, and even more not to smack the smug look off her face when she realized I'd seen it.

"Oh!" She pouted. "Well, I never had a chance to call him back last night. It seemed important"—she lowered her voice in a conspiratorial whisper—"but part of me assumed it was just another booty call, so I thought I'd make him sweat a little."

My stomach knotted at her words.

She winked at me, looked around the kitchen, and shrugged. "I can wait."

I took a step toward her, trying to block the entrance. "He won't be back for a while. I'll just tell him you stopped by."

She smirked, arching an eyebrow. "Does he know you're here waiting for him?"

I smiled at that. "Yeah. I live here now."

The news didn't appear to bother her at all. "I told him he'd need a roommate once I moved out."

I was about to inform the smug little bitch that I was Matty's girlfriend when she turned and bounced down the stairs.

She turned at the bottom, lifting sunglasses to her eyes. "Don't get too comfy, Joey. From the way Matty was talking yesterday, I'll be back before the weekend is over. And we don't need a roommate. Three's a crowd and all that…"

I was rooted to the spot, watching her get in her little car and drive away. Before I could stop them, every doubt I had about us, from Taylor's claim on him, to Will's stupid packet of secrets, to everything I'd learned in Boston, came flooding to the surface. I sat down, frustrated, my thoughts whirling. I dialed his cell, wanting only to hear his voice. Only Matty could make all this bullshit worth it.

TWENTY-NINE

Matty came home late that night. It was unexpected, and I couldn't hide my relief when he walked through the door. I ran to him, practically jumping in his arms, grateful when he picked me up. Forgetting to ask about his day or find out how Ian and Ellie were doing, I threw my arms around his neck and pulled him down for a suggestive kiss that promised there was a lot more coming.

He carried me to the bedroom, leaving every light blazing and the eleven o'clock news anchor talking to the empty living room. The mattress dipped under our combined weight as he lowered me to the bed, standing only to peel off his jacket and shirt, kicking his boots to the wall. I leaned up on my elbows, watching as he unbuttoned his jeans and slid them over his hips. He was so beautiful it hurt to look at him, and I bit my lip to keep from sounding like a blubbering idiot and telling him exactly what I thought of his body.

He smiled down, seeing my expression. "Jesus, Joes, if this is how you're going to welcome me home every time I go away, I'm gonna go away more often." His sexy, lopsided grin appeared as he crawled up the bed toward me, parting my legs with his knee. "But just so you know"—he kissed my knee—"I missed you all fucking day." His tongue traced a wet trail up my thigh, making me shiver, "I'm never"—his teeth bit into my hip, and I groaned—"ever"—he looked up, locking his eyes onto mine—"leaving you"—his tongue danced over my stomach, circling my belly button, and I arched— "ever again."

"Matty, please," I begged, my voice barely audible. I needed him to touch me, to make all my worries go away.

He raked his teeth over his bottom lip, the simple action causing every ounce of my flesh to catch fire, and braced his arms next to my shoulders, looking down at me.

"Get used to begging, beautiful," he growled. "I spent the last three hours thinking about those sweet sounds you make, and I plan to spend just as many hearing you make them." He lowered himself slowly, aligning his body with mine.

I woke up to a cold bed. Sitting up, I searched for my phone, trying to figure out what time it was. Then I remembered it was out on the coffee table. I'd forgotten it last night when I'd heard Matty's bike pull into the driveway.

I rubbed the sleep from my eyes and grabbed a T-shirt to cover my nakedness before I went in search for my own personal heater, hoping that I could find some way to lure him back to bed. I smelled coffee, but the kitchen was empty. I paused outside the bathroom door, listening for the shower, but it was silent. Heading down the hall, I heard the shuffle of papers on the sun porch.

I turned the corner, smiling at him as he sat in the middle of the floor, paperwork scattered around him, the early morning sun giving his bare chest a bronze glow. He was scowling at whatever he was reading, obviously engrossed. I leaned my cheek against the door frame, content to watch him. His eyes glanced up and he looked away before doing a double-take and snapping his baby blues back to mine.

He tried to cover his surprise as he hastily gathered up the papers, a move obviously aimed at keeping whatever it was from me.

"Morning." I watched him reach out, grabbing mindlessly, not caring if he kept the piles organized. "What's all this?" I wasn't sure I wanted to know, but my curiosity got the better of me.

He shook his head. "Nothing."

I took a step into the room before I realized that he was shoving everything back into a familiar manila envelope.

He looked up, offering me a small smile that didn't reach his eyes. "Morning, babe! I didn't think you'd be up yet."

Obviously. "Matty, I..." I wasn't sure what to say, how to tell him.

He shook his head again. "It's nothing, Jo." His voice was hard. He moved himself from the floor to the chair, never making eye contact, and sighed. "I talked to Tay yesterday, told her I wanted her to come get her shit out of my garage so we'd have a place to park."

I snorted. His head snapped to me, and he waited for an explanation.

I shook my head. "She was here yesterday. She claimed that you kept calling her and that she assumed it was for another booty call." I laughed again. "I could have gotten her stuff out for her. But, she didn't ask."

He rolled his eyes. "She... she's something else, isn't she? She told me she had left some things and asked me to pack those as well, said she'd be here first thing this morning. I want her gone, completely, so I started gathering the leftovers. Then I found this." He picked up the envelope. "It was an interesting read to say the least." He looked at me, pain evident in the way he held his body. "It's a—"

"I know what it is, Matty."

His brows knitted together as he silently questioned me.

"It isn't Taylor's."

The color slowly drained from his face, but he didn't say a word. His whole body was erect, stiff. I moved into the room and sat across from him.

Taking a deep breath, I explained, "I don't know what it says, but Will gave it to me before I moved in. He hired a private investigator. I was going to tell you but didn't want to start a fight."

His jaw clenched, and he took several deep breaths, eyes never leaving mine. "You didn't want to start a fight?" He worked his jaw. "Your husband somehow manages to dig up records from my childhood that are sealed, and you don't tell me because you don't want to start a fight?"

I opened my mouth to respond, but nothing came out. I shook my head at him, and I could feel my eyes widen. "I didn't know what was in it!"

"I'm not your fucking husband, Jo! You and me, we argue— always have. You have no problem telling me exactly what you think of me, even when I'm being a prick and I tell you to buck up and stop being a bitch." His nostrils flared. "We don't keep shit from each other because we're afraid of a fucking fight."

He pushed himself off the floor and stalked around the room. "What else haven't you told me? Oh no, don't you give me that fucking deer-in-the-headlights look! You aren't telling me something!" He pointed at me. "I won't do this, not with you. We don't have secrets, and we're not gonna start now. What else?"

He spun around at the door, glaring at me when I didn't say anything. "Nothing? Fine. I've got my own list I've been carrying around. I'll start." He was yelling, and I forced myself not to jump at his words. "Why didn't you call me when you saw Will at the hotel? And why in the fuck did you stop me?"

My mouth fell open. "Because I don't need you to save me! I told you, I had it under control."

His eyes narrowed. "Don't need me to save you? No, 'cause you can do it all on your own, can't you? How about the fact that he'd already had his hands all over you once? Or have you conveniently forgotten that?"

My temper flared. "He's my husband, Matty. He—"

"No!" he screamed. "He gave you up, remember? He broke your heart! He doesn't get to come back and say 'oops, I made a mistake' once you've moved on! You're mine, and I don't fucking share. If I have to beat his pansy asshole ass into oblivion to get that message across, I'll fucking do it!"

I gaped at him. "I can't believe you're mad about that!"

"Well, I'm fuckin' pissed." He turned around and started pacing again. "Any other secrets I should know, Joes?"

"You're one to talk, Matty! Your whole life is a secret. I say I fell in love with my best friend, but then your friends are constantly looking at me like I'm crazy because I don't really know anything about you."

Matty slowed, turning back to me. "You know me better than anyone!"

I raised an eyebrow. "Really? That's why I knew you were rich, that you belong to some bike gang, and that you are covered in tattoos?"

He rolled his eyes, exasperated.

"I don't know a fucking thing about you, not really!"

"Yeah, 'cause having a little money, a few hidden tats, and friends really changes who a person is." He turned, grabbed the manila envelope, and hurled it onto the floor at my feet. "There, read that. That will tell you every single thing you want to know!"

I kicked at the packet. "I don't want to read that shit! I want you to tell me. I want to know the you that Rob knows."

He took a slow breath and shook his head. "No, you don't. Not really. You're too much of a social worker to let the past go. You think that once you have all the pieces, you'll understand me. Well, sweetheart, those pieces aren't as important as you think."

"Matty, I just want to know you."

"You do!" he exploded. "You don't need to know the kid in that file." He nodded toward the floor. "He was lost and angry, looking for something to make sense. He needed someone like you, someone who would make him laugh, call him on his bullshit. But I can promise you, even if he'd had you, he would have hurt you, because that's who he was. That's who he had to be."

I listened to him, watching the man in front of me transform into a cold, tough stranger. His shoulders pulled back, his face lost all trace of humor. He was right—I didn't like this Matty. I didn't want to hear any more, but he continued anyway.

"My parents didn't beat us, they didn't starve us, they didn't hurt us. In fact, they loved us enough to walk away from their screwed up lives and then their shitty marriage. Nothing lasts forever and love is never enough, so my dad moved on. When he left though, my mom was fucked. She was sad, didn't think things through. So I did what I had to do. I was fifteen, Cris was twelve, the day I came home and found my mom's boyfriend perping on her. She said it was the first time, but it sure as hell was gonna be the last. I made sure the fucker would never touch a little girl again.

"I got sent to the youth center and met Rob. His life had been shit since the beginning, but he was determined to make things right. I got out and went back more times than I remember. And you know what? I'd do every single thing over again! I told you once that I was a monster and I fuckin' meant it."

"For Christ's sake, Matt, you were a kid! He breaks my heart, but I don't give two shits about him. I want to know you—the you who seems so happy to have me one minute, asking me to come to Boston, then seems ashamed of me and won't let me come the next. The you who had me get all dressed up to go out to a club, then I find out it was only so he could spy on some asshole. I just want you to talk to me!"

He looked as though he was ready to explode again. "I know you don't fucking get it, but I'm trying to keep you safe."

There was that stupid phrase again, and I groaned in annoyance. His eyes narrowed. "She may not live, Joes. Ellie might die! Do you know how fucking helpless Ian feels? He couldn't do anything to stop them. By keeping you here, away from that shit, I can keep you safe!"

"Do they know who attacked them?"

206

He shook his head. "No, but that doesn't matter right now. All that matters to me is you!"

I walked toward him and put a hand on his chest. He tensed at my touch. I needed to fix this, make the last few minutes go away. "Matty. I'm right here, I'm safe."

He looked down at me, searching my eyes with his.

I sighed, my voice soft. "I love you, and I'm so sorry I didn't tell you about the envelope. I promise, from now on, even if it starts a fight, I'll be honest." I chuckled. "Except when the kids are here. I will hold it in until they're gone." I winked, but Matty closed his eyes and turned his head.

"Joes"—he was gritting his teeth—"what was Will going to do with that information? What did he want it for?"

I tipped my head. "To use it against me in the custody battle, I'm sure."

His shoulders sagged, all fight suddenly gone from him. "Jesus, Joes! You can't bring the kids here." He closed his eyes. "I'm sorry, Jo, but your kids can't live here. I don't think you should either."

I gasped, pulling away, sure I'd heard him wrong. "What?"

He didn't answer, just turned and walked into the house.

THIRTY

I heard his footsteps as he walked down the hallway, but I didn't turn around, not even when I felt him in the doorway. I'd avoided him while I gathered my things from the rest of the house and had been in the bedroom for the last half hour, emptying the drawers he'd given me onto the bed. I wanted to make sure that I didn't leave anything behind when I left. I didn't want any reason to have to come back.

I didn't understand what was happening, how he could tell me he loved me one second then break up with me the next. I wondered if it was Taylor. She'd said all that shit about him wanting a booty call. Maybe she'd been serious and I'd misjudged Matty. Maybe Will and my mom had been right. Maybe I wasn't enough.

I hadn't dated anyone since high school, but knew there should be more closure. I needed more. I felt a pang of empathy for Teagan and her numerous heartbreaks. I couldn't do this again. It hurt too much.

"Where are you gonna go?" His voice was strained but I couldn't tell if it was because he didn't want to ask or because he didn't want to know the answer.

"What the fuck do you care? I'm doing what you want— leaving. That's all that matters." I knew I was being a bitch, but I couldn't stop myself.

"There's the hotel. I know you can't have the kids there, but until you could get an apartment..." he trailed off. When I didn't respond, he cleared his throat. "You could go back home. It's what Will wants."

I couldn't look at him. His tone was enough to make my breath catch, and if he looked as sad as he sounded, I'd break down and beg him to change his mind.

"Joes, I know you don't understand, but I just need a little time. To figure shit out. This isn't the end, it's just a step back."

"Why in the hell would I go back to Will?" I demanded, his earlier question infuriating me. "So I can spend the rest of my life pretending I love him? Counting down the days until the kids are old enough for me to leave? Do I just forget how he's treated me lately? Yeah, I'm good, thanks." I started transferring my clothes from the pile on the bed in front of me into my bag. I heard him moving toward me, but I couldn't look up.

"I didn't mean go back to Will. I meant that you could move back home." He pushed my half-packed bag out of the way. "Joes, we'll sort this out eventually, I swear. You know I'll take as much of you as I can get. Maybe we can stay at the hotel a few nights a week—"

I shook my head, interrupting him. Visions of Taylor living here again while I got him a few nights a week drifted across my mind. "No, Matty." I couldn't say more.

He sat down abruptly as if he'd been expecting a different answer. "Joes?" He shifted on the bed, and I knew he saw the look of confused bitterness on my face. "You're not going to give me time to figure this out, are you?"

The shock in his voice ripped me apart. I couldn't find my voice. I bit my lip, shaking my head.

He put a hand on my chin, turning my face toward him. "I'm not Will, Joes. I love you." He sighed. "There isn't someone else."

I hated how he could read my mind, how he knew I was worrying about Taylor.

"I just need some time."

I searched his eyes. "Time? Wow, that's a new one, even for you! Why, Matty? What is there to figure out? I love you; you say you love me. How is that confusing?"

He didn't answer, only raised an eyebrow at my questions. The image of Taylor standing on our front steps, telling me she thought Matt was calling her for another booty call, filtered through my mind. My old insecurities just wouldn't die.

"Who am I kidding? This was never gonna work." I laughed bitterly. "We've been acting like stupid kids for months. It's time we face reality. I'm married and have two kids. You have Sammy and so much going on that I don't even know where I would fit into your life. We're adults! No one falls in love like this when they're our age. You're right. We walk away now, and no one gets hurt."

"Jesus, you're so fucking melodramatic!" He closed his eyes for a brief moment, as if praying for patience. Suddenly they opened back up, locking onto mine. "No one gets hurt?" His eyes narrowed, and his jaw clenched. He flexed his cheek muscles, and I could tell he was trying to control his temper. "It's too fucking late for that, isn't it?" His voice was cold. He let go of my chin and pointed at me. "I told you I didn't want this, that it was a line we couldn't cross. As usual, once you get an idea stuck in that beautiful brain of yours, you don't fuckin' listen to anyone. Now we can't go back. No matter what you do, Jo, someone gets hurt. It's nice to know it won't be you though."

That's not what I meant, and he knew it. "For crying out loud, make up your fucking mind! You tell me one minute that we can't be together, the next you tell me you love me and want me forever, and now? Now, you need time and want some sort of relationship, but I just can't live here." I glared at him, feeling my nostrils flare as I debated what to say next. "What about me? What about what I want? I can't do this anymore, Matty! I'm done." Sighing, I nodded. "You're right, we can't go back. But we can do the right thing now. Can't we just be friends again?"

His face hardened. "Friends? That's really what you want? To have me come into work with stories of my latest girlfriend? 'Cause I can guaran-fuckin-tee there will be girlfriends. Plural. Do you want to hear how amazing she is in bed, or wanna talk about our latest trip to the Caribbean, 'cause you can bet your ass she'll have a fuckin' passport!"

I felt the color drain from my face as I let his shittiness get to me.

"I told you I needed some time. I won't keep asking you to give me one simple thing, and I won't spend my life alone just because you're terrified of the unknown. I'm not a fuckin' monk."

"Ha! That's the fucking truth!" I spat at him. "Maybe you should tell the next girlfriend about the mountain of skeletons before she falls in love with you. Might save you some trouble."

It was his turn to laugh bitterly. "Now you worry about me? That's disgustingly sweet."

"Oh, don't fool yourself. I'm not worried about you in the least. Like you just said, you'll move on and fall in love, no problem. And why wouldn't you? You're God's gift to women, right? I hate to break it to you Buddy, but some of us want more than half-truths, empty promises, and romance whiplash!"

God! Why did he have to be so infuriating? I never would have pictured us ending like this—two pissed off people hurling insults at the other. I stared at my best friend, wondering what in the hell had happened to us. Only hours ago we'd been happy.

He shook his head. "Think what you want, but I never said a thing about love. I said there would be someone else, but we both know you are it for me. You are the love of my life." He reached a hand out, grabbing mine. "I will be in love with you until the day I die."

His tone was so sincere, it tugged at my heart and I wanted to believe his words. But his history was blatantly obvious.

"Now who's being melodramatic?" I threw my free hand in the air, annoyed. "You said the same thing about Becky, but that only lasted until the next bimbo came along. Poor Matty can't be alone."

"The fuck I did!" He jerked his hand away, narrowing his eyes dangerously. "I didn't want to lose Sam, but Bex and I... we were together for him. Yeah, the rest of them were because I didn't want to be alone. But you? I fucking love you! Now that I've had you, I can't imagine you being with anyone else! The thought of you being with Will, letting him touch you... Jesus, it makes me want to kill him." He stood, walked around the bed, and raised his arm, clearing his dresser with a crash. I jumped at the sound of bottles breaking as numerous scents filled the air. "Don't you have any fucking idea how hard this is for me?"

"No! I don't," I whispered.

"I want to wake up with you every day for the rest of my life. But right now... that asshole prick hasn't given us much of a choice." He was yelling at me again. Jackass.

"Will is an ass, I'll give you that, but right now, he's worried about his kids. I know for a fact that if you hated the man Becky was with, you'd do the same fucking thing! You would dig up every bit of his past to see what kind of man he was, to see if you could trust him around Sam. And if you thought you couldn't, you aren't above threatening and scheming to keep him away."

"I'd be pissed, yeah, but I'd trust her instincts."

"Bullshit! You don't trust my instincts, and you're my best friend. Why would he? You know the Bastards are dangerous! You're dangerous! You beat up Will in a parking lot. If I hadn't stopped you..." I looked up, shocked to see his face pale. I couldn't finish my thought. "And mixed with your history, why would any dad let his children live with you?"

"I don't give two shits what that asshole wants. All I care is that you want me, that you trust me. Those Bastards would kill to protect you and the kids. Think what you want of me, but know I would die before I'd let anyone hurt you!" He ground his teeth, obviously fighting for control.

"Really? Tell that to Ellie! Do you really think Ian wouldn't have died to protect her? You just told me that he's never gonna be okay. He's going to be broken for the rest of his life!"

"You're scared, and I get it. I'm fuckin' petrified. There's a reason most of us don't have families. I never know when my past is gonna catch up. Until now, I thought I was safe here, that building a life here kept the ones I love away from everything else. I just need time to make sure you're still safe. Don't end this, Joes, because if you do..." He trailed off, leaving his threat to my imagination.

"Are you listening to yourself? I can't do this, Matty! I can't leave today and sit around waiting for you to change your mind. I can't be with another man who puts me last."

His eyes roamed my face, but then he looked away.

I couldn't breathe. "You're asking me to give up everything in order to maybe someday be a part of your life! I'd never ask you to do that!" I hollered.

"Bullshit!" he yelled back. "I'm not asking you to give up anything but time. I would give up everything I have, every fucking thing I own, to make sure you didn't have to lose anything, Joes!" He raked his hands through his hair.

I narrowed my eyes, taking a deep breath. He just didn't understand. "I can't do this. It's so much more than how I feel about you! I can't live like this. Wondering if the day is going to come when you decide you need more than just a little space." I shook my head and felt the tears sting. "I can't give you time, because I won't be that person again—waiting on the back burner for someone to get his priorities straight. Because after the last fifteen years, I deserve more than the sporadic fifteen minutes. And because I love you and can't even fathom a life without you in it, I can't have only part of you. We deserve to be happy, and as much as I want to, we can't do that together."

"What does my happiness look like exactly? Taylor?" he sneered. "And you? You deserve some boring-ass guy who works nine to five? Someone who will never push you? Someone who will put you up on a pedestal and never let you live? Guess what, sweetheart, you already had that and hated every second! You are so fucking stubborn," he screamed at me, fists clenched.

"Here's a fucking newsflash, Matty, so are you!" I screamed back.

He took the two long steps to me, bending his knees so we were eye to eye, an emotion I couldn't read on his face. "We don't work as a couple? Well, baby, that's the only way we'll ever be anything again. It's all or nothing. I can't be a bystander anymore. I won't sit back and pretend I'm your friend. You've thought it all through, huh? Fuck!" His voice broke, and he started to shake. "The one thing you're missing, the one thing you can't get through that god-awful thick skull of yours, is that you are my everything, Joes! By leaving me, you are taking my everything."

I saw the water pool in his eyes, and my heart broke. "Matty."

I fell into him, a lump in my throat preventing more words, and wrapped my arms around him. I loved this man more than I could even comprehend. After a few minutes, he shifted and opened to me, pulling me in. I could feel the tension radiating through his body, and I wanted nothing more than to take it away. For a long time, he held me to him, tighter than he'd ever held me before, as if he knew if he slackened his grip, I'd slip away.

I swallowed at the lump, not wanting to believe the words I was about to say, but it didn't budge. We couldn't be ending this quickly, over something so small. But here we were. "We were always going to end up here."

"Don't you know that I would do anything for you?" His voice was full of emotion.

Anything except ask me to stay.

I knew that was his way of telling me he would let me go. There would be no ploys, no threats, no begging—because he wasn't Will. I knew that even if it killed him, he wouldn't call me tomorrow to see if I'd changed my mind or to tell me how much he loved me. This was how we ended eleven years of friendship. This was our good-bye.

He tensed, and I knew he felt the finality of it too. Pulling back, he closed his hands around my face, rubbing his thumb back and forth across my cheek. I wanted to remember this moment forever. His scent, the cold metal from his ring, the quick beat of his heart echoing against my chest.

His lips brushed mine softly, and I forced my eyes open, needing to see him. The thumb moved to my lips, gently tracing them as if he too was memorizing this moment. "I'll miss you, Joes."

I couldn't tell him I'd miss him, or that I loved him, or that I'd changed my mind and would do whatever it took to stay in his life, because my mouth wouldn't form words.

He gave me his lopsided grin, and my heart shattered. "Plato said that we each have a soul mate—one person we share a spirit with. That person can be a friend or a lover, but it is someone to whom we are bonded for eternity." He eyes bore into mine, showing me how much pain was behind those beautiful blue depths. As if on cue, a single tear pooled from his eye and rolled down his cheek. "I want you to know, to remember, Joes, that you have always been mine."

He dropped his hands and turned, hurrying from the room. I fell onto the bed when I heard the bike roar to life. Just like that, he was gone, and my life would never be the same. I sat on the bed, clutching the T-shirt I'd claimed, until the tears stopped running.

THIRTY-ONE

I grinned at the little blue-eyed blond in front of me. Today had been a perfect day. Yes, it was sleeting ice cold sheets and the dreary February weather seemed never ending, but none of that mattered. Today had been perfect because the family in front of me was now whole.

I'd begged Connie to let me have Todd's case when Matty left. I was invested and needed to see it through. She'd been hesitant at first, but after talking with the Smiths, seeing how devastated they'd been at Matty's decision to transfer to another office and how worried they were over the appeal, Connie had given in. Over the last several months, I'd grown very close with Teddy and Pam. Fighting for something Matty had wanted was therapy. I felt as though I was giving him something that no one else could, repaying him, even if he'd never know.

I'd been right—after he'd left that day, he hadn't contacted me. He worked out his two-week notice but conveniently was never in the office at the same time I was. I didn't go to his good-bye party, allowing Teagan to tell everyone I was just too sad because my best friend was leaving. And in true Matty fashion, he played along, making our co-workers promise to keep me busy. He still talked to many of them, and they'd bring me tidbits of news, thinking I already knew.

I missed him. Every day. At first, whenever I heard something funny or needed to vent, I'd grab my phone before catching myself. I had replayed our last conversation in my mind a million times and realized what an idiot I'd been. I'd made a big deal about the fact that I wanted to know him and then shut him out when he tried to let me in. I needed to find the right way to apologize and ask for forgiveness, but it was easier said than done, and I let the days drag by.

Right before Thanksgiving, Teagan came back from training with a serious expression marring her beautiful features, announcing she had something awful to tell me. She'd been at the Portland office, and had heard some of the workers talking about Matty. Teagan said it was very clear that he wasn't single. So he'd done what he'd promised. He'd moved on.

I didn't cry. I'd left him, not the other way around, so I had no right. I still longed for him though. His touch, his voice, his presence. I didn't think I'd ever get over it.

Will had the kids for Thanksgiving weekend, so Teagan took me out. Three shots in, I escaped to the bathroom and called Matty. He answered on the second ring.

"Joes? What's wrong?" His voice was groggy. I'd obviously woken him.

"Nothing. I miss you." I knew the sadness in my voice came through, even though I tried to hide it.

"You're drunk." He cleared his throat and I heard a rustling in the background. "Where are you? I'll leave now."

Something in his voice stopped me from telling him. I shook my head. "You can't. I'm so sorry. I shouldn't have called."

"Tell me where you are," he urged, his worry was clear.

"Will you take me home and make love to me? Let me make this right?" I regretted the words once I said them, but I held my breath for his answer. "I miss you."

"Joes," his voice was flat, "I'll get you home safe."

"I love you. You know that, right?"

He took a deep breath as if he was going to launch into a long speech. Instead, he blew it back out. "Let me come get you and take you home. Okay, hun?"

Being doused in ice water wouldn't have been as sobering as that word. Hun. I'd never been Hun. That was the name reserved for people who annoyed him. The universal term he used for women who called after their one night together and wanted more. And, how he spoke to his exes. The thought hit me hard, leaving me breathless. He really had moved on.

"Never mind, friend. I've got a ride." I hung up, hearing him call my name as I did. Part of me hoped he'd call me right back, but I knew Matty wouldn't play those games.

But he had. My phone rang seconds after I disconnected.

"Who are you with?" he demanded, all sleep gone. "I swear to fucking Christ, Jo, I will drive around all night until I find you if you don't tell me."

"T. I'm with T." I finally mumbled.

"I'll talk to you later." He hung up.

I texted Cris, knowing she'd still be awake, simply asking if he was happy.

Her reply was quick and short. *With Ursula? Never!*

The thought of him with Taylor, kissing her the way he'd kissed me, making love to her, building a life with her, destroyed me. The nausea that hit made me glad I was in the ladies' room. Teagan found me there not long afterward. Matty had called her and insisted she take me right home.

That night cured the problem though. I hadn't been tempted to call him since. There was no need to. I'd wanted to fix us, to apologize for being stupid and running away. Matty, on the other hand, had gone back to the one woman I hated.

"You look sad." Pam sat in the seat next to me, interrupting my thoughts.

I smiled and shook my head. "Not at all. I was just thinking about Matty and wishing he could be here for this."

Pam nodded. "Me too." She stood up, eyes twinkling as she smiled down at me. "We're going to have cake and pictures in a little while. You'll stay, right?" She didn't give me a chance to answer before she walked away. I wouldn't have left anyway.

I was overseeing a rousing game of hide-and-seek when I felt him. I sat up straight, the hair on my arms standing on end as the electrical current that could only be coming from one person drifted over my body. I heard him give a low greeting to the Smiths, and my body reacted instantly, heart pounding, palms suddenly sweaty. Before I could move, Todd realized he was there and ran across the hall, screaming excitedly. I wiped my hands down the front of my pants, eyes darting around the room trying to find the closest exit, debating whether I could sneak out the back door without being seen.

"Congratulations, Jo. You had a big win today." His voice was low and steady as he sat in the chair next to me, draping his arm over the back of mine as if it hadn't been six months since I'd seen him.

"Thank you," I finally managed, without looking at him. I couldn't. Just having him this close to me was too much. I needed to move, to get away before he saw what he was doing to me. "I didn't know you were going to be here, but I'm glad you made it. If you'll excuse me... " I leaned forward, ready to stand, but he shifted, almost touching me, and I froze.

"How are the kids?"

Before I could answer, Todd ran over to us, gave us each a giant hug, then ran off again. I silently groaned. I didn't want to sit here and make small talk, but seeing Todd's face when he looked at Matty was enough to keep me rooted to the spot and be nice.

"They're well, thank you. Ben decided to try basketball." I forced a laugh. "Thank god he's got Will's height. Lily wants to try softball in the spring, but I'm not sure another sport is a good thing right now. Will got offered a promotion."

"I didn't ask about Will, and I don't give two fucks if he got promoted or not," he growled, just loud enough for me to hear him.

Out of my peripheral, I saw his body turn, his knees touching my thigh, but I stared straight at the wall ahead of me.

"I heard he turned it down anyway," he said absentmindedly, "because he couldn't guarantee the nights and weekends it required, now that he shares custody of his kids."

How in the hell did he know that? Taylor and Will must still chat. The idea annoyed me. I swallowed a little too loudly.

"Now, how are the kids really?"

Once again, I despised the fact that he knew me so well. "They're good. Better." I shrugged. "It was a struggle at first, but I think we're almost there. Most of the time I think they like having the undivided attention of each parent." I took a deep breath, not sure what to say. I didn't need to ask about Sam; I saw him during Becky's weekends and he spent a lot of time at my house. "How's Cris?"

He snorted. "You talk to her more than I do. I should be asking you that." He was still staring at me, but I refused to look back. I was going to tell him that I hadn't really talked to her in months, but he continued. "She's still pissed at me. So how—"

Pam interrupted, having everyone line up for the celebration picture.

I jumped at the chance to get away from him. Without thinking, I looked over as I stood up, meeting his eyes; other than small bags under them, he looked exactly the same. The realization irritated me. I was ragged and worn out, and he was none the worse for the wear. He smiled, seeing me stare at him, and stood, walking close to me as we approached the family. When we posed for the photos, Pam put Matty right next to me and he moved his hand to the small of my back in a familiar gesture. I fought to keep from melting against him, reminding myself over and over that we were done.

After a quick bite of cake, I made my excuses to the family and sped from the party. I couldn't spend another second in the same room as Matty. His scent, his laugh, the way he looked at me every time I glanced up, it was all too much.

I felt as though I could start sobbing any second. I'd be damned if I'd let him see me cry, not after everything I'd done the last few months to start over without him. I'd forgotten how much I missed him.

I made it to my car, lost in thought, before a hand curled around my upper arm, making me lose my balance, and I fell against a steady chest. Struggling to stay on my feet, I braced my hands on his shoulders. Immediately, I realized the mistake as both his arms circled around me, pulling me close.

"Joes..." He chuckled as he steadied me. "Christ, I miss you and your klutziness." His eyes widened at his words, as if he didn't know he was going to say them out loud.

The freezing rain had drenched me, and a cold wet trail was running down the center of my back, but all I could feel was the warmth of his body against mine. The scene was eerily familiar and reminded me of another time we'd gotten caught in the rain. I shook my head, getting the damp hair out of my face, and threw back my head to meet his eyes.

"Get your hands off me, Matty!" I seethed. "Just let me go."

"So you can run again?" He glared at me. "I've had enough of this bullshit. You're gonna stop bein' stubborn, and you're gonna talk to me."

"Really?" I could feel my temper flare. "You've had months to call me and you decide to wait until now?"

"See?" He tipped his head sideways, searching my face. "Stubborn pride. You always make the worst decisions when you're mad. The phone works both ways, you know. You never called me."

"I had no reason to call you! You crawled back to the sea witch just to spend eternity being tortured because you were lonely and pissed at me. That trumps any stupid decision I've made because of stubborn pride. We have nothing to say to each other anymore."

He raised an eyebrow at my bitchy tone. "Sea witch?" Suddenly recognition crawled over his face. "Taylor." His lips thinned in a hard line, and he leaned in close. "I told you I wouldn't be alone. You left anyway."

I inhaled sharply, looking over his shoulder, avoiding his eyes. He swore and moved, and I thought he was going to let me go; instead, he lifted me and carried me to his car.

"What? Matty, put me down!" I demanded but couldn't struggle as the cold finally caught up with me. I started to shiver, my teeth chattering.

He didn't answer, just opened the passenger side door and dropped me on the seat before closing it again and running over to the driver's side. Starting the car, he turned in his seat to look at me. I didn't know what he wanted. I'd given him so much of me, and he'd let it go. I sat rubbing my hands together, waiting for him to start talking.

After a few minutes, he switched the fan to full blast and I sat stationary, letting the heat blow over my skin, thawing me. I sighed, sitting back once the numbness in my limbs started to disappear. I wanted to apologize, to tell him I missed him too. I turned, meeting his eyes, and swallowed my words. He wore a look I hadn't seen before.

"I'm not with Taylor, Jo. I told Cris that to piss her off." He smirked, rolling his eyes. "Long story." He shook his head. "I went on one date. One. With a friend of a co-worker. It didn't work 'cause she wasn't you." He offered me a small smile. "I told you, you're it for me. I meant it. But you were right—we don't work right now."

My breath caught, and I looked away, unsure of what he would say next. His hand grabbed mine, holding it tight.

"You're not the only stubborn idiot here." He smirked. "I want to be with you. I want to get back to where we were, but right now..." His empty hand grabbed my chin, and he pulled my face toward his. "Right now I miss you. I was wrong." He shrugged giving me the lopsided grin I loved. "I need you, Joes. I don't care how I have you, just as long as you're in my life."

I closed my eyes, trying to will away the tears that were burning the backs of my eyes. Emotions warred inside me. Pride instructed me to tell him to go to hell, that I was fine without him. Love told me to tell him exactly how I felt.

I opened my eyes, stared into the baby blues I knew so well, and used every ounce of energy I had to respond. "It won't be easy. We're both such stupid assholes."

He threw his head back and laughed. "Yeah, we are. That's one reason I love you."

I nodded as relief flooded through me. I wanted to crawl into his lap and have him kiss away the last few months, but that wouldn't get us anywhere. Instead, I squeezed the hand that held mine. "You really think we can fix us?"

His eyes burned into mine. "I think we owe it to ourselves and each other to try. It's not gonna be easy. Shit, between our exes and kids and the Bastards, we're gonna be on our toes constantly. We're gonna argue, I'm going to annoy you, and you're gonna piss me off. But I'm not gonna let you run away again just because life gets tough. And you're gonna tell me when I've got my head shoved up my ass. It'll be one hell of a ride, Joes, but you're worth it. You're my best friend, and that's all I need to get through anything."

I didn't know what to say. There were so many issues that wouldn't resolve themselves in a day, or hell, even a month. But he was worth it. We were worth it.

I leaned into him. "I love you too, Matty."

HONEY WHISKEY

For **MI MADRE** -

Even though she hates it when I call her that.

I know I haven't been an easy child,

But the greatest things in life never are.

I love you, **MUM**!

PROLOGUE

MATEO

A giggle floated across the room, snagging my attention from the conversation a few of the guys were having around me. I didn't have to look up to know who the contagious sound was coming from—Joes had a laugh like no other. It always made me smile.

Then again, Jo had an uncanny ability to make everyone around her react that way. I'd once bet a co-worker he couldn't spend the entire day locked in a car with her without laughing. The crotchety old bastard was adamant that she was annoying as fuck and he wouldn't as much as crack a smile. He'd even rolled his eyes at her as they were leaving, scowling at whatever story she'd been sharing.

I didn't gloat—much—when he walked up at the end of the day and put a fifty in my hand. I did laugh loudly as I walked to my car, but that was only because I'd been in his shoes. Easiest money I'd ever made.

I may have been a member of the Josephine Walker fan club, but after that day, Robert Pappas became the president. Any time one of our co-workers complained about the new kid, Bobby—as Jo affectionately called him—was quick to put them in their place.

Another laugh pulled my thoughts back to the present, and I looked up, watching her with our work friends. A group of us had come out for our monthly "Babes and Booze" night; I inwardly cringed at the God-awful title it had been given. It was the one evening every month when we grabbed our significant others and went out drinking to forget that we were responsible adults, a night we all looked forward to for weeks.

There was only one rule: no talking about work. It might sound simple to follow, but at least one of us broke it every time. We couldn't leave the job at the office, no matter how hard we tried. A bad case stayed with you long after you'd gone home. We all had 'em, but some of us were a lot more fucking unlucky than others. Sometimes you just needed to lift the bottle, drown the memories, and depend on your friends to get you home.

Tonight, that was my plan. As much as I loved my job, some days I wished I'd stayed a carpenter. A bored housewife who wanted to flirt with the help was a hell of a lot easier to forget than the case I'd been assigned this week. Todd, a tiny toddler, had been beaten bloody because his mom didn't have one fucking ounce of maternal instinct and lacked even the smallest amount of motherly love. I'd seen some fucked up shit—hell, we all had in this job—but I'd never forget his bruised face, eye swollen shut, and the fear that made every inch of his body shrink away when I walked into his hospital room. He would never remember the words I had whispered or even begin to understand what I meant when I promised him he'd never go through it again.

I'd never forget.

That kid had gotten to me. Part of me wanted to scoop him up and take him home, spend the rest of my life making sure he never missed another meal or bath and proving to him that he could be a kid, a real kid, without fear of physical harm. Another part of me wanted to call Rocker and have my brothers come take care of the parents, just to make sure they never got him back. Instead, I did my job. I let the law work the way it was designed and prayed that it wouldn't let me down. Because I sure as shit didn't know how I would react if his parents got him back and hurt him again. I wasn't sure I could do my job if there was a next time.

I could rest easier knowing that one of the best foster moms I had ever worked with was staying at his bedside until Todd was discharged from the hospital. Then she would take him home and love him like her own until his parents could get their shit together. She would hold him, and scare away the monsters in the night, tell him he was adorable and funny and sweet, and give him lots of kisses. She was a fucking saint, the kind of mom every kid deserved. The idea that she might save him only to have me take him back to shitty-ass parents pissed me off.

Three days later and I was still infuriated. I could feel the tension flow through my body, as if it was just waiting for someone to goad me so I could use my fists and get out some of this anger. I took a long drag off my bottle, hoping it would help.

Joes picked that moment to look over at me, her smile slowly fading into a frown as she caught my eye. Shit! I hadn't even realized I was giving her the death glare until she raised an eyebrow and tipped her head in silent question. I shook mine, hoping she would understand that she wasn't my target, and sent her a quick smile. Our friend Teagan grabbed Jo's arm, dragging her eyes away from mine, and said something that made everyone crack-up.

Jesus, she was gorgeous when she laughed. My mouth was suddenly dry, and I took another gulp of my Sam Adams, unable to tear my eyes away from her. She'd pulled her dark hair back, giving me the perfect view of her face; her usually pale skin had a pink tone tonight, probably from all the alcohol she'd consumed, but it suited her. Even from halfway across the bar, I could see the pale blue-green of her eyes. She was beautiful all the time, but when she laughed...

No. I shook my head, scowling at my thoughts. She was taken. Seriously fucking taken. Happily married taken.

I ground my teeth at the idea. Married to a fucking douchenozzle who didn't even begin to deserve her. I may have some serious shit buried deep, but compared to that fucker, I looked like a prince. I took another swig, pissed at my thoughts. She was my Joes, my best friend. That was it. That was all she could ever be, and any other ideas that filtered through my mind, I'd blame on the booze or my miserably fucked up week. Just another reason for me to be pissed off at the world.

I needed a shot. Screw one—I needed ten. Chased by a couple glasses of Jack. I turned back to my buddies, made my excuses, and headed to the bar.

"You okay?" Jo's voice was full of concern as she slid up to the counter next to me.

I nodded, threw my head back, and swallowed, hissing as the harsh liquor burned its way down my throat. "I will be."

"Wanna talk about it?"

I could feel her heated gaze but refused to look at her. I didn't need to see the concern I was sure was etched all over her face. Instead I shook my head and lifted the next shot in line. She chuckled, and I turned to her in surprise.

"Jesus, you are a stubborn ass!" She shook her head, but I couldn't tell if it was in annoyance or humor. Then she smiled and stepped in closer, wrapping her arms around my hips. "I'm sorry you had such a rough day."

I sighed, moving my arm around her back and pulling her close. If she didn't care that Billy or our friends saw us like this, I didn't either. Fuck 'em. Half of 'em thought we were already screwing, and the other half knew she thought of me like a big brother. I couldn't care less about any of their opinions. As for Billy, he could suck it. I leaned my chin down to rest on the top of her head, enjoying her soft body against me, while she gave me a quick squeeze then pulled away.

I let her back up but kept my arm over her shoulders. My mood instantly improved. "What was that for?"

She smiled up at me then shrugged. "You needed a hug." She laughed lightly, as if embarrassed by her actions. She tipped her head back to meet my eyes then wrinkled her nose. "I like her."

One of the many reasons she was my best friend, Jo was a master at changing the subject and could distract me from even my worst thoughts. "Yeah?"

"Yeah." Jo smirked. "I mean, obviously she's gonna wake up in a few weeks and wonder why in the hell she's dating an old man who looks like you, but in the meantime, she seems pretty great."

"Old man, huh? Last time I checked, you were about a minute younger than me."

"Dude, you turn thirty-five next month and that's ancient!" Her eyes grew wide in exaggeration, and she laughed. "And what is she, like, twelve?"

I snorted. Tay definitely looked a lot younger than twenty-six. "Yep, something like that."

"Seriously though, she is beautiful. You weren't exaggerating; I think she may be the prettiest woman I've ever met." A frown crossed her features, but she cleared her face before I could say anything.

I raised an eyebrow, sure I was missing something.

"And she's nice. I can't believe I'm going to say this, but I think you've finally found it."

"It?" I didn't want to know what she meant, but I had to ask.

"Your future." I wasn't sure how to respond. Jo shrugged knowingly. "You don't have to say anything, but it's been written all over your face all night. You're distracted because of work, yeah, but you've got this goofy surprised look too. As if you just realized something important. Kind of like the one you had when you realized you were in love with Becky." Jo moved her attention to the bar, as if avoiding me, and grabbed my glass of whiskey. After taking a giant gulp, she turned back to me. "I was worried. After Bex..."

She bit her bottom lip and "hmphed" the way she did when she was debating something. That habit always distracted me and pulled my thoughts to places they shouldn't be, like wondering what sounds she would make if it was my teeth sinking into her. Forcing my mind to clear, I raised the third shot and downed it fast.

"I just worry about you."

"I know." I'd been a screwed up mess after my divorce; there wasn't a bottle of booze I didn't like.

Joes had come to my hotel a few weeks after I'd left my house, and she made me sober up. She stayed with me for days while I acted like a pathetic loser, whining and crying and telling her I didn't have a future without my wife or kid. It was an embarrassing time, and I'd wiped most of it from my mind—of course she'd remembered.

I swallowed hard. "You really think Taylor's future material? 'Cause she's obviously too good for me."

Jo chuckled. "Obviously. But she's young and you're... well, you're you. She's probably convinced she's the lucky one." She shook her head again. "You be nice to her!"

I'd been seeing Taylor for a few weeks, and even though I'd told Jo all about her and Tay all about Joes, I'd been dreading introducing them. Becky hadn't been bothered by the fact that my best friend was a woman; she trusted me, and I never would have betrayed that trust. But some—hell, most—of the women I'd dated since the divorce didn't feel the same way.

My last girlfriend had been convinced that I was going to leave her for Jo one day. Instead I broke it off because she wouldn't stop obsessing and wanted me to stop seeing Joes anywhere other than work. I apparently needed to come with a warning label: *Hot female best friend included. Petty, self-centered, and jealous women need not apply.*

Taylor wasn't jealous of anyone; she knew she was damn close to perfection and didn't have a problem letting everyone know she was God's gift to men. Yet not only was the threat of another woman still there, I would do anything for the other woman in this scenario. I just didn't know how Tay would feel once she figured out how close Joes and I really were.

I was worried about Jo too. She'd been crushed after my divorce. She would tell everyone that I was her best friend, but there were times when it seemed that she and Bex were closer. When I'd mention it, she'd laugh and tell me it was the "girl code" that made her take Becky's side in arguments, but that I was still her best friend.

I'd complain about it, but secretly, I liked the fact that the two of them were cohorts, because it meant I got to spend more time with my two favorite girls. When Bex left me though, she'd dropped Jo too, devastating my friend. I didn't want to be the cause of that pain again. If she and Taylor got close, and Tay and I didn't work out, Joes would be left once more.

It had been almost two months since I met Taylor, a month since we'd started dating, and I'd known it was time for me to introduce the two most important women in my life. Figures it would happen at such a fan-fucking-tastic time, but the week had already been shit, and if they didn't like each other, that would be par for the course my life had taken lately. I may not have shown it, but I was relieved that bomb had been avoided and happy that at least Jo liked Taylor.

"When am I not nice?"

Jo answered with an angry one-eyebrow look.

"Hey!" I held up my hands in defense. "I'm nice to her!" I laughed.

"Who are you being nice to?" Pretty Boy Billy Boy came up behind Jo and wrapped his arms around his wife possessively.

There wasn't a single man in the bar still wearing what they'd worn to work except for him. Everyone else had gone home and changed into jeans. But Billy's pompous ass needed the entire world to see he wore a suit and tie; he needed everyone to think he was important.

Fucking asshat. I reached for my glass and took a long drink as he slid his face into Jo's neck. I fucking hated him with every fiber of my body, but I nodded my hello. "Billy."

"Matt." His voice was just as cool as mine; there was clearly only one reason we needed to talk to each other, and she was standing right between us. He gave Joes a quick squeeze, making her squeak. "You ready to go, Pudge? I'm exhausted!"

My hand tightened on the glass when I heard the nickname he still used. *Fucking hate him.* I clenched my jaw, remembering the promise I'd made to Jo last year about minding my own goddamned business. As much as I wanted to beat his ass into oblivion for the sly way he constantly talked down to her, I had to hold it in. He was Jo's choice, not mine. My job was to support her.

Pudge, Joes told me once, was his term of endearment for her. I didn't understand how a name like that could ever be anything other than an insult. And only an absolute selfish fuck would not be able to see how much it bothered her; it freaking bothered me for her. She wasn't fat. I hated the word curvy—since it had been overused in the last few years to explain away obesity—but that was exactly what Jo was.

She reminded me of the 50s pin-up girls in Uncle Liam's workshop—full and round in all the right places, tight and toned in the rest. Lately she'd gotten too thin for my liking, a fact I blamed on Billy and his insulting nickname. I tried to keep my face blank but knew my repulsion must show.

Jo caught my look, and for an instant, shame drifted over hers and she broke eye contact. Patting Billy's hand, she nodded.

"Yeah, babe. I'll be right there. Go get the coats?" Billy grumbled but retreated back to their table, and she turned eyes that vaguely reminded me of the Caribbean Sea to me. "You sure you're okay? 'Cause if you need me to, I can stay." She smirked suddenly. "I'm not sure how your girlfriend would feel about me hitching a ride home, but..."

I fought the urge to haul her into my arms and instead cupped the softness of her cheek. I stared into her eyes, getting lost for a minute as I thought about what I really wanted to say. *Fucking right I need you to stay. I need you to come home with me, need you to make this entire week fade into oblivion.* Reality crept in, and I shook my head.

"No. Go home. I need to go save Taylor from Teagan anyway."

She reached a hand up, covering mine. "You know I'm here if you need me, right? I'll always be just a phone call away."

I nodded. There wasn't much I was sure about anymore, but that fact was clear.

She dropped her hand to my chest as she stepped into me, stretching up on tiptoes, and kissed my cheek. "Love you, Matty." She smiled quickly then backed away, my hand falling from her.

229

"See you tomorrow!" Jo called over her shoulder as she made her way to Billy.

I finished off the whiskey before I turned and leaned back against the bar. Taylor was lost in conversation with a group of clerks from work, not even noticing that I wasn't where she'd left me earlier. I watched her laugh with my friends, waiting for her to realize I was staring, hoping she could feel my eyes on her. She never gave me as much as a glance.

Jo was wrong; Taylor wasn't my future. I had to be honest with myself, as much as I fucking hated the idea.

There was only one woman I wanted to be with for the rest of my life, and she was taken by a dickwad who thought he was too good for her. If she was mine, I'd do anything to keep a smile on her face, make her happy, and keep her safe.

I glowered at that thought, knowing I'd never have the chance. The ball-busting truth was that Billy wasn't the only one bad for her; the skeletons in my closet terrified even me and were hidden away for a damned good reason. If Joes knew a quarter of my shit, the secrets I kept, she'd run away screaming. I'd never be able to let her in because once I did, she'd leave and never look back. That was not a chance I was willing to take.

No, Jo would never be mine.

That cold hard fact pissed me off more than everything else that had happened this week. *Fuck my life.* I turned back to the bar and ordered another round.

ONE

JO

I tried to be a good, attentive friend and listen while Teagan talked about her day. However, I couldn't keep my eyes from drifting to my phone, and I only heard a few words as my mind wandered. I was determined not to turn the cell over and look to see if anyone had called. What was the point of silencing the ringer if I was just going to drive myself nuts by checking it every five minutes? Keeping my resolve intact, I leaned back against her headboard, making myself concentrate on her voice.

"Just so grown up, ya know? It blew me away. He isn't even close to being the same kid he was five years ago; I really think that this placement will decide to adopt. As long as he can keep himself out of trouble." She laughed. "I had to lay down the law again, gave him the old 'I love you, but if you are a brat and screw this up, I will kick your butt!' speech. You know?"

I nodded even though she couldn't see me. Teagan seemed to have the worst-behaving teenagers on her caseload. Thank God she had the patience of a saint and loved them all.

She pulled out another armful of purses and balled up clothes, shoved them into the already giant pile, and pushed her mahogany hair out of her face. "It's in here, I swear. I just never wear them, but they will be so cute with that top you bought."

She'd been in her closet for almost half an hour, searching for a shoe that she insisted I had to wear out, while I sat cross-legged on her bed, drowning in misery.

I couldn't care less about the shoes. There was only one thing weighing on my mind, and it didn't have a thing to do with what I was going to wear later. Hell, I didn't even want to go out anymore. If I hadn't promised half my co-workers that I'd meet them, I'd stay in my pajamas and sulk in my room.

I wondered, once again, if Matty was going to make an appearance. I gave in, picked up my iPhone, and groaned when I saw I didn't have one single missed call or unread text. Sighing, I tossed the phone angrily back down. I didn't know what annoyed me more—the fact that he hadn't called or that I was upset about it.

Teagan leaned back on her haunches, concern etched on her beautiful face. "You sure you don't want me to cancel?"

I smiled at my dearest friend, trying to offer reassurance. I didn't know where I'd be without T. She'd not only offered me a constant shoulder over the last few months, she'd taken me in and given me a place to stay. Her boyfriend, Tom, was finally coming home after three weeks away for work. Both her daughters were gone for the night, and with me going out, they had the apartment alone for the first time ever.

"Don't you dare. You and I can go out drinking any time. You need to enjoy Tom while he's here."

She gave me a skeptical frown but turned back to the closet. A few minutes later, she yelled, "Aha!" and picked up a sexy, red spike-heeled stiletto that looked way too dangerous for me to wear. "Found it."

She beamed, but her face fell when her eyes met mine. Pushing her giant frame off the floor, she joined me on the bed and leaned her head back next to mine. The bed tipped slightly under her weight, and I adjusted so I didn't roll into her. I wasn't a tiny woman, but Tegan dwarfed me by a good ten inches and roughly sixty pounds.

"Oh, honey. He's probably got a million and ten things going on right now. It was a crazy week! He'll call."

I didn't argue. Teagan had always adored her "biker boy" and told me once that if she'd been a little younger, he wouldn't have known what hit him. She loved us both, but she'd never thought we were a good match.

Even though she didn't like us as a couple, she'd been extremely supportive of me. I knew she must be tired of me moping, especially after the last few days. Instead of snapping at me or telling me that she knew this would happen, she only smiled and told me we'd get through it. I couldn't bear the thought of telling her how badly I'd screwed things up this time.

I hadn't spoken to Matty since Tuesday, and that conversation hadn't gone as planned. There were so many things I wanted to tell him, but instead we'd argued. Feeling bad because I had been such a bitch during the call, I'd sent him a text apologizing and telling him where I was going tonight. I asked if he wanted to meet me. He hadn't responded. I sighed and closed my eyes.

After what felt like years of radio silence, the two of us had reconnected two months ago; well, if you could call Matty picking me up and carrying me to his car, demanding I talk to him, reconnecting. We'd talked hundreds of times since then and exchanged a few thousand text messages. However, every time we'd made plans to get together, life always got in the way and one of us had to cancel. I was desperate to see him; I needed my boyfriend to be more than a voice on the other end of the phone.

That's if he was my boyfriend. I wasn't sure what we were anymore. Matty had said I was his forever but that we just didn't work right now. When I asked if he thought we could fix us, he said we could, but that it wouldn't be easy. He was worth the effort, and I was willing to do almost anything to get us back to where we had been last summer. I believed that our declarations of love after Todd's adoption party was the closure each of us needed in order to put the past few months of hell behind us and move forward, to work on mending whatever was broken so we could be together.

The funny thing about closure was that once you felt as though you had it, once you were finally healing, the last thing you wanted to do was rip the scab off the wound. That's what I felt like we were doing. Our problems didn't go away just because we wanted them to, and underneath it all, we were the same people we'd been just a few months ago.

He was determined to keep secrets from me, to shut me out of God knows what, and that was something I wouldn't tolerate if we had any hope of a future. And as much as I tried not to be, I was bitter; without any explanation, he'd been ready to let me go and expected me to run back to the man who had hurt me, the very man Matty had sworn he'd kill if said man ever touched me again. Every time we tried to talk about that day, we picked at the scab a little more. It was painful and would only leave us scarred if we couldn't figure it out.

I knew that Matty didn't really want me to leave and that neither of us meant a quarter of what we'd said. However, he refused to talk about it. I didn't understand how he could be amazing and possessive one day then weak and pathetic the next. I was positive there was some underlying reason, but no matter what I said, he refused to let me in.

Without realizing it, I'd fallen back into my nasty passive-aggressive pattern. I knew I needed to break the mold and just tell him how I felt, but instead I found myself getting angry for no real reason and feeling annoyed with him for little things that normally wouldn't bother me.

It was excruciatingly clear that neither of us was sure how to move on. When we talked, we avoided any serious topics as if we'd come to an unspoken mutual understanding that we didn't get much time and we'd be damned if it was going to be ruined by an argument. Leaving things unsaid seemed to breed mistrust though. He'd been distant, almost cold, over the past week, and it hurt me that he wouldn't tell me why. Plus, I'd worked myself into a tizzy trying to figure out how to tell him about everything that was going on in my life, making me overly snappy.

The last time we'd talked, I took offense to his cold shoulder routine and suggested that we should quit while we were ahead. I told him I thought we would always work better as just friends and that the friendship was what we both missed the most. He claimed that we'd get to the point where we could forgive each other, and eventually everything would fall into place. I yelled back, telling him I hadn't done anything wrong and didn't need his forgiveness. I couldn't remember much more of what was said, but I knew it had gone south quickly. I would probably never forget the relief in his voice when I told him I needed a break and he had agreed.

"Maybe this time it really is over."

"Jesus, you two are way more dramatic than any teenagers I know—and believe me, that's saying something. Maybe you are. I seriously doubt it, but maybe. You have some crap to work through, but so does every other couple. Divorcees come with crazy amounts of baggage." She twirled her hand over her head. "Most men can't handle all this, let alone my two monsters. But I'd go through all the bullshit all over again just to find Tom." She smiled. "If you're over, you are. Stressing over it and getting depressed won't make him come back. It will only make you feel like shit. So you're gonna get up, get dressed, put on my stripper shoes, and go dance your ass off." She shoved me off the bed. "Tomorrow's a big day."

Teagan was right. I'd done everything I could do, and now the ball was in Matty's court. I needed to let it go, at least for tonight, and have a great night with my friends. My life was about to change.

TWO

ROCKER

The bar was full, the music loud, and the dance floor crammed with people grinding and laughing, drunk off their asses. Thankfully, we were the only ones filling the stools at the bar. I sat, listening to Hawk and Fred shoot the shit, grumbling responses when they were required.

The two of them kept trying to drag me into the conversation, but all I cared about was finishing the beer in front of me and downing the next. It had been a long-ass day full of nothing but shit I didn't want to deal with. If I hadn't promised the guys we'd stop at Hooligan's to see Fred, we'd be halfway back to Boston by now.

Thinking of my buddies, I scanned the room for Dean; he'd taken off with a tasty little piece a while ago and I hadn't seen him since. A loud group came up to the other end of the bar, and I turned toward them out of boredom. One of them, a tall blonde in a barely-there outfit and a "come fuck me" mouth, offered me a knowing smile. I ignored her, not even close to being interested, and moved my eyes over the rest of her group, settling on the short one who had her back to me. There was something familiar about her, and I searched my mind, struggling to place her.

She wasn't my type, so there was no reason I should stare, but an uneasy feeling settled in my gut and I couldn't pull my eyes away. Her hair was short, barely touching her shoulders, and I knew I'd remember those colors. It was all three—brown, red, and yellow—in alternating chunks—and unless it was the lights from the strobes, there were also streaks of blue and purple. Dancing in place, shaking her ass to the beat, her clothes left very little to my imagination and showed the world just how curvy she was.

Nothing about her interested me, except that fucking nagging feeling that I knew her. A couple of guys joined her group, one draping his arm around her shoulders in a gesture that showed everyone he was staking his claim. I lifted my bottle, ready to turn back to Fred, when I heard the laugh. I froze, hand in the air, bottle almost at my lips, staring. The douche with her had leaned in, but she'd stepped away from him, leaning her head back and giggling.

No fucking way in hell.

I felt my whole body tense and took a swig, squinting to see if it could really be her. This chick was similar in height, but that was about it. She was different—from the way she dressed to the undeniable curves to the crazy hair. But no one else in the world had that laugh. I'd know it anywhere.

My fist squeezed the bottle as the douche ignored her signal, slid his hand down her back and grabbed her ass. She was free now; the divorce was final. Mateo had screwed up and let her walk away, but that didn't mean she should be there and letting some pansy-ass wimp fondle her. She didn't move into the ass wipe, which was his intention, but instead stepped forward, moving her arms wildly and forcing him to let go. The entire group laughed, apparently finding whatever she'd said hilarious.

And I knew. It was her. I started to stand, but Fred's voice kept me back.

"Leave her be, Brothah." It was a low, threatening tone.

I turned to him, jaw clenched, eyebrows raised, trying to determine if he knew how he sounded. He stood directly across from me, on the other side of the bar, towel slung over his shoulder, thick arms folded over an equally thick chest, watching her.

I lifted my chin in her direction. "She come here often?"

The jackoff raised his hand in the air, trying to get the attention of one of the barkeepers. Fred shook his head and snorted, as if my question was absurd, and walked to them before one of his employees could.

Seconds later, Jo screeched Fred's name and practically jumped over the counter to give him a hug. He laughed, wrapping himself around her, and I felt an instant pang of annoyance. Obviously the two of them had gotten close.

I didn't jump as a familiar hand smoothed my back in comfort and a soft warm body curled against mine.

"You promised no trouble," Darcey purred in my ear.

I looked down, smiling. "Me?" I shrugged. "Hawk's the one you gotta watch."

Darcey laughed, giving me a hug. Fred's wife wore a tight tank—the word Hooligan's spread across her perfect tits—and an apron around her tiny waist. Setting the empty tray she carried on the bar, she turned to me, giving me a pointed look.

I shifted, uncomfortable under the gaze. "What?"

One eyebrow arched at my tone, but she shook her head, looking down the bar toward Joey. "She's a regular now." She sighed sadly, turning back to me. "In here whenever she doesn't have her kids. She trusts him."

Watching Fred joke with her, I knew Darcey meant her husband, not the prick still trying to touch Jo.

"She's been through hell and is just starting to come out. She doesn't need more," Darcey informed me, as if I didn't know.

My jaw clenched at the assumption that I'd cause trouble. I didn't want to Joey to have any more problems; she'd been through the fucking wringer. Cris told me she'd been worried, that I should check in and let Jo know I was there if she needed me, but I hadn't seen the point. Joey had her own friends.

She wasn't the only one who had been left a fucking mess. I'd had my hands full trying to deal with the fallout she'd left behind. Now I was sitting here on a Friday night, staring at the back of the woman I hadn't stopped hearing about. And my best friend was no where to be seen. Fucking perfect.

As Joey and her entire group headed out to the dance floor, I realized that I needed to leave before she saw me. I turned back to the bar, ready to tell Hawk we had to go. Instead, he handed me a shot of whiskey and slid another over as soon as the first was gone.

"Don't you ever get sicka cleanin' up his messes?"

I shook my head in warning. This wasn't the place or the time. I stood, knowing I had to go—but out of the corner of my eye, I saw her dancing. I turned out of habit, and the image of her, obviously pretty tipsy and surrounded by sleazeballs, made me freeze.

Fuck! I couldn't leave without saying something.

Darcey stepped in my way, giving me that mom look she enjoyed pulling on me, but I moved around her, ignoring the warning Fred hollered at my back. Nothing he could say would stop me from yanking her ass off that dance floor and shaking some sense into that pretty little head of hers. I was the last person he should be protecting her from.

The rage rolled off of me in waves, and most people, sensing danger, moved out of my way. I was behind her in just a few steps. The pussy that had started to move toward her slid away fast when I narrowed my eyes at him. Joey still hadn't seen me, but her tall blond friend stopped the hideous jerking she considered dancing, mouth falling open at my presence. The target of my annoyance was oblivious though, moving to the beat.

I didn't think; my hands reached out, flat against her soft stomach as they circled around her, and pulled her back into me. I could feel the change immediately. She tensed, looking up at her friend. The blonde nodded—as if since she approved of my face, I was worthy to dance with her friend—and Jo relaxed a little, her body moving backward into mine. The action infuriated me to the core. I could be anyone, any sick prick, but because her friend thought I was hot, she was gonna grind with me? Fuck, no.

I'd forgotten how short she was—the top of her head barely reached my chest. She'd gained weight in the few months since I'd seen her, giving her body a softness I hadn't realized was missing. I leaned over to put my head on her shoulder, and the scent of vanilla hit me. I tipped my head toward her ear and felt her stiffen as if she sensed I was after more than a quick dance. She attempted to pull away, but my hands held her close.

As her breath quickened in panic, I couldn't stop the smirk. She should be scared. She was a grown-ass woman who should know when she dressed the way she was tonight, she'd attract attention. Maybe she thought Freddy would save her; I had no doubt that the giant softie would break his fists on anyone who tried to touch her without her permission. But he wouldn't be able to save her this time—not from me.

Using every ounce of patience I had, I didn't drag her off the floor. I didn't knock out the teeth of the douche who was still eyeing her like she was dessert.

Instead, I yanked her hard against me and growled in her ear, "Hello, Lil' Kangaroo."

THREE

JO

"Rocker?" I turned around so quickly, I made myself dizzy, almost falling.

Thankfully his arms were still around me, and he held me upright. I braced my hands on his chest just to be sure I stayed on my feet in T's pathetically high heel. His whole body was tense.

"What the hell are you doing here?" I yelled to be sure he heard me over the music.

Instead of answering, he let go of me, stepped back, and tipped his head toward the side of the bar. I nodded, knowing he wanted me to follow him, happy that he did. Walking behind him brought on serious deja vu. It hadn't been that long ago when Fred led me off this dance floor and walked me over to the tables Rocker was headed to now. Yet it felt like a lifetime ago.

I sat across from him, his large frame making the small square table seem almost miniscule. I'd only spent a few days with this man, but I genuinely liked Rocker, and knew my feelings reflected in my smile. I waited a few minutes for him to say something, but he just stayed silent, his dark eyes surveying me.

I'd once imagined the Hulk every time I thought of Rob; now the image of a green monster was the last thing on my mind whenever Rocker entered it. Rob was huge, and by huge I meant monstrous—he towered over me by at least a foot and couldn't weigh an ounce less than two hundred and sixty pounds—but he was hilarious and a loyal friend. I was happy to see him but surprised he was here alone.

The thought struck me hard as I realized that he probably wasn't alone. If he was in Maine, it was either for a job or to see... my eyes snapped over his shoulder, searching the bar patrons for the familiar face. Maybe he had come after all.

"He's not heah, Lil' Kangaroo." The voice was low and gruff and proved without a doubt that he hailed from South Boston.

I tried to hide my disappointment and fought the urge to ask where Matty was. This wasn't his weekend to have Sammy, and before our argument, he'd mentioned he was probably going to hang out with friends. I'd assumed he meant the Bastards.

If he wasn't here with these friends... my mind wandered to a place I didn't want it to go. The only reason I could think of that would keep him from spending time with Rocker was a date. I hated that I was that insecure and that I automatically assumed the worst. But I had told him to move on, and Matty was who he was.

I definitely hadn't made the greatest choices over the past few months, especially where Matt was concerned, so it was probably a good thing that he wasn't here. I wasn't sure how to tell him about all the changes I'd made. Or even how to explain what I was feeling.

Part of me had been so sure he would show up though, because Matty was always there when I needed him. Or at least he always used to be. Regret settled in my gut, and I closed my eyes, trying to make the nerves go away.

"Jesus, Joey, you are wicked pale. Did you eat supper before you came out and decided to get shit-faced?"

The irritation in his voice surprised me, and I snapped open my eyes to find him glaring at me. I would probably never get used to the gruff attitude that seemed ever present in these crazy Bastard boys. They were either ordering me around, telling me exactly how to live my life, or bitching about how I lived it. They all seemed to need to lecture me constantly about the dumbest stuff and jump to conclusions. This time, Rob was way off. I took a deep breath and raised an eyebrow.

"No," I started slowly, "I haven't had anything to eat yet. I was," I cleared my throat, searching for words. "Busy before we came out, and we're going out for breakfast after we leave here."

Rob swore and muttered something sexist about women like me not being able to take care of themselves.

I chuckled then talked over him. "As for being shit-faced, the last time I checked, you can't get drunk off water. I guess we can always check with Fred to make sure that's all that's been in my drinks."

"Wait. What?" Rob stopped short, shaking his head as if he didn't believe me. "Water? You're tellin' me you've only been drinking water? Not countin' all the shots, right? I think you are forgettin' that I saw you out there dancin'."

I smiled. "Yeah, I kinda figured that when you came up behind me and started to cuddle." I couldn't help the giggle that escaped at the disgusted way his features twisted. "It's called having a good time, silly. You should try it—it'd do you some good. I'm letting loose and having fun, yes. But I am painfully sober."

Rocker sat back, his dark eyes traveling all over my face as if trying to decide if I was lying. "You must be wicked hungry." His tongue wet his bottom lip. "I haven't had anything either. Is there anywhere near hear we could go?"

I nodded without really thinking about it. "There's the Little Hole in the Wall down the street. Do you like Mexican?" I wasn't sure if I wanted him to say yes or not.

He nodded. "Let's go then." He must have seen my hesitation and gave me a toothy smile. "I'll bring ya back in one piece."

I looked over his shoulder, trying to see where my friends were dancing. They didn't seem to miss me, all having a good time swaying with each other. I shrugged then nodded. Why not?

Rob stood suddenly, pulling me to my feet. "I've gotta tell them, then we'll go."

Them? I took a deep breath. I didn't know which ones were there, but I was pretty sure I wasn't up to facing any of them. Most of Matty's friends hadn't liked me to begin with, and after the way things ended, I was positive they hated me now. I tugged back on Rocker's hand. "I'll stay here and wait for you."

Rob turned back to me, his dark thick eyebrows raised in silent question. "The hell you will." He tightened his hold on my wrist as if he thought I was going to run away, and dragged me behind him toward the bar.

"Wait!" I tried to pull my hand away again. "I need to tell my friends that I'm leaving."

Rocker stopped suddenly and spun around. "Friends?" He sneered. "They never once came over to check on you to make sure you were okay with me. Those aren't friends." He turned back just as abruptly and pulled me to the bar.

Hawk shook his head when he saw me trailing behind Rob, but he did offer a smile. "Hey, LK."

I lifted my hand in a silly wave. "Hi Hawk."

"We'll be back before last call." Rocker snapped, not offering any more information.

Hawk didn't hide the look of shock on his face. He leaned towards his friend, and even though I couldn't hear the words he whispered to Rob, I was positive he was pissed at the idea. Rocker simply shook his head and pulled me towards the door and outside into the cold early spring air. He stopped suddenly at a giant black Ford.

"This is your truck?"

He only offered me a nod as he unlocked the front passenger's door then pulled it open for me. I eyed the tall step, wondering if I could make it up in the dangerously high heels and too tight jeans Teagan had insisted on. I must have hesitated a second too long because Rocker grabbed my hips and lifted me as if I didn't weigh a quarter of what I did.

"Yeah, it's mine." He lifted a shoulder as he backed away. "Big Little Man Syndrome." He shut the door.

I contemplated his words as he walked around the front of the obtrusive vehicle. Little Man Syndrome, or Napoleon Syndrome, I knew, but Big Little Man Syndrome was lost on me. I reached over and opened his door, not sure if I wanted to know what he meant.

He laughed at my look as he slid into the driver's seat. Raising an eyebrow, he held up his half-bent pinkie finger. "Ya know, the luck o' the Irish?" His voice took on a Celtic accent that was spot-on.

I didn't have a clue what in the hell he was talking about. What did the luck of the Irish have to do with anything?

I was about to ask when he burst out laughing. "Jesus, Joey, you fuckin' kill me!" He cleared his throat and tipped his head. "I guess you would say that I'm overcompensatin' for life's shortcomings."

As realization hit me, I could feel my face flame and I couldn't stop the snort. Leaning my head back, I stared at his ceiling, letting the laugh subside. "But what does that have to do with the luck of the Irish? Wouldn't life's, um"—I cleared my throat—"shortcomings be bad luck, not good?"

Rocker didn't just laugh at me that time—he tipped his head back and howled. I didn't want to join him, but it was too hard not to.

When he finally got control of himself, he wiped his eyes and looked at me with a smirk. "Lil' Kangaroo, the Irish have the worst luck of any people ever. When someone says they have the 'luck of the Irish,' it means they're anything but lucky. I'm Irish to the core—third-generation American, but as Irish as they come. Matty likes to tell people I drive a big truck to make up for the fact that I have a little dick." He shrugged. "Big Little Man Syndrome." He turned to look at me, smiling. "So where is this place?"

He turned back to the windshield as my face flamed red, and I was relieved he couldn't see me. I gave him directions as he turned the key, and the beast of a truck roared to life. A few minutes later, he pulled into the tiny parking lot.

"Little Hole in the Wall?" he asked, reading the hand-painted sign on the side of the building. "I thought you were telling me that this place was just a crappy little restaurant, a dump. Not that it was the actual name."

I smiled as I opened my door. "It looks sketchy, but it's the best Mexican food around."

The tiny, dimly lit restaurant was almost empty. The only other patrons were a young couple huddled together at the corner table. We ordered, Rob refused to let me pay, then we sat by the window to wait for our food. I was about to ask him how he'd been over the last few months when he broke the silence.

"What in the hell are you doing?"

I stopped trying to fold the napkin into different shapes and glanced up, the look on his face confusing me. "Sorry?"

He scowled, looking away. "With your life, Lil' Kangaroo. Why in the hell are you dressed like that? Why are you out with people like that?" He nodded toward the window.

He didn't say "instead of with Matty," but he didn't have to. I knew exactly what he meant.

"He's fuckin' miserable, you know that, right?" His voice dropped as though he didn't want to say the last few words.

There was no reason to lie. "I was saying good-bye."

Confusion crossed his features.

"I've made some seriously screwed up decisions over the last few months, Matty included"—Rocker nodded eagerly, and I narrowed my eyes at him— "and I need to start over." I tried to figure out how to explain it. "One morning, after the divorce was final, I was lying in bed, feeling sorry for myself. I had gone from having everything to practically nothing in a matter of weeks. Hell, I don't even have my own apartment; when I'm not with the kids at the house, I stay with a friend. I only have my kids two weeks out of the month, so for the other two weeks, the only thing keeping me going was a job I dreaded going to." I took a sip of my Coke. "I realized that morning that this was a chance for me to find myself, to start over and do things right this time. So, I did."

Rocker leaned forward. "And what did you do?"

The food arrived, saving me from answering. I dug into my enchilada quickly, almost moaning at the taste. I hadn't realized how hungry I was. If Rocker heard me, he didn't say anything; but then, he was too busy shoveling food into his mouth to notice much of anything. We ate in comfortable silence.

It wasn't long before Rocker sat back and smiled. "You were right. Best Mexican ever." He finished off his soda then met my eyes. "You gonna tell me this big thing you're celebrating?"

"I'm not. I'm saying goodbye." I shrugged, "I decided I don't want to be a caseworker anymore, that I need something more *me*. So, I applied to and surprisingly got accepted into grad school. But I had to take some undergrad refresher courses this semester, just to be prepared next fall."

Rocker looked disappointed, as if he thought my life change was going to be much more interesting.

I swallowed my amused smile. "I talked to Will, and he's on board. He thinks I should focus on the kids and school, not work. I quit my job." I ignored Rob's frown. "I'm actually going down to your neck of the woods tomorrow to look at apartments. I'd like to start moving no later than Monday, because commuting all the time sucks and I need to find a part-time job."

"My neck of the woods?"

I nodded.

"Why?" His brows knit together. "Joey, where in the hell are you goin' to school?"

"Boston College. They have the best psych grad program around." I smiled at the blank look on his face. "Yes, Rocker, I'm moving to Boston."

"Holy shit." He dragged out the words in complete surprise. "Fuck, Joey." Then the surprise turned to look I couldn't read. "You haveta tell Matty."

FOUR

JO

I wasn't sure how long we sat in front of Hooligan's Pub, but the silence made it feel like hours. I didn't know what to say to him, but since he'd left the truck idling, the heater on, and hadn't attempted to get out, I could tell he didn't want me to head back into the bar yet. I was more than happy to sit there in the quiet and avoid life for a few minutes.

Rocker was right. I did have to tell Matty, because I didn't want him to find out from someone else. Things with him were still so screwed up though. I couldn't simply pick up the phone and drop the bomb that I was moving to the one city he wanted me to stay away from. If he found out from anyone other than me that I had quit my job—the job he loved and valued—and that I was moving to a city he thought was dangerous, he'd be furious.

Although, it didn't matter how he found out. Matty was going to be livid and wonder why I hadn't told him sooner, why I had kept it a secret for so long, especially when I was so adamant that we should tell each other everything. I didn't have the answers.

I snuck a peak at Rocker. He was staring straight ahead at the building, his triangular face covered in shadows, thick fingers tapping a soundless beat on the steering wheel as if trying to work out some giant puzzle, and I knew he was thinking about his best friend. Rob was more loyal than anyone I'd ever met. Fear hit me suddenly.

"Please don't tell him before I can." The words were a whispered plea.

He didn't look at me, but I could see his teeth working his bottom lip as if he was lost in thought. He shook his head. "I ain't telling him shit. Not my business." He snapped his head toward me. "You drivin' down or takin' the train?"

I started; that was the last thing I'd expected him to ask. "Train. I'm staying with a friend tonight, and she's dropping me off in the morning. Cris is meeting me at the station."

"Where are you lookin' for apartments?"

I shook my head. I actually didn't know. "Cris set them up. I guess one of her friends is a realtor, and since I'm just looking to sublet for a while, she offered to help. My budget is pretty small compared to what some people want for rent, so we'll see." I sighed, stressed over all the things I had to do. "I also need to find a job, so I'm dropping off a ton of applications."

His eyes narrowed. "What about your kids? You're just gonna leave 'em here?"

I frowned at him for a minute before I realized he didn't know. "Oh! I assumed Matty would have told you... sorry!" I offered him a small smile before explaining. "Will, my ex, and I have joint custody, and we agreed that it was unfair to have the kids get uprooted. The kids live at the house all the time, while Will and I alternate. We tried doing the every-other-week thing, but it was just too much for everyone. Now the first two weeks of every month belong to him, and the last two weeks belong to me. If there's a five-week month, I keep the kids an extra few days and he moves in a couple days early. Divorce sucks, but we want the kids to have as much stability as they can. They shouldn't be punished because Mommy and Daddy can't live together anymore."

"That's..." He glanced back at the bar before meeting my gaze. "That's a really great thing to do for your kids. Most parents only worry about themselves after a divorce."

I couldn't have agreed more. "The only thing Will and I ever did right was those kids. We're both determined to make sure they don't get hurt. I've seen how hard it is for Sammy when he has to go home after spending the weekend with Matty. I couldn't imagine doing that to my babies. It'll be a struggle once I'm settled in Boston, but we'll make it work."

Silence filled the cabin again as Rocker seemed to lose himself in deep thought but never took his eyes off me. The steady stare made me nervous, and I turned to look out my window, watching people leave the building. Last call was getting close. I needed to go inside and find my friends, but I couldn't bring myself to open the door. I felt like there was more to say.

Rocker cleared his throat, apparently feeling the tension in the air. "Come home with me."

I jerked in surprise, hoping the gasp I'd let escape wasn't as loud as it sounded in my head. I looked over my shoulder at him, my eyes huge. "I'm sorry, but I think I missed a step. I... uh, I'm not..." A slut. Someone who would sleep with her ex's best friend. Jesus, I knew I hadn't met Matty's friends under the best circumstances and most of them thought I was a whore because I was still married then, but wow. These guys had a really shitty opinion of me.

"You didn't." Rocker interrupted my thoughts—I'm not sure if he realized where my mind had gone. He tipped his head and looked at me. "We're drivin' home tonight. You can come with us. By the time you find your friends and go get food, it'll be time to catch the Downeaster. It's stupid to pay for a train when I'm drivin' back."

I slowly released the breath I'd been holding, feeling like an idiot but relieved by his explanation. I thought about his offer for a few minutes, not sure it was a good idea. "I'm not sure I'll be able to get Cris to meet me then... it'll be early tomorrow morning by the time we get there. And I don't have any of my stuff."

I could just make out his frown in the parking lot lights. "Ya know that I have tons of room, right? You can crash at the apartment for the night. We'll stop and get your shit on the way." He seemed to sense my hesitation. "Joey, Cris knows where I live. She can come get you there—after you've had a decent night's sleep." He shut off the truck. "Go say good-bye to your friends while I grab mine."

He slammed the door after he got out. Apparently, the discussion was over, the decision had been made. Riding with him would be more convenient than riding down on the Amtrak tomorrow. I just didn't know how I was going to survive a three-hour ride with Matty's friends; hopefully I'd fall asleep quickly.

Rocker waited and followed me into the building. As soon as we were inside, he headed toward the bar in search of Hawk and God knew who else, while I stopped and scanned the crowd. I found the girls quickly—on the dance floor, almost right where I'd left them. Mere only laughed and jumped excitedly when I told her I was bailing on breakfast and heading home with Rob. I shook my head, denying her implications, but she smiled and winked. I was slightly irritated as I turned and went in search of my ride.

The music suddenly quieted, and the lights came on—last call was over. I groaned, realizing just how late it was. We wouldn't be back to the apartment before sun-up.

Rob wasn't hard to spot; a man his size was generally given a wide berth by most sane men. He was leaning against the bar, talking to Fred and Hawk. I was half surprised the three of them didn't have a bunch of drunk nitwits hanging off them, begging for attention. They were all very handsome—if you liked that tattooed, rugged, dangerous biker look.

I smiled, thinking of the one tattooed biker I definitely found beautiful. Thoughts of Matty invaded, and I shook my head, trying to clear it. Now was not the time to get my libido all wound up. I walked toward them slowly, dreading finding out who else had come up with Rocker.

"I haven't seen him in hours. Should be back by now."

Fred rolled his shoulders, clearly annoyed. "Did ya call him?"

Hawk nodded. "Yeah, a few times."

"If he's not back in ten minutes, he can find his own fuckin' way home." Rocker's voice was low and gravelly, obviously irritated.

I stepped up next to Hawk. "Who are we missing?"

"Dean," Hawk said before anyone else could.

Out of the corner of my eye, I saw Fred glance at me, but I met Hawk's eyes instead. He smiled, giving his face a softer look. The man had intimidated me when I first met him, and I had no doubt that he had the same effect on many others. Not as tall as Rob, Hawk still towered over most men. His broad shoulders combined with his height made me feel much smaller than I actually was, something a girl my size could seriously appreciate. The top half of his shoulder-length blond hair was pulled back, allowing me an unobstructed view of his wide nose, thin lips, and adorable dimple in his chin.

One dark eyebrow suddenly shot up as he watched me inspect him. "Like what you see?" His voice was full of humor, but I could feel embarrassment creep in and my cheeks flame just the same.

"Jesus, leave her alone." Fred's deep voice interrupted as he slammed a massive fist on the counter. "Joey, are ya really gonna ride all the way to Beantown with these assholes?"

I chuckled nervously, but nodded, stull unsure. I was about to tell him that I'd be fine when Rob swore.

"It's about fucking time. Where in the hell have you been?"

Dean just smirked, shaking his head, as he strolled up to our group. "You're wicked smart brother. I'm sure you can figure it out."

He winked, his eyes twinkling, and I didn't have to see more than the untucked shirt or messed up hair to know exactly what he'd been doing. I didn't want to know where—or with who. He looked like he was going to go into detail though, and I groaned at the idea. Dark green eyes snapped to me, widening in surprise.

"Joey?" He looked uncomfortable, glancing between Rocker and Hawk.

Rob leaned toward Dean. "You're lucky ya got back when you did. Five more minutes, and I was leaving your ass here. Your date woulda had to bring ya home." He slapped the bar twice, tipping his head toward the door. "Let's go." He pointed at the door. "Later, brother," he spoke to Fred as he passed.

I stopped to give the massive barkeep a quick hug, kissed his cheek good-bye, and followed Hawk out the door.

"Joey's got shotgun!" Rocker hollered from behind me as Dean yanked open the passenger door.

Dean jerked back as if the handle had burned him and turned slowly, surprise written all over his face. "What? Last time I checked, we weren't a fuckin' taxi." He waved at me as if to shoo me away. "Go find some other dumbass to rescue you, 'cause we don't give two flyin' fucks."

Rocker stopped next to me abruptly, handling landing on the small of my back the way Matty's always did. "Last time I checked," he spit out, "it was my fuckin' truck, so you don't tell me who can ride and who can't. Joey's family. She's coming with us." Dean looked as if he was going to argue, but Rob shook his head. "Shut. It."

I tensed, not wanting to cause a problem, wondering if it was too late to catch my friends. Rob moved his hand from my back to my upper arm, gripping it tight as if he sensed I was thinking about bolting. Hawk's lips twisted into an amused smirk, obviously used to seeing his friends rant at each other, and climbed into the backseat on Rocker's side.

Dean didn't move. "You know Matty will throw a shit fit if he finds out you're takin' her home." He glared at me as if I was public enemy number one. "Don't do it, brother." His low voice held a warning.

"And you don't know shit. Get in the truck and shut your fuckin' mouth or find another way back."

I tried to pull away from Rob, but he refused to let me go. Of course, he'd be here with Dean; the man had barely tolerated me when I was dating Matty and clearly loathed me now. I groaned. I wouldn't survive three hours with these men.

Dean gave me a nasty look but climbed in beside Hawk, leaving me alone in parking lot with Rocker.

"That goes for you too. Get in the truck." Rob's command left no room for argument.

I tried another angle. "Instead of stopping to get my stuff, you can just drop me off at my friend's, then I'll catch the train tomorrow as planned."

Rocker walked toward the black beast, shaking his head and pulling me along. "Naw. You're comin' with us. It'll be fine." He opened the door and lifted me up again.

It was anything but fine. The tension in the cab was so thick I could feel it crawling up my arms. I could almost feel Dean's glare burning a hole in my seat. Pulling out my phone, I sent a quick text to Teagan to let her know I'd be stopping by and she and Tom better be decent, then I gave directions to Rob.

The silence was unbearable. Music. We needed music. Without thinking, I leaned over and turned on the radio, surprised when "Midnight in Montgomery" filled the air. I couldn't stop the smile that formed.

"Alan Jackson?" I turned to look at the giant man next to me. "Really?"

Rob didn't take his eyes off the road. "Yes, really." He didn't sound annoyed, just curious. "You got something against Alan Jackson? Or is it country music in general?"

"No." I shook my head. "I love country. I just pictured you listening to... something else."

"Such as?" I couldn't see his face in the dark truck, but the humor in his voice was unmistakable.

"I dunno... Godsmack. Disturbed. Marilyn Manson, maybe." I shrugged. "You know, loud, scary, 'stay the hell away from me 'cause I'll seriously fuck shit up if I don't get my own way' music."

Rocker chuckled. When he stopped at a red light, he turned toward me. "Why would you think that?"

I just stared at him, taking in the whole picture. His scuffed-up work boots were hidden beneath jeans that showed serious wear around the knees, a beat-up tee layered over a long-sleeved gray waffle-knit said he'd come to the bar right after work. He looked like a man who had spent his day laboring hard.

If you looked harder, though, you'd see so much more than that lingering right below the surface.

His sleeves were pushed back to the elbows, showing the ink that danced down his muscular right arm. A ring graced his middle finger on the left hand he had draped across the steering wheel, and he wore two more on his right. The scruff around his jaw told me he hadn't shaved in a few days, and while it would make most men look sloppy, it only made him look more precarious and appealing. A black beanie was pulled low so I couldn't see his hair, adding to the overall picture. He was the epitome of dangerous.

Looks had never been more deceiving, but he wanted to know, so I gladly shared.

"Gee, I don't know." My sarcasm was hard to hide. "Maybe 'cause you look like you're ready to beat someone to death." I smiled. "Seriously, you dress like a badass biker thug."

Hawk's hoots filled the truck as the light turned green. "Badass biker thug? Fuckin' perfect."

I was half-relieved when Rob turned the truck into Teagan's driveway, because I needed to get out of the truck and away from the three of them. The other half was nervous though, wondering if I could go inside and lock the Bastards out just so I didn't have to go with them. I jumped out of the cab as soon as Rob stopped, somehow managing to stay on my feet, and walked as quickly as I could on the ice-covered ground in heels. I was halfway up the front steps when his words stopped me.

"You've got ten minutes, Joey. If you're not out here by then, I'm comin' in to getchya." His voice was low and full of warning. "I may listen to country, but I will fuck shit up if I don't get my own way. Remember that."

FIVE

JO

Someone nudged me. I didn't want to wake up—my dreams were too good. Matty and I were sitting on a couch, me leaning against him, his strong arms snug around me, as he kissed my temple lightly every few minutes. He was singing along to the music, laughing. He was happy, and when his eyes turned to me, they were full of affection.

I wanted to stay in this moment forever, wrapped up in nothing but Matty, loving him for eternity. Another nudge made me open my eyes.

"Hey, you awake?"

I sat up a little and leaned forward, trying to figure out where I was. I blinked against the bright street lights and wiped my mouth, ashamed when I realized I had a line of spittle working its way toward my chin. I couldn't stifle the yawn that escaped. God, I was tired. Tipping my head back, I fought the urge to close my eyes again.

"You snore, ya know that, right?"

I started, almost yelping, at the voice right next to my ear.

Rocker laughed then cleared his throat. "Sorry." He moved underneath me, making me jump again. "Jesus, you are wicked jumpy!"

I blinked again, realization slowing dawning. My memories played like a movie: the bar, a late supper with Rob, then he took me to Teagan's, I'd changed my clothes, packed, and gotten back in the truck. After listening to the guys banter for what seemed like ages, I must have fallen asleep. I rubbed my eyes, slowly becoming aware that I was leaning on him. I sat up quickly, pulling away.

"Sorry!" My voice was raw, and I had to swallow to make the word come out, not sure if I was apologizing for the fact that I fell asleep or that I fell asleep on him. I stretched my neck, trying to get the crick out. When I tipped my head to the left, my eyes landed on the instrument panel, where a picture of a little curly brown-haired girl beamed back at me. I couldn't keep my curiosity to myself. "Who's that little beauty?"

"My daughter." The love and pride evident in his voice.

"Daughter?" The answer shocked me more than it should have. Rocker didn't seem like a dad, and I couldn't remember Matty ever telling me that he had kids. Unless she didn't get to see her dad, which would be awful and would explain Rob's earlier attitude toward me moving to Boston.

Out of my peripheral, I saw him nod. "Yeah, Hannah Jean." He smiled at the words.

Hannah Jean? Hmm. I'd expected a Kathryn or a Mary Kathryn, something that sounded Irish.

"She's way too cute to be your kid," I teased. "How old is she—three?" I had similar pictures of Lily where she was that tiny, and a sudden pang of lost time hit my gut. I missed my kids.

Rob cleared his throat. "She'd be twenty now. But she's two in that picture."

My blood ran cold at his words. *She'd be twenty now.* Meaning she was gone. My heart broke for him, for the loss no parent should ever have to face. Without thinking, I grabbed his hand. "I'm sorry!"

His only answer was to give my hand a quick squeeze then let go. I sat where I was, even though I felt like staying in the middle seat might be invading his personal space. Jesus, if she'd be twenty now, then he'd just been a kid when she was born—only fifteen or sixteen. I looked out the window, wondering where we were, at a loss for words.

Rocker seemed to read my mind. "We're in the city, L.K."

I looked at him. "L.K.?"

He chuckled. "Yeah, Lil' Kangaroo is a mouthful, so we decided to shorten it after ya passed out."

Realizing it was too quiet, I turned around and scanned the backseat, laughing when I saw both men out cold. Dean, his mouth wide open in slumber, was leaning over the middle onto Hawk. I needed a picture. I grabbed my cell and snapped one, ecstatic when the flash didn't wake them up.

"Blackmail?"

I nodded, laughing again, and moved away from Rob into the passenger seat. "You never know when it might come in handy." I shrugged. "So L.K.? I like it." It was catchy, different than any nickname I'd ever had. This move was all about new beginnings, and the new name fit perfectly.

We drove the rest of the way in silence. When Rob punched in his code and pulled into the garage under his townhouse, the butterflies hit. I'd only been here with Matty, and the house held some of my best memories of our relationship.

It was here that he'd let me in, let me see the person he really was, told me some of his secrets. Here that he'd told me he loved me for the first time, on a roof lit only by candlelight. Here that he'd made love to me in a way that only Matty could, his body telling mine that I was the only one for him. If I had realized that a house, this perfect and beautiful apartment, could make me miss Matty more than I already did, I wouldn't have come.

Rocker didn't let me lose myself in memories or wallow though.

"Hey, shitheads," he yelled as he turned off the truck, "Time to wake up!"

Before I could move, Rob slid from the truck, grabbed my bags from the tool-body bed, and strode toward the elevator door. I practically ran behind him, not wanting to be caught alone with Dean, especially not a Dean who had just woken up and looked pissed. When the elevator stopped, I followed Rob off, surprised when the other two stayed on.

A quick glance told me that we were on the second floor of the building, the bottom floor of the apartment—the bedroom floor. Large muscles rippled under his shirt as Rocker lifted my heaviest suitcase, even though it had wheels, and walked straight toward the familiar door – Matty's door.

"No. I'll take the spare room."

Dark eyes turned to me as he hesitated in the doorway. "Cheech and Chong are upstairs, and there's no way I'm letting the three of you bunk together."

I hesitated for a moment, wondering which one was which. It didn't matter. At that point, being alone with Hawk and Dean actually didn't sound like a bad idea.

"L.K., this is your room. You'll sleep here." Without another word, he carried my bags into Matty's bedroom, around the bed, and set them on a chest under the windows that were just starting to show the break of dawn.

I didn't follow him. "No. This is Matty's room." I scanned the room quickly, looking for changes, but it was the same as it had been months ago, right down to the picture of the two of us on his

254

nightstand. I swallowed, meeting Rob's eyes. "What if..." I licked my lips, not wanting to ask and definitely not wanting the answer. "What if he's had other guests here?"

Rob quickly joined me in the hallway and stared down at me. "Joey, there hasn't been anyone here but you." His voice was low, serious. "He's been goin' out of his fuckin' mind." He shook his head, and I thought he was going to say something else. Instead he offered me a half smile. "It's late. Get some sleep."

Then he walked across the long hallway, toward his room, and shut his door before I even had a chance to thank him for the ride.

Sighing, I walked into Matty's domain and closed the door slowly. He was everywhere in this room, from the pictures on the mantel to the scent of his cologne in the air, to the clothes he had left draped over the chair near the bed. I pulled open his middle drawer, changed into one of his T-shirts—still my favorite thing to sleep in—and crawled into the giant bed. I took one last look around the room and at his beautiful face smiling back at me from the pictures, grabbed his pillow, and hugged it tight, thankful it still smelled just like him.

SIX

JO

I tossed and turned for what seemed like hours. Visions of Matty were mixed with nightmarish images of a beautiful little girl, who looked just like her daddy, leaving this world too soon. In the weird way that your mind sorts through the day's events, the toddler in my dreams was my Lily, and I could hear Matty's voice telling me that Lily and I needed to stay away from his hometown, that he needed to keep us safe.

Danger found us anyway, and I watched helplessly as the dream me cried at a tombstone housing her husband and daughter. The nightmares seemed never-ending, and I wasn't sure when I finally passed into a dreamless slumber.

When I woke a few hours later, the sun was shining bright, giving the room a warm, cozy, lazy afternoon feel. My entire body ached, and I wasn't sure if I should blame it on the dancing, the shoes, or the restful sleep. I lay back against the pillows, smelling hints of the cologne I loved so much, and sighed, trying to sort through the dreams. Remembering that Lily Belle was safe at home with her daddy, my mind settled on Rocker and his horrific loss. I hadn't handled his revelation very well, and that made me feel bad. I wondered if Cris would tell me what had happened to Hannah.

Cris! I sat upright, searching for my phone. I groaned, remembering I hadn't charged it last night. I crawled out of bed and searched through the pockets of my jeans. Teagan had called me a few times and sent me a text checking to make sure I was okay. I smiled, typed a quick response, promising I'd call her later.

The fact that I didn't have any missed calls or texts from Cris surprised me. It was almost noon; I'd expected no less than ten angry messages from her. As if on cue, the cell vibrated in my hand, notifying me I had a text from the last person I expected.

Will: Hey! Just checking to make sure you made it okay. I know you're busy & I'm on my way out so I can't chat. Remember my parents have the kids tonight so you'll have to call them to say night. Good luck apartment hunting.

I typed a quick reply, just to let him know I was safe and sound and that I did remember his parents had the kids. He and his girlfriend were going away for the weekend, and even though I'd volunteered to stay an extra few days at the house, his parents were back in the state and wanted the time with their grandbabies.

Things with Will and me were good—not great, but definitely good. We talked more now than we had when we were married and seemed to understand each other better than we had in years. For the first time, we were actually co-parenting our children peacefully. He had genuinely supported my move and insisted that he wanted to help any way he could. Most of his behavior was probably driven by guilt, but at least he was trying.

If only everyone else could be on board.

Pushing myself up off the floor, I dialed Cris, annoyed when it went right to voicemail. Maybe she was pissed I hadn't called. I needed caffeine, then I'd try again. Worst-case scenario, I'd take a cab around town to try to find a job, and maybe Rocker would let me stay one more night. I climbed the stairs groggily.

"What in the hell did ya do to your hair?" Cris shrieked as I rounded the corner on the top floor.

Crissia Murphy was almost the twin image of her big brother, with Aphrodite looks that I envied: long, curly dark brown hair, defined cheekbones, and bright blue eyes that seemed like they could see into your soul. Those eyes were now glaring at me as she sat across the table from Rocker, coffee cup in hand, gaping at me, completely appalled.

"You ruined it!"

I chortled as I took a seat at the head of the table between them and ran my hands through my hair. "You don't like it? Teagan's girls decided they want to be hair stylists, so I let them practice on me. You're the one who's always telling me to try something different."

"No, I don't like it!" She tipped her head and pursed her lips. "It looks like your hair has gone manic and can't make up its mind which color it wants to be."

Rocker gave me a wink and tugged on a chunky blond piece. "I like it. It fits her."

"Yeah, only 'cause its crazy hair and she's fuckin' nuts." Cris rotated her finger next to her temple.

Rocker chuckled as he pushed away from the table.

Cris's lips twisted in a killer smile that reminded me so much of her bother. "It's about time you dragged your lazy ass outta bed. I was getting bored."

I stifled a yawn. "I guess I was exhausted. Sorry."

She smirked. "I knew where to find ya."

"When do we meet your friend? I just need to take a quick shower, then I'm good to go."

Cris shook her head. "We don't. I already found you a place."

"What? Really?" I scowled. "But I haven't looked at any apartments yet."

"This place is perfect, trust me. Cheap rent, nice neighborhood, secure building, furnished, no bugs." She held up her hand, lifting a finger as she checked off every one of my requirements. "All the stuff you listed. I figured you'd rather spend your time trying to find a job."

"Thanks?" I wasn't sure if I should be grateful or not; knowing Cris, I should be terrified. "When can I see it?"

Rocker sat down again, sliding a mug of coffee in front of me. "You're in it."

My mouth fell open. "Here? I can't live here!" I looked from Cris to Rob and back again. They were obviously being assholes. "You're kidding, right? Nice try, guys."

Cris watched me closely for a minute before she spoke. "I'm serious, Joey. Why can't you live here?"

All words left my mind. She knew why I couldn't live here, why it wasn't even close to being an option.

Before I could form an answer, Rob added his two cents. "He's never here, L.K." He straightened in the chair, his face taking on a serious expression. "I know that's why you wanna say no, but he is never fuckin' here. And even if he was, you two are gonna have to face each other at some point and figure out what ever shit you two have goin' on. There's plenty of room for both of you. I'm lonely as fuck by myself. If you stay here, you'd be doing me a favor."

I stared at my coffee while I let his words settle, realizing that he had some really good points.

He was smiling at me when I looked up. "Definitely no bugs."

"Where would I sleep? I can't stay in Matty's room..."

"Cris wants to remodel the spare room for ya. When your kids come visit, you can have the living room, or they can bunk in Sam's room."

I glanced around the room, feeling my resolve slipping away. I loved this place and all its charm, plus it would be nice to have a home that I knew was safe as well as a roommate I trusted. I could see me spending hours on the deck, studying in the sun or just enjoying the view.

However, I had desperately wanted to prove to everyone, myself included, that I could move to a new place and start over and that I could do it myself. I needed to figure out if living here would be taking the easy way out or if it would be a blessing in disguise. "How much is rent?"

Rocker gave me one of his condescending looks, as if to say, "like I'm going to charge you rent." I stared him down, daring him to say the words and give me a reason to say no.

He tipped his head back, staring down his nose at me. "Five hundred a month—everything included but food."

We both knew that number was way too low. I didn't couldn't prove it, but I had no doubt that his mortgage was at least four times that. Add in all the other expenses, and five hundred dollars wasn't anything compared to what he paid out monthly. On the other side of the spectrum, I could pay that much and still have money for my bills and the kids. It would be nice not to have to be a starving college student again.

"Okay. Get me a lease, and I'll sign it. Roomie."

Rob only gave me a nod, but Cris clapped annoyingly in excitement. "Yay! I've been dying to do something to that room for years."

I rolled my eyes. Cris's style wasn't anything close to mine, and I dreaded what it might look like.

"We can go look at paint samples and new furniture today. It's a huge room once we take out one of the beds, and with the right colors, we can make it look even bigger. The bathroom needs to be completely redone too. Less frat boy and more relaxing day at the spa..." she trailed off, lost in her thoughts.

My eyes slid to Rocker. "I'll move my stuff up when we get back."

"Stay in Matty's room until after yours is finished." His tone left no room for arguments. "The guys will be gone before you know it, then you two can make all the changes you want."

"Guys? They're still here? I thought they were crashing last night because we got back so late."

Rocker shook his head. "No. They're here for the weekend."

"You could kick 'em out and make 'em go to the club," Cris suggested as she picked at her fingernails.

Rocker's eyes held fire as he stared at her. I had no idea what I'd missed, but it was clear her suggestion was not welcomed. Rob stood, grabbing his cup. "I'll get a rental agreement printed today." He reached into his back pocket and threw a piece of plastic down onto the table in front of Cris. In the meantime, make yourself at home. Try not to max out that card, Princess." He walked away without another word.

Cris held up a credit card and gave me her boxer-dropping smile, the one that I had no doubt could bring any man to his knees. "Let's go shopping!"

The day had been crazy. Cris dragged me from store to store, grabbing samples of paint, looking through special-order catalogs, and taking pictures of furniture. I was relieved when I realized she was going for a comfortable, coastal cottage chic—a style, she claimed, that was perfect for me. Even more surprising was that she had some great ideas. I was excited to start the renovation.

We got back in late afternoon but Cris didn't stay. She practically ran out of the apartment as soon as she dropped me off. I wasn't sure if she was avoiding Rocker or if she really had somewhere to be, but it seemed like a combination of both.

I changed into one of Matty's T-shirts and a pair of shorts, called my kids and talked until they had to go, then I flopped on the couch to study.

Rocker strolled in a while later, and after I signed the lease, he declared it a lazy night. He changed into basketball shorts and an old beat-up tee—which made him look completely out of place—ordered takeout and settled onto the other end of the sofa to watch a movie. It was relaxing and comfortable, and I felt as though we'd been friends for years.

I barely glanced up from my textbook when the elevator pinged in arrival.

"Don't you think you two should change?" Hawk asked as he strolled in. He leaned back against the counter with a sneer, surveying us as if the fact that we were lying around in comfy clothes was a crime. Next to him, in his jeans, gray T-shirt under a flannel, and leather Bastards jacket, we were seriously underdressed. "They're gonna be here any minute."

Rocker tensed. "I told you to move the fuckin' thing to the clubhouse or to Tiny's."

Hawk pushed away from the counter, eyes narrowed at the accusation. "You didn't tell me to move shit," he spit, "or I would have."

Rocker swore. "I told Dean to do it and to tell you."

Hawk looked pissed. "Yeah, well, he didn't. I just talked to Tiny, and almost everyone is on their way here." His eyes moved to mine. "It's too late to cancel now."

I got the message. Rocker was cancelling whatever it was because I was here. Trying not to feel like the outsider that I clearly was, I cleared my throat. "You don't have to change your plans just because I'm here. I can go study in my room. It's no big deal. Pretend I'm not here."

"That's not it." Rocker's eyes slid to me, agitation evident in his movements. "It's not your kinda party, L.K."

"What kind of party is it?"

They both answered at the same time.

"A welcome home party," Hawk informed me.

"A release party." Rob's eyes searched mine. "Tank got out early. Good behavior or some shit."

Oh. As in released from jail. A "welcome back to real life" party. I could only imagine why these two thought it wasn't my scene, and I didn't want to stick around to prove them wrong.

I stood, gathering the takeout containers, and offered them both a smile. "Let me grab a drink, then I'll hide in my room." I tapped Rob's knee on the way by. "You should go change."

The tension between the two was obvious, but they apparently weren't going to talk until I was out of earshot. I hurried around the counter, opened the fridge, and stacked our leftovers on a shelf before grabbing a bottle of water. I was closing the door when I felt someone come up behind me.

"Joes?" The voice was full of confusion and disbelief.

My heart hammered against my chest and I forgot to breathe. I turned slowly, taking in every detail I could. I hadn't seen him in weeks, and somehow, he was even more beautiful than he had been—edgier than I remembered. Even though I'd stared at his picture and memorized every line of his face, now that he was in front of me, I didn't feel like I'd ever get my fill.

Faded blue jeans clung to his waist and made his legs look longer than they were mixed with the tight T-shirt that showcased his muscles under his leather cut, he was every bit the badass biker I tended to forget he was. His dark hair was shorter than I'd seen it in years, styled in a mess that made me want to grab hold and let him take me for a ride. He hadn't shaved in a while, and a thick layer of hair ran along the sides of his square jawbone, down his chin, and under his bottom lip. Full black eyebrows wrinkled at me over electric blue eyes as he watched me study him.

"Jesus, you look good." I felt my eyes widen at my confession, barely resisting the urge to roll them when he chuckled. I seriously had no filter where this man was concerned.

"I was thinking the same thing about you." He gave me that signature smirk of his before biting his bottom lip as his eyes trailed over me. "What is it with you and my shirts?"

I swallowed, remembering the first time he'd caught me wearing one, and a warmth began to grow deep in my core.

He gave me a smile but couldn't mask the confusion etched on his face as he stepped closer. "What are you—"

The elevator ping interrupted his question, and the silence that had surrounded us was filled with loud voices and laughter. I glanced to my left, surprised that Rocker and Hawk were still there, watching us cautiously. I'd forgotten all about them as soon as I'd seen Matty. Turning back to him, I was about to explain that I needed to talk to him when my thoughts were interrupted.

"There you are! I waited, but you didn't come back!" The voice was soft and silky, and as the owner moved in next to Matty, hand resting on his arm, fake pout on her lips.

His eyes never left me, indecision crossing his features as I watched them together, and every insecurity I had flooded forward. My thoughts betrayed me as I wondered if she was the woman who would be keeping his bed warm because I was a stubborn idiot.

I couldn't meet his eyes, not when it felt like he could see straight through me. Instead I turned my attention to her. Of course, she would be a tall, beautiful blonde with legs that went on forever, totally rocking her mini skirt, black halter cut low to show her perfect breasts, and stilettos that I couldn't even begin to walk in. I suddenly felt extremely underdressed and was very aware of every single ounce of fat I'd gained over the winter.

She caught me staring and gave me a genuine smile that could light up any room. "Hi." She held out a hand. "I'm—"

"Well, fuck me!" Tiny shoved himself between Matty and Legs, staring at me as he dropped a giant keg on the counter and lifted me into his arms. "It's about fucking time you came back!"

I smiled at his excitement, hugging him back. At least Tiny was always happy to see me. He let me go but didn't release me completely, keeping an arm around me as he pulled me from the kitchen to the other side of the island, asking questions about my kids and life in general until Rocker interrupted him.

"L.K., this is Jessie." Rocker smiled warmly at the blonde without giving an explanation of who she was. "Jess, this is L.K." His eyes held mine. "My roommate."

I offered her a small smile then gave my full attention to Rob, hoping he'd rescue me from this awkward moment.

As if reading my thoughts, he moved his hand to the small of my back and leaned in close to my ear. "We should go change."

It was a simple, supportive gesture, and I sighed in relief; it meant the world to me that he was trying help. I could hear men talking behind me and the clink of bottles as they got ready for the party. I knew we needed to get downstairs before anyone else showed up.

I glanced at Matty, intending to say good-bye, but the look on his face made my breath catch. The easy-going smile he'd worn earlier was gone, and he was clenching his teeth so tightly that the muscles in his jaw were ticking as he glared at Rocker. I half-expected Rocker to move away; instead he held Matty's angry stare. For a few uncomfortable minutes, I watched the two of them have a silent conversation.

Finally, Hawk broke the silence. "Everyone will be here before w—"

"He's right," Matty interrupted, looking at me. "We'll have plenty of time to catch up in the morning, L.K." He practically spit out my new name.

Rob moved then, practically pushing me out of the kitchen and down the stairs before I could hear if anyone responded.

Matty's never here, my ass.

SEVEN

JO

"Where in the hell am I supposed to sleep now?" I seethed at Rocker once we were downstairs. "I can't stay in Sam's room either!"

There was no telling how thin the walls were; I knew firsthand just how loud Matty was during sex, and I would not spend the night listening to the two of them. No fucking way. I fought the tears, pissed at myself for insisting Matty move on and heartbroken that he had. I paced the hallway. I needed to leave; there was no way I could face them in the morning. The train didn't run this late, but maybe Teagan would drive down to get me. She wouldn't get here for hours though.

I turned back to Rob, desperation filling my voice. "Will you take me home?"

He gave me a sympathetic look but crossed his tree-trunk arms over his thick chest. "You are home, Joey. You signed the lease and wrote me a check earlier. Remember?"

"Well, tear them both up, and we'll forget all about this shit show!"

"No."

"No?" I was practically screaming, my voice getting louder with each word, but I didn't care if they heard me upstairs. "You"—I jammed a finger into his chest above his folded arms— "told me he was never here. *You* told me he'd never had anyone else in that room."

"Jesus, you two are frustratin' as hell. Don't you ever talk?"

"Yes!" I snapped, suddenly pissed off at the world. I had told myself that I would be fine without Matty, repeating it hundreds of times since we'd broken up. But the last few weeks had put a glimmer of hope back in my heart.

Even though I'd told him to move on, I had clung to that little sliver, believing that one day we'd find our way back to each other. I was such a moron. I didn't fight the tears anymore. Instead, I sank to the floor and let them flow.

Shaking his head, Rob leaned back and watched me cry it out. When the tears had dried, he offered me a hand and pulled me up. Without saying a word, he led me into his room. It was very similar to Matty's, with two large windows and a giant marble fireplace. Instead of hardwood though, my feet happily sank into a thick plush rug. The room was practically bare: two rocking chairs sat by the windows and one bedside table flanked the giant bed. It was immaculate—no clothes on the chairs or glasses on the table— and I wondered if Rob was a neat freak. My favorite thing about this room though was that once the door shut, every noise from the rest of the house vanished.

He took one look at my tear-stained face and rolled his eyes. "I have never seen two people jump to conclusions like the two of you." Shaking his head, he gave me an annoyed look. "L.K., you really need to talk to Matt and figure this shit out."

Rob was right of course, and I knew that Matty and I would have to talk in the morning. I didn't want my new roommate to be angry with me on our first night though, so I changed the subject. "I'm sorry you're missing your party."

"I'm not. It's not my party, and I told Dean to move it because I'm fuckin' beat. It'll go half the fuckin' night. I'm too old for that shit."

"Tank won't be upset?

"Nah. I saw him today. He gets it." He smirked as if he was trying not to laugh at a private joke. "He won't be there long anyway. As soon as he sees his ol' lady, he'll forget the rest of us and go make up for lost time."

I didn't know a thing about Tank or why he'd been in jail. That was that line, the one that Matty had drawn a long time ago to separate me from this part of his life. The idea made me sad. "Why was he in jail?"

Deep blue eyes met mine. "Prison, Joey. He was in prison." I didn't know there was a difference, and Rob must have seen the confusion on my face. "Prison is jail for big boys." He smirked. "How can I explain it?" He paused, frowning. "You get bagged doing somethin' stupid, like driving drunk, and the cops throw you in jail until you can get bailed out or until you go to trial. Prison is serious shit. Think maximum security, convicted killers that would like nothin' more than to shank you in your sleep or beat you until you are bloody if you piss 'em off or just 'cause they don't like the color of your skin, and guards that don't protect you unless they have a monetary reason to do so. Jail's a fuckin' joke, L.K. Release from prison is somethin' to celebrate."

"Oh. Have you ever...," I looked away, swallowing. "I mean, you sound like you know the difference firsthand."

"Are you askin' me if I'm a convicted felon?"

I nodded, not really sure I wanted the answer.

"I am. I've been to both, lived inside both for longer than I woulda liked, and have no doubt I'll see the inside of both again."

My mind went into overdrive. I couldn't imagine the Rocker I knew doing anything that would land him in prison. I debated with myself for all of two seconds before I asked, "What did you do? To get sent to prison."

He didn't blink. Didn't hesitate. "Felony assault. It would have been voluntary manslaughter, because I meant to kill the prick, but the DA pled me down."

Meant to kill him. Rocker had murdered someone. My mouth went dry.

"Matty didn't tell you any of this?"

I shook my head.

Rob shifted, eyes surveying me wearily. It was clear he wasn't sure if he should tell me more or not. "How much do you know about the Bastards?"

"Not much." I cleared my throat. "I didn't even know Matty was part of anything like that until I came down that weekend last July. Ian explained the backs of the jackets. He said you protect the innocent, but that's all he'd say."

He sighed, a long painful sound, and rubbed his forehead. When he met my eyes again, an internal struggle was clear on his face. "Matty..."

A loud banging on the door cut him off. I turned, amazed to see the wood shake on the hinges.

"Speak of the devil," Rocker said, his voice full of humor, "and he shall appear."

EIGHT

MATTY

The voices on the other side of the door quieted instantly, but no one opened the door. I pounded my fist against the thick wood again, sounding like a mad man, but I didn't give a flying fuck. I'd checked my room first, just to make sure, but I'd known she wouldn't be there.

I could barely breathe as I walked to Rocker's door, half tempted to just burst in. If I found it locked though, I'd lose my shit and kick the fucking thing down. And I'd end up beating my best friend to an inch within his life.

It was better for me to just knock. Telling myself there was a perfectly logical explanation for Jo being in Rocker's room, I took a deep breath. The last twenty minutes filtered through my mind while I waited for someone to answer my knock.

I clenched my fists as I watched them rush downstairs, using every ounce of self-restraint I had not to follow them. Jo was the last person I'd expected to see, and by the look on her face, she hadn't planned on seeing me either. I stood there like a fucking idiot while she smiled at him the way she used to look at me. I didn't know why she was there or why Rob was in such a hurry to get her downstairs, but I had a few ideas.

I'd glared at Hawk, clenching my teeth so I didn't say something I'd regret. He met my stare, only raising an eyebrow in challenge. I wanted to demand he tell me what he knew, but Jessie picked that moment to lean on the island next to me.

"That didn't go quite like I'd pictured." Her eyes slid from me to Hawk, oblivious to the tension, and sighed. "I'm missing something, right? Is L.K. his girlfriend and he's trying to spare my feelings by saying she's his roommate? I mean, none of my roommates ever looked at me like that." She shook her head, dejected. "Maybe I shouldn't have come."

I laid a hand on the counter, fighting my anger. If she'd picked up on it too, then I wasn't imagining it. The only thing keeping me from running down the stairs and beating Rocker into oblivion was the fact that Tank would be here soon.

"Tonight is about your brother. I thought you wanted to be here for him, not Rocker." Hawk pointed out.

"I do." She laughed bitterly. *"But you know damn well I didn't dress like this for Tank."* She rolled her eyes as she gestured at her barely outfit. *"You can tell me, you know. I'm a big girl."* She chewed on her bottom lip, waiting for one of to respond. When neither did, she tried again. *"It's not like I'm just some piece of ass that comes to these things hoping to get one of you to notice me. I'm as much of a Bastard as either of you."*

No one could argue with that. She might not ride with us or wear the jacket, but Jessie was one of us. She had been since the beginning.

"I know who he is and don't expect more than he's able to give." She narrowed her eyes at the prospects who were setting up a makeshift bar, but I knew it wasn't them that had upset her. *"He's been so distant lately, pulling away again."* For a fleeting moment her face twisted in pain. *"I get it. She's very distracting."*

Hawk shifted, clearly uncomfortable with the topic, and he looked everywhere but at me. Finally, he shook his head. *"You're readin' way too much into it. They're just friends. L.K. needed a place to stay. There's room here. Nothing else."*

"Ahh." Jess nodded as a light bulb went off in her mind. *She's one of his rescues. Do you know what she's running from?"*

Hawk narrowed his eyes at me, crossed his arms and waited for me to answer. I had nothing to offer because the answer was me. Jo was running from me.

We'd had that fucking fight. A stupid bullshit fight. I never called her back, not even after she apologized, because I was still pissed. I half expected her to run, because that was who she was. But I hadn't expected her to run straight to Rob. And he was the last fucking person on earth I thought would catch her.

Realizing I was going to stay quiet, Hawk finally answered. *"Nothin' that I know of. She's friends with Cris and goes to BC. Seriously, Barbie, they're just roommates."*

Jess snorted. *"Of course, she would be linked to Cris somehow. I wonder how the princess feels about the way Rocker looks at L.K. and how much longer they'll stay buddies when she realizes there's a fox in her cock-house."*

It was no secret that Jess and my sister hated each other, and under normal circumstances, I would have defended Cris. But I was far too distracted. *"BC? She's going to grad school?"*

Hawk nodded.

No fucking way. *She'd done it. I was so damn proud of Jo. We'd talked about her going back to school, but she was so sure she'd never get in. BC had a tough grad program, and admission was wicked selective. I wondered why she hadn't told me. Big news like that, I would have shouted it from the rooftops. Then a nasty thought hit. She'd known but kept me in the dark.* "When did she move in?"

Hawk glanced over his shoulder. He walked to the table, grabbed a bottle of Jack, and poured three shots before coming back to the island. He handed one to Jessie, slid one to me, and raised the third in silent salute. "Last night." He grimaced and waited for me to swallow mine before finishing. "We brought her home with us last night."

My mind reeled. Jo had been at Hooligan's last night—she'd asked me to meet her there. I couldn't because I'd been on my way back from Pine Knot, Kentucky. The Bastards had wanted to greet Tank in style, so I took vacation time and a bunch of us rode down on Wednesday to bring him home from McCreary Penitentiary.

I'd had nothing to do for thousands of miles but replay my last conversation with Jo. She wanted answers, so many more than I could give; I wasn't ready to let her walk away forever yet, but I would do anything to keep my secrets a little while longer. I had planned to call her, to try to figure out the shit that was dragging us down, but I couldn't just pull out a cell phone and talk while on the back of a bike. When we stopped for the night, there was no privacy to have the kind of talk we needed to have.

They must have found her at Fred's. I slammed the glass down, startling Jess. *Memories of the last time I was there with Jo assaulted me.*

Jo had a low tolerance and was a messy drunk. I should be relieved that it was Rob who found her like that and not some stranger, especially since she had been there because of me. Instead, all I could imagine was her coming onto him the way she had me. She'd torn off her clothes and demanded I sleep with her. She was so sexy that I couldn't have said no if I'd wanted to.

Hawk tipped the bottle into my glass, filling it again while Jess watched us, scowling in confusion. *I needed to calm down and get a fucking grip.* I swallowed the shot in one gulp, feeling it burn. A ping announced the elevator's arrival, and suddenly the room was filled with a roar of voices.

All I could think about was my girl and my best friend. Were the two of them downstairs screwing right now? Was she showing him how wild and crazy she was? Was he enjoying taking what was mine?

If he had touched her, I'd kill him. Best friend or not, I would murder him with my bare hands. The two of us had scuffled a few times over the years, and each time it'd been an even fight. But this time, he didn't stand a chance. I turned, fists clenched, and stomped across the room and down the stairs, only one thought in my mind.

If he had touched Joes, I would decimate him.

NINE

MATTY

Rocker's face was the first thing I saw as he pulled open the door and leaned onto the frame, blocking my view of the room.

"Hey." His voice an eerie calm, "Everything okay?"

My entire body was on alert, as if recognizing a threat, and my fists ached to knock that smug look off his face. Rocker never missed a thing; I knew he saw my reaction. He didn't take the bait though, and instead, scratched his head lazily. The movement gave me just enough of a view to see Joes, leaning against the end of the bed, fully clothed.

The sight made me relax as I met her eyes. "It is now. What are you doing?" I sounded like a prick, but I couldn't help it.

Her eyes narrowed slightly at my tone. When she inhaled sharply, I knew I was in for one of her tongue lashings. Without waiting for an invitation, I shoved past Rob. She didn't move, and as I reached her, my arms circled around her, yanking her into me, as I claimed that sassy mouth of hers.

It wasn't one of the gentle, sweet kisses she loved; it was rough and full of emotion, and after a few seconds, I felt her lose control as she tangled her hands in my hair and moaned into me. There wasn't anything sexier than her reactions to me. I pulled away, my teeth tugging at her bottom lip.

Just having her that close to me made all my blood flow south. Jesus, I wanted her. Instead of tossing her onto the bed and proving to her just how much I missed her, I ran my hands down her arms and twined my fingers with hers.

"Wanna go get coffee?"

She arched a perfectly groomed eyebrow then glanced at her wrinkled clothes and bare feet. "Can't we have coffee here?"

I shook my head. "There're a lot of people here, and we need to talk."

Rocker cleared his throat, reminding us that we definitely weren't alone yet. "No one will bother you in here."

I glowered at him. "I don't fuckin' think so."

I wanted to get her as far away from him as I could. Turning back to Joes, I gave her the full once-over, taking in her bare arms

271

and legs. I thought about all the places in the apartment that we could go, and only one seemed feasible. She wasn't dressed for it, but if I didn't take the chance now, I might not get another.

I let go of her hands, grabbed her waist, and in one fluid movement, I threw her over my shoulder. She didn't fight me as I had assumed she would, and I couldn't resist slapping her perfect round ass, making her yelp. I spun, carrying her out of the room.

As we made it to the end of the hall and turned up the stairs, I heard the prick laughing.

Unfortunately, there were people everywhere already. Bastards and half-dressed women spilled into the stairway and were scattered throughout the living room. A few spoke to me, but I only grunted responses when absolutely necessary. If anyone was surprised by the sight of me carrying a woman around, no one said a word. Then again, they'd been to these parties before and had seen much worse.

I stopped by a couch long enough to grab a blanket—Jo would need one. After prying open the giant window with one hand, I stepped out into the night air and eased Joe to her feet. She looked around the fire escape, obviously surprised. We kept a wooden bench and table out here so people could take smoke breaks if they were on this side of the house, and sometimes I came out here to clear my head. I closed the window, muffling the music and noise from the party.

The temperature was warm for April, but there was a nip in the air, and I shrugged off my jacket and held it out to her just as a breeze blew across us. "Put this on."

She giggled slightly as she slipped it on and held up the sleeves; it dwarfed her, reminding me how fucking tiny she was. She walked to the bench, pulling her knees up to her chest as she sat. I couldn't do anything but stare.

I opened the blanket and covered her before dropping down beside her. "It feels like it's been forever since I've seen you."

She nodded. "It has been."

I slipped an arm around her shoulders, pulling her close. When she was with me, sitting like this, everything else faded away. When it was just Joes and me, it was perfect.

I stared at the skyline, searching for the right words to say, while trying to figure out how we had gotten so screwed up. Only a few short months ago we'd been inseparable, together whenever we could find the time. So much had changed since then, and I missed her more than words could explain. I brushed a few flyaway strands of bright pink hair behind her ear. "This is new."

She gave me a tight smile. "Yep. I needed a change, something that wasn't..."

"Expected." I finished for her, knowing exactly what she'd been about to say. "Something different, something you never would have done before, right?" She didn't have to answer, because I knew that was why she'd done it. "You always said you wanted pink and blue hair." I chuckled, remembering all the times she'd told me she was going to shave her head and dye it blue. "If I'd known it would look so fucking hot, I would've begged you to dye it months ago."

"Thanks." She smiled in the slow sexy way I adored making my dick harden in response. "I'm dying it back to mundane brown tomorrow."

"Why?"

"Because I'm too old to pull it off. I need to find a part-time job and I'm pretty sure this won't help. And Cris hates it."

Her reasons surprised me. "You're not too old—in fact, I think you rock it better than someone half your age could. It's sexy as fuck. Any job where you can't have your hair the color you want isn't worth your time or energy. As for Cris, fuck her. Didn't she give you pink hair extensions last year?"

"I forgot about that!" She rolled her eyes.

"Her opinion doesn't matter either. It isn't like you're gonna see her all the time." I pointed out.

The smile disappeared and she sighed, turning her head away from me. The way her hands were fidgeting told me she had something to say, and whatever it was, she was worried.

"I will see her all the time because I live here now. I quit my job, enrolled in a grad program, and Rocker offered me the extra room so I could save on rent." Her words came out in a hurried whisper, and she glanced at me, wringing her hands. "I tried to tell you a few weeks ago, but I just didn't know how."

She looked terrified, and I reached for her, wanting to do anything to take that fear away. "I know, Joes."

"Wait." She narrowed her eyes, pulling back from my touch. "What? How'd you know?"

I smirked at her tone. She was like a tidal wave of emotion—from worried to pissed in point five seconds flat. "I have my sources."

"And you're not angry?" Her cold tone sent off warning bells.

I needed to figure out a way to backtrack. I didn't answer right away; I wanted to be honest, but I didn't want her to leave. "I'm irritated that you didn't tell me. I mean, fuck, we've been talking for weeks and there were plenty of times you could have. So yeah, I'm pissed that you didn't."

She watched me, eyes wary, and I rushed to finish. "But I'm so fucking proud of you for getting accepted into BC. That's a big fucking deal with some seriously tough competition. Good job, kid!" In that instant, I realized I would never get enough of her. I pulled on a few pieces of blue hair, vocalizing my thoughts. "If I come down on the weekends I don't have Sam, we'll get to do more than text. I fuckin' miss you."

Her entire body tensed, and she jerked back from me. She stared at me for a few seconds as if struggling to understand my words. Then she practically ran to the edge of the porch, gripped the railing hard, and took deep breaths.

"You are so fucking unbelievable!" she snapped.

It was my turn to glare. She'd been completely dishonest with me for god knows how long, then I found her here, with Rob. She wasn't turning this around on me. I leaned back, hands rubbing my thighs, trying to keep my temper in check.

"Yeah." I'd conveniently forgotten this part of her—the one that made me want to throttle her and kiss her senseless at the same time. "Sometimes I tell myself that there's no way in hell you are really as frustrating as I remember, that I must have made it up." I forced a laugh. "Good to know I didn't."

As her eyes narrowed even more and she stood a little taller, I knew I was in for a fight. About fucking time.

"Oh, I'm frustrating? You know what pisses me off? The fact that you are suddenly fine with the idea of me living not only in Boston but in your apartment, even though just a few months ago, you didn't want me within a hundred-mile radius and wouldn't even let me come with you."

"Are fucking serious right now?"

She talked over me. "So let me get this straight. It's okay for me to be here because I'm not your girlfriend, but when I was, it wasn't safe enough for me?"

We stared at each other for a few minutes until I finally shook my head. "Oh, is it my turn to talk now?" The look she gave me left no doubt that she would have slapped me if I was close enough, and I almost couldn't contain my laugh. "Why are you really mad right now? Is it 'cause you expected me to be pissed over something stupid and I'm not? Or is it something else entirely? Like maybe the fact that you're hiding shit from me and want to turn it around? I'm having a hard time figuring it out."

I'd never seen her look so frustrated, and I almost felt I should have been easier on her. Almost.

"Who the fuck is Jessie, Matt? Does she know you're out here with me?"

Jesus, she was all over the fucking map tonight—the very definition of a hot mess. But she was my hot mess, and I'd rather have her fighting with me than shutting me out. And at least it seemed as though we were getting closer to the real issue.

"Jealous, sweetheart?" I sneered, making her growl in exasperation. "Don't worry, she's Rob's girl, not mine."

I realized after I said it that I was waiting for a reaction, half expecting her to show jealousy over the woman who shared Rocker's bed. When the only thing that showed on her face was relief, I felt like an ass. But I was a thankful ass.

I loved the passion she had when we fought, but I needed to fix us so I could see the other side of that passion. "Just so you know, I never had a problem with you being *here*, Joes. In fact, if I remember correctly, we had one hell of a weekend in this apartment just a few months ago. Boston was never the fucking issue. Yeah, I told you I wanted you stay away, but I never meant I didn't want you here. It was me." I slapped my chest, hoping she'd understand. "You weren't safe with me!"

You're still not safe with me! The thought made me sick, and I forced it out of my mind.

I walked toward her, never taking my eyes off hers, even though I was sure she could see right through me. "Will was out for blood as long as I was in the picture. I barely had a handle on my own shit and wasn't about to drag you down with me. I told you that I'd do anything to protect you, and I fucking meant it. I still do. Don't think, not for one fucking second, that I would let you stay here if it wasn't safe."

"Where I live is none of your business, Matty." She tipped her head back to see me, her voice almost sad. "We're just friends, remember?"

I stepped into her, completely invading her space, grabbed handfuls of hair, and tipped her head even farther back so I could lean my forehead against hers. "We've never been just friends, Joes," I growled.

The lust in her eyes made me want to strip off her clothes and take her right there, not caring who saw. Instead, she pushed me away. "Stop it, Matty!"

I stepped back letting her think she was in control.

"Fine, we're not just friends. But I'm not your girlfriend, remember? You don't have to protect me anymore."

I cupped her cheek. "Yeah, I do. I'll protect you until the day I die—from everything." *Including me.* Needing close I wrapped one arm around her back, yanked her into me, and leaned down to kiss her forehead. "You are mine, even if you don't realize it. I'm not moving on, no matter how much you push. I'll be here when you're ready."

She didn't say a word as she melted into me, letting me hold her as we stared at the city. This was where she belonged—in my arms, in my hometown, and sooner than later, in my bed. I didn't know how long I'd have with her, especially if she was living here, but I was determined to enjoy every single second.

I never knew when my past would come back to haunt me, but at least in Maine, I had kept it at bay. It was only a matter of time before someone here let something slip and Joes left me for good. I couldn't explain, not even to myself, why I loved this woman so fucking much, but she was my entire world. I hadn't been strong enough to let her walk away last time and knew it would be a fight next time too.

All I could do was pray it didn't kill me.

TEN

JO

The window slid open with a noisy squeal, but Matty didn't move. When the intruder cleared his throat, Matt only gripped me tighter, either ignoring the interruption or not caring. As long as I got to stand right there and have him hold me for a few minutes longer, I didn't care.

I closed my eyes, focusing on the heartbeat under my ear and the fingers massaging my scalp. He leaned down and gave my temple another lingering kiss. It was such a tender gesture, and nothing was clearer to me in that moment than the fact that I was completely in love with Matthew Murphy and would walk through fire for him.

I tipped my head back quickly, catching his lips before he could step away. He groaned into my mouth, sliding his hands down to hold my face still. A calloused thumb drew circles on my cheek as he deepened the kiss. I balled his shirt in my hands, hoping he would understand that I wanted more.

The throat cleared again, but this time he spoke. "Mateo, we need you."

Matty broke away, sliding his nose up along the side of mine. Staring into my eyes, he gave me a wink and whispered, "Two seconds, babe." He straightened, letting go of me, and turned to face the man trespassing on our very awesome, but private, moment. "What the fuck do you want, Prospect?"

I cringed. His voice was full of irritation and extremely intimidating. This was a Matty who was quite scary.

The young man paled a little under Matt's angry glare. "Sorry to interrupt, but I was sent to find you."

"Why?" Matty barked.

The kid swallowed and looked at me as if I was the unwelcome visitor.

"Oh, for Christ's sake! She's with me. Spill it," he growled.

"Wiz just got word there's about to be a BOLO issued. Rocker wants everyone at the clubhouse. Now." His voice broke.

Matty swore under his breath and glanced over his shoulder at me. "Tell them to give me twenty minutes."

277

He jerked his head toward the window once, dismissing the young man, and turned back to me. Stress was etched on his features, and he looked as though he was struggling to figure out what to say. I didn't know which of his friends was in trouble or what was going on, but I did know that whatever it was, it was important. We'd been sharing a great moment and Matty would never leave for anything trivial. When the muscle in his jaw ticked, I knew I had to lighten the mood.

"'Cause twenty minutes is all it'll take, right?" I stepped toward him with a mischievous smile on my lips, repeating the words he'd said to me after our first night together.

He didn't react for a second, confusion showing in his eyes as he looked at me. As realization dawned, his lips quirked with laughter. "Oh, babe, you do inflate my ego. Don't kid yourself though. It's been so long, I won't even need five."

"Really?" I asked in mock horror. "I thought guys were supposed to last longer after a dry spell?"

"Dry spell?" He scoffed. "Nah, two days is a damn dry spell. The last few months, I've been in a sexual purgatory."

I giggled, stepping into his open arms. "That's just depressing."

He nodded. "No worries, kid." He leaned down, whispering into my ear, "I'll make sure that five minutes is worth the fuckin' wait." His breath was hot on my neck, sending tingles down my spine and making me shiver. Mistaking it, he rubbed my upper arms. "You're cold. Let's get you inside."

I didn't argue as he pulled me in the window, through the living room, then down the stairs. The party, while apparently still going, seemed a lot less crowded than it had been just a few minutes before, and there weren't any men in sight. I couldn't help the bitchy smile I sent toward a few of them when they gave the two of us double takes or sent suggestive smiles toward Matty.

I wanted to shout, "That's right! He's taken, girls. Move along!"

Once we were shut into his room, I pulled his jacket off my shoulders and held it out to him, trying to find something to say. Butterflies invaded my stomach, and I wasn't sure if I was nervous because I was alone with him or if it was because he was leaving and I didn't know why. I wanted to ask for details, but I worried his answer would ease my nerves.

"Hey." His voice was soft. "I've gotta take care of this, and then I'll be back. It's club business—nothin' to worry about. I promise." He tucked hair behind my ear. "I don't know how long I'll be, but can I come join you when I get back? We don't have to..." He cleared his throat. "I mean, I just want to be with you. I don't expect you to—"

"Rescue you from sexual purgatory?" I asked, amused at how flustered he was. Tipping my head to the side, I ran my hands up under his jacket. His stomach muscles tensed beneath my fingers. "I better be the only person you plan on ending your dry spell with." I chuckled at his uncomfortable expression. "I'll be here when you get back, Matty, keeping the bed warm."

He gave me a quick peck on the lips, then a longer kiss on my forehead. Backing up a step, he grabbed my chin. "I'll be back as soon as I can. And tomorrow, we'll talk. Yeah?"

"Yeah."

He lifted his chin toward the bed. "Go warm my bed, woman."

He was gone before I could come up with a witty reply. I didn't know where the clubhouse was, so I wasn't sure how far Matty had to go, but I wanted to be ready when he got back—for whatever our night had in store. After locking the door, I headed into the bathroom. I was almost through with my shower before I realized I was still smiling.

"Good morning, sunshine."

I opened my eyes to find Cris sitting in the overstuffed chair next to the bed. I slid an arm over the space behind me, hoping to meet warm flesh, but I was disappointed to feel only cold sheets. I'd waited up until I could no longer keep my eyes open, but apparently Matty had never come back.

Before I could greet her, Cris leaned forward, bracing her elbows on her knees, and pointed toward a Dunkin' Donuts cup on my nightstand. I sat up, swept my hair out of my face, and reached for the Styrofoam cup. After a couple of sips, I smiled.

"Morning."

"Last night was quite the rager, huh? I won't even tell you how many people I had to climb over to find that."

I followed her glance to my phone next to where the coffee cup had been. I'd completely forgotten it last night. I scrolled through my missed calls, relieved that the only ones were from Matty and Cris.

"He couldn't reach you, so he called me," Cris volunteered. "He'll call you later to explain."

"Is everything okay? He was supposed to come home and—"

"He's fine. Whatever they're doing took longer than he thought." She arched an eyebrow. "It's about fucking time you two ended your little spat. I was getting worried." She smirked. "Tell me everything."

I smiled. "There isn't much to tell really." My mind drifted back to seeing him yesterday, and within seconds, the tall beautiful blonde entered my thoughts. "Cris, who is Jessie?"

Irritation darkened her face while her eyes flared in anger. "Biker Barbie was here last night?" The way she ground out the words had me wishing I'd never asked. "That explains why I wasn't invited. I wondered why they weren't havin' it at the clubhouse, but I figured they were tryin' to keep it small to not overwhelm Tank. Shit! I knew I shoulda blown off my date and come anyway!"

"Biker Barbie?" I only had a first impression to go on, but the name actually seemed perfect. I stifled my laugh as soon as I saw the disgusted look on her face.

"Fucking bitch." Cris spat out. "Was she glued to Rocker all night?"

"No, he barely spoke to her."

She spiked her eyebrows, silently asking me to continue.

"He was with me." I shrugged as if it was no big deal and sipped my coffee. When she didn't speak, I explained exactly what had happened the night before.

Her amusement took me by surprise. "I bet Matt loved that! Rocker should be grateful they aren't kids anymore. A younger Mateo wouldn't have waited for an explanation; he'd have just kicked his ass."

"It's not like that!" I snapped. "Rob was just being nice."

"You and Rocker know it's not like that. I know it isn't like that. But my brother?" She shook her head. "Matty doesn't play well with others, Joey. He never has. He only ever shared with me when he absolutely had to, and never, ever let me play with his favorite toys. In this case, you are his favorite toy, and if someone

280

else tried to play with you..." She shrieked in surprise and caught the pillow I threw at her.

"Are you calling me his plaything?" I demanded angrily.

She snorted. "Ugh, yeah." I turned to grab another pillow, and she rushed on. "When we were little, he had this stuffed dog that went everywhere with him. He loved that thing more than anything. Copper scared away the ghosts and rode in the basket on his bike. He'd play with other toys, but Copper was always his favorite. I got mad at him one day and hid Copper. Matt couldn't sleep and he refused to eat. All he did was mope around until my parents panicked and bought a new one. But it wasn't the same, and he never got attached. He needed Copper to be happy."

The moment turned serious very quickly. I swallowed as her words sank in.

"You're more than his plaything, Joey. You're his Copper." She stood, looking uncomfortable as though she'd said too much. "Get dressed, and we'll go get breakfast."

The restaurant was beautiful, with crystal on the tables and a breathtaking view of the Charles River. I scanned the menu, trying not to laugh at the way the waiter hovered over Cris. His face fell when she ordered and handed the folder back to him without a glance in his direction.

"So how was your date last night?" I asked as soon as we were alone.

She sipped her mimosa, shrugging. "It was okay." At my concerned look, she continued. "Caleb is great, really. He's very sweet, very proper. He's every girl's dream—tall, dark, and handsome with the most adorable dimples. He works out constantly, he's never even lived with a woman, and he's a lawyer."

"You're right. That sounds truly awful." I deadpanned.

"I only went as a favor for a friend." She looked out the window, lost in her thoughts. "He's not my type."

"You mean he isn't moody, covered in tattoos, and often mistaken for the Hulk."

Blue eyes met mine quickly, but her face remained blank. I chuckled at her lack of a response. She was only that quiet when she was hiding something.

I poked the bear. "So, Rocker and Jessie, huh?"

I could practically see the flames leaping in her eyes. "Barbie's a Brat, a club whor—" She cut herself off mid word and cleared her throat before she glanced around the room full of people in their Sunday best. Sitting back, she hid her shaking hands under the table. For a moment, she worked her jaw. "Barbie's a club girl, working her way through the guys until someone claims her. She holds on to one until the next best thing is single. She's had her sights on Rocker for years, since we were kids. I never thought he was dumb enough to go for it. Over the last few months, he's done nothing but prove me wrong and disappoint me."

"I'm sorry." Cris was a strong woman with a chip on her shoulder. I'd seen many different sides to her, but this sadness was not one I was used to. Rocker had hurt her. I didn't want to think about Matty moving on, and I knew I'd never be able to see it every day. I didn't know how Cris was coping. Slowly, the rest of what she said sank in. "She and Matty weren't a thing, right?"

Cris snorted as if my question was the most absurd thing she'd ever heard. "That's not even a no. It's a hell, no!"

I let out the breath I hadn't even realized I was holding.

"He wouldn't have looked twice at her," she scoffed. "Not only is she Tank's sister, God knows who's been there already."

I hoped she was right. I hated the idea of having to face other women who knew him like I did. Something told me that as long as I lived down here though, I'd have to deal with a lot of them.

Matty called when we were halfway through our meal, and I hurried out into the hall, excited to talk to him.

"Hey, beautiful." I smiled at his greeting. "I'm sorry that I didn't get to come back last night."

"It's okay. Cris told me you couldn't get away." Someone spoke to him in the background, but I couldn't understand the words; the roar of motorcycles coming to life was almost deafening. "Is everything okay?"

"Fuck, I thought I had more time. I'm not gonna make it back today, Joes." He practically yelled in my ear. "I'll explain everything when I see you, okay? I'll call you tonight."

I didn't know what to say. Questions swirled through my mind.

"Babe? I gotta go, but I'm not getting off this phone 'til you tell me we're okay."

"I miss you."

"Fuck. Not as much as I miss you."

I grinned at the wall. "We're fine. Ride safe, Matty.

ELEVEN

JO

Disappointment settled in after the call, and even though I tried to force it away, I got cranky. Blaming it on lack of sleep, I convinced Cris to let me take a rain check on her plans for the day. She dropped me off at the apartment before noon, lending me her key fob until Rob could order one for me. I was relieved that everyone had cleared out and I had the place to myself.

Sinking onto the couch, I attempted to read the chapter I had due tomorrow. After a few hours, I gave up and settled on flipping through channels on the TV. It was better than staring at the phone and waiting for Matty to call.

The quiet of the house was unnerving. When the elevator arrived, I was off the couch in an instant, excited to not be alone. A smiling Jessie was not at all what I'd expected. Jeans, a baggy T-shirt, and sneakers made her almost unrecognizable as the same woman from last night.

She lifted up a paper grocery bag. "I brought food."

"Oh." I hadn't even thought about the fact that we didn't have anything here. I could have just ordered delivery, but after eating in restaurants and having takeout for the last few days, a homemade meal sounded heavenly. "Thanks."

She started pulling out ingredients, filling the counter.

"Anything I can do to help?"

Her smile was kind as she set a pot of water on to boil then pulled out a skillet. "Nope. Cooking is how I unwind after a long day." She popped open a bottle of beer and took a long sip. "I'd love some company though."

I pulled out a stool and sat, watching her, not sure what to say. She moved around the kitchen with ease, proving that she'd been there many times and knew it a hell of a lot better than I did. I wondered if she was here to cook for me or my roommate.

"Rocker isn't here," I said.

She looked up, surprised. Her eyes moved over my face. "I know. He called and asked me to come by. He was worried about you being alone all day. I thought it'd be a good chance to get to know each other."

I sat up a little straighter, suddenly worried. Was Matt the man she planned on going after next? My voice was cold when I asked, "Assessing the competition?"

She stared at me for a moment then burst out laughing. "If you had asked me that last night, I'd have said yes. I didn't know what to think about a woman I'd never heard of suddenly not only moving in but also disappearing from the party. But today Rob called me at the same time Mateo called his ol' lady. I'm gonna wager that was you on the other end of the phone, L.K. Or should I call you Joey?"

"Jo is fine."

She dumped a box of rigatoni into the boiling water and stirred it. "You're different than I thought you'd be. I'm not saying that's a bad thing, I'm just surprised. I thought he'd end up someone like..." She paused, lost in thought. "Well, something different. He needs a woman who will keep him on his toes. I've heard the stories and have no doubt you can do it. And more." She met my eyes. "You and me? We're gonna be great friends."

I paid close attention, trying to see any evidence that she wasn't being genuinely nice. There wasn't any. This woman was completely sincere. "Stories, huh? Should I be worried?"

She shook her head, obviously not willing to share what she had heard.

I picked at the counter in front of me. "I'm not his old lady. I'm not sure what we are, but we definitely aren't married."

Her mouth fell open as she stared at me, her eyes wide, her shock evident. I wasn't sure what I had said that would cause that reaction. I sat up uncomfortable.

She recovered quickly, turning back to the stove. "Dean told me how civilian you were and that you didn't know a thing about us, but I just assumed, since it was Dean, that info was a bit exaggerated." She took out a package of hamburger and broke it into the skillet. "It doesn't matter how you label it. No matter how you look at it, that man is head over heels in love with you."

My heart fluttered a little faster. "I hope so, 'cause I'm crazy about him too." I sighed. "He and I seem to be worlds apart right now. I can't guarantee what tomorrow will bring." She'd hit the nail right on the head when she said I didn't know a thing about them. Once again, I felt like an outsider looking in.

"Jo," she said sympathetically, as if she could read my thoughts, "do you know why they call him Mateo?"

I shook my head.

"It means 'God's gift'. As in God's gift to women. They've been calling him that for as long as I can remember—at least eighteen years. He used to be horrible—a different lay every night."

I stiffened. If she was trying to help, she was failing. I remembered that man all too well.

"That all changed about ten years ago. He suddenly wasn't interested in the club girls. He'd talk to everyone, act like the Mateo we all knew, but it was obvious that he was taken. Everyone knew he was unobtainable, and it just turned 'em on even more. He became the ultimate challenge—who could get his attention away from this mystery girl he was wrapped up in?"

Seriously not helping. The burger sizzled as it fried, and she took turns scrambling it and swirling a spoon around the pasta. I half wanted her to stop talking, half hoped she had a point to this story.

"Then he came back one weekend with a wedding ring. There were plenty of broken hearts and even more shattered dreams. After a few months though, we realized he wasn't bringing the wife around. She was a separate life for him. That meant he was still fair game."

It was my turn to be shocked. "What? He was married. How does that make him an option?"

The look she gave me made me immediately want to eat my words. Of course she would know that I'd slept with Matty while I was still married. I was a judgmental asshole.

"Yeah." I held a hand to my chest. "Kettle, meet Pot."

She laughed again, grinning. Becky, Matty's ex-wife, was amazing, and I prayed Jessie wasn't going to tell me that he'd cheated. As hypocritical as it would be, I didn't know how I'd feel about him if he'd done that to sweet Bex.

"The Bastards don't typically do it, but it isn't unheard of for a man to have a wife outside the club as well as an ol' lady inside the club. Two different women for two different lives. He had no interest. A few years later, when the ring disappeared, the girls got excited, thinking the old Mateo was back and they'd have a shot." She carried the pot to the sink and drained it.

"What none of us realized was that it was never his wife that had stolen him away. It was you." Adding pasta sauce and the meat to the pot, she mixed it all together. "You may not realize you're his ol' lady. Hell, he might not have even said the words yet. But I can promise you, there isn't a single man in this club who doesn't know you're his. He's claimed you. You're off limits. Soon, the women will know too."

After opening one of the cupboards, she pulled out two pasta bowls and came back to the stove to fill them. "You're not my competition, Jo. Even if I wanted Matty, which I don't, I couldn't begin to compare to you in his eyes." She grabbed forks, came around the island, and sat with me. "You're one lucky bitch. I'd kill for someone to love me that much."

After a few bites, she continued. "You're always going to have problems, whether you're with Mateo or someone who lives in your world. And none of us know what's coming tomorrow. But he loves you. Enjoy it."

The meal was delicious. We made small talk while we ate, and I told her about my kids. I was surprised when she told me she thirty-three; she seemed so much older than I was, but she looked so much younger. She'd said she'd known Matty for eighteen years—that meant that she'd known him since she was a young teenager. I couldn't help but wonder how long she'd known Cris. They were the same age. Had they been friends?

After dinner, we sat on the couch and talked more, not touching on any serious topic. Jessie was funny and sweet, and as much as I felt like I was betraying Cris, I could totally see her and Rocker together. Talking to her was like catching up with an old friend. I was a little sad when she told me she had to go, but she pulled me into a hug and promised to check on me later in the week.

I called my kids, listening to them on speakerphone tell me how much fun they'd had with their grandparents. After we said good night, I cleaned up what I could, left on the lights in case Rob came home, and took the stairs down to Matty's room. I hoped he would call me soon, because I needed to tell him that Jessie was right. I was ready to start over.

TWELVE

JO

Two days. Forty-eight hours. Well, forty-seven hours and thirty-nine minutes.

I waited. But the call never came. I had gotten a text message from an unknown number that said *I'm so sorry!* I assumed it was from Matty, that his phone had died sometime over the last few days and he borrowed one to send a text to me.

Perhaps that was wishful thinking and it was actually a wrong number. Maybe someone out there was wondering why their loved one had never apologized. Or a groveling husband was wondering why his beloved wife never responded after he'd apologized. Maybe by not writing back, I'd broken up a nice, innocent couple.

Or maybe my imagination was running wild because I'd been alone for two days. Cris and Jessie had taken turns visiting me, trying to keep me entertained. Neither of them had heard anything either, but apparently that was nothing new. The Bastards, Jessie explained, were known to take off for days at a time at a moment's notice.

I honestly couldn't figure out how Matty had been able to do that. Sam had been sick a lot over the years, and it always seemed like Matty or Bex caught it right after, making Matt miss another day of work. Now I wondered if any of them had actually been sick. One more question to add to the pile, one more answer I hoped I would have one day.

I talked to Teagan every day but hadn't filled her in yet. I tried to keep things generic, wanting to wait until I had something definite to tell. Her stories were a great distraction and made me a little homesick.

My Boston friends called me every night, but they both worked, so I was on my own during the day. If I didn't have class, I'd probably have gone crazy.

I missed my car. I'd taken a cab to school, walked to the grocery store, and had food delivered. If I'd had my car though, I could have gone exploring. Getting reacquainted with the city I used to love was nice; so much had changed in such a short time.

I was beyond lonely though. I shook my head at the realization. Obviously, my original plan of finding an apartment by myself would never have worked. I would have gone mad in within the first week. Hell, if the guys didn't come home soon, I knew I might still go crazy. I pulled my casserole out of the oven before checking the time once again.

Forty-seven hours and fifty-two minutes.

"Somethin' smells delicious."

Startled, I almost dropped the pan, then I paused, not sure if maybe I'd moved on to the next level of loneliness and was now hallucinating. I turned slowly, just in case he wasn't real.

He looked like shit. Wearing the same clothes he'd had on Saturday night, except now they were filthy and covered in road grime, he was in desperate need for a shower. His beard had grown in even more. It was the most hair I'd ever seen on his face, and it gave him a sketchy mountain man look. Worst of all was the pure exhaustion that couldn't be hidden.

I wasn't sure if he'd slept at all in the last few days, but if he had, it wasn't for long periods of time. All that mattered to me right now though was that Matty was here. Right in front of me.

I ran across the room and jumped onto him, not caring how dirty he was. I just wanted to hold him.

He smiled, leaning down to kiss me. "Christ, it's good to see you!" Pulling me into him, he held me tightly, arms locked behind me. I could feel the tension flowing from his body. Something was wrong, very wrong. I tried to pull away, but he was too strong. "Just let me hold you a minute. Please, Joes?"

I stopped struggling, but my mind scrambled in a thousand different directions. Was it Rob? One of the others? Had someone gotten hurt?

Matt sighed, but I couldn't tell if it was in annoyance or frustration. "Jesus, Joes, I can practically hear you thinking." He grabbed my shoulders, holding me at arm's length so he could look in my eyes, then he sighed again—sadly this time. "I can't stay long, but I needed to see you."

Of course he couldn't stay long. It was early evening, but he was still three hours from home. He didn't look up for the drive, and I was tempted to ask him to stay with me. But after missing the last two days of work, he couldn't miss a third. I couldn't let him leave this tired though.

Racking my brain to think of something that might wake him up before he left, I smiled. "Do you have time for a shower with me?"

His entire face perked up, "I'll make time."

I grabbed his hand and yanked him down the stairs, determined to make the most of however long we had together.

As soon as I was through the bedroom door, I started to strip. My shirt was over my head in seconds, and I started to wiggle out of my leggings before it hit the floor. By the time I'd made it to the bathroom door, I was as naked as the day I was born, and a trail of clothes was laid out like a treasure map to lead Matty right to me. He hadn't followed me; instead, he was leaning back against the closed door, one foot propped up behind him, biting the knuckle on his index finger as he watched me.

Before I could ask what he was waiting for, he groaned. "I've had dreams like this." He pushed himself off the door and swaggered toward me. "Where you come here, take off all your clothes, and tease me. I always wake up before I get to touch you."

He ran fingers along my collarbone lightly, as if to make sure I wasn't a dream. The fingers trailed down my chest, between my breasts, over my stomach, and onto my hip. He stood so close that I could feel his breath on my face while he looked over every inch of me, and I fought the instinct to cover myself and hide.

There was a lot more meat on my body than there had been last summer. I'd let the irritation of the divorce and the stress of losing Matty get to me, and I'd packed on an extra fifteen-ish pounds. I was curvier than I'd been in a long time, and a lot more woman than I was sure he was used to.

His eyes met mine, watching me carefully for a few minutes. "You are so fuckin' beautiful, and you don't even know it, do you?" His voice was low, practically a whisper. He reached out his other hand and, following the same trail slowly, ending up on my other hip. "Joes?"

He bit his bottom lip as his eyes met mine again, and I knew he was asking if I was sure I wanted this. I nodded.

He picked me up, and my back hit the wall before I even realized we'd moved. His hands skimmed down my hips, onto my ass, then to the undersides of my thighs, pulling me as close to him as I could get while he was still fully clothed. I wrapped my legs around his waist, desperate for contact. His mouth moved up my neck, his tongue drawing a line and his lips blowing on it, his beard tickling me—the combination sent shivers down my spine and made my muscles clench.

I tangled my fingers in his hair, trying to pull his head back, needing to kiss his lips. He was stronger though, and he continued his tantalizing journey—lapping, blowing, and sometimes nibbling—up to my ear and back down the front of my neck. Helpless to do anything else, I rocked my center against his jeans, the denim providing just enough friction to make me moan.

He ran the tip of his nose back up my neck, onto my face, and his mouth closed over mine, claiming me. All too soon, he pulled away, releasing me and backing up. My feet weren't ready to hold me, and I leaned against the wall, confused.

He grinned proudly as he looked me over once more. "Fucking amazing."

Shrugging off his jacket, he let the leather drop stiffly to the floor before he reached over his shoulders, grabbed his shirt. I inhaled, appreciating the view. While I had packed on the pounds, Matty had apparently exercised his stress away. He'd always had a fit runner's body—muscular in all the right places with a six-pack, and that V that drove me crazy. Now, all of him was toned and well-defined. Thick pec muscles rippled with every move he made, his abs belonged on a model, and even his stomach looked as though it would feel like solid rock. Amazed by the differences, my fingers ached to touch him and explore this new Matty.

I'd forgotten how beautiful the art that decorated him was. The words "Only God Can Judge Me," above a heavily shaded cross, were in the middle of his chest. Below it to the right was an odd drawing I had never asked him about. A giant anchor started right below his belly button and stretched over the middle of his stomach. A large angel, hands clasped and head hung in prayer, filled up his right side. A Claddagh covered the front of his right shoulder, surrounded by tribal knots that wove down his arm into a sleeve. A single word, Trust, ran beneath his heart.

I'd only gotten a few of the backstories, but the pictures made me want to know why he'd chosen the things he had. I skimmed each tattoo quickly as he unbuttoned his jeans and kicked them off. A moment later, I could see my favorite tattoo because he was just as naked as I was. I tore my eyes away from the words "Suck My" on his pubic bone. All my insecurities snuck back in as I saw him in all of his glory; I didn't know how I could ever be enough for a man like him.

His gaze darkened as I met his eyes. He knew exactly what I was thinking. Somehow, he always knew.

Before I could do anything, he reached down, eyes still on mine, and wrapped a hand around his gloriously large erection. He moved his hand up and down, slowly pumping himself.

"Look at me, Jo." Growly and deep, his voice held a command that I couldn't disobey. "Watch me."

I glanced down, fascinated as his thumb swirled over his tip.

"You do this to me. Every fuckin' time I think about you, I'm hard for hours. Watching you strip off your clothes, knowing that it was for me..." He went back to the slow pumping. "Drives me fucking nuts."

I swallowed, not sure if I should reach out and touch him.

"Get on the bed, Joes."

I didn't hesitate, didn't think twice. I didn't remember climbing up, lying on my back, or Matty crawling up behind me, it all happened so fast. He lay next to me, his head propped on an elbow next to my mine. He smiled down at me, a small sexy smile that grew into a giant seductive grin as his free hand traced circles around my belly button.

Slowly his hand drifted lower, running over the curve of my stomach and onto the top of my thigh. "So fuckin' soft." Bending his head over mine, he nipped at my bottom lip. "Open for me."

As I moved my legs apart, giving him access to my most secret spot, his lips pressed against mine. Fingers light as feathers tickled down the inside of my leg then up to my folds. A thumb found my clit, massaging in a slow circular motion, and I moaned into his mouth. He smiled against my lips and pushed his cock against my leg so I could feel just how hard he was.

He slid his entire body down, so that his face was level with my chest. Keeping his thumb moving in a steady pace, he kissed a trail from one nipple, down the valley, and up to the other. Expecting him to bite me, I was surprised when he sucked the hardened point while his other hand gently fondled me.

Pinching and pulling at the nipple, making me cry out, he smirked. "God, I fucking love the noises you make." Moving over me so that our feet were tangled together and his torso was pressed into mine, he whispered, "I need to taste you." His thumb was still teasing my clit as he growled. "I'm gonna lap every inch of you. I'm going to feast on your pussy until you beg me to stop."

Before I could process his words, he slipped down the length of my body. I gasped and arched in surprise as he nuzzled his bearded chin against the sensitive skin on my inner thigh. Taking advantage of my reaction, he moved his mouth onto me and swirled his tongue gently around my clit. I grabbed his hair, pulling handfuls as I moaned.

One hand joined his tongue, adding pressure, before he pushed a finger into me, finding that special spot almost immediately and making me cry out again. He added a second finger, and my muscles automatically clenched around him as his tongue and lips worked over my upper core. He sucked my clit, letting it go only to lick it roughly.

His other hand grabbed a nipple, twisting and pulling, and I realized I wasn't going to last long. There were fireworks behind my closed eyelids, and I started to pant, mumbling incoherent words. It felt so good that I couldn't think straight.

"Oh, God! Matty," I pled when I found my voice.

His only answer was a chuckle that sent vibrations through my extremely sensitive area, making me gasp again.

Lifting his head for a minute, while his fingers continued to thrust inside me and yank on the opposite nipple, he found my eyes and commanded, "Come for me, baby. I want to taste how much you want me."

Putting his tongue back on me, he increased the pressure as he lapped up and down. That was all it took before I tumbled off the edge.

"Oh, my God, I love your tongue!" I gasped over and over as I fell apart.

While I rode out my orgasm, he stayed propped between my thighs, lapping and sucking until I had nothing more to give. I tried to push him away, unable to handle more, but he wouldn't budge. After a few excruciating minutes, and lots of begging from me, he sat back on his knees and pulled out his fingers. I was wrecked. I might not have been an expert, but there was no denying that Matty not only knew how to go down on a girl, but he excelled at it.

I watched as he put his fingers in his mouth and sucked them clean. My face flushed scarlet when I realized what he was doing, and he smirked in response.

"I love how you taste." He moved quickly, leaning above me once more, kissing me as he pushed into me agonizingly slow, letting me feel every inch of his hardness. "Fuck. You feel good."

His lips moved against mine, nipping and licking, as my hands pulled on him, trying to get him to hurry. I needed him to fuck me hard, and I needed him to do it right then.

He pulled out just as slowly, and I growled in frustration. He moved his mouth next to my ear and chuckled. "Something wrong, babe?"

"Matty... please!" I could hear the desperation in my voice.

He bit my ear and whispered, "Always so greedy!"

Then he pushed himself onto his knees, lifting my legs to his shoulders. Every thought I had disappeared when he started to move quickly, pounding into me over and over. My sounds of pleasure joined the sound of flesh slapping against flesh and Matty's panting and moans. I was desperate to touch him, to drag my fingernails over his back, but every time I reached out, he'd shake his head and grin.

"Come on, baby. Let go. Give me all of you." He never broke from his rhythm, and it was too much, I couldn't handle the intensity. "Joes!" He growled, "I can't wait." He bit his lip and adjusted his angle but didn't slow down. I tightened my muscles, squeezing him. "Christ, woman," his voice broke, "I fuckin' love you!"

Hearing those words on his lips, I let go, giving him everything I had. "I love you, Matty."

He swore again, collapsing on top of me, still pumping. His hands grabbed my hair, tilting my head back roughly, and his lips captured mine. I dug my nails into his back and wrapped my legs around his hips. He came with a hiss of pleasure, and after his thrusts slowed to a stop, he didn't pull out. I hugged him tightly, not wanting him to ever move.

I ran my fingertips up his sweat-soaked back. "I missed you." My voice was no more than an exhausted mumble, but I had to tell him. "I can't live without you, Matty. Promise you'll never leave."

I couldn't keep my eyes open to hear his response.

THIRTEEN

MATTY

I needed rest. My body was begging me to lie back, close my eyes, and drift off into the void that only sleep could bring. As much as I wanted to, I couldn't give in.

I didn't have much time before I had to leave her. Once I was gone, I would never get this moment back and I'd be damned if I was going to lose it now. We both needed it too much for me to let go. I trailed my fingertips over the roundness of her hip, enjoying the feel of her warm, soft skin.

She sighed softly in slumber—a satisfied, happy sound that spread a warmness through my chest and put my mind at ease. She was right here next to me. Jo was safe.

I hadn't planned on fucking her senseless. I had needed to see her with my own eyes, to hold her in my arms and make sure she was okay. From the moment I'd left her, she'd been at the front of my mind. I knew I wouldn't be able to function this week if I went straight home. The second she'd taken off her shirt there had been no other option for me—I had to have her.

The fearful look in her eyes almost killed me. That look said so much; she expected me to take one look at her beautiful body and criticize her curves or walk away. It told me that she was still unsure of my feelings for her. Somewhere along the way I had failed to explain the magnitude of my feelings. I knew the moment that her eyes met mine that there was no way in hell I was leaving until I'd shown her how much I fuckin' loved every single inch of her.

I was nothing like the douche canoe she'd been married to. He'd done one fuck of a number on her self-esteem. I knew she would deal with the lasting effects for years. But he was gone. She was mine now. It was my job to help her see herself through my eyes.

Now that she was finally asleep, I should join her. It had been a long week and I was fucking exhausted. Lying next to her, watching her, was far more important than rest.

The last few days had been nothing new for the Bastards. For almost twenty years, we'd made it our job to chase down scumbags before they could get off the grid. We never knew how long a job would take, where we would end up going, when we'd be back.

There was no planning these trips. When we got the call, we packed our shit and left. It was fine for the single brothers, but it got old for those of us with families.

I couldn't change a thing though. It was what we did. It was what we needed to do.

Over a month before, Wiz had intercepted a police report about an abused child in critical condition. Mom had dropped him off at the hospital, right at the door for fuck's sake, and gone on the run with her sleazy-ass loser boyfriend. Stupid fucking cunt. Any woman who hurt her child, or allowed someone else to do it, deserved whatever punishment we'd give.

Before the police could issue a public statement, Rocker had called our other charters and every affiliated club while Wiz faxed and emailed pictures of mom and her deadbeat boyfriend along with details of the assault to everyone we knew. The warning was out. The Bastards wanted these two, and we'd do whatever we could to find them and bring them the punishment they deserved.

For over a month they'd been able to hide, which meant someone was helping them. When the mainstream media picked up the story, the general public wanted blood, and we knew it would be only a matter of time before someone saw them. Wiz tapped into every available database he could, and we knew that when they surfaced, we'd be there.

And we had been. With a few hours heads-up, we'd gotten the information from the BOLO on their new vehicle before it went nationwide. We knew what car they were in, had a license plate number, and had a good idea of where they were headed.

The fuckers thought that their biggest fear was the police and that the worst thing that would happen to them was dealing with other scum in prison. They were wrong. They should have been terrified.

If they knew about us, about what we would do to them when we found them, then more abusers would turn themselves in. I hoped one day that the idea of us, of what we were capable of, would scare parents straight. That one day, even in a blind rage, the name Bastards would halt a batterer's fists.

Until that day, we'd hunt them down like the animals they were. And I would enjoy the fear in their eyes when they realized what was about to happen. In those few moments, I wanted them to experience the terror they'd inflicted.

It had taken us longer than I'd wanted, but we'd finally caught up with them in Maryland. When our group of bikes drove up next to them, they blatantly ignored us, laughing as if they were on a damn joy ride. My rage was almost uncontrollable, and I knew we couldn't wait for them to stop on their own.

When I swerved in front of the car, making Mom slam on her brakes, the only thoughts in my head were of her broken four-year-old. My heart hammered in my chest, not in fear, but out of anger, as we boxed her in. Half the guys stayed next to her, making it impossible for her to move into the passing lane, half followed me. With our truck behind her, she had no other option than to stop.

The wannabe gang-banger boyfriend and a couple of his buddies jumped out, guns waving, shouting at us as if we should be afraid. The fight was over before it began—kids who couldn't even figure out how to make their pants stay around their waists shouldn't play with guns, and they really shouldn't threaten a group of pissed off bikers.

In minutes, Mom and her boyfriend were cable-tied and forced into the back of her car and their friends were beaten unconscious, duct-taped, and thrown into the truck. Someone who helps an abuser is just as fucking guilty as the abuser.

That had been Sunday night. When the newspapers hit the stand in just a few hours, the world would find out that Mom had walked up to a police officer and turned herself in. If she went to trial in a few months, we'd be sitting front and center—a gentle reminder that she needed to accept responsibility and take the punishment, or we'd give her one of our own. I hoped she'd just plead guilty and save the state the money a trial would cost. Either way, she was headed away for a long time.

As for the other three, no one would ever find their bodies. The friends had told us everything we needed to know, hoping to save their own skins. Their deaths were merciful.

An easy death was not in the cards for the prick boyfriend. He got to experience what the sweet little boy went through—every single bruise, every single burn, every single cut. His last few moments were filled with pain, and before we sent him to meet his maker, remorse filled his eyes. It was never enough for me.

CARINA ADAMS

Ridding the world of one sleazeball at a time should have made me feel better, but it didn't. We weren't able to help the boy until it was too late. I wanted more. Needed us to do more.

We were doing what we could now. Until he was healthy enough to go back to his grandma's, Bear and the prospects would take turns sitting at the hospital, silently watching over the little guy. Not only would their presence show our support and hopefully make him feel secure, we wanted to make sure no one else had a chance to get near him. Rocker had talked to the Grandma, and she knew that we were always just a phone call away – no matter what they needed. They weren't alone; he had hundreds of Bastards at his back.

I rolled over, pulling Jo with me. I'd made peace with who I was a long time ago. I'd always be the monster hiding behind a polite smile and a respectable job. As a Bastard, it was my responsibility to put a pretty face to the rumored "bad men" so we could show that we weren't evil at all. Jo had only seen that façade.

I didn't want to let go of her, but I didn't know how she would cope with this part of me. Earlier, with three little words gasped as she came apart beneath me, she had given me hope. Maybe if she loved me as much as she claimed, she'd stay. As much as I wanted her next to me, no secrets between us, I wasn't sure she could handle it. She was full of goodness, and I couldn't guarantee that this life wouldn't suck it out of her.

I'd never brought anyone in. Becky knew just enough to realize she wanted no part of it and was happy being my escape. Taylor, growing up the daughter of one of the most corrupt senators imaginable, knew who I was before I could tell her. A man who looked like me and had the money I did was great arm candy for a spoiled Daddy's girl, but it was the dangerous Bastard who turned her on. She knew I was a jealous prick who would kick a man's ass just for looking at her the wrong way, and she loved it even more than the designer clothes, luxury cars, and any other expensive present I could give her.

But Jo—my funny, loving, crazy Joes—didn't want me for any of that. The money made her uncomfortable, the club made her nervous, and my physical characteristics intimidated her. She'd told me once that if we hadn't had to work together, she never would have looked at me twice because she thought I was out of her league—that someone like me would never be friends with her. It amused me that someone who was obviously way too good for me felt unworthy, and it only made me love her that much more. She might not know the Bastard, but she knew a part of me that no one else did—the real me that I hid from everyone else. However, I was almost positive this part of my life would push her to her breaking point.

Anger coursed through my veins at the thought, my arms tightened around her. I wished I could let her go. I never would be able to.

As long as she'd been with Billy, I was content to be on the sidelines watching from a distance. After she'd left him, though, I couldn't handle being away. The idea of her with some other asshole, one who might take her away from me for good, made me furious. This was where she belonged, right here in my arms, where I could watch over her, keep her safe, and love her.

Her eyelashes fluttered against my chest, and she wiggled as she opened her eyes, leaning her head back to see my face. She smiled.

I couldn't resist leaning over and nuzzling her neck. "Hey, baby."

She sighed into me, pressing her lips to mine. "Honey, you need to sleep."

The words were no more than a half-awake murmur. Kissing me once more, she pushed her tits into my chest, groaning into my mouth when my hands cupped her. She moved quickly, settling into my side and leaning her head onto my chest, her hand holding mine. Within seconds, her breath was once again deep and even. Enjoying her wrapped up in me, knowing she was right, I closed my eyes and let the quiet take me away. I could worry about the rest later.

FOURTEEN

JO

I reached for Matty, only half awake, needing to know he was close. His skin was hot under my hand and I instinctively moved toward him, hoping he would wrap himself around me. I smiled as he rolled toward me, strong arms enveloping me, and his lips found my forehead.

It seemed like only seconds later when he moved again, this time sliding me to the pillow, the cotton cold against my cheek. I tried to force my eyes open, mind scrambling.

Matt shushed me as his hand ran down my back. "Sleep, baby." The bed moved slightly as he leaned over and kissed my forehead, whispering, "I love you, Joes."

When I finally woke up, threw on some clothes, and stumbled to the kitchen for caffeine, I was disappointed to find him not only gone but already at work. I had wanted to talk to him while he drove, just to help keep him awake. I also longed to hear his voice for more than a five-minute conversation. Being around him made me miss the friends we used to be.

He'd sent me a very sweet text message, telling me he wished he was still in my arms but that his meeting couldn't wait. I smiled, thinking about the "I love you more" that he'd ended the text with. It would be enough to tide me over.

I sat at the table, sipping the burning hot liquid and staring off into space until Rocker joined me. I glanced up, concentration broken, surprised at his disheveled appearance. I smiled my greeting, unsure of what to say. He nodded back.

"I'm glad you're home. It's quiet here without you."

"Glad to be home." He mumbled. "Fuckin' sucks, right? I hate bein' here alone." He turned his coffee mug around, staring at it thoughtfully. "'Course, I hate it when it's crowed too." Looking up, he caught my eye. "How's the job hunt goin'?"

I scowled. "Not good." Shrugging, I added, "I'll find something, but I..." The elevator arrived with a loud ping, and we both looked toward the door. "Must be Cris." I mused. "She has the day off. We're going shopping."

Rocker turned his attention back to his coffee, relaxing a bit. The blonde who came around the corner was definitely not Matty's little sister. I smiled at my new friend and tried to keep the confusion out of my voice.

"Good morning, Jessie."

Rocker stiffened. It was only for a moment, and I wondered if I imagined it. His eyes closed briefly before he took a deep breath and stood, kissing her cheek warmly. "Everything okay at the shop?"

She nodded, putting her hand on a strong forearm, her perfect face scrunched in worry. "You didn't call me last night, and when Tank told me you were back..." Her voice was full of concern, and the look on her face made me feel as if I was intruding on a very private conversation. "I called, but you..."

"I'm fine." Rocker stepped back, obviously putting distance between them. "Want coffee?"

Jessie hesitated, confusion clear on her face. Nodding, she sat in the chair next to his. "Good morning," her voice was soft as she greeted me. "Did you have a chance to see Mateo?"

I couldn't keep the smile off my face, or the heat from my cheeks. "He came home last night."

Jessie lips slid up in a smile that didn't reach her eyes. She was clearly happy for me but she also had a sadness that told me she wished Rocker had gone to her when he'd gotten home. I wanted to hug her and slap him simultaneously.

"Cream and sugar?" Rob asked interrupting my thoughts.

"Yes, please."

The elevator arrived with another ping as soon as the words were out of her mouth. I stood abruptly, hoping I could run into the entryway and cut off Cris before she came in, but she was too quick. Rock star sunglasses in place and her phone pressed to her ear, Cris strode into the kitchen as though she owned the place, throwing a giant smile at me.

I saw the exact moment she realized that Jessie was with me, her steps faltering for just a second. The smile never left her face though, and she threw herself into the chair next to me as she ended the call, laughing at whoever was on the other end. Pushing the glasses to the top of her head, dazzling blue eyes twinkled at me, and I sat back down, mentally preparing to be a buffer between the two.

"Good morning!" Her voice was sing-songy, immediately putting me on edge. She was too happy. She turned to Jessie, the smile widening in faux enthusiasm. "Barbie! How are you?"

Jessie had straightened in her chair, ready for battle. One eyebrow arched perfectly as she smiled the way one does before it devours its prey. "Princess!" Her over the top excitement made me even more nervous than Cris's fake happy. "Now that the boys are back, I couldn't be better. How are you doing?"

"I'm great. To be honest, I'm surprised to see you here. I forgot that little job of yours allows you to come and go whenever you want." Cris waved her hand dismissively.

Jessie laughed. "Oh, that's just one of the many perks of sleeping with my boss."

I clenched my jaw to keep my mouth from falling open.

Jess didn't stop there. "Are you still pretending to work hard at that gym teaching men how to do that thing? What's it called again? Mai Tai?"

Cris tensed next to me, the smile never leaving her face as she opened her mouth. I knew we were in for more than an earful, because not only was her job as a personal trainer difficult, she co-owned the academy where she taught. It was her baby.

"It's Muay Thai, Barbs. No need to pretend you don't know the difference; we all know how much you like your booze. But don't worry about it. All you need to remember is that you can't handle either Mai Tais or Muay Thai; both will kick your scrawny ass."

Rocker picked that moment to practically slam two mugs onto the table, and as he slid one toward Cris, he glowered at her. It wasn't lost on me that while he'd had to ask Jessie how she took her coffee, or even if she wanted one, he'd never asked Cris either question. It was clear which of these women he knew better.

The uncomfortable silence that surrounded us made me remember why I didn't like being around women. It wasn't that I disliked my gender. I had some of the best friends anyone could have. I loved my girl time with Teagan and her daughters, my lunch dates with Becky, my one-on-ones with Cris, and even looked forward to expanding my friendship with Jessie. In most situations though, I would take being stuck with a hundred men over being stuck with ten women any day of the week. We were such a catty species; everything was a frigging competition.

I inwardly rolled my eyes at the looks Jessie and Cris sent each other whenever Rob looked away. He was not a stupid man, so there was no way he hadn't realized that they hated each other and were acting this way because of him. I felt awful for all three of them.

Rocker's discomfort was clear, but I was fascinated. I wished I could read minds, because I wanted to know what he was thinking. After a few minutes of near silence, I stood and grabbed my cup as well as the one Cris was using. I ignored her quiet complainants as I carried them to the sink, beckoning her to follow me.

"We'll catch you guys later, okay?" With that, I bounced down the stairs.

Cris and I were able to get in some great retail therapy as well as some hot boy ogling. After spending the morning shopping for nothing in particular, and listening to her hate on Jessie, I convinced her to go to the movies to see the new Marvel flick. I knew that no hot-blooded female could be stressed after watching Chris Evans look adorable while saving the world.

Once back at the apartment, Cris sat at the table while I prepared dinner, and we gushed over the men in the movie and how kickass Scarlet Johansson was. That woman was more terrifying than half the men I knew. She didn't have to depend on someone else to save her, and I was just a bit envious. I wanted to be that strong—emotionally and physically.

"It really wouldn't take that long, just some dedication." Cris shook her head when I opened my mouth to argue. "Seriously, you should know how to protect yourself."

I twisted my lips as I scraped the chopped onion into the salad bowl. "I do know how to protect myself, silly. It's called mace, and I carry it everywhere. But I'd love to be just as scary as Black Widow."

It wasn't the first time I'd said it today, and ever since I mentioned it, Cris had been trying to get me to go to her gym. She claimed her type of kickboxing would be a good sport for me to pick up, and if I didn't want to learn it, then I should at least take a martial art or two. I just wanted to know how to throw a punch and have it hurt my intended target without breaking my hand. Being able to defend myself wouldn't be a bad thing either.

"Why don't you come with me tomorrow?" she asked.

"I will as long as you can promise me that there will be hot men I can stare at."

"There will be tons! Why do you think I love my job?" She shot me a look that said I was crazy. "Hot, sweaty, beautiful, and kicking the shit out of each other while I yell at them. What more could you want?"

The thought was so obnoxious that I couldn't hold in my laugh, and she joined me, shaking her head.

Rob came into the room, stopping dead. "You're cookin' supper, L.K.? No shit!" He smiled. "Thank god. I couldn't handle takeout again." He grabbed a beer from the fridge then pulled a chair from the table, turned it, and straddled it as he sat. "What are you two hens cackling about?"

Cris rolled her eyes, trying to look annoyed, and smirked. "I want Jo to come down to the gym tomorrow. I started a new class last week and think she should join us." She winked at me. "I think I'm wearing her down."

"Not happening."

I looked up from the tomato I was slicing, sure I'd missed a step.

Cris jumped in before I could, the glare in her eyes matching her icy tone. "I'm not gonna put her in the ring against a pro on her first day out—just teach her the basics."

Rocker took a sip from his bottle and shook his head. "Over my dead body."

"Fuckin' Christ, Robbie. The girl doesn't even know a single defensive stance, let alone any of the aim points." Her eyes narrowed farther. "You really don't think it's a good idea for her learn what to do if someone attacks her?"

After taking another sip, he swirled his bottle as he listened to her. His eyes rolled as her arms flew through the air in her dramatic fashion, and he leaned toward her as he answered. "I said no."

I slammed the knife on the counter, and they both turned to look at me. "I don't remember anyone asking you."

He shrugged dismissively. "You think I'm gonna let ya go get your ass handed to ya and then explain to Mateo why his woman is covered in bruises? I don't fuckin' think so."

I picked the knife up and pointed at him. "Fine, then you can take me to your gym and teach me."

A look I didn't recognize crossed his features, and he swallowed hard as Cris broke into hysterics. Once she'd composed herself, she grinned. "That won't work, Jo. Rocker doesn't hit girls." Her voice took on an odd tone as she turned to look at him, eyes sparkling. "He refuses to hit anyone with a pussy, even if they are really, really naughty and begging for it."

Not backing down like I thought he would, Rob shrugged again. "You knew I wasn't into that shit, that it's not my thing. I told you if you wanted someone to tie ya up and spank ya, you shoulda been with Hawk, not me."

Cris answered with a laugh that was sharp and didn't hold a speck of humor. "And I told you I needed *you* to do it. I didn't want Hawk, dammit, I wanted you. But no! You didn't trust me enough to even try." She slammed a small fist onto the table. "Besides, I'm pretty sure I lack what he requires in his partners. Do I look like one of his chubby subbies?"

Chubby subbies? Good Christ! I would never look at Hawk the same way again, and I let my thoughts wander to a place I didn't want them to be as I wondered if I was Hawk's type of chubby.

"Oh, my god! How would you even know that?" I groaned, closing my eyes and trying to fight the embarrassment I felt flooding into my face. "Thank you both for that wonderful image! Unless I can figure out a way to boil my brain, I'm gonna be stuck with it for the rest of my life! Jesus, is nothing private anymore?"

Leaning my head onto the counter next to the cutting board, I let the coolness of the marble soothe my warm cheeks. Some things, you just couldn't unhear. They were both looking at me when I stood and opened my eyes a few seconds later. Rob was trying to hide his amused smile behind his bottle, but Cris was gaping obnoxiously as if I had two heads.

"What?" I snapped, harsher than I meant to.

Cris shook her head and cleared her expression, making her face go almost blank.

Rocker, on the other hand, gave me a shit-eating grin, his dimples deep. "Hate to break it to ya, kid, but I've lived with Mateo in one way or another for over half my life. Not all of those places had two bedrooms, and if they did, the walls were pretty fuckin' thin." He took a long swig while I scanned my mind, vaguely worried about what he might have heard. His eyes met mine. "I can promise you, L.K., I know more about him"—he stole a glance at Cris— "and his..." He cleared his throat, obviously uncomfortable in front of Matty's sister. "Preferred activities than I ever wanted to."

I felt the color drain from my face, embarrassment momentarily replaced with shock.

Surprisingly, Cris snorted, not looking uncomfortable in the least. "What he means, Joey, is that we all know just how kinky my brother likes to get. At least, we've all heard the stories."

Stories? Christ! What was it with these people and their stories? I felt my lips purse in agitation, the knowledge that I didn't know what she was talking about leaving a sour taste in my mouth.

Pausing for a second at my response, Cris smirked and raised an eyebrow. "While I obviously don't know for sure, I think it's pretty safe to assume"—she held up her hands in surrender, rushing on— "by the fact you're still together, that you also like a bit of kink. There's no need to get embarrassed by a little BDSM talk."

"So, I'm guilty by association?" I glowered at her. "And I'm not embarrassed," I added childishly.

She giggled. "The way you're acting like a sheltered and innocent schoolgirl is a little amusing. In fact, I think it's fuckin' hilarious." She wiggled her eyebrows suggestively and beamed at me.

Rocker tipped his head as if trying to work out something she'd said, and he spoke before I could form a retort. "No. That's not what I meant." He gave her a dirty look, obviously as irritated with her as I was, before turning to me. "It's more than that. I don't ever want you to think that anythin' in this club is private, because it ain't. We all know things about the others that they feel they have to hide from the rest o' the world. That's how we build trust, how we survive. We may give each other a hard time, but we'll defend each other to the grave."

He sighed and sat back. "There ah some things about us that you'll learn early on 'cause no one tries to hide 'em. Hawk likes to dominate fat women, and his job is to protect the club and its members at all costs. Yet he hates violence and is always the first to try to talk me down. Princess"—he jerked a thumb toward Cris— "wants someone to tie her up and give her the spanking she obviously deserves, but if a man messes with her any other time, she'll fuckin' wreck him and make him cry like a little bitch. Tiny is anything but, and I mean that in every way. Bear is a cocky fuck who'll screw anythin' that shows interest 'cause he's trying to forget his ol' lady walked, but he hates it and wants to find a woman to go home to. And me? I'm a miserable fuckin' prick that won't hit women"—he looked back at Cris, the corners of his lips quirking in teasing laughter— "even when they're begging for it but won't hesitate to throw the first punch any other time."

Emotions warred within me. I didn't know if I was shocked at how he listed off their eccentricities as if they were normal things everyone talked about all the time, intrigued to know more about these people who meant so much to the man I loved, or if I wanted to laugh because every single thing Rob just said was pretty frigging funny. They may be freaks, but even I had to admit that they were fascinating.

"If I'll learn all that early on, what juicy tidbits will I pick up later?"

I felt eyes on me, and I looked up, surprised to see that Rob's face had hardened a bit, all trace of humor gone. "Some secrets you may never know, L.K. It isn't personal, so don't take it that way. We're a tight group. Most of us have been Bastards since we were kids. With that history comes severe loyalty. Not one of us will tell someone else's story unless we're told we can."

I remembered Matty had said almost exactly the same thing last summer. Loyal to the core. These men—hell, this whole group of people—were hard to figure out. They surprised me at every turn. I was relatively certain they would never act how I expected them to.

FIFTEEN

JO

I tried to convince Cris to stay for supper, since that had been the original plan after all, but she swore she was exhausted. I didn't buy it; the tension between her and Rob was so thick it would take more than a knife to cut through it. I didn't know who seemed more relieved as I walked her to the elevator, but they both acted as if a huge weight had been lifted from their shoulders.

"I'll see you tomorrow. Wear comfortable but form-fitting clothes. Work on him tonight, will ya?" she said just as the doors closed.

Then Cris was gone and I was alone with my roommate for the first time in days. I hummed to myself as I walked back into the kitchen. Rob had taken my place by the stove, searing the chicken cutlets. He didn't look like a rough-and-rugged biker, but an off-duty chef instead.

I walked around the counter, grinning at the sight. "I'm sorry. When I planned dinner, it was just for Cris and me. If I'd known you would be home, I'd have cooked something else."

He looked at me quizzically. "What? Meat and potatoes?" I could hear the humor in his voice. "Real men eat salad, L.K."

I held in my laughter, but barely. "Oh, really? Is that why I found our crisper bare—you ate all the veggies but left the frozen junk and processed foods for me?"

He nodded vigorously as he flipped the poultry once more. "That's exactly what happened."

I rolled my eyes in amusement. "Makes complete sense."

"Hey, I left you beer." He turned off the burner.

"No, you didn't!" I argued, "I bought that yesterday!"

"I don't know about that." He frowned. "How'd ya know what kind I drank?" He transferred two pieces of chicken onto our plates, grabbed forks, then lifted both onto the counter in front of me. He turned to grab a couple bottles of said beer.

"Jessie told me."

He paused at the mention of her name but recovered quickly, easing onto the stool next to me.

"I thought you'd stay with her tonight," I probed quietly.

308

He opened my bottle, dropped the cap onto the counter, then did the same to his before taking a sip. He shoveled a few forkfuls of greenery into his mouth before answering me.

"That's what she figured too." He looked up, staring into the empty kitchen as he chewed absently. "She take good care of you?"

"Yeah. Thanks for sending her over. She's really sweet and very funny. I like her."

"She's great." He tipped his bottle back, taking three or four swallows, before lowering it and meeting my eyes. "I've known her since she was a kid. I used to call her Jailbait, 'cause that's what she was." He paused, lost in thought of a distant memory. "She fuckin' hated that name. She was all of fourteen or fifteen, even though she thought she was a lot older, when she decided she was gonna marry me. I was wicked fucked up still, so I didn't pay any attention, except for the fact that she was Tank's little sister. She was just an annoyin' pain in the ass who wouldn't go away." He rubbed a hand over his face, as if struggling with something.

"Never thought she'd end up working for me or bein' part of the club. She was too good for this shit. She shoulda stayed away and married some yuppie who would be home every night by six. One who could give her a normal life." His voice was full of regret.

I didn't know what to say to that, since I was positive she'd already told him that wasn't what she wanted, so instead I focused on something else he'd said. "Pretty fucked up? Did you have a motorcycle accident?"

He shook his head. "Naw." He didn't offer more.

After finishing off his food, he stood, grabbed my plate, and carried them both to the sink. Realizing the conversation was over, I picked up my bottle, ready to head downstairs, but he walked back to me, two new bottles in his hand. After handing me one, he tipped his head toward the living room in silent beckoning. Sitting in the easy chair next to the fireplace, he watched me sink into the couch, lean back onto a pile of pillows, and stretch my legs out onto the cushions.

"I asked you before, but we were interrupted before you could answer. How much do you know about the Bastards, L.K.?"

I felt my forehead wrinkle in surprised confusion. "Not much more than I've told you. Jessie told me a few things about Matty, but nothing significant."

He nodded, a look of determination crossing his rugged face as he lifted one shoulder. "I thought Mateo would tell you eventually. But I think you should know who you're livin' with, don't you? You should have a say about who you're spending your time with. And I don't want you to hear it from one of my brothers."

I wouldn't turn down any information he was willing to give me, especially if it helped me solve the mystery of Matty. Yet, anxiety washed over me at Rocker's words. My palms began to sweat.

"To understand the Bastards, you need to know my history." He leaned forward, bracing his elbows on his knees, and rolled the bottle between his hands. "I was a wicked wild kid. My parents were shanty Irish and didn't give two shits what happened to us as long as we stayed outta their way. I was the oldest of four: Katie, Meghan, and little Colin. He was the tiniest five-yeah-old I'd ever seen."

He swallowed apprehensively, his eyes narrowed on the throw rug at his feet. I could tell he was uncomfortable by the way his thick accent had crept back into his words. I opened my mouth to tell him he didn't need to tell me anymore when he continued.

"We were hungry all the time, never warm enough, and if we whined or asked for food, my father would beat us. I'm not talking back-handed slaps or spankings. No, if he came after ya, you spent the next few days lyin' on a bare mattress in the corner 'cause ya couldn't fuckin' move. I can't tell you how many times he went after one of the babies only to have me or Katie get in the way. I wanted it to be me he hit, I could take it, but sometimes I wasn't there.

"I started stealing shit when I was five or six—just food at first, that the four of us would eat once our parents passed out. I was fast, and being as small as I was, I could get into a store and out before anyone even knew I was there. Megs loved melon. She had a piece of watermelon at school one day, but our parents wouldn't buy it. Katie liked anything fresh—veggies, fruit, as long as it didn't come in a can, she loved it. Colin, well, he wanted peanut butter. I'd make a couple runs a week, grabbing some bread and peanut butter, sometimes jelly, whatever veggies I could, and always a melon for Megs."

My heart ached for the little boy who'd had to steal food in order for his family to eat the most basic meals.

"Then I got a little bolder, and I started on the bigger shit. Jackets for us, shoes for the babies, and this stupid teddy bear that Megs saw one day and swore she and Colin needed. I told my dad they came from school, but he was pissed because we'd taken charity. He threw everything out. When I stole more, he beat me worse than he ever had.

"Social services was a fuckin' joke. They'd come talk to my sisters, brother, and me at school, take pictures of our bruises, but my parents would just move us to another shithole, and we were forgotten. It was a never-endin' cycle. Until I was ten." He set the beer on the table next to him and sat up, putting his palms on his thighs as if bracing himself for what he was about to say. "I had a new baby sister. Elizabeth was the prettiest thing you've ever seen. Dark curls, chubby cheeks, and her smile melted my heart.

"Katie and I took turns feedin' her and makin' sure she was dry. Kate's a year younger than me, and we did what we could to help the little ones. I worried from the time we left for school until the time we came home, not trustin' my parents to be alone with my Lizzie girl. It was a warm spring day when we came home and found her all alone, sleepin' peacefully. The fuckers had left her on the couch, under a pile of blankets, not even a chair propped up to keep her from rollin' off." Emotion made his voice crack.

"I had Katie go pick her up while I grabbed her bottle. I didn't know how long the deadbeats had been gone, but I figured she'd be hungry. I opened it to rinse it out and gagged. I knew the smell well enough—dear old Da reeked of it all the time. Just then Kate started screaming to me 'cause Lizzie wasn't waking up. I ran to them, desperate for her to open her eyes, but she wouldn't. I picked up Megs and Colin, and we ran straight to the nearest hospital.

"I'll never forget the look in the nurse's eyes when we ran through the door—full of pity and disbelief. I set the little ones down and handed the lady the bottle, begging her to save my Lizzie girl." He stopped, clearing his throat.

I wiped at the tears I couldn't stop from streaming down my face.

"We never went back home. Child services came not long after and took us, split us up. They found an uncle I didn't know I had in Maine and took me up the next day."

"Lizzie? Was she okay? Did they save her?"

He looked away. "She survived, I know that. I think they pumped her stomach. They told my uncle later that she was adopted by a good family, one that would give her the best of everything, even if she had problems because of the alcohol."

I was horrified. "You don't know?"

"I can't find her. Colin is now Colton, and he and Megs were adopted together. Great fuckin' family. I see 'em as much as I can. He's an artist. Lives in Florida with his wife. Works for fuckin' Disney." He beamed, the pride clear, but his eyes were full of sadness. "Megs is a school teacher in New Hampshire. She got engaged a few months ago and asked me to walk her down the aisle next fall. Told her adopted dad that she needed me to do it, because I saved her." His smile was deep enough to show his dimples, but his eyes started to glisten.

"Katie was sent to Maine too, to another uncle. Turned out her abuse was worse than any of us knew." He bit his lip. "I never saw it. She never told me. If I had known..." His voice was low, just above a whisper, his eyes full of hate. Then he cleared his throat. "She's a veterinarian. Never married, never had kids because she was afraid she'd repeat the cycle. She spends all her time with animals. But we never found Lizzie."

"I'm so sorry, Rob!" I didn't know what else to say. He was barely keeping it together, and even though I knew how beneficial a good cry was, I didn't know how to comfort him or how to make it okay. "You don't have to tell me anymore."

After everything he'd been through as a kid, a group like the Bastards, protecting children and trying to help, made complete sense. I understood now and didn't need to hear more.

He didn't act as if he'd heard me. "My uncle Liam was a decent guy, but I was just too pissed off at the world to care. I missed my brother. I missed my girls. I wanted to be back with them more than anything, even if I had to go back to the hellhole my parents lived in. I wanted to rock Lizzie to sleep one more time, to scare the monsters away for Megs, to knock out the kid bullying Colin, to tell Katie I loved her. I worried about them all the time, not sure if they were hungry, cold, or scared... not sure who was taking care of them."

"You were just a kid, Rob. Those weren't your responsibilities!" I interrupted, aching to help the child he'd been.

"I know that now. But then? I was fuckin' miserable. By the time I was a teenager, drugs were the only thing that numbed the pain. They made me forget how much I missed 'em, how I'd failed 'em." He shook his head sadly. "I got in a ton of trouble from the day I moved in with Liam, but as I got older, it got worse. He tried to help, and at first he was able to cover for me, to make excuses to the world. But by the time I was fourteen, no amount of money could help me, and I was sent to Longcreek. My uncle came to see me every visitor's day. And every visitor's day, I'd yell, tell him I hated him, that I didn't want him there. He'd still come back the next time. He told me once that he was a stubborn bastard, which meant that he was passionate, that he loved me more than I loved myself, and he wasn't gonna stop 'til he saved me.

"I got out after a few months and was headed right back to the old me when my uncle forced me into his car and took me to see Megs and Colton." His voice broke. "I hadn't seen 'em since a social worker dragged me away from the hospital. Megs was ten, Colton nine, and they were fuckin' beautiful! So fuckin' healthy. And so fuckin' happy." He smiled. "Their house was huge, with a backyard and a tree fort, and they had their own rooms and more toys than fifty fuckin' kids needed. They remembered me and gave me the biggest fuckin' hugs. It was the happiest day of my life." His eyes watered, and I bit my lip to keep from interrupting. "That was it for me. I wanted them to know me, to be proud of me. On the way home I promised my uncle that I wouldn't touch another fuckin' drug. And I never did.

"I met Allison that summer."

I held my breath, not knowing who he was talking about but sure it would be another devastating story.

He turned his eyes back to me, and the sadness I could see broke my heart. "She was perfect. A straight-A student, beautiful, funny, tons of friends, and I couldn't believe she wanted a loser like me as much as I wanted her. My uncle tried to warn me, told me she came from a rough family, but all I cared about was her. I had started writing to Katie, got to see Megs and Colton every month, and Ali filled the rest of my time. I was happy."

The way he said the words made my hair stand on end, and I knew something awful was coming. I shook my head. I didn't want him to tell me more. I didn't want to hear how this story would turn any more horrific. He didn't stop though.

313

"I'd seen bruises on her, but she always laughed 'em off. We were so close that I knew she'd tell me if something was wrong, but she never did. We'd been together for almost a year when she came to me, crying. She was pregnant, almost four months.

"We were fifteen, both just kids ourselves, no idea how to be parents. We talked about running away, but I couldn't leave my family, not when I'd just gotten 'em back. We talked to Liam, and he told us we could live with him, that he'd help us. Ali's dad had other plans, though, and decided since it was too late for her to have an abortion, he'd beat the baby out of her."

I gasped.

"Turned out she'd been his punching bag for years. I never would have let her go home if I'd known. It didn't work.

"Hannah was a fighter, even in the womb. Ali though, she wasn't as strong as our daughter. Her dad was charged with child endangerment, and when she got released from the hospital, her family wouldn't let her go home. It was a small town, and a fifteen-year-old pregnant girl was not the kinda kid most parents wanted their daughters around. Suddenly she was the shunned girl, not the shining star.

"As she drifted away from me, I watched helplessly, hoping after the baby came that Ali'd be okay. She wasn't. I suspected that she was using. I was terrified for Hannah, pissed off that Ali'd do that shit after I told her about my childhood. The day I caught her dealer in my house, with my very pregnant girlfriend, both shooting up, I snapped. I fuckin' came unspun. If my uncle hadn't come home and stopped me, I'da killed him.

"I was sent back to the youth center, this time as a violent criminal. I missed Hannah bein' born, missed her first cry, her first smile." He swallowed hard as the memories clearly became too much for him to bear. "I only got to hold her a handful of times, but I loved that little girl with every part of my soul.

"Liam had her for a few years and would bring her when he came to visit. She reminded me so much of Lizzie—dark curly hair and chubby cheeks. The most beautiful baby girl on the fuckin' planet.

"I was determined to be a great dad, to be everything mine wasn't. More like my uncle. I had this need to be someone my baby girl could be proud of, to right other's wrongs, and stand up for the kids who couldn't stand up for themselves. There's a lot of shitty stuff that happens in a correctional facility, L.K., even when you're in there with kids as young as ten. Matty and I had become friends, and he always had my back, even when he thought I should mind my own fuckin' business. But everything good I was doin' didn't matter 'cause I was still stuck inside.

"And when Ali came back, after two years of being a fuckin' lowlife, to take Hannah, my uncle had to give her back 'cause she was the mom. She had the fuckin' nerve to come to Longcreek and gloat. Told me I'd ruined her life and that I'd never see Hannah again.

"I was in the middle of a fuckin' science class when the guards and my counselor pulled me out, haulin' me to the office liked I'd done something wrong. When I saw Matty sittin' there, looking like he was ready to burn the place to the ground, I knew." His voice broke again. "I fuckin' knew there was something wrong. They brought him in to soften the blow." He shook his head, a tear streaming down his cheek. "There is nothin' in this world that will help you when someone tells you that your daughter is dead, that her mother's boyfriend killed her. There is no pain that comes close to knowing you failed the people you love again, or that you didn't save her."

I didn't think, just pushed myself off the couch and flew at him. I pulled him against me so hard that he didn't have a chance to resist. Even sitting, he was almost as tall as I was standing. I held him tightly, my body shaking as sobs wracked his body, letting him know that he wasn't alone. It was heartbreaking and I couldn't stop my own tears.

Jesus, this evening had not gone as I planned it. I had no idea that this was where our conversation would take us, and if I had, I would have stopped it before it started. I wished I could take it all back.

I waited until Rocker's breathing had returned to normal before I eased my grip.

He cleared his throat, sitting back and pulling me onto his lap. "You asked me if I ever killed anyone." He shrugged before he wrapped an arm around me. "I meant to kill him because he took her from me. I got off 'cause I had a brilliant attorney who had an even more brilliant plan. I would do it again, even if it meant spending the rest of my life locked away."

I understood perfectly. I would kill for my children, without a second thought. I turned my head to look at him. "And Alison? What happened to her?

He met my gaze, face hardening in resolve. "She took the coward's way out and ran. Just disappeared. I haven't found her yet. For all I know, she could have died in an alley with a needle in her arm."

The fierce look in his eyes was too much, and I had to look away. "And the Bastards? You started the club, didn't you? Right after that?"

"Matty and I started it together. I don't know what he's told you about his time locked up or why he was there, but when we got out, I came home to Boston to get away from the memories of Hannah. I needed to channel my energy into something else or I knew I wouldn't survive. Mateo's my best friend, so he came too. We fell in with a rough club and were prospects. It wasn't enough for me though. The prez was the one who told me to start the Bastards, and he lent me some money and gave me a list of contacts. We had friends who wanted in, and they had friends. It didn't take long before we were an official club.

"MC's are fuckin' risky, L.K. Starting a new one and getting the AMA - American Motorcyclist Association - to sanction you as a real club isn't easy. We wanted to be aboveboard—completely legal, so everyone would take us seriously. But to them, we were just a bunch of criminal kids. The cops called us a gang, other clubs ignored us or picked fights whenever they could, and the AMA wouldn't even acknowledge our existence. One day Mateo and I were talking about what the Bastard's were and what we wanted them to become. The answer was simple. We protect the innocent, are passionate about what we do, and we're not gonna stop 'til we save 'em all."

As the words sunk in, I realized that had been his uncle's definition of a bastard. It all made sense.

"To do that, to be who we want to be, we have to step outside the boundaries of the law. We can't hold people accountable, or save the people we want to save, if we don't. We spend ninety-five percent of our time inside the gray area. We may not sell drugs or do illegal shit to make money, but we're still not welcome by the AMA because we're not law-abiding citizens. We decided that they could all go fuck themselves, and we happily accepted our roles as outlaws. We wear those one percent patches with pride."

"I told you that people are afraid of us for a fuckin' reason. Like you said last summer, the general consensus is that we're vigilantes. Some see us as heroes, others think we are sadistic fucks. We all have our own demons, stories that are worse than mine, and we'll do anything to keep other kids from going through the same shit we did. We try to protect the ones who have no one else to keep them safe, to watch out for them. And we shelter the ones we love at all costs, including keeping them in the dark because our secrets will hurt 'em."

I didn't know what to say. This group of broken men, all tough and scary and freakishly weird in their own way, were the most amazing people I'd ever met. I wanted to support them in any way I could because I knew they were helping more people than they were hurting.

And even though I didn't want to, I could understand Matty's insistence to shut me out. Whatever secrets he was still keeping weren't important anymore. Whatever it was that he'd done that he thought was so horrible didn't matter to me.

SIXTEEN

JO

I didn't want to get out of bed. I wasn't sure what time it was, but by the amount of sunshine invading Matty's room, I knew it was late morning. I needed caffeine, to pee, and to get dressed before Cris showed up—not necessarily in that order. I couldn't find the energy to move though.

I'd stayed up with Rocker well into the night. We'd talked about my kids, my future plans, and anything else I could think of to keep his mind off of what he'd told me. He'd been so deflated, nothing like the man I'd come to know, and I wanted to distract him for as long as possible. He'd finally given in though, telling me he had early appointments today, and he hugged me and kissed my hair the way Matty did before he headed down to his room.

I'd sat up for a long while after he left, trying to process everything I'd learned, before I gave up and headed to bed. I should have stayed up. I'd only tossed and turned, begging for what seemed like hours for sleep to come. I'd gotten up and taken a steaming hot shower at one point, hoping it would quiet my mind and relax my body into slumber. It hadn't.

I stretched, my muscles screaming in agony as they protested any movement. My phone rang, and I grabbed it begrudgingly, not even looking at the screen. Only Cris would be calling me at this time of day. She probably wanted to know why I wasn't ready.

"I'm still sleeping," I growled, breaking into a yawn.

"Morning." The low, sexy voice drawled, full of amusement, and I could almost hear the smile on his lips. "Sleep well, sunshine?"

"Not really." I stifled another yawn. "I sleep better when you're here with me."

"God," Matty groaned. "I'd do anything to be there with you right now. I guarantee you wouldn't be so grumpy."

I smiled and chuckled.

He sighed. "I didn't mean to wake you up, Joes. I'm driving to a visit and thought we could talk for a while."

I sat up, instantly awake. We used to do that all the time. Whenever one of us was on the road, we'd call the other and chat.

"We can talk later if you want to go back to sleep."

"No!" I practically shouted.

Matty laughed. "Good." He let out a tired sigh. "I'm sorry I didn't call last night. Sammy's game ran late. Did you get my texts?"

"I didn't." I pulled my phone away from my ear and frowned at the screen before putting it back. "But I didn't look either." I hesitated, not sure if I should tell him. Biting my lip, I decided to be honest. "Rocker kept me awake most of the night, and I didn't even think about checking my messages. I'm sorry!" The silence that answered me made me think he'd driven into a dead zone. "Hello?"

"Sorry, it sounded like you said Rocker kept you up all night."

I nodded to my empty room. "Most of it, yeah."

"Doing what?" The voice was cold and agitated and held none of the warmth it had only minutes ago.

The memory of me sitting on Rob's lap flittered through my mind. At the time it had been purely innocent, one friend wanting to comfort another. But if someone had seen us, would it have looked that way? I swore under my breath.

"Joes?" The tone of his voice sent shivers up my spine. This was scary Matt.

"Not like that!" I snapped, irritated. "We were up talking."

He waited a few seconds for me to continue, but I stayed silent. "About?" he finally bit out.

"The Bastards." I took a deep breath, trying not to read too much into his silence. "He told me about his childhood, about Hannah and Ali, and how the club got started."

"That's a lot of fuckin' information to take in at once. How you holdin' up?"

I didn't know what I thought he'd say, but it wasn't that. I smiled, loving him even more. "I'm fine." I shrugged. "I haven't had a chance to process it all yet. I was more worried about him than anything."

"You don't need to worry about him, babe. He's been dealing with that shit for a long time."

I could hear him take a sip of his drink. I smiled, picturing him with his Dunkin Donuts coffee.

"I wanted to tell you all of it, Joes, but I wanted to do it in person. There hasn't been time." He sighed. "That mind of yours

319

must be running at full speed. I have about fifteen minutes before I get to my appointment, if you want to ask me anything."

My smile grew. He knew me better than anyone. I had so many questions I didn't even know where to start. Rob had told me a lot, but one thing worried me more than anything else, and I had focused on that most of the night. "The things you don't want to tell me..." I swallowed, not sure how to continue. "I don't need to know whatever it is. I love you. I trust you." *I can't handle the thought of you breaking down the way Rob did.* "But is it always gonna be like this? Will I ever know what's going on?"

"Fuck, Joes. I want to be looking at you when we talk about this." He sighed. "There are some things I'll never be able to tell you. Club business is for members only."

"Okay. How do I become a member?"

"You don't."

"Why not?"

He snorted as if my question was absurd. The sound pissed me off. "Answer the question."

"Because you can't. Women aren't members. Let's talk about it when we're together, okay?"

I ignored his last question, hating that he was trying to pacify me. "That's archaic and sexist!" He didn't argue, irritating me even more. "Fine," I seethed. "Then what exactly is a woman's role?"

"Well," he started slowly, and I couldn't tell if it was amusement or apprehension in his voice, "there are a few."

I waited patiently, expecting him to continue. He didn't.

"You're saying that the women who hang around the Bastards are either club whores or old ladies. All those women who were here Saturday are one or the other? That's it for women? I don't fit into either category, so what, I don't have a role?"

"That's not what I'm saying." His voice was calm but hard. "There are those women, yes, but there are others too. Like the women who work for us and th—"

"As in prostitutes and strippers?" I interrupted angrily. "I know I'm pretty clueless about this whole MC thing, but I'm not an idiot. I've seen *Sons of Anarchy*. You made me watch it with you after you got snipped, remember? So, unless I decide to swallow my pride and become a whore or take my clothes off for money, there isn't a place for me in your stupid club?"

"Yeah, that's not gonna fuckin' happen, so don't even fuckin' think about it. The only man seeing you naked is me. And no more HBO for you."

If I hadn't been so pissed, I would have laughed.

"The Bastards don't own a strip club, even though I can see how that might be a great idea." He laughed when I growled. "We're not pimps. What I meant was the girls like Jessie, who work for one of the businesses. Some are moms of the kids we've helped, some are friends. They come over and clean or help us organize charity runs. There are the female friends who enjoy hanging around. And there are sisters, like Cris."

I huffed, not sure I was going to accept his explanation.

"Ah, fuck, babe. You kill me." I could hear the amused humor in his voice. "The Bastards aren't your typical MC. We like to do things a little differently. But you're right. There are club whores and ol' ladies too. Nothing to worry about though. Jessie's tight with those women, and they'll love you. Like I do."

"You don't get it!" I snapped. "Cris and Jessie, they have separate code names, just like the rest of you, and they know all about the club and what to expect when you go on a ride. Jessie called me a civilian, as if she's a member of some super-secret cool club. Which apparently she's not. Because she's a woman!"

The jackass laughed hysterically.

"Really? I'm glad you find this so damn amusing! I like your friends—well, most of them," I corrected myself quietly, "but I... goddammit, I hate the fact that I have no fucking place in your life! Okay?" I threw a pillow across the room in anger.

"You're mine, Joes. That's your place."

I groaned. "I'm not your property, Matty."

"You wanted to know your role, Joes, and I'm telling you that's your role in my life and in my club. You. Are. Mine." He enunciated each word. "That's all you need to worry about. Everyone else knows it too." I started to snap back, but he interrupted. "I'm here, Joey. We'll finish this tonight, okay?"

I scowled. It wasn't okay. I wanted answers, but I knew he had to go. "Fine. I'm going to the gym with Cris today and need to get ready anyway. Call me later?"

"Absolutely. I love you like crazy, even if you are a giant pain in the ass."

I smiled, all my irritation gone. "Love you too."

SEVENTEEN

JO

"Am I dressed well enough?"

Cris grabbed her gym bag from the back and slammed the door of her Jeep Wrangler before coming around to my side and sweeping her eyes over my light gray yoga pants, unzipped hooded sweatshirt, and black exercise tank that proclaimed, "Sweat is Fat Crying," in bold letters over my chest. With a sassy smile that mirrored one I'd seen from her brother at least a thousand times, she nodded.

"It's a gym, Joey. How else should you be dressed?"

I rolled my eyes as we turned toward the building. "Well, considering the vehicles I see in the parking lot, I just wanted to make sure I wasn't underdressed." I cast an apprehensive glance at the row of cars that contained two Jags, a Mercedes S Class, and a Porsche mixed in with another wrangler and Volvo.

Cris snorted as she swiped a card in front of the security panel and beeped us in. Looking down at her miniscule sports bra and boxing shorts, she smirked. "If anyone's underdressed, it's me." She held open the door for me, dropping her voice. "They're a bunch of nerds who made their millions and now they need to come here to keep their trophy wives happy. Trust me. You're fine."

The beginners' class was exactly how it sounded. I joined a group of five men, all dressed in baggy T-shirts and shorts, and we concentrated on learning stances and footwork. Muay Thai, we were told, was the art of eight limbs. It had an eight-point fighting system and used every part of the body. Unlike traditional kickboxing, we could use our fists, feet, knees, and elbows to hit our opponent. First though, we had to learn how to control our bodies and work on core strength.

Cris taught the class, standing with her back to a wall of mirrors that reminded me of a dance studio so that we could see ourselves and watch her at the same time. The school's co-owner, Nick helping us move our bodies into a new pose and offering suggestions. My fat was most definitely crying—I was sweating buckets.

The class ended with us watching a sparring match between Cris and Nick. She was tiny compared to him, even with her headgear and boxing gloves. He was a few inches taller, maybe 6'1", and had a good fifty pounds of pure muscle on her. They were obviously not trying to hurt each other, explaining each move as they went, laughing and taunting each other. Someone could do serious damage with this method of fighting though. I was impressed.

After she climbed out of the ring and pulled off her gear, she dragged Nick over so she could introduce us.

His dark brown eyes sparkled at me. "When Cris told me she was bringing her friend Jo today, I assumed he'd fit right in with the rest of the class." He shot her a dirty look. "Thanks for the warning! I'da shaved." He ran his hands over his chin.

"It's nice to finally meet you." I gave him a small smile.

He winked in reply, a beaming smile splitting his cheeks. Nick was every woman's fantasy, dressed only in silky red boxing shorts, his tanned, toned body glistened from the workout. He wasn't as tattooed as Matty, but he had plenty of ink running along his arms, and a giant minotaur dressed as a boxer ready to pounce took up his entire back.

"So whatchya think?" He tipped his head toward the studio part of the building, where class had been held. "You comin' back?"

I nodded. "I had so much fun! I may never get to the sparring level, but I'd like to know more."

Nick nodded. "Good." He leaned his upper body toward me, eyebrows waggling friskily. "If not, I'd have to beg ya not to leave until you'd given me your number."

Cris groaned, playfully annoyed. "God, you're an idiot!" She snorted, pointing at me. "This is Joey."

"Yeah. You said that." Nick didn't take his eyes off me.

"As in Joes." Her tone turned snappy.

Nick raised his eyebrows, clearly not understanding.

"As in Mateo's girl."

Nick's eyes widened, and he jerked back. "Oh!" He met my eyes. "Sorry. Didn't realize."

It was like flipping a switch as he went from flirtatious to polite and accommodating instantly. I turned my attention to Cris, raising an eyebrow, sure I was missing something.

She just smirked and nodded at him. "Jo, meet Neo. Matty's brother."

I scowled, confused for a split second. Matty didn't have a brother, unless you considered the club. Then the reaction made sense—Nick was a Bastard.

After chatting for a few more minutes, I explained that I really wanted to learn self-defense tactics. Nick happily took me back to the studio and showed me a few easy moves to use to ward off would-be attackers while Cris went up to her office to deal with paperwork. He promised that the next few classes of Muay Thai would help, but he spent the good part of an hour teaching me how to punch.

"No." He laughed when I showed him how I would make a fist. Opening my hand, he pulled out my thumb then closed my fingers. "If you keep your thumb on the inside, you'll break it."

It took a few tries, but I was finally able to line my knuckles up the way he wanted. Next, we worked on wrist alignment and where I should aim.

"You're a little thing," he said, laughing when I gave him a glower. "It's not a bad thing. It just means that you're going to have fewer targets than most. Aim for the throat. The nose, if the guy is short or sitting. But the throat any other time."

"Make sure you're following through. It's the most important thing when you're punching someone." He was in the middle of a demonstration when Cris rushed in, freshly showered and looking fantastic in tight jeans and a tank.

"I'm sorry to cut your session short, but we gotta go, Jo."

I dropped my arms, turning to her. "Everything okay?"

She only shook her head before hauling Nick up to the office.

Five minutes later, we were in her Jeep.

"Do you have time to drop me off at the house first?" I asked.

She zoomed through a yellow light as she shook her head. "No. Unfortunately, we've both been summoned to 'Bury."

"Summoned? By who?"

She gave me a sideways glace, her tone bitter. "Who do you think?"

I scowled. Rocker. I wondered what was so important that he needed us in the middle of the day and couldn't wait. I watched out the window, trying to keep my bearings as I wondered if we were going to his office. Cris headed toward South Boston, but then turned again toward Roxbury.

I tensed a little when I realized we were headed into the part of the city Will and our college friends had called Glocksbury. I couldn't remember ever being here—it was supposed to be scary as hell. The apartment buildings were nice though, not at all what I expected, and as we drove, they started to disappear, replaced by businesses and warehouses that got farther and farther apart. The property on my left was huge, but I couldn't see much more than a building or two through the privacy fence surrounding it. Cris slowed suddenly and put on her blinker.

"Where are we?"

She turned into a paved driveway and stopped at a camera that sat outside the fence. Opening her window and reaching out toward a security keypad, she finally replied, "The clubhouse."

There was a loud beep, then the gate swung inward. I glanced around, trying to take it all in. It was a large parking lot, with one huge building and two smaller ones. Between the smaller buildings was a giant playground and a picnic/grill area with deep green grass that seemed out of place amidst all the asphalt.

She parked in a space near the large red building and sighed. "I forgot you haven't been here." Her eyes skimmed the lot then nodded. "You'll be fine. There aren't that many people here."

"I can't go in!" I exclaimed, shocked, staring at the sign that took up most of the wall in front of me. It matched the back of the Bastards' jackets. A silver Itus held two blood-red swords in his hands, ready to viciously slay anyone who threatened those he protected. "Bastards MC" arched above him in bold red print, and "Boston" curled below him in the same red letters. It was intimidating as hell. I searched for a feasible excuse. "I'm all sweaty and gross. You changed. I didn't."

She pushed open her door and pointed at me. "Out. Now. If I have to face him, you do too."

I glared at her but got out.

"This used to be an elementary school," she explained as we walked toward the door. "The city sold it when they upgraded. Perfect place for the club. Tons of space for everything they want or need, and easy to get to."

We walked into a dimly lit space, and once the door closed behind us, and my eyes needed a minute to adjust. If I hadn't known better, I would have sworn we were in a bar. Everything about it reminded me of Hooligan's.

The room was decent-sized but full; at least twenty-five high tables, each surrounded by three or four black padded bar stools. In the corner to my left were a few black leather couches and a couple of chairs set up in a large square. In the opposite corner, four pool tables. At the end of the room, straight ahead of me, a long wooden counter set in a U. Behind it, lining the walls, were hundreds of bottles of liquor and a stainless-steel refrigerator. Above them, stretching the length of the room, was a sign that proclaimed to the world, **"GOD FORGIVES. BASTARDS DON'T."**

The bottoms of the walls were wood, the tops painted a light silver. Everywhere I looked, the Bastards insignia seemed to be present. The walls held framed newspaper clippings, pictures, and framed leather jackets. Everything was either black, red, silver, or polished wood.

"Wow."

Cris gave me a disgusted look and rolled her eyes. "I need a fuckin' drink." She strode behind the bar and grabbed a glass. "You want?"

"It's two in the afternoon!"

"Exactly!"

I shook my head in exasperation and took a seat, leaning onto the counter. "Water?"

She grabbed me a bottle from the fridge then downed her shot. Bracing her arms on the counter, she leaned forward and gave me a wry smile. "I better go back. Stay here. I won't be long."

She walked back around the bar and down a hallway that I hadn't noticed earlier before I had a moment to respond. I wondered what was down it, half tempted to go exploring. There were two closed doors: one right behind the bar and one by the pool tables. She'd told me to stay here, but I wasn't really leaving if I just peeked in them.

I turned in my chair, awed by not only the size but by how different it was from the image I'd had in my mind. I thought a clubhouse would be dirty and dingy, with bike's torn apart and greasy parts littering the floor, and classic rock to be screaming from the speakers. I'd expected half-stoned women, clad only in bikini's, to be stumbling around trying not to spill their drinks, stopping only to make out with a random biker. I was relieved that my imagination was overactive and not a reality.

I slid off my stool, ready to go explore, just as a man walked out of the hallway. He had a glass tumbler in one hand and held a phone up to his ear with the other as he talked loudly. He slowed when he saw me, curiosity making him stare. I smiled and offered a pathetic wave. He returned the grin, then walked toward the couches.

I turned back to the bar, feeling like an idiot. I stood, tapping my foot and sipping my water as I replayed everything I'd learned earlier, trying not to listen to his conversation.

"Babe? I said I need a refill."

I jumped when a hand touched my arm, my hand flying to my chest.

His eyes followed the movement and lingered on my breasts as he smiled sarcastically and held up the empty glass. "My glass is empty."

"Oh!" I laughed at my jumpiness and tried to ignore his scrutiny. "I'm sure they won't mind if you get yourself another drink." I gestured at the bar and turned back to my water.

He chuckled, a low deep sound, and stepped closer. "First time heah?" He had the same South Boston Accent that I was used to hearing from Rob.

I nodded, turning slightly to make eye contact. He practically oozed "Bad Boy Biker," from the way he leaned his beefy frame confidently against the counter to the intense and dangerous look in his hazel eyes.

"Yeah. I'm waiting for Rocker."

He pulled out a pack of Marlboro Reds and held it out to me. I declined. As he shook one out and lit up, I took the opportunity to scan him. Next to Tiny, this mystery man was the biggest Bastard—if he was a member of the club—I'd met. His arms were veiny, as if he spent every second he could working out. His plain black T-shirt was tight, showing a wide and muscular torso, but it was tucked into a pair of baggy blue jeans that looked as if they hadn't fit him right in years. The thick belt he wore was barely keeping them from slipping off his waist. I stared at his buckle a second too long, trying to figure out what was on the large bronze circle. It was Itus. The man wasn't wearing a vest or jacket, but I doubted he'd be able to wear the symbol if he wasn't a member.

When my eyes moved back to his face, I realized that he was giving me the same kind of once-over I'd just given him. I shifted, uncomfortable.

"I thank God every damn day for the man who invented yoga pants," he mumbled to himself more than to me.

Feeling extremely self-conscious, I slid away from him a little. Nothing about him scared me, but better safe than sorry. "You don't have to wait with me. I'm good."

I gulped another sip of water and, aware of his eyes glued to my ass, turned around, backing into the bar. It was the wrong move. He seemed to take it as an invitation. Instead of moving away, he stubbed out his cigarette and stepped in front of me, boxing me in with his arms.

"I'm sure Rocker will be out to get me any minute." I tried to mask the irritation in my voice but knew he heard it.

He only smiled coyly, leaning down and invading my space, moving his head to my ear. "Naw, babe. He's got his hands full right now. Won't be out for hours."

I pushed against him but would have had better luck moving a boulder. He acted as if he didn't even notice my hands on his chest.

"I have the whole fuckin' afternoon free." He lifted his left hand and ran a thick knuckle down my cheek. "I bet we could think of somethin' that would fill the time."

I moved quickly, squeezing out from under him. The hand slapping my ass didn't hurt, but it made me yelp and jump, moving my hand to my butt as I whirled on him. I rubbed the spot gently, trying to numb away the sting. "What the fuck was that?"

I got a glimpse of teeth that were so white they looked out of place as he grinned at me mischievously. "Babe, rule number one—if you're gonna have it on display here, it's gonna get touched." He twisted his lips and took a step toward me. "Why don't we go back to my room and you give me a sneak peek before you go audition for Rocker?"

I stepped back, trying to find a way to tell him to go to hell without causing trouble. Not taking the hint at all, he reached his hand out, and without giving it too much thought, I knocked it away. Deciding that flight was my best option, I turned quickly, but fingers wrapped around my left wrist, pulling me back and spinning me around. I didn't think, just balled my hand into a fist like Nick had shown me and stepped my weight into the punch.

I aimed for the throat, as instructed, but the brute in front of me lowered his chin when he saw the hit coming. I didn't know who was more surprised when my fist actually connected. He grabbed my right wrist as I tried to back away, amusement, not anger, filling his eyes. Yanking me flush against him, he laughed and ran his other hand over his jaw.

"You're a feisty bitch, aintchya?" The hazel eyes twinkled. "That's not somethin' we see too often in here. It's fuckin' sexy as hell." His voice was low and rough. Moving his hand from his chin to my backside, he rubbed the spot he'd slapped earlier and ground his front into me so I could feel just how much of a turn-on he thought it was—he was hard as a rock. "Don't worry, sweetheart, I give just as good as I get. If this is your idea of foreplay, I'm all for it."

Ignoring the way my stomach soured, I lifted my face to his to show him I wasn't afraid, I glared at him. "Back off, buddy." I shoved at him again, but he didn't budge. If he didn't let me go soon, I was going to murder him with my bare hands.

"Fuck, you are hot!" he muttered absently and buried his face in the side of my neck, closing his teeth over the bottom of my ear.

I narrowly avoided the urge to gouge out his eyes. My hands curled into fists instead. I started counting silently, giving him a few moments to get his head on straight before I kicked his ass.

"Mmm. I want to taste every inch of this body." He picked his head up, licking his lips as he starred at mine. "My ol' lady won't be back 'til tomorrow. Give me the word, and I'm yours for the night. Let me be your first Bastard." His voice held a pleading tone.

I couldn't fight the look of disgust. He thought I was a club whore. Not just that—this jackass had a girlfriend, or wife, he was going to cheat on. "I don't fuckin' think so." I sneered, "Let me go."

His grip began to loosen, but the sound of catcalls and whoops had us both looking across the bar. A handful of bikers, all wearing Bastard jackets, were watching us as if we were putting on one hell of a show. He swore and turned us, so his back was to them, sheltering me from their view, and pushed my head down into his chest, hiding me.

"Fuck off," he barked. I couldn't hear their replies because his thick hand was over my ear, but a few seconds later, he startled me by roaring, "Now!"

A few minutes later, his arms released me, and he stepped back, but enormous hands cupped my cheeks and tipped my face toward his. "Sorry. Fuckin' prospects," he admonished, obviously annoyed. "You good?"

I gaped at him. In the last few minutes, this man had spanked me, manhandled me, propositioned me, and implied I was a slut. Now he was worried about how I'd handle a bunch of obnoxious men staring at me? I giggled at the absurdity of the situation.

He arched a concerned eyebrow and shook me slightly, as if trying to get me to focus. "Babe?"

I couldn't answer, the giggles turning into breath-stealing, side-hurting laughter. His mouth closed over mine before I realized what was happening. I reacted instantly, laughter gone, recoiling violently and slapping him hard across his face.

He grinned. "There you are."

He stepped toward me, but I held up my finger. "Don't you fuckin' come near me again."

"Holy fuck." The words were dragged out in a slow, surprised drawl, stopping both the moose and I dead in our tracks.

EIGHTEEN

JO

I jerked my head toward the door. A man stood in the shadows, watching us. All I could see of him was a thick dark beard and wide shoulders.

My companion turned too, nodding a hello. "Got it under control brothah."

The man shook his head, "The hell you do!" In just a few steps, he was in front of me, inserting himself between the giant and me, gently grabbing my chin between his thumb and finger and pushing my head back. "You okay, ma'am?"

The familiar face and low voice made distant memories filter through my mind. "Ian?"

He looked as if he'd aged ten years in the last few months. I knew he was almost young enough to be my son, but the innocent twinkle in his eyes had been replaced by a cautious wariness that he shouldn't have acquired for years, and dark black smudges underlined his eyes. His lips split in pleased surprise, and for a second, I could see the handsome kid he'd been.

"I wasn't sure I'd see you again, Joey."

It had only been for a few hours one night the summer before, but the time I'd spent with this young man had touched me. I'd been out with Matty and the Bastards when a brawl had broken out, Cris and I smack-dab in the middle of it. Ian had put himself between danger and me, carried me outside, taken me home, and spent the night trying to keep my mind off Matty. He was brilliant and insightful and sweet. He'd entertained me with stories of his girlfriend, Ellie.

Then only a few weeks later, he and Ellie had been viciously attacked. I'd often wondered what had happened to him and, until this second, didn't even know he was still a Bastard. Thinking about it made my heart ache. Not just for him and Ellie, but for Matty and me. That had been the worst weekend of my life—the one where Matty walked away, breaking me.

"C'mere!" He dropped my chin and pulled me against him. A nasty scar ran up his throat and disappeared under his beard. I wondered if it was a souvenir from that awful night last August.

331

Without thinking, I traced the red line gently with a fingertip. I felt him tense immediately.

I took a deep, shaking breath, fighting tears. As much as I tried to, I couldn't stop them. He ran his hand up and down my back, muttering words of comfort.

"I don't even know why I'm crying." I sobbed against him. "Are you okay?" I mumbled as I backed away from him.

He searched my eyes. "Are you?"

He glanced over his shoulder, and I could see the other man watching us, confusion clear on his face. I nodded as I wiped away the last of my tears and looked around. The room was still empty, except for the three of us.

"No one's gonna hurt you here. I promise." Ian vowed.

"She's fine," Gigantor snapped.

Ian's eyes flashed, and his face hardened before he ground out, "I asked her, not you."

The other man stepped toward us, fury written all over his face.

Ian spun around, going toe-to-toe with the much larger man. "Some things never change, do they, Brothah?"

The look of rage that crossed the other man's face was enough to tighten my stomach in knots.

"I know I've been gone a long time, but you're outta line, kid. I don't have to force women to do anythin' they don't wanna do." He glanced at me, and his face softened slightly. His nostrils flared when his eyes moved back to Bear. "If you wanna talk about this more, we can go out back."

I stepped toward my friend, but kept my eyes glued to the stranger as I answered. "It was a silly misunderstanding, that's all."

Out of the corner of my eye I watched as Ian altered his gaze from me to the other man and back, before he visibly relaxed a bit. He turned, grabbed a stool from the table closest to us, and pulled it out before gesturing for me to sit. He took the seat beside me then kicked the third chair away from the table slightly, pointing at it as he glared at the other man.

"Why don't you two tell me what the hell I walked in on?" He turned back to me. "'Cause after what I heard outside, I never expected you to be the one I found in here."

I blushed and stared at the floor as the other man grunted. "I thought she was a new girl and lookin' for some fun. I'll talk to

Rocker when he comes out and take whatever punishment he gives."

Punishment? The words made me snap my head up in surprise.

"I'm sorry if I scared you," the man told me sincerely.

I shook my head, trying to convey that it was fine. He didn't need to apologize. He ignored me and continued.

"I'm sorry, Bear." I could hear the sincerity in his voice. "I didn't realize she was yours, Brothah."

"I'm not his!" I snapped, breaking my confused silence.

A scowl crossed Ian's features as he sent me a scathing look. "You two don't know each other?"

"No," I answered, sighing. I turned my attention back to Mr. Massive, offering him a hand. "I'm Jo."

He took it, swallowing my fingers with his firm grip. "Tank."

My eyes widened in surprise. Immediately, everything made sense. Now that I was looking, I could see the resemblance to Barbie. I offered a small smile, trying to convey that everything would be fine.

"If you aren't the new girl and you aren't Bear's, what's a tasty little thing like you doing here darlin'?"

I opened my mouth to answer, but Ian cut me off, clearly annoyed. He tipped his head toward me. "Tank, meet Mateo's Jo. Or as Rocker calls her, L.K."

Tank snorted. "That's fucking fucked, Brothah. Quit screwin' with me 'cause I'm not that fuckin' stupid. I've seen pictures of Mateo's girl. She's not you." He winked at me, looking over my tight tank and dyed hair. His eyes roamed my face for a few seconds, then they grew large and he sat back, paling a little. "Christ, I'm a dead man."

"That's what I'm sayin'!" Ian nodded, crossing his arms smugly.

"You are not!" I snapped at them. "For God's sake, you didn't do anything some stranger at a bar wouldn't do. And you didn't know who I was—even though I could have told you numerous times." I waved a hand in front of my face, dismissing their argument.

"We're not in a bar, Joey. What happens out there doesn't happen in here. We don't fuck with brother's ol' ladies, simple as that. We view it the same way the rest of the world views stealin'.

Tank tried to take somethin' that wasn't his, and he'll go to court to answer for it."

Court? What? And back to jail. The thought infuriated me. "I wasn't scared of him in the least!"

Ian didn't believe a word I was saying. "Then why were you cryin'?"

I sighed, exasperated. "I don't know! Adrenaline? Seeing you for the first time since..." I trailed off, but Ian understood. I swallowed. "No one will talk about you! I don't know if Ellie recovered. I didn't even know you were still here until I saw you ten minutes ago!" I rolled my head, trying to work out some of the tension in my shoulders. "You were the last person I expected to see."

Ian sighed. "Doesn't matter. In this house, you are protected above all else. It's club business. When somethin' like this happens, there are consequences."

"It's club business," I mocked childishly. "Jesus, you sound just like Matty!" I sat a little straighter in the chair. "In case you hadn't noticed, I didn't need you to run in and rescue me." I shifted my gaze to Tank. "You're not telling Rocker shit. He doesn't need to hear your version. I'll take care of it."

Tank shook his head. "L.K.," he started cautiously, "you can't just—"

My fists curled in anger. "You just met me. Don't for one second think that you can tell me what I can and cannot do, or I will kick your ass!" I practically shouted, suddenly pissed at him. "What kind of man cheats on his girlfriend when he just got home from prison?" He started to speak, but I slammed my hand on the table. "Seriously? And why in god's name would you think I was a club girl?" He started to answer, and I slammed my hand again. "No! Don't fuckin' answer that!"

His eyes had grown wide, and he looked as if he might be fighting a smile.

I narrowed my eyes. "Let me give you a little advice. You may have gone to prison, but your girlfriend, wife, old lady, or whatever the hell you call her was also punished. Being without the man you love sucks. You have a free afternoon 'cause she's not coming until tonight? Awesome. Spend that time doing something nice for her instead of doing a club whore. Maybe think about a nice gift you could give her instead of giving her, oh, I don't know, chlamydia!"

A look I couldn't read passed between them, and they both burst out laughing.

"Little Kangaroo with boxing gloves," Ian mumbled, as if explaining away my behavior.

Groaning in frustration, I slid out of my chair, grabbed my water off the bar, and stomped to the couches. I wanted to leave and get the hell away from all things Bastard, but there was no way I was going outside alone. Ian had said he'd heard about Tank and me, which meant the men from earlier were out there. I had no desire to see them, and until Cris and Rocker were done, I had nowhere else to go. Sinking down onto the couch, I leaned my head on the arm rest and closed my eyes.

"She got your cards."

I heard the unmistakable sound of someone sitting on leather as the hushed voice spoke to me. After Matty had left me, I'd been a mess, but Ellie and Bear had always been at the front of my mind. It had given me months of nightmares. I'd sent cards to Cris, asking her to deliver them for me, because I wanted Ellie to know people were praying for her.

I desperately wanted to know how she was.

As if reading my thoughts, he continued, "She's fine, Joey." He sighed. "Physically, it was a quick recovery. Mentally took her a little longer. But she's fine."

I sat up, turning toward his voice. Leaning back in the chair across from me, he looked defeated. His dark jeans were stained with what looked like grease, and I could see the steel on the toe of his boot where the material had worn away.

"Will I ever get to meet her? Or do you keep her away from the club?"

He swallowed and tipped his head back, staring at the ceiling. "We're not together anymore. I still see her sometimes. Ya know, just to check in. I want to make sure she's safe. But, we're not together." He shrugged as if it wasn't a big deal, however I could see the pain etched on his face. "You're a lot more naked than the last time I saw ya."

I hesitated, thinking about my outfit before following his eyes to my empty hand and the finger that used to hold my wedding ring. Last summer Ian had taken offense to the fact that

Matty was sleeping with me while I was still hitched. Amusing, considering all the things I'd heard about these men since.

I looked at the bare hand and smiled. "Yeah. I feel like I've lost a ton of weight, too." We were quiet for a moment. "Bear, huh?" He nodded absentmindedly. "What should I call you?"

"Whatever you want. Most of the club calls me Bear, but my closest friends can call me either one." He stood. "Have you gotten the tour yet?" I shook my head as he held out a hand. "Come on, I'll show ya."

NINETEEN

JO

The clubhouse was huge.

The door behind the bar led to a commercial-grade kitchen that any chef would be proud of. Next to the kitchen was a communal eating area that was once the school cafeteria. Ian explained that at least quarterly they had giant "family" gatherings where every club member brought his family and friends. It was also the room where the club gathered before charity events.

The hallway to the left of the main room was long and made several turns. No way in hell I would find my way around without getting lost. Not only did they have the main common room, there was a TV room, a game room, a quiet room, a giant playroom for the kids, offices, and an entire wing dedicated to the dorms and sleeping quarters. It felt like a compound where you could wait out any natural disaster.

Some of the sleeping areas made me chuckle. Once classrooms, they had been divided in half and now housed two sets of bunk beds. They looked just like college dorm rooms, each with two bureaus and a desk. There was one bathroom for every four rooms and a communal shower. I had a hard time picturing any biker staying in them, let alone four sharing the tiny space.

The rest of the sleeping quarters were private. No bigger than the shared rooms, they at least had a single queen-sized bed. Some had bureaus, some had closets, and all the of ones Ian showed me were decorated uniquely by their "owner." Another perk to having a private room, Tank told me, was that each of them had originally been classrooms for lower grades or teacher's offices, so each room had its own bathroom.

"Why do people live here?" I asked as we were leaving Tank's room.

"They don't." At my arched eyebrow, Ian rushed on. "Sometimes it's easier to crash here than go home—after a party or a late-night run. Other times, it's a place to catch a few hours of shut-eye while you're on duty. And sometimes you need a few minutes of privacy."

I tried to ignore the last comment, knowing he meant a place to take women to sleep with them. "Does Matty have a room?"

Tank nodded. "All the officers have rooms."

Officer? One more question to add to the pile. "Can I see it?"

They both hesitated at once.

"Oh." My voice was soft, but my heart started pounding. The apartment was literally twenty minutes away. There was only one reason Matty would have for keeping a room here. It wasn't a place for him to sleep. "Oh. Can you take me to Rocker's office? He and Cris must be done by now."

Tank put his hand on the small of my back, steering me down the hall back toward the main room. As soon as we turned a corner, we heard voices. Angry voices raised toward each other, having one hell of a disagreement. Tank grabbed my arm right above my elbow, preventing me from going any farther.

"Mommy and Daddy are fighting again," he muttered to Ian. "I hate when they fight." He turned to go, but I didn't budge.

"It's two nights away, Princess! You've known about it for how long? Why in the fuck would you wait to tell me until now?"

"I called Jessie as soon as I knew!" Cris screeched back. "Caleb just surprised me with the trip, you ass. You're the one who told me to get close, to do whatever it took. That's what I did! I can't help it if I'm a good lay and he wants me all to himself this weekend!"

"Cancel the trip. You're not going!" I couldn't hear her reply but knew she must have said something because Rocker started screaming again. "Because it defeats the fuckin' purpose, doesn't it?"

"No!" Cris bellowed back. "I've spent weeks working on him, and I'm not losing it now. Go to the fuckin' benefit yourself. Better yet, I'm sure Barbie would be more than happy to play dress-up for you."

"Is that what this is about? Jessie? I moved on to somethin' better. Get over it! Petty jealousy doesn't suit you, Crissia!"

"Fuck you!"

"Already did that, sweetheart. You're not that good. No desire to do it again!"

Silence surrounded the three of us for a moment, then all hell broke loose. Something shattered, Cris started screaming, Rob was yelling back, and there was loud banging. I yanked my arm away from Tank, ran for the door, and burst through, concerned for my friends. My entrance went unnoticed.

A giant wooden desk took up the majority of the room. On one side, Cris danced around, grabbing and chucking whatever she could get her hands on while she yelled incoherently. On the other, Rocker was trying to dodge or catch the objects flying his way. The window was broken, and the floor behind him was littered with debris. I slammed the door, hoping to get her attention.

Instead, it was Rocker's head that turned toward me, distracting him just long enough so that he didn't see the stapler Cris aimed at his head. It hit his cheek with a meaty wet *thunk*, and his head snapped to the side with the impact. Blood gushed down his face.

Ian and Tank rushed in behind me. Tank grabbed Cris around her waist and carried her out of the room, still screaming obscenities, with Ian right behind them. I hesitated for a minute, not sure if I should follow them or stay.

I stayed. Hoping to help, I rushed toward Rob, but he raised a hand, stopping me.

"No! There's a shit ton of glass over here and I don't want you cut!" Rocker stepped gingerly around the wreckage.

"What was that all about?"

When he got close enough, I got a good look at him. "Do you have a first aid kit?"

He beckoned to me as he left the room and I followed him down the hallway into the dorms then into a private room. This one was painted a deep red. I waited by the bed, looking at the pictures scattered around the while he disappeared into the bathroom. He came out a few moments later, carrying a white box. He dropped onto the bed and handed it to me. I cleaned the already swollen flesh as gently as I could, then I sat next to him.

"She may be a little angry with me." He sounded lost. "It's possible I said the wrong fuckin' thing."

I fought a chuckle and lay back on the bed. "I'd say that's a good assessment, smartass." The bed was extremely comfortable, and I wanted to do nothing more than close my eyes and forget about this awful and strange day. Then I thought of Tank's casual mention of Rocker "auditioning" the new girls and jumped off the bed. "Eww!"

"What's wrong?" He watched me closely, alarmed.

"How many women have been naked in here?"

He gave me a look that clearly said he thought I'd lost my mind. "I swear to God, every single woman in my life is fuckin' spastic!"

"We're crazy?" I narrowed my eyes. "I've only been here a few hours, and I've been hit on, mistaken for a club whore, kissed, punched someone, watched my friend lose her shit, tended a wound caused by a fuckin' stapler, and discovered that you personally audition all the women who hang out here. It's not the women in your life that are crazy, Rob—it's your club!"

As I rattled off my list, Rob's face grew angrier and angrier. "What?" He spit the word and if I was someone else, I'd be afraid.

I shrugged.

He closed his eye briefly, moving his hand up to rub his face on the uninjured side. "L.K., I have a bitch of a headache. I need you to slow down and explain that all to me."

"Fine. When you tell me how many naked women have been in here. And when you washed your sheets last."

He tipped his head from side to side, snapping his neck. "That's none of your fuckin' business and I'm not tellin' you shit. But I will tell you my sheets were washed last week, and the blanket is new. I haven't had anyone here since then."

I wrinkled my nose. "You're sure I won't catch anything?"

He rolled his eyes, exasperated. "Sit." I hesitated a second too long. "Now!"

I joined him on the bed again, pulling my feet up and sitting cross-legged, leaning my elbows onto my thighs. "Do you really audition all the club whores?"

He raised an eyebrow.

"Yeah. Club business, right? So, you won't tell me."

He didn't argue.

"That's disgusting, just so you know. I'm relatively sure I've lost all respect for you."

"Christ, you're a pain in the ass. You know that, right?" he said.

I nodded.

"Between you and Cris, I'm gonna end up killin' someone." He sighed. "Who did you hit?"

"Tank."

"Fuck." He growled. "Why?"

"He kissed me."

Rob clenched his teeth so tightly, his jaw started to tick.

"Before you ask why, it's because he thought I was here to audition for you. Because he thought I was a club whore." I glared at him. "Awesome, huh?" I ignored his string of curses and mutterings about kicking Tank's ass. "You're not gonna do a friggin' thing about it. I handled it!"

His eyes narrowed at me. "'Scuse me?"

I heard the warning tone and ignored it. "It's done. Over. No harm, no foul."

"Joey," he gritted between closed teeth, "I'm tryin' to cut you some slack, but you don't make it easy. The only person who handles shit in this clubhouse is me." I pffted, waving my hand at his absurdity, but he continued in a controlled voice, accent gone. "There is a clear set of rules that we all follow, and no one breaks them without punishment. It's how we keep order in the club.

"I should have explained it to you earlier and not waited for Matty to do it. As far as the Bastards are concerned, you belong to Mateo. It is his job to protect you and take care of you. Because you are his, you have our respect and our protection. We will take care of you when he isn't around to do it. We don't touch our brother's woman sexually. Ever. And if one of us is stupid enough to break the rule, even if she wanted it or initiated it, punishment for the member is severe.

"And it's Matty's job to keep you in check. When you do anything with the club, here or out in the community, your behavior is a direct reflection on Matty. You misbehave, whether it's by mouthing off to a member or being disrespectful, he gets punished. You're feisty and sassy as fuck, which is great 'cause you keep him on his toes. But if you don't pay attention, Matty's gonna pay the price."

I felt the blood drain from my face. "That is the dumbest thing I've ever heard! It's not 1912 anymore. Women have just as many rights as men."

He shook his head. "Not in this club they don't."

I swallowed hard. "What's gonna happen to Tank?"

"How many people saw you two?"

I told him the whole story, telling him about the group of men and Ian.

He shook his head. "Probably not much. He didn't know who you were, and you hit him because he grabbed you. Both he and Matty should get out of it with no more than a warning. I'll argue that point on their behalf at court."

"I don't understand." My voice was quiet, brain on overload. "What does court have to do with the club?"

He chuckled. "Court is a meeting that all patched members need to attend. It's where we talk about problems, like this one, and vote on policies. I wouldn't worry as much about Tank as I would about what's gonna happen to you when Mateo finds out."

I snorted sarcastically. "What's he gonna do? Spank me? He'd have to be here to do that. Plus, I'm pretty sure you've already figured out I like that." I fought a smile when comment made him look away, uncomfortable. "Besides, Matty would never do anything to hurt me."

"Joey." His tone was cold and harsh. "It's not about hurtin' you. It's about teachin' you your place and keepin' you safe."

I groaned in frustration, making his eyes snap back to mine. "God, he doesn't need to keep me safe! I'm pretty sure I've proved I can handle that on my own!"

"That's his fuckin' job. Stop emasculatin' him, for fuck's sake!"

"I'm not emasculating him!" I snapped back.

"You are! Every fuckin' time you say shit like that, you're telling him you don't need him. You're sayin' you're too good for his life!'

"I am not!" I yelled, thoroughly pissed off. "The life he lives with you here is so different than anything I'm used to. I'm struggling to figure out how in the hell the man I love can be okay with the ass backward rules you have in place. I'm not property—no one owns me, and no one is responsible for my actions but me!"

Rocker tried to interrupt, but I held up my hand. "I get that this is your life. I fucking get it! But you need to understand that I fell head over heels in love with a geeky social worker who loves to run, listens to the worst music on the planet, and can make me laugh even when I want to cry. I'm trying to accept that he's..." I trailed off, unsure what I was trying to say. Sighing, I pushed myself off the bed. "I love him, Rob. I'm just trying to figure out where I fit in. And where this new man fits in my life."

TWENTY

JO

The sounds of traffic coming in through my window and a few smutty books on my Kindle were the only things I had to keep me company that night and the next morning. That was perfectly fine with me—I was in a foul mood and didn't want to talk to anyone. I preferred to mentally beat myself up without an audience.

Matty had called a bunch of times last night after I'd sent him a text telling him I had a headache and was going to bed early. This morning, he'd blown up my phone. His last voice message was simple.

"Babe, you've gotta talk to me at some point." Long audible sigh. *"Rob told me what happened. I love you, Joes. Just call me back."*

I would. as soon as I figured some things out.

I would never ask Matty to leave this life, because I understood the appeal. Being a member of a motorcycle club meant belonging to something bigger than yourself, a fraternity of brothers who would support you and always have your back. It wasn't like MCs were the only groups like that. There were the Masons, actual fraternities at every college nationwide, and the boys' club many women had to face at work. The Bastards were as big a part of him as anything else, and I wouldn't change a single thing about the man I loved.

If I was determined to be with him, I had two choices: accept the role as "his" and whatever that entailed, or take the same stance Becky had and be his "other life." I didn't know if I could handle having just a piece of him though. For a decade, we'd been inseparable. I couldn't imagine a life with anything less.

The politics of the club pissed me off. I could understand the "can't tell you 'cause it's club business" attitude. As a caseworker, I'd been bound by strict confidentiality laws and there were many days when I'd been called out on an emergency only to say to my family "Mommy's gotta work." They didn't know what I was doing or how dangerous of a situation I was walking into. The fact that Matty couldn't discuss club business with me was the same thing. The club was almost like a second job. I was no longer a case worker, so he couldn't discuss either job with me. It took a few hours to get

343

my head around that, but it really did make sense. If I didn't know what he was doing, I couldn't be forced to tell anyone else.

There was more to my negativity toward the club than that though. I had never been labeled a feminist, yet I felt like one now. Women should have the same rights as every man in that club, as long as they earned them. The fact that they looked at me as nothing more than property made my stomach churn.

If I succeeded or failed, I wanted it to be on my own merits, not because of Matty. But most of all, I didn't want Matty to be judged by how I behaved. I was my own person, and after everything with Will over the last few years, I felt like I needed to know I could depend on myself.

Realizing I could never make the decision alone, I longed to pick up the phone and talk to Teagan. She'd never understand any of this though and would tell me to get my ass home. Cris was out too—she'd gone away with her boy toy for the weekend. That left just one other person who may understand where I was coming from. Taking a deep, calming breath, I grabbed my phone and dialed the person I knew would give it to me straight.

"Jo!" Jessie gasped, out of breath. "I was just gonna call you!"

I groaned. "About the Tank thing?"

She was quiet for a split second. "Tank thing?" I could hear the confused curiosity. "No. I needed to ask you a favor. But now I'm a little worried. What Tank thing?"

I quickly relayed yesterday's events. Halfway through, just as I'd gotten to the part about him kissing me, she started to laugh uncontrollably. "Oh, my God!" She chortled. "He must have been mortified! I'm sorry, I'm afraid that's partly my fault. I told him he needed to find a girl and enjoy himself for a little while."

I finished the story, leaving out Cris, to more laughter. "I need to talk to you about it all though. Can you meet for coffee in a bit?"

"Ummm..." I heard the hesitation in her voice. "I'm actually on my way out of town. That's why I was going to call you. I'm supposed to go to some fundraiser with Rocker tomorrow night. He got tickets at the last minute, and he needs help schmoozing someone. It's a black-tie shindig that is extremely 'high society.'"

I smiled at her fake British accent. I couldn't believe Jess would pass up a date with Rob, especially one that sounded so elegant. "Why can't you go?"

She sighed. "Long story short? Tank's girlfriend is a fuckin' piece of shit. I talked to her last week and told her about his welcome home party. She promised she'd be there but never showed. Since he's been back, she hasn't answered her phone. She sends him a text every now and then, but they're cryptic at best. She told him she'd be at the clubhouse first thing this morning. Still hasn't shown. He's going looking for her, and I'm not letting him go alone."

I didn't know what to say. Guilt flooded me as I remembered how mean I'd been yesterday. "Do you think she's just avoiding him?"

"I fuckin' hope so. He went away to keep her ass safe, so I hope to Christ we don't find her in trouble again. Will you go with Rob for me?"

"Yeah, um... about that..." I searched for words. "We had a little bit of a squabble yesterday, and then he didn't come home last night. He may not want me to go with him."

"Jeez, you're fighting with everyone, aren't ya? I already talked to him though, and he told me that if I could convince you to go, he'd happily take you."

"Okay... what in the hell should I wear?"

We spent a few minutes talking about the details, and I grabbed a pen and paper from the nightstand, trying to write down all the places she had appointments to get beautiful tomorrow.

"I have a couple of extra minutes... you know, if you wanna ask me what you called to ask me."

I fumbled for words. "From a woman's perspective, is it worth it? The club, I mean."

She didn't even hesitate. "Yes." I heard her zipping what I assumed was a suitcase. "I'm a young, pretty, single woman living alone in a city, and I don't have one fear. Those boys will protect me from anything. I've dated many of them over the years, and I've dated men from outside the club. Bastards are a special breed. I was treated like a fuckin' queen, worshiped like a goddess, and respected by all of them. If one of them makes you a promise, he keeps it. If for some reason he can't, his brothers do. I know that if

I'm scared or need help with anything, they will be by my side in minutes. They are the best family anyone could ask for."

"You don't think their views are a bit..."

"Outdated? Discriminatory?" She laughed. "I do. But tell me where you've been that isn't that way. At least the Bastards have rules they follow. Out in the world, if a man touches you and you say no, you can file charges against him, maybe claim sexual harassment. Then it becomes a 'he said, she said' nightmare and every decision you've ever made is questioned. In the Bastards? A member who touches you when you don't want him to gets his ass beat or loses his colors.

"I know that I could be drunk off my ass and work one of the boys up and then say no, and that Bastard would let me walk away without so much as a scratch. I'd probably have to pay a fine or lose club privileges for a while, but that man would not hurt me. Granted, I would never pull shit like that because if they're going to treat me with respect, it's gonna get returned." She paused, and I heard a loud thump. "I gotta hit the road. Call Rocker, tell him you're gonna be his date, and clear the air while I'm gone. Okay?"

I loudly cursed my skirts the next evening as I rode the elevator up to the top level of my apartment. There was no way in hell I'd be able to navigate the stairs in them. They weren't extremely bulky, but they were a horrific combination of full and tight and long. Whenever I moved, I had to yank a handful of the material off the ground, and then take small steps to avoid tearing. I swore the slit up my left side had ripped a little higher already, and I'd only had the dress on for fifteen minutes.

I had assumed that searching for a formal gown on the day before I had to wear it would be difficult. I couldn't have been more wrong. After I called Rob to tell him I'd go, Hawk had showed up at the apartment with Rocker's credit card in hand and taken me to a designer boutique. Twenty minutes after I walked through the door, I was standing on a stool in the middle of the shop, being fitted into one of the most beautiful gowns I'd ever seen. The sales staff had taken one look at me and told me it was the perfect dress for my figure.

Wearing it was another story though.

The sea foam wrap gown was more daring than anything I'd ever owned. Thin sparkly material made an X over my upper back and continued over my shoulders and onto my chest, making another X, each side holding a breast and continuing onto my hips, before the left side wrapped back around my back, met the other on my right hip, and was tied. The bottom half was made up of layers of silk and had a slit that went almost up to my left hip. The dress, combined with all the pampering I'd had done, made me feel like a princess.

I hadn't just spent the day getting pretty—I'd also been researching. The Bastards, it seemed, needed a new lawyer. They had one on retainer, but after Tank had been convicted, Rocker had started looking for another. Jonathan Greenwood, Esq. was the best criminal attorney in the state, Rocker had explained when he came home Friday night, and he hadn't lost a single case. However, he was very selective of his potential clients and wouldn't return Rob's calls.

Mr. Greenwood had a soft spot for smart and strong-willed women. Cris had been the first option. That was where Caleb came in. He was a partner in the firm Greenwood owned and couldn't resist her advances after one of her classes at the gym. Something told me that him walking into her studio hadn't been an accident. However, after weeks of dating, Cris still hadn't met Caleb's boss.

Now it was my turn. Rob had friends everywhere, and one of them had made sure we would share a table with Greenwood at the benefit. I would sit right next to him, making small talk and charming him until I had him wrapped around my finger. Or until I could show him that the Bastards were worth his time.

No pressure.

I pushed a hand against my stomach, trying to will away the nerves as the elevator opened.

My date stood in the hall, waiting for me and holding out an arm. "You look absolutely stunning, Ms. Walker."

I grinned. "You don't look half bad yourself, Mr. Doyle."

He looked rakish and as dangerous as James Bond, dressed in a tux that had obviously been made specifically for him. It hugged his hips and long legs perfectly, and the jacket accented his wide shoulders and large biceps. A gigantic man any day of the week, Rob usually looked like the quintessential biker or the carpenter he was. Tonight though, his giant frame in that monkey suit would make every other man at the benefit look like they were playing dress-up in Daddy's best.

"Hawk and his girl will be here soon," he promised as he pulled me into the kitchen.

Hawk had told me as we looked through dresses that he went to this benefit every year in order to placate his father. He was sharing our limo and table though, to offer support.

"You feeling prepped?"

I pushed my hand into my stomach once again as I sat at the table. "Yes." I nodded. "Well, I think so."

Rob walked to the island and poured us each a shot.

"What if I screw it up?" I asked.

He handed me a glass and smirked. "You won't. But even if he doesn't bite, at least you tried." He tipped his glass back and strode back to the counter to refill it.

I turned my glass around, looking at the amber liquid, too nervous to drink it. I felt as if something was going to go wrong, which usually wasn't a good sign. The elevator came back to our floor with a *ding,* and I heard laughing.

Laughing from more than two people.

A low whistle sounded from the hall. "Holy shit! Someone cleans up nice," the familiar voice joked. "And I'm usually the one who's overdressed." He laughed. "You're taking pictures, right? My sister is gonna flip her lid when she sees how you look with Barbie tonight."

I'd done a ton of preparation for tonight, but nothing could have gotten me ready for this development.

As Matty walked into the kitchen, Hawk and his date behind him, and leaned against the counter opposite my date, Rob scowled. "What in the hell are you talking about?"

Confusion crossed Matty's handsome face. "I thought Cris went away and you were taking Jess."

Rocker didn't answer. Instead, he turned his entire body toward me, arms crossed, face hard. His eyebrows were raised in question, but he looked pissed.

Matty's head turned to follow Rocker's glare. As soon as he saw me, his entire body stiffened. The look of confusion mixed with fury made me nauseated. I pushed myself to my feet, needing to touch him and make everything better. I was almost to him, walking slowly in the death traps some designer had decided was stylish, when I offered him a small smile.

"I didn't know you were coming tonight." It was a pathetic grasp at conversation, but I had to say something to break the tension.

Matty inhaled sharply, his eyes widening showing me the dark blue storm clouds in them. "Yeah. I can see that."

TWENTY-ONE

MATTY

It had been a long fucking few days. I thought things were good between us when I left Wednesday morning. If I hadn't had to get back for work, I would have stayed in our room, wrapped up in her all day. Now I wished that I had just called out sick and stayed put, because things weren't good—they were fucking falling apart.

When Rob called and told me about what happened at the club, I was pissed. My first call had been to Jo, but she didn't answer, so I dialed Tank, just to let my brother know that I was going to kick his ass next time I saw him. He apologized and told me everything that had happened; not only had he kissed her, but he'd fondled her and slapped her ass. My girl had stood up for herself like a fucking champ, but she shouldn't have had to. It was my fault I hadn't been there to stop it.

I called her every chance I got from that point on. She sent me to voice mail or ignored every call. Of course, she was pissed, and she had every right to be. She'd been telling me for days that she missed me, and I'd promised her last year that no one would ever put their hands on her again. It only made it worse that it was one of my brothers who had.

I had to get to her, just to hold her and tell her how sorry I was. I'd had Sammy the night before and all day, but I explained to Becky that I needed to drop him off early because I had to get to Jo. She'd understood. Hell, she'd been in my life long enough to know that I wouldn't drop everything if it wasn't important.

I drove as fast as I could, imagining I'd find Jo dressed in one of my tees and her ratty sweats, eating ice cream and lying in bed. I had so many ideas on how the rest of the weekend was going to play out—all of them involved the two of us not leaving the bedroom. I was going to love every inch of her until she forgave me.

The woman in front of me wasn't moping in bed missing me. No, her makeup was flawless enough for a magazine cover shoot, and her hair was up with curls dangling everywhere. She was a walking wet dream. I wanted to pull her out of her chair and carry her downstairs, not letting her leave my bed until both of our bodies were satisfied.

I saw the panic in her eyes as she stood and walked toward me, giving me a full view of her dress. If you could even call it that. There was more skin showing than anything else. Material crisscrossed over her chest, barely hiding her nipples, her breasts bulging out over the top of them. Every single one of her sexy curves was on full display. The bottom wasn't much better. A long slit up one side flashed her leg with every step she took, and the material just managed to cover the crack of her ass.

She smiled at me, dark red lipstick making me think about how the only place I wanted those lips to be right then was wrapped around my cock. "I didn't know you were coming tonight."

"Yeah. I can see that." I was pissed. She would have known if she'd picked up her fucking phone. I felt my anger growing as I watched her. She was every man's fuckin' fantasy, and there was no fucking way she was leaving my sight in that. "Go change."

She raised an eyebrow as if she needed an explanation for my bad mood.

"You're not leaving here dressed like that!"

"Excuse me?"

I shook my head, annoyed. "I didn't fucking stutter." I felt my lips curl in disgust. "You're not fucking wearing that!"

She inhaled at my tone. The entire atmosphere of the room shifted, the air suddenly full of tension. Hawk and Tabby's quiet conversation came to a screeching halt. I heard the uneasy shuffle of feet as they tried to figure out how to ignore us.

Jo tipped her head back slightly, meeting my eyes with an angry glare. "Yeah, I am."

Trying to force my agitation down, I took a couple of deep breaths then stepped toward her.

"What the fuck is your problem?" she hissed, taking a single step back.

"Right now, you are. You and that pathetic excuse for a dress! I've seen hookers who had more covered than you do!" I pointed at her so she would understand that the coming threat wasn't an idle one. "Either you go change, or I'm gonna carry you down those stairs and strip you myself."

I wanted nothing more at that moment than to do just that. In fact, I had never wanted to take a woman over my knee as much as I did right then. She swallowed hard, but her eyes stayed on mine, defiant.

I leaned in, lowering my voice even further. "And when I'm done with you, you won't be able to walk for a week."

Color rose in her cheeks, but Joes was never one back down. "The last time I went out with you and your friends, I looked like a cheap-ass whore, and you didn't have a single complaint!"

"Yeah, well, at least you weren't half naked. I didn't have to sit around fuckin' worryin' about who was looking at you and who might try to put their grubby paws all over you 'cause we were right there, weren't we? No one was gonna look twice because it was obvious who you were goin' home with and even more obvious who you belonged to!" My eyes narrowed even further as I leaned closer and realized that she wasn't getting the point. "Go. Change."

She pulled back her shoulders, straightening herself as if readying for a fight. "Oh, for Christ's sake! Rocker's one big dude, Matt!" The sarcastic way she said my name had me fuming again. "I'm his date! No one is going to even look twice at me. And unless you have other plans, you'll be here when I get home."

My jaw clenched. "Joes." I hoped she knew by the way I growled that that I was barely controlling myself. "You're wearing somethin' else!"

"My date said I look fantastic." She copped a major attitude, jabbing a finger into my chest. "If you don't like my dress or how I look in it, then don't fucking look at me."

"You're all anyone is going to be looking at!" I snapped back, done having this ridiculous conversation.

"Thanks!" she snarled back. "I'm gonna take that as a compliment." Her eyes slid to Rocker. "Now if you'll excuse me, my date is waiting."

She tried to move by me, but I wrapped my fingers around her bicep. "He's gonna keep waiting!" I looked over her head at my best friend, hoping he could see how dangerous an interruption would be right now.

He held up his hands as if in surrender, backing up. "We're gonna go see if the car's here yet and give you two a minute."

Jo snapped her head toward him, but not before I could see worry crashing over her features.

Rob wisely ignored her. "I'll see you later tonight Mateo."

I waited until I heard the elevator doors close before I yanked her back, so she was facing me. "What the fuck, Joes?" was all I could spit out. I had so much to say, but I couldn't process a single thought.

"Exactly! What the fuck?" she yelled back, shoving at my chest with her free hand. "Let me go, or I will kick your ass."

I leaned close to her ear. "You wanna get rough, Joey? I fuckin' love rough."

"Ugh!" She screamed in frustration, and I had to fight not to laugh. "Let. Go. Matty."

I released her arm. Instead of stepping back, she stepped into me, shocking the shit out of me. Grabbing my shirt, she pulled herself into me. My body, already tense from our argument, reacted instantly, and I felt myself harden against her. I would want this woman until the day I died.

She tipped her head back, looking at me with perfectly made eyes. "I have to go, Matty. If I had a different gown, I would change. Just for you. I don't so I have to wear this."

I searched her eyes. "Why didn't you tell me you were going tonight?"

Her frown told me she hadn't even thought about letting me know, that she hadn't thought I'd be concerned.

"It's club business." She shrugged sardonically, and I suddenly hated that fucking term.

"And I'm a member of the fuckin' club, Joes. So, I can know!" I paced into the hallway and back. "Don't go. Stay here with me."

She reared back, as if I'd slapped her. "You know I can't do that. Your club needs me to do this." She walked over to the elevator and pushed the call button. "It's only a few hours, then we'll have the rest of the weekend."

Vibrations of anger ran through my arms. "My club doesn't need you to do this shit! We've got it fuckin' handled. You're doin' this for Rob!" I sneered, fisting my hands at my sides. "I could make you stay, you know that, right?"

She turned to me, eyeing me coolly, then pushed her shoulders back, making her breasts jiggle and proving once again how fucking skimpy her dress was. "Yeah, I do. But I also know you won't."

The elevator opened, and I reached for her, stopping her as she stepped in. "Jo." Even I could hear the hard warning in my voice, the ultimatum there, left unspoken.

She stepped around my hand, facing me with pleading eyes. "I have to go, Matty. I have a quick job to do, then I'll be back. We'll talk about this later."

Then the elevator doors closed, and she was gone. My fists clenched at my sides. I wanted to hit something. Fucking beat the shit out of something. I turned around the empty foyer, mind frantic.

I needed a drink. No. I needed ten, and to get drunk. Fucking shitfaced. Can't-even-walk-let-alone-think-straight drunk. I slammed the call button, and when the elevator came back up, I pressed the basement button angrily.

There was no doubt where I needed to go. After throwing my leg over my Harley, I fired her up and headed for the clubhouse, tires squealing angrily on the pavement. I needed to sit my ass on a stool and drink until I forgot that Jo had just left me.

TWENTY-TWO

JO

I sagged against the wall as soon as the elevator door closed. I hated fighting with Matty, but the look of disbelief and wrath he'd just given me was enough to make me want to cry. I knew he wouldn't believe it, but nothing sounded better than taking off this contraption and crawling into bed with him. It was as if he thought I was choosing his friend over him. I wasn't.

When the elevator opened on the bottom floor, I didn't move. I could easily press the button and go back upstairs. Except, I realized as I debated with myself, that I didn't have the key fob. Well, fuck it—the decision was made for me.

A stretch Lincoln Navigator was parked in front of our building, and my three companions were standing on the sidewalk, chatting with the driver as I hobbled down the stone steps. I knew my face must reflect my shock at such an obtrusive vehicle, but Rocker ignored it as he walked to me and held out his arm once more, leading me to the car. He stepped into the limo then turned back, offering me his hand, and pulled me up.

A long curvy black bench seat down ran the left side of the vehicle and curled into a cozy loveseat at the back. On the right side was a bar. Rob sat in the first seat and tugged me down next to him. Hawk helped his date climb up into the cabin, laughing and joking as they took seats. We'd barely pulled onto the street before Hawk moved toward the bottles and filled a glass. He took a single sip before holding it out to me. I shook my head. Alcohol was the last thing I needed.

Hawk didn't pull it away but arched an eyebrow instead. "Trust me, L.K., you're gonna need it to get through tonight."

I took it, sipping gently. After a few minutes it was clear that Hawk had been right—I had needed a drink to calm my nerves. By the time we arrived at the venue, I felt much better.

We got stuck in a long line of limos. The time gave me a chance to watch Hawk and his date, Tabby. Hawk surprised me at every turn. Tonight, he was attentive, cuddly, and looked at Tabby with eyes full of love.

The term chubby subby seemed even more obnoxious now. Yes, she was chubby, but no bigger than I'd been a few years ago. I guessed that she maybe wore a size sixteen. She looked exquisite in a black mermaid-style gown that clung to the top half of her body, showing off an incredible hourglass figure, then flared out into gorgeous skirts.

It was the subby part I was having trouble buying, because she was the furthest thing from submissive. In fact, the way Hawk fawned over her, one would think he was a submissive. Not that I knew much about either lifestyle.

After more than a half-hour, our car finally rolled to a stop. As Rob helped me from the limo, flashbulbs erupted around us and I was shocked to see a large group of men with cameras. I hesitated, but Rocker wrapped his arm around me protectively and guided me up the carpeted walkway. They snapped photo after photo as we walked by them, calling out to Rob by name, asking about me, but he only smiled before guiding me into the building.

"What was that?" I asked as soon as we were inside the lobby, my voice wobbly from both stress and excitement.

Tabby didn't let Rocker answer. Instead, she looped her arm through mine and pulled me close, whispering in my ear conspiratorially. "They're always outside at galas like this, hoping to catch Boston's elite doing something they shouldn't. Whenever you feel out of your league, just nod, smile, and offer a random compliment. The men will love you."

"And the women?" I whispered back.

"Hate themselves." She answered before Hawk tugged her away.

I couldn't begin to remember all of the faces and names of people I was introduced to. While I was chatting with a very sweet woman in her sixties, a man in dress blues approached our group and grabbed Hawk, pulling him into a hug. I sent Rob a nervous glance.

He leaned in, close enough so no one else could hear him, "Hawk's dad, the Superintendent in Chief of Boston's finest."

I watched them closely, surprised to see how happy he looked to see Hawk and how he genuinely seemed like a proud papa. Hawk returned the sentiment. I had not expected his father to be a police officer.

For an hour before dinner, we mingled over cocktails and chatted with the other hundred guests. When Jessie had told me it was exclusive, I hadn't realized that meant small and private. Everyone seemed to know everyone – except for me.

I'd just come back from the bathroom and was scanning the small crowd for my friends when an older gentleman stepped up beside me. "You look absolutely bored, my dear."

"Not at all." I smiled up at him politely, trying to remember if we had already met. "I don't know that many people here, but I am most definitely not bored."

He held out a hand and gave me a mischievous smile. "Henry Butler." After I put my fingers in his palm, he pulled my hand to his mouth and gave it a quick peck. He didn't let go. "My friends call me Hal."

"Hal? Not Hank?" I asked, trying politely to get my hand back.

He wrinkled his nose aristocratically and dismissed my question as if I were a silly little girl. "No. Hank isn't any good for politics. Would you vote for a Hank Butler?" He chuckled. "Maybe if we lived down south."

"Oh? You're a politician?"

"Something like that." He finally let go of my hand, but only to snatch two glasses of champagne from a waiter's tray and offer one to me.

I took it, happy to have my hands filled with something other than his.

"And you are? Who can I say kept me entertained this tonight?"

"Look who I found walking around like a lost puppy," a voice I never thought I'd hear again purred, and I stiffened as Taylor put her hand on Hal's shoulder and gave him a peck on the cheek. "Hi, Daddy. Sorry I was late." She was out of breath, as if she'd just run across the venue.

Before I could react, a familiar hand found the small of my back, and Rob's voice filled my ears. "Senator, I'd like to introduce my date, Josephine Walker."

Senator? Internally, I rolled my eyes. I knew that Taylor came from what Matty called "Boston royalty," which in reality meant "old Boston money," but I hadn't known her father was an elected official. My eyes roamed from father to daughter, and I realized not only how beautiful Taylor really was, but also that she got both her height and striking features from her dad. Too bad she hadn't inherited his charm.

Dressed in a form-fitting sparkly black gown that showed off her perfect figure, she oozed sophistication. Her platinum-blond hair was pulled back in a knot, and she'd chosen to forgo jewelry, leaving her long neck bare. The look would have been plain on anyone else, but on her, it was elegant. Her makeup brought attention to her large purple eyes—the only indication she wore contacts—and her adorable heart-shaped mouth. Not for the first time, I compared her to Helen of Troy in my mind. Taylor had a face that would make men fight battles, and a rare beauty that would launch a thousand ships. She was simply stunning.

Taylor slid around her father and offered me a genuine smile. "Jo. How nice to see you."

I almost forgot why I hated her. Almost. Then she stepped toward me, put hands on my shoulders, and kissed each cheek. I could have sworn I heard her hiss the word, "Please," but I was too distracted. The move made the giant engagement ring on her finger reflect the light. I hadn't seen that ring in a few months, but there was no denying it was the same one she'd shown me last July.

Before I could react, she'd stepped back and was looking at her father. "Jo is a close friend of Matt's, Daddy. But I hadn't realized that the two of you were dating." She gazed inquisitively at Rob, whose hand was gripping my back, fingernails digging into my flesh.

"A woman like Jo is a rare find." His voice was steady and sincere. "She has the ability to make a man forget every other woman he's ever been with. She understands that not everything is how it may seem, and she waits to make a judgment until she has all the facts, because she knows that when a man loves her, he would do anything to keep her safe."

I raised an eyebrow. Considering that didn't sound a thing like me, I got his message loud and clear—there was more to this than what met the eye. I didn't know why Matty's ring was still on Taylor's finger, but I knew Rob would explain it later.

Rob's hand drifted up to my face, and he cupped my cheek. "We aren't dating and we don't like labels. But Jo has moved in with me." Conveniently leaving out the fact that we had a strictly platonic relationship, he continued, "I'll gladly take every bit of her I can get." He had a part to play. Apparently I did too.

358

"I never thought I'd see the day Robert Doyle would settle down!" Hal's voice was full of humor. "Darling, I think you may be rubbing off on him!" He turned from his daughter to me. "You and my son-in-law are friends? I'm sorry to say I don't remember meeting you."

"Future son-in-law, Daddy," Taylor corrected. "And Jo is always invited to our parties, but she's had some difficulties over the past few years."

His features wrinkled, and I could tell he was skeptical. I glanced toward Taylor, seeing the worry that she was trying hard to mask. I was missing something, that was obvious, but she seemed concerned that I was going to ruin their charade.

I stepped closer, hoping to ease his curiosity. "I've been going through a nasty divorce." I gestured toward Taylor and Rob. "They like to try to protect me. To be honest, I haven't been up for parties."

Hal seemed to accept my explanation and offered his condolences before moving on to lighter topics. But I didn't miss the look of relief that passed between Taylor and Rob, or the way that Rob stole me away from Hal as soon as he could.

As he led me toward our table, Rob leaned in, grinding out just one word, "Later."

Jonathan Greenwood was not at all what I'd expected. He didn't look like how I thought a lawyer would, even though he was clearly more comfortable in his tux than the rest of the men at my table. He had accented his with a gray homburg hat and matching wool scarf, making him stand out from the sea of black-and-white clad men. He was a solid six feet tall with wide shoulders, a thick chest, large arms that proved he worked out, and was shaved bald. If I didn't know better, I would say he was hiding some serious ink under his formal wear and liked to ride a Harley on the weekend.

Thankfully, we hit it off immediately. He laughed at my jokes that no one else seemed to understand, and he winked at me when he told me he was also fluent in sarcasm. His easy smile put me at ease. We chatted all through dinner, and I almost forgot that we were at a table filled with other people.

During the speeches and the start of the silent auction, he slid his chair closer to mine and kept me entertained by pointing out guests and gossiping about each one in a way that proved he knew everyone's secrets. By the time the last plate had been cleared away, I felt as if we'd been friends for years.

Once the first chord of music had been played, Greenwood stood and held out a hand. "Would you do me the honor?"

I walked with him to the open floor. "I can't dance very well. No rhythm."

"I don't believe that for a second! But, in case you're correct, just follow my lead." He pulled me closer. "There's this little village in the south of France..."

I was so engrossed in the story of how he learned to dance that I completely spaced everything else, including my nerves and my awkwardness. Well into our third song, he moved his mouth to my ear, voice low. "Which one do you belong to?"

I pulled my cheek off his chest and found him peering down at me. "I'm sorry?"

He smiled, but it didn't touch his eyes. "Which Bastard do you belong to?"

My face fell.

"There are many things I am, but naïve is not one of them," he scolded, eyes gleaming with something I didn't recognize. "I always do my homework, Ms. Walker. The Bastards have been trying to snag my attention for months, and I have no doubt that you, as absolutely delightful as you are, are another attempt to plead their case."

I didn't argue. There was no reason to when he had hit the nail right on the head.

He gave me a small smile and continued. "I know you aren't a club whore. You've too much education and class to reduce yourself to that." I wasn't sure if I should thank him or be offended, but he continued thinking out loud before I could interrupt.

"You're here with Rob, but I can't imagine he'd let me monopolize all your time if you were his. Even if he wants you to get close to me, the Bastards are a jealous lot. He'd rather die than let me hold his woman like this. If you're not Rob's, and you definitely aren't Jeremy's type, I can't help but wonder which one has claimed you."

"I don't belong to anyone. No one has claimed me." I shook my head when he began to argue. "It's complicated."

He chuckled. "It always is, isn't it?"

I sighed, watching the other couples dance around us. "I fell in love with one of them before I knew he was part of the club." I lifted a shoulder, deciding to stay with the truth as much as possible. "Then my life fell apart and I needed to start over, so I came down here to go to school. Rob's been a great friend."

"And the one you love?"

I hesitated, not sure how much to say. "Is taken."

Without meaning to, my eyes found Taylor twirling around the floor with Rob, both looking serious as they had a quiet conversation. Jon, as he'd insisted I call him, followed my eyes.

"Ahh." After a few minutes of silence, he shifted, moving my head back to his chest. The song ended and another began before he spoke again. "I've met Matt a few times."

I stiffened. If there was a connection between Matt and Jon already, why in the hell was I there?

Mistaking my reaction, he apologized. "I didn't mean to upset you."

"You didn't." I forced a smile, but the look he gave me told me he knew it was fake. When the music stopped, I pulled away.

His hand found the small of my back, and he leaned toward my ear once again. "If it makes you feel any better, I won't be going to the engagement party." He looked toward my date. "I've suddenly realized that something will come up that day, a schedule conflict that I can't avoid." His eyes twinkled as they looked back at me. "I would love for us to have dinner that evening, maybe show you around the city."

I nodded, half numb as my heart thundered wildly. I'd done what I was supposed to do. I'd created a bond that would hopefully lead to the end result Rob was so desperate for. However, I was more confused now than I had been in months.

I didn't know what engagement party he was talking about, but it made my skin prickle with fear. I had no idea what in the hell was really going on, or why no one had told me, but a part of my mind nagged at me, telling me I wasn't going to like it.

The ride back to the apartment was filled with tension. I wanted to demand answers, but the warning look on Rob's face told me I would have to wait. As our driver weaved in and out of traffic, I felt my annoyance grow.

There might be a perfectly good explanation, but the jerk could have at least warned me. At least it was clear why Matty hadn't wanted me to go. He was going to give me some answers, and he was going to give them to me immediately.

I stormed out of the limo and into the building behind my date, barely offering Hawk and Tabby a terse good-bye. Rob tried talk to me once the elevator began to move, but I crossed my arms over my chest.

"No," I snapped. "Save it! Matt and I need to have a chat."

Rocker nodded and pulled his cell from his pocket. I heard the chimes of the phone coming to life as I stepped onto the lower level of our house, and I marched straight for Matty's room. I didn't care if he was sleeping. His ass was getting up and finally answering all the questions I had. There was no escaping it this time.

But Matty wasn't in his room. And there were no signs he'd been there all night. Groaning in frustration, I yanked the bobby pins out of my hair, letting the curls cascade down around my shoulders. I'd go upstairs and face him, but I refused to do it in this damn dress.

The sharp double-knock on the door startled me.

"Jesus, Matty, it's your room too. You don't have to knock!" I yelled as I started to untie the knot on my hip. The knock came again though, and I hurried around the bed and pulled the door open in frustration.

Rocker, jacket off and bow tie undone, stood in the hall. I inhaled sharply, ready to give him a piece of my mind, but he held up a finger. "No, we're on our way. Just keep him there!" he snapped into the phone before jabbing it with a finger. He jerked his head toward the stairs. "You're comin' with me. Let's go."

"What's wrong?" Panic started to rise. "What did you do now?"

"Me?" he asked incredulously, holding up the phone before shoving it into his pocket. "Eighteen messages. That's how many I have, but I only needed to listen to one to get the fuckin' point." He grabbed the edges of the door frame, leaning into the room, every line of his body stressed with tension. "Matty is at the club, totally fucked." Dark eyes narrowed at me. "I'm thinking that has more to do with you than me."

Well, that explained why my boyfriend wasn't at his house. I turned back into room, exhausted, intent on changing into pjs and falling into bed. "He's pissed at me."

"Yeah," Rob snorted. "You could say that. You didn't tell him you were coming with me. Why the fuck not?"

I spun around, irritated at his accusing tone. "Are you freaking serious right now? It takes seriously large balls to be irritated with me for keeping a secret after all the shit you've been lying about! But, to answer your question, I didn't tell him
because I thought you would! You tell him everything else I do!"

"I don't know if you've noticed, but my plate's a little fuckin' full right now!" he bellowed. "Is that really why you didn't tell him, L.K.? Or was it some sort of screwed up payback?"

My mouth fell open in shock, but I couldn't form the words to argue back.

The asshole took that as a sign of guilt. "You need to stop fuckin' with his head or so help me god, I will..."

"What? What are you gonna do?" I cut him off before he could finish his threat, white-hot anger scorching through my body as I stepped toward him. My eyes flared. If only looks could kill. "We had a fucking argument! Wasn't our first, sure as hell won't be our last! Couples do that every now and then. I'm not some weak-minded little twit who's going to roll over and do whatever the fuck he wants me to do, whenever the fuck he tells me to do it. He doesn't own me! I am my own person, and just because I make choices on my own doesn't mean I'm fucking with his head!" My fists balled at my sides, all exhaustion gone.

He watched my rant, unimpressed. "I like you, L.K. But Matt's my best friend. Yeah, I would take a bullet for any one of my brothers, but Mateo and I have been through the fuckin' wringer together. There isn't a friggin' thing I wouldn't do for him." He pulled himself up straight. "There is a lot of shit goin' on right now, and I need Matt thinkin' straight, not fucked up over you." He pointed at me. "You are gonna go over there and straighten this shit out. And you're gonna do it right now!"

It was my turn to snort. "Oh? And what am I gonna do—stroll in there and take the bottle away?" I'd done it once before, and it hadn't been easy. Matty was a mean drunk. "Have one of your whores do it."

His nostrils flared as he glowered, making me step back, momentarily terrified. "That's exactly what you're gonna do." If possible, his face got even darker. "You say you wanna know the secrets he's keepin'? Well, I've watched him drink himself half to death over the last few months. We don't sit around bitchin' and moanin' about our feelings, but it doesn't take a rocket scientist to figure out what's wrong with him."

I shook my head, feeling the blood drain from my face. No. Matty had drunk himself into oblivion once before, a long time ago, when he and Becky got divorced. I'd been so sure he was going to kill himself, either with alcohol or by making a stupid decision because of it. Getting him sober had been hell, and I doubted he remembered the days I'd spent with him or the things he'd said while drunk. He'd promised me that he would never let anything get him that low again. That idea scared me more than anything else.

"You are his whole fuckin' world. You're always so quick to remind everyone you don't need to be saved. Did you ever stop to consider that you're the one who needs to save him?"

TWENTY-THREE

JO

The atmosphere outside the club was completely different than it had been two days before. The parking lot was filled with motorcycles, the music loud as it drifted out every time someone opened the door, and tough-looking men stood in small groups while a few scantily clad women competed for their attention.

Most of the men acknowledged Rocker, some throwing a laughing insult, others nodding in greeting. Their eyes were glued to me, some curious, others skeptical. Not one of the women offered me a smile, most scowled. It was clear that even though they didn't know jack shit about me, I wasn't welcome.

As Rob pulled open the door for me, I wiped my sweaty palms down the front of my jeans, nervous. I was thankful that he'd given me a few minutes to throw on pants and a T-shirt. I couldn't imagine coming here in my dress from earlier, but either way, I was scared as hell to see Matty.

I found him almost immediately. Tons of people were inside, scattered along the couches, huddled together at the high tables, or playing pool. Matty was sitting on a stool at the bar, hunched over his drink, oblivious to the fun going on around him. One of the prospects was leaning against the other side of the bar, talking to Dean. It looked as though they were trying to include Matty, but he only had eyes for the glass in front of him.

He looked so sad that my nerves vanished immediately, and my heart tore a little.

"Oh, Matty!" The words came out as a whisper, but I had a feeling Rocker heard them anyway. I took a step forward, ready to hurry over and rescue my beautiful boy, but a hand closed over the top of my arm.

"Wait," Rob growled in my ear, not giving me a chance to speak. "These boys don't know you yet. Let's not give Mateo a reason to start a fuckin' fight. Yeah?"

I nodded, letting him pull me toward the bar. After the confusion with Tank, Rob wouldn't get any argument from me. He was offering the protection I welcomed.

We were almost to the other side of the room when a short, curvy redhead slid onto the empty stool beside Matty and slid her arm up his back and over his shoulders. It was a comforting gesture that seemed all too familiar, and butterflies invaded my stomach as I realized that Matty didn't move away from her. Rocker stopped abruptly, almost making me fall. I glanced up and saw the scowl, but he didn't look at me.

"What are you doing?" I hissed, prying at the fingers that were now squeezing my bicep painfully.

He didn't pay me any attention, and he didn't loosen his grip. Instead, he turned his head as if looking for someone. Finding whomever he was searching for, he started moving us sideways.

I peeked back toward the bar. The woman was still there, and Matty had sat up a little and leaned in to talk to her. It was painfully obvious that they knew each other, and I saw, rather than heard, him laughing at something she said.

We stopped as suddenly as we had started. I couldn't hear what Rocker was saying, but the quick jerk of his head toward the bar and the way his free hand sliced through the air told me he was pissed. Before he'd finished speaking, Tiny and another man moved away and weaved through the mass of people.

Within seconds, Tiny wedged his giant body between Matt and the redhead. He spoke roughly, and whatever he said made Dean, the woman, and the prospect turn to look at us. The woman scowled, daggers shooting from her eyes straight at me. With another word from Tiny, she uncrossed her legs and pushed herself off the stool, throwing me one more nasty look before she stomped away.

The prospect had enough sense to turn around and pretend to be busy.

Dean, however, didn't try to hide his annoyance. "What the hell, Brothah?" he asked Rob as we approached.

I didn't know if he was talking about bringing me to the club or about forcing the other woman away. Rocker ignored him, instead tipping his head once more, and without a word Tiny and Rob disappeared leaving me alone with Matt and Dean. I swallowed, not sure what to do. I shoved the stool out of my way and stepped next to Matty. He didn't even turn to look at me.

"That's Rebel's seat," he slurred, four sheets to the wind. "She'll kick your ass when she comes back."

Groaning to myself, I forced a joke. "Let her try. I've been told I can hold my own."

His head rolled toward me as soon as I started to talk. Blood-shot eyes squinted to see me through his drunken haze. "Joes?" The disbelief in his voice chilled me to the bone.

"Matty." I palmed his cheek, enjoying the feel of stubble under my fingers. "Why don't you come show me your room?"

He swallowed, eyes searching my face. Then he turned, breaking our connection, picked up his glass, and downed it in one gulp. "Naw. I'm good. Thanks." He held the glass in the air toward the prospect.

I felt my eyebrows rise in surprise. The prospect immediately refilled the amber liquid.

Keeping my voice level, I asked, "How much have you had, babe?"

Matty's only response was to turn to Dean and laugh as if I was the most hilarious thing on the planet. In seconds, the glass was empty, and he was holding it in the air again.

I covered it before the temporary bartender could fill it, and I glared at the kid. "He's done."

The prospect's eyes moved between Matty and me and then to Dean. The poor kid swallowed, obviously not sure what to do.

Matty turned back to me, but this time his glare was full of anger. "What the fuck is your problem? Didn't have fun on your date so now you're ruinin' my night?"

I didn't move my hand. I'd seen him a lot worse and sure as hell wasn't going to back down. Trying another angle, I leaned in closer, making my voice soft. "I'm worried about you. You're a fucking mess right now."

He scoffed but set the glass on the bar. "I'm just havin' a good time." Then he turned back to me, voice sarcastic as he spit the word, "Babe."

I laughed bitterly. He really thought he had an option here. Fuck being nice. "*Were* having a good time. Now you're done."

Dean twirled his finger at the prospect, motioning him to fill up the cup.

I wasn't fast enough, but I snatched it away before he could half fill it. Glaring at the kid, I tried to sound as threatening as possible. "You give him any more, and I swear to Christ, I will ruin you." I blocked Matty's attempts to reach the drink as I slid it down the bar, away from him. "Come on, honey. Let's go sleep it off."

"Fuck off!" he spat as icy-blue eyes filled with indifference turned to me. "Why are you even here right now?" His voice was filled with emotion. "You left me, Jo. So, no. You don't get to worry. You don't get to ask how much I've had to drink. And you sure as hell don't get to take my glass away. Honey, whiskey is all I got."

I pushed my face into his. "I'm not sure if you're talking about tonight or not." My anger rose with each word. "But I didn't fuckin' leave you, you giant stubborn ass! I'm right here, and I'm not leaving until you do. We can go now or in a few hours, but either way, you're not drinking another fucking drop tonight."

"I'm not your fuckin' constellation prize!" he sneered, jutting out his chin and moving his shoulder to push me away.

I swallowed my smile but felt the corners of my mouth quirk. "No, Matty, you aren't the consolation prize. You're the whole fucking package."

He held my glare and I could see the fight he was forming in his mind. If I couldn't calm him down, there was going to be one hell of a brawl, with lots of yelling and broken bottles—and whatever damage Matty could do in response to mine. He wet his lips with his tongue, and inspiration struck.

Last time, we'd both been married to other people and I hadn't been able to use sex to persuade him to leave the bar, but I knew it would work. Now, he was mine. He wanted me as much as I did him, and I would use whatever tool I could. My hand slid from his knee up the inside of his thigh, massaging gently. He inhaled sharply, and his whole body tensed.

"Come on, Matty." My voice was as low as I could get it, eyes pleading with his. "I've missed you. I need you to take me to your room and show me how much you've missed me." I bit my lip and closed my eyes, the way he loved. Then I leaned in and nipped his ear.

"God, Matty," I moaned seductively, or at least I hoped it was, then kissed his ticking jaw. "I need you right now."

He groaned, a noise so raw and filled with pain that it physically hurt my heart. I could see the struggle, his brilliant mind trying to fight through the Jack Daniels' fog. His pupils darted back and forth in crazy rhythm, desperate to figure out if I was sincere. Then he pushed himself up and stumbled toward the hallway, yanking my hand roughly. I followed him hurriedly, looking over my shoulder to see if I could find Rob.

Instead, my eyes landed on an obviously irritated Rebel, hand on her hip, hatred clear on her face. I'd been too worried about Matty to pay any attention to her, but I had a feeling I'd see her again soon. *Get in line. He has a fiancée too.*

Matty's room looked just like Rocker's, or at least what I could see of it was the same. Matty didn't turn on a light when he pushed through the door, and I didn't try to look for the switch. I hadn't realized just how drunk he was until I followed him to the bed. I pulled his boots and socks off after he flopped onto the covers and remained immobile. Somehow I got him stripped down to his boxers and lying under the covers on one side.

"You're not leavin', right?" were the only words he mumbled.

I promised him I wasn't, but he asked over and over, as if he'd forgotten the answer. I piled his clothes in the chair and stripped off my flip-flops and jeans before crawling in next to him. The warm scent of his cologne and the sound of his even breathing calmed me, and it didn't take long for my eyes to close and sleep to call.

The last thing I remembered was him moving next to me, throwing a heavy arm over my middle, and burying his head in my neck. "I love you so fuckin' much, Joes. So much it hurts."

TWENTY-FOUR
MATTY

A fucking freight train was running through my head. No. I took that back.

I was stuck on the goddamn Gravitron with a freight train running through my head. My world was spinning so fast that I couldn't begin to figure out where I was, and the locomotive was pounding a loud path from temple to temple, screeching as it bounced back and forth like a Ping-Pong ball. I forced one leg to move, knowing I needed to find the floor before either would get better.

Instead of hardwood though, my toes met ice-cold concrete. I ignored the chill, planting my foot flat, and almost immediately the room stopped moving. I opened on eye cautiously, then the other. There was no head-splitting pain, which surprised me. Then I realized the chugging engine noise was actually coming from the soft warm body next to me. I smiled—only one woman made that much noise when she slept.

The night before was a vague memory. I'd been so angry with Joes that I'd come to the club. Dean and I had drowned our troubles with the Three Wise Men: Johnnie Walker, Jack Daniels, and Jim Beam. I hadn't had a night filled with so much whiskey since—fuck, I couldn't remember.

We were in my room at the clubhouse. Jo must have come to me. I could remember seeing her, and she looked pissed, but that memory merged with visions of Rebel. I couldn't sort reality from the tricks my mind was playing. Christ, I could only hope that I hadn't been a douche and Jo hadn't been on the receiving end of it.

As if sensing I was awake, she stretched next to me, and a hand flattened itself on my chest. She pushed herself up on one elbow and leaned over me, lips turning up in that sexy smile that made every part of me jump to attention.

Ignoring my sour stomach, I grinned back. "Good morning, beautiful."

"Is it? A good morning, I mean. How are you feeling?" Her hand went to my forehead, as if checking my temperature, then drifted down to my cheek.

"Don't you know by now? Waking up next to you always makes everything okay."

She rolled her eyes and slapped my chest playfully. "Whatever. Want me to go get you a water or a cup of coffee?"

I grabbed her hand before she could sit up and pull away. "No. All I need right now is you."

I gave her a tug, pulling her body on top of mine, and found her lips. Screw morning whiskey breath and hangovers. All I wanted right now was to be buried inside her. She kissed me back and lost herself in me, responding with an intensity that I'd never gotten from anyone else. I rolled us over, her back to the bed and me on top, and pushed my upper body off her as my knees moved her thighs apart.

"Matty, what the..." Her voice was full of shock as her fingernails dug into my breast bone.

"What?" I stilled, looking down, half afraid of what I might see.

"When did you get that?" Her eyes were wide with surprise as her hand moved to the Claddagh tattoo on my shoulder, but it was the ink surrounding it that she was tracing.

"Last fall." It was a simple trinity, winding in and around the symbol of love, loyalty, and friendship that meant so much to me. But somehow I knew it wasn't just the trinity that had stolen her words.

"August 9." Fingertips light on my flesh traced the dates as she whispered them. "July 26." Her eyes moved up to mine, questioning. She had no idea what they meant, but I knew they seemed familiar and her mind was churning, trying to figure it out.

I grabbed her hand, not taking my eyes off hers, and moved her finger back to the first date permanently etched on my heart. "Not the day I met you, but the day everything changed. That's the day I told Rob what a pain in the ass you were, how fucking insane you made me. He laughed and told me that I was obviously crazy about you. Lookin' back, that's the day I fell in love with you." Tears filled her eyes.

I slid our fingers to the second date. "It took almost eleven years, but this is the day that you told me you loved me back."

A single drop fell from her eyes, and my thumb caught it, stroking her cheek. She needed to hear it all.

371

"When you left, I had to find a way to carry you forever. I needed to remember that it took eleven long, miserable years for you to realize you loved me too and that no matter how long it took, you'd remember again. Until then, I needed to see a piece of you every time I looked in the mirror. These were two of the best days in my life."

Her face was soft, and she was biting her lip, driving me insane, but I needed to finish this. Then I could nibble on her flesh all I wanted.

"And this"—I pulled her fingers to the bottom of the trinity, the dateless band— "this is where I'm going to put our wedding date."

Her eyes grew huge, and she yanked her fingers away. "What?"

Not wasting another second, I slid the ring form my pinkie and held it up to her. "This was my mom's."

She knew the story—I'd told her years ago—but it didn't seem right to not tell it again.

"It was her dad's. And his dad's before that. It goes back for generations." The ring showed serious wear, but it was still beautiful. Crown, heart, and hands etched into the thin silver band, darkened by age. "When the eldest son came of age, his father would pull him aside and tell him that when he found a woman who he would stay loyal to, one he would love for eternity, and most importantly, a woman he would be friends with until the end, and as long as she would return all three, then he was to give her this ring immediately and marry her."

Jo looked confused, but I continued. "I married Becky because she was pregnant with my kid and it was the right thing to do. I never offered her this ring because I never knew if I would be able to stay loyal to her." I swallowed, knowing what an ass that made me sound like. I could see the question on Jo's face and needed to answer it before she asked. "Taylor never would have gotten this ring either, because she is none of those things."

A look of anger passed over Jo's face, and I leaned down, pushing my lips against hers.

I pulled back and planted a quick kiss on the tip of her nose. "This ring has been meant for your finger for the last twelve years, Jo. I will be loyal to you until the day I die, I will love you for longer than eternity, and you will be my best friend until the end of time.

You don't have to take it now, but I'm gonna ask anyway. Just know, even if you say no, I'll hold onto it until you're ready." I could feel her heartbeat pounding wildly beneath me, but she didn't move a muscle. "Joes, my beautiful, hilarious, stubborn Joes... you have always been mine. Let's make it legal. Marry me?"

She was going to say no. I could see it in the scowl that wrinkled her forehead and the unvoiced concern in her eyes. I fought down my disappointment. Even though I'd known it was a possibility, I hoped that she wouldn't fight the inevitable, because we were always going to end up here one day. She took a deep breath, ready to launch into whatever lecture she was going to give, and I had to force myself not to kiss her senseless.

Instead, I cut her off. "I know you have tons of questions, and I promise I'll answer every single one. You're scared about the club, my life, and worried there isn't a place for you here. You are my life. I'm a dick with a bad attitude, and I'm gonna do stupid shit. But I will never let you go again. I told you, I'll be here when you're ready. Take as long as you need."

Tears filled her eyes, and the tension left her face. "I love you more than I ever thought it would be possible to love someone." Her voice was a whisper.

I inhaled. *Here we go.*

"I want nothing more than to be yours forever." I held my breath as she bit her bottom lip and closed her eyes. When she opened them, they were filled with nothing but love. "Of course I'll marry you."

I stared at her, almost afraid to breathe again because I was sure she was going to change her mind. But she only stared back. I couldn't breathe. Somehow I found her ring finger and slid the circle on, almost surprised that it fit. It was a little loose, but we'd figure it out. Right now, there was only one thing I wanted to do.

I paused, mesmerized as I looked down at the beautiful woman in my bed. I was terrified that if I blinked, she'd disappear, that this would all be a dream. I couldn't really be this lucky, right? I had done nothing to deserve someone like her. In fact, I'd done just the opposite, and at any moment, fate was going to step in and say, "Ha-ha, just kidding!" The thought scared me shitless, freezing me in place.

She watched me as intently as I was her, then smirked. "Well..." Her fingertips climbed up my arms. "I thought I'd at least get a kiss when I said yes."

I laughed, leaning down to press my lips against hers. I met her eyes, knowing that she'd see the hunger mine were barely containing. She shifted her legs to the outsides of mine and thrust herself against me. She'd seen the look, all right, and she wanted what it promised.

There were still way too many pieces of clothing between us. I pushed away, sitting back on my knees, and yanked her shirt up and over her head. She pulled her knees to her chest, as if giving me permission to remove her panties, but I was too impatient and ripped them off instead.

She yelped in surprise then giggled as she wrapped her legs around my waist and tugged me down on top of her. "Better?"

Her words held a teasing note, but I couldn't do anything more than grunt in response. Her hands had wound themselves tightly in my hair, fingers digging into my scalp, and her heels were grinding into my ass cheeks as if she was trying to make sure I didn't move.

I framed her head with my forearms, trying to hold some of my weight off her. The move made my chest push into her perfect tits, her nipples hardened in anticipation. I fucking loved feeling her like this. Skin on skin was the only way I ever wanted to be with Jo. "So fuckin' much!"

Wrapping my fingers in her crazy curls, I started in on her neck, licking and nipping, finding the perfect balance between soothing little kisses and the sharp sting that made her fucking crazy. I moved up to her ear and over to her lips and back down. I feasted on her skin, enjoying the salty taste and the scent of vanilla, while she squirmed beneath me. Her hands traced my back, my biceps, and my head as she begged me for more.

I pushed myself off her slightly, arms flexed—knowing how much she loved the feel of my muscles under her hands—and kissed my way down her. I didn't consider myself a breast man; then again, I wasn't an ass man either. I was simply a man who worshiped every inch of the female form. Jo's body though called to me in a way no other woman's had. Every inch of her held a secret that turned me on.

I loved her tits. Fuck, I could easily spend an entire night just worshiping them and giving them the attention they deserved. Each filled up a palm, and I had big fucking hands. They were soft and perfectly round, crowned with little pink nubs that grew when I sucked on them. I pulled one into my mouth while my fingers rolled and squeezed the other. Using just the tips of my teeth, I added enough pressure to make Jo cry out. Chuckling, I dragged my mouth away from her and kissed down the valley and back up, closing my teeth over the other nipple.

"Matty!" Joes groaned, fingers jerking my head back harshly. "God, Matty! Kiss me!"

I couldn't deny her even if I wanted to, and I abandoned my post to find her mouth, warm and inviting. Sometimes I forgot how much my girl liked to kiss. If she had her way, we'd make out like horny teenagers every chance we got. I didn't have a thing against kissing—I fucking loved kissing her. Right now, though, there were other lips crying out for my attention.

After a quick battle of our tongues, Jo sighed as I backed away again, biting her lip lightly as I did. She was coming apart beneath me, making those noises I loved, the same ones that had haunted my dreams over the last few months without her. None of that mattered now, I reminded myself, because she was mine and was never leaving again.

Legs wrapped tighter around my waist, she shifted again, trying to get my dick where she wanted it. I smiled against a breast. Jo was eager, but she was gonna wait. I tweaked a nipple on my way down, and leaning all my weight onto my knees and her center, I reached around my back to unhitch her legs. She whined an argument, but I ignored it and slid farther down her body before she could stop me.

Realizing what I was doing, she jerked and tried to clench her thighs together. I was already between them, so her efforts were pointless, but she tried to sit up and push me off her anyway. I found a shoulder and shoved her back down.

"Matty! No! I haven't shaved... I didn't take a shower..."

I "Mmhmm'd" against her most sensitive skin, knowing the vibration would make her wetter than she already was. It worked, and she seemed to lose all conscious thought, even though she continued to babble and try to stop me. As if either of those excuses would prevent me from tasting my piece of heaven. She was going to be my wife. It was time for her to realize that this body was mine, and I would never have my fill of kissing it, fucking it, or eating it.

Her weak attempts at discouraging me turned to loud moans of ecstasy as my tongue swirled around her clit before I sucked it then found a punishing rhythm. It was only seconds before she was moaning and crying out, bucking beneath me, unable to keep her first climax at bay.

"God, Matty!" she squealed, hands trying to force my head away. "Stop. Stop! I can't take it!"

I didn't stop. Instead, I inserted a finger, then two, finding her spot almost immediately. When I said her body called to me, I meant it. Most men couldn't find the fucking thing if they had a road map, but it was as if Jo's had a magnet that drew me right to it. My bedroom was filled with screams as she came again, this time gushing all over me. I wiped my chin on the insides of her thighs, proud as a peacock. The stubble rubbed her sensitive skin, making her cry out again and milk the fingers I still had inside her.

No one else has ever made her feel the way I do. No one else has made her come the way I do. She never had, and never will, love anyone the way she loved me.

Her gasped words weren't just a boost for my ego. They set my heart flying and made my dick harden even more. She was mine; her body belonged to me. It was about time she realized that there wasn't another soul on this planet who could do to her what I could. I would fucking destroy anyone who tried.

The thought pushed its way into my mind and wouldn't leave. Were there other men who lusted after what was mine? The realization that there were had me pulling my fingers out of her, shoving my boxers down, and quickly repositioning myself. I drove into her hard.

I stopped, groaning at the soft wet heat that engulfed me. "Christ, Joes!"

She lifted her hips below me, trying to get me to hurry, but my hands grabbed them and held them down. If she kept moving, this would be over a lot sooner than either of us wanted. I leaned onto her again, kissing her with more restraint than I realized I still had. Teeth gnashed against teeth, lips crushed against lips as we lost ourselves in each other.

Her muscles tightened around my dick, as if taking his hand and begging him to come out and play. I backed out a little before driving myself back in roughly. Her eyes opened slightly, and she smiled at me as she tipped her head back into the pillow as far as it would go, looking every bit the sexy little temptress I knew she was. I swiveled my hips, and instantly she was moaning, teeth sinking into her bottom lip in an effort to hold back some of her sounds.

I had wanted to go slow, to drag out this moment for as long as possible and be as gentle as I could. But seeing the love in her eyes, mixed with pure carnal need, I couldn't hold back anymore. Grabbing her hands, I entwined our fingers, smiling to myself as I felt my ring on her, and forced them over her head, pulling out and thrusting again.

She struggled against my hands for a few seconds, trying to get free so she could no doubt rake those nails down my skin. Fuck, I wanted her nails to dig into me. The thought of the stinging pain that only came from sex with Joes made me pull out all the way before I slammed back in.

She responded, thrusting in perfect time. That was all it took. Suddenly, I wasn't celebrating the fact that she'd agreed to be mine forever and I wasn't a man fucking his girlfriend senseless. I was an animal in heat, pounding relentlessly into the bewitching creature under me, needing only to release into her and mark her as mine forever.

"This pussy belongs to me, Joes," I ground out as I hammered into her. "You hear me? It's mine."

She half nodded, as if agreeing with me, but that wasn't enough.

I pushed every inch of me into her and stopped, leaning over her. "Jo, who does this tight little pussy belong to?" I was out of breath and my voice was low, but the look she gave me said she heard me just fine.

The little minx cocked an eyebrow. "Right now, it belongs to you."

The words drew a feral response from somewhere inside me, even though I could see the glint of challenge in her eyes. Fuck that. It belonged to me. Always.

I forgot I was trying to keep her hands off me and moved mine to her ass, grabbing her hard and yanking her butt off the bed, driving into her until I couldn't go any farther, so that there was absolutely no room between us. The sound of my hand colliding with her flesh cut through the room, making her spit out a moaning laugh while her insides clenched me tight.

"Who does this perfect cunt belong to?"

Her lips moved into a grin as fingernails dug into my lower back and clawed their way up. She bit the front of my shoulder, hard enough to make me jump, while clamping onto me on the inside again. Then, smirking, she challenged me with a honey-smooth voice.

"Why don't you show me who my perfect"—clench and release— "tight"—harder squeeze— "little"—release, grasp, release— "pussy belongs to, Matty."

I shuddered, closing my eyes and biting my cheek, desperately trying to hold on. I never came until my partner was satisfied, usually more than once, but Jo and her kegelcunt were destroying every ounce of self-restraint I had. I felt as if I was getting the best blow job I'd ever had, while being fucked senseless at the same time. The sensation was beyond words. I wasn't ready to come yet, but if she kept it up, I'd blow.

Leaning down, I kissed her. Not like earlier, but slow and tender. I hoped it told her how much I loved her, how there wasn't a single thing I wouldn't do for her. She sighed happily, then her hands were back in my hair, holding my face to hers.

I moved back just enough to rub my nose against hers. "I love you."

"Matty." It came out as a plea, but she didn't have to say more.

I'd calmed down enough that I could get back to my task and show her exactly who she, and every part of her anatomy, belonged to. Teeth bit, fingers grasped, and I moved in and out of her fast and hard.

Jo wasn't quiet. Neither was I. We were lost in a sea of feeling, every touch igniting a response that couldn't be tamed.

I didn't care that my room was in the middle of the clubhouse, with thin sheetrock walls that allowed my brothers to hear a whispered conversation, let alone the pounding of my headboard and the screams of my fiancée. Let them listen to what I did to her, know what she did to me. She was mine, and I was staking my claim.

She came with a strangled cry, and I followed seconds later, pumping every last drop into her then collapsing onto her, utterly spent. We were soaked, her hair plastered to her head as if she'd just run the fastest mile of her life, and our skin was red and sticky. I'd never seen her look more beautiful than she did that second.

Reluctantly, I pulled out, making us both groan at the loss of contact. I dropped my head onto the pillow next to hers and yanked her into me, arms tight around her. I was exhausted, but I wouldn't let my eyes close. I'd never felt like this - completely satiated, but I wanted to do it all over again, just to have her body under mine, just to have her respond the way she did.

I had felt this way once before. Last summer, when I'd made love to her for the first time, this same eternal need for her had lingered, but I'd blamed it on the alcohol. She'd stumbled home from Hooligan's, drunk as a fucking skunk, and had started to strip off her clothes before I had a chance to lock the door. I hadn't had as much to drink, but with her being so close, thinking clearly was a challenge. When I managed to push her away, telling her that we couldn't have sex, she threw her shirt back on and told me if I wouldn't fuck her, she'd find someone who would. That was all it took.

The thought of her with another man had made me see red. I'd pushed her against the wall and kissed her. I'd considered walking away, but I didn't have enough fight in me, and I wanted her more than I'd ever wanted anyone. When she took off every inch of clothing she had, I carried her to the bed and fucked her so carefully and slowly, it was almost painful for me. I'd been afraid she'd realize what we were doing and make me stop. But she hadn't.

Instead, the touches, kisses, and words we'd exchanged set the night on fire. I couldn't get enough of her. She begged me for more, and I was more than happy to give. We spent the entire night forgetting that we were supposed to be just friends and that she was married to someone else. I should have realized that our reactions to each other, that the amazing sex we had over and over that night, was not a side effect of great whiskey. No, it had been the evidence of two people so in love with each other that we couldn't do anything but show it.

Or it had been Jo's magic pussy. I'd found the fucking illusive perfect pussy. I snorted as that thought filtered across my mind.

I'd laughed when one of my brothers had coined that term a few years ago, and I'd said there was no way in hell any bitch's twat was so amazing that I would overlook every single flaw she had. I understood now though. There wasn't one annoying trait Jo had that I wouldn't ignore. Not a single thing I wouldn't do for her. *Or it*, that perfect magical pussy. I chuckled again, running my hands over the softness of her stomach and down to the spot that had me hypnotized.

"What's so funny?" she asked sleepily, opening her legs for my fingers.

I shook my head but leaned down to kiss her temple. "I can't get enough of you, you know that, right?"

She nodded, shifting her body to reach for me, voice suddenly husky. "I don't want you to."

TWENTY-FIVE
MATTY

The quick double-knock halted her warm, wet mouth mid-bob, and I instantly lifted Jo off me, tossed her onto the bed, and was on top of her, sheltering her naked back from whoever was stupid enough to throw open my door before I called them in. Jo's eyes were wide, alternating between surprise and humor, as she looked up at me over her shoulder, waiting for our uninvited guest to say something. We both knew whoever it was had seen more of our nakedness than they bargained for.

"Jesus." Rob cleared his throat, his disgust clear. For someone who had just walked into my room without an ounce of warning, he sounded extremely offended. "I figured it was so quiet that you two had decided to take a much-needed break. Maybe you'd even passed out or some shit. Christ, how do you have so much energy as hung-over as you must be?"

I shrugged, keeping my eyes on the incredibly sexy back in front of me and the ink next to her spine. I hadn't even begun to explore that part of her yet today, and I wanted to trace those words with my tongue.

"I've got my own version of Red Bull right here, 'cept she tastes a helluva lot sweeter. I could eat it all day."

Jo's cheeks turned beet red before she buried her face in the bedclothes, and Rocker groaned quietly in repulsion.

I leaned down and kissed her bare neck, wanting to get back to what we'd been doing before he'd barged in. "What the fuck do you want?"

"We have court."

"Now?" I started tracing her shoulder blades and was rewarded with a shiver. How would she react when it was my mouth?

"Yeah."

I lifted my head just enough to turn and look at him. "It can't wait an hour?"

He snorted. "Bein' a bit generous, arentchya?"

I answered him with a middle finger.

"No. It can't even wait the five minutes your Mr. Wiggly will need, Minuteman."

"Twenty." Jo spoke meekly, almost muffled by the pillows, "He needs twenty minutes." Then she started giggling. "'Cause that's all it'll take."

I was never going to live that down. Her laughter was contagious though, and within moments, I'd joined her. "I gotta go, baby. We'll pick this up later?"

She nodded, offering me her lips. I moved to the edge of the bed, careful to pull the blanket over her as I did. Once she, and every glorious piece of her, was covered, I stood and faced my best friend.

"Missing something?" His eyes moved over me, unimpressed. He'd seen me naked plenty of times, in so many different situations I couldn't begin to recall them all, and now he didn't even pretend to turn away.

"Here." The uncontrollable laughter coming from the bed made me turn.

If I didn't know who I'd buried under my comforter, I wouldn't know it was her. All that stuck out was a slim hand holding the boxers she'd yanked off me just a few minutes ago. A hand that wore my grandmother's wedding ring on the fourth finger.

I took the underwear, stepped into them, and pulled them up slowly, trying to decide how to play it. Turning, I found my jeans from last night in the chair. Maybe Rocker hadn't seen it. I didn't bother throwing on my shirt, because if I had my way, I'd be back in bed with Joes before she even knew I was missing.

"I'll be right back. Don't move," I growled as I kneeled on the bed and kissed the blanket where it covered her lower belly.

"Bye, L.K.," Rocker called.

Another giggle and a wave was the only response she made before I shut the door.

He took a few steps down the hall before turning back. "Really?"

I stood straight, arms crossed, and stared back. There could be so many things he was talking about right now, but I knew it was only one. "Really."

"And Taylor—"

I didn't give him a chance to finish. I knew what he was going to say, because we'd had this argument before. "Has no bearing in this at all. This is my life. One I can't live without the woman in there, and I shouldn't have to."

"No one said a fucking thing about living without her..." He stopped when a look of fury crossed my face and narrowed his eyes as he watched me. After a few seconds, his face cleared, and he nodded. "Congratulations, Brothah. She's a fuckin' handful."

I laughed. "You don't know the half of it."

Tiny came around the corner, stopping abruptly. "There you are. We're all waitin'." Without missing a beat, he asked, "Rough night, Mateo? Looks like you mighta forgotten somethin' somewhere." He tapped the side of his cheek as if wondering what was different about me, checking out my bare chest and feet.

I smiled. "Yeah. Jo's holding 'em hostage until I go back and finish what we started. This way I can't run away."

"Why in fuck's sake would ya wanna run away?" Tiny whistled. "Ya better hurry. You don't wanna keep a screamer like her waitin'. Fuck me! I'm gonna be dreaming of her moans for weeks."

I chuckled as I followed him to the common room. Jo was going to kill me when she realized everyone knew what we'd spent our morning doing. I couldn't have been happier. Even if they hadn't heard it, news traveled fast, and now every single one of these assholes knew that if they touched her—hell, if they even thought about touching her—they would have their ass handed to them.

I was surprised at the amount of people hanging around our main room. It hadn't seemed as though that many people were home last night. As we navigated our way across the room, I nodded to a few ol' ladies and smiled at a couple of the girls. But when a short redhead bounced off her stool and wandered toward me, a feeling of dread hit.

Fractured memories played like a movie: a hug, laughing as we took shots, a hand on my thigh, stolen kisses that made my blood hot. Every single one was a blur, a mixture of Rebel's voice, hands and face and Jo's hands, face, and tits and her silky voice telling me she loved me.

I couldn't tell what was real. Fuck!

"Mateo, you don't have time," Rocker grunted, almost bumping into me when I stopped dead, but I only held up a finger.

"Mornin'." I never took my eyes Rebel. She smiled brightly in answer, and my blood turned to ice water.

I'd known Rebel for a long time, almost as long as I'd known Joes. She'd been the comforting arms I'd fallen into more than once, and even though I knew she wanted more, I'd still taken what she offered and promised nothing in return. That was her job, but thinking about it now made me feel like a dirty old man. At one point, I had wondered if the two of us could have a future, but that was before I met Taylor, back when I was still struggling with the fact that I was in love with a married woman I didn't think I'd ever have.

Even after I started dating Taylor, Rebel had made it perfectly clear she still wanted me. I ignored it, thinking she'd move on eventually. She hadn't. I prayed to Christ I hadn't given her false hope last night. I was a lot of things, but I would never intentionally hurt her that way. And I sure as shit would never cheat on Joes.

"I don't have time to talk right now. Later, yeah?" I said.

She put her hand on my arm, stopping my escape. "Was that her, Mateo? The woman here last night?"

I nodded, not needing her to explain. I hadn't fucked one of the Brats–how the club whores referred to themselves–in years, and even though they still tried to steal my attention, they knew I had someone special. Searching her green-and-brown eyes, looking for any sign that she was going to drop a bomb and blow Jo and me apart, I offered her an apologetic smile.

I couldn't have been so drunk that I blacked out and did something that fucking stupid. I could count on one hand the amount of times I'd had so much booze that I'd blacked out and woken up the next morning not remembering the previous night night—or the woman in my bed. I hadn't had that much last night.

At least, I didn't think I had. I remembered Rebel leaning in close, asking me what was wrong, and offering comfort. The next clear memory was a hand sliding up my thigh and grabbing my junk. But I couldn't see that woman's face.

Fuck, fuck, fuck! I'm never drinking again!

Hoping I remained calmer on the outside than I felt on the in, I nodded again. "Yeah. That's her. She's in my room now." I wasn't sure why I felt it necessary to add the last part, yet something told me it needed to be said.

Rebel let out a resigned sigh, twisting her lips as if she had something to say. Then, thinking better of it, she shook her head sadly. "So that's Jo?"

I nodded.

She pursed her lips. "She's not at all what I pictured." Why did everyone say that? Before I could ask, Rebel gave me a fleeting smile and let go of my arm. "If she hurts you again, I'll kick her ass." Then she let go of my arm and fled toward her friends.

Shaking my head, I turned toward the end of the room, relief flooding me. If I had kissed her or let her touch me, she would have said something. That meant the memories I had were all of Jo. I practically whooped in relief but saw that Rob was holding the door open for me, the look of annoyance barely masked on his face.

The back room where we held court was filled to capacity, bikers squished in like sardines. I pushed through my brothers to get to my empty seat at the table, Rocker right behind. The whole room silenced as he took his spot next to me at the head.

Scanning the room, I realized that all eleven officers were here for the first time in years, and almost every patched member of the Bastards had crowded in around us. Dread pooled in my stomach - I'd missed something. Something big.

My heart pounded frantically as I realized my brothers looked as worried as I felt. Across from me, Hawk shifted when I met his eyes, the panic clear. Next to him, Tank was flexing his jaw muscles and kept clenching and unclenching his fists. He was supposed to be with his ol' lady, that was why Jessie had cancelled on Rocker the night before. I didn't know if he was pissed because we'd called him back early, or if he knew more than I did.

I half expected that we were about to find out about a job that would take us away from our loved ones for a long period of time. I didn't want to leave Jo already. Yet, that wouldn't require all hands-on deck.

Rob called the meeting to order, his speech brief and to the point. Tinkerbelle, Tank's ol' lady, was missing. No one had seen her for more than two weeks.

Tink's neighbors said she left for work one night and hadn't been home since. The hospital where she worked as a CAN claimed she'd called that same night and told them she had a family emergency out of state. She hadn't given them a date when to expect her back.

Robbery was out. Her house hadn't been trashed, and it also didn't look as though she'd packed any clothes. The only thing

Tank and Jessie found missing was her cell phone. Even her iPod and laptop had been left on her desk.

Tiny cleared his throat. "I hate to be the one who says it, 'cause you all know my history with Pixie." His eyes narrowed on Tank. "Maybe she just didn't want to see you, brotha'. You got out early. She wasn't ready."

History was a nice way to put it when the rest of us called it like it was – drama caused by an attention seeking whore. Tiny had taken one look at the crazy bitch and staked a claim. She lived it up, enjoying being his, until she'd realized Tiny already had a wife outside the club and he was never going to leave her.
Tinkerbelle denied him and chose to stay a club girl.

Tank had been smitten with her from day one, but never wanted an ol' lady. It took a while, but he moved in once he realized he couldn't handle the idea of her screwing any of us. They'd been together since.

Seeing the pint-sized woman bring two giant men to their knees had been entertaining for a bit. After a while, though, it had been clear she was the wedge that would drive the two apart. Anything that caused a rift between brothers was a problem. And, Tink had proven to be more than a problem.

I nodded at Tiny's point. "You didn't exactly leave things on the best terms. Maybe she needed a little more time."

Tank's murder filled gaze slid my way. Instead of engaging, I turned to our prez, curious as to why this was important enough to call court. Rob read my look instantly, jutting his chin in Tank's direction.

Tank swallowed hard then pulled a picture from inside his cut. "This was the only thing out of place. She always kept it next to the bed—even when we stayed here. I found it on the counter in the kitchen, like it was left out so I wouldn't miss it." Hatred crossed his features as he held the photo out to me. "I grabbed it before Jess could see."

The picture had been taken on a Toy Run a few years before. Tink and Tank stood in front of his bike, the White Mountains in the distance, smiling at the camera.

The image had been mutilated, an X was crossed over his face, while Tink's had been scratched away, a giant number 2 in its place. Every ounce of humor left me as I realized what this was saying, and I thought of another number etched into a woman's face. My fists clenched, and I reluctantly handed the picture to my left. Bear tensed, hands gripping the edge of the table as he saw the message.

There were murmurs around us as the print was passed around. Thoughts about Pixie hiding herself or running from Tank evaporated as reality struck. They'd said they were coming for us, and apparently they were coming now.

No one knew who the elusive *they* was.

Last summer, Bear had been out with his girl when they'd been attacked. He wasn't wearing colors, and there was no way to know he was a Bastard—unless someone had been watching him. A group of men jumped them, dragged them into a van, and beat Ian while holding a gun on her. Then they'd taken turns brutalizing Ellie while forcing Ian to watch. He'd fought them with everything he had, but they'd only beaten him more.

When they were done taking turns with her body, they left the ultimate memory ingrained on her skin. A giant number 1 carved into her forehead. Then they dropped them off the same place they'd taken them, with a warning for Ian—they were coming for us, and we'd never know when they'd hit again.

I could still hear his voice telling us the story, and that, mixed with the image of a broken young woman in a hospital bed, made me sick to my stomach still.

The reality was sobering. Rocker tried to keep order, but there were panicked questions and angry declarations. Should we go into lockdown? Could it be a copycat? Why Tink and Ellie—what made them targets? Were the rest of the ol' ladies safe? What else did we know?

We needed to figure out who was behind this and take down these pricks before anyone else got hurt. We would find them, and we would kill them. Slowly.

Rob raised his voice, talking over everyone. "We can't fight a fucking ghost. That's what this enemy is. From now until I call it off, we're on alert – ol' ladies, sisters, mothers and the protected are not to be left alone. Every child will be escorted to and from school and they'll be here during non-school hours. The Brats will buddy up, even if they object. The will not go anywhere alone. We will all be vigilant and aware of our surroundings."

His words were stern, but we trusted him and would do whatever he said. The eleven officers sat as the rest of the club filed out, everyone somber and in a hurry to get home and hug their loved ones or pull one of the girls into their room and release some tension.

As the door closed, Rob leaned forward, worry etched into his face. "Tell me we've got somethin' on this prick. Anythin'."

Wizard, our computer whiz who could find anything about anyone, shook his head. "I have her drivin' through a traffic light on the way to work. She's alone in the car. She never made it. So somewhere from the light on Western Main to Elm, she went missin'. There isn't a single security camera in the area. Whoever got her knew they were in a blind zone." He sighed, tapping a few more keys on his tablet before adding, "The security system in her house wasn't triggered. But it was disabled ten minutes after she went to work, right about the time she was drivin' through the light where I got a time-stamped picture. Twenty minutes later, whoever was in the house left and reactivated the alarms."

"Do any of you have any idea of possible perps?" Hawk asked, sounding like his dad. "I can't plan an attack if I don't know who I'm goin' after. Give me somethin'. Anythin'."

King shook his head, typing hastily away on his own iPad. "We're still diggin'. We're lookin' at anyone who has a grudge. Every dad, husband or boyfriend who's got an ax to grind. Each sleaze ball we've run off. And every mom. So far, the only one who's made parole hasn't bothered to go home or even call his family."

Wiz sighed. "If we just had one single clue, I'd blow it out of the water."

But we didn't. Whoever this was, they were smart. They knew we'd be watching. By breaking into her house while Tink was very obviously somewhere else, they proved that she hadn't defaced the picture herself. By letting her drive under the one traffic light with CCTV, they had ensured we would be able to see her before they abducted her, fucking with us.

Just like with Ian and Ellie, this had not been a spur-of-the-moment attack. It had been well thought out, and the only evidence had been intentionally left. We wouldn't know who did it until they got careless or until they came forward.

I hoped it was the latter. Because if they got sloppy, it meant they were panicking, which meant they would kill. A ransom demand would be much better.

As Rob closed the meeting and dismissed us, Neo caught my eye. He hadn't said much during the meeting, but sitting between Tank and Wiz, he probably hadn't had a chance. Now though, he nodded to the side of the room.

"Drop L.K. off at the gym this afternoon. I'll be there in an hour, and I'll stay as long as it takes."

I didn't need him to explain more. He knew she was the only woman involved in this who didn't know how to take care of herself. I nodded. I could only hope it would be enough.

As I walked into the main room, I was still numb. This was how we lived. When you were the vigilantes, you took on someone else's fight as your own, and you fought their battles because they couldn't. But it brought the war to your front door.

I hated that Joes was here in the middle of this shit. I needed to get to my room, pull her into my arms, and prove to myself she was safe. To remind us both I would move heaven and hell before I let someone hurt her.

Then I needed to call my boss. There was no way in hell I was going back to Maine and leaving Jo alone. Yeah, my brothers would keep an eye on her, protect her if she needed it. But if something happened to her... I couldn't even let the thought finish because it made me too sick. Maybe it was time for me to give my notice anyway. Jo was building a life here, and I needed to be where she was.

TWENTY-SIX

JO

I waited until long after I heard the two of them walk down the hall before I slipped from the bed and sprinted into the bathroom. I didn't want anyone else to walk in and see me buck-ass naked. My cheeks were still burning.

I'd never been caught going down on anyone before. Not even my unpredictable roommate in college had seen me doing that to Will, and she'd come home at the most random times and found us in many compromised positions. Of course it would be Rocker who would literally catch me with a dick in my mouth.

Laughing to myself, I grabbed a cup of water, wrapped a towel around me, and walked slowly back to bed. I needed coffee, but Matty had told me to stay here, and that was exactly what I was going to do. I'd had enough trouble to last a lifetime by walking around this clubhouse alone, and I had absolutely no desire to repeat that mistake.

I propped myself against his pillows, smelling his musky scent on the bed, and smiled. I felt so happy that I could seriously scream. It didn't feel like it had just been over a week before that I'd told Teagan I was sure Matty would never forgive me. I'd been so convinced that I had blown it. Now that I was in his room, in his bed, I could finally admit to myself that I was most definitely his.

Looking around, I realized that his room was exactly what I would expect—simple and tasteful, even in the middle of a motorcycle clubhouse. It was clean, unlike some of the other rooms I'd seen, which had empty alcohol bottles strewn everywhere, and the light blue walls made the room seem larger than the others. A giant Bastards flag hung on one wall, and pictures of Sammy were on every available surface. Except for next to his bed. That held "our" photo. The one I had kept on my desk for years, the same one he had on the nightstand at our apartment.

In it, we were young. I'd been maybe twenty-five and he'd been around twenty-eight—just babies compared to now. His arm was thrown around my shoulders in that brotherly way he used to hug me, and we were laughing at whoever was taking the picture. We looked like a happy couple without a trouble in the world. It made me miss the kids we used to be.

I picked up my left hand, staring at the ring, and twirled it on my finger. Yes, it was real. Matty had really proposed, and I'd really said yes. Holy shit! Young, womanizing whore Matty would never have asked me to spend eternity with him, so maybe I didn't miss our younger selves as much as I thought.

We needed to talk about so many things, so many secrets that were still buried. I had been ready to demand answers, but seeing him at the bar, devastated and drinking his pain away, brought back every memory I had of him ten years before, when Bex left him. That reminder was as effective as a sharp slap in the face—my life would be nothing without him, and I could not lose him. While I was still very curious about everything, I wanted to push it away and just be happy, at least for a little while.

Looking at the ring made me realize that, for the first time in years, I wasn't worried. Being with Matty was so different than being with Will. I didn't have to wonder if I was going to come home to a husband who rejected me and made me feel as though I was hideous inside and out. Matty would spend eternity helping me battle those demons. And I would do the same for him.

Over the past few days, I'd come to the conclusion that even though I might not look like Taylor or that beautiful girl who'd been with him last night, I was what Matty wanted. Me. Cellulite, stretch marks, pudge, and all. It was my body that made him hard, my figure that had him gasping in pleasure for hours on end.

It was my mind he loved. I was awkward, geeky, stubborn, and had the tendency to say the most inappropriate thing at the most inappropriate time. And he loved me anyway.

He wanted to marry *me*. Matthew Murphy, the sexy-as-sin, wet-dream-inducing man that hundreds of women lusted after, loved me. Matty, my annoying but hilarious best friend in the entire world, had said that he would want me forever. Mateo, the badass Bastard, had asked me to marry him. And I'd said yes.

I smiled as I turned and cuddled his pillow, smelling him again. I couldn't remember a time when I was this content. I drifted off to sleep, happier than I'd been in a long time.

Strong arms lifted me back into a wall of muscle, and a deep sexy growl pulled me away from dreamland. I managed a small sigh and a smile as I reached over my head and tangled my fingers in his hair. The move pulled my breast off the bed, earning me another growl as Matty cupped me. I wiggled my ass against him in response.

He leaned into my neck and bit me gently. His fingers found mine, twining between them and tugging them away from his head, moving them to the headboard, where he urged my fists to close around the wooden slats. Teeth and tongue burned a trail over my shoulder and down my back. Fingers slid down my sides, up and over the outsides of my breasts, skimming my ribs, and onto my hips before curling into my flesh and holding on tight.

Each breath was ragged. I was so turned on that I was sure I'd die of combustion if he didn't offer me relief soon. He shifted his body over mine slightly, using a knee to part my legs, as his tongue left a wet trail around the knobs of my spine, tracing the words on my flesh.

"You are. You know that, right?"

Lifting my head off the pillow, I glanced over my shoulder, trying to see him, but his *tsks* at my movement made me immediately drop back down.

"I am what?" I asked, completely breathless and distracted.

"Enough the way you are." As he repeated the words of my tattoo, his voice was husky. "You are more the enough." He moved behind me, and entered me slowly. "You are everything." He insisted, pulling out slowly, he leaned over and kissed the words.

I bit my lip as I felt every inch of him ease himself back inside me. Nothing had ever felt as good.

"Tell me," he demanded, slowing down his pumps even more. "Tell me how much you're worth to me. I know what you think of yourself. I want you to tell me how much you think you're worth to me."

My mind processed the words for a moment before I realized what he wanted to hear. "I'm worth everything to you."

"That's right." Matty growled back before nipping my neck. "You are enough the way you are." His hand grabbed a handful of flesh before backing out and slamming in at a mind-numbing pace. "You. Are. My. Everything." He accentuated each word with a deep, hard thrust.

He was so honest and raw in that moment that it almost distracted me. Almost. Then all thought was gone as he picked up the tempo, in and out, fucking me stupid. The hand on my hip shimmied back up my skin, grabbing my boob just rough enough. His thumb and finger pinched, pulled, and rolled my hardened nipple, and I couldn't hold on anymore.

My muscles tightened around him, trying to coax out his release so we could have it together. His low grumble of appreciation pushed me over the edge, and I gasped for air, every nerve on alert. His fingers moved quickly, finding a home at the apex of my thighs. Expertly, they moved to my clit, flicking and massaging. I'd stayed relatively quiet—the fact that it was the middle of the day and there were people around always in the back of my mind—but I couldn't hold back a second longer. I cried out loudly as his fingers pulled another orgasm from me.

Matty laughed happily, as if he was beyond pleased with himself, and never missed a beat. He slammed into me over and over at alarmingly fast speeds. Though he bit my shoulder roughly to mute his cries, I heard his moans of ecstasy perfectly. It was beautiful.

"Fuckin' Christ, baby girl." He gasped as he found his release. "Those sounds undo me, every single time."

I groaned as he pulled out, feeling how sore I was. Then I let go of the headboard and turned over. I needed to touch him. Dropping onto his back, head next to mine on the pillow, he seemed happy to let my fingers roam. Within minutes though, once his lungs had had a chance to catch up, Matty turned onto his side, propped on an elbow, captured my hand in his, and looked down at me.

Normally I'd want to hide, knowing that the cellulite on my thighs and the stretch marks on my belly were giant turn-offs. But the look in his eyes held only love, and I watched in wonder as his fingers trailed down over my body, around my belly button, then over the roundness of my tummy. Keeping his hand there, cupping my Buddha belly, he leaned over and gave me a kiss so hot that it could melt the polar ice caps.

"Do you have any idea how much you glow when you're pregnant?"

Romantic mood gone, I sat up on my elbows and watched him cautiously. "Matty?"

I wasn't sure what to say. If his idea of marriage meant more children, we were going to have a very unpleasant conversation. We had agreed that we were both too old to start over, and he'd gotten a vasectomy for Taylor.

His eyes flicked to mine for just a second before they looked back at my stomach, mesmerized. "Just because we can't have babies doesn't mean I don't wish we could." His fingers traced one of my faded lines, a souvenir from being a mom. "Did I ever tell you that you're to blame for Sam?"

My forehead wrinkled, and I wondered if he'd been drinking while he'd been out in the great room. He didn't notice, too busy following my stretch marks as if they were going to lead him to the largest gold mine ever found.

"I wasn't sure I even wanted to have kids. But watching you carry Ben, seeing how your belly grew a little bit every week and how much you radiated happiness, did something to me. When you pulled my hand here"—he pressed two fingers into my lower abdomen— "and made me feel him kick, I was a goner." He smiled at me. "From that moment on, I wanted nothing more than to be a dad."

Fingers moved again, tickling as he danced them to the other side. "Then with Lily, I watched you glow all over again, expanding a little more and more every day as you housed a life. At that point, I didn't want to just be a dad; I wanted to be her dad." My heart paused, his words having more of an effect than they should. "I would give anything to watch you grow a miracle that we create together."

"Matty," my voice was soft, and I was almost afraid to admit the next part. "I don't want any more kids."

He smiled wistfully. "I don't either, Joes. I wish we'd figured us out ten years ago. We could have had a baseball team by now." He let his hand slip off me and gave me a quick peck before pushing himself off the bed. "Come take a shower with me. We have somewhere to be."

TWENTY-SEVEN
JO

"Go in, babe. I'm right here." Matty held the ropes apart so I could climb up into the ring with Nick.

I felt like an idiot in all the protective gear I had on, and I was still reeling about the fact that I was there. When Matty had told me we had somewhere to be, the gym was the last place I had imagined. After Rob's reaction to Cris bringing me here, I never expected Matt to agree to it, let alone arrange a private session.

There I was though. Nick smiled that killer smile of his and went over what we were doing once more. Self-defense was more about avoiding a hit than it was anything else.

"Don't stand still," Nick instructed. "A moving target is harder to hit. Someone comes after you, you're gonna wanna freeze or back into the wall. It's a first gut reaction. Don't do it. Move."

He also showed me the pressure points to target: eyes, nose, throat, knees, and groin. If I was backed into a corner, he said, I was to use my knees, elbows, fingers, and feet and aim at those pressure points. The goal was not to kill, but to get the attacker down long enough for me to get away. He had me practice by cornering me and having me try to get by him.

Next, he taught me how to take a punch. Unfortunately, instructions could only go so far. After he'd walked my body through each maneuver and reminded me to constantly keep my eyes on my attacker so I could react appropriately to where the hit would land, he asked me if I was okay with him hitting me.

I hesitated for a minute too long. He looked relieved and suggested we leave this part of the lesson for another time. I shook my head—I didn't want to postpone learning.

The stomach hit drove me back into the ropes and earned me a nasty remark from him about paying attention, keeping my eyes on him, and tightening my stomach muscles. I not only didn't tense up, but I didn't roll with the punch or keep my balance. Epic fail.

The next few blows weren't much better. My cheek had started to bleed and my lip felt puffy, my side ached when I took a deep breath, and my eyes watered from the pain I felt all over the rest of me. But I refused to give up. Each time Nick knocked me to my knees, I got back up and faced him for more. He was taking it easy on me; an attacker would not.

For the first part of the session, Matty stood patiently next to the ring. Every so often he'd holler words of encouragement to me, or shout something to Nick, asking him to remember to show me another technique. Now though, he seemed to be struggling. He hadn't said anything in a long time, other than asking if I was okay after the first hit to my gut.

At one point, after I didn't avoid an elbow to my cheek and I'd fallen flat on my ass, I glanced his way. He had his back to the ring and was leaning over, hands on his knees, as if trying to catch his breath. The next time I looked at him was after I forgot to keep my chin down and I'd gotten jabbed so hard it made my teeth snap on my tongue. The enraged look on his face terrified me, and I turned away quickly.

I didn't know how long Nick beat the shit out of me, but it felt as if it lasted years. I wasn't even sure I was getting any better or if poor Nick was just taking it even easier on me than he had when we started. Every part of my body was begging my mind for a break when Cris started yelling to me.

"Jesus, Jo, move! Just because he's showing you how to get your ass handed to you doesn't mean you should make it easy on him!"

I didn't have time to acknowledge her, but relief washed over me. I knew this was all just pretend and that I could tell Nick to stop at any time, but it was nice to feel like I wasn't alone.

"Watch him! Keep your eyes glued to his every movement!" she screamed.

As Nick advanced, she walked me through what to do. Slide right. Duck. When he closed in on me again, she told me to watch his hands, move, and react. I jerked my head to the left, throwing all my weight onto that foot, and aimed my heel for his knee. Nick stumbled back, surprised, while Cris shouted excitedly on the floor behind us.

"That's it! Fight back."

Nick smiled and shrugged. "I think that's a good way to end our first class, don't you?"

I nodded, groaning when even that hurt, and climbed out of the ring. I looked everywhere, but my fiancé seemed to be missing. "Where's Matty?"

Cris grinned. "I sent him outside. Wicked sore?"

I didn't even bother to nod, just closed my eyes. "I think my bruises have bruises."

She gave me an understanding look and pulled me to the locker room. I was too tired to object when she removed all my gear for me then stripped off my tank top and shorts. There was no doubt in my mind that I'd never be able to get my arms to cooperate enough to get the shirt over my head. Then she stepped into a cool shower with me and helped me wash away the blood and sweat. The temperature was frigid, and I wanted to ease my aches and pains with heat, but she insisted cold was better.

As soon as I was clean, she snapped off the water and led me to a massage table. "I need to rub you down. It'll help, you'll see. Plus, I need to make sure nothins broken."

Expert fingers trailed over my body, rubbing gently at the spots where I was still tense and inspecting each and every spot where I'd taken a hit. Not only was I exhausted from the workout, but her hands were soothing, and I had to fight to stay awake.

"Why'd you send Matty outside?"

Cris snorted. "Really?" I waited for her to continue. "My brother is a lota' things, Jo, but a bystander is not one of 'em. He has a white knight complex. If someone is in trouble, he has a psychological need to save 'em." She laughed. "He still has a hard time comin' to my fights, and I could kick his ass in the ring. I think watching the woman he loves gettin' beat to a bloody pulp was a little more than he'd bargained for. I was half convinced that he was gonna jump in there and rip Nick to shreds."

I groaned, rolling my eyes. "This was his idea, not mine."

"Right. So, he was not only watchin' you take a beatin' and not able to help, but it was him who put you there to begin with. He needed a time-out. I'm glad I got here when I did."

That made sense. I'd have to make sure Matty knew how much I appreciated his self-restraint. "Oh! How was your weekend away?" Closing my eyes again, I let her hands do their magic as she gave me all the details.

She sounded like a girl falling in love—a very happy and spoiled girl who was realizing the man she was dating could actually be something more than an occasional hook-up. It was so different from her normal view on relationships that I knew something must have changed over the last few days. I didn't tell her I'd gone to the dinner in her place, or that I knew why she'd started dating Caleb, and I didn't mention Rob. Cris deserved to be happy, and I didn't want to be the one who took it away from her.

My injuries weren't that bad. I was sore, yeah, but my ribs weren't broken. My lip was a little swollen, but I could easily cover it with dark lipstick. My cheek was the worst. The crack in my skin was bright red and stood out on my pale skin, even though it looked worse than it felt. Concealer was an option, but the cut was too sore to touch, so I bought big sunglasses that covered it instead.

Matty refused to go anywhere with me. Well, he insisted on going everywhere with me, but he wouldn't hold my hand or cuddle me in public. He said my face made me look like a battered woman and that people would assume he'd beaten me. I rolled my eyes and asked what kind of idiot would automatically come to that conclusion, considering I could have had an accident of some sort. The look he gave me made it clear that *he* was that kind of an idiot. Whenever we left the apartment, he was more like an annoying shadow who would shake his head when I tried to talk to him. If Secret Service agents were like that, I felt bad for the president and his family.

It was actually nice having Matty around all the time, even if I wouldn't admit that to him. When he'd told me he'd taken a leave of absence from work, I had panicked. I didn't want to be the reason he lost a job he loved, and I was worried about being with him twenty-four, seven. The last time we'd lived together hadn't exactly ended well. Not to mention the fact that we'd gone from barely talking on the phone to engaged and living together in a little over a week.

We spent every second we could together. I had class and my one-on-ones with Nick, and Matty had to drive back to Maine to meet with his boss and go to Sammy's games, then he had a ton of meetings at the clubhouse, but other than that, we were together. Sometimes he'd just sit and hold me while I studied. Other times we'd sit on the roof, enjoying the sun while catching up and laughing like we used to. Others he'd pull me out to the bike and we'd ride for hours.

If possible, I'd fallen in love with him a little more every day.

The need for answers was always in the back of my mind. Each time I thought about suggesting we sit down and have a serious conversation, something more important came up, or Matty would smile and I'd talk myself out of it.

I wanted to think that we were strong enough to handle anything, but as the days went by and he didn't mention Taylor, I let worry settle into my gut. An engagement ring on another woman was a big thing to forget to tell your current fiancée. I told myself that he was giving us extra time to fortify our relationship.

Pushing the nerves away, I focused on our happiness.

The days merged into a blur. We were cuddling on the roof, Matty lying with his head on my lap and feet dangling off the other end of the couch, enjoying the late afternoon sun on a Thursday, when reality hit. As much as I was looking forward to seeing my kids—and I missed them more than words could explain—I didn't want to leave Matty.

I brushed the hair off his forehead and pressed my lips against his skin. "I'm gonna miss you."

He opened his eyes, looking up at me sleepily. "When?"

"Tomorrow's Friday. I'm headed home."

"Shit!" He sat up abruptly and turned, looking at me in concern. "I forgot." He swallowed and chewed the inside of his lip. "It's vacation week."

I nodded, confused. A shit-eating grin transformed his face, and he turned and lay back down.

"Matty?" I'd missed something.

He smirked. "You don't have to go home. We'll go up tomorrow, get the kids, and bring all three of 'em back for the week. A week with my girl and our brood? I can't think of anything better."

"All three...? Do you have Sam next week?"

He shook his head. "No. But Bex will let me have him." He opened his eyes, looking into mine. "Come on, babe. It'll be a blast! We have the room, plus it'll show us what our future will be like. And that way, I don't have to worry about how I'll sleep without you."

I smiled back, his enthusiasm catching. "Okay. I'll tell the kids tonight."

My kids were ecstatic. There was a Jack and Annie light show going on at the planetarium that Ben "just had to see," and

Lily asked if we could visit the aquarium so she could see her beloved Rockhopper penguins. Even Will seemed happy about it—but that might have been because he had the next two weeks "off" and had something planned with his girlfriend.

Unlike most divorced couples, I didn't have to get his approval to bring the kids down here. Part of our parental rights and responsibilities agreement specified that since neither of us had full custody, during the two weeks we had the kids, we did not have to ask the other parent's permission to take the children over state lines. Our PR&R was pretty in depth, but we felt it would protect us from having to go back to court and argue over the kids later. We'd fought enough over the last few years and were done.

At least until he found out that I was marrying Matty.

I promised the kids I'd be at the house when they got home from school the next afternoon, told them I loved them, and hung up. Glancing up, I found Matty leaning in the doorway, watching me.

He smiled and sauntered across the room, climbed onto the bed next to me, and pulled me close. "We'll pick Sam up on the way back here, and I promised Becky I'd have him home by seven next Sunday. For the next week, we get to be a real family. I can't wait to tell them we're getting married!"

Matty's unbridled happiness brought out mixed emotions. On one had I felt the same – I couldn't remember being this happy and hopeful about anything in years. But, on the other, unease had started to settle. I could only hope this time we'd make it.

TWENTY-EIGHT

JO

"No. Not happening." I seethed again.

Matty simply crossed his arms and tipped his head back slightly. "Get in the fucking car, Joes."

"No."

"Look"—he leaned in close, hissing— "you promised the kids you'd be there when they got off the bus. If you don't get in the car this fucking instant, we're gonna hit traffic and be late."

I took a deep breath, torn between not being home when I promised and standing my ground. I glared at the man I loved. "I'll call T and have her go up. Tell them I got stuck. Want me in the car? Get him out."

Matty shook his head. "He's coming too."

Dean opened his door and gave us both an annoyed look. Then he turned his icy gaze on me. "I don't want to be here either. But my president gave me an order to stay with you, and I have no choice. The quicker you accept that, the faster we can get on the damn road. You wanna take the train up instead? Fine, I'll get my shit and take the damn train too. Just make up your fuckin' mind already!" He slammed his door as if to accentuate the last word.

I raised an eyebrow at Matty, his lips quirking with amusement. "You heard him."

I groaned, rolled my eyes, and stomped to the passenger seat. We were taking Rocker's Expedition, because it could fit all three kids, their gear, the two of us, and apparently Dean. I slammed my door, mimicking Dean's behavior, and closed my eyes as I leaned back into the seat. Our fun family trip had just turned into a nightmare.

Until fifteen minutes ago, I'd thought Matty and I were driving to Maine alone. Matty had gone to get the car, leaving me to pack us a lunch and some snacks, and I had been singing along to the radio as I looked forward to a great day with my favorite people.

Then Dean had walked into the kitchen carrying a duffle bag, his eyes narrowed on me nastily. Rob, it turned out, had decided that with the three new additions, we needed another set of hands. Apparently he thought the number of kids should never outnumber the adults with them. Out of all of the Bastards, he'd assigned Dean.

"Come on, babe," Matty had crooned as Dean settled into the SUV. *"He really isn't that bad. He's great with kids, and he's like the little brother I never had. It'll be fine."*

I heard Matty get in and start the car, then we were moving. His hand slid to my thigh immediately. I wasn't angry with him, just the situation. I laid my palm over his hand, hoping to convey that message.

That didn't mean I was going to sit up and make small talk with someone who hated me. Or to pretend that I was fine spending time with a man I'd grown to resent. Instead, I let sleep call me.

I woke a few hours later to the two of them laughing uncontrollably. I listened for a few minutes instead of opening my eyes and sitting up. It took me moment to realize they were talking about fishing and Sammy.

Dean surprised me when he sobered. "Can't wait to see him, man. It's been what? Three or four months? I miss that kid."

The way he talked about Sammy stunned me, but then again, Sam was an amazing kid. Yet, hearing a total douchenozzle talk about the little boy that I adored as if said little boy was the coolest kid in the world wasn't something I expected. Dean gave off a weird vibe - one you'd expect from someone who only tolerated women and children because he had to.

I was sure I'd never understand these Bastards.

"Mom! Mom! Mom!" Lily screamed as she ran off the bus and straight into my arms. "You're here!"

I laughed, hugging her little frame tight. "I'm here, Lily-Belle." I leaned down and kissed her curly blond head. "You ready for a week in Boston?"

She nodded vigorously, tipping her head back to see me. Her smile faded. "What happened to your rock star hair?"

I laughed, running a hand through my curls. "Yeah. Mommy needed a change."

"Hmm." She crossed her tiny arms. "I liked it. I didn't think it made you look like you were trying to recapture your youth like Nana said. I agreed with Daddy—it was fun, and you need fun."

I raised my eyebrows as she talked, trying not to laugh as she parroted a conversation she'd obviously overheard. Pushing my sunglasses to the top of my head, I contemplated her words. I wasn't sure how to respond to that and wondered which Nana had commented on my hair, but it sounded more like something my mom would say than Will's. Thankfully I was saved when the last of the neighborhood kids filed out of the big yellow vehicle.

"Mom!"

I looked up as Ben jumped off the bottom step and shuffled away from his friends.

"Did you get a new car?" he asked as he got closer to me, eyeing the Ford parked in front of our house.

"That's the first thing you wanna say to me after two weeks away?"

My mini-me shook his head and threw his arms around me.

"It's not mine. It belongs to a friend of Uncle Matty. We've got it for the week in Boston. Nice, right?" I hugged him tightly. Hugs from him were few and far between now, and I never got one in public. "Geez, did you grow another two feet while I was gone?"

He might look just like me, but he got his height from Will. At eleven, he was only an inch shorter than me.

"I did actually." He giggled, a rare sound that reminded me of his toddler years. He pulled back, and his laughter died instantly.

The look he gave me was another thing he'd obviously inherited from his dad. It was horror mixed with rage, and though I hadn't seen it in a few months, I almost took a step back.

"What happened to your face?" His voice had gone ice cold.

Out of my peripheral, I saw Lily squinting at me to see what he was talking about. Instead of letting him go, I tucked him under one arm, pulled Lily under the other, and turned them toward the house. Ben hesitated, obviously irritated that I hadn't answered him.

"She's decided to learn how to box."

The voice from the doorway had them both glancing up. When they realized that their favorite uncle was standing there watching us, they forgot all about me and ran to him. I couldn't decide who I enjoyed watching more: the kids or the love of my life.

He greeted them the same way he always did—kneeling down and pulling Lily into his arms, then picking her up while ruffling Ben's hair before pulling him in for a hug while dropping a kiss on the top of his head. The scene would have made a beautiful portrait, one that reflected the love a father gave his children. There was no doubt in my mind that they would never feel unloved or unwanted by their soon-to-be stepfather.

"Box? Like Muhammad Ali?" Ben asked, awed.

I laughed as we ushered them inside, trying to answer all of the questions they kept throwing at us while directing them to get their school bags to their rooms and grab anything they might want. Within ten minutes, we'd loaded them in the car, locked the house, and were on our way to get Sammy and Dean.

The ride took a little longer than the normal half hour, but with the two chatterboxes in the backseat, it passed quickly. Ben talked about his upcoming science fair and how he still wasn't sure what he was going to do for a presentation, while Lily kept interrupting to tell us all about her drama club and how they were going to be performing *Charlie and the Chocolate Factory*. Matty jumped right into the conversation, never missing a beat, and corrected the kids when they were mean to each other. I sat back and watched the three of them. Life with Will had never been this laid-back or exciting. I was one lucky girl.

Once we pulled into Becky's, the kids jumped out and ran around back, headed straight for the playground, Matty hot on their heels as soon as the car was in park. Before I'd had a chance to make it to the front door, laughter and shrieks of enjoyment filled the air. I fought the urge to join them. There would be plenty of time to play over the next few days.

Becky was in the kitchen, piling snacks on a tray. The idea of this woman doing anything domestic, like baking, amused me. But then again, she'd always been a conundrum. Just like the rest of the women Matt had slept with, Bex was built like a supermodel, with pale golden hair, legs that went on forever, and dimples that could convince anyone to do anything. That was where the similarities between her and the others ended though.

Becky's long hair was in dreads, her arms were colored with tattoos of flowers, her favorite poems and song lyrics, and she had more piercings than I wanted to know about. Even the way she dressed set her apart. It was only mid-April, but she was wearing corduroys, a tiny tank that showed off her ink, and was barefoot.

I smiled at her eccentricities. She stopped and came around the corner to greet me with a giant hug. We'd been friends before the divorce, but I'd been Matt's friend first, so he kept me when they split. Over the past couple of months though, she and I had spent some time together and were finally getting close again.

As she pulled back from the embrace, she grabbed my left hand. "I hear congratulations are in order." She beamed. "It's about freaking time, don't you think?"

"Thank you." I couldn't keep the smile off my face. The fact that she was happy about my engagement meant the world to me. I took off my glasses and set them on the table. "What can I do to help?"

Bex scowled, grabbing my chin in a way only another mother could. "Those bruises the reason Dean's sitting on my deck?"

I shook my head, pulling back slightly and not understanding the connection she was trying to make. She turned, grabbed a pitcher out of the cupboard, and began to make iced tea.

My curiosity got the better of me. "Why would Dean's being here have anything to do with my bruises?"

She turned back to me, brown eyes so intent I was frozen in place. "Please." She rolled her eyes. "You don't have to pretend around me. I've been living this life a long time, Joey, and I can handle the truth. I know that when Dean shows up here, something serious is going on. Maybe you can't tell me what, but don't insult me by acting like nothing is happening. Especially when you look like you've been beat to a pulp. Matty better kill whoever touched you."

I tried not to gape at her, but my mouth wouldn't close. Her eyes searched mine, and I could tell she was angry with me, but I had no idea why. "I think I've missed a step."

"You don't know." Her face went blank, but she couldn't mask the surprise in her voice. "You really don't know."

It wasn't a question, but I shook my head. "What does Dean have to do with anything?"

She bit her lip, playing with the hoop in the middle. She sighed before she answered. "Dean's an enforcer, Joey. Whenever the club has trouble, he comes to stay with us. Whatever is going on, it's bad enough that they want to have eyes on Sam."

"Enforcer?" My voice sounded weak even to my own ears.

She tipped her head and raised an eyebrow, as if to say, *"How do you not know this?"* Instead, she swallowed and clarified. "For the club, Jo. He does security, amongst other things. He doesn't have a family of his own, so it's his job to protect us if Matt can't be here."

Suddenly it all made sense: Dean telling me that he had to come because Rocker had sent him, Dean acting as if he'd known Sammy his whole life, Matty telling me he'd trust Dean with his.

"I don't know about any of that," I assured her. "My face looks like this because I'm taking a self-defense class."

She smirked. "You actually have balls enough to get in the ring with Cris?"

I snorted. "God, no! Nick's teaching me."

"Your fiancée's brave." Becky looked behind me just as hands grabbed my shoulders.

They pulled me back into a familiar body, and lips found the spot where my neck met my shoulder. Wrapping his arms around me tightly, he inhaled, making me shiver. Then he was gone, crossing the kitchen in two strides, and grabbed his ex-wife in a bone-crushing hug.

"Don't hug me!" she admonished as she hugged him back. "I'm pissed at you."

"Me? Why?" He stood, looking from me to her and back.

I knew the look on her face too well and excused myself before they started arguing. I wanted to hear what they were going to say, but they needed a few minutes to talk in private.

Wandering out onto the deck, I saw Dean. He didn't turn when he heard me, just sat in his chair, watching the kids as he sipped a bottle of beer.

I plopped down on the edge of a chaise lounge next to him. "Are you really here to be our security guard?"

He nodded absentmindedly, not looking at me.

"So, you're just gonna follow me and Matty around?"

He didn't turn. "Not you and Matt. My job is to protect them." He tipped his head toward the kids, still playing and screaming away. "I'm gonna follow them, stay with them, play with them, and make sure nothing at all happens to them."

"Really?" I asked, my tone cool. "You're just gonna spend all your time with kids? And how exactly are you gonna keep them safe?"

"I like kids. I'd rather spend time with them than adults; we have more in common."

Makes sense, since you're about as emotionally mature as they are, I thought snidely.

"I'm good at my job. You don't need to know how I do it, just that you can trust me with the lives of your children."

I swallowed and looked back at the kids. The silence stretched between us as we watched them play Capture the Flag and chase each other. Lily got the advantage and shot up the ladder before either boy could stop her. Once the flag was in her hands, she twirled and hooted, doing a victory dance.

"She's beautiful."

"Did you seriously just tell me my eight-year-old is beautiful?" I don't know why I said it other than to get a rise out of him. His words didn't come across as creepy.

He scoffed. "Jesus, Jo, I don't belong to the Bastards just so I can be a pedophile and fly under the radar myself. We kill sick fucks who have those thoughts." He sounded pissed at me, and without giving me a second to process the words he'd just said, he continued. "I'm saying that she's a beautiful little girl. And if she's that pretty at eight, we're gonna be fucked by the time she's a teenager and starts realizing boys are not the enemy and that they definitely don't have cooties. She is gonna be a world-class beauty, and we're gonna haveta scare the vultures away."

I laughed, taking the compliment for what it was and trying not to read too much into it. "She is. She gets her looks from her daddy."

Dean turned toward me then, shaking his head. "Not from what I can see. She looks like her momma."

I felt the blush rise in my cheeks. No one ever looked at Lily and saw me. Even though I had been blond as a child, everyone assumed she got her hair from Will. Her skin was a blatant contrast to mine, darker than I got when I was completely tan. And she was a tiny speck of a child, short and skinny for her age, where no one had ever accused me of being skinny.

As if reading my thoughts, he continued. "She's not always gonna be a little girl. Then you'll see. Although, that'll probably be the day Mateo decides she can't leave the clubhouse without at least three brothers watchin' her every move."

"Four. And that's when we let her out of the clubhouse. I say we send her to an all-girls' boarding school." Matty's voice was full of humor as he walked to my chair, swung a leg over, and sat behind me.

"We may have to." Dean nodded as if taking Matty's absurd idea seriously. "She's gonna be trouble. Does Cris know the club has a new princess?"

Matt laughed. "Jesus, don't tell her. Then poor Lily will be her new pet, and we'll have two of 'em on our hands. Naw, we'll just let Lil grow up and see where time takes her."

"Better the Princess than a Brat." Dean mused.

No. Uh-ugh. Never happening. Absolutely not.

"You two are wrong. My daughter is not going to grow up and be the next club princess, or a club whore, or an old lady, or anything else to do with the club. She's going to go to college, have an adventure, and find herself. Away from men who tell her that she doesn't have a say and that she has to belong to someone."

Matty tensed behind me, but Dean just laughed like my words were hilarious. "You're right, Jo. She's not gonna be any of those things. 'Cause that little beauty right there?" He pointed the tip of his bottle at Lily, "She's gonna have every single brother wrapped around her little finger. One day, she's gonna be the motherfucking club queen."

TWENTY-NINE

MATTY

I listened to Dean's spiel, half amused until I felt Jo tense a little more with each word. He didn't wait for either of us to respond, just set his beer on the floor next to his chair, stood, and strode down the stairs toward the kids. Jo and I sat in silence, neither sure what to say.

I wondered if she realized how accurate his words had been. Dean was a lot of things, but he knew what he was talking about and seeing how beautiful Lily was worried him. She was going to be a shitload of trouble for us in seven or eight years.

I wrapped my arms tighter around Jo's waist and leaned in, my chin was on her shoulder. I could feel the stress coming off her in waves and knew that it might have absolutely nothing to do with Dean's opinion and everything to do with her own. I hated that she felt like I was trying to oppress her.

She was wrong. Not every woman had to belong to someone—there were plenty of women in the club who didn't. Jo was mine, yeah, but shit, the ring on her finger showed everyone that she owned *me*. When it came right down to it, she had more say in my life than I did.

If she wanted me to walk away from this life, I would. I'd be fucking miserable, but I'd do it and I'd understand where she was coming from 'cause being an old lady wasn't for everyone. I would do anything to be with her, I was that much of a pansy-assed asshole.

If she decided to leave me, I'd do everything in my power to change her mind, but I couldn't make her stay. It was her choice, and when she finally had all the pieces of the puzzle, there was a very good chance I'd be all alone. I fucking hated the thought.

"We're gonna have to talk about this shit. It's not gonna magically disappear just because we ignore it." I didn't need to explain further. I'd tried to bring up the subject a few times over the last week, and Jo had shot me down every single time.

She leaned back into me, turning her face to mine. Giving me a quick peck on the cheek, she shook her head once. "No, it's not going to disappear. But I don't want to know. I've told you, I made up my mind, Matty. The past is in the past."

My chest ached. "It's not. It will never be that fucking simple, and you know it. Pretending it is will only make it harder for you." I resisted the urge to lean into her and kiss away the worry line that appeared between her eyes. "I'm not talking about the past right now. There's a lot going on, and I don't want you to feel like I'm keeping things from you." *Even when I am.*

"But you are." Jo sighed and turned away.

I followed her gaze. Dean was chasing the kids in a game of tag, and all four of them laughing.

"Let's not do this now. Not here." I started to agree, but she cut me off. "There was a time when that was all I wanted—you to let me in, I mean. To tell me the secrets that it seems everyone else knows. I'd like to think that if you love me as much as you say you do, then I'd know everything important about you and the rest of it is just BS. But every time we go somewhere, it seems like something else I don't know pops up."

I let out a breath I didn't even know I was holding. Finding her hand, I gripped it tight. "You said there was a time when you wanted to know all my secrets. What about now?"

"You." She pulled her hand out of mine and pushed off the chair. "Now, I just want you. I'll take you whatever way I can." She turned and jogged down the stairs as she adjusted her sunglasses back on her face.

Watching her go, I leaned forward, putting my elbows on my knees, and steepled my hands. My mind was still reeling from the conversation with Becky, and now I had even more to contemplate.

When I'd walked into my old house a half hour ago, it had been to say hello and finalize my week with Sam. The look on my ex-wife's face as she talked to Jo had made my stomach knot though, and I almost turned and hurried out before they saw me.

"Your fiancée's brave," had been the first words Becky uttered when she spotted me in the door.

As soon as she'd said the word fiancée, I realized Jo had told her before I'd had the chance. Of course, Becky would be angry. We never, and I mean never, made decisions like that without talking to the other and making sure that it was the best thing for Sam.

I pulled away and grabbed her chin. "I'm sorry, Bex. I should have talked to you before I asked her. It happened so fast—"

"Fuck you!" She pulled away, smacking my hand back as she did. "You seriously think I'm mad about that?" She turned her back on me and slammed a dish into the sink.

Leaning a hip against the counter, I gawked at her back. Becky never swore, and if she did, something was seriously wrong.

"If I'd known Jo was going to tell you," I started cautiously, not sure what to say. "I'd have come in and we'd have done it together."

She turned, glaring. "Jo didn't tell me, you ass! Dean did. It's about damn time that you two got your shit together and agreed that you're madly in love. Don't you think? Twelve years is a long fucking time, Matt. I was sure I was going to die from old age before you two figured it out." Crossing her arms, she gave me the death glare. "This has nothing to do with Jo."

I was at a loss then. "Okay, what'd I do this time?" Even though I tried to cover it, the question was filled with irritation.

Instantly her body was on alert and she pulled back her shoulders. "Fuck you and the horse you rode in on, Matthew Murphy!"

"Rebecca Murphy!" I scoffed playfully. "I'm not sure what I've done, but I can guarantee I deserve your attitude. My poor horse though? What did he ever do to you?"

She tried to keep a straight face, but it cracked slightly. "You are such an asshole."

"We established that on our second date." I agreed. "What in the hell is going on, Bex?"

She sighed and looked sad. "Dean is in my backyard, Matt. There is only ever one reason for Dean to be here. You haven't told me anything, and we both know I know better than to ask. But worse than that is that Jo doesn't know there is anything going on. Why in the hell are you keeping her in the dark? She didn't even know what he does!"

I could feel my irritation growing, and I needed to nip it in the bud before I blew. "Jo knows what she needs to."

"Exactly!" Becky threw her hands in the air. "That's what I'm talking about. I thought you learned from our mistakes and you weren't going to make them again."

My eyes narrowed. "I'm not making the same mistakes. You knew about the club. You knew about my life. You chose to stay out of it. I'm making the choice for her."

"I chose to have a baby and stay safe. You aren't giving her a choice. You act like she's some dutiful little thing who will follow you around and never question it. What happens when the cops show up? I at least knew enough so when they started to spin their lies, I could laugh and tell them to go to hell.

"What's she going to do when they show her pictures of a man beaten bloody and tell her that you're the one who did it? Or if some of those skeletons really come out, and they claim you're a murderer? Will she lie and give you an alibi, or will she pack her crap and run?

"If you aren't telling her anything, then she won't be prepared for the shit that will get thrown her way. And how is she going to handle lockdowns? You think she's just going to willingly lock herself in the clubhouse with your whores while you ride off with your friends to do God knows what?"

"They're not my whores!" I snapped back.

"Out of everything I just said, that's what you got out of it?" She snorted disgustedly. *"And yeah, they are. She's been your friend for years! Do you honestly think she magically forgot how you used to act once you started sleeping with her? Jesus, Matt! Just because you haven't been that man in a little while doesn't mean she doesn't remember!"* She shook her head. *"You need to tell her what's going on. And you need to do it soon."*

I slammed my palms on the tile. *"When I tell her, she's gonna leave me!"* The fear that had been in the back of my mind for the last week came shuffling forward. *"She won't stay. She'll give me back my ring, tell me what an evil cunt I am, and she'll never talk to me again."*

Becky's face softened a fracture and she sighed. *"No, she won't. That woman loves you. But if you don't tell her, and I mean tell her everything, she will leave you. Secrets have no place in a marriage, whether you want to keep her safe or not. Jo is not me. She won't be happy with just pieces of you. She wants you all. Jo isn't stupid – she'll figure it out eventually. And, she'll hate you for keeping her in the dark."* After pulling me into a quick hug, she backed away and met my eyes. *"Go talk to her."*

"Now? Here, in the house I used to share with my wife? With our kids around? I think I'll pass."

She smirked. *"No, not here, you ass. I've got the kids – Dean's with me. We'll feed them, you take Jo for a drive and talk."*

I shook my head. "She won't leave the kids—"

"Stop making excuses. Go."

I'd gotten sidetracked by Dean when I first came out, but remembering Becky's words now, I stood and headed straight for my woman. Grabbing Jo's hand, I started to pull her around the house. She didn't put up much of a fight, more surprised than anything.

"We'll be right back," I called over my shoulder.

That made her dig her heels in though. "What? Where are we going?"

I pulled open the passenger door and pointed at the seat. "Get in the car, Jo."

She shook her head and yanked her hand from mine before crossing her arms defiantly. The sunglasses she wore were large and dark, covering half her face and hiding her eyes. I had no doubt she was glaring at me behind them.

"We just got here! I can't leave my kids."

I hardened my stare, letting her know she had no choice in the matter. "They're with Bex and Dean. They're fine."

She twisted her lips, a sure sign she was barely containing her anger.

"We'll be right back," I promised, my tone softer than it had been.

"Whatever." She huffed then gave me what I assumed was supposed to be a nasty look before she slid into the seat.

As I dropped into the driver's seat, I was half surprised that she was still in the vehicle. Part of me had expected her to act like a petulant child and run as soon as I made it halfway around the hood.

I didn't know where to go. The last time we'd been at my house was the day we'd broken up, and I didn't want that hanging over our heads. Her house was out because it was too far away. It took a few minutes, but finally inspiration struck. When we pulled into a local park ten minutes later, she looked around, surprise and confusion mixed on her face.

I shifted the car into park, unbuckled, and turned my body toward Jo. I wanted her to be able to see my face for this talk, to look me in the eyes and tell me that she hated who I was, if need be.

After looking out her window for what seemed like forever, she followed my lead and mimicked my movements, unbuckling and turning toward me. "I haven't been here since Memorial Day."

I hadn't either. That had been a good day. We'd had a great meal with good friends and lots of laughs. Not even a year had passed, but it felt like a lifetime ago. Jo had been here with Will and the kids; I'd been here with Tay and Sam. This place held tons of great memories. Jo and I used to come here on our lunch break, or after work, to run, and we'd talk about everything.

I reached over the center console and pulled the sunglasses off her eyes before tucking a piece of hair behind her ear. I needed to see her without anything in the way. She could never keep her feelings from being reflected in her eyes, and now more than ever, I needed to see what she was thinking. All I could see now was love and trust, and I cursed myself for not having a better plan.

Taking a deep breath, I just said whatever came to mind. "My name is Matthew Murphy. I'm thirty-six-and-a-half, have a ten-year-old son, am engaged to the most amazing woman I've ever met, and I live a double life." I twisted my lips. "By day, I'm a social worker who lives in a tiny little fixer upper and drives a piece-of-shit car—the same one Adam Sandler sings about." I winked, hoping for a laugh. She didn't disappoint. "I like to run because it helps me de-stress. I enjoy staying at home on Saturday afternoons, lounging in my sweats, watching the Sci-Fi channel, and gorging on junk food. My best friend is the most important person in my world, and I will drop everything when she calls, no matter who I'm with or what time of day."

Jo's face had softened, and she was biting her bottom lip. I stroked her cheek then pulled her lip free. I wanted to end here, reach over and kiss her then spend the next hour fogging up our windows.

I pushed on. "By night, I'm Mateo Murphy, reformed man whore, VP of the Bastards of Boston. I ride a Harley and own a monstrous apartment. I inherited a shit-ton of money when my grandparents died, which I invested wisely, and now I co-own a cabinet company called Beautiful by Design."

Her eyebrows rose with that. She'd been surprised when I told her about being the Bastards' veep, but Rob's company being half mine wasn't common knowledge.

"A lot of people think BBD is a cover for the club, that we filter money through it. But it's legit. I worked my way through college next to him, building the business into what it is today. And even though a lot of the guys work for us, it is completely separated from the club."

What it was now was a nightmare. Over the last few years, it had become *the* company to have remodel your kitchen, bedroom, or bath. Anyone who was anyone within the city limits had custom cabinets from us.

"The club isn't a normal club. We don't sell or transport drugs or guns. In fact, we don't allow any of our members to use any illegal substance."

Her features relaxed.

"That doesn't mean we don't break the law, because we do. In order to become a Bastard, you have to take an oath to protect those who can't protect themselves. In order to do that, I've done a lot of things I'm not proud of. I've also done things that should keep me up at night. I sleep like a baby."

She opened her mouth, and I knew what she was going to ask.

I shook my head, not giving her a chance. "Things that I may never be able to tell you. Not because I don't want to, but because it's club business and if you knew, you'd be a liability. I'll be as honest as I can, but will never tell you any specifics. I have hurt people, Joes. I have tortured men."

Jo's face lost all color, but she didn't turn away.

I didn't want to say more but knew she needed to hear it all. "I've killed."

She shook her head. "Stop. I don't want to hear any more." Still shaking her head, as if she could rid her mind of everything I'd just said, she swallowed hard. "That's not you, Matty."

"It is me, Joes. You've seen the same fucked up shit I have. You know what it's like to see a child who's been broken by the one person who shouldn't ever hurt them. You've felt the same rage knowing their parent is going to get away with it, yet the kid will carry those scars for life. I'm not ashamed of what I've done. We take away the boogieman so kids can sleep at night, so that a mom can leave her house without fear of her fucktard of a boyfriend attacking her and dragging her into hell with him. We help those families take back something that was stolen from them."

415

I couldn't believe she was still sitting in front of me. She looked horrified, but she was still there. I'd take that as a good sign.

When I reached for her hand, she didn't resist. Her eyes never left mine as I talked, telling her as much as I could about the ins and outs of the club and how it worked, and who did what within the club. I mentioned that once we saved a kid, or a family, they became our family and we protected them forever. I didn't want to tell another brother's story, but I did say that sometimes those kids grew up and joined us. If Dean or Bear wanted her to know that Rocker and I had saved them from hell, it was their tale to tell.

I explained how we took the "jobs" we took, and that some required us to leave at a moment's notice, often for unknown periods, but that there would always be someone left behind to watch over her and our kids. I finished with lockdowns and how, even though we were trying to help, we had made hundreds of enemies over the years. I finished with the fact that while we weren't on lockdown now, we'd beefed up security, just in case, and that was why Dean was with us.

"Whenever there is a threat, I'll make sure you're never alone. If you're up here, I'll send someone to you. But if you're home, then you'll need to stay at the clubhouse. As my ol' lady, you're in more danger than most." She was irritated by that, and I knew her pathetic arguments about being able to take care of herself weren't far from her mind. Needing her to listen, really hear my words, I pulled our linked fingers to my mouth and kissed her wrist. "If someone is out for revenge, they'll come after you. I know you're not going to want to go, but I can't keep my shit together if I have to worry about you. If you want me safe, you need to do what you're told and move into the club."

She rolled her eyes but nodded anyway. My throat was dry, and I felt as if I'd been talking forever. I was positive I'd never seen her quiet this long—not even when we watched a movie. Her color had come back, and she hadn't run from the car screaming.

"Say something."

Her eyes searched my face for a minute. "Wow."

I snorted. "Wow? That's all you got? No questions?"

"Oh, I've got questions." She wet her bottom lip and adjusted in the seat, staring out the windshield instead of meeting my eyes. "How come you never get caught?"

I scowled at the radio. That was a good question, one I wouldn't be able answer completely. My hesitation spoke louder than any words I could have said.

"Hawk's dad." She said the words as if she already knew the answer. "Corruption at its finest."

I could feel the judgment from her side of the car. I raised an eyebrow. "No. There's no corruption. We have some people in the department who keep us informed and help us out when we need it. And yeah, we have someone with pull looking out for us. But we're still a target. You were there when we were all hauled into the station last summer. Tank just got out of prison. We have to keep our train on the tracks or we're in deep shit, just like everyone else. I am smarter than your average bear, and a lucky son of a bitch, and have been able to avoid the inside of a cell."

She sighed and turned her attention to something out my window. "What was in the envelope, Matty? What was so horrible that you couldn't tell me last summer?"

And there it was. The question that, when answered, would have her telling me to get the hell away from her. And demanding I stay away.

I swallowed. "Jo." I had to look away. I didn't have the balls to look her in the eye right then. "I don't know who Billy paid to find all that shit, but whoever did it was pretty fuckin' thorough. My juvie records, things I thought were sealed—it was all in there."

And Providence. I couldn't bring myself to say the words, knowing it would be the end of us. So, I told her what I could, what I'd told almost everyone else who knew. I pulled my hand away from hers and sat back in my seat.

"A few years back, a job went south. Tank, Bear, and I walked into it before anyone else, thinking we were going to bust up a sick fuck and take his stepdaughter home to her mom and real dad. Wiz had tracked this pig down, and we were the closest. We should have waited for our brothers, but we wanted to get it over with and get home. We weren't prepared for what we found."

No. Not prepared at all, although nothing could have gotten us ready for that. Young women and teenaged girls, some as young as thirteen, being held in dog kennels and used in the most horrific

417

ways. If I closed my eyes, I could still see the fear in their eyes and smell burning flesh and the horrifying conditions. Tank had told me that he still had nightmares too, and would spend hours replaying the scene in his mind. Bear had just been a prospect, and he never talked about it; it was as if he couldn't tolerate what had happened, so he blocked it. Could we have done more? Yes. I wished I could go back and redo that day. But we couldn't, and I'd be damned if Scott Dyer took one more thing from me.

I looked back at Jo, hoping she'd understand what I was about to say. "I'm not ready to talk about it yet. I may never be ready. I became someone else that night. We did what we had to do. I push it away because I don't want to think about it. I didn't know evidence even existed, but the day I opened that envelope, it all came flooding back." I stopped, not sure what else to say.

I'd been terrified, seeing the proof all over my sunroom floor. Pictures that would not only put me away for life but would make anyone who mattered to me a target. I'd found the packet the day after Ellie's attack, and with those visuals fresh in my mind, the fact that someone had connected me to Dyer and had also been watching and taking pictures of Jo and me over the last few weeks was just too much. In that moment, I'd thought someone was coming after me, and the only way to protect Jo was to push her away. Wrong move. I'd panicked for nothing; we'd never been able to link Ellie's attack to Providence.

Jo didn't turn and jump out of the car. Instead her eyes glistened in understanding, and she pulled my hand back between both of hers and squeezed it. Tightly. "Okay." Meeting my eyes, she gave me a small smile. "The names? Hawk, Bear, Tiny, Tank. Rocker. Where did they come from?"

I took a deep breath. She was changing the subject, turning to something light; for that, I was grateful. Leaning forward, I whispered, "Promise you won't tell?"

She nodded.

"They're actually nicknames that just stuck. Dean, for instance, is insane. He rides like a mad man and does total James Dean shit. So, Dean. Ian's the tamest guy in the room unless you fuck with him. Then he'll tear you to pieces. Like a grizzly bear. Jeremy never misses his target, so I called him Hawk Eye. It became Hawk over the years. Tiny's Tiny, 'cause, well, he is anything but. Tank will plow through anything and seriously fuck shit up. Rob always rocks the boat. Preach sees the good in others and prays for our souls. Neo, if you see him fight, you'll see has serious kickass reflexes. Watching him is like watching *The Matrix*. And me—"

"Yeah, no." A smile tugged on her lips as she shook her head, interrupting. "I already know that one."

I smirked, trying to cover my laugh. "What's wrong? The fact that you're engaged to God's gift is a little hard to handle?"

Her smile faded instantly, and her grip lessened. I knew I'd said something wrong.

"Why is Taylor still wearing your engagement ring?"

THIRTY

JO

I immediately regretted opening my mouth.

Matty had finally gotten his signature smirk back, and we were joking, then I opened my big fat mouth. Same problem I'd had all my life—open mouth, insert foot. I could have smacked myself.

When we pulled into the park, I'd known he was going to finally open up to me. God knew the talk was long overdue, and I'd been mentally filing away questions for the last few weeks. Some had been in the back of my mind for months.

When he started talking, all I felt was relief. I wasn't an idiot; I'd figured out the Bastards were more than what I'd been told. There were signs—some blatantly obvious, like the ones hanging in the clubhouse saying that Bastards didn't forgive—and some were subtle, like the fact that after the boys went on their ride a few weeks ago, a woman who had abused her child just happened to walk up to a sheriff and turn herself in the day they came home. Maybe I was playing connect-the-dots with random events, but it all seemed to fit. Add in Rob trying to get the best defense attorney in the state to take the club on as a client and it seemed like even the blind would see the trail.

I wanted to think that I'd overlooked all of it because I was so caught up in my drama of Matty, but it was really so much more. The truth was that Matty wasn't the only Bastard I loved. Rob—even though he was moody, gruff, and took his role as the president way too seriously—had quickly become one of my favorite people, even with his tendency to talk down to me. Ian was a great kid who I felt connected to on various levels, and part of me wanted to hug him and ruffle his hair the way a mom would. Tank made me laugh. Hawk always greeted me with a hug and a sexually inappropriate conversation that would make most people blush, but our banter suited us.

The men who made up this club were kind and loyal. And good. The club's thoughts about women annoyed me, but my feelings about the members easily made me turn a blind eye to what I'd known all along.

As Matty talked, I learned more about each one of them, and my suspicions about the club became fact. It was one thing to think I knew something; it was a beast of another color to actually know it. I didn't want to have the image of Matty hurting someone, of him taking a life that wasn't his to take. I didn't want to think about my friends being the judge, jury, and executioner.

I'd spent the last decade of my life doing casework. Matty was right—I'd seen the worst of the worst. Kids who were destroyed because their parents were selfish assholes. And yes, there were times I'd wished for a different sort of justice for some parents. I had always believed in the system. The one that teaches us that bad people do bad things and that if you do something wrong, you go to jail.

Life was never black and white though. Sometimes bad things happened to good people. Child abuse was just one example of that. To combat that, this group of burly men did what they could. Sometimes good people did bad things for the right reason. If they'd maimed or killed to help save or protect an innocent, I couldn't blame them.

I felt the anguish rolling off Matty as he talked. He wasn't bragging about the things he'd done, and he sure as hell wasn't enjoying talking about it. It was painful to watch, and I wanted to take all the hurt away from him. When he was finally done, I asked questions that I thought were neutral.

When he'd started to talk about the packet Will had given me, he bit his lip, ran his hands through his hair, and turned away from me. He whispered just one word, and I didn't think he even knew he'd said anything.

"Providence." It had come out as a wistful breath.

I'd heard them talk about it before. Last summer, Tiny had mentioned that Matty was angry, "Providence angry." Whatever had happened in Rhode Island was horrible, and I didn't want Matty to think about it now. I tried to change the subject again, asking about the road names. It worked, and within seconds, my playful, fun-loving man had returned.

Then he'd made a comment about being engaged, and my mind worked in that annoying way it did. I immediately thought about the woman wearing the giant diamond and throwing a pretentious engagement party, and I asked about her without even thinking. I wished I could take it back.

"You've seen Taylor."

It wasn't a question, but I nodded anyway. His hand was still between mine, and I held it tightly. I wanted him to tell me that it was all a misunderstanding, that they weren't really engaged, but deep down, I knew that would be a lie. Right now was the time for truth. "I did."

He sighed a long, sad sound and looked around. "That is a very long story. It's getting late, and we need to get the kids back to Boston. Can we talk about this later?"

My heart had already been pounding, but now it felt as if it would jump out of my chest. Disappointment curled in my gut. I could only nod because if I spoke, I'd be cruel.

Sensing the change in me, he pulled his hand free and cupped my cheek. "Hey. I promise it isn't what you think. I love you. You are the woman I want to marry."

I nodded again and forced a smile. Turning, I put both feet back on the floor, and buckled my seat belt. We'd just had the talk I'd been saying we needed to have for months, and he'd told me some of the darkest, scariest secrets I'd ever known. He was a vigilante who had committed numerous crimes and could potentially go to prison—not jail, but prison—at any time. A ring on another woman was hardly the biggest issue we were going to have. Yet, the feeling lingered that the worst was still to come.

The kids were ready to get on the road when we got back to Becky's. They'd had a good supper then played video games with Uncle Dean, as even my kids were calling him now. They all kissed Bex and climbed into the car, excited to be away on our adventures.

Lily was the first to fall asleep. After making us listen to the *Frozen* soundtrack on repeat numerous times, and helping Matty make fun of the fact that I couldn't hit the notes on "Let it Go," she gave in and leaned on Dean's shoulder. We'd barely made it Portsmouth before Sammy was snoring in the backseat and Ben was trying to figure out how to make him quiet down. Finally, Ben plugged in his headphones and played his 3DS.

Matty's hand barely left me. If we weren't holding hands, it was on my thigh or his thumb was rubbing circles on the side of my neck. A few times he'd grabbed my hand and kissed it before telling me he loved me. I knew he was grateful that I was still sitting beside him after what he'd told me and was also trying to make up for the fact that Taylor was still hanging over my head. I smiled, told him I loved him back, and took every ounce of comfort he offered.

When we pulled into the garage, Ben sat up, intrigued. Dean carried Lily, Matty lugged Sam, and Ben and I grabbed the luggage as I tried to explain how close we were to everything.

"I'll give you the tour of the house tomorrow," I promised as we stepped off the elevator. "And we'll go explore the city."

Ben smiled as he stepped through the walk-in closet into Sammy's room. "Awesome! It's like a secret room with a hidden door and everything!"

I nodded. I'd never actually thought of it like that, but yeah, it was.

"This week is gonna be so much fun!" he insisted excitedly.

I rushed him out of the room before he could wake up the others, showed him the bathroom across the hall, and pointed out that Matty and I were right next door.

That earned me two hands on his hips and an arched brow. "You're sharing a room?"

I groaned. It was too late at night for this conversation, and I wanted to have it with him, his sister, and Sam all at once. "We are. I wanted to tell you, Lily, and Sam at the same time. Matty asked me to marry him, and I said yes."

Ben tipped his head back, surveying me in a gesture that proved once again he was growing up way too fast. He sighed. "Dad's gonna have a shit-fit."

"Benjamin Andrew Walker!" I hissed. "You watch your language!"

Ben just shrugged. "What? He is. And Nana will freak."

I narrowed my eyes. "That is an adult conversation. Your father can talk to me if he has a problem, and you will stay out of it. The same goes for your grandmother. If she has something to say, she can say it to me."

"Whatever." He shrugged again. "I love Uncle Matt. He makes you laugh."

Before I could say another word, he walked into the bathroom and shut the door. I waited for what seemed like forever for him to come back out. Leaning against the wall on the other side of the hallway, I smiled when Dean and Matty came out of the kids' bedroom.

"They're both still out cold," Matty whispered as Dean nodded his good nights and headed for the stairs. "Do you wanna tuck Ben in then go up to the roof to finish our conversation?"

I shook my head. I didn't want to talk about Taylor on a normal day, and I sure as hell didn't want to even think about her as tired as I was. I'd learned more than enough to make my head spin already. "No, I'm exhausted. Tomorrow night maybe?"

Matt nodded, but I could see his disappointment. I was too mentally wrecked to try to fix it tonight.

Blue eyes met mine, then he nodded again. "I'm gonna go find Rob, okay?" Leaning in, he kissed my temple. "I'll be down to cuddle in a little bit."

I rubbed his arm as he passed, not sure if I was trying to comfort him or myself.

Ben came out a few minutes later, teeth brushed, face washed, and all ready for bed. I followed him back into his room, and just as I had almost every night for the past ten years, I helped him say his prayers, told him I loved him, tucked him in, and kissed him on the nose. I reached over to turn out the light, making sure the nightlight was plugged in, when he called me back to his bunk.

Slim arms came out from under the covers and snaked around my neck. "I love you, Mom. I missed you." Then he kissed my cheek and fell back onto his pillow.

I made it back to my room and managed to strip before I gave in and dropped into bed. I didn't have any time to process the day's events before my eyes closed against my will. I never heard Matty climb into bed later.

We'd decided to take the kids to the museum on Saturday and the aquarium on Sunday morning. Even though they were visiting, Matty insisted that I keep my training schedule with Nick, so I planned to do that on Sunday, Tuesday, and Thursday afternoon. I had a quick test that I couldn't miss on Monday, but the rest of the week, I was going to play hooky from school and have fun with my family.

Matty and the kids were awake long before me on Saturday. He and Sammy had already given them the tour, then they'd broken into pairs. Sam and Ben were playing in their room and Lily was helping make breakfast when I finally dragged my lazy bones out of bed. Rocker and Dean were helping get the food ready too, but what shocked me speechless was that all three men were wearing makeshift crowns. Dean's was incredibly girly—all pink and purple sparkle pipe cleaners.

"Wow," I murmured from the doorway, not sure whether to laugh or be impressed. "Those are some nice crowns!"

Lily turned and gave me a gapped-tooth grin as she continued to stir whatever was in the bowl in front of her. "Good morning, Mumma. I made you one too!"

At that, she jumped down and ran over to the table, pulled a pink-and-blue tiara off the table, and thrust it at me. I leaned down, telling her how beautiful it was, and slipped it over my hair. She beamed before running back to Matty to offer more help.

"I ran to the craft store this morning," Dean told me quietly as he handed me a cup of coffee. "We didn't have a lot for girls, so I called Cris and Jessie and they told me what to get." He nodded at the desk on the other side of the room that was now covered with bags of arts and crafts.

"That should keep us busy." My smile was genuine. "Thank you."

He waved as if it was nothing, adjusted his very unmanly crown, and sauntered off to help Lily stir. I watched as my daughter did exactly what Dean had predicted she'd do. With a few giggles, sweet smiles, and very silly jokes, she'd managed to wrap three large and surly bikers around her little finger. I was so screwed.

Breakfast was filled with laughter and lots of eye rolling from me as I realized it didn't matter how old a man was because fourth-grade humor was enough to bring out the kid in them all. There wasn't a straight face at the table. Even I had to give in and giggle at the way they snorted and carried on.

Lily caught my eye once and whispered, "Silly boys!"

I could only nod and grin back.

Rob declined our invitation to the museum, but Dean tagged along, telling Ben and Sam that the lightning show was his favorite thing in the world. I knew why he was really there, even if they didn't, and was actually impressed by his ability to keep a constant visual on them while managing to survey the crowds for threats and play with them. Lily stayed with Matt and me for the most part, holding my hand and letting me act like a little girl with her when we were in the butterfly exhibit.

It was an amazing day, and even though we were all dragging our feet, we were all smiles when we stepped onto the elevator. We'd been discussing dinner ideas, and the general consensus was pizza delivery. Followed by movies and popcorn in our pajamas. Maybe ice cream sundaes if the kids were really lucky.

Matty hurried out of the elevator before the rest of us, heading to find the takeout menu for the local Italian restaurant. I wasn't really paying attention to him, focused more on Ben's explanation of the way the human heart works, when I realized more than one voice was coming from the kitchen. And one of them was very feminine.

As we headed across the foyer, I struggled to hear the other voices, trying to figure out if it was Jessie with Rob, or Cris. The kids kept rattling on, making it impossible to tell for sure, and Dean was hanging on their every word, so I couldn't ask them to be quiet.

The face that greeted me as we turned the corner surprised me. I hadn't thought I'd see Senator Henry Butler so soon, and definitely not standing in my kitchen. He wasn't alone. His daughter had her arms wrapped around my fiancé and was leaning in for a kiss.

THIRTY-ONE
JO

Whomever said the devil wore Prada hadn't come face-to-face with the beauty clad in an adorable Dolce and Gabbana black-and-white polka dot sheath dress and mile-high patent leather wedges. She should look overdressed next to the man wearing a plain white tee and blue jeans; instead, they looked perfect together. The way they were snuggled together gave me flashbacks, and I couldn't even pretend the jealousy wasn't there.

Knowing my face would show my true feeling if I looked at them, I ignored the duo and smiled at the senator instead. Then I glanced around the room for Rob. Anything to keep myself from glaring at Matty and Taylor.

"Senator." I glanced back at him, struggling to keep my voice level. "What a surprise. If I'd known you were stopping by, I would have made sure to be here."

"Josephine." Hal smiled at me warmly, closing the gap between us as he reached for my hand. "I won't lie. I had hoped to run into you." His thumb trailed over my knuckles. "We came to speak with Rob. He told us you were out with Matthew and the children."

I pulled my hand away and gestured toward my offspring. "Yep. My kids are visiting for vacation week. This is Benjamin and Lily."

The senator said his hellos to my kids, then he patted Sammy on the back, asking them about their day. The whole exchange took maybe five minutes, but I could feel Matty's eyes boring into my back, willing me to look at him. Dean, understanding the glance I sent his way, ushered the kids downstairs. The kids, especially Sam, seemed in a hurry to get away from us. I had no doubt they could feel the unease in the room.

Hal didn't waste any time once the four of them had started down the stairs. "I didn't know you were in town, Matthew." Suspicion made his voice cold.

I glanced at Matty then and found him staring at Taylor instead of me.

"You didn't? Why didn't you tell your dad I was in town, Tay?"

She smirked, only making her features look even more alluring. Pushing her hair back off her shoulders, she winked at him before dropping her lips into a fake pout. "If he knows you're here, he tries to steal you. Is it so awful that I wanted some time alone with my man?"

I rolled my eyes, instantly feeling like the unwanted third wheel.

Hal chuckled at his daughter. "You'll have plenty of alone time in just a few months."

Matty cupped Taylor's cheeks then kissed the middle of her forehead before returning his attention to Hal. "It seems that Miss Taylor didn't fill me in either, Senator, because I didn't realize you hadn't gone back to D.C. I'm in town for vacation week. Sam's very close with Jo's kids, and we wanted them to spend as much time together as they could." Turning back to Taylor, he smiled and moved his thumb along her cheek in a move that made me feel as if I was intruding on their private moment. He'd done the same thing to me numerous times. "We missed you today."

His tone was soft and seemed sincere. I couldn't watch another instant. I thought about joining Dean and the kids, but I didn't have enough self-preservation. Telling myself it wasn't real, and instead of saying something that could destroy their whole sham, I turned to the table and sat just as Taylor excused herself to use the bathroom. When I glanced up, Hal was watching me intently.

I forced myself not to glance away and smiled up at him instead. "The kids wore me out today. My feet are killing me!"

Hal chuckled. "You need a foot massage."

He started toward me when Matty demanded, "What's going on, Hal? Why were you coming to see Rob and not me?"

Hal's eyes left mine and moved to Matty. He pursed his lips in thought, tucking his hands in his pockets, then jingled the change in his tailored khakis. "Taylor is being followed."

"What?" Matty's tone was abrupt and full of disbelief. I heard him step toward the island, but I still didn't turn to look at him.

Hal raised an eyebrow, and the change rattled more. "I knew she wouldn't tell you. That girl thinks she's untouchable. Always has." He shook his head, sighing. "Three separate times in the last week, my security caught someone tailing her." He nodded to a manila folder on the counter.

Out of the corner of my eye, I saw Matty rush around the counter and grab the file. Shuffling through it, he demanded, "Have your men made contact?"

Hal shook his head. "No. They didn't want to spook him. He hasn't come any closer, but she hasn't been alone either."

Matty swore and slammed the file onto the counter. "Why didn't you tell me about this before now? What'd Rocker say?" His hand curled into a fist as he demanded answers.

"I said we'd look into it, but that Taylor needed to tell you what was going on from now on," Rocker answered, coming in off the patio, slipping his phone into his jeans and sliding the door shut.

He headed straight for me and kissed my hair before pulling out the chair next to mine. His hand found my shoulder, and he pulled me back into him before I could object. I balked for a moment before I remembered that Rocker was supposed to be interested in me. Awesome. I inhaled slowly, preparing to play my part.

"How was the museum?" Rocker asked, his fingers drawing pictures on my skin.

I turned to him, not even bothering to hide my irritation with the whole damned mess. "It was a great day. Then we came home." To find the blonde bombshell I wanted to hit.

"You must be exhausted."

Ah, yes. Speak of the devil, and she will appear.

"I can't imagine running all over the city with three kids!" Taylor's eyes went wide in revulsion as she joined the men at the counter. "Ugh." Then she shuddered dramatically, as if the thought of traveling with kids was absolutely horrific.

Everyone else ignored her.

Hal moved to the table and leaned down across from us. "Any luck?"

Rob shook his head. "Wiz is running the picture. As soon as we know something, I'll call you. In the meantime, she needs to have someone with her."

Taylor scoffed. "You are all making something out of nothing. I'm sure it's just some paparazzi freak hoping to dig up some dirt before the wedding. It is going to be the social event of the fall." Her eyes twinkled happily, as if the idea of being stalked by a man with a camera was exciting.

"Taylor, this isn't a game. We don't know how serious it could be," Matty warned.

She rolled her eyes. "Daddy, you talked to Rob. We should get going."

Hal nodded at her before turning toward Matty. "Why don't you ride with us? We can talk more about the plan to keep our girl safe, discuss options. Someone will bring you home in the morning."

Before Matt could answer, Taylor interrupted, "Daddy! Sam's here. Matty can't just leave!"

Hal gave them a condescending look. "I don't know why you two act like I'm old-fashioned. Or an oblivious nitwit." He laughed at his daughter. "It's very obvious that you've been sneaking over here every weekend. And now that we know someone is following you, it would be safer, and make me feel better, if you two stayed at our house. It sounded like the kids had plans tonight, and I don't want to make my future grandson dislike me by forcing him away while his friends are here. I'm sure Rob and Josephine won't mind him staying with them."

Three sets of eyes turned to us.

"Uh..." I didn't know what to say. There was no way in hell Matty would take off with Taylor and leave Sam here, even if we weren't a couple, but I needed to have some sort of reasonable excuse for refusing. My mind whirled, trying to find something – anything to say.

The fingers on my shoulder tightened, as if warning me to be quiet. "Absolutely. He'll never know you're gone," Rob's deep voice answered.

I snapped my head toward my friend. "What?" I hissed at but Rob just shook his head slightly. My eyes narrowed at the giant man, and I was sure I'd never been as surprised by someone as I was at that moment.

Until Matty spoke. "If you're okay with it, it sounds like a plan. Let me go say good-bye to the little man."

My eyes closed automatically, and I exhaled slowly. No. This was a sick joke. Matty would never choose to go spend the night with *her* instead of being here with Sammy and me. I was dreaming and would wake from this nightmare soon.

"Joey?" The voice in my ear startled me. Matty was suddenly standing right next to me. "Did you hear anything I just said?"

I shook my head pathetically agitated by his scolding tone.

"I asked if you wanted to come downstairs with me. I thought you might help soften the blow of me leaving."

Looking up at the face I loved, I let the hurt flow through my veins. Even though they should have been buried deep, the words Taylor had flung at me last summer came flooding back, and every single insecurity came bubbling to the surface. I could practically hear her sneering, '*Have you looked at yourself lately? Honey, I can promise you, if you can't keep your own husband in your bed, you sure as hell won't be able to get mine there.*'

I studied him for a few seconds: square jawbone that was filled with scruff and ticking in frustration; heart-shaped lips twisted in concentration as he watched me; perfect long, thin nose; and bright blue eyes, surrounded by a thicket of black lashes, that were staring into mine.

Yeah, she was right. He was far too beautiful to belong to me. Then I chastised myself for being a fool.

Fuck her. Matty was mine. He was in my bed every single night while she had to lie about where she'd been. *Sorry, sweetheart, he doesn't want to marry you, regardless of what the ring on your finger tells the world. He wants me. I have his grandfather's ring and, most importantly, his heart.*

If I had just let him explain the whole situation last night, I wouldn't be so confused right now, I realized angrily. Well, now was really as good a time as any to get to the bottom of this shit pile.

I nodded and stood. "Taylor, you really didn't get to say much to Sammy earlier. Why don't you come with us?"

Three sets of eyebrows rose, and I had to fight to keep from laughing at the disgusted look on her face. I didn't wait for an answer. Instead, I patted Rob's head and practically skipped across the hall to the stairs, happy with my plan.

I heard them behind me—one set of footsteps heavy and hurried, the other slow in her annoyingly stylish shoes. Matty called to me, but I didn't stop at the landing because I didn't want the kids to hear what was going on. This was a long overdue conversation for just the three of us.

Matty's long legs caught up with me before I reached the last step, but he waited until we reached the bottom before he grabbed my arm and pushed me back me against the wall.

"Jesus, Joes!" He was slightly out of breath, but my chest was heaving; I didn't know if it was from the exercise or because of anger. "Would you wait a fuckin' minute?" Twisting a hand into my hair, he pulled my head back, forcing me to look at him, and pushed his body into mine, preventing any sort of escape. "Talk to me."

Taylor's heels click-clacked on the steps as she carefully made her way down to us. I ignored the sound, focusing on the livid sky inside Matty's eyes. A hundred thoughts filtered through my mind as I tried to figure out what to say to him. Without thinking, my hand snuck under his shirt, and I dragged my nails up his back.

He groaned and leaned in, nipping at the soft skin between my neck and shoulder before moving his empty hand to my chin. He leaned back, just enough to meet my eyes again, then his lips were on mine.

"This isn't what you think," he managed as his teeth moved to my ear and sucked on my lobe. "You don't get to run away anymore!" Teeth sank into my bottom lip almost painfully before his mouth was crushing against mine, punishing me. The hand in my hair tightened as he leaned back once more, his eyes demanding attention. "You are wearing my ring. That means you are mine. It means I'm yours. You. Do. Not. Run. Away!"

His mind was working on overdrive, and he was just as scared as I was. But he'd totally misunderstood. When I shook my head, his face fell.

"I'm so sorry Joes. I didn't know she'd be here. Didn't know you'd have to see that. So fuckin' sorry!" And he captured my mouth again.

Taylor cleared her throat at least twice before the sound sank in and I remembered that we weren't alone. Matty must have heard her at the same time I did, because he moved away slightly but kept his forehead pushed against mine.

"As charming as this little public display of affection is, we really do have to get going." Bitchy Taylor was back. I was surprised she was making an appearance in front of Matty.

"I'm not fuckin' leaving, and you damned well know it!"

Taylor sighed, obviously annoyed, and tapped her foot loudly. "And just how in the hell do you plan to get out it?"

Matty shrugged. "I'm going to be honest. My kid doesn't want me to leave, and since I only get a few nights a month with him, you are gonna stay here with us. If your dad asks, I'm sure Jo has something you can wear. Then Rob can drive you to your boyfriend's house."

She inhaled sharply. "First of all, if anything of Jo's fit me, I'd kill myself. Second, I don't have a boyfriend! Is that jealousy talking, Matt?"

Matty stepped away from me and turned on her. "Oh, get over yourself. The only reason you're minutely smaller than Jo is because she isn't afraid to eat more than a handful of veggies."

His words and hateful tone shocked me. Something had happened between these two, something bad.

"Make no mistake, if you insult my fiancée again, you will regret it," he snapped.

I was off the wall and moving between them in a flash. Holding up my arms, I pushed Matty back from getting any closer to her. "Hey!" I snapped. "Back off!"

He backed up but only marginally, shooting daggers at the beauty behind me. "How stupid are you?" he seethed at her. "Sneaking out of the house? What's gonna happen when your father's goons follow you and realize you aren't coming here?"

Taylor raised her chin defiantly.

"Holy fuck. You've planned it all out, haven't you? You're meeting him at a hotel or some shit so you can say you're meeting me." His tone was now one of surprise. "Good Christ, Tay! Tell me you're not fucking a married man!"

She straightened her back. "As opposed to you, the man who was fucking a married woman?"

Ouch. That hurt a little.

"You're such a selfish, miserable bitch!" Matty snarled.

"Oh, I'm selfish and miserable? Funny how you'd see it that way considering you're the only one in this room who fits both descriptions!"

"I see it the way it is!" he snapped. "I bet you know who's following you and you're the little boy crying wolf to get some fucking attention."

Feeling very much like the monkey in the middle, I put my hands up and jumped up and down, trying to get their attention before she could reply. "Seriously? Stop!" Looking from one to the other, I realized I had their attention. I pointed at the closest door. "Matty's room. Now!"

Once we were all inside and the door was closed, I motioned Taylor to the chair and pushed Matty onto the bed. "What in the hell is going on?"

Taylor's eyes narrowed at me, making Matty glare at her in return. Finally, she answered, "It's club business."

I laughed. Of course it was. Fucking, stupid, pathetic club.

"Fine." I sighed, realizing I wasn't going to get anywhere. "I'm gonna say it's safe to assume that neither of you are happy and that this fake engagement has gone on long enough. Can you break it off?"

Matty sighed. "I don't know. Can we, Taylor?"

She shook her head. "Not yet. He's getting close. Especially after he met Jo." She motioned at me with her chin. "But he's still not there yet."

I turned to Matty, hoping he'd fill in the blanks.

"Senator Butler and Jon Greenwood are old friends. They grew up together," Matty said.

"Are you kidding me right now? This whole thing has been one more ploy to get the lawyer you want?" All this drama for something so stupid. So very anti-climactic. I was disgusted.

"Not really." Matty leaned forward, grabbing my hand. "Taylor first had the idea to keep our breakup a secret last fall, after she found out you and I were no longer together."

"Please," Taylor interrupted. "It was a win-win for both of us. You got to have a popular senator support you and the club. He's a powerful ally to have. All you had to do was pretend to date me. Every man in a hundred-mile radius wishes they'd been so lucky!"

Matty ignored her. "The senator knows everyone, and everyone owes him a favor. I won't lie—it's nice to have that connection. Tank got out early thanks to him. A few of our kids were spared the trauma of testifying because he golfs with a few judges. Plus, we've gotten some huge donations."

"Plus, we've been able to give numerous families a new start. That money goes a long way toward new identities and relocation costs," Taylor added.

"Like the witness relocation program?" I asked, confused.

"Along the same lines, but funded by the Bastards rather than the government," she clarified. "And, we've managed to clean up the Bastards' image. Put a founding member with a pretty little Daddy's girl, and people start sucking up to the club. Everyone who owes my dad something wants to help us out, just to get in his good graces. We haven't landed Jon yet. That's my main concern right now."

Now I was really confused. "Your main concern?"

Taylor's face was blank when she looked at Matty. "This is my job, Jo. I run welfare for the club. I make sure that kids and parents have what they need until the trial is over, if there is a trial, and then I find them a new life. Whether it's here or in another part of the country, I find them a home, a counselor, and a job, get them furniture and clothes, then check in on them every couple of months. And I work with Rob to make sure everyone is protected."

"What's that have to do with Jon?"

"If the Bastards go to prison, my families aren't protected. If they go to prison, the image I've worked so hard to perfect becomes tainted and we won't have the help we do now. I need the boys to stay out of trouble. In order to do that, we need Jon. We need him to feel a camaraderie, a connection to the club. It's there, I can see it, but he needs that final push."

She rolled her eyes at the look of bewilderment on my face. I was impressed but shocked that this Taylor was so dedicated.

"You don't know me, Jo, you never did, so don't look so surprised. What I do for the club is important, and I'm not going anywhere. So as long as you're around, you're just going to have to put up with me." Standing, she smoothed down her dress. "I think we've been gone long enough, don't you? Let's go tell my dad that I'm staying here with your delightful little group. Yay!" She gave me a fake excited smile then left the room.

"She won't be here long, babe, I promise. I'll have Rob take her to wherever she wants to go as soon as the old man is gone."

I honestly didn't care about that right now. I swallowed, trying to wrap my mind around everything. "Why do you hate her? It seems like she did you and the club a pretty big favor, and she's helping as many people as she can."

"I don't hate her. I don't want to be alone in the same room as her because she's a lying, manipulative wench. But I don't hate her."

"You were so cold and mean to her!"

"Just because I don't love her anymore doesn't mean that I hate her. I didn't treat her any different than I treat anyone else in my life." Grabbing my hand, he pulled me out of our room and up the stairs. "I'm really sorry, Joes. Forgive me?"

I nodded. I'd already forgotten why I was mad. Now all I could think about was how he'd never treated me with as much disgust as he had Taylor. Not once, even before we'd gotten together, even when he'd been a dick when we'd first met. The thought made me speechless.

He really had loved me from the beginning.

THIRTY-TWO

MATTY

What a fucking day.

I opened the door to our bedroom and looked in on Jo one more time. I'd just double-checked the kids, covering Ben back up, tucking Lily's much loved Pooh Bear in next to her, and turning Sam around so that his head was on his pillow instead of both feet. Hearing Jo's snores, I smiled at how normal this felt—her in my bed and the kids here with us.

I had the sudden urge to yell, "Eleven o'clock and all is well!"

Chuckling to myself, I shut the door and climbed the stairs. After grabbing a bottle of Jack's Tennessee Whiskey—my favorite after a hard day—and a couple of tumblers, I joined Rocker on the deck. It was a warm spring, and the city was alive beneath us. I didn't even ask him if he wanted a drink, just poured three fingers and handed it to him.

We sat for a few minutes, enjoying the burn.

"L.K. sleepin'?"

"Yeah. She's been overloaded with information the last few days. She's fuckin' exhausted, man." I didn't mean physically.

"You come clean and tell her everythin'?"

"Everything I could."

"And she stayed with your dumbass? Huh." He smirked behind his glass. "Must be the great sex I keep hearing."

I flipped him off. "Did you get Taylor where she needed to go?"

"Interestin' change of topic, from one fiancée to the other."

Fucker thought he was funny.

He took a long pull off his whiskey. "Yep."

"You're not gonna tell me where you dropped her off, are ya?"

Another sip. "Nope."

I swirled the amber liquid. "Which brother is it?"

He arched an eyebrow.

"She's obviously been goin' to the clubhouse in the middle of the night. No way in hell the senator's security wasn't on her like white on rice. Only place she'd go that'd make them think she was meeting me is the clubhouse. So which brother is she fucking?"

Rob stared at me, expressionless. "Does it matter?"

"No. I just want to shake that motherfucker's hand and warn him she's seriously crazy."

He pursed his lips. "He already knows."

I leaned forward, glass still in hand. "Holy shit! It's you, isn't it? I knew you two were getting close!"

Rob choked on his drink. "Fuck no! I've got my hands full with the two I've got. Every brothah knows she's bat-shit crazy, and whoever he is, he's gonna have his hands full."

I laughed. I let the humor surround us for a few minutes before I asked what was really on my mind. "Anything on the stalker?"

He shook his head. "Not one damn thing. We talked about it, and Taylor promised that for the next few weeks, she wouldn't go anywhere alone. I put Preach on her."

I tipped my head, concerned at his choice of a guard.

He rolled his eyes. "No, I don't think she's fucking Preach. But he's the only one who won't kill her in the meantime. She's a wicked pain in the ass."

"Someone's really following her?"

"Yeah, it's real." He finished off his whiskey. "I'm calling court first thing in the mornin'."

I swallowed the last few drops in my glass then refilled it. "You think it's related?"

"It could be. Fuck, Mateo. Ellie was attacked. We have one missin' ol' lady. Now Taylor's being followed. There are no such things as coincidence. I'd order a lockdown, but we have nothin' to go on. Not a single threat, not one fucking lead. I'm goin' crazy trying to figure this shit out."

"Should I send Jo and the kids home?"

"No. They're better off here with us. Especially until we figure this out."

I nodded, agreeing completely. "You headed to the clubhouse tonight?"

He turned back to the city before answering. "Naw. I need to think. The answer is right there, just out of my reach. I know it is."

I leaned back into the cushions, getting comfortable. "Okay. Let's figure it out then."

I stifled a yawn as Jo refilled my coffee mug and offered a sexy smile that made me want to throw her over my shoulder and hustle down the stairs. It had only been a few nights since we'd been together, but it was too fucking long for me—especially when I'd found her brushing her teeth dressed in nothing but my shirt this morning. The thought of it riding up the backs of her legs as she bent to spit was enough to make me hard, and I tried to adjust discreetly.

Dean caught my eye as Jo moved on to fill his cup, and he gave me a knowing smirk. A quick look around the table assured me that no one else had seen it. The kids were laughing and talking amongst themselves, and Rob looked as exhausted as I felt.

We'd stayed on the deck until the sun came up, going over every single enemy we'd made and trying to figure out who could be behind this. All the threats we'd gotten over the years had been clear—they'd either been stupid enough to leave tracks or brave enough to claim responsibility. There was something we were missing now, and we both knew it.

I had the kids clear the table after we were done eating while I pulled Jo into the roof stairway so we could have a few seconds of privacy. She giggled and hooked her arms over my shoulders as I yanked her close, leaning down to run my tongue over her collarbone. I wanted to kiss every square inch of her, but I knew that if I started, I would never stop. I pulled back and held her close to my chest.

"Are you sure you're okay taking the kids without me?"

I felt her head move. "It'll be fine, honey. Cris said she'd meet us there, and Dean will be with us. We'll miss you though."

"I shouldn't be long. I'll meet you at the gym this afternoon, yeah?"

She backed up slightly and put her chin on my chest. "Yeah. Stop worrying!" She laughed. "We'll be fine."

I couldn't stop. Rob had called court, and as VP, I had to be there. Jo and the kids had decided not to wait for me and to go to the aquarium with Cris instead. Dean had wisely informed us he was missing court because he didn't want Jo taking all three kids by herself, and for that, I was thankful. I didn't think anything would happen to my family in broad daylight, but that didn't make the uneasy feeling go away. Pair that with lack of sleep and all the demons Rocker and I had dredged up last night, and I was on edge.

The meeting wasn't much better. There was still no sign of Tink, and Tank was ready to go off the fucking rails. The fact that Taylor had been followed spread panic around the room like wildfire; we all knew the chances that she was the only one being tailed were small. Even though we weren't ordering a lockdown, most of the brothers decided to move their families into the house anyway. When the people you loved most in the world were in danger, there were never enough precautions to keep them safe.

We did have some suspects, people that thought we'd wronged their loved ones: a group of dirty cops we'd gotten fired five years ago, and Carlos. Everyone around me was wound up as we decided to break into groups and track each one of those fuckers down until we had answers.

Dean would stay on my kids, unless they were staying at the clubhouse. Tank would be stationed here to keep an eye on things—he was too unpredictable to go out in the community right now—and the rest of us would stagger shifts. I didn't want to leave Jo, not for even a minute, but I knew she'd come to the clubhouse and be okay.

I hadn't thought about it before, but when I realized that Taylor was a target because we had a very public relationship and that there was no reason for anyone to connect Jo to me, I was immediately relieved.

As the meeting closed and the brothers filed out, Bear kept the officers back. He waited for the door to close then faced us all. "There's one name not on that list." He stared at me then at Tank. "I know you don't want to hear this, but first El. Then Tinkerbelle. Now Tay. The marks on the forehead. How do you not see the pattern? He's coming after the three of us, not the club."

"Because of Providence?" Tank asked as my stomach dropped. "No way in hell."

I'd thought about it but hadn't wanted to be the one who made the connection. I didn't want it to be a possibility. Because I wasn't sure how it would end if it was him.

Rob looked down the table. "Wiz? Is there any way to look back through security footage to see if Tink had been followed? Maybe if she was, we will finally have the connection."

Wiz looked thoughtful. "There might be, depending on how long the city keeps their files. I'm on it." He turned his attention to the tablet in front of him and began tapping away.

I looked at the men sitting around the table. We were all wearing the same irritated expression. That dick had been a source of worry for us for years. Outside of this room, only a handful of people knew what had really happened that night. Yet everyone here knew, and they all supported us.

Scott Dyer was the grandson of some down-on-his-luck immigrant who moved to America, struck gold, and became an oil tycoon. Not much older than me, Scott had been born with a silver spoon in his mouth and grew up entitled and spoiled. Unfortunately, he was also a demented soul.

We'd dug up file after file of cases that were buried because good old grandpa threw money at them, paying every injured party off instead of having his beloved heir face the consequences of his actions. Even his parents had gotten fed up at some point and sent him to boarding school in Europe to scare him straight.

The plan backfired though, because Dyer became friends with men just like himself and some who were much worse. When his grandfather finally kicked the bucket, Scott inherited millions and moved back home. Men with his sadistic tastes couldn't just quit cold turkey and forget the life they'd once led. On the outside, he looked like a model citizen. He donated to every charity Boston had, hob-knobbed with the local celebrities, and was friendly with the most powerful men in the city.

When he married a middle-aged single mom, their rags-to-riches fairy tale made the gossip sites. When he beat her the first time, no one batted an eye. When it happened the second, third, and fourth time, the police failed to respond to the frantic 9-1-1 calls her daughter made, and when the woman was rushed to the emergency room, all evidence conveniently disappeared. No one would help her. Until her ex-husband came to us.

Almost a year later, when she finally met with us, her once-beautiful body was marred with the scars Dyer's treatment had left. She was shaking when we walked into the room, but I didn't know if it was because she was afraid of us or terrified for her teenaged daughter. According to his friends, Dyer had taken his stepdaughter on a dream European holiday while her mother got the psychological help she needed because of all the lies she'd told about him. It was a great cover story.

Funny thing though. To get to Europe, one needs to fly. Dyer's private jet hadn't left the airstrip in months. We started digging, knowing that whatever we found would have to be dealt with internally. The police would be no help.

It was hard to dig up, but what we discovered made us sick. Not only did he have all his grandpa's money, but he'd made his own fortune in an international sex slave trade, selling women to the highest bidder. Most of his sales came with a guarantee that they'd been "tested out" and listed how much pain they could handle. There were even pictures that caused more than one of us to lose our lunch. I'd taken a peek at just one and my stomach had revolted instantly.

Hawk had called his dad, convinced that this was something that needed law enforcement's attention. But once again, Dyer's money slammed doors in our faces. There was no way to help those girls, no way we could get them all back, but we were determined to stop him before his victim list grew larger.

Wiz ran each girl's photo through every missing child database there was, because we wanted a name to go with the face. He wanted closure for the families. The rest of us had broken into groups, each going to one of Dyer's properties in the city. We wanted to find him before his stepdaughter disappeared for good.

Every place we checked was empty. But then Hawk's dad came through and sent Hawk and Rob to a detective's house. A detective who knew more about Dyer and his activities than he should have because he'd been too involved. After a little friendly persuasion, he'd given them an address - an old abandoned warehouse, and since my group was the closest, we went to check it out.

We assumed it was going to be another dead end. But if it wasn't, the plan was to go in, grab her, and bring her back to her mom. And put a bullet in his head on the way out.

Instead, we found the heavily guarded American hub of his trade. The same place he'd held, and tortured, every single woman and girl he'd kidnapped over the last few months. As well as the bodies of the ones who couldn't withstand the pain he'd caused.

I didn't know how many people I killed that night or how many magazines I went through. I could say, without a doubt, that we rescued seven women. Seven out of fifty. I wished we'd been able to save more, but I would always look at the seven as a success. And I'd forever mourn the loss of the women I couldn't save.

When we realized what we'd walked in on, Bear started breaking the locks on the cages while Tank and I searched for the stepdaughter. Some of the women were too weak to walk on their own, others were too terrified to leave because the threat of punishment was greater than the idea of freedom, and worst of all were the ones who were severely injured and begged us to kill them. Bear took it on himself to carry them out, one at a time, promising the others that he would be back. Torn between helping him rescue them and looking for the girl, I'd only managed to lug two to safety before the screaming started.

Tank found the daughter, but he also found the men abusing her. His gunshots brought men running in herds, all armed to the teeth and ready to kill, or die, protecting not only their boss but his high-profile customers.

From that point on, the memories got fuzzy. I could remember holding a woman as she took her last breath; in her chest was a hole that had been intended for me. I pulled another from a kennel, even though she screamed, kicked at me, and clung to her cage. Once she was out, I wrapped her in my arms, assuring her everything would be okay, and carried her out. I could see the faces of women we couldn't rescue, and the ones I saved with a bullet instead of my hands.

I would never know if those memories were real, or if they were brought on by the pictures that had fallen out of that envelope last summer. Photos from Dyer's surveillance cameras. Proof that I never knew existed.

Unfortunately, we'd only been able to wound Dyer before he locked himself in a safe room with some of his clients. For years I'd hoped that he had gotten a flesh-eating bacterial infection and died a slow, painful death. Or that he'd gotten stuck in the fire that we could only assume he'd set to destroy every ounce of evidence that he'd been there. He'd left America that night and never come back. But a few years ago, Wiz found him in Russia, running another slave trade.

That thought brought up a great point.

443

"We'd know if he was back, wouldn't we?" I asked the group in general.

"It's not him." Turning his tablet around, Whiz pointed at the picture on the screen. "Dyer's jet landed in London three days ago. He hasn't been stateside."

"Wouldn't matter if he was," Tank pointed out. "There is no way in hell he'd be coming after the three of us. We weren't wearing our colors, and nothing on us told the world we were Bastards, let alone who we were. He doesn't know who in the hell broke in that night, or he'd have come after us before now."

"But there is proof!" Bear snapped back. Then as if realizing that Tank wouldn't know because he'd been serving his sentence, Ian sat back. "Sorry, brother, I forgot." Looking at me, he added, "Mateo's seen it."

I nodded and explained to Tank the pictures that were in Billy's satchel of secrets.

"Where'd he get the pictures?" Tank demanded.

I didn't have an answer because I'd never asked which private investigator he'd hired. There hadn't been a reason, because I'd felt as though the damage with Jo had been done.

"That's a good fuckin' point," Rob murmured from his seat beside me. "Call that asshole and ask him. Tell him we need to know. Then you and Ian track the PI down to see where he found them. The rest of us will look into the others. We'll meet back here Wednesday night and report."

I had to meet Jo and the kids at the gym, then I was going to have a great night with my family. But first I needed to call her ex-husband and have a little heart-to-heart that. And somehow resist the urge to tell the miserable fucker that he'd lost. It didn't matter how dirty he played, Jo was mine, and she was never going back.

THIRTY-THREE

JO

THE things I loved most about the Boston aquarium was that there was something for everyone to do and it didn't take all day. In only a few hours, we'd seen every fish and exhibit, played in the touch tanks, watched Lily's penguins, and sat for a sea lion show. After a quick trip to the gift shop, where all three picked out something they absolutely had to have, we were off to the gym.

"You guys don't have to watch me if you don't want to," I assured them, not knowing how they'd handle seeing me go up against a much larger man and take a few hits.

Yet, they all wanted to see, making me more than a little nervous than I already was. I was surprised to see Cris instead of Nick as we approached the ring.

She smiled warmly as I squeezed between the ropes and moved close so no one else could hear her. "I thought it might be easier for the kids to see you spar with another woman instead of a man. Listen to Nick the same way you did me. He's gonna walk you through the moves." She backed away but snapped, "Listen to Nick!" once more before throwing a punch.

For the next forty-five minutes, Cris and I circled each other, avoiding flying fists and feet as much as we could, although we both landed blows. I was physically wiped when it was over, yet not as sore as I had been. Cris had apparently taken it extremely easy on me, but I wasn't going to complain.

Dean and the kids clapped and hooted when I stepped out of the ring, and I felt the blush rise on my cheeks. Even though I laughed and waved off their silliness, I appreciated it. Lily beamed at me as though I was her hero, and both boys were impressed. One member of my fan club was noticeably absent however, and I quietly asked Dean if Matty had stepped outside.

He shook his head, his face blank. "Haven't seen him. Probably thought we'd take longer at the aquarium?"

I frowned at the door. Maybe. This was the time I always came to the gym and he knew that. Court must have run over. I tried to shrug off the worry and headed for the showers.

Matty still hadn't shown by the time I was clean, so we headed back to the apartment. I'd invited Cris for dinner and was glad she'd agreed to come. It was Mexican night in the Murphy house, and I was making all the kids' favorites: quesadillas, enchiladas, taquitos, and Spanish rice. I figured having Cris there and cooking a giant meal would be a great distraction for me in case Matty didn't come home.

"What can I do to help?" Lily asked not long after we got home.

"Hey! I wanna help too!" Sam shouted from the other end of the room as he ran toward us at full speed, desperate to be included.

Dean leaned against the doorway, watching with sparkling eyes. "I have an idea. Why don't we cook supper? That way, your mom and Aunt Cris can go visit on the patio?"

I turned toward him, surprised. "No, that's okay. I'll cook with the kids now, and Cris and I can visit later."

Ben shook his head. "Good. I don't want to cook."

"That's fine. We need someone to set the table."

I gave him my silliest smile, but he just rolled his eyes and sighed in the way preteens do. "I don't want to do any woman's chore."

"Hey!" I glanced up, startled by both Dean's tone and his angry expression as she scolded my son. "Don't give your mom a hard time! You only get one mom, kid, and I promise you, you'll regret your attitude when she's gone." He sounded as if he was speaking from experience, and my heart ached for him. "There are no such things as woman's chores and men's chores. We all help out in this house. Real men don't say shit like that."

We were all quiet for a moment, Ben's eyes round in surprise, Lily and Sam glancing at the three of us to see what would happen next. Before any of us could speak, Matty walked through the door.

"I don't know what I missed, but Dean's right. You show your mom respect always, but especially while you're in my house, boy." Matty's tone wasn't as harsh as the other man's had been, but it gave no room for argument.

Ben quickly moved to the cupboard to get plates.

Matty watched him for a moment before he rushed to the stove and pulled me into a hug. "Sorry I missed the gym. How'd you do?"

"She was up against me." Cris snorted as Matty snapped his head around. Motioning to me, she moved her hand up and down. "She's fine. See? I didn't hurt her."

Matty turned back to me, his gaze moving over me slowly as if to make sure I really was fine.

"I'm fine," I assured him quietly, but he didn't look convinced.

Supper was a crazy experience. Food filled the center of the table, and it seemed as if everyone was having a conversation with someone across the table from them. Rob made it just in time, and although I could see something was bothering him and Matty, I was happy everyone was home. The eight of us laughed and ate until we'd had our fill. Then the men pushed Cris and I out onto the deck with a bottle of wine while they took care of clean-up.

"So," I demanded as soon as we were alone, "how was Friday night?"

After an amazing weekend last week, most of which she wouldn't go into detail about, it was clear that Caleb and Cris were starting to become serious. I had yet to meet the man she described as "devilishly handsome," but I was hoping that would change soon.

"It went great, but no, that's not what we're talking about right now. I want to know what you meant when you said he told you everything."

I shrugged. "Exactly what I said. He came clean and told me about his past. I think we're finally in a place where we won't have to worry about secrets. He doesn't have to keep things from me because he knows I'm not going anywhere, and I don't have to be afraid of what he might be keeping quiet, because he's going to tell me everything." I took a sip of my wine. "Well, everything that he can. It's a good place to be."

Cris squealed excitedly. "It's real now. I can finally be excited. We're gonna be sisters!" She fell back against the cushions and sighed. "When are you tellin' the kids?"

I turned to look into the house. The six of them were sitting around the table, engrossed in what looked to be a serious game of Monopoly.

I reached for the ring hanging on a slim chain around my neck. "Tomorrow night. We wanted to give them a few days to get used to being around us and each other. Ben already knows, but he's keeping our secret."

"I'm gonna have a niece!" Cris squealed again. "And another nephew!" Instead of screeching again, she bounced up and down like a child excited about the idea of a new puppy.

I pulled my feet up and tucked them under me, grinning at her. I understood exactly what she meant. Matty and I had done our damnedest to sabotage ourselves along the way, as if one of us was always pulling away because we thought we didn't deserve to be happy. We'd learned our lessons and were clinging to it this time. If, or when, one of us started to drift away, the other was going to hold on tight with everything they had.

Once we told our kids, there was no going back, because even though we'd hurt ourselves and each other, we wouldn't ever break their hearts. She was right—it was real now. We were finally grabbing onto our happiness, and each other, and not letting go.

Cris stayed just late enough to do the bedtime routine with the kids. She took Ben into the living room, I took Sammy into my room, and Matty took Lily into the kids' room, and we each read stories. After we made sure teeth were brushed, prayers were said, and they were all tucked in, we turned out the lights and cuddled with our respective kiddo until all three were asleep. It was my favorite moment of the weekend.

Once they were asleep, Cris quickly made her excuses to leave. As excited for us as she was, and as great as things seemed to be going with Caleb, she couldn't hide the sadness in her eyes when she glanced toward Rob. She could deny it all she wanted, but I knew she was rushing away so she didn't have to spend any more time with him.

Matty insisted that she couldn't drive home alone and suggested that Rob take her. She immediately declined, saying she was fine. Thankfully Dean interrupted, ignoring her arguments, and simply informed her that he would take her because he needed to stop by his apartment to get clean clothes.

I knew she couldn't see it, but Rob's eyes followed her every move and he always looked a little lost when she was around. He seemed genuinely disappointed when she refused the ride from him. As soon as she left, he said his good nights and retired for the evening.

Matty and I took another bottle of wine onto the deck and snuggled on the loveseat.

"I wonder who he'll choose," I said more to myself than to Matty.

"Hmmm?" he asked, tracing the alphabet onto the back of my arm.

"Rocker. I hate love triangles, but I wonder who he's going to pick."

Matty pulled his arm off my shoulders and sat up. "Love triangle? I think you have outdated info, babe. There's only Jess right now."

"Right now, maybe. But when he realizes he loves Cris as much as he thinks he loves Jessie, more even, there'll be hell to pay. That boy is knee-deep in love triangle angst."

Matt frowned, "No he isn't."

"Yeah. He is," I argued with a snort. "And she feels the same."

Matty's lips twisted angrily as he turned my words in his mind. "She can't."

"Oh, but she does." I laughed at his obvious discomfort over the news of his sister and best friend. Then I gulped down the rest of my glass in the most un-ladylike manner there was. "Speaking of, I need to call Jessie to make sure we're still on for coffee tomorrow."

I stretched for my phone, almost falling off the couch, before Matty shout out a hand to steady me.

"It's late. Call her in the morning." I giggled at his commanding tone. His eyes immediately turned amused. "How much have you had to drink? I think you may be a little drunk."

I shook my head too fast and had to sit back because the world started to spin. "Nah. I've only had four or five glasses."

"Four of five?" He laughed, voice full of humor. "Yeah, you haven't had much at all. What time are you meeting Jess?"

"Tenish. Right before class. I have a test at eleven."

"I have to work tomorrow." He pursed his lips. "Is Dean staying here with the kids?"

I shook my head, slower this time so I didn't get sick. "No. We're taking them to the clubhouse to play in the tree house." I giggled. "Why is there a tree house in the clubhouse?"

He grinned, tucking hair behind my ear. "It's a fort in the playroom that's wicked neat. Sam loves it there."

"Ah. Well"—I cleared my throat— "we're taking them there and then Jessie and I are going for coffee and then she's going back to there to stay with 'em and then I have a test and—"

He kissed me, cutting off my words. "And tomorrow night we make it official. We tell the kids, and you put my ring on your finger where it will stay the rest of your life."

I nodded, my grin as large as a jack-o'-lantern's.

He sobered a bit. "I'll ask Rocker to send someone with you. Stay with him, yeah?"

I agreed then cuddled into his side and looked out onto the city skyline. It took me a few minutes to realize the smile was still in place. I was so happy I couldn't wipe it off if I tried.

The sun was streaming in the windows, but I desperately wanted to ignore it. Matty rolled over next to me, moving in closer so that we were arm to arm on our backs. His hand moved, sliding under the covers until it found mine. The romantic gesture made me happy—until I realized that he wasn't twining his fingers into mine but instead moving my hand back toward him. His intentions were made clear when I found him erect.

I yanked my hand away, scolding quietly. "Our children are next door, Matthew!"

Tugging me back to his morning wood, he chuckled, his sleepy voice deep, the sound sexy as sin. "We can lock the door."

I groaned. I wanted him, but the thought that our kids could possibly hear us was just too much. I made a mental not my myself. When we bought a house, I needed to make sure that the kids' bedrooms were on one side of the house and ours is on the other.

My thoughts came to a screeching halt. I hadn't thought about us buying a house before. We couldn't continue to share the house I owned with Will, and Matty's house couldn't hold us all. It would only make sense for us to buy our own house.

"Hey? Where'd you go?" His face was full of concern.

"Sorry, lost in thought." I leaned up, kissing the tattoo I'd claimed as mine - the trinity and Claddagh over his heart.

He pushed back my hair, keeping his hand on the back of my head. "Fine. If you don't want to fool around, give me a back rub." With that, he let go of my hand and turned onto his side.

"A back rub? Oh, are you hurtin', old man?" I joked but started to massage the muscles anyway.

His back was fantastically toned and as much a work of art as his front. High on one shoulder was a Jedi symbol, and a Sith symbol was in the same place on the other—Matty's version of having an angel on one and a devil on the other. Stretched across his shoulder blades in large bold letters was the word FAMILY. Under that, right smack dab in the middle, was a profile of a man who resembled a roman gladiator, complete with a metal hat on his head. He was wielding a shield that looked just like the backs of the Bastards' jackets and holding up a sword as if ready to strike. I now knew that he was Itus, the Greek God of protection and the symbol that the Bastards had adopted. Low on the right side, right above his ass cheek, was a white wolf with striking blue eyes. Sitting back on its haunches, his head was thrown back as if getting ready to howl at the moon.

"Okay, so I get the others, but why a wolf?"

"It's my sign," he murmured into the pillow. "Lower. Harder."

I moved my hand down a little and worked at the knot I felt just under the skin. "You're a Scorpio. How'd you get a wolf from a scorpion?"

He chuckled. "Oh, yeah, right there. Celtic sign, not zodiac."

"Oh. What's it mean to be a wolf?"

"Hound. It's a hound. I'm fiercely loyal and enjoy helping others." He groaned as I finally got the muscle to relax. "I'm handsome and large and tough and built like a horse and—"

His obnoxious list was cut off as I pounced onto him, moving my fingers to his sides and tickling. He bucked, trying to throw me off, but I held on tight, my attack merciless. I didn't stop until we were both breathless from laughter. Sliding off his side of the bed, I headed for the shower.

"Joes?" Matty's voice called just as I walked into the bathroom. "You make me happy. I can't wait to spend every morning like this. I fuckin' love you."

I blew him a kiss before closing the door.

451

THIRTY-FOUR
MATTY

When I walked into the clubhouse, I headed straight for the play room. I didn't know how long Jo's test would take or if she had other things to do once she left the campus, but I needed to see if my kids were still there – needed to put my eyes on them.

No matter what I'd done all morning, I couldn't shake the feeling that something was wrong.

Sam and Ben were acting like pirates with a few other young boys. They'd turned the tree house into a ship, had swords and bandanas, and had even hung a Jolly Roger. A couple of the Brats were pretending to be their prisoners and offered me knowing smiles when they saw me leaning on the door.

Dean and Lily were sitting in chairs in the corner and were either having a tea party or playing dolls. I almost pulled out my phone so I could get evidence to show Joes. It wasn't every day that you saw a tattooed biker playing dress up with a little girl, which was a damn shame. People would look at us in a different light if they did. I knew Billy loved that little girl, but she'd been glowing from all of Dean's attention and I had to wonder if her dad ever spent this much time with her.

Jessie was nowhere to be found. Maybe she'd realized she wasn't needed and had gone to work. Assuring myself that everyone was not just okay but also having fun, I pushed off the door frame and walked to the bar. Bear had a beer ready for me.

"Any luck?" Tank asked from the other side of the great room.

Bear shook his head. "Nothin'. Until Jo's husband—" My growl stopped him, and he smirked before continuing. "ex-husband answers his goddamned phone, we're flyin' blind."

I'd called Billy five times. Left five messages. The fucker hadn't called back.

"I'm ready to drive up there and beat it outta him," I admitted. God knew he had it coming. "Anyone else back yet?"

"Tiny, King, and Clutch are still out. Hawk and Rocker are back in the office. Pain, Dirty Dan, and Preach came in earlier with nothin', and I think Rocker sent 'em back out. Neo's with Princess, one prospect is with L.K., another with Barbie."

"Preach?" I repeated, turning toward my friend. "He's supposed to be with Taylor."

Tank's face flashed in surprise before he forced it to go eerily blank. "I dunno, brotha'. Prez sent him out this morning."

"Fuck!" I slammed my beer down and rushed down the hall to Rob's office. I didn't knock, didn't care that I could be interrupting, just shoved open the door and demanded, "Why is Preach not with Taylor?"

Rob looked up from the computer screen, hands paused on the keyboard. "Because she ditched him. She snuck out. That was after she told me I could shove my watch dog up my ass."

"Fuck!" I exploded, sinking into the chair next to Hawk.

Of all the dumb shit she'd done over the last few months, this was the worst. She knew she was being followed and she knew how worried the club was. That spoiled, selfish bitch.

I would have gone on ranting in my head, complaining about the woman I'd once cared for since it was easier than focusing on everything else, but all hell broke loose. Screaming from the great room had me standing, pulling my gun, and sprinting toward the commotion, Hawk and Rob hot on my heels. Pushing through the people stupid enough to stand in my way, I got a good look at what was causing the commotion.

My blood ran cold.

Neo had my sister in his arms, carrying her toward one of the couches. She was hurt, that much was clear. Her face was cut to shit, blood smeared across one cheek. She was holding her right arm, which was draped across her chest, with her left. I shoved my gun into the back of my jeans and rushed to her side.

"Someone find Ratched!" Rocker shouted above the noise.

I sank to my knees, trying to assess the damage. "Cris, talk to me. What hurts?" I practically whispered, fighting to keep my voice calm.

Memories drifted through my mind as I ran my fingers over her cheek as I saw the little girl she'd once been. I'd known from the moment my dad sat next to me, with a teeny bundle of pink in his arms, that she'd been mine to protect. For years I'd loved her more than anyone or anything. I'd tried to protect her, even though she never made it easy. I'd done the unthinkable to keep her out of danger.

Our relationship had shifted over the years, but I still loved her almost above all. There wasn't a thing I wouldn't do for her. When she hurt, physically or emotionally, I felt it, the urge to protect her strong in my veins.

I'd fought her when she told me she wanted to be part of the club. I hadn't wanted this life for her – I still didn't. I had hoped that she'd have the fairy tale ending that she deserved with a man who put her first in a way my best friend never could. She'd refused to listen, and I'd given in instead of losing her.

I'd supported the Muay Thai. Had been excited when she'd purchased the gym, hoping it was her first step in healing. I'd been to almost every one of her fights, my heart stopping as I watched helplessly those times she had her ass kicked.

I'd seen her broken and bloody more than once. None of those times compared to this. The spark she always had in her eyes - sometimes a mischievous twinkle, others a shot of rage - was missing.

This woman wasn't just my baby sister. This was a victim. This was someone who had been savagely attacked.

"My arm." She lifted her uninjured hand and wiped at her cheek, only managing to smear blood everywhere. "I think it's dislocated." Her voice was hoarse, fighting through the pain.

"It's okay. We're gonna get you fixed up." I promised. Her face had been used as a punching bag, numerous spots had already started to swell, most turned a horrible shade of blue. I wanted to kiss her, to offer some sort of comfort, but I didn't know where to touch her without causing pain, so I just patted her hand weakly like an asshole instead. "What happened?"

Before she could answer, Ratched appeared at our side. "Let me clean her up, okay?" Her voice was soft but full of authority. "Call Doc. Right now."

Ratched had been a trauma nurse in Iraq before coming home and deciding to settle in the OB field. She said that being King's ol' lady was more than enough excitement for her; she just wanted a normal job and to cuddle babies. She'd gotten plenty of action over the years with us, always stepping in to sew a cut or tend to us when one of us was hurt. She was kind and gentle, nothing like cold-hearted tyrant she was named for.

If she wanted us to call Doc, then it was bad.

"I already called him. He's on the way," Hawk assured me as he led me to a table where Neo, Rob, and Cris's boyfriend, Caleb, stood.

"Princess was attacked," Rocker filled me in, ignoring the 'Thank you, Captain Obvious' glare I sent his way. "She finished a session and went out back to take a call. She hadn't said good-bye to Caleb, so he went looking for her..." his words drifted off, as if what he had to say was too painful to spit out.

"There were two guys." Caleb spoke to no one, his gaze glued to the other side of the room. Where Cris lay. "One had his arm around her neck in a sleeper hold while the other beat her."

"Thankfully Caleb left the door open and the gym was empty, so I heard him scream." Neo picked up the story, eyeing Caleb with worry. "They were trying to force her into a van and had worked her over. But they obviously didn't know who they were dealing with, because she wasn't goin' without a struggle and took one down right as we got out there."

"And the other?"

Caleb paled at my question.

"Fuckers broke her arm. He tried to pick her up but she kicked at him, distracting him, but I could tell she was too hurt to keep fighting. So, could he. He dragged her toward the ally. I couldn't reach her, and I wasn't gonna let that fucker get her in the van, so I did what I had to do. I didn't stick around to see if anyone heard the shots – we needed to get her here."

Rocker shoved away from the table, most likely to send someone to do cleanup, and Hawk grabbed his phone. Two dead bodies in the middle of the city in broad fucking daylight in the back of a building owned by a Bastard was bad news.

Before I could ask any more questions, the door opened and I turned, hoping to see Doc. Instead, Jon Greenwood strode in, acting like he'd been here a thousand times before, like he owned the place.

"Did you call him?" I asked.

Beside me, Caleb dug nervously at the dried red splotches on his hands. Blood that wasn't his. I didn't know if it belonged to Cris or one of her attackers, but Caleb was not a Bastard, and he was having a rough time handling what had just happened. Seeing his boss only made it worse, and a look of panic crossed his face. "I didn't. But if he's here, they must have found the bodies."

I caught Jon's eye as he surveyed the chaos in the room but once he found me, he headed straight for our table. A master at hiding his emotions, I couldn't get a read on him. Until he saw the man next to me and his eyes widened slightly in surprise. He hadn't expected Caleb, which meant he didn't know about Cris.

Jon didn't bother with pleasantries. "Matthew," his tone and use of my full name meant to show me he was in charge of this conversation, I was too tired to argue, "Where's Taylor?"

I shook my head. "She slipped the guard I had on her."

"When was the last time you talked to her?"

I didn't like the accusation, and I narrowed my eyes. "Saturday night. What in the fuck is going on, Greenwood?"

The lawyer matched my angry glare. "No one has seen or heard from her since Sunday morning. Her father is worried."

No. No fucking way. My mind spun on hyper speed.

"Tank?" I screamed to be heard over the commotion. "Call Jessie right now!"

He didn't hesitate, just pulled out his cell and dialed.

I grabbed my phone and hit Becky's number.

"What's up, buttercup?" She laughed as she answered.

"Where are you right now?" I demanded.

"At home. Matt, what's wrong?"

"I need you to grab Grams and take her to Katie's. Right now." A few years ago, we'd developed a code so that I could tell her when things were bad without a chance of someone overhearing us. Grams was the gun she kept loaded.

"Katie's, or Fred and Darcey's?"

Fred and Darcey were family friends who would keep her safe, and that was usually where I sent her.

But Katie, Rocker's little sister, owned a fucking fortress. After she'd had a nasty bout with an abusive boyfriend a few years before, Rob had made sure she could fend for herself and had a state-of-the-art panic room installed. It was where we sometimes sent kids who needed extra protection before a trial. Katie and Becky had gotten close over the years, and Kate owned a veterinary practice with Becky's fiancé.

"Katie's. Then I want you two to take Grams to the vet's." It was important that she know she needed to get her fiancé out too.

"I'm leaving right now," she said, and I heard a door close in the background.

"Call me when you're both there, yeah?"

She promised she would and hung up, not saying goodbye. I let my eyes close in worry for a brief moment.

When I turned back to my friends, Rob was back, standing next to Jon. His face was a thundercloud of anger, but he'd pulled out his phone as well. He lifted a finger and pointed at me.

"I'm checking with the prospects. Ian, call Ellie. You, call L.K."

My phone was halfway to my ear when Wiz appeared in front of me.

"We've got a problem." The kid's voice was shaky and his hands unsteady as he set the tablet onto the middle of the table so we could all see. Slowly, he scrolled through a group of pictures.

The first was of Taylor. She was in a store, looking through a rack of clothes, laughing at something or someone out of the frame. The next was of Jo and Jessie sitting outside a little bistro and laughing. I recognized the outfit Jo had put on that morning—I'd told her the jeans hugged her ass perfectly and that she needed to take them off and come back to bed. The next picture had been distorted, but each woman was looking at the camera and now had a number where their face should have been.

The final picture was of Taylor. She was tied to a chair, bloody and beaten. The number three had been carved into her forehead.

Wiz swiped sideways one more time, and there was a black screen with blood red block letters: **AN EYE FOR AN EYE? NO. A LIFE FOR EVERY YEAR YOU STOLE.**

They had them. Whoever it was, they'd taken our girls. The noise Tank made sounded more like a wounded animal than anything else. A bottle went flying across the room, and I heard someone swear. I didn't realize my legs had given out until I fell to the floor.

THIRTY-FIVE
JO

The room where they had me was pitch black, cold, and damp. I could smell the mildew, so I assumed it was a cellar. My arms, pulled tight over my head, had fallen asleep ages ago, and now they were just numb. I felt something crawling on my stomach and tried to convince myself that it was just my mind playing tricks on me, or maybe a breeze blowing against the hair that made it feel like something much more. I struggled against the cuffs that kept me spread-eagled and tied to the top of the bed, but it was still no use. I couldn't move.

If I closed my eyes and concentrated really hard, I could feel the sun on my face as Jessie and I sat outside, soaking up rays and catching up over a Danish and java. It had been such a fantastic day, from waking up next to Matty, breakfast with the kids, seeing Jess, then realizing I hadn't needed to study because I was going to ace my test anyway. Nothing was in the correct order though, and when I thought back, it seemed as if I'd gone to school first.

I still wasn't sure how I'd been grabbed. The fire alarm had gone off, and I'd followed my professor and the other students to the back of the campus instead of leaving via my usual exit – the exit where I'd left the prospect, making him sit on a bench in the shade to wait for me. There had been hundreds of people around me as we hurried out of the building. I couldn't figure out how someone not only found me in the large crowd, but managed to get me away without anyone stopping them.

I'd felt a hand on my arm and heard someone say my name, so I turned to see who it was. Then someone put a hand over my mouth, and I felt a prick in my neck. I had tried to scream, to fight back, but then I'd woken up here.

With a man on top of me. A man who, in my drugged state, had Matty's face. Even though I knew better, I knew it wasn't Matty, he was all I could see. I couldn't remember any other features of the man who had hurt me.

Every inch of me ached. I'd been roughed up, I could tell that much. Slivers of memories came through the fog, and I remembered someone asking questions, hitting me when I didn't know the answer, or it wasn't what they wanted to hear. Most of my clothes were gone, and I refused to acknowledge what that could mean. I couldn't remember it, so it hadn't happened.

I was parched, my lips aching and dry. Yet, I was more sore and confused than I was damaged beyond repair. It was nothing compared to whoever was being held with me.

Wherever we were wasn't soundproof. I'd heard the screams for what seemed like hours on end—horrible, blood-curdling screams that came only from someone suffering badly. It was another woman, I could tell that much. I'd tried to hum over it, to retreat into my mind, but it was too loud, no way for me to ignore it. Instead I spent the time praying her pain would end soon.

I spoke to God, begging and bartering with him to let me see my kids again. I longed to see Matty smile at me - just one more time, the way he did that made me feel like I was the only woman in the world. And, my final mumbled plea, that if I was taken out of this room, that I'd survive long enough to bring vengeance on the men hurting her.

Minutes stretched into what felt like years. My body begged me to let it give in and sleep, but I fought against it. I wanted to be awake when the man came back in. I focused on happy memories, trying to bring anything to mind that would drive away the fear.

Matty. My kids. Rocker and Tank and Bear. And, yes, even Dean playing with my kids. Happy moments I would cling to.

The pop-pop of fireworks startled me into the present, and for a minute, I imagined that Matty and the Bastards had found me and were rescuing me from this hell. Then the screaming started again. Another pop-pop echoed through my room, then it was suddenly very quiet.

The eerie silence thundered around me. No voice, no echoes, not even the scurry of rats in the corner. The quiet was so loud it made my entire body shake in terror.

Then, the scuffle of footsteps. My teeth chattered, every one of my senses was on alert, fear so real it wrung the air from my lungs. Before I could prepare myself, the door flew open and the room was filled with light that made me squint against the brightness.

The man in front of me was definitely not Matty, even though I could see why my mind had connected the two. He was roughly the same height and build, but that was where the similarities ended. His hair was lighter, and the expression he wore was pure malice. When his lips turned into a leer, I wanted to hide.

"You're lucky da boss man wantsta see ya," he mumbled as his eyes drifted over my body, "or you and I'd have some more fun."

The man unlocked the cuffs then dragged me from the bed before I'd even gotten my feet under me. I scrabbled to stand, the sudden rush of blood to my limbs painful, but he took my struggles as an attempt to fight back. Digging his fingers into my arm painfully, he hauled me up then backhanded me.

"There's nowheres to go, so don't fuckin' bother," he growled, tugging me along a hallway without putting my clothes back on.

We stopped in a large open room where seven or eight men, all dressed in the same dark shirts and jeans and all wearing gun holsters over their clothes, stared at me with various levels of disgust and hate. I tried to ignore them and searched the room, hoping for a sign of easy escape. In one corner, there was a jail cell with a cot in the middle. In the corner opposite was a tool bench and a large metal chair that reminded me of a dentist's office. In the section between the two was a desk filled with things I couldn't make out.

In the center of the room, four chairs sat in a large circle, a man stood in the middle looking like the proud ring leader at the circus as he surveyed the three women in them. The goon with me hauled me to the only empty chair, roughly pushed me down, and tied me in, making the prickly rope cut into my ankles and already raw wrists. I was half afraid to look up, not wanting to see the evidence of the torture I'd heard and not wanting to observe what I was about to face.

A familiar voice made me whip my head up, instantly pissed.

"What the fuck is she doin' here?"

"Let's call it a little extra incentive. We haven't had any real fun with her yet." *Yet.* A wistful, regretful tone spoke more than his words could convey. They were going to hurt me. "She's the whore fucking your man, right? You must despise her," the man goaded her. "I figure it can go one of two ways: we can hurt her for you, and you tell me what I want to know, or you can tell us, and we won't hurt her. That way, you can be the hero."

"Save your time and go ahead and kill me," Taylor snapped. It hurt me to look at her. Her beautiful face was almost unrecognizable, filled with cuts and bruises, one eye swollen shut. She somehow managed a glare with her open eye in a gesture that said she didn't believe he would. "I'm not gonna tell you a fuckin' thing, you piece of shit."

When she spoke, I noticed that she was missing at least one tooth. The man with the gun tipped his head at another, one I hadn't seen. The second man stepped out from the shadows and brought his large fist to her beautiful face. I winced for her.

She spit out a mouthful of blood and laughed – a cold, brutal sound. "If you think for one second that Mateo didn't put that little boy on the first plane out of the States, you're a fuckin' lunatic. He's not going to let you get your grubby hands on him."

The fist flew again. Then again. Hard enough to knock her sideways. It took a second, but she sat back up and shook her head. I wasn't sure if it was to clear it from the beating or in defiance.

Crazy Man smirked. "Fine. We'll play harder."

Then he lifted his chin in my direction and I noticed that the man who had brought me out was standing between me and... oh, my God! My heart stopped. Jessie was tied in the chair next to me.

Almost unrecognizable, only the tattered shirt, the one she'd had on during our date, told me who she was. Now shredded, it hung from her shoulders, open in the front, showing her bra. Down the arm closest to me were hundreds of bright red lines, almost like little scratches. I inhaled sharply when I realized they were cuts. Someone had taken a knife to her—repeatedly. The patches of uncut skin I could see were filled with marks: red puffy perfectly round spots, jagged angry pink marks, and good old-fashioned bruises.

They had tortured her.

The man next to me, stepped forward, and at least had the decency to hesitate before backhanding Jessie's already beaten body. I struggled against the ropes holding me, trying to get to her. Blood came flowing out of her nose and she started shaking, yet her eyes remained closed.

If Jessie, Taylor, and I were here, then... terrified, I turned to the third chair, positive I would find Cris strapped in it. Relief flooded through me when I realized it wasn't her, but instead a tiny speck of a woman I didn't recognize. Not that I would want my worst enemy to be here and going through this, and I felt awful that she was here, but I was elated that it wasn't my soon-to-be sister.

"Where would Mateo send the kid?" The man in the center asked Taylor again.

"Fuck off!" She screamed in return.

The man raised the gun and pointed it at me. For a brief moment, I stared down a barrel. Without any warning, he spun, turning it on the little woman. He didn't hesitate before pulling the trigger.

The loud noise reverberated around the space and made me jump. Silent tears ran down my cheeks as the life slowly drained out of her. I hadn't known her, but brutalized and tied in this hell hole was no way to die. Jessie opened her eyes and muttered to herself, head moving up and down in a rocking motion. Taylor didn't react at all.

"You will tell me what I want to know," the man's voice was clear, full of conviction. "I want to know where the boy is. Stop protecting the man who didn't even bother coming after you!"

When none of us said anything, a sadistic look crossed his face. He smirked at the man closest to Taylor. "Blowtorch."

Taylor reacted to that. Her whole demeanor changed as she shrank into herself and the color drained from her face. I glanced toward Jessie, not understanding. I thought she'd been quaking in fear before, but now her whole chair was shaking, which made it rattle against the cement floor.

"Ah, fuck!" the man between Jess and I muttered, before grabbing a handful of her hair, yanking her head back forcefully. "This stupid cunt pissed herself again." He pushed her head down brutally as he leaned down next to her. "You're gonna clean that up!"

The men around us laughed, amused greatly by our terror. As one came back with the lit torch, the gas hissing and spitting, Taylor's eyes grew huge. He didn't stop next to her, but headed straight for Jessie.

I pulled against my ties with every ounce of energy I had, the ropes slicing my skin, making blood run down my fingers. I couldn't handle it anymore.

"Stop!" The word came out hoarse, but I knew the man in charge heard me when he stalled and turned slowly. I swallowed, begging my body to release some saliva to help my burning throat. "I can give you what you want."

Taylor reacted instantly, my words tugging her from her anxious state. She screamed at me, swearing, calling me a liar.

The man ignored her, yet scoffed at me. "You?" He sauntered over, twirling the gun on his finger as if performing a parlor trick, and dropped to a squat in front of me. "You're going to tell me that the great Mateo Murphy would come after a club whore but not his rich fiancée with the famous daddy?" He laughed bitterly. "You're nothig," he seethed. "No matter what lies he fed you, you're just a stupid cow that he uses for his own pleasure. He's going to discard with yesterday's trash."

I raised my head, summoning every ounce of courage I had, and met his eyes. Surprise had me biting my lip sharply, trying not to react. Before I'd left to meet Jessie, Tank had pulled me aside and shown me a picture, asking me if I recognized him as a friend of Will's. I hadn't at the time, but that was before.

This was him. Scott something or other. He'd gained weight, his eyes were cold and dead, which I hadn't noticed from the picture. Charles Manson eyes. But it was, without a doubt, the man in the photo. He cocked the gun and moved before I could say a word, the cold metal biting into my flesh. Jessie whimpered.

I laughed. "I'm not the stupid one here, Scott." I leaned my head against the barrel, trying to prove that I knew him, that I had something none of the other women had.

"Someone remind me why you grabbed this one instead of his sister?" he challenged the group as a whole.

The voice that answered wasn't near me, and I couldn't see a face. "The sister fell through. We went with plan B and grabbed you the next best thing—the whore he spends all his time with. Figured she'd be easy to crack."

Scott pushed the gun into me harder. "Even to us you're just a backup, something that'll work in an emergency."

"You heard what he said—I'm always with him. But that's okay. Pull the trigger." My eyes challenged him. "Kill the valuable one."

He thought for a moment, and I knew he was replaying the reasons they'd grabbed me. He didn't lower the weapon, yet tipped his head in thought. "And why are you so valuable to him?"

I wanted to lick my lips. They were so dry I was afraid the next words I spoke would crack them. Instead, I ignored the urge and watched Taylor over his shoulder. "Because she may be marrying him, but I'm the mother of his child. He would move heaven and earth to keep me safe."

The gun moved so fast I didn't see it before it was slicing across my face.

"Lying cunt!" Scott spit, wetting my face with saliva before grabbing a handful of hair and forcing my head back up. "You've been around those dumb fucks too long if you think you can fool me," He snarled. "You're not her."

Jessie started to sob. Taylor screamed at me, her hoarse voice demanded me to shut up. I'd started this, I'd gotten his attention, couldn't stop. I drowned them out.

I forced a laugh, hoping it sounded arrogant, that my fear was buried deep. "You're an idiot." The fist in my hair tightened, and I knew he could rip it out with one tug. "I'm not Sam's mom, no. But I'm not the decoy that crazy bitch is either."

I didn't take my eyes off Taylor, even though the gun was back at my temple.

Matty had told me once that I was the worst liar on the planet, that my face gave me away every time. This prick didn't know me. I only had one chance to sell this lie, and I knew I could make him believe it.

Worry tugged at my mind. Once it was out, there was no going back. If one of the girls lived to tell Matty and I didn't – if I wasn't here to explain, he would never understand. That was a chance I was willing to take.

Turning back to the madman in front of me, I said the words I suddenly wished were true. "We have a daughter."

Taylor gasped, her obscenities quieted for a moment. Jessie was shaking her head and rocking again. The man in front of me narrowed his eyes and inspected my face intently, looking for any hint of a lie.

"Get me the pictures," he demanded of no one in particular.

The guy between Jess and me lunged toward the desk. A heartbeat later he was back, handing over a folder. Scott, pulled the cool metal away from my skin and holstered his weapon long enough to shuffle through it, grabbing one and holding it close to his face. Then he grabbed another and held them side by side. As he lowered them, my eyes darted to them, my heart cracking.

My loves. He had pictures of the kids. One was a school photo of Sammy and the other was Lily and Matty at the museum. He had his arm around her and was beaming at something she'd said.

I knew what he was seeing. I'd held their pictures next to each other numerous times over the years. Sam was the spitting image of his dad, a mini Matt, but with brown eyes and dimples. Lily, with her bright blue eyes, tanned skin and crooked smile appeared to have inherited the Murphy traits Sammy hadn't.

It was like two people who had been married a long time— when you watched them, you could see similarities. When you looked, really looked, at the three of our children, they appeared to share the same blood. Sam and Ben easily passed as cousins. Sam and Lily had been mistaken for siblings more than once. They had similar heart-shaped lips, thick black lashes, dark eyebrows that covered bright eyes, and the soft features that most children had. Give them five years and the similarities would be gone. Right then, they both looked like Matt's children.

Scott stared at me with such glee, as if he'd just won the lottery, it made me want to hide. "Where is she?"

It was quiet, too quiet. The others had stopped crying, stopped pleading with me. Even the blowtorch was out.

I shook my head. "You want Matty. I can get him for you."

He sneered, sliding out his gun. "Where. Is. She?"

I had him. Relief washed over me. He'd bought it. I didn't even think, just let more lies fall off my tongue. "At the safe house. If she isn't there yet, she'll be there soon. You let them go"—I lifted my chin toward the others— "to prove I can trust you, then you promise me that you'll let my daughter and me go, and I'll take you there. It's an old family camp, and I can promise you, you'll never find it on your own."

Taylor was hollering again, screaming at me again. Swearing and throwing whatever insults she could. I ignored her.

Scott's eyes narrowed. "I'm not letting them go."

I wasn't backing down. "Then you might as well kill me, because I'm not telling you anything. It won't be long before Mateo and the Bastards track you down. But for whatever reason, you seem to want just Matty. I can deliver him to you wrapped with a giant red bow. Or you can wait for all of them to come get me."

"I tell ya what"—he dropped in front of me once more— "I'll put them in the back room, leave them here safe and sound with a few of my guys. After I get Mateo, I'll let you go. You can come back here and get 'em."

I pretended to think over his offer. I knew he'd never let them live, he'd kill them as soon as we left. "If you kill them, I won't help you."

He smiled snidely. "Oh, little girl. I'm saving all my bullets for your baby daddy."

A man cut Jessie's binds and yanked her into his arms. I saw her wince and try to avoid his touch, tears rushed down her cheeks. Taylor, on the other hand, fought like a cat being forced into a bathtub, spitting, clawing, and biting the man that freed her. Scott sliced my ropes and let me walk, keeping a firm grip on my arm, and led us to the room where I'd been held. He grabbed my clothes and shoved them at me. I tugged them on, thankful to have something between me and their roving eyes.

They tied Taylor to the hooks that hung from the ceiling and laid Jessie on the bed in the corner, securing her wrists to the bedposts. Stretched out on the bed as she was, I saw all the damage that had been done, and bile rose. If Matty didn't kill this sadistic fuck, I would.

I wished I had a way to convey to them that all they had to do was hold on a little longer. Help was going to come, all they had to do was cling to that hope.

The door was closed and locked, but even as my captors dragged me down the hall, I could hear Taylor's screams, telling me I was stupid, before they turned to wordless shouts. I wished I could tell her that there was no safe house, that Matty wouldn't let my kids go to the woods in the middle of nowhere when the club must be searching everywhere for us and was probably on lockdown, that I would never risk my child, and that I was only doing this to give the club time to find her and Jessie. Maybe if they made it out of this alive, they would be able to tell Matty where I'd taken Scott.

I wanted to believe that neither would tell him what I had said about Lily, that they'd be so grateful to be rescued it wouldn't even cross their minds. I wanted to not worry about something so simple right now, because chances were that I wouldn't make it out of this alive. I tried to tell myself that in the grand scheme of things, it wasn't that important. But it was. If he believed the lie, it would life-altering for the man I loved.

Scott's fingers dug into a bruise, bringing me back to the present. "Where are we going, Baby Momma?"

I hated everything about this man, and the way his mouth was close to my neck, his breath blowing on my skin when he talked, made me want to cry. I didn't know where we were, so how was I supposed to give him directions? I didn't dare question him, because I knew he'd only hurt me.

"Take the turnpike to Gray, Maine, then get on 26 North. I'll give you better directions once you get there."

Scott opened the back of a big blue box van with tinted windows, and I stepped in willingly, desperate to get away from him. I sank to the floor and leaned my head back against the cold metal side. All I could do was pray that the Bastards found Jessie and Taylor soon.

THIRTY-SIX
MATTY

They say that after twenty-four hours, the chances of getting your loved one back alive are slim to none. If that was the case, why couldn't you report someone missing until after that much time had passed? A lot could happen in a single day.

I paced around the great room once again. I should be in court with my brothers or home holding my kids, but I couldn't sit still. So, I walked in circles.

Jo had been gone almost twenty-two hours. We'd gotten the exact time of the fire alarm from the prospect. He had still been sitting on some fucking bench where Jo left him, waiting for her to finish her test, when we called.

They said he was devastated. Terrified I was going to murder him with my bare hands. He didn't have to worry though, 'cause I didn't have the time or energy to punish him. All I wanted was Jo back, in my arms.

Billy came out of court and stopped short when he saw me. I would never get used to seeing that fucktard in my home, but I knew he was trying to help. We needed him. That didn't stop my violent hatred for him. This whole fucking mess was his fault, and one day I would make him pay.

After my brothers had dragged me off the floor yesterday and forced a few drinks down my throat, I'd called the twat again. I used the club phone instead of my cell, and he actually answered on the second ring.

"This is Will."

"Billy." It had been the only word I could manage without flying into a rage.

The phone muffled as I heard him ask whoever he was with to give him a moment then a door closed before he uncovered the mouth piece. *"Matt, I'm at work. This better be important or, so help me Christ, I'll file a restraining order on you."* The agitation in his voice was nothing compared to how I felt in that moment. I would rip his fucking throat out.

"Shut up, Billy. Just stop fuckin' talking. Jo's gone."

He laughed bitterly. *"Yeah, I know she's gone. She moved to get away from you. How's that feel?"*

"She moved to Boston to be with me." I snapped, seconds away from ripping the phone from the wall and driving to Maine to murder him with the cord. *"I need to know who you hired to spy on me last year."*

"I'm hanging up now."

"No!" I screamed into the phone. *"You don't understand. Jo is really gone. Someone has her. He took her. You dug into shit you shouldn't, and now they took her."*

I'd lost it then, the words sinking into my thick skull as I spoke them. This wasn't Billy's fault—it was mine. My past had put her in danger. Rocker had taken the phone from my hands and finished the conversation.

To his credit, Billy had left work and driven straight to the club. Then he'd helped as much as he could. The investigator he'd hired was also missing, but Billy had all the emails they had exchanged, as well as all the digital files of the shit he'd dug up. Wiz had been busy, running prints off the men Cris and Neo had murdered behind the gym, searching video footage to see if Pixie had also been followed, and rifling through my history to see if I was the target.

Hawk's dad had some of his buddies working on it, talking to their CIs on the street. Greenwood and his team were talking to every sleazy client they had. Rob was sure we'd find something.

That was before they'd kicked me out of court. It had been late last night or early this morning—I wasn't sure because time had run together—when Doc came in to give us the final word on Cris. She was stable and sleeping. He'd had to relocate her shoulder and set a broken wrist, so he'd given her pain meds and knocked her ass out. She had a few broken ribs, a few sprained fingers, and lots of bumps and bruises. But she was alive and would heal.

I was ecstatic that my baby sister was going to be okay. Yet, I couldn't celebrate until the others were home safe. Rob and the others didn't seem to be as worried as I was. They were taking their time finding Jo, as if she was an afterthought. When Rob told me I needed to calm down, I'd lost it.

"Are you fuckin' shittin' me right now?" I'd screamed. *"You have no fuckin' idea what I'm going through. She might not come back; don't you get that? I don't know what they're doin' to her, how badly they're hurtin' her! I'm about to lose my fuckin' mind! I*

don't wanna calm down. I wanna get on our bikes and track this fucker down!"

Rob had slammed his fist onto the table and stood. "You're not the only one worried! You're not in this alone. We all want them home. We all understand what you're going through!"

I sneered at that. "Don't you fuckin' tell me you understand! The love of your life is safe and sound fifty fuckin' feet away. It's not Cris out there—it's Jo! The priority isn't as great as it would have been, is it? You don't have one fuckin' iota of a clue what I'm goin' through!"

He grabbed me and shoved me against the wall, getting in my face. "Shut the fuck up, Mateo! Jessie is out there too! I thank Christ that Cris is here, that she'll heal quickly. But I have a prospect MIA. Tank's ol' lady is still missin'. I don't know if Jessie is dead or alive and bein' hurt. I love her!" He hissed. "I fucking get it. We fucking get it." He let go of me and backed up. "Get the fuck out! Don't come in here again until this shit is over."

I had nothing to do but pace the room and stare at the dickhead Jo used to be married to. We didn't need more bloodshed, so instead of butchering him, I grabbed a bottle of water and threw myself onto one of the couches.

Bear woke me up later. I didn't know how long I'd been out, but I sat up in a panic.

"Wake your ass up, Mateo, we got something!"

I was off the couch in seconds flat, following him into court. It had been turned into a command center of sorts. Papers and pictures lined the walls, laptops and tablets covered the tables, and someone had set up a projector so everyone could see what Wiz was looking at.

Rob stepped up to my side. "Scott Dyer died three years ago."

I snapped my head toward him, shocked.

"After Providence, he never came home because he was convinced someone was looking for him. His little brother, Seth, inherited everything when he died."

"There was no record of a little brother," I said.

Rob looked at the wall where Wiz was using his finger to draw a circle around a building. "His parents sent him away when he was young 'cause he had the same issues as his brother—a sadistic fuck from the word go. They even went as far as changin' his last name so that he wasn't associated with them."

That way no one in their high society social circle would know.

"A few years ago, the Dyers were killed in a car crash. The police ruled it a homicide, but there were no suspects. Seth never came forward to collect his inheritance and no one could find him, so they ruled him out. It's still an unsolved case.

"We only found him 'cause he flies back and forth between here and Moscow couple of times a month. Flies coach, never draws attention to himself. But in Europe, he's big-time, runs all of his brother's businesses. He looks enough like his brother for Wiz's facial recognition to flag him though."

"And we think he's behind this?"

"We know he is." Grabbing a file off the table, Rocker grabbed a picture of me I'd never seen. It was grainy and beyond blurry, but it was definitely me. And behind me was Bear. "A few years ago, right after Scott died, Seth hired a PI to find you. The only lead he had was this girl." He handed me another picture, one that had been used as a sales ad for one of Scott's girls. One of the women I'd carried out that night and given another chance on life.

"She was no help, not really. But she was able to tell the investigator that there were three of you: one named Tank, one named Bear, but she never caught your name."

I swallowed. He'd been trying to track us down for years.

"Tank and Bear are common road names, so the PI couldn't narrow it down. Until last spring when Will hired him to dig up dirt on you."

I clenched my fists at my sides. Fucking Billy. I'd known it.

Rob ignored me and continued. "Once he had that picture and your name, the rest was easy. He got more pictures of you from Dyer, gave those to Will, then focused his attention on the club and the three of you. His first attack was Ellie."

I looked back at Bear, who was watching Wiz with a fierceness I hadn't seen.

"It looks like he had business that dragged him away, or we'd have been doin' this last fall and not now."

"Where is he?"

Rob nodded at the projection on the wall. "He has a warehouse in Manchester. We think he took the girls there."

471

Manchester? That was an hour's ride. Shit! Fuck! "Why haven't we left yet?"

My friend tipped his head. "We're goin'. Just trying to figure out the best way in. This dick's got heavy hitters on his payroll. This isn't us goin' up against Jo Schmo and his gang-bangers. This is serious shit. As soon as we have a route, we're gearin' up and hittin' him hard."

It took forever to get loaded up and on the bikes. Tiny drove the Expedition, because while we didn't know what condition we'd find the girls or the prospect in, we doubted any of them would be able to ride. I spent the entire trip imagining how slowly I was going to kill the men who had taken her.

We parked a half mile away, not wanting the sound of fifty Harleys to tip Dyer off. The warehouse was quiet as we approached, and I didn't see one guard. Either he believed we'd never find him, or he was already gone. The door was down in seconds, and we were in, guns ready.

As my brothers swarmed through the rooms like ants out of a nest, I stayed back, searching for any place they could be holding Jo. There were only four guards and none of them had expected an attack, so it wasn't really a challenge. Rob and I broke down every door, but there was nothing. At each empty room, my heart sank. She wasn't there.

"Here! They're back here."

The space was already filled with Bastards when I stepped in. I wasn't prepared for how the girls would look; seeing them was worse than a kick in the balls. Taylor had been beaten so badly I wasn't sure she was even coherent. Jessie... fuck. Jessie was almost unrecognizable. They'd survived the worst kinds of torture. Rob shoved me out of the way to get to his girl, Tank not far behind.

"It's bad. She needs to be taken to the hospital," Doc was telling them. "I don't even want to move her."

"Prez! You need to see this." someone shouted.

My heart stopped. Jo wasn't here. I grabbed Taylor from Bear's arms, shaking her hard. "Where's Jo?"

"She's been through enough, Mateo! Leave her." Bear snarled at me.

"Rocker!" Tiny's voice boomed into the room. "There are bodies out here!"

I fell against the wall as two hands grabbed my shoulders, holding me up as I fought to stand on my own. No. It couldn't be Jo!

Before I could make it out into the hall, Hawk appeared by my side. "It's not her, Mateo. It isn't her!" He shook me, as if to make sure I was paying attention. "It isn't her."

"Who?" I demanded, needing to prove to myself it really wasn't my girl.

"The prospect and Tink." Hawk's voice was close to my ear. "We'll keep looking."

"They took her, Mateo." Jessie's voice was small and weak, coming from the bed in the corner. "They took her because she said that you'd send the kids to the safe house."

I turned to Jessie, sure she must have heard wrong. The poor girl was hurt badly enough that I couldn't bear to see it. I had to look away.

"She said that it was an old family camp. That she'd have to show them the way," Taylor spoke from behind me. "I tried to get her to shut up, but the stupid bitch wouldn't stop."

Taylor started to cry, and I closed my eyes against the sound. She never cried. She clung to Bear as he carried her out to the truck.

I swallowed. I knew where she'd taken them—her family's summer place. It was out in the middle of nowhere, and there was no way we'd be able to sneak up. They'd hear our bikes from miles away. I didn't understand why she'd do something so fucking stupid.

"Mateo," Jessie's voice was so small, and I knew she was using all her energy to talk. I braced myself before sinking onto the floor next to her. Tears streamed down her cheeks. "She did it to save us." She whispered, fear contorting her face. "He'll kill her when he realizes she was lying. What Tink when through- Jesus, that won't be anything compared to what he'll do to her!"

I only had one option right now. Save her or die trying. And I couldn't do it alone.

THIRTY-SEVEN
JO

My plan seemed like such a great idea at the time. Probably because I didn't think it through. My mother had always said my tendency to act on impulse would get me in trouble one day. Of course, I was relatively sure that when she said that, she didn't imagine I'd have a scary-ass dirtbag with the word PAIN tattooed across his knuckles pointing a gun at me. Well, maybe—that woman did have quite the active imagination.

The ride had been long when there was music blaring or a friend to talk to. When all you had to keep you company and help pass the time was your conscience verbally kicking your ass, it took forever. *Why couldn't I have come up with another lie?* I was still half surprised it had worked.

As the miles sped past, realization set it. There was no reason these men wouldn't kill me once I got them to my camp. When they realized that it was not a meeting place, or that Matty wasn't coming for me or Lily, they would have nothing but reasons to butcher me. I worried myself sick until a barking voice demanded that I crawl closer to the front and give directions.

When the van finally turned onto the one-lane dirt road that was used so rarely it looked more like a deer path than anything else, reality hit hard. I'd once told Matty that this was where I came to make sense of life, my peaceful spot. I never anticipated it would be the place I came to die. As the building came into view, fight or flight kicked in. I wondered how far I'd get before they shot me if I was to push open the door and run.

There was nowhere for me to go. The closest neighbors were "summer" people and wouldn't move in for months. I knew the woods, had spent hours of my childhood traipsing through them, and might be able to hide once night fell, but I had no idea what time it was. It could have been the middle of the day; I'd never be able to get away if they could see to follow me.

I was no closer to figuring out my escape when van came to a screeching halt, parked in front of the camp. The door slid to the side and I was hauled out, my captors not caring that the sharp rocks of the driveway sliced into my bare feet. A black SUV pulled in behind us, surprising me. I had been naïve enough to think it was just Scott, his two goons, and me. The four men that piled out of the other car, armed to their teeth, told me escape was not an option.

"Where's the key?" Scott demanded.

I pointed at the flower pot next to the door.

"Go check it out," Scott commanded his crew.

They filed into the house, guns drawn, leaving me with Scott and a guard, the latter's hand clutching my arm tightly.

After assurance that the house was "all clear," they pulled me inside. It wasn't a huge cabin, but it had enough room for a family to be comfortable during an extended stay. Downstairs was an open concept kitchen/living room with a bathroom and two bedrooms. Upstairs had three more bedrooms, a small closet, and a small bathroom. My hope was that they'd shove me into one of the bedrooms upstairs and leave me. My grandmother had left rope ladders in each room, and I knew how to use it to sneak out because I'd done it more times than I could count when I was dating Will.

The thought of Will made me see his smiling face, visions of my children danced before my eyes. I couldn't allow myself to think of them. If I did, I'd remember how much my arms ached to hold them, just one more time. What I would do to kiss them and hear their voices. I pushed the thoughts out.

I couldn't afford to think of things that may never be. It was a risk I couldn't take. I needed my mind clear so I could come up with a way out of this mess.

I zoned out while Scott walked aimlessly around the house, as if searching for some piece of evidence. He pulled a chair away from the table, scrapping its legs against the floor as he dragged it to the middle of the living room. He simply pointed at the chair, and the man who held me forced me toward it.

"No one is here," Scott said simply, as if I hadn't noticed. I didn't know if he wanted me to respond, so I stayed silent. "Where are they?"

I met his eyes. "Can I have some water?"

The question was answered by Pain, the guard's fist. I saw it coming this time though and was able to move with the impact the way Nick had taught me. The connection hurt like hell, but it could have been much worse.

"Why isn't anyone here?"

"I don't have my cell phone." I lifted my eyes toward the man in charge, regurgitating the lies I'd weaved on the way to the cabin. "There's a solid plan in place. Once the club goes into lockdown, my daughter's guard grabs her and keeps her safe. Once he thinks it's not dangerous for them to travel, he brings her here. I come here as soon as I can. We stay here until Matty can get us. Then we head to Canada, where there is another safe house. He has a route that we take where we don't get stopped by border patrol." I was rambling on purpose. I knew from experience that sometimes people in stressful situations gave way more away than they should, just because they're nervous.

"So now we wait." He narrowed his eyes. "Get her a drink and take care of her." The way he said the words made a shudder run down my spine.

Someone handed me a glass of lukewarm water and I gulped, hoping my stomach wouldn't revolt. As soon as it was gone, another man grabbed my arm, jerking me to the smaller of the downstairs bedrooms. Closing and locking the door behind him, he gave me a sinister smile.

I shook my head at him as I backed away from the door. "No. I brought you here. My daughter will be here soon!" I cried, grasping at anything I could to sway his mind from what he was so blatantly thinking.

He only laughed as he pulled out a cigarette and lit it. "Oh, don't you worry. Boss man'll take care of your daughter."

His implication made my stomach heave, and I knew the water was coming back up. He closed the distance between us, and I pressed myself up against the wall.

"I'll scream," I whispered, unable to talk any louder.

Maniacal laughter filled the room. "God, I fucking hope so. I like it better when you scream."

Something was going on. I listened for a few minutes, trying to hear bits of the excited conversation over the hurried movements of the men in the other room. A car? I pushed myself off the floor with a painful groan, positive one of them had said a car was coming. A car that could hold anyone from Matty to the police.

I limped to the dresser, praying that someone had left clothes in one of the drawers. I didn't care what it was, but I needed to cover myself to hide the marks from my last few encounters with Scott's men. My jeans and shirt had been destroyed. It wasn't just that I didn't want other people to see what had happened to me, it was harder to ignore it and act as if it hadn't happened if I could see them.

I almost cried with joy when I found a man's T-shirt and flannel pajama pants. They were too big for me, but if I pulled the drawstring tight, they'd stay up. The slicing pain of the rough fabric as it slipped over my wounds made me grab the bureau for support. I closed my eyes and focused on my breathing.

Then the door barged open.

"Look who's awake." The now familiar voice snarled.

I was surprised this one had come to get me; he'd barely left the room since we'd gotten here, his boss finally forcing him out only a few minutes before. I apparently was his personal plaything. I swallowed and tried to back away from him.

"Oh no, you don't. Boss wants you out here!" His long bony fingers curled around my arm, and he hauled me into the open room just in time to see headlights drift over the ceiling and onto the walls.

Someone had come.

As the car drifted slowly around the bend and up the hill toward the house, I closed my eyes in dread. When I opened them again, I surveyed the room quickly. It was just the two of us, everyone else must be outside, or hiding in here, waiting to attack whomever was in the single car. I was pushed toward the window.

"Let them see you," the man demanded, releasing my arm but cocking a gun in my direction.

I did as he commanded, not recognizing the large light-colored SUV that had pulled in. The door opened, yet no dome light came on, preventing me – all of us – from seeing whom was inside. I wanted to beat on the window and scream a warning, telling the driver to get back in and drive fast in the other direction.

When Will stepped into the light, and I cried out, unable to keep the shock and horror contained. No – not Will! He was not supposed to be here. He needed to be somewhere far away, somewhere safe, because if I was going to die, my kids needed a parent. He smiled at me and gave me a half wave.

"Who is that?" The cool, evil voice sent shivers down my arms.

"My ex-husband," I breathed.

Will walked calmly up the path and opened the door without hesitation. "Jo?" he called as he stepped inside, as if he hadn't seen me through the window.

I turned, not sure if I should call to him, to try to warn him, but before I could respond, men invaded the room, guns drawn, screaming at him to get on the ground. He shook his head, not understanding what was going on, before one of them struck him and forced him to kneel. Had Matty sent Will to check on me? He probably didn't even know he was walking into a trap.

Where were the others? Was no one really coming? Every hope I had of rescue died as I glanced out the window. The men who had been inside only moments before swarmed the car, guns drawn.

Will shouted my name. I turned my eyes to him, feeling like I was somewhere else. That I was someone else.

His eyes bore up into mine. "Move!" One word was all he managed to get out before he was silenced with another blow.

My body reacted, and I moved so quickly that the man next to me didn't have a chance to grab me. The sound of glass shattering made me shriek, but it was the thump of the man next to me falling to the floor, and the expanding puddle of blood underneath him, that had me sprinting across the room, the long pajamas tripping me.

Moments turned into seconds and seconds stretched into minutes as pure pandemonium broke loose.

My ears rang as guns fired too close to me, men running everywhere. An arm wrapped captured my waist, lifting my feet off the ground, and I shoved at it, digging my fingernails into the uncovered skin, kicking whoever had me. I needed to get outside and make a break for it. My pants slipped down, tangling my legs and making it harder to struggle. Another shot went off, making me grab my ears, shrieking in pain, as the man holding me went lax. I glanced behind me, prepared to see a face I hated.

Will's form slumped on the floor at my feet was my breaking point. I sank down next to him, lost in the chaos that surrounded me. Tears burned down my cheeks as I shook him, screaming at him to open his eyes until my voice was gone.

I had nothing left to fight Scott when grabbed my hair. I stood simply to ease the pain he was causing, my bottoms falling off completely. We were alone in the room, but I could hear the guns and shouts from outside and knew there were others around.

"You lying bitch!" he growled. "You'll pay for this."

The look in his eyes told me that I was as good as dead unless I fought back. Without his goons, he was just one man. One man currently without a gun.

"Did you think I'd actually lead you to Matty?" I scoffed. "He'll kill you." It was a promise I hoped my love would keep after I was gone. The one thing that would bring me peace.

His hand moved fast, poised to strike me, but I ducked and brought the heel of my palm up under his nose.

Scott cackled as he wiped away the gushing blood with his sleeve. "Never thought you'd be a fighter." He charged again.

Nick's words came back. *Keep moving. Use what you can.* I kicked at Scott's knee at the same time I aimed a fist for his throat. I just needed to get him down long enough to get out the door. He yelped in pain or surprise, I wasn't sure, but he managed to get a good punch in, and I reeled backward. He was over me in a second, kicking my already bruised side. I rolled onto my stomach, scrambled to my knees, and sent an elbow into his groin. He fell back, but not before kicking me in the back, making me fall forward onto the flagstone of the fireplace.

The rock sliced my cheek, yet I was beyond feeling pain. Turning over, I lifted my legs and kicked his knees again. He fell forward onto me, not backward as I had planned. His hands closed around my throat, but I wasn't giving up. I grabbed his head, shoving my thumbs into his eyes. He let go of me, attempting to knock my hands away, and I took the chance to slam my head into his nose. His hands were back around my neck instantly, as he smashed my head onto the fireplace.

Nausea hit. For a second, I couldn't see straight and there were three of him instead of one. I didn't want to give up, yet I was so woozy that it took me a second to remember what was going on. Using my fingernails as claws, I dragged them down his cheeks hard enough to bring blood. He refused to ease up, and I realized too late that he was winning—I couldn't breathe.

I didn't want to die struggling. I let my eyes drift closed, summoning images of happier times. Matty and the kids at Disney

479

the summer before, Matt and me on the back of his bike, the feeling of freedom as the wind drifted over me. For a few moments, I was at peace.

Reality hit hard when Scott was lifted off me and thrown across the room as if he didn't weigh more than a sack of potatoes. Tank loomed above me, saying words I couldn't hear. I struggled to sit up, pulling my shirt down to cover me, but I couldn't muster the energy.

Tank dropped to his knees, kind eyes meeting mine before he ran hands over my bare legs, avoiding the recent gashes. Then he was gently tugging my arms away from my sides, seeing the cigarette burns. Finally, he moved his fingers under my hair, over my scalp, and I was surprised when one came back bloody.

I didn't understand, but my lips refused to form the words I struggled to say. He spoke again, but I could only stare because I couldn't hear a thing he said. Slowly, as if not to spook me, he leaned closer and slipped an arm under my knees. Then I was in the air, supported by a giant teddy bear who kept dropping quick little kisses on my temple.

I leaned into him, feeling the beat of his heart against his chest. I was safe. He would die before he let Scott get to me again. I lifted my head, suddenly terrified, wondering where the evil creep had gone. Rob and Matty were on the other side of the room, Scott kneeling before them. There were Bastards everywhere, and I honestly didn't know how or when they'd gotten there.

Matty turned toward us, speaking inaudibly, but he didn't come to me. His eyes traveled over me but never connected with mine. He nodded to us then turned back to the man in front of him. Tank kept moving, and I closed my eyes, not wanting to see Will's body. I felt as if I was floating through the air, suspended on a cloud. Suddenly we stopped and I was lowered a little, but Tank's arms never left me. A door slammed, making me jump, and I opened my eyes in panic. We were in the safety of the car, where it was blissfully quiet and dark, with only the dim glow from the outside light.

Tank's voice broke through. "I got you, L.K. You're safe. I'm gonna get you help."

The sobs that wracked my body hurt, but I couldn't keep them in. I cried for Taylor and Jessie and the pain they'd endured. I cried for the woman I'd seen murdered. I cried for Will - I had loved him for almost twenty years, and even though we'd had our problems, he was a part of me. I cried for my kids, because I didn't know how to make everything okay ever again.

And I cried for me, because Matty hadn't come to me. I didn't know what I looked like right now, but I'd seen the horror on his face. He would love me forever, but after this, how could he ever want me again? I grabbed Tank's shirt, fisting it, and let it all go.

THIRTY-EIGHT

JO

I stood pressed against the cold glass of the window as I slid the ring back and forth over my necklace. Hawk had found the ancient Claddagh somewhere in the camp and had bought me a new chain so I could have it with me. Playing with it had become my new quirk, my nervous tic as my mom called it, to help pass the time.

I loved this view, especially at night. The Portland skyline was gorgeous all the time, but after dark, the lights came on and gave the city a whole new look. It was peaceful.

I was being released in the morning, and I couldn't wait. Not that it was awful – I'd been allowed to wear my own clothes instead of a hospital gown, and the food was more like catered room service than anything. I was ready to go home and see my kids, my family.

I'd been allowed to have visitors—hell, I'd had a steady stream of them over the past seven days. My parents had been here when I'd finally woken up, my dad crying with relief. Teagan had come and read to me from her gossip magazines every day. At least two Bastards had been here around the clock, barely giving me five minutes to myself, and they barged in even when it was just a nightmare making me cry out. Cris, her arm in a sling, had made the trip up twice. Even Will had been wheeled in by a nurse, making me break down when I saw him for the first time and realized he wasn't dead. But the four people I wanted to see most in the world hadn't come.

Becky, much to my mother's displeasure, had all three kids. Dean was with her and hadn't left my kids' sides through the entire ordeal. He had taken a break once they were back in school and brought me down the get-well cards they'd made. He and Bex had told them that Will and I had been in a bad car accident, and while we were going to be okay, we needed time to heal. I had gotten to talk to them on the phone a few times, but I didn't want to scare them with my ability to just start crying for no reason.

Even the police had visited me. I'd told them what I could remember. My memory got a little sketchy around the time the Bastards showed up, but I didn't feel the need to tell them that. I simply explained I couldn't remember any more, and they didn't push. I was sure the fact that Jon Greenwood and Hawk were in my room at the time encouraged the detectives to be gentler than they would normally be.

I didn't want to discuss what had happened, not even with the hospital psychologist. The problem with her was that she was trying to social work the social worker. There was a reason shrinks didn't go to other shrinks, and it wasn't because they didn't need help. It was because hearing the words you said to clients repeated back to you didn't help. I knew what I had to do to heal and that wasn't going to change because someone else told me to do it.

I moved slightly, sliding my body sideways, and caught the reflection of a man leaning in my doorway behind me. I whirled, seeing the face I'd missed dreadfully. "Matty." A mere whisper.

He didn't move, just raked his eyes over me.

"How long have you been there?"

He shifted and stepped into the room, shutting the door. His body was tense, and he seemed as if he was going to come to me, but then he stopped himself. Crossing his arms, he demanded, "What the fuck were you thinking, Jo?"

His tone didn't surprise me. I'd known his first words to me were going to be something angry. He was still Matty, after all. Cris had explained that her brother had stayed at my bedside until I'd woken up, and he'd camped out in the waiting room ever since, wanting to be close but needing space. She'd promised Matty just needed some time, that he was angry with himself, but that he'd come to me when he was ready.

Cris hadn't needed to justify it. Most of Matty might have been a mystery to me lately, but there were still parts of him I knew better than I knew myself. First, he'd beat himself up, focusing on the worst-case scenario, the 'what could have happened' instead of on the positive. Next, he'd get angry at everyone involved. Finally, he'd be sad.

Usually he'd let me in, and I could help transition him through the phases. He could be as angry with me as he needed to be, I'd take it, because it meant that he was here and that he'd finally moved on to the second stage of healing.

He looked as bad as I knew I did, and a hell of a lot worse than I felt. His clothes were clean yet wrinkled, as if he'd been sleeping in them for days. His hair was disheveled, the whiskers on his chin had almost grown into a full beard.

I desperately wanted him to come hold me. Knowing he wasn't ready, I simply took a deep breathe. "Are you okay?"

"You don't want me to answer that right now." He paced, finally stopped in front of one of the chairs, and dropped into it, one leg bouncing repeatedly. "I wanna know what thoughts passed through that brain of yours that made you think going somewhere alone with a sociopath was a good idea."

I hobbled to the other chair and eased myself down. My body was healing fine, however some of the bandages that covered my wounds pulled at my skin when I moved just right. I sighed, not sure what to say. I knew the answer because I'd asked myself the same question a thousand times, yet no one else had asked me. Not even the detectives.

I swallowed, trying to get rid of the lump. "I was thinking I'd heard the screams of that monster torturing them for hours on end. I was thinking that I'd just seen a woman shot in the face and that I would do anything to keep him from doing the same to Jessie." I closed my eyes, willing images of happier times to replace those from that night.

"I was thinking that I was tied to a chair and forced to watch as they beat Taylor, even though she was already hurt and didn't have much fight left. I was thinking that Jessie was so terrified she was shaking." I opened my eyes, but I couldn't look at him, so I focused on the worn gray tiles on the floor, pushing my hands into my stomach to help ease the butterflies that had taken up permanent residence.

"I was thinking that a sadistic fuck was coming after Jessie with a blowtorch, probably not for the first time, and that I couldn't sit there and do nothing." I didn't realize I was crying until the tears fell on my hands like rain drops. I swiped at my face, and my voice broke. "I was thinking that he was just going to keep hurting us if I didn't do something. I was thinking it was my only chance to save us. I was thinking that you would risk your life to save them, so why shouldn't I?"

"Joes." Matty's voice was soft, suddenly full of unbridled emotion.

I didn't stop. "If you're asking if I thought about you, the answer is yes. I thought about how much the idea of never seeing you again terrified me. I thought about how if I could just give them a little while longer, that you would find them, because you would move heaven and earth to get to me." I swallowed painfully and tucked my hair behind my ear before I brought my eyes back to his. "I thought about you every time I closed my eyes, praying you'd come rescue me, because I wanted you to tell me you loved me one more time. I know I scared you, Matty. But I didn't do it to hurt you."

He lurched forward, attempting to come for me, but my raised hand stopped him before he could reach me. The pain in his eyes almost unbearable to see. If he touched me now, I would break. I needed to stay strong, to make him understand.

A broken bone would heal, but if it wasn't fixed properly, it would always be bent. We'd move forward no matter what, but in order to be what we once had been, we had to clean the wound and set the bone. We needed to have it all out in the open.

Matty sighed and sat forward, bracing his elbows on his thighs, halting his restless leg, and rubbed his palms together. "I can't begin to tell you..." He stopped, looking at the window.

Silence surrounded us, but I refused to prompt him. He needed to say whatever was on his mind, and he needed to do it in his own time.

After what felt like ages, his eyes turned back to me. "I could have lost you."

"But you didn't." Was my only reply. "I'm right here."

"Lily." He wet his lips. "I immediately wanted to dismiss it, to think that you were just using what you could to get him to take you out of that warehouse. But I can't stop thinking about it. I looked at the calendar, Jo."

I raised my eyebrows in confusion then vaguely remembered worrying about this exact thing before I had been taken to the camp. It seemed like a lifetime ago. I hadn't thought about it since. Lily. I'd lied about Lily.

I opened my mouth to apologize, but Matt cut me off. "Lily came early—thirty-eight weeks." I pursed my lips, hoping he wasn't connecting dots that weren't meant to go together. "I looked at a calendar, counted back forty weeks from her birthday, and you know what I found? She was conceived around the time you came to my hotel room and stayed after Becky kicked me out." I shook my head, but he ignored me. "I know I was out of it, that I said and did a fuck-ton of terrible shit that week. I've wracked my brain for days, trying to piece together the timeline, trying to remember anything at all."

I shook my head again, cutting off any further argument from him. "You won't remember something that didn't happen." I adjusted slightly in my chair, trying to relieve some of the pressure from my ribs. "I would never have kept your daughter a secret from you while letting you be an adoring uncle, Matty. How could you think that?"

He raised an eyebrow and gave me a cold stare. "You had me help name her! You talked me into going to ultrasounds whenever Billy couldn't make it! You made sure you showed me videos of every one of her firsts, and invited me to every party, play, and school event. You had me involved just enough so that I would never miss anything. Why?" He hissed.

"Because you're my best friend. You were struggling and needed something to distract you. You're her godfather and it's your job to be involved! Do you really think I'd keep something that important from you?"

He looked away. "I don't know what to think, Joes."

"Think I loved you enough to concoct a lie I thought I could sell, no matter how wild it was, just so I could see you again." He still wouldn't look at me. "I hoped I'd be the one who told you what I'd said. I'm sorry if it caused you more pain, but I said the most believable thing I could come up with." I sighed. "Taylor wouldn't stop screaming at me to stay quiet," my voice broke as I remembered how hopeless and terrified I had felt in that moment.

"She was trying to stop you because she thought you were telling the truth. She knew that if our daughter was taken, the Bastards wouldn't stop until we got her back."

"You weren't going to stop until you got me back. Until you got us all back," I bit out. "I knew that. I needed to buy you some time. She needed more faith."

"In her mind, Bear wouldn't risk his life to save you. But he would do whatever it took to get Lily back."

"Bear? Why in the hell does she care what he does?"

"They're together."

"What?" I stared at him in disbelief. I couldn't picture the young man I adored sleeping with Taylor. Ellie was sweet, innocent, and kind—everything that Taylor wasn't. How in the hell had he ended up with Tay? Apparently the world really had gone crazy while I'd been locked away. I lifted my hands and scrubbed gently at my face.

The sound that came out of Matty was something a wounded animal would make. I jerked my hands away in surprise, desperate to see what was wrong. His eyes were glued to my arms, his fists clenched tight.

I'd forgotten I had on a tank top. When I lifted my arms, the marks were visible. I lowered them as fast as I could, bringing up my hands to hug myself, covering what I could. They didn't hurt anymore, and I'd forgotten they were there because I didn't have to look at them.

Matty pushed out of the chair, falling to his knees in front of me, his hands landing on the arms of the chair, boxing me in. Bending over a little, he leaned down so we were eye to eye. "I would give anything to take away what you went through, anything to make it all just a bad dream. I want to kill him. I want to do everything he did to you to him. But, most of all, I want wrap you in my arms and never let you go."

"Matty." I lifted my hands to his cheeks and moved my thumbs over his whiskers. I didn't think he'd shaved since the day I was taken. "I'm okay. I'm alive. I'm right here," I whispered, trying to soothe the sadness oozing from him.

"What can I do to make it better? Tell me what you need, and whatever it is, I'll get it."

"I need you, Matty. Just you. Tell me I have you."

He pulled back a little, surprised. "You'll always have me. You own my heart. My soul." His hand closed over mine, lifting it to his chest. "I'm not me without you. I would never be ok if you were..."

His voice broke and he swallowed roughly, as his eyes moved over my face, taking in the stitches over an eyebrow, the split lip, the swollen cheek, and the bruised chin before drifting lower. His growl told me he was seeing the light gray-and-green handprints that wrapped around my neck and hadn't quite faded completely. Then the baby blues I loved moved lower, over my chest and down my arms, stopping often, as if cataloging each mark and every contusion.

I'd seen my reflection and knew how bad it was. But I needed him to look past the image in front of him, to see me. I wasn't a client or a job. I wasn't someone who he needed to feel quilt over. I needed him to see *me*, to remember that it was me in here.

"Kiss me, Matty. Make me forget."

His eyes snapped back to mine, and he shook his head once. "I don't want to hurt you."

"Matty—" It was a plea.

His mouth fell on mine gently. After a minute, his arms came around me.

He moved back slightly, sliding his face to my neck but not loosening the grip he had on my body. "I was so scared, Joes. I've never felt like that before. He hurt you because of me, and..."

He broke off, crying soundlessly. Every so often he would babble, apologizing for putting me in that spot, vowing to never let anyone hurt me again, or just telling me he loved me.

I let him cry, running my hands over his head and back, whispering words when I could. A nurse peeked in at one point, but I waved her away. Matty and I needed this moment, because without it, we would never heal.

My funny, caring friend needed reassurance that I was okay, that I was still here with him. My scary, commanding biker needed to release the tension and fear he'd been carrying around. I was going to do what I did best—sit and hold him, loving him until the end.

THIRTY-NINE
JO

I could see him watching me out of the corner of my eye, yet I kept reading. We'd been playing this game for a solid twenty minutes. He'd stop what he was doing and stare at me, I'd glance back at him, and he'd quickly look down at the paper in front of him. I finished the article and turned the page of the *Martha Stewart Weddings* magazine Jessie had picked up for me. This time though, I just skimmed the pictures of a beautiful reception.

Unable to take it anymore, I laughed but didn't look up. "Why are you staring at me?"

"I'm not."

I lifted my eyes to his, catching him in the act.

Matty only smirked. "Maybe I was."

"Mmhhmm." I nodded, scowling at him. "What's wrong?"

He shook his head but winked. "Can't a man stare at a beautiful woman?"

I wanted to roll my eyes, or point out that I was wearing a pair of his old sweats that were three sizes too big for me and stained with god knows what, or bring attention to the fact that my face still looked as though I'd been used as a human piñata and I hadn't washed my hair with anything but dry shampoo in three weeks, but instead I tipped my head and smiled. He always knew the right thing to say to diffuse my irritation. "Well, you'd better enjoy the view while you can. I'm getting married soon, and my future husband is tad bit possessive."

"No!" He grabbed his chest playfully. "You can't marry him! I won't let you." He stood abruptly, moved from his chair to the loveseat where I was stretched out, picked up my feet, slid under them, and put them on his lap. He didn't move his hands though, and they massaged my calves absentmindedly. "What's he have that I don't?"

I raised one eyebrow, playing along. "A better taste in music. He knows Modest Mouse and Green Day are so yesterday."

"Now that's just mean." The hands on my legs slid to my feet and started to tickle.

My magazine fell to the floor as I thrashed against him, giggling uncontrollably. He was laughing and saying "Tickle, tickle, tickle," in a high-pitched voice that made the whole thing even more amusing, and I was certain I was going to pee my pants before he let me go.

The thought immediately generated memories of Jessie, and my face fell as my heart started to pound. I recovered but not quickly enough. Matty pulled his hands away from my feet, sat up a little, and in one simple move, he transferred me so that I was straddling his lap, his hands limp by his sides. This was our "safe zone."

Over the last couple of weeks, we'd discovered that certain situations brought me back to those days. When I'd been discharged, the doctor and the psychologist both explained the effects of PTSD to us. I laughed it off, telling them I was educated enough to know all about post-traumatic stress and that I was fine.

For the most part, I was.

However, there were moments when anxiety hit or panic set in. The hardest part for Matty was that we never knew what would trigger an attack. And once again, he was helpless.

Once it was as simple as him rushing through the bedroom door, late to a meeting. I'd been on the other side of the room, but it wasn't Matty I'd seen—it was another man who had rushed through another door. I collapsed in a fit of tears, terrifying Matty. Another time it had been the smell of Tank's cigarette, which he immediately threw over the edge of the balcony and then spent twenty minutes holding me while I sobbed into his neck.

Matty had been so sure that physical contact would be a trigger, but we'd avoided that bomb so far. In his arms, I was safe and felt protected. Even so, whenever I had an episode, he very quickly became submissive, making sure I knew on every level that I controlled our contact. We would go as slow as I wanted, and he would be right there, supporting me, not pushing.

Which was exactly why he'd pulled me onto his lap and wasn't touching me. When I was on top of him, I could get up and leave anytime I wanted. I was not a prisoner here; no one was going to hurt me.

The sweet gesture brought tears to my eyes. This man was trying so hard to make everything okay, to let me know that he was here, and to give me whatever I needed. I loved him even more for it, even though I never would have imagined that being possible.

I moved my body closer to his and leaned down to kiss the little patch of hair below his bottom lip. I heard him swallow, and I moved my lips up onto his. He sighed but didn't move his hands from the cushions. I sat up, intending to smile down at him, but I lost my train of thought when I felt his reaction to my closeness. He was hard as a rock beneath me.

We hadn't been intimate yet. My body had been too sore to do much more than walk from one chair to the other at first, then I'd been very aware of how I still looked. It wasn't that I wasn't physically ready, even though my doctor hadn't given me the green light yet. No, it was Matty who was holding us back from crossing that line. He hadn't even attempted to do anything more than kiss me.

"Jesus, I'm sorry, Joes," he whispered, moving his hands to my thighs to halt my movements.

"Why?" I shifted again, grinding against him lightly.

He groaned and gave me a dirty look, making me giggle.

I leaned down, lightly kissing a line down his jaw. "Matty?" I slid my hands down his chest, loving the hardness I felt beneath his shirt. He'd been exercising again, sweating his stress away and toning up the muscles I loved so much. "Why don't we..."

His hands wrapped around my wrists, preventing any further exploration, and he leaned his head away from mine. "We can't, Joes." His voice was stern but not angry.

There was no arguing with him when he had that tone, so I just nodded. We didn't have to have sex right now—there'd be plenty of time later—and I technically should wait until I'd been cleared by a medical professional. But he wanted to. I'd felt the evidence; I'd turned Matty on.

The thought brought a smile to my lips. Deep down, so deep I refused to acknowledge it, I'd been worried. The look he'd given me the day the Bastards rescued me was one I would never forget and made me believe I was too damaged for him to ever want again. And there were times I'd felt as though he would never forgive me for putting myself in that situation.

I'd never been so happy to be wrong in my life. Matty's body wanted mine. I grinned like a madwoman and planted another kiss on his lips.

"Sorry, kids. Didn't mean to interrupt."

Tank's deep voice startled us, and Matty quickly moved me back to my side of the loveseat.

Tank laughed—a deep, throaty sound. "Jesus, Mateo, you're acting like you just got caught jerking off. Chill, man." He held up his hands as he walked to the chair. "Prez wantsta see ya."

Matty hesitated a second too long, so I nudged his arm. "Go! I'll be fine. Tank'll stay with me."

Matty had been spending way too much time with me, and I knew he must be aching to get on his bike.

Tank laughed again. "Ooo, brotha' just got dismissed by his lady love."

Matty's middle finger shot up in Tank's direction, but his eyes never left me. "I'll be right back."

I nodded, puckering my lips for a kiss. He gave me a quick peck as he stood, and within seconds, he was gone, nodding to Tank as he went. We sat there, staring at the city until the roar of Matty's bike faded down the street.

Tank immediately moved to the spot next to me. His face was serious now, all humor gone. "How we doin' today?"

I sighed, leaning the side of my head against his shoulder. I loved my sessions with Tank. He came over almost every day, and we would sit here, talking. He'd promised me that anything I said to him stayed with him, unless I wanted him to tell Matty. The few minutes I got to spend with him were much more beneficial than any I would spend with a therapist.

"He still won't touch me."

A thick arm draped over my shoulders. "Give him time. I can't tell you what's goin' on in that mind of his, but if it was me, I'd be afraid I'd get too rough and hurt you. Or touch you in a way that would bring on a flashback. Think about it, L.K.—if you two are in the middle of gettin' busy and you have an attack because of the way he touched you, neither of you would get over that anytime soon. It's better to wait."

"I don't think Jessie and Rocker waited," I pointed out without thinking.

I expected him to chastise me about his sister, but Tank cleared his throat instead. I knew we were about to delve into serious topics. "She had a different experience than you did, babe. I don't know what they're doing or what they're not. But, I do know that Rocker is doing whatever he can to drive her bad memories away."

I shuddered. Jessie had had a much different experience. When the girls first started opening up about what had happened in the warehouse, everyone expected that I'd share too. But I hadn't felt the need to talk to anyone, so I stayed quiet.

When she'd admitted the fucker had brutalized her, every Bastard took the news hard. Bear had hired a top-notch counselor to go to the clubhouse and help Taylor work through her memories. When they learned that she'd suffered the same way Jessie had, the Bastards started looking at me with pity and tiptoed around me even more.

I couldn't handle the way Matty was always staring at me with his sad puppy-dog eyes, so I finally broke down and clarified some things. I didn't tell him what had happened. As strong as he was, there were just some things I knew he couldn't handle, and my treatment fell into the "lose his shit" category. Instead, I put all their minds at ease and made it very clear that I had escaped the ordeal without losing that part of myself.

Tank knew what had really happened though. He'd told me that I needed to tell someone. He didn't care who it was as long as I told someone, because if I didn't, it would eat away at me until I snapped. One day, not long after I got back to Boston, he'd come to visit after a particularly rough anxiety attack, and I let it all out.

He'd sat next to me on the loveseat, just as we were now, and listened as I told him they'd held me down and hurt me for no apparent reason other than they were sadistic fucks. They didn't ask me any questions about the Bastards or Matty, or demand to know any secrets. No, instead they taunted me, saying horrible things, and did their best to make me scream. I'd bitten my lip and cried until I had no more tears, but I never gave those pricks the satisfaction of a scream.

After I was finished my tale, Tank hadn't told me he was sorry it happened. He didn't stand up and rush off so that I wouldn't see his tears. He didn't get angry that they'd hurt me or say that I'd brought it on myself.

No, he'd lifted my chin and given me a giant smile. "You are fuckin' tough as nails, you know that, yeah? I'm so fuckin' proud of you, kid!"

Then he'd pulled me against him, and we sat there in silence until Matty came out. I never asked if he'd given me those compliments because of what I went through or because I'd finally let someone in. It felt as though he meant them for both.

Every day after that, he'd come back. Some days we processed my memories, some I listened while he reminisced about Tink, others we worried about Jessie together or talked about the latest club gossip. He filled me in on the legal ramifications the club was facing and told me stories that would make me laugh until I cried.

We literally could talk about nothing and I would come away with a smile. Tank was so much more than the man who had fondled me all those weeks ago. He was the friend who was helping me find myself again.

"So," he asked, pulling the conversation to happier topics, "how's wedding planning going?"

"Ugh!" I rolled my eyes. "Matty wants a massive gathering. Apparently the Bastards negotiate with terrorists, because he'd giving into her every demand."

Tank chuckled. "Your mom?"

I shook my head. I doubted my mom would even come down for the ceremony. "No, worse than her. Lily."

That made him laugh until he coughed. "Yeah, Dean says she's a little firecracker like her mom," he managed to get out.

I shook my head. "Oh, no. This goes beyond me. I wanted it to be just us, the kids, and a couple of friends. But Miss Lily-Belle and Cris decided that it would be mean to leave out anyone. The two of them are bad enough, but once Jessie jumped ship and joined the enemy, I was screwed." I may not have wanted a large wedding, but it seemed to be just the distraction most of my friends needed. "Now I'm stuck with three bridesmaids, two junior bridesmaids, a maid of honor, and a flower princess, because flower girl sounds too babyish."

He chuckled again. "Mateo asked me to stand with him." He sounded surprised, and I looked at him, questioning his tone. "We've known each other forever, but we haven't been close in a while." He shrugged. "Didn't expect the honor."

I smiled, cuddling into his shoulder. "He loves you, and he knows that you are one of the reasons I'm smiling again. Did you say yes?"

His shoulder nudged me forward. "Fuckin' right I did. Mateo Murphy is marrying the woman of his dreams and throwing a big-assed bash afterward. I wouldn't miss that for the world. Plus, I wanna see him cry like a baby when he sees how beautiful you are walkin' down the aisle. Great blackmailin' opportunity."

We talked about the wedding until Matty came back. I'd hoped Tank would stay for dinner since Rocker was never home anymore, but he turned me down. He stayed with Jessie at night, and he was in a hurry to get back. I didn't blame him.

"You seem awfully chipper tonight."

I glanced up from my plate, trying to fight the smile. "Chipper?"

Matty nodded. "Yes, chipper. Like cheerful, happy for no reason." He smiled. "It's nice to see."

I set my fork down and sent him a cool look. "Aren't you just a little curious why I'm so happy? I mean, you have been gone all afternoon and when you come back, your girlfriend is all happy and you're not the least bit curious?"

His mouth quirked, fighting a smile. "Now that you mention it, my interest has been piqued."

"Hmmm." I picked up the fork and stabbed at a cucumber. "Let's go for a run."

"You think you're up for it?"

I nodded vigorously.

He turned his head, watching me closely. "We haven't gone running together in almost a year. I'm not sure you can keep up."

I laughed at his challenge. "Listen, old man, I'll keep up just fine."

We left the dishes on the table and dinner on the stove and changed into running gear.

Ten minutes in, I was gasping for breath and my ribs ached, but I felt better than I had in weeks. Matty refused to let me push through the pain, turning us around instead, and we walked with my hand in his.

"Are you going to tell me?"

I didn't need clarification. He wanted to know why I was happy. "Because I have you. Because I'm yours."

He stopped walking, pulling me back when I tried to keep going. "You've always had me. And you've always been mine."

I nodded, standing up on my tiptoes to kiss him quickly. "Yeah, but now I'm ready to make it official. Let's set a date and start planning."

"Yeah?" His arms circled around me, pulling me in and holding me tight. "I fucking love you, Joes."

I pushed away, smiling mischievously. "Good. Then you'll let me win." I took off running.

"Not a chance!" he countered, keeping my pace. "Hey, I have 'Float On' on my iPod if we want running music." He laughed. "I say winner tonight picks tomorrow's playlist."

I growled at him and swore, damning his horrid taste in music. As we laughed and raced back to our apartment, I forgot all about the bullshit of the last few weeks. I forgot everything except how much I'd missed those moments with him—the ones where we could be carefree and ourselves. This was who we were, and it was time we get back to us.

FORTY

MATTY

Another nightmare pulled me from sleep. I kicked at the covers in a panic, sitting up and sliding back until I was leaning against the smooth wood of the headboard. My heart pounding, my naked chest covered in sweat. They were so vivid, it always took me a few minutes to remember they weren't real.

I ran my hands through my hair and absently scratched at my scalp, trying to force the images away. Once the haze started to clear, I moved one hand to the miracle sleeping next to me and placed it softly on her back, just to make sure she was real and that she was really here with me. Her steady breathing moved my arm up and down, and I knew for a minute I could rest easy.

Jo was here. Jo was safe. Jo was mine.

The dreams—terrors, really—had started the night she'd been discharged from the hospital. We'd spent the night with the kids in the home she'd once shared with Billy, and I initially thought the dreams were caused by the noises of a strange house. The second night there, I had another, but I blamed that one on Billy.

I hated sharing a house with him. I might not hate him anymore, because the jackass had gotten shot while helping save the woman I loved. He'd volunteered to drive a vehicle full of Bastards, all packing serious heat, up to the camp, and he did risk his life by walking into that same camp to try to get Jo out. For that, I would spend the rest of my life being civil. But I didn't want to be around him for more than five minutes.

That was almost two months ago though, and every night, without fail, I'd woken up terrified. Every single one was the same. I'd hear Jo screaming for me, begging me to help her, but all I could do was watch them hurt her.

I never got to her, and I stood helplessly as they sucked the life from the woman I loved. It was enough to bring any man to his knees and beg for mercy. Rob had them too, but he thought that once my mind could comprehend that she was really safe, they'd go away.

I wished now that we'd drawn out that fucker's death, made him pay the way our girls had. When I'd seen my injured fiancée in Tank's arms, covered in welts and blisters and bleeding from more than one spot, I'd lost it. I stayed patient as my brother carried her out of the house, waited just long enough for the dick to answer Rob's questions, then I'd pulled my gun and shot the miserable son of a bitch right between the eyes. And again, in his chest for good measure. When I emptied the rest of my magazine into his body, it was purely out of hatred.

The sleaze had had Ellie and Bear attacked, abducted and murdered Tink, and hurt our girls all as some fucked up plan to avenge his narcissistic demonic brother. A brother who hadn't even died at our hands. And that was a fucking pity.

I sighed, remembering how bad Jo's face had looked the day we rescued her. She still wouldn't tell me what had happened. Fuck, she wouldn't tell anyone for that matter.

We all knew, of course. The emergency room doctor had told us quietly that he had found possible internal injuries as well as two fractured ribs, a dislocated toe, a broken finger, dozens of burns, over a hundred puncture marks caused by numerous objects, countless bruises, sections of scalp where her hair had been ripped out, and she had been severely dehydrated. She'd been through hell and back in the two and a half days they had her.

The other women were opening up little by little, recalling their time in the warehouse. The stories Jessie had were enough to make any human being sick and vow revenge. Taylor's didn't focus on what happened to her as much as on how she refused to break. Jo wouldn't say a peep though. I'd catch her staring out into space sometimes and wonder if she was reliving her time.

Jo hadn't been with them the longest and she apparently had avoided some of their more vicious treatment, but she had put herself on the line, risking everything to save the others. She refused to acknowledge it, because she was stubborn like that. Instead, she insisted that Cris, Jessie and Taylor were the ones who needed our love and support. I knew she'd open up one day when she was ready, and until that day, I'd be there waiting.

I did feel as though I was smothering her a little. I'd barely let her go to the bathroom alone those first few days. I still wasn't at the point where I could let her leave the house without me, and I wasn't sure I'd ever get there. I might not have been able to keep her from getting taken last time, but it would never happen again. Jo didn't seem to mind my constant presence.

I wasn't the only one being overbearing. Rob was with Jessie every waking moment and only left her with Tank when it was time for bed. Tank, still struggling with the fact that he hadn't saved Tink, visited Jo almost every day, sometimes just sitting with her on the deck, then he guarded his sister every night. Bear was worse than any of us. He'd moved Taylor into the clubhouse, barely letting her leave the compound. The time would come when we would relax a bit, let the women we loved have some freedom. But probably not for a while.

I had too much on my mind to sleep, so I just watched Joes. Even in slumber, she was beautiful. It always took me a few minutes to remember that I was the lucky son of a bitch who would get to have this view for the rest of his life. If someone had told me two years ago that I'd be here now, I would have told them that Jo would never be with a man like me.

When she rolled over a few hours later, she found me staring at her. She stared at me for a second then gave me that breathtaking smile of hers, filled with nothing but love. "Morning."

The bruises were gone now, most of the wounds healed. Some of them had scarred, which killed me, but she ignored the pink puffy skin. She would laugh and say that men thought scars were sexy, so I'd better watch out because I was going to have some serious competition. In reality though, she'd chosen tattoos to cover the noticeable marks and had gotten her first one a few days ago.

I thought it was a great idea, not only because I didn't want to see the scars forever on her skin, but because I was a man who thought ink on a woman was sexy as hell. The more, the better. In fact, we'd agreed to get our wedding rings tattooed on after the ceremony. That way, there was no chance they'd ever come off.

"Good morning, beautiful!" I leaned in for a kiss.

"God, I didn't wake you up, did I?" She covered her mouth as if her breath would offend me. "Is the snoring getting worse?"

I shook my head, smiling as I scooted down into the bed next to her. "No. You're fine." I pulled her upper body onto my chest. "What do we want to do today?" My hand slid down her hip. "I was thinking that maybe we could spend the day in here, order takeout, and you could show me that new tat again."

Before she could answer, the door flew open and three kids rushed inside, all talking at once. I needed to learn how to lock the goddamn door.

"I told them that you were still in bed!" Lily stomped her little foot. "Why don't you two ever listen to me? Ugh!" she hollered, putting her tiny fists on her waist. "Mommy, Datty, tell them I'm right!"

Suddenly three voices were yelling at each other, but I couldn't help but smile.

Datty.

The kids had been excited at the news of our engagement. Lily wanted to help us start planning the wedding right away, and she had a list of demands—like the fact that she would wear a princess dress with a tiara. Not long after that conversation, she'd asked what she should call me. Sam called me Daddy and Ben called me Matt, so Lily decided Datty would work for her. I fucking loved it.

I eased Jo off me, jumped out of bed, and shooed them, still hollering at each other, out of the room. Apparently the honeymoon was over, and they were back to being real siblings—ones who argued over what to watch on TV and disagreed about when to wake up their parents.

Turning the lock, I leaned against the door and smiled at the love of my life. "So, Lily... we're really sure she's not mine?"

Jo sat up, laughing as she pushed the hair out of her eyes. "That demanding little monster out there with the bad attitude and the smirk?" She pointed at the door where we could hear our little princess still barking orders. "Oh, she's all yours. She might not have your DNA, but she apparently doesn't know that."

I laughed and thumped my head back, sighing. "When do they go home? I want you to myself again."

She giggled, sliding over in the bed and opening her arms to me. "Come here, babe."

I didn't think twice, just climbed into bed and pulled her into my arms.

She sighed. "They are home, Matty. You're stuck with us. This is what the rest of our life is going to be like. I hope you're prepared."

I smiled down at the woman who was still by my side, even though she knew the darkest truths about me and had almost paid

500

the ultimate price for my decisions. I still didn't deserve her, but I would never stop trying to be the man she saw in me. She was right—my family was home.

The Bastards would heal and continue to fight for those who couldn't. Jo would marry me in a few months. We would raise our crazy threesome as best as we could.

And I would wake up next to my Joes every day for the rest of my life. I'd never know how I'd gotten so fucking lucky, but I was going to enjoy every second of it. She was finally mine, and I was never letting her go.

NOTE FROM THE AUTHOR

Everyone says you should write about what you know.

Years ago, I was sitting at an outside cafe with some friends chatting about a horrific local case that had been all over the news and social media. I remember saying that my husband and his friends would never stop searching for me if I disappeared because they protect me and my kids at all costs. I made some comment about how I wished everyone had that—a group of men who would do whatever it took to protect the people they love.

And, The Bastards were born. They're fictitious, yet each Bastard (and Brat) is based on a real person—someone I know.

Always Been Mine was my first book, Honey Whiskey my second. They're far from my best work. I had no idea what in the world I was doing. In fact, I wrote ABM to prove to my husband that I *couldn't* write romance. Joke's on me.

If you made it through them, you're a rock star. I can't tell you how many times I've tried to read them and given up. Jo bugs me. Even though at the time I loved her and there was a lot of me in her. Maybe I'm too hard on myself. Maybe I've just grown a lot...

Books are like children; you're not supposed to have a favorite. An author invests hours, leaving bits of their sole on the pages. I should love each story equally. I don't.

ABM and HW are definitely not my favorites, however, the characters are. I love these vigilante thugs. They own me. And, like a first born, these books taught me how to be the author I am today.

I've been asked a lot if there are more Bastard books coming. There are. I want Tank's story. I want Jessie to get her HEA. However, I don't have release dates.

If this was your first introduction to the Bastards of Boston, I highly recommend Unfinished Business—Rocker's book. It took me four years to write it for a reason. It's my favorite.

Thank you for coming on this journey with me. I hope you stick around.

ACKNOWLEDGEMENTS

It has been a crazy few years, eh?

Nothing I do would be possible without my husband—or as pe FB knows him, The Hubs. He keeps me laughing when I want to cry—or kill him. Humor, it saves lives.

To my always amazing (now ex) PA's. It really is too bad that you quit right before this was supposed to be published. I'm pretty sure you made it into the acknowledgements the first time around, so it would have been awesome to see your name in print again for the boxed set. Right, Samms and June? I hope one day we can forgive each other and move on. No? Yeah, didn't think so. You can go and love yourself. 'Cause, God knows I do love you both. Oh, and did I mention that you can't quit me? LOL Thank you for everything. Always.

Sommer, at Perfect Pear Creations, the cover is more than beautiful – it's perfect!

Cassie, at Joy Editing, You took my babies and were both gentle and kind while making them better. I appreciate you more than I can express.

The readers that have fallen in love with Matty, Rocker, and the rest of the Bastards—thank you for coming on this journey with me! I read each of your emails, Facebook messages, and reviews. I love that you love these vigilante thugs as much as I do. More is coming, I promise. I want to know which one is your favorite (mine is Tank), so make sure you message me and let me know.

Jenn, from Read and Share Book Reviews and Jen, from Three Chicks and Their Books—If it wasn't for you two, I wouldn't still be writing. New authors don't always get support, especially from bloggers. I will always count you two as my biggest blessings. I have a career because of you. I won't ever forget that!

DHHS friends, you are truly astounding. Not only do you spend more time with me than anyone else, you work in an environment that can break your heart and leave you jaded any second, but you keep fighting for the kids. It makes sense that my first book was about social workers, because you are my heroes. Thank you for all that you do!

Printed in Great Britain
by Amazon

79942963R00292